CROWNS OF STARS & TIDES

The Five Realms   Book Two

Jenessa Ren

Copyright © 2024 by Jenessa Ren

All rights reserved.

No part of this publication may be reproduced, distributed, or transmitted in any form or by any means, including photocopying, recording, or other electronic or mechanical methods, without the prior written permission of the publisher, except as permitted by U.S. copyright law. For permission requests, contact authorjenessaren@gmail.com

The story, all names, characters, and incidents portrayed in this production are fictitious. No identification with actual persons (living or deceased), places, buildings, and products is intended or should be inferred.

Book Cover by Marcia Godfrey @plusinfinityart

Chapter Illustrations by Athena Bliss @chaotictired

Map by Lindsey Staton @honeyy.fae

Editing by Allie Crain

First edition 2024

Paperback ISBN: 979-8-9891050-2-1

Hardcover ISBN: 979-8-9891050-3-8

For those who still feel trapped in the mosaic of their grief,
may you remember that healing isn't linear, but that it will come with time.

For a quick recap of Heir Of Sun And Moon, as well as the pronunciation guide, please scan this QR code and enter the password:
THEFIVEREALMS

Content Warnings

This story contains depictions of:
    Physical abuse
    Mental, verbal, emotional, and psychological abuse and manipulation
    Depression and depictions of grief
    Sexually explicit scenes
    Sexual coercion
    Forced sexual acts (off page)
    Vulgar language
    Adult content
    Gore
    Death including that of a shifter child and animal

Each topic has been approached sensitively and written with the utmost respect and care, but should any of these topics be triggering for you, please do not read.

Your mental health matters.

-Jenessa

Prologue

BEFORE THE WAR OF FIVE KINGDOMS

"REMEMBER WHAT I TOLD you, Amari," my mother states, her voice low and hushed as if she doesn't want anyone to overhear. "The future of our kind rests on your shoulders. You mustn't fail."

"Yes, Your Majesty." It's the same speech that she has given me for the past year as she prepared me for this very moment. Queen Zola Malika, ruler of the Siren Queendom, floats in the water next to me, her closest friend, Themu Adanna, flanking my other side. We stare in the direction of the Mortal Kingdom, where King Fionn and his son, Prince Erik, are waiting to greet us. The meeting details were laid out as the rulers of each realm had spoken through their respective magical Mirrors.

"I do not like this plan," Themu expresses, her third time doing so since we left the capital of Lumen. I glance at her from the corner of my eye, trailing over her dark umber skin and the way her bright green braids gleam beneath the sunlight above. "It could be a trap."

My mother grips her golden trident so harshly that her knuckles lighten in color. "Themu, have you no faith in your queen?"

"I have every faith in you, Zola. In Amari as well. It is the *men* I do not trust. You see the looks they give us when we walk in their cities. The *leering*."

"I do not trust them either. However, we need a pliant king. Once Amari is welcomed into the palace and our people into the kingdom freely, then we can enact the rest of our plan," my mother says as she narrows her eyes keenly towards the coast. "For too long, we beings of two worlds have been forced to stay relegated to one. Sirens deserve the land as much as we do the sea. Once Amari is married to Prince Erik, she will help us gain what we are *owed* and I will rule over two realms."

I lift my chin up, keeping my fingers relaxed at my sides despite my mother's declaration. I am her eldest daughter; rule of the Siren Queendom will one day fall to me. I merely have to pretend to love the mortal prince until I can get him under my thrall and order him to do my bidding. Then we will finally have a space above land to call our own that isn't a small island. *Power is nothing but a tool for you to take, Amari. Do not hesitate to claim it.* My mother's words ring soundly in my mind.

"Men always have ulterior motives—secret plans of ways they think that they will gain the upper hand. All we need is to feed into the king's ego until Amari is married, and then no one will be able to deny our rule when the king and prince die."

"And if the mortals fight against it? We cannot take on an entire mortal army," Themu growls, her bright green tail swishing angrily beneath her.

"Enough, Themu. It is time to go," my mother snaps before darting towards the coast in a flash of deep blue scales and braids.

"You better hope that she is right, or we'll be dooming our queendom."

My top lip lifts in a snarl as I show Themu my teeth. "You better hope that she doesn't grow tired of the way you constantly undermine her." Then I join my mother in swimming to the Mortal Kingdom's beach.

Warm air brushes against my skin, my eyes drawing down my body as we emerge from the ocean and step foot into the soft, dry sand. My dark purple scales retreat into my skin, their leftover luminescence a faint glow in the sunlight. Soft ringlet curls drape down to my hips, covering my breasts. The first few moments of walking on feet are always jarring, my toes flexing in the sand with every step I take. My mother and Themu transform as well, and together, we head towards the small gathering of royals on the beach.

"Greetings, Queen Zola. Welcome back to the glorious land of the Mortal Kingdom." King Fionn's voice is grating against my skin, and I fight the urge to sneer in his direction. He's a portly man, his round belly stuffed tightly into a tunic of rich blue with gold adornments. His crown glints under the sun, the ruby-red jewels and diamonds laid within it large enough that I wonder if its weight hurts his head. He wears a sword of gold strapped to his hip, and as we step closer, I see a gold pin formed to look like the head of a roaring lion placed just below his collarbone on the right side.

He runs his hazel eyes over us, lingering on our naked bodies much too long. When he catches sight of my mother's crown—one made of spiraling seashells, pearls, and aquamarine diamonds—he smirks, as if she's nothing more than a child playing dress-up. He, at least, pays more respect to the diamond-tipped golden trident she holds in her hand. Despite us possessing magic that could bend him to our will, King Fionn looks at us like the trident is the only weapon worth being wary of.

"Your Majesty, the honor is all mine." My mother's voice is serene and lovely, holding no hint of the brutal power I know lies beneath her skin. "This is my daughter, Princess Amari, and my advisor, Themu." Advisor isn't a word we use in the Siren Queendom. There is the queen and her court; sometimes, my sisters and I serve as the right hand to the queen in matters that require her attention. But no one *advises* Queen Zola. She does as she wants. Her word is final.

I dip my head and hold it there in a small bow for five seconds, each one feeling much too long for a show of respect towards this imbecile. When I lift my gaze again, I wait for the king's eyes to rise up from the lower half of my body. They do, only briefly meeting my gaze before his attention goes back to my mother. As he speaks to her, I look past him to the men lining the beach. Most look like guards, their armor a heinous gold that covers them from head to toe. Standing directly behind the king is another man wearing a much smaller crown. *Prince Erik.*

He's handsome enough. His light brown hair is neatly trimmed, the top strands longer but styled in a way that leaves his face unobscured. Hazel eyes match his father's, while a short beard frames the lower half of his face. His eyes snap to mine, and there is nothing but bored interest laid bare within them. My lips curl up at the corners as I roll my shoulders back and clasp my hands behind me.

My mother often laments on the simplistic nature of the male brain. *They want to rule, and they want to fuck, and there is not much in between that they care about.* So I push my breasts out farther, my curvy body on display for his consumption. Yet the prince looks almost *appalled* and directs his focus forward again.

"That is *not* what we agreed upon," my mother says sharply, her tone sending a chill over me. I turn my head to look at her, the breeze coming off the water gently rustling her hair. Themu stands on her other side, her lips flat in a grim line.

"I know, I know. You wanted official land for your kind. But you women are already welcome to walk the streets and spend your coin here any time you like! That won't change."

"Females," Themu seethes, her light green eyes flaring. "*Women* is not a siren word."

King Fionn chuckles as he shakes his head. "Of course. In *any* case, the truth is, my son has informed me that his heart is already spoken for by another. So marrying the princess is no longer an option."

Dread curdles my stomach, but I keep myself still as my mother takes a small step forward. The guards in gold follow suit, only stopping when the king lifts his hand. Prince Erik's eyes widen as he seems to recoil in on himself. *Fucking coward.*

"We had a *deal*—"

"We had a verbal discussion at best, and one that was not set in stone. My son is in love with someone else, one more fit to be the future queen of the Mortal Realm than a being who has spent her life beneath the surface." His smile is cruel as he adds, "A *female* of half land is still part fish."

My mother growls, her talons growing out from her fingertips. The hair on the back of my neck rises as she opens her mouth to start singing. One of the guards snaps his arm forward, and something whistles through the air, a quick glint in the sunlight before pain flares to life in my thigh. I scream, my fingers framing my leg where the multi-colored jeweled hilt of a dagger sticks out.

"We must go," Themu snarls, wrapping her hand around my arm tightly. Pain pricks there too from where her talons are threatening to come out.

"You *dare* attack my daughter?" my mother shouts, her dark blue eyes fixated on King Fionn. He flicks his hand, and more guards step forward, all of them drawing their golden weapons and pointing them at her.

She opens her mouth again to reach for our song, but Themu stops her. "No, Zola! This isn't the time."

Queen Zola lets out a frustrated growl but glares at the king as she backtracks into the water. "You will *pay* for this." He says nothing as he watches us retreat, our bodies changing as soon as we are deep enough in the water.

Pain flares as my scales replace skin and my legs morph into my tail. My hair returns to braids, and I brush them away from my face, my hand going to the hilt of the dagger.

"Wait, Amari," my mother says, swimming over to me with calculated slowness. I wince from the pain as she positions herself in front of me, handing her trident off to Themu. Placing her hand on my shoulder, she grows her talons until they pierce my skin. I grit my teeth together but do nothing else, used to her brand of punishment. "I asked you to do *one* thing." Her other hand wraps around the dagger's hilt, and her jerky movements send a wave of blinding pain through my body. "For an entire *fucking* year, we have prepared for this! This would not have happened had you done your duty and seduced the prince! Had you presented yourself in a way that he could *not resist*." She yanks the dagger out of my tail, my whimper pathetically loud as she lets me go and my body curls over itself. "You have failed me, Amari, and if I didn't need you to prepare for the war I'm about to bring to the Mortal Kingdom, I would kill you now."

Dark blue blood leaks from my wound, my mother letting the dagger fall from her grasp as it descends towards the ocean floor. Gripping her trident once more, she angles it towards me, the diamond-encrusted tips scraping at my chest and making me flinch.

"You will get me that kingdom one way or another. Even if it costs you your life in order to do it."

Part One

Grief is like trying to fight an invisible enemy. There's no way to prepare for it—no lessening of the savage way it further pulls me apart. It's a scar ripped open over and over again.

Chapter One

RHEA

The sun's warmth bears down on me like fire from above though it does nothing to melt the ice that begins to settle in my veins. Like the waters of a lake touched by bitterly cold winter air, everything in me stills.

Tell me, was your mission in the Mortal Kingdom successful? The older mage's words pelt into me one by one until I struggle to take a breath.

"Mission?" I question, peering up at Flynn.

His fingers twitch from where I've dropped his hand while his dark gray eyes flash with panicked surprise. When the silence stretches on between us, the older mage clears his throat and mumbles something about catching up with *His Highness* back at the palace.

"Highness?" I whisper, looking back out over the gathered crowd. Most have their attention on the interaction happening beyond the Spell at the edge of the beach, but a few have turned to look our way. To look at Flynn—or is it Nox? "Who are you?" I breathe, confusion gripping my throat as I turn back to look at him.

A few tendrils of his wavy black hair move in the breeze, the sunlight glinting off his sharp cheekbones. He opens his mouth to speak, but nothing comes out.

"More lies?" My tongue feels like lead in my mouth, and I can't stop tripping over each thought and emotion that is boiling up inside me until it nearly renders me mute. He had confessed all his lies at the inn. He had—

"Rhea, let me explain," he pleads, only loud enough for me to hear.

Your mission.

Was this whole *thing* between us nothing more than a façade? A way to get me to his kingdom? My chest rises and falls harshly, but the air isn't reaching my lungs. I'm back in that stone tower, the walls slowly pushing in as my reality continues to suffocate me. My own fears of him seeing me as an illusion have been thrown back in my face, the irony of it all like a sharpened dagger slowly driving in between my ribs.

"Who are you?" I ask again, feeling pressure build behind my eyes.

He quickly closes the distance between us, faster than my spiraling mind can comprehend, and though he doesn't touch me, he leans down close enough to keep his voice barely above a whisper. "I know you're confused and you have questions, which I promise to answer. *Anything* and *everything* you want to know, I will tell you." He pauses, turning his head as figures approach us from the water's edge. "I just need a few minutes here first. Please."

Please.

The word bashes my grip on my anger and, instead, lets it slip through me, filling my body with something acidic. With his honeyed words and even sweeter lips—ones that had nearly devoured me two days prior—what parts of him are real? How many of his declarations could I comb through and find a hidden meaning for? If I looked hard enough, could I pinpoint the spaces between his words that held the truth of what he *wasn't* saying?

"Sunshine, please," he begs again, leaning in even closer to me.

My options are truly limited; I am in a foreign kingdom and outside of my tower for the first time. If I take Flynn out of the equation, I am completely and utterly *alone* again. My chest clenches at the memory of a white bundle of fur, of pointed ears that always twitched in warning. Those things are gone now—*she* is gone now. So what choice do I have but to stand by this man who clearly lied to me *again*, despite proclaiming he'd confessed nothing but truths? The sickening thought that I'd rather have his betrayal and still have *him* than have nothing but solitude bleeds into my mind. How *pathetic*. Still, I nod in agreement.

The figures that were on the other side of the Spell reach us, two women and one man. Up close, the women look almost identical while the man—*king*—looks exactly like Flynn. His black hair is longer, down to his shoulders, and his stature slightly shorter, but there is no mistaking the identities of these people—his father, mother, and sister.

Flynn hugs his father, and I turn my attention out to the ocean. Though I have never been to the beach before, I had read enough about it to be able to picture it in my mind. I could imagine how it moved, how the crystal-blue water was powerful enough to consume anything and everything in its path. There have been so many times in my life where I felt overwhelming emotions crest over me, exactly like how I pictured those waves moving. Right now, as I stand at the side of the only person my heart has ever truly spoken for, I *feel* like I'm being crushed by waves of shock and confusion. As if I'm standing out in the middle of the vast waters ahead of me, waiting to be swallowed whole.

Flynn and his father separate, his mother stepping up next to embrace her son while his sister eyes me curiously. She's taller than I am, and the dress she's wearing does not hide her strong physique. I meet her gaze, her irises the same as Flynn's though they are missing the tiny specks of silver that reside in his. I begin to wilt under her inspection and the way she looks at me like she already knows every secret I carry. Flynn moves in front of me and says something to his sister, but I can't hear anything above the rapid beating of my heart in my ears.

His head abruptly jerks to the side, a *thump* accompanying the movement, as his mother gasps and his father lifts a brow in question. *His sister just hit him in the face.* I take a step back, needing space, and bump into something hard. Turning my head quickly, I see Cassius—Flynn's best friend—smiling widely, his hand gently pressing between my shoulder blades to steady me. His white-blond hair is pulled back from his face, its length falling past his shoulders. The color is stark against his rich dark skin, which is mostly hidden under the thick dark brown leathers he is wearing.

"Careful, Blondie," he whispers, winking before removing his touch.

My heart batters my ribcage, my stomach growing more uneasy as the reality of the past few minutes catches up with me. A warm, tingling sensation starts to accumulate in my palms, drawing my gaze from Cassius and down to my hands where my magic is glowing. I quickly make fists, hoping that the brightness of the beach under the sun hides the white light from anyone who happens to be looking. Cassius shifts on his feet behind me, and when I look back over my shoulder again, his smile has lessened and a line has appeared between his brows.

What if he saw?

I don't know what Flynn's plans are for me anymore or if he intends to tell anyone about my magic, but my innate response is to force it back inside of me, like everything else I either don't *want* or *know how* to deal with. I cross my arms over my chest, my fists tucking under them as I focus on trying to breathe through the swelling emotions roiling within.

A throat clears, fingers caressing my arm and causing me to flinch as I turn away from Cassius. Flynn stands in front of me, his face stern while he stares at his best friend. I look down at the way he is touching me, his large hand gently laid on my forearm, and have to swallow back tears that threaten to spill. It was only *this morning* that I would have let him touch me anywhere he wanted. It was mere hours ago that his presence was the only thing I had needed to feel like I was home.

"Sunshine, we can go now." Flynn extends his hand and then drops it when he realizes I'm not giving him my own. "I know you're angry, and you have every right to be, but I promise I can explain." He tilts his head to the side, trying to catch my gaze, and when I finally give it to him, all the effort of holding my tears back is for nothing. His eyes gleam with an eager anxiousness, but it's the other emotion that I see in them that has my own eyes overflowing.

Love. Pure, unfiltered love looks back at me. And it isn't fair because I may have never been in any sort of romantic relationship before, but I *know* that you don't lie to people you love. The juxtaposition of the look in his eyes and that of his secretive actions leaves me feeling completely suffocated.

I nod my head, unsure of what else to do or say, and follow Flynn as he leads us off the beach. I keep my gaze down, looking only at his steps ahead of me, while inside my mind, I'm screaming in frustration. In panic and confusion. *In anger.*

Once we are off the beach, walking on a path in the shade provided by the abundant trees, I blow out a breath, tugging my loosened braid over my shoulder and nervously twisting the strands. Flynn walks beside me now, so closely that our arms graze with each step, Cassius taking his place behind us. His parents' voices sound farther back, but I focus on the light wood carriages up ahead and am reminded of the conversation we had on our way to the beach.

After we see what is going on at the beach, I will introduce you to my parents and we can talk more, Flynn had said. Did he know his supposed truths were about to be exposed for what they actually were—polished lies? Gods, I had even *felt* like he was on the verge of telling me something before pulling back.

Flynn opens the door of the carriage we originally arrived in, allowing me to step in first. I take a seat on the dark green velvet bench, squeezing myself as close to the glass window as possible and giving the door my back. He sits across from me, the distance feeling so much larger than what the tiny space of the carriage actually measures. I can feel his stare, but I don't look at him as we sit in stilted silence. It's heavy and *ugly*, and I wish more than anything we could go back to the night of my birthday. The night when his lips devoured mine and we were poised to do much more. I ache fiercely to go back to when he gave me that journal and a note that left me feeling like no one could possibly love another soul as much as I loved him. As I thought *he* loved me. It was a love worth exposing my magic for. One worth following him into an unknown kingdom for.

I now wonder if it is one worth enduring his lies for.

With my attention focused on the window, I take in the beauty of the forest as we move. This kingdom truly is a marvelous wonder; the varying shades of green and the immense amount of plant life outside is almost enough to draw some happiness out of me—though I'm unsure if that emotion will ever come easily again.

A tear drops down onto my arm, more flowing over my cheeks as I squeeze my eyes shut and burrow deeper into myself. *So naive. So incredibly naive and stupid to assume that someone could actually love me as I am.* The carriage jostles, and then I feel him right behind me, his warmth doing nothing against the bitter numbness hardening me from within.

"I'm so sorry." His voice is a rasp, like it's been scraped along jagged rock.

"Who are you?" I ask again, the words barely a harsh whisper between my lips. Those already full mental boxes—brimming with grief and hopelessness—rattle inside me, reminding me that I don't have the capacity to hold anymore. Flynn was supposed to be a *reprieve*. He was supposed to be the one person that I could trust—*and I did*. I trusted him with everything that I was.

"I'm still me, Rhea."

My breath feels trapped in my throat, my lungs struggling to get air in that won't come. It's reminiscent of how I felt the first time we reached the town of Celatum, where panic replaced my thoughts and imaginary mountains crushed my chest. I ball my hands tightly in my lap, my nails digging into my palms.

"Breathe. It's going to be alright," he says, though uncertainty paints his voice the same way it frays my soul.

My eyes close, and I focus on following his commands, working to steady the erratic beats of my broken heart. To pull that invisible shield inside of me up and over myself so that I don't have to bear witness to the feeling of there being a stranger in this carriage with me.

"There you go, Sunshine. We're almost at the palace."

"Why are we going there?" I ask between gulps of air.

He is silent for a while, just the noise of the carriage wheels over the stone pathway and Cassius humming a tune from where he sits outside playing between us. "Because I am the crown prince of the Mage Kingdom."

The crown prince. He is royalty, and yet he paraded around in another kingdom as one of their guards. Why?

"Please say something," he whispers behind me.

"What would you like me to say?" I murmur back, keeping my gaze to the window as we slow and come to a stop. I hear the door open, and then Cassius' voice trails in.

"Let's take Blondie to the tavern and—" He cuts his question off, and I tense, feeling his stare on me.

"We're going to need some time, Cass. I also have to say goodbye to Bahira before she leaves," Flynn states quietly.

"Okay, then," Cassius drawls.

"I'll come find you when I can. Thank you, Cass."

"Anytime. You know that." There's a pause, and then he adds, "Are you home for a while?"

"I'm home for good." It's silent again, and I don't know why, but that causes me to grit my teeth while an ache forms in my chest. Turning around to face the door, I see that Cassius is already gone, and when my gaze then finds Flynn's, it's a struggle not to crash my body into his. The way his eyes plead with me to... To what, I don't know this time. Listen to him? Believe him? *Trust him?*

He must see the indecision in me because his eyes close for a moment as he tilts his head down. One of his hands runs through his hair, pushing the strands back and holding them there. I study his face closely, the way his mouth is bracketed with tension and how his brows are drawn down and in. He looks tired, dark circles visible under his eyes. Even with all of those things, he is still the most beautiful person I've ever seen. Which only unravels me further. Here, in the painful quiet, Flynn blows out a deep breath and forces his eyes to meet mine.

"I want to tell you why I was really in the Mortal Kingdom."

Chapter Two

BAHIRA

"Bahira," Daje rumbles again, his fingers stretching towards me on the other side of the iridescent wall of the Spell. Between his wide eyes boring into me and the shifter king's domineering energy behind me, I'm pinned into place. *Three months.* Three months to try to fix another kingdom's magic problems—to hope it helps more than hinders the solving of ours as well.

"Deal," I say firmly, keeping my gaze on the man that's held such an important part of my past but speaking my answer to the looming male who represents my now-immediate future. "Three months." Daje sucks in a breath, his head jerking back as his hand falls to his side.

A rumbling, dark laughter makes my hair stand on edge. "This will be an interesting three months, *Princess,*" King Kai says, his deep voice laced with amusement.

Though the blue sky above is free of clouds, I swear a shadow passes over me as I turn to face the exasperating ruler of the island kingdom. "Can't wait," I say through a fake smile. "Being that you can't pass through the Spell, I assume you will want to leave soon?"

Only one side of King Kai's mouth lifts as he half smiles, half snarls at me. "How perceptive you are. I can see now why—"

"Say another word, Your Majesty, and I will kick your balls so far inside you, Tua here won't be able to find them."

Tua lets out a sigh while the shifter king leans forward, all pretense of an attempted grin gone from his expression. "That would be considered an act harsh enough for me to declare war," he grits out, his advisor shifting closer until his shoulder bumps the king's.

I smile—my own flashing of teeth—as I take a step towards him until our bodies are a mere hand's width apart. "And yet you've just given a blood oath to protect our people. Your threats are as pathetic as you are."

The shifter king growls low in his throat, and I laugh. A flicker of surprise passes through his earthy brown eyes, but then it's gone and is replaced by animosity.

Good, the feeling is fucking mutual.

"Return here with whatever you need for your stay in my kingdom within the hour, or you'll swim to the ship." He turns around, and I'm about to retort with something entirely unladylike, when my father steps up to me and gently guides me away.

"Let it go, Bahi. Something tells me that the shifter king has never met a woman who could rival him in insults," he says with a small chuckle as we step through the Spell. That silky bubble feeling washes over me for half a second, and then we're back on the other side.

Daje is waiting for me, and based on his bitter expression, I know he wants to have a conversation right this very second about what just happened, but there is someone else who draws my gaze away. My parents and I trudge across the warm sandy beach to greet Nox, our first time seeing him in person in a year.

All I can see is his side profile as he speaks to the blonde woman I saw him with earlier, though their conversation looks mostly one-sided. When we're only a few feet away, Nox meets my eyes with a pained—near panicked—expression before turning back to talk with the woman. She gives him a nod, facing us as we reach them.

"Son," my father rasps, bringing Nox in for a hug. The tension melts from their shoulders as the crown prince and his king reunite. My mother patiently waits her turn, stepping into my brother's embrace the moment my father has vacated it. Where the two men hugged with the intensity of too much time spent apart, the hug with our mother is softer. Like caressing a delicate rose, Nox rubs her back in soothing strokes as she cries tears of joy at having her only son back home.

My attention is drawn back to the woman beside Nox. Though she looks a little travel worn, it's impossible to ignore how classically beautiful she is. Each of her features looks as though they were hand-picked and placed with the utmost care.

Nox angles himself in front of her, and though sadness pulls on the edges of his eyes, his smile is bright as he says my name and starts to reach out to hug me. Instead, my fist connects with the side of his jaw. The sound of the impact causes a reverberation of gasps amongst the crowd still gathered at the beach. My parents' heads snap towards me, their gazes ranging from utter shock to confused amusement. Nox's head jerks to the side where he stays for a moment, his lips pinching together before he turns back around to glare at me.

"What," he growls, "was that for?"

My arms fold over my chest, the corner of my mouth lifting with delight. "*That* is for writing such vague letters, you idiot."

Nox lets out a strangled laugh before pulling me in for a hug that I don't fight. "I missed you, nerd," he says into my hair.

"I missed you too." His arms tighten around me to the point of near suffocation before he lets go, stepping back. "Who is she?" I ask, gesturing with my chin to the woman behind him now standing with Cassius.

His entire body tenses, fists clenching, as his eyes dart to the council members standing off to the side before coming back to mine. "Not here," he says quietly, turning towards our father. "Did you get my last letter?" There's an odd insistence in his voice, his body poised as if he's preparing for an attack.

My father nods in response to Nox's question. "Bahira was chosen by the magic of the Continent to leave for the Shifter Kingdom," he says, his gray eyes finding my own. "We only have an hour before she is to sail with him."

"Why are you going there to begin with?" Nox questions.

"I'm going to help them with a magic problem," I reply. They can hash out the details of the deal my father made with the shifter king later, once I'm gone. "I need to go pack my things and stop at my workshop. Shall we go home?"

Nox nods before giving our parents one last glance and then turning to face the woman. They speak quietly before walking towards the carriages, and I move to follow them when Daje calls my name.

"Bahira, wait!" he yells, running up to my side.

"Ride with me to the palace?" I offer, brandishing what I hope is a placating smile.

He nods his head and motions for me to lead, an awkward and rigid silence descending upon us as we walk. We get into the carriage behind the one carrying my parents, and once we're in motion, Daje leans forward, resting his elbows on his knees.

"Can you please explain to me what the *fuck* that was?" I squash down the immediate quell to bite back and, instead, observe him. The last time we talked—at the Summer Solstice celebration—he had left with a hopeful glint in his eyes. Like maybe I would actually stop my pursuit of trying to fix the magic issues that plagued our kingdom and settle down with him as his agreeable wife. Now they are narrowed in accusation and his shoulders are hiked with tension.

"I was *chosen*, Daje." I hold his stare, those intense blue eyes moving over me like he's seeing me in a different light—like I'm someone new. I suppose that's the issue: this is who I've been for my entire adult life, what I've been trying to get Daje to see and understand. He's my best friend, but when was the last time he truly *listened* to me? We can joke and have fun together, but when was the last time we focused on learning something new about each other? I wasn't stupid enough to think that *I* was the only one who had changed over the years. "What is it about me being chosen that you do not like?"

Daje sighs and looks down at where his hands hang between his legs. The carriage softly rocks side-to-side on the stone road as we near the palace. When his silence lingers, I tilt my head back and look up at the canopy-filtered sky. A hint of bright sunshine peeks through the dark green and blue leaves and entangled limbs. Summer's warmth wraps around us, and I'm just now realizing how being in the sun uncovered at the beach for so long has left my skin feeling hot to the touch.

"I feel like you're using it as an escape," he finally says, drawing my attention. He sounds resigned, unprepared to live up to the terms of the ultimatum *he* put into place. Or at least most of him does—a small glimmer of defiance and resolve shows in the way he rolls his shoulders back and sits up taller.

"An escape from what?" I dare to ask.

"Everything. My proposal, and your answer. The issue with the magic and your failure to—" His eyes widen as he sucks in a breath.

Failure. Your failure. I'm unable to stop myself from wincing.

"I'm sorry, Bahira. I didn't mean—"

"You did," I interject as the carriage slows to a stop. He looks as if he's teetering on the edge of a cliff and I have the ability to either pull him back or push him over. I lean forward and grab one of his hands in mine. One of the guards opens the door to the carriage, but neither of us makes a move to leave. "But you're wrong. I'm not running away from you or from answering you. This is an incredible opportunity. A grand experiment to see if I can fix our kingdom's magic—if the answers might have been found elsewhere all along." Daje's eyebrows furrow in confusion as he stares at me, his fingers growing lax in my own. "By working on theirs, I might find a solution to ours—"

"Bahira," he groans, yanking his hand back.

"Please, Daje. Don't make me answer you when we'll be separated for the next three months. Let me focus on only this, and if you still care about me in this way when I return, we can talk more about it then." It's the best I can do, the only concession I can make. I don't want to lose him as someone important in my life, but I also can't promise myself to him until I know for sure that I've exhausted every avenue. That I've overturned every rock in my search for a solution. That I truly have *failed*.

"I don't know, Bahira. I just—I don't fucking know." He exits the carriage and walks away from the palace. Away from me. I squeeze my hands into fists while walking up the white dragon stone steps to the palace entrance. Guards clad in the traditional mage leather armor open the large double doors for me, bowing as I pass. Inside the foyer are my parents and a few of the council men and women, including Daje's father—who looks past me and then narrows his eyes when he sees his son isn't here. I fight the urge to scowl at him.

"We must speak with him at once and see what he has learned!" Councilman Osiris bellows, raising his voice with each word spoken. Apparently, he still does not understand that being the loudest person in the room doesn't equate to having the king's ear.

My father, who has now removed his ceremonial robe and placed his hands casually in his pants pockets, simply shrugs his shoulders. "Nox will speak with us when he's ready to share the information he has. For now, we will let the crown prince enjoy his first moments being back home with some rest." Our eyes connect, and with a small jerk of his head, he signals for me to head to his private office, leaving the chaos of the chattering council members behind. "Your brother said he'll be down to say goodbye to you shortly."

My father closes the door and takes a seat next to my mother behind a wide desk that is centered in the room. This office is a newer edition to the palace, comparatively speaking. When our family took over as rulers after The War Of Five Kingdoms, my ancestor added an office to this wing. Three of the four walls are lined with white and gray stacked stone, while the last wall is primarily made of three large windows. They curve halfway up, forming an arched point, and are lined with the dark wood of the banya tree. Carved into the stone on the back wall—behind where my parents sit—is the celestial sigil of the queen of Void Magic.

My father taps his fingers on the desk idly as he studies me. "How are you feeling about all of this?"

I take a seat across the desk from my parents, my back stiff as I grip onto the armrests. "I'm fine. I'm ready to do this." It's not completely a lie though, if I were being truthful, I'd admit that I'm apprehensive to go to another kingdom and attempt to solve their magic issues, and part of the feeling stems from not having solved our own.

"My rose, you know that you can be honest—" My mother is interrupted when the door opens and Nox walks in.

He takes a seat in the chair next to mine, an ankle resting on top of his knee casually, as though we can't feel the tension rippling off of him. My mother looks back to me, and I can practically hear the words she wants to say—that I can tell them that I'm fearful, that perhaps I'm even feeling like Daje is correct, *that I am the wrong choice.* But I know she also has questions for Nox, and I'd rather not dwell on my feelings of inadequacy when there is nothing I can do with them anyway. I nod at her, and she smiles in response before looking at my brother.

"So," she begins, cocking her head to the side as her lips pull into a smile, "who is that beautiful woman that was with you?" I snort and roll my eyes though it is odd that he's brought someone home. As far as I knew, his dating life was practically non-existent due to the fact that he was in a foreign kingdom. *Which is where I'm about to be as well.*

Nox takes a breath and blows it out slowly, one of his fingers nervously tapping on his knee. He looks *reluctant* to speak about her. My eyes dart to my father, who watches Nox with concern. "Her name is Rhea," he finally says.

My father interlaces his fingers together on the desk, his chin dipping in contemplation. "Where is she from?" His question lingers, the insinuation behind it causing Nox's shoulders to tighten.

A prickling of agitation travels down my spine. It has nothing to do with Nox and who he's speaking of but everything to do with my own anxieties about leaving my home. My grip on the armrest of the chair tightens. "Look, I don't have a lot of time before I'm climbing aboard a ship for the first time and sailing away for three months to a different kingdom. Can we please get to the point before I have to go pack?" Nox and our father share an incredulous look while our mother stares at me like I've just thrown tea in her face. Shrugging, I gesture towards Nox to get him talking again.

"She is from the Mortal Kingdom," he supplies.

Surprise floods my system as I frown. How did she cross through the Spell if she is mortal?

"And does she have information regarding the magic we felt?" my father asks. Long and quiet seconds pass, and I'm about to yell at Nox again to hurry the fuck up, but his next words choke off my own.

"Dad, she—she *is* the magic we felt."

Chapter Three

Bahira

SILENCE, THICK LIKE SYRUP, suffocates the room. My mother glances at my father quickly, a language all their own expressed in just one look.

"What do you mean?" I ask, staring at my brother's profile as he wipes his palms on his thighs and shifts in his seat. "Is she mage?"

"She must be. She wasn't even aware she had magic until she accidentally called on it." Nox swallows roughly and adds, "Four years ago."

Realization forces me back into the chair. *Four years ago, when we first felt the wave of magic.* I shake my head, trying to organize and work through the questions that are firing off in my mind. "I don't understand. If she is mage, how did she come to be in the Mortal Kingdom?"

"She was born there—as the princess," Nox answers, and if I think it isn't possible to feel more shocked than I already was, *I am wrong.*

"I wasn't aware that King Dolian was married, let alone had children," my mother muses.

"She's his niece." And there is that fucking shock and silence again.

"So she is the daughter of the late king and queen. If memory serves me correctly, her parents died sometime after her birth, yes?" my father asks, looking to Nox.

He nods in confirmation, and my stomach twists at the thought. "She doesn't know anything about them. She was held captive by her uncle."

My mother's mouth twists into a frown. "Held captive? How long?"

"Since she was born. She was forced to live secluded in a tower, and I do mean *secluded*. She had no one except for a guard who treated her like his own until…" He shakes his head, as if in disbelief. "Until the king killed him in front of her."

"Gods," I gasp, echoing my mother.

"How did you convince the king to let her leave the castle? Is he aware of what she can do?" my father queries, a line forming between his brows as he leans his elbows on the desk.

Nox tilts his head back and drags a hand down his face. "I didn't. I helped her escape, and we ran. He didn't know she had magic until he caught her using it to heal me." My parents bristle in their chairs before Nox holds up a hand. "I'm fine, just took a sword to the side."

My mother lets out a squeak of protest as my father's eyes widen. I do the only reasonable thing and burst out into a fit of laughter. "Are you fucking serious? Gods above, Nox—"

"I'm fine, and we have other things we need to discuss," he argues, cutting me off. "We need to keep her magic and identity a secret."

My father scratches his jaw, looking at my mother and communicating again in a way that only they can understand. "I wish you guys wouldn't do that," I grumble, folding my arms over my chest.

"We can feel her magic, Nox," my father confesses with a sympathetic smile. My eyebrows draw up in surprise.

"Her magic is *strong*, perhaps even as strong as yours is. At least, that is what it feels like," my mother supplies gently.

"Then I will leave with her if she isn't safe here," Nox growls, his voice a sharp knife cutting into the air as his anger rises to the surface.

A knock at the door interrupts the moment, and my father beckons the mage in, halting our conversation.

"Highnesses, the princess' bags are readied in the carriage as you commanded," Leyah, one of the palace staff, says.

I blow out a breath, standing up and forcing myself to be steady despite how my nerves threaten to rattle me. I think if I had time to prepare for this endeavor—longer than an hour at least—I wouldn't find myself so nauseous with the thought of leaving. "I guess it's time."

My father's eyes are soft as he grabs my mother's hand and walks around the desk. "We'll ride with you."

Nox stands as well, a hand running through his hair as he looks at me. "I'm going to stay here. I'm sorry, Bahira—"

"I understand," I interrupt, stepping up to him and wrapping my arms around his torso. If we are truly harboring the *stolen* niece of the mortal king, then Nox is needed here.

He tightens the embrace, taking a deep breath before pulling away. "It feels a bit like fate is playing a joke on us to take you away as soon as I get back. Will you be able to use their Mirror to talk with us?"

"I'll make sure of it. You focus on acclimating to being back home for good. And perhaps figuring out where your new girlfriend gets her magic from."

He snorts, but the sound is forced. With one more squeeze, he quietly excuses himself from the room, his tall figure exiting the open door of the office and into the bustling hallway.

"He'll be fine, Bahi," my father says, gesturing for me to walk out. Luckily, the council members have all dispersed, leaving just the palace staff as they attend to their duties. I take in the white stone walls decorated with tapestries and paintings that depict important events and portraits of rulers from the past. Looking up to the large five-tiered golden chandelier lit with spelled flames in glass orbs three stories above me, I feel myself getting *emotional* over a damn light.

I wonder if that's the thing about leaving the place you've called home your entire life—suddenly the colors of everything are sharper, the details more finely tuned. A slight panic that this may be the last time I'll be here, in this room with these people, overtakes me, and there is nothing I can do to stop the tears that finally well in my eyes.

"Oh, my rose," my mother says, drawing me in for a hug. "Remember who you are, who you've always been. Regardless of what happens over the next three months, you were *always* worthy of this. You, Bahira Rose Daxel, may be the princess of the Mage Kingdom by title, but you are, and always will be, so much more than that."

I hug my mother fiercely, my hand cupping the back of her head and all that curly dark brown hair that is twin to my own. "I love you, Mother."

"I love you too." She pulls back, wiping my fallen tears with her fingers and cradling my face as she kisses my brow. Time suspends when I turn to look at my father. He stares at me with such adoration, such *love,* that it leaves me feeling as if I might not be able to do this. Maybe I'm not truly the person he thinks I am. I lay my cheek on his chest, the scent of leather and cinnamon strong with my deep inhales while we embrace.

"The first mage in two hundred years to be invited—more or less—to visit another kingdom," he ponders, pulling back from me and tilting his head to the side. "And I can think of no one else more worthy of going, my Bahira. Your name means 'brilliant beauty,' and you are those things. But it's your resilience and your pursuit of knowledge that will make this journey one that will be recorded in history books across all of the kingdoms one day. I know it." His hold is firm, love and strength pouring out of him, and I greedily accept it for myself.

Agreeing to meet them back outside at the carriage in ten minutes, I dart up the stairs to the third floor, passing a few guards on my way.

"Safe travels, Your Highness," Barron, a longtime guard, says from his post at the top of the stairs.

"Thank you, Barron. You keep this place from falling apart until I get back, alright?" His warm chuckle draws a slight smile from me while my heart pounds to the beat of my steps as I walk the long hallway to my room. Muffled voices sound farther down the hall, coming through the door of Nox's room. Curiosity briefly has me taking a step towards them, but when the voices grow more tense, I enter my room instead. Rifling through my closet first, I change into a fitted black top with shortened sleeves tucked into tailored dark blue trousers and sandals that tie around my ankles.

On the nightstand next to my bed is a pile of mage journals that I hadn't finished reading through yet. I grab those as well as my personal journal, bundling the collection into a leather pack I snagged from my closet. Giving my room one final scan, my eyes catch on something leaning against the wall.

"Why not," I mutter to myself, walking over to my spear and sliding my hand down its shaft before grabbing it and heading out of the room. I don't look back as I shut the door and make my way down to join my parents outside.

We stop at the library first so that I can grab another set of journals to bring, as I'm sure I will have ample reading time on the ship at the very least. Walking past Elisha with a wave of my hand, I quickly climb the stairs and make my way to the back shelves where the ancient journals of the king's council are kept. Sliding a ladder that is attached to a track on the wall, I climb up to the top shelf and gather as many of those older journals as I can without tipping over.

When I have all I can carry, I carefully climb down and make my way to the exit. Elisha warns me that the magic that protects the journals may falter in the Shifter Kingdom, as it's been a long while since they've tested such a thing. Promising to keep them in excellent condition, I say goodbye and head back out to the carriage, carefully laying them in my trunk and wrapping my clothing around them to ensure they stay safe. My parents cast me an amused look as I climb in before I shrug my shoulders and the carriage takes off.

My last stop before we go to the beach is my workshop. Opening the door to the place that has held so many failed attempts feels almost cathartic. Maybe because now, mixed in with all of those failures, there is a new discovery. With the intent of grabbing my magnifier, I walk to the back of the room. I am wrapping my hands gently around it when my attention is drawn to the counter that holds the glass bottles containing my experiments. I peer at the one that somehow had a delayed growing reaction. Perhaps I can still study it, and though I don't exactly know what else I'm expecting to find, an intuitive feeling says to bring it with me. Grabbing a cork, I close off the top of the bottle and then race back to the carriage, packing both items carefully into my trunk.

I allow myself to really take in the landscape of our kingdom one more time, knowing it will only be three months until I return yet still feeling like things might change before then. My parents talk quietly, their voices working to settle some of my anxiousness as I watch the trees pass by quickly through the window.

The briny scent of the ocean fills the air as the carriage comes to a stop, one of the mages who sat out front opening the door for us. I move first, grabbing my spear and my backpack, and exit the carriage with a jittery step. Looking out to the water's edge, I can practically *feel* King Kai's eyes on me though he is too far away to make out his features. *I do not cower to anyone, let alone an arrogant, egotistical ass of a king. I will be strong at this moment. For my kingdom and the people in it, and for myself.* Standing up tall, I slide my spear into the loops at the top of my back, the leaf-shaped tip reaching over my head. My father carries my trunk as he and my mother lead the way, walking through the remaining crowd still gathered at the beach. I'm nearly to the Spell, marked by its iridescent shimmering magic, when Daje calls out my name. He pushes his way through the throng of people, his eyes wide when they collide with mine.

"Bahira," he says again as he stops right in front of me, his hand reaching out to grab my wrist. The emotional toll of the past hour feels even heavier when he speaks. "I'll wait for you. I'll wait, and when you come back, we can talk about what it means for us." The words come out on a ragged breath, his fingers flexing against my skin. The familiarity of his stare, of his unwavering dedication, momentarily snaps the mask I've donned in half. The tip of my finger caresses the inside of his own wrist, but where I imagine there should be heat or longing or desire of *some* sort, there is nothing.

"I'll see you in three months," I say, quickly turning around and walking through the Spell.

Chapter Four

Aria

*T*HREE HUNDRED AND FORTY-SEVEN.

That's how many things I have collected from the ocean floor. I clutch a small jeweled dagger in my hand, the silver metal glinting against my dark brown skin in the sunlight that streams in through a hole in the rock at the top of the cave. The green and purple gems catch the light and reflect tiny colorful flares—it's how I had found the small weapon partially buried in the ocean floor's sediment.

My small cave of keepsakes is tucked between an outcropping of ancient coral and rock, hardened and leached of color by time. I discovered this place by accident nearly two years ago, when my mother had made me take my first life. *When she had forced me to—*

I stop the thought before the memory can replay again in my mind. I lay the dagger on the naturally indented rock shelf next to a golden pin fashioned into the head of a roaring lion. Though the metal is rusted around the edges from its time in the water, the bright green of the emerald eyes still shines. My ruby-red braids float around me as I study my refuge, my one safe spot in the entire ocean because it is known only to me. Here, I don't have to pretend to be anything harsher or scarier. I can honor those whose lives were cut short by my sisters and me. By my mother. By my *kind*. Though no one else—let alone the dead—will ever see it, I still feel a sense of duty to preserve their memory in *some* way.

To appease some of the guilt I feel.

The water is warm thanks to the summer sun, and though siren skin is made to withstand all temperatures under the surface, this time of year is my favorite. The warmth caresses my soft curves when I swim as opposed to the more piercing waters of winter. Plus, the need to change into my mortal form means that going onto the beach in the winter is extremely unpleasant. I shiver merely from the thought.

I wish I could stay here all day, basking in the sense of security this hidden cavern gives me, but I am due back in the capital for a *party*. Gritting my teeth, I cross a pouch made of deep blue woven eelgrass over my shoulder, its weight digging into my muscles, and slowly turn towards the sea kelp growing high from the ocean floor that hides the small second entrance to the cave. I prefer to enter and leave through this one, as it is less conspicuous than the hole in the rock far above. My hips undulate, working my red to yellow to green gradient tail in smooth motions to keep me hovering in place while I tentatively peer through the kelp.

When I see that no other sirens are nearby, I dart out, traveling quickly to a valley between two smaller seamounts that reach up about halfway to the surface. I propel myself with the help of the current back towards home.

Home.

It is the only place I have ever known, yet I often wonder if perhaps I am not meant for this world. It feels like a volatile, dangerous place, and I've never once known what it is to fully relax here. I may have been raised in a palace of gorgeous coral and seashell, but my soul often feels like I am entering a battlefield with zero advantage every time I go near it. And if the palace is a battlefield, then the other sirens who reside there are split into two hugely unequal groups: the too-few allies and the many I have no chance of befriending.

A passing school of zanclus fish draws me out of my thoughts, and I dip my chin in thanks to their thin black and yellow striped bodies as they separate so I can swim up the middle of their grouping. While siren magic doesn't give us the ability to *speak* to the creatures of the sea, they do seem to know what our intentions are—good or bad. It is the way of all beings who inhabit the ocean, an instinctual understanding of not only the water we call home but the others who live here as well.

Some sirens have even made companions with different creatures. Like my sister Allegra, who managed to capture a delphinidae—the largest of its species and with a mean temperament that matches her own. With a sleek gray body and a long snout full of razor-sharp teeth, the delphinidae are nearly impossible to domesticate. Allegra had somehow not only *caught* her delphinidae, whom she named Mashaka, but she had also trained him to obey her every command. Together, they prowl these waters, ruthlessly striking fear into any and all who might challenge them or our queen.

There is no escaping what we are as sirens, what we are *forced* to become. It is beaten into us by words and decrees and sometimes by actual fists. In this queendom, compassion is a weakness and benignity a death sentence.

The miles that separate my secret cave from the capital city of Lumen are eaten up quickly with the current doing most of the work. Moving out of the valley and into more open waters, my eyes can't help but scan along the ocean floor. I doubt I'll find any new treasures this close to the city, but I still look on the off chance that I might. The ocean floor here is closer to the surface, the soft dark sediment of deeper waters turning to granular tan sand. Coral and anemones in tones of bright pink and sharp yellow dot along the sea bottom, interspersed between the bright green of the seaweed and deep red of the algae. Flowering enhalus plants dance in the undercurrent, their white and purple petals fanning open with the movement.

A deep thumping sounds in my ears as I see Lumen near. At first, I think it might be thunder from a storm overhead, but as I look up at the clear blue sky through the shimmering Spell, I realize it is the sound of my heart. My hands ball into loose fists, stopped short only by the sharp black talons that tip each of my fingers. *No one knows where I was. It is not abnormal for me to explore the ocean.* I remind myself over and over again.

The capital, Lumen, isn't the only city in our realm, but it is by far the largest and where the majority of sirens reside. Scattered around the outskirts of the

Continent are a few small towns and outposts, mostly there to serve as stopping points to rest on the journey north to the only land mass that is part of the Siren Queendom—the Northern Island.

Centered in Lumen is the palace where Queen Amari Malika and her five daughters live, as well as a menagerie of nobles and friends close to the Crown. Beautiful homes decorated in crushed pearlescent seashell and colorful sea glass surround the palace, lush plants and water flowers growing in between them. On the edge of the city live sirens who were unable to keep their homes in the chaos that occurred after the Spell was put into place, when they were labeled as traitors. They have carved homes into the inclines of the looming seamounts, the dwellings crude in comparison to the finery at the center of Lumen.

The shimmering veil that floats at the surface above has left our people more secluded than those above the water. Though I am much too young to know what life would have been like before the Spell separated the kingdoms, many sirens—my mother included—have vivid memories of sauntering down the streets of the lands above in their mortal forms. Those that remember tell their stories in bitter detail, loathing and longing both woven into their voices. I have never known a world where I can traverse another realm without dire consequences—and that includes the one I am currently swimming in.

I feel the eyes of the sirens in the seamounts as I advance past, their jewel-toned irises boring into me intensely, as if they can see down to my very soul. Perhaps they can. I am not like other sirens, and sometimes I feel it is very obvious exactly how *different* I am. If that were the case, however, my mother would have disposed of me long ago. Diving deeper towards the base of the mount, I watch a group of siren offspring playing in a small circle on the ocean floor.

The females here were skittish when I first arrived, but once they realized that I wanted to help them in the only way I could, most of them turned a blind eye to my visits. That doesn't mean there aren't a few that hate who and what I represent—the oppressive monarch that is forcing them to live in rudimentary caves instead of in the city like every other siren. But at least they don't try to hurt me for it.

"Aria!" The small shrill voice brings a smile to my face as the rest of the young sirens turn their colorful heads towards me.

"Hello, young ones. How are you all today?"

"We're playing naughts and crosses, and I have the most wins!" Tiana, a siren of eight, says. My knuckle gently brushes her cheek, making the dimpled smile there grow. Her hair is of similar color to mine, but where my reds are deep and rich in color, hers are bright with undertones of orange. They gleam beautifully against the soft dark brown of her skin.

"And you are playing fairly?" I ask with a mock serious tone and a lifted red brow.

She scoffs, crossing her little arms over the burnt orange scales on her chest. "I always play fair!"

"Not always! Yesterday you cheated!" I look over to the little female hovering above the ocean floor, her short yellow braids dangling above her ears. She watches me with wary eyes, a look that I'm not unfamiliar with. I force a smile to my face, hoping it conveys that, while I may live in the palace, I am not like the majority of those who reside there.

Tiana draws my attention back to her, her voice high-pitched as she asks, "Can you play one round with us?"

"No, I don't have—"

"Please? Please, Aria?" They all start to chant loudly, surrounding me with their excited voices.

"Okay, okay. Just one round." I don't have time for even that, but staring at these young sirens—forced to live in near isolation for things that are no fault of their own—temporarily quells the need to make sure I am at the palace with more than enough time. If I swim fast enough, one game shouldn't matter.

Except one game quickly turns into five.

"I really have to leave," I say, rising from the ocean floor. "But before I go, will you give these to your mothers? And anyone else who needs it." Reaching into my small satchel, I begin to pull out little bundles of gold coins wrapped in large blue kelp leaves. Each young siren eagerly lines up, the pouches barely in their palms before they are swimming away.

My anxiety builds as I race away from the seamounts, a line of more finely crafted homes appearing beneath me. The residences sparkle, their outsides made of coral, seashells, sea glass, and rock. Bright green seaweed and waxy-leafed waterweeds grow tall from the sand between them, providing a sense of privacy. Bathed in light, it's easy to see how Lumen got its meaning: "a glow in the dark." The city itself is an illuminated beacon.

My gaze is drawn back up towards the white palace ahead. There is a celebration tonight to honor the birth of my eldest sister. I swim high above the capital for as long as possible until I can no longer avoid my destination. Gliding through the water, I descend into the chaotic center of the main waterway that we use to traverse the city. Merchants line both sides, selling and bartering for goods. I think briefly about browsing the merchant stalls for *something* to gift Allegra, but

I might as well slap myself in the face instead. It's what she would do if I presented her with anything. Internally sighing, I pick up my pace, knowing that, though the party hasn't officially started yet, I can't afford to be one of the last ones there.

Water glides along the red scales that cover my breasts and sides, the shiny colorful crescent shapes going down and changing in color from yellow to green as they near the end of my tail. *Nearly there.* The grounds surrounding the palace are free of homes, instead filled with small hills of flowers, anemones, and coral reefs. I swim up to the palace entrance, meeting the members of the Queen's Legion that are guarding it.

"Well, well, well. Look who is late again," Sarina sneers at me. She looks menacing in the legion's armor, which is carved from the tritonelli seashell—the largest and thickest seashells in our ocean. A breastplate in sandy tones protects her front, while spiky shoulder plates connect it to a back piece. Horns made from white and brown striped conch shells stick out on the top of her helmet, giving her a deviant appearance. I will my face into neutrality, having to work at putting on the mask of indifference that seems to be ingrained in every other siren. Through the small opening of her helmet, Sarina's topaz eyes seem to glow as she lifts her lip in the smallest hint of a snarl.

I force my body to relax as I tell her to let me pass. Sarina doesn't move, and Hova, the other legionary guarding this post, rolls her eyes at my command. My heart flutters fast as I force myself to look down my nose at them. Silent moments slide by, and though I can't exactly sweat in my siren form, the anxiousness building within me makes me believe that I will be the first to do so. *Finally,* they both move out of the way, uncrossing their spears so I can pass under the arched doorway.

"Enjoy the party, *Your Highness,*" Hova deadpans. Sarina snorts, grumbling something quietly that I am happy I can't hear.

I focus on my breathing, relaxing each part of my body as I go farther into the glimmering white palace. *Jaw and shoulders relaxed, lips flat, spine straight, and attitude vicious.* Over and over, I repeat the instructions my sister Lyre taught me as I approach the large blue and purple sea glass door. A handful of legionaries glance at me quickly before turning their attention elsewhere.

Pushing the door open myself, I dart down a long hallway, the floor made of crushed seashells. It is open to the waters above, but only those given approval by the queen can swim within the palace itself. Stone pillars line either side, leading to corridors that branch off into various different rooms.

I swallow, the salty taste of the sea lingering in my mouth as I begin to pick up the low murmurs of voices beyond an opaque yellow sea glass door. Running through my list one last time, I roll my shoulders back and push through the door as though arriving at this exact moment was absolutely intentional. As if I decided to grace those here with my mere presence. Lyre had made me practice this cold face of apathy relentlessly, but I've never been the best at pretending and, somehow, the queen can always tell.

The throne room is brimming with sirens—all laughing and moving languidly about. They fill most of the space, their shiny scales sending small flares of light all over the chamber from how they reflect off the glowing crystals embedded in the walls. I brush past them all without a second glance as I make my way to the stone dais. The room is lavishly decorated, no corner left unadorned. Long strands of silky sea kelp painted with bioluminescent bacteria wrap around every pillar, glowing bright neon green and blue. Vines of red and orange are strung above me, their large yellow cup-shaped pondily flowers hanging heavily every few feet.

Despite the fact that I am one of the five daughters of Queen Amari, I am still expected to bow before my mother as if I was no better than someone born without a title. It's not the show of respect that bothers me; it's how she makes me feel like I'm doing it *wrong*. There is neither love nor regard freely given by my mother. I have to *earn* her affections by being as wicked as Allegra or as cunning as Sade, both sisters my mother favors feverishly above the rest of her offspring.

Queen Amari sits upon a wide throne of aged brown bones and decayed gray coral. Seashells in tan and yellow dot between the dead minerals, the only bit of color to be found not on the queen herself. The macabre mixture of the *extravagant* chair towers high into the water above, the sight of it making my stomach churn.

"Greetings, Your Majesty," I say, bowing deeply at the waist and keeping my gaze drawn down. Her dark purple tail fin whips back and forth harshly, disturbing the water and creating swirls of small bubbles. I stay bowed, my upper body completely still and my abdomen muscles straining, as I wait for her to release me. Though the revelry of the other sirens still sounds around me, I can now feel the heat of their gazes searing through my scales and skin.

Still, I remain submissive.

"You may rise now, Aria." Her voice, like all of our kind, is melodic though her tone is deeper—more amplified by the ancient power coursing through her and stronger than any other siren here. The hair rises on my arms as that magic washes over me in a sickly wave. "I'm so happy you decided to arrive, even if you are late. I must know, what took your attention so thoroughly that you nearly missed your eldest sister's birthday?"

It takes all my effort—all the training Lyre worked on with me in secret—to remain completely relaxed. To not show any weakness like a quivering lip or trembling fingers. I am right on time, the party having only just started. However, I can't say that. I can't question the queen or suggest that she is wrong in any way. So I dip my chin and draw my gaze down again.

"Nothing more important at all, Your Majesty. I simply lost track of time." I force the embarrassment from my cheeks as the chuckles of the partygoers behind me claw at my back. The foolish, weak youngest daughter of the siren queen, that's who I am to them.

But it is better than them all finding out the truth.

With a tap from her massive golden trident—each tip adorned with a large jagged cut diamond—my mother silences the crowd's ridiculing. I finally let my gaze rise again to meet her deep purple eyes, the color so dark it looks obsidian. Her thick black braids, each one embellished with gold beads stacked in various heights, writhe around her head like sea snakes. Her dark skin glows with the light of the neon sea kelp, making the gradient shades of purple on her scales stand out in stark contrast. Like all sirens, her form is supple and soft, giving the illusion of a gentle creature. It is part of how we lure others in. Yes, our magic makes it impossible for any males to resist, but being beautiful also calms victims. It makes them less afraid of us than they should be.

My mother smiles, her bright white teeth looking sinister as she flashes them at me.

"Do *try* to keep your mind under the surface where it belongs instead of in the clouds, yes?"

"Of course, Your Majesty. My apologies," I concede before movement draws my gaze to the space next to my mother. Allegra treads the water gracefully, her dark blue tail undulating like a predator lurking in the shadows. She watches my interaction with our mother hungrily. Deep sapphire eyes set within rich dark skin meet mine, her lips tugging up to the right in a sharp smirk. "Happy birthday, sister. May you be blessed by all the queens that have passed," I tell her. She narrows her eyes, her half smile dropping quickly.

"Today is a lovely day!" my mother shouts, lifting her trident high in the air as she raises both arms. While the words spoken are joyous, the underlying lilt is one of warning. I spot Lyre and my other sisters off to the side of the dais and swim their way quickly. The crowd turns rapt attention to their queen, all of them wide-eyed and eager for her words. With another tap of her trident, the yellow sea glass door I came through swings open. Every head turns to look, the room falling into complete silence. "Not only is it Allegra's birthday, but we have even *more* reason to celebrate."

A few of the party attendees bristle with movement as someone travels up the center aisle. I glance at my mother, and the feral glint in her eyes causes my stomach to bottom out. Whatever is about to happen, it makes my mother *happy*, and that means we are going to witness something horrific.

"My dear subjects, we have found a traitor in our midst."

Chapter Five

ARIA

THE CROWD COLLECTIVELY MURMURS as bodies move to give the middle aisle a wide berth, letting the supposed *traitor* through. A siren with dark green braids matching her emerald-colored eyes is led to the bottom of the dais, held up by two legionaries. Purple and blue mottles the light brown skin around one of her eyes, and blue-tinted blood trails from the corner of her lips.

Zahra.

She keeps her gaze down, but I'm not sure if it's out of respect or because she is too injured to fully tilt her head up.

With a tap of her garish trident, my mother silences the soft mumbling of onlookers. "My subjects, you know as your queen that I do *everything* possible to keep you safe." The crowd voices their agreement, some even clapping and cheering as they praise my mother. "And part of keeping you safe—of keeping this queendom thriving *despite* the limitations those on land have forced us to live with—is what we do with the males we capture."

My stomach revolts, my last meal threatening to come up before I squash the sensation down. The way of the sirens has always been to lure males of all species to us with our seductive song. Before the war, the custom was to release them after we used them for our purposes—to make offspring. Some would even forego their song altogether and simply ask the males if they wanted to have sex.

As an all-female race, we were *created* to be dependent on the other beings in this world to sustain our kind. Luring males had been easy before the Spell descended—or so I had heard—but things have changed since then. With the Spell in place, it limits the overall amount of people on the water. Along with that, our magic has grown weaker over time, taking more females to lure in a ship than ever before. There are even some who have lost their voice altogether. Those unlucky few have been forced to join the females that live in the seamounts, my mother deeming them all *unworthy*.

"Zahra is being accused of releasing a male instead of killing him, *as the decree I have given states.*" Sounds of condemnation ring out in the throne room, tiny bubbles lifting into the water from the crowd's energetic tail movements. Queen Amari smiles from where she's once more seated at her throne, her pointed canines glinting in the glow of the crystals. My gaze is drawn back to Zahra, her arms pulled tautly behind her. "I am a fair queen, am I not?"

Fair. Hardly a word I would ever use to describe the queendom I live in—*definitely* not one I would ever choose when referring to its ruler. The queen's *decree* forces all sirens to use our magic in horrifying ways.

Our eerie song immediately captures the mind of any male that hears the notes, and once under our influence, they are ours to command. Most draw their victims into the water, the magic within us giving the males the ability to survive under the surface when our lips seal with theirs. Holding them captive, we are told to sink until we reach a reasonable depth without the pressure killing them. There, we partially shift, our lower halves morphing into our mortal forms while our gills remain in place. Once the act is complete, we are supposed to break the kiss and watch as our magic fades. They can attempt to swim back to the surface, but none have ever survived the distance before they begin to drown. It's a cruel and barbaric tactic, and I've never truly understood why my mother has put it into place since crossing through the Spell equals their death anyway.

"Though I know many of you would disagree and opt that I kill Zahra right now for her indiscretions, I will instead offer her the chance to defend herself. To explain to her fellow sirens and her queen *why* she would defy my orders and risk our safety."

Zahra tries to straighten her spine as she half-heartedly attempts to tread the water. *Gods below—her tail.* My eyes hone in on the puncture wound near her hips that I hadn't noticed before. Blue blood trickles out of it at a steady pace, mixing with the water as it does. Siren magic has a small healing ability, enough to scab a cut quickly, but her wound must be large to still ooze with blood as it does.

I force my palms flat against my own scaled hips, my sharpened nails gently scraping them. Lyre settles in close to me, and from the corner of my eye, I can see her own mask frozen in place. Her lips are in a firm line, a bored expression shaping her lavender-colored eyes and brows.

Zahra bares her teeth, more blood spewing from her mouth as she speaks. "It is not true," she rasps slightly, her voice giving evidence to the pain she must be in. "I have not let a mortal man go."

A deep, sinister laugh booms from Queen Amari as she rises from the throne. Her voice trails off before she looks down her nose at Zahra. "I have another who says you have. Bring her in!" All of our heads turn to the back just as another female is led through the middle aisle though she remains free of any legionary's hold.

"Darya?" Zahra says quietly, shock widening her eyes as she stares at the female. *Her sister.* "What are you doing? What did you say?"

"I told Her Majesty the truth of what I saw last month. You, fucking that mortal man on the edge of the beach and then letting him go!"

Snickers of disgust and hissing sounds ring out, the mob moving closer to Zahra before the legionaries push them back with their spears. Commanders in the legion have smaller tridents fashioned after my mother's, while everyone else carries spears, both are made of different colored sea glass.

"What do you have to say to that, Zahra?" At the queen's words, everyone's eyes shift to the green-haired siren, waiting for her to confirm or deny. I'm not sure either answer will change her fate.

"It is true," she growls, hanging her head low as her body struggles to maintain its floating.

"You think the life of this mortal man is equal to ours?" my mother asks, her head tilting to the side. When her question goes unanswered, the legionaries pull back Zahra's arms more harshly, her grunt of pain causing a ringing in my ears.

"I think it's unfair to punish him for the crime of two hundred years ago. I think he did not *ask* to be a victim to our song, and therefore, he does not deserve to die for it." Faster than Zahra—let alone those holding her—can react, my mother darts down the dais and backhands her so severely that her head snaps to the side, the sound echoing out over the room.

"We are trapped down here, unable to enjoy the land we were promised, *because* of his kind. His ancestors, whether they be blood to that wretched king or not, started the war when they denied us what should have rightfully been ours. You dishonor our own past queens with your self-righteous pity on those who deserve *none*."

"*You* dishonor our ancestors by pursuing vengeance that you are not owed," Zahra says quietly—though the words might as well have been a scream with how they echo in the following silence. If there were *any* chance that my mother would let Zahra go with only a warning, something I have never seen happen, then those words changed the trajectory of her fate. The queen stares at Zahra, her hardened gaze relentless before she softens her features. Backing up, she turns to those gathered.

"Do you see the delusions she is under? To think that we should show *mercy* to the men who attacked us all those years ago? I was there! Where was *our* mercy?" Her voice booms off of the palace pillars and walls.

Zahra slumps between the guards, unable to hold herself up anymore.

"One day, this Spell will fall, and when it does, we will take what is ours. What should have *always* been ours. For we are beings of two worlds, something no other creature can say in Olymazi!" The crowd cheers, pumping their fists in the air and swimming around each other in chaotic swirls that temporarily cloud the space in bubbles. My mother revels in the way they lap up her words, in how they believe without a doubt that they are *owed* more than what they have. I don't know what to believe.

According to our history books, The War Of Five Kingdoms started when the Mortal Kingdom betrayed my grandmother and tricked her into thinking that they would make her daughter—my mother—their future queen, wed to their crown prince. Princess Amari Malika was only twenty-seven when the resulting war started, young by our standards with a siren's lifespan averaging three hundred and fifty years. Our aging slows down at twenty-two years, which means my mother was barely on the cusp of adulthood when she was forced to fight in the war caused by the Mortal Kingdom.

Queen Amari bangs her trident on the dais, the clanging sound resonating in the air and causing me to wince. The congregation stops their wild movements immediately, vicious eyes all turning to face the throne.

"Zahra, you are accused of treason by disobeying a direct order from your queen. You put this queendom at risk for your own selfish and misguided morals. You have been turned in by a witness to your crime, and thus, we have evidence to proceed with your punishment."

I count to ten, willing ice to fill my veins and begging with the gods to help keep my face neutral in the wake of what is to come.

"I am a fair queen, my dear subjects. I do not want to hinder you as they do above. I do not want to *take* from anyone that does not deserve it. I simply want what I was promised—what you beautiful beings and your ancestors were *promised!*" she bellows, her voice taking on a magical cadence though our abilities don't work on other sirens. I can *feel* the power of the queen as she delivers her final remarks. "And this betrayer"—she points to Zahra with her trident—"would risk you all in the name of saving a *mortal man*. Does that seem like someone we want in our midst?" The question is rhetorical, yet the crowd shouts out their answer all the same.

"No!"

"Is this someone we want near our precious offspring?"

"No!" their screams grow more frenzied. Though my gills draw water in for oxygen, I still feel my throat constrict.

"Is she someone who deserves to stay alive after her treachery?"

"No!"

"Allegra, come here." My sister moves down the dais and to our mother's side quickly, her delphinidae, Mashaka, right behind her. "As the future queen, I believe you should show everyone what we do to those who betray their own kind." Allegra's hungry smile somehow transforms to one of begrudging pity. She almost looks convincing too, like she really doesn't want to do this but knows she has to. As I struggle to keep my composure flat and unresponsive, Allegra battles to keep the murderous glee inside her from showing. Her only tell is the grip she has on her silver trident. The weapon, smaller than my mother's but larger than any of the commanders', seems to vibrate with her energy. Three opal gemstones lay flat across the front, while dark blue eelgrass is wrapped around the trident's long body, trailing off like fluttering ribbons at the end. An addition Allegra added on herself.

The legionaries holding Zahra swim out to her sides, extending her arms so that she resembles a cross. She manages to lift her head to look at my sister. The crowd surrounds Zahra in a crescent shape, their colorful hair floating all around them so at odds with the menacing darkness threatening this moment. Allegra casually swings her trident side to side as she stares Zahra down, her cold eyes unforgiving and calculating.

"I have no regrets about what I've done," Zahra heaves out between her teeth. "And you—"

My body jerks involuntarily when her words are cut off as the trident pierces her heart. Allegra drives it farther into her, the legionaries straining to keep their hold on Zahra from the force.

"Traitorous bitch," Allegra seethes before ripping the trident out, a squelching sound following. Blood eddies with the water, my eyes frozen on watching how slowly it blends in.

"Take her body and cast it off Tula Ledge. Let the creatures of the deep have her," my mother commands with a flick of her wrist. The legionaries turn, dragging Zahra's lifeless form behind them as they head to the door.

Mirth starts to sound again in the throne room, as if nothing happened at all. My mother swims back up the dais, taking her seat on her throne of bones and leaning back—completely at ease.

"Let's go," Lyre whispers as my other sisters who are floating next to us begin to disperse into the crowd.

A shriek cuts through the revelry, followed by a quieter grunt of pain. I scan the space, finding Allegra as she stares down at Darya, her trident pierced so deeply into the siren that none of the three prongs are visible above her body.

"What is the meaning of this?" Queen Amari asks casually, sounding *bored*.

"She waited weeks to tell us that her sister had betrayed us. She should have come right away, but instead, she chose a liar over the safety of her queendom. She deserves death as her sister did." Allegra yanks the trident from Darya's now dead body, smiling as Mashaka uses his bottle nose to poke at the dead siren's scales.

"A fair judgment, my daughter. Come now, everyone, the time for celebration is upon us!" Two more legionaries in seashell armor swim up to grab Darya's body, taking her quickly through the partygoers and out of the throne room.

Drums are brought out as well as conch shells and string instruments, and a band begins to play, the melody seductive and rhythmic. I shoot Lyre a quick look—one that says I'll meet her in my room in a little bit—before I pretend to mingle with the crowd.

No one attempts to talk with me, as everyone I pass either gives me space or stares at me like I'm the next one that will be called a traitor. What they don't understand is that I don't want to betray my mother or this queendom. I don't want to put anyone at risk or see anyone hurt.

Keeping my chin high as I swim towards the back of the room, I'm startled when Mashaka abruptly appears, his gray rubbery nose poking at my chest painfully as he lets out a high-pitched noise.

My heart leaps into my throat as I try, and fail, to get around the delphinidae. Panic tears at my insides knowing that if Allegra sees me trying to leave so soon, she'll force me to do something horrific to prove my loyalty to our mother—to *her*. Eyeing the door, I watch as a small group of sirens swims towards it. Knowing I have to time it perfectly, I feign moving to the left just as the group reaches the door. Mashaka falls for my bluff, and I immediately take off to the right, darting between sirens as I race towards the door.

He lets out a screeching noise, but *luckily*, I am able to squeeze through the door before it shuts, slamming it closed in front of Mashaka and holding it there until I hear his retreating squeaks of frustration. Relaxing my shoulders, I hastily proceed to my room, propelling myself through the winding, open tunnels connecting the floors of the palace.

While only those with royal blood are able to swim past the first floor—an ancient enchantment keeping them from doing so—I don't like being out of my room on my own at night time. I am not a beloved daughter of the queen, and Lyre is the only one of my sisters who is actively *kind* to me. The rest either view me as competition for the throne or ignore me completely.

I don't want the throne, nor do I even want to stay in the palace. What would it be like to not have to be a part of this world? To not have to pretend to be something so cruel? As I reach my room, a ruby-red jewel placed in the middle of the door, I wonder how much longer I can continue on before I turn into the very thing I'm afraid of.

Chapter Six

Rhea

I walk over to the windows in Flynn's sitting room and look down at the palace grounds outside. Set atop a small hill and surrounded by some of the biggest trees I have ever seen, the palace is nothing short of marvelous. Despite being three stories, it still *blends* into the surroundings. What I've seen so far of this kingdom is so vibrant, the plants and trees integrated into the structures and not merely pushed out of the way to make space for buildings. Even inside, multiple potted plants dot each corner—varieties which I've never seen before.

Flynn had brought me to his bedroom on the third floor before leaving to say goodbye to his sister as she embarks on a journey to the Shifter Kingdom. The sitting room is indeed very *princely* with its dark wood floors and rich-colored accents. A deep blue and gold oval rug lies in the middle of the space while two green couches face each other across it, a wooden table between them. To the right of where I stand, in front of a wall of windows and a sliding glass door that leads to a balcony, is a square table with four chairs. A bookcase stacked neatly with different tomes lines a wall to my left, a fireplace with a light wood mantel next to it. There's a door on the adjacent wall, one that must lead to Flynn's bedroom.

The whole space reminds me of him—elegant, unexpected, and confident. I'm angry that it even smells like him, and more than that, I hate that I'm comforted that it does. *Stupid, naive woman.*

It's everything my tower wasn't, and still, my body seems to feel the needles of confinement creeping in. I'm no longer locked in a prison—not even locked in this room—but it doesn't seem to matter as my lungs struggle to inhale deeply enough. Time creeps by while I'm lost in my thoughts before Flynn returns and I feel him come up behind me, my eyes shutting as I try to focus on taking a full breath.

"Rhea, please talk to me. Let me try to explain everything. I swear to you, I—"

"Just tell me," I insist, turning away from the window to face him.

His face falls before he drags a hand down it and gestures for me to take a seat on one of the couches. He doesn't join me, though, opting to stand.

"Four years ago, we felt a burst of magic come from the Mortal Kingdom. We had never felt magic radiate like that before and certainly would have never expected it from a kingdom that was supposed to be magicless." A line forms between my brows as I think his words over. I was unaware of any sort of event that might have caused such a thing, but of course, I wouldn't know unless Alexi or King Dolian told me. "It was you," he continues, adding to my confusion. "Four years ago, you used your magic on Bella to save her life, didn't you?"

I start to shake my head but stop short when I realize that he's right. It had been four years since that fateful night when Alexi had brought Bella to me and it was revealed to both of us that I had magic.

"I don't understand how you could have felt my magic from all the way in a different kingdom," I protest, digging my nails into my thighs. "Can you sense other mages' magic?"

"Yes. I can feel their magical *signature*. It's like a slight vibration in the air when they are near."

"But I wasn't *near*," I emphasize.

"No, you weren't, but it was you, Rhea. Your magic—it's *strong*."

Something about those words makes my panic flare higher, coursing through my veins with icy trepidation. The dark, ancient otherness inside of me swirls as if at attention.

"You're wrong. I may somehow be a mage and have magic, but I'm not strong with it. I'm not strong at anything." The idea that I had yet another thing that made me stand out amongst everyone else, another *flaw*, is a burden I don't want to bear. There is already *so much* stacked upon me, waiting to crush me with one false move, how can I possibly add anything else? How can I *survive* anything more?

Flynn's eyes soften when he recognizes the fear roiling in my own. He takes a step towards me and then kneels on one leg, both of his hands resting tentatively on my knees. "Rhea, it *is* you. I can sense you. My parents can sense you. And your strength"—he drops his voice low, tilting his chin down slightly—"is something I admire about you. It's one of the reasons I love you. That you haven't allowed the things that would normally cripple anyone else to do the same to you. Your strength has very little to do with your magic and everything to do with what is in here." One of his hands lifts and comes to rest above my heart.

My breath catches, the trickle of air I'm able to get in barely reaching the depths of my burning lungs. My heart pumps wildly under his palm, but he keeps his hand there as if he can *will* me to believe him. "Then what happened?" I ask, looking away from him.

Flynn removes his touch before standing and taking a seat next to me on the couch.

"Then, I volunteered to go to the Mortal Kingdom to search for that magical pulse. To see if it was something we needed to prepare for."

"Your parents didn't object to you going?" I ask, knowing how it feels to watch someone I love leave. I wonder if leaving me would be as easy for him to do. If perhaps that is something he is planning.

"Oh, they did," he answers, a small amount of amusement in his voice. "But they didn't have a choice. I was going to go whether they liked it or not. My kingdom was the most important thing to me at the time."

"Was? What is the most important thing to you now?"

"You are, Sunshine. Only you. I would—" He pauses, swallowing as he turns to face me fully. "I would do *anything* for you."

I close my eyes, forcing warm tears to escape from their corners. "Except tell me the whole truth." When my eyes open again, they meet his, and it's like two shooting stars colliding in the night sky—the explosion is both brilliant and devastating. "Why didn't you tell me *everything*?"

"I wanted to wait to tell you until we arrived here. I was hoping that if you saw what I was protecting—where I had come from— you would understand my need to hold on to more secrets." The words come out rushed, a sharp inhale following them.

Swallowing is difficult as my gaze searches his, looking for the lies between his words—for a false truth. But all that is there is that unrelenting devotion.

"I didn't tell you I was the crown prince or that I was pretending to be mortal because I didn't want to scare you. I hated the idea that you would think that all this is, all *we* are, is a mission. That you are some *thing* to be captured or taken back to a different prison. I swear to you, Rhea, the moment I realized you were the magic we felt, my plans changed. I was going to leave you alone and come back home."

Gods, I do believe him. My foolish shattered heart beats harshly to each word he says like he's the lifeline to my soul.

"So you knew the whole time that I had magic?" I ask.

He nods slowly, his shoulders rounding as the tension in the room thickens. I think about how, when I used my magic for the first time, he hadn't looked surprised or shocked. How he had coaxed me to call it back in with language that—looking back now—clearly spoke to his familiarity with how magic is wielded. He never got angry with me for hiding it from him because he knew it was there all along. *And because he was hiding secrets of his own.*

Like arrows firing off in my mind, each thought stabs into me with ferocity. I'm so shocked and angry by what he hid from me, but I'm also deeply and overwhelmingly in love with him. How is it possible to be entirely encompassed by that love and still hurt like I do? How can I look at Flynn and know that he's lied about so much and still feel like there is no one else that my heart is ever supposed to belong to?

Flynn shifts on the couch, closer than before but still not touching me. Just like how he used to visit me in the beginning, always so conscious of my wariness around touch. "You have every right to be angry with me," he says softly, halting my scattered thoughts. "I will spend every godsdamn second on my knees for you, begging for your forgiveness, if that's what it takes."

For some inexplicable reason, my heart beats faster at the imagined scenario. As if sensing it, Flynn's pupils widen, heat and desire fusing within them as we look at each other. *Focus, Rhea.*

"What is your real name?" I ask with a breathy whisper, trying to calm the baffling flutters in my chest. "I don't know what to call you." The cold reality of that truth douses the flames that had begun to spark. The past months I've gotten to know *Flynn*. There is no other name that I could possibly think of to call him by.

"The only thing I want you to call me is *yours*, Sunshine," he says, his voice low. That tension between us begins to shift, but doubt still lingers like a chill in the air. "But my full name is Nox Flynn Daxel."

So Flynn is his middle name, then. I do find relief in that revelation. Maybe we could try to start over. We could try to rebuild our foundation from a place of total honesty instead of a mashup of broken truths. Perhaps here in a new kingdom, where freedom is something we both now have, we can truly discover what it is to be with each other. In all aspects.

"I do have something else I need to tell you." The heat previously in his eyes dwindles until it's replaced with an emotion I never thought I would see from him. One that makes the apprehension building a ravine between us wider.

Fear.

Chapter Seven

RHEA

"What is it?" I ask quietly, afraid to move. Flynn has never looked at me like this before, like I might actually break from what he's going to say. "Flynn, what is it?"

He swallows, slowly running a hand through his hair as he says, "When I came to the Mortal Kingdom, I could feel that the magic was coming from somewhere in the castle. It's how I knew to enlist in the King's Guard—so that I could have more access to search." His fingers tap his knee in a staccato pattern as he takes a deep breath before continuing. "Moving up through the ranks was an incredibly slow process. King Dolian was paranoid about who he allowed to be in the guard for the castle, even more so when it came to which ones would get near you. After nearly four years, I had narrowed down that the magic was coming from the tower specifically, but I couldn't get anywhere near it without raising suspicions. I needed a way in."

Dread begins to prickle over my skin as my magic coils tightly within me, poising to strike, but the only threat is what Flynn will say next.

"You have to understand. I was *desperate*. Four years of pretending to be someone I wasn't had slowly chipped away at me. I wanted to keep my people safe, and in order to do that, I needed to get into the tower and figure out what the king had that was emitting so much magic. I needed answers so that I could *finally leave*."

"What did you do?" I ask, but it's not really a question so much as an accusation. And Flynn doesn't miss the connotation in my words.

"I began to spy on the guards for your tower. To see if there was a weakness I could exploit to get inside," he says, the cadence of his voice laced with regret.

A fear I had never even thought to consider begins to take root within me. The words are said a bit harsher when I again ask, "What did you *do*?"

"I noticed that Alexi would often leave his post in the middle of the night. He'd go into the tower for about an hour and then come back out. A few times a week he would do this, but you already know that."

My mouth parts as breathing becomes difficult again. Blood rushes into my ears, my throat constricting like the very grip of *death* is on it, squeezing until there's nothing of me left.

"Please, tell me you didn't," I whisper, forcing my gaze to stay on his. Begging, *begging* to be wrong in my assumption of what he is going to say next. *Please, no.*

"I knew King Dolian wouldn't tolerate a guard, no matter how tenured they were, leaving their post for any length of time. Anyone who paid attention could see that he was obsessed with you, and—"

"No." That single word is all I can manage between the tight pains in my chest.

"I reported to my commander that I had witnessed Alexi leaving his post—"

"No," I whisper again, shaking my head vehemently. As if doing so will reverse time and make Flynn's words untrue.

"And he started observing him too, until—"

"No!" My hands dig into my hair as I stand and begin to pace in front of the couch.

"I didn't know that my actions would lead to his death, and that is a regret I have carried with me since I learned who Alexi was to you," he insists, his voice a shaky murmur as he stands. "*I didn't know.* You have to believe me when I say that. Please, tell me you believe me." I hear his words, but they do not resonate.

"You—you *lied* to me!" The imaginary shields and walls I built for my own mental and emotional protection crumble completely, leaving raw turmoil to devour me fully in their wake.

Memories of the night of my failed escape—when Flynn confessed his feelings for me—come to the forefront of my mind. He had said those things *knowing* what he had done. To Alexi. *To me.*

I never want you to doubt anything when it comes to me.

"You let me fall in love with you knowing that *your* actions led to his *death!*" I scream.

The truth is, I find you so captivating...

"You consumed me, as if I was nothing more than fuel to your fire, and I—" I fall to my knees as the ringing in my ears intensifies. My body *aches* with this betrayal, and my magic within me hums coldly in response.

The truth is that when I look at you, it's like peering into a blazing sun.

"Rhea, *please*," Flynn begs.

The truth is, I feel that there is no limit to the things I would do for you...

Lies. Lies. Lies. *Lies.*

Looking up at him—his eyes red and filled with anguish—I let my anger power my next words. "I *burned* for you, and now, all that's left of me is ashes at your feet. I don't want your words, *Flynn.* They mean *nothing* to me now."

He stills, looking more pained than when a sword was driven through him. Dark, foreboding power explodes from my heart and down my arms and fingers, the icy tingling unstoppable as I scream and scream *and scream.* Distantly, I'm aware that Flynn is kneeling before me, but it is like someone has placed a dark veil over my eyes. All I see is infinite inky black. Sounds echo around me as the world shakes, and I hover over my knees.

"Rhea!" He shouts my name, but it sounds so muffled—so far away. How could we ever move past this? He used Alexi as nothing more than an opportunity—a pawn in a game neither of us asked to be a part of.

I love Flynn with everything that I am—every *single* shattered part of me. Even now, I can still feel that love trying to prod its way through the swirling oppressive *nothingness.*

But I don't know if it's enough anymore. And that realization... It fully wakes whatever that dark beast inside of me is. My body feels completely numb, my heart a frozen chamber hidden behind more layers of ice than ever before. I am no longer Rhea Maxwell; instead, I am whatever this pain that dwells within molds me to be. Hadn't that always been the case anyway?

I hand over control to my magic and sink down deep within myself. While I cower in a corner of my mind, the consuming darkness wraps its icy, sharp talons around me. The screaming continues, but I can't tell if it is me or Flynn.

"Hello, Rhea."

My eyes flutter open at the sound of her voice. Her ethereal cadence instantly calms my heavily beating heart. I hadn't been to this place—the Middle—since I had nearly drowned in the river.

"That was a terrifying day indeed," she says softly, as if speaking the words too loudly will make the memory of the ice water filling my lungs real again.

Coming up onto my elbows, my head tilts back as I search the sky, but it's like shadows are obscuring my view. The stars and galaxies of blazing color I've become used to seeing here are muted, distorted. When I don't answer her—knowing she can either read my mind or hear my thoughts—she sighs.

"You have expelled some of your other *magic," she says, causing me to jerk as I look around for her.*

Able to sit up fully, while simultaneously floating in this space, I turn around in all directions, but I see nothing but those half-lit dots and swirls of light. "What do you mean other *magic?" I whisper, looking down at my hands.*

"There are two halves to your magic. Now that you are somewhere safe, you need to learn how to wield both, and he can teach you."

"Safe," I say with a scoff, shaking my head as I hug my knees to my chest. "I am not safe there." A gentle breeze laced with the scent of jasmine caresses me, the feeling like a tickling of fingers on my shoulders. "I don't want him to teach me anything else—not anymore." The words taste bitter as they leave my mouth, but I pretend that I believe them anyway.

"He loves you. Even those not of this world can see it. Feel it."

"You do not lie to the people you love! Not about something like that."

"Sometimes, even with the best of intentions, we end up hurting the people we care for most." There's a sadness to her voice, heavy even in this wide expanse of space. "Did you not lie to him as well?"

"That's different. I had to lie. I had to protect myself."

"Hmm. And what do you think he was doing?" she asks.

My fingers curl in on themselves, anger rapidly replacing any moment of reprieve I had from my spiraling thoughts. "He knew he was a part of Alexi's death, no matter how unintentional it was, and he didn't tell me! That only protects himself from my anger; nothing more."

"He **was** afraid. Certainly, you can relate to that. He speaks true about his remorse. His regret."

"And yet that cannot bring Alexi back," I seethe, the universe around me going even darker than it was before. I sigh, rubbing my hand over my chest.

There was a part of me that had hoped a future with Flynn meant leaving behind the pieces of myself that were damaged. As if I could sort through my fractured memories and that pitiful existence in the tower and handpick the things I wanted to bring with me to this new life. I realize now that this might have been my biggest dream of all: not escaping the tower or hoping to find love or a family, but pretending that I could sift through the mess that I was and find enough parts of myself that I felt were worthy of something better.

"Unfortunately, there is no locking up and simply forgetting about the experiences that we'd rather not relive. Each event and memory and story you have—good and bad—makes up who you are, Rhea. Like threads on a tapestry, they weave together to form a larger picture of the person you will become. But only *you* can choose how you will let them define you."

I huff another breath, playing with the ends of my hair. "So many nights I had looked up to the stars and wished with all my might that I could be free. Free to leave the tower. Free to make my own choices. Free to fall in love. Free to live a life for myself."

"I know," she says softly.

"What if being here—being with him—isn't the freedom I thought it would be? I already feel like everything between us is untrue."

"But was it not your plan to leave? If he had told you all of these things upon your first meeting, would you still have gotten to know him? Still gone east with him?"

"I—" I stumble over my response because I don't know. *If I had learned everything about who Flynn was and all the secrets he had kept, would we have been able to work through it? He was persistent in the beginning—showing up and making sure that I knew he was thinking about me. Was that truly just him, or was he still trying to piece together why he could sense magic coming from me? I feel like I have to question everything between us now. How can he possibly love me without motive when he didn't love me enough to tell the truth? When I don't even love myse—*

"Rhea," she interrupts. The feeling of something warm settles over me like a comforting hug. Inside, however, I'm still numb. Frozen. "You are suffering. You have been for a long time."

"Yes, well, I'm not sure what you are aware of from this magical world in which you exist, but my life only ever afforded me the opportunity to suffer." I was stunted in every way that made a person, well, a person. I was denied everything I lusted after until—

"Until he came into your life. And he saw who you truly are."

I stay silent, unsure of what to say to that. The woman, her voice still achingly familiar to me in a way that I don't understand, chuckles.

"It is true that he lied to you by hiding things. Not a move I would have used, personally, to woo someone. But sometimes, men can be quite dense."

A shocked laugh scrapes out of me as I, again, look around. "Unfortunately, my experience in that area is basically nonexistent," I say though I suppose she already knows that. Wait... "Can—can you see what I do on Olymazi?"

"I can."

I cringe, thinking about all of the intimate moments I shared with Flynn.

"You needn't worry about that. I can block things from my view at any time."

"Am I the only one you can speak with?"

Steady and calm moments pass before she replies. "I'm afraid that I cannot tell you that."

"Why can't I see you?" I ask, the flickering of the stars above me brighter than before.

"Because of a deal I made a long time ago. Not being able to show my face is the price I pay for being able to share my voice."

"I do remember you saying that before," I answer, extending my legs out in front of me as I lean back on my hands. Silence falls between us—one that feels far too easy to share with this stranger who is not quite a stranger. The breeze around me begins to pick up, the tendrils of hair loosened from my braid snapping against my cheeks. "I'm not ready to leave. I can't— I don't know if I can face him. After learning everything, I don't know if we can fix this."

She hums as sparkling stardust floats in front of me.

"Can't I stay here for a little longer?"

"This is not supposed to be a place for you to linger," she responds, firm but not unkind.

"Please." The word is a heartbroken plea, a desperate attempt to try and stay in the one existence that hasn't shown me any pain or heartbreak.

The woman sighs though the sound isn't one of annoyance. It is more resigned, as if she had known this was going to happen. "Rest here for a little while, Rhea. And then you will have to return."

I nod my head, lying down on my side and curling in on myself. And though I know I am not in the world of Olymazi anymore, and that she cannot reach me here, I still wait for my white fox to settle in next to me. But Bella never comes.

She is dead because of me.

Chapter Eight

Bahira

"It's well over the hour mark," King Kai growls, holding my trunk as we make our way to the rowboat at the edge of the water.

I ignore him, my gaze steadily fixed on the expanse of ocean in front of me. The lapping deep blue waves move in rocking motions, the sunlight sparkling off of the Spell lying at the water's surface.

The king sets the heavy chest down in the middle of the long wooden boat, his arms folding over his chest as he faces me. Rolling my eyes, I turn to glance over my shoulder one last time, meeting the stare of my mother and then my father through the Spell. He tilts his lips up, quickly nodding his head in a show of support that squeezes around my heart. I dip my chin in response, the breeze blowing off the water moving my curly hair wildly about my face. Finally, my gaze falls to Daje. His hands rest at his sides, his face contorted into a concerned grimace as our eyes meet.

"You'll see your boyfriend in three months. We need to go now."

Slowly, hoping it will piss him off, I turn back around and face the annoying male. Tua walks to the opposite side of the boat and leans down to grab its edge, waiting for his king to do the same. King Kai just stands there instead, his towering frame incredibly imposing even with the entire ocean behind him. Still, a sharp thrill runs through me at the thought of riling him up. So I again ignore him and walk up to the vessel, leaning down to grip it as I raise an eyebrow at him in question.

Grumbling under his breath, King Kai turns around and grabs the boat roughly, his strength causing it to tip his way. He looks as if he could carry the entire damn thing by himself. I let my eyes roam over the width of his shoulders and the way his muscles bulge and flex with his movements.

Once we are far enough away from the shore that the rowboat is somewhat floating, Tua and King Kai hold it steady so that I can get in. My abdominal muscles flex as I try to balance myself while the craft rocks steadily side to side from my weight. Once it evens out, the king and Tua step in, each grabbing an oar and pushing us the rest of the way off the sandy embankment and fully into the water. I peer over the edge as they row, looking down through the thick layer of the Spell that extends a few feet beneath the water's surface.

The king looks over his shoulder at me, studying my face and then moving up to my hair where he lingers before focusing on a point above my head.

"What?" I snap, folding my arms over my chest.

"I'm just curious if you know how to use that spear. And I'm wondering why you brought it at all." The boat rocks slightly, poor Tua doing all the work of rowing us while the king asks stupid fucking questions.

"Is it against some sort of shifter custom for a visitor to bring a beloved gift with them when they travel?" I ask, grinning when I see his hands tighten around the dark wooden handle of the oar.

"Of course not. Bring whatever gift you want. Though it would be a foolish thing to advertise if you don't know how to wield it, *Princess*."

That thrill within me at riling him up sparks brighter—fiercer—as I lean forward, planting my hands on the bench in front of me. "Keep offering up unwanted, idiotic advice, and perhaps you will find out, *Your Majesty*."

The king observes me for a moment longer, wicked amusement sparkling in his dark brown eyes, before he makes a noise of derision and turns back around. Tua laughs quietly as the rowboat finally nears the hull of the ship.

It is so much larger up close, towering many stories above me while its white sails loosely flutter in the wind. My head cranks back even farther as I try to take in the ship fully. Masts loom tall from its center, built from a light brown wood.

Tua and King Kai guide the rowboat up to the side of the ship, near where a rope ladder is now hanging flanked by two single ropes. My thoughts run wild as I look at my trunk, wondering how in the world I'll be able to climb the ladder while holding it.

Seeing my unvoiced question, Tua grabs one of the ropes hanging from the ship and begins to loop it through a metal eye hook sticking out of the top edge of the rowboat. "We'll attach the ropes to the boat for them to haul up, and then we'll climb the ladder."

I give him a genuine smile as I nod my thanks for his explanation. King Kai sees the entire exchange and decides to add another tally to the total I'm keeping in my head of things he says that make me want to punch him.

"Worried all your pretty dresses might get ruined?"

"Prick," I mumble under my breath as I check to make sure my spear is secure on my pack before moving to stand closer to the ladder. My shoulder hits against his arm as I pass, eliciting a dark chuckle from him. When Tua tells me that it's safe to climb, I begin the ascent to the deck of the ship.

When I was a child, I was terrified of heights. For a young girl who already felt like the world's biggest target, I decided that I would make sure there was one less thing that the other children could pick on me for. Near the palace is a hidden garden only accessible from the third floor, where my room and Nox's room are. Deep within that garden, anchored at its center, is an ancient banya tree. Its trunk sprouts out into many smaller limbs, growing wildly up towards the sky in wide arcs. Every day as a child, I would go to the garden and climb that tree as high as I could until my fear took over and I could move no farther. It took hours of climbing—weeks of digging my nails into the bark to stave off a panic attack—so that I could then climb my way back down. Finally, I reached the highest point of the banya tree and was able to look down at the kingdom from a place of conquered fear.

Now as I climb the side of the massive ship, the rope ladder feeling far too flimsy for my weight, I wonder how much longer I will have to fight my inadequacies before I am rewarded with my magic. It also doesn't elude me that the shifter king might not be aware that I do not possess any magic at all, and that may prove to be problematic. Grinding my teeth together, I place my foot on the next rung and push up, reaching my hand above me when a crack sounds and my foot falls. I yelp, my left hand holding the side rope of the ladder while my right barely misses the rung I was reaching for. My grip tightens on the rope as I slide down, a burning sensation flaring to life in my palm as my right hand finally grips onto a lower rung to stop my fall.

Shouts from the males above and below rend the air as my feet dangle beneath me. My heart pounds against my ribcage as I struggle to find purchase on a rung below the broken one. I force a deep breath into my tight chest and nearly scream when a hand guides my foot to an unbroken step of the ladder. A moment later, the scent of sandalwood and citrus envelops me in addition to the chiseled muscles of a large male.

"Careful, Princess." His deep voice rumbles against my back. When I don't respond, he gives a mocking laugh. "I could carry you the rest of the way if you're too frightened to go on alone."

"I'd rather fall to my death," I hiss, beginning to climb again as his laughter trails behind me. The pain in my hand stings with every movement as blood streaks along the rope.

I feel King Kai's eyes on me the rest of the way up the long ladder like a heavy wool cloak under the intense sun. When I finally reach the deck, helped over by a short male with black hair and amber eyes, sweat beads at my temples and a full throbbing ache has started radiating in both wrists. With my gaze on my shredded palm as I step forward, I don't see the animal in front of me until it's too late. My sandaled foot steps onto the toes of a black and silver *gorilla*. It growls, the sound vibrating the wooden planks of the deck beneath me and making the hair on my arms rise.

"Shit!" I screech as the gorilla slowly turns its head towards me; its golden eyes lock onto my own as I take a step back. I expect it to bare its teeth at me or, at the very least, fully face me and prepare to attack. Yet, after a few more seconds of intently studying me, the gorilla simply turns and leaves. I release a breath, folding my arms over my chest and focusing on slowing my racing heart.

Looking around the deck of the ship, there aren't nearly as many shifters aboard as I thought there might be. There are a handful in their animal forms including a jaguar, a small black bear, and a snake. I wonder if all the other males in their mortal forms will shift once we prepare to leave—so that they aren't susceptible to the sirens' song should we be attacked. And if they do shift, who will steer the boat?

"Bahira, your finery has made it safe and sound."

Plastering on what could barely be called a smile, I turn to face King Kai. My façade morphs to horror as I watch him drop the trunk onto the deck with a sickening thud. All I can think about is my magnifier lying within and the glass bottle holding the experimental leaves I still needed to study. Not to mention the *ancient* journals with magic that may falter and not keep them protected. Outside noises fade away, replaced by a ringing in my ears. My vision goes red, and before I realize what I'm doing, my feet are closing the distance to the shifter king.

His infuriating smirk wobbles as I near, but he makes no move to defend himself from the fist I send crashing into his jaw. Immediately, the hands of several males are on me, pulling my arms behind my back.

"I will only give you one warning. Get your hands off of me, or you'll find out what it feels like to be *without them*."

Their grips only tighten, one of them squeezing my injured wrists so tightly that I hiss out in pain.

"Release her," the king commands, his hand massaging his broad jaw as his dark eyes lock on to mine. When the crew doesn't obey, King Kai's eyes change colors to a molten amber for the briefest of moments before he steps forward and looks behind me. "I said, *release her*," he growls deep in his throat.

They finally listen, and I immediately move to grab the trunk, my biceps bulging and hands stinging as I lift it up to my chest. The king extends his hands out to help me, but I twist to move out of his grasp. His eyes narrow as they find mine, while my lips lift into a sneer.

"If you touch anything of mine again, I will make you *beg* for mercy." Our eyes hold while something rough and jagged forms between us.

Tua moves from behind the king, gently placing a hand on his shoulder—which is immediately shaken off—before King Kai turns on his heel and walks towards the front of the ship. Tua offers to help with the trunk which I promptly refuse.

"I can at least show you to your room if you'd like," he offers.

I nod, feeling some of the tension ease at the sound of his voice. His smile is real, if a little tight, as he leads me past the glaring men who held my arms behind me. I hold their gazes, pouring my anger into it until I've walked past them.

"I am sorry about them," Tua says, voice low, as we head in the direction King Kai went. "They were simply protecting their king."

I don't respond as Tua leads us past the helm and down a set of stairs off to the right. The steps creak with our weight, and I follow him to the first landing, where he continues down a long hallway. Flame gems in hanging glass sconces line the otherwise-dim space, no windows anywhere to let in natural light.

"Your room is the last one on the right," Tua says as he reaches the door and opens it.

The hinges creak, and though I didn't exactly know *what* to expect upon entering this room, it certainly isn't this. Lush, exotic plants hang from the rafters above and line the sill of the small square window that lets the bright afternoon sunlight in. The entire room—floors, wall, and ceiling—is made from red-hued wood. On one side of the room is a large bed, framed with the same wood on the head and footboards. Light blue linens are pulled taut across it.

"We should be raising anchor at any moment. The evening meal is served as the sun is setting. I can meet you on deck to show you to the dining hall if you would like, Your Highness?" Tua asks, clasping his hands in front of him as he lingers by the door.

"Sure, that would be great. Thank you, Tua. And it's just Bahira." I turn to look at him, to nod my head in thanks, and find that he is already studying me with an amused grin.

"Of course. There's a pitcher of fresh water and some light food on the table there," he says, gesturing to a small cabinet next to the bed. "If you need anything else, head to the deck. Otherwise, I'll see you later." Tua shuts the door quietly as he leaves.

I pour myself some of the water, gulping it down before walking over to the small window to look out onto the ocean below. I can't explain the feeling that is bubbling up in my chest the longer I watch the soft rolling waves, the Spell lying atop the water shimmering with the movement. Apprehension, yes, but perhaps dread too. Lingering anger for the shifter king is most definitely present as well, but there is also a feeling of curiosity and *excitement* and... hope.

As the ship turns slowly and the border of the Mage Kingdom comes back into view, I close my eyes and take a deep breath.

Hope. That, perhaps, is the most unnerving feeling of all.

Chapter Nine

BAHIRA

WATCHING THE SKY SLOWLY morph to bright pink and orange with the setting sun, I get ready to meet Tua on the deck. To say I have been avoiding going out because I don't want to see King Kai again is only a partial truth. The full reason is because I am *uneasy* being here, and I recognize that I did not make the best impression with the shifters above when I assaulted their king.

My stomach twists in on itself.

With shaky legs, I clear my throat and walk to the door. It creaks loudly, making my shoulders rise towards my ears, and after stepping into the hallway, I freeze when a particularly strong round of nausea barrels into me. Leaning against the doorframe, I close my eyes and try to take deep breaths through my nose.

"The unshakable princess appears to be uneasy on the water." *Fuck me.* His powerful voice fills the hallway and makes my stomach clench again in response.

My hand goes to my lips as I swallow roughly. "How do you know it isn't just your presence that makes me feel sick?" I weakly retort as saliva starts to pool in my mouth. His chuckle skitters along my skin, making goosebumps rise in its wake.

"I make females feel many things when they are with me, but sickness has never been one of them," he taunts.

That does get me to open my eyes as I stare at him incredulously. He leans on the door across the hall and down a little from mine, his large arms crossed over his chest. The black lines of his tattoo stand out in the golden light pouring from the flame gems. He's changed, wearing a short-sleeved black tunic and dark green trousers that tuck into well-worn calf-high brown leather boots. He's impossibly muscular—every single *inch* of him strains against the confines of his clothing. It isn't until my eyes make their way back to his that I remember what he said.

"For both of our sakes, I'm going to pretend you didn't say that."

"You can try."

My eyes narrow, and I'm about to tell him that I would prefer it if he jumped off the ship and into the churning waters below, when I'm forced to turn and sprint to the bathroom. His laughter follows me as the battle against keeping the food *in* my stomach is lost.

When I finally feel well enough to walk up the stairs and onto the deck, it's mostly empty, only a few males at the helm talking—one of them had held my hands behind my back after I punched his king. Their eyes immediately shift to mine as I walk past them, a low growl dancing in the space between us. I keep walking, my shoulders rolled back and spine as straight as I can make it while the weight of their stares follows me across the deck.

My hands latch on to the rail on the edge of the ship to steady myself as I stare out over the vast water. Under the colors of the setting sun, the ocean takes on a teal hue.

"I was worried that perhaps you had gotten lost," Tua jokes as he steps up to me, running a hand over his short hair. "It is a big ship, after all."

I snort though the sound makes my raw throat feel worse. "Not lost. Just sick," I scrape out.

"It can take a few days to feel comfortable on the sea."

"And by then, we will already be on the island," I counter, enjoying how the cool breeze coming off of the water feels on my clammy skin.

"Indeed."

Although a comfortable silence settles between us, uncertainty twists within me at not knowing much about the kingdom I am going to. I have learned the basics from the records that had been kept by mages up until the Spell was put into place. Everything written after that time is either repeating what we already know or merely speculation. Relations were obviously strained when the Spell was cast during the war, but making it a death sentence to cross into another kingdom hadn't done any favors with repairing them. Of course, mages are exempt from the effects of the Spell—a fact King Kai *somehow* knows. I wonder how hard it will be to pry from him how he found out. In any case, I need something—*anything*—that might help me feel like I am not so unprepared to step foot in a foreign land.

"I do have a question," I say finally, looking at Tua. He moves and faces me, keeping one hand on the rail as the other goes to his hip. "What can you tell me about life on the shifter isle? Anything I should be aware of?" I watch Tua as he chews on the inside of his cheek, debating his answer.

"It is a beautiful island. I'm sure everyone thinks that of their own home, but ours truly feels like paradise. Most of the people are kind—helpful towards each other. There is unrest on the island though," he says slowly. My brows furrow as I move a few strands of curly windblown hair out of the way.

"Kai—His Majesty—hasn't been king long, and many are not happy that he was crowned as his father's successor. There is a small but growing group who want to see another replace him as king."

I study the king's advisor—his tense shoulders and tight grip on the railing. Unrest in one's own kingdom seems like it should be an impossibility in the wake of a post-war world. Maybe that is naive of me to think, especially coming from a kingdom where peace has always been something to strive towards—not actively hinder. Tua finally looks my way, his brows shooting up as he sees whatever look I've contorted my face into.

"You needn't worry, Your Highness. You will be staying on the palace grounds where it is safe," he says, mistaking my contemplation of the situation for fear.

"I'm not worried about my safety, Tua, though I appreciate the reassurance. I am just thinking about how different it will be to stay somewhere that isn't happy with their appointed ruler." And based on my—admittedly little—knowledge of the king so far, I'm not exactly sure I blame them. "And again, please call me Bahira."

His smile grows wide, the sun-kissed skin around his eyes crinkling with the movement. "Yes. Something tells me you can take care of yourself, Your H—Bahira."

I laugh, some of that pressure easing from my chest. When our voices dwindle, the only sound again is that of the ocean below, another thought unburies itself. "Who else knows that I am both princess and mage?" Tua looks at me, reading my face once more, and nods his head gently at the words I'm not saying: *who else will know that mages can walk through the Spell?*

"Only His Majesty and I know you are the mage princess. This is a bare bones crew, exactly what is needed to operate the ship, and I've handpicked them all because of their loyalty. So besides them and myself, only the king is aware that mages can pass through the Spell."

"And how *did* His Majesty become aware of a secret such as that?" I ask, tilting my head to the side.

Tua blows out another long sigh, avoiding my eyes as he speaks. "I'm afraid that is something you'll have to learn from King Kai himself."

Great. "And the magical blight affecting your island?"

His lips twitch. "Better seen firsthand."

I snort, turning to face the water again. "Okay, what about this: are you related to King Kai?"

Tua chuckles. "That I am. His father was my eldest brother."

"And were you *his* advisor as well?" I ask as footsteps sound on the deck behind us.

"I was." It's all he says before he turns away and bows deeply.

"I told you not to do that," the shifter king grumbles from behind me. I keep my gaze on the ocean in front of me as I smirk. Darkness has fallen fully now, the Spell shimmering under the silver light of the moon on the water's surface as the waves crash up against the side of the ship. My stomach twists in protest again.

"My apologies, Your Majesty. If all is well, I think I'll grab some dinner and retire for the evening," Tua says.

I look over my shoulder to him, dipping my chin slightly. "Thank you for the conversation, Tua."

"Of course, Bahira. Goodnight."

I turn back to face the water, my hands gently gripping the railing as his footsteps fade away. My palm and wrists throb, reminding me that I need to keep the injuries hidden from the king standing silently behind me.

"Why are you lingering behind me like a ghost?" I swear the deck itself shakes as he takes a few steps until I can feel him looming nearer. "An annoyingly close ghost," I grumble. He snorts but doesn't answer me, and my frustration rises until I turn around and fold my arms over my chest, leaning my back against the railing. Even then, I still have to tilt my head back to meet his gaze. "If you're going for an annoying *and* creepy ghost, well done. You've achieved it."

"I'm wondering if perhaps staying silent is safer. Wouldn't want to get punched again," he drawls, lifting a dark brow. My eyes narrow, hands instinctively closing into fists before pain flares and I have to grit my teeth to hide my reaction. "I'm still unsure of what I did to have warranted such a hit in the first place."

I scoff, my head jerking back with the movement. "You're joking," I reply flatly. When he continues to *stare* at me, I open my mouth to list all the reasons he was due that punch and honestly even another, when he takes a step closer. His hands brace the railing on either side of my body as he leans down to get on my eye level.

"I must admit, you hit much harder than I would have thought. It makes me think that you do in fact know how to use that spear you brought." His eyes catch the scant moonlight above, his irises appearing to *glow*, and I'm unable to look away from him as I push myself farther back against the ship's railing. The next inhale I take mixes his scent with the salty ocean air around us. My stomach tightens in response, and I'm positive that I have the seasickness to blame for that.

"You need to back up before you find out what it's like to get hit on the other side of your jaw," I grit out. Ignoring the slight breathiness to my voice, I observe said jaw, disappointment flaring when I note how his golden skin is unmarred.

The corner of his mouth tugs up while his eyes flick briefly to my hair. They linger there for a breath before they are back on mine. "You do not act like how I imagined a princess would."

"Well, you act *exactly* as I imagined a male who is half beast would." I attempt to straighten my spine and force him out of my space, but he is as immobile as the mast of the ship behind him. "*Move.*"

His powerful stare lingers another moment, both of us battling silently against one another before he finally pushes up from the railing and steps back. I have to temper the sigh of relief I want to draw in as I step around him and walk back to my cabin, my stomach still too upset to consider eating anything.

But I feel the heat of his gaze scorching my skin the entire way.

Chapter Ten

BAHIRA

I HATE SAILING. THE thought rattles around in my brain as I throw up again and again into the toilet.

Wiping my mouth with a cloth, I lean against the edge of the tub, the cool stone biting into the skin at my temple. We've been on the water for three days, an estimated few more to go, and I've managed to avoid King Kai since our last interaction that first night. But it's only because I'm too sick to leave my cabin. Tua has come by to check on me a handful of times each day, offering food and water which I manage a few bites and sips of. Most of it ends up coming right back out.

My head feels heavy, and my skin clammy, as my stomach continues to churn. Distantly, I hear what sounds like knocking, but I don't register what it is before I'm unconscious.

"Princess, wake up," a stern voice rumbles near me.

I go to speak, to move, to do *anything*, but my body feels as though it's weighed down by lead. Even my tongue is too heavy as I try—and fail—to remove it from the roof of my mouth.

"Bahira," he says again, closer this time. His voice sounds distorted through the ringing in my ears, the dizziness in my head swirling until I start to feel nauseous again.

I force my eyes to open, the world spinning around me as I reach out to grab the toilet. Hauling myself up with barely any strength, I start to dry heave though there is nothing in my stomach to actually purge.

"Fucking gods," the king mumbles before I feel my hair being pulled back from my face.

For a long while, my stomach cramps and spasms in its effort to expel something that isn't there. *Finally*, it settles enough for me to sit back, my forearm coming to my mouth as I try to focus my eyes. The glow of a flame gem silhouettes his figure where he squats down in front of me. His hair looks ruffled, the strands on top pushed back and off to the side. A few days of scruff peppers his jaw and cheeks and surrounds his lips, which are currently in the shape of a frown. I meet his eyes, unable to decipher what I see in them before they narrow.

"When was the last time you ate or drank?" he asks accusatorially, as if being debilitated my first time on a boat is my fault. "It shouldn't take you this long to overcome your seasickness."

I do my best to roll my eyes, but based on the way his brows draw together in confusion, I doubt I succeed. Clearing my throat several times, I rasp out, "Sorry, Your Majesty. I'll make sure to relay your unhappiness to my stomach."

He grumbles something under his breath before standing and bracing his hands on his hips. "Do you think you can stand up?"

I look myself over, my eyes still half-closed, before meeting his gaze above me. "What the fuck do you think?" I grate out. I can't even move my legs from the position they are in. *How long have I been asleep on the floor?*

"Does everything have to be an argument with you?"

"Only when you ask stupid questions." I place my hands on the floor, pushing onto my palms to try and sit up but only managing to cause pain to flare where my injuries from the rope ladder are. My arms give out, but somehow, the shifter king's hands are on me before I hit the floor as he hauls me up to a sitting position. My heart beats heavy and loud in my ears, my eyes finding his in the haze. His jaw is clenched, a muscle there thrumming with his pulse while his fingers tighten around me a little more.

"Here is what's going to happen. I'm going to pick you up and move you to your bed. Then you're going to drink some water and try to eat something so that you don't die." His hands leave my body while he repositions his arms under my knees and around my back.

"I distinctly remember telling you not to touch—"

"You can yell at me about it later," he snaps, and before I can get another word out, I'm crushed against his chest. One of my arms wraps around his shoulders, his muscles there flexing, as he turns to walk back into the bedroom. My lips pinch together, and my head is much too heavy to keep upright, so I let it loll to the side and right onto where his neck meets his shoulder. King Kai tenses, faltering for just a step before he's at the edge of the bed. Carefully, in a manner that is much more gentle than I ever would have expected, he lays me down. "If you die, then the deal between our kingdoms is null. So eat and drink," he commands, gesturing to the end table at the side of the bed.

"I can't," I rasp, turning onto my side and closing my eyes.

"What do you mean you can't?" he asks, his tone exasperated.

My eyes open back up, the king blurring in front of me. "I mean, *I can't*. I can't eat or drink anything. I can't even fucking move on my own."

Panic blooms, my chest tightening like I'm trying to breathe through a straw. I have *never* been this weak before, never been this sick. I'm completely vulnerable right now, and the thought has my pulse racing wildly. King Kai is silent for a long while, his stance unmoving.

"Why don't you heal yourself?"

I'm too ill to come up with a retort, so I close my eyes and stay silent, hoping he thinks I've fallen asleep. He sighs, long and full-bodied, before I hear the clattering of glass and metal. I open my eyes again to see that he's poured some water into a cup on the nightstand and is now squatting down in front of me. I'm caught off-guard by his closeness, by the way his gaze blankets me.

"I'm going to help you get some water in and, hopefully, something to eat, and then you can sleep."

Surprise flows through me when he delicately wraps an arm around me and helps me up to sit, one hand staying on my shoulder to hold me upright. He reaches back for the glass and brings it up to my lips. I'm so disoriented by what's happening that I don't move to drink it, and his huff of frustration tickles the hairs at my temple.

"Please, do not fight me. Just drink the fucking water." I force enough focus to open my mouth and let the cool liquid in. It slides down my throat slowly before King Kai pulls it away, setting the cup back on the side table. "Not too much too quickly, or you'll be back at the toilet." My eyes close again, my fatigued muscles cramping as I try to stay upright and losing the battle as I lean into him. "Why didn't you tell anyone you were so sick?"

"Tua has been coming in to check on me." And he had apparently been keeping that information to himself. An awkward silence stretches between us, heavy and filled with a tension that makes it impossible to relax.

He reaches over to grab the cup again, bringing it to my mouth where I gently sip from it. "Do you think you can eat?"

"No," I answer quietly, my throat still raw and inflamed.

When seconds pass and he doesn't respond, I clear my throat and push his hand off of me. "What are you doing?"

"I think I just want to go to sleep." I all but flop backwards on the bed, my legs still hanging off of the edge.

He exhales roughly before inelegantly working to try and move me into a more comfortable position. I decide not to fight him as sleep beckons me, darkness already prodding at my consciousness, when he speaks again. "Try to eat when you wake up."

Then I hear the door close and fade away into oblivion.

King Kai checks in on me multiple times throughout the day and into the night. His grumpy demeanor grows each time he arrives to see I haven't eaten anything. On his last visit, he pulled me carefully upright, put a glass of water to my lips, and then laid me back down.

It isn't until the next morning that I finally find relief in the battering of my seasickness. The first thing I force myself to do is shower, washing off *days* of clammy skin, and brush my teeth. My thick curly hair is nearly too tangled to comb through, but after an hour or so, I finally get it under control.

A new tray of food was brought to me this morning, fresh fruits and soft rolls laid out next to a pitcher of water and a smaller container of what looks like fruit juice. Sitting on the bed, I reminisce on the way the shifter king took *care* of me, but before I can even chastise myself on it, the door to my cabin unexpectedly swings open.

"Gods!" I shout, coming up to stand as a hand flies to my chest. King Kai walks in, his golden tan skin gleaming in the sunlight. His dark brown eyes find mine, narrowing slightly, before they dip quickly to look down my body. My fists tighten at my sides. The only benefit to being so incredibly sick for so many days is that the wounds on my hands have almost completely healed. "I guess you're just barging into rooms now?" I ask, sitting back down on the bed.

He snorts as he walks around to my side, his arms folding over his chest. "You're awake," he states, ignoring my question as his piercing gaze once again lingers on my hair, before adding with a flare of his nostrils, "And smelling better."

A shocked laugh barrels out of me as I gawk at him. "Yes, I truly believe you *do* know how to entice women, Your Majesty," I retort, remembering his words from the first day. "How does anyone *not* succumb to your charms?"

"You would see how irresistible I can be *if* I was trying to entice you. Unfortunately for you, I am not. And it's *females*. Not women."

I narrow my eyes as I take a bite of the soft roll. He's right, but I'll never give him the opportunity to correct me again. "What do you want?"

He takes a step closer to the bed. Too close—citrus and sandalwood reaching me easily as I take my next inhale. *Why does he have to smell so fucking good?* I hate myself for wanting to lean into it.

"I suppose a 'thank you' for making sure you didn't die is too much to expect?" he rumbles, his head tilting to the side.

"Stop being dramatic. I wasn't dying." I scowl, though the memory of how weak I was is one that will be forever burned into my mind. I have never been that vulnerable around *anyone*. "And besides, as I remember you so *eloquently* saying, if something happens to me, our deal is null and void. So don't pretend your care of me was anything more than ensuring a business transaction stayed intact." I stand from the bed, my arm brushing his as I grab the pitcher of water to pour myself a drink.

"You had no problem with me coming into your room unannounced before," he says, as if I had a choice in him coming to *help* me.

I sigh heavily, tilting my head up towards the plants hanging from the rafters. The room starts to feel sweltering with him so near to me. "Let's assume that anything that happened over the past few days was a once in a lifetime moment for you. Barging into my room unannounced, holding my hair back as I purge my guts, and"—I hesitate, swallowing a drink of water—"any other care you provided will *never* happen again."

"Fine," he growls from behind me. "Don't expect such *generosity* from me again, however. I'd sooner turn this ship around and drop you right back off in your kingdom than have to deal with trying to get you to fucking drink water again."

"I would expect nothing else from you, Your Majesty. Now, if you'd so kindly leave, I'd like to get some more rest," I say through gritted teeth, my heart pumping against my ribcage in frustration.

King Kai chuckles, the sound sliding down my spine. His booted steps echo out in the room as he walks towards the door, opening it before pausing. I turn to look over my shoulder at him, his glower set deeply into his face.

"You might want to open the window in here. You may have been able to shower, but the room cannot." He slams the door shut before the roll I hurl at him makes contact.

Asshole.

Chapter Eleven

Aria

"Aria, wake up! You're going to be late!" Lyre's panicked voice makes my eyes fly open, my heart racing in my throat as I haphazardly swim to the door to unlock it, swiping my ruby-colored braids away from my face. "Stars above, Aria! How could you sleep in so *late*? You only have five minutes to get ready!"

"I'm sorry!" I scrape out, moving to my white coral and pink sea glass vanity. "I stayed up late doing glass art."

While most of my sisters had taken up sparring as their hobby, I had never wanted to learn combat. I wasn't interested in reading about the histories of our world either, like my sister Dyanna, so I spent my free time making art out of sea glass.

I study myself in the mirror and grimace. Dark bags hang under my eyes, dulling their hazel glow. The usually rich darkness of my skin tone is wan, making the even darker freckles sprinkled across the bridge of my nose more prominent. My full lips pull down in a frown, their color matching my skin's pallor.

Knowing my appearance is a lost cause, I motion for Lyre—who is nervously pacing back and forth—to go through the door.

"We have to hurry," she practically yells as she takes off down the winding hallway, her lavender tail leaving little bubbles in her wake. I rush behind her, going through my mental list as we near the throne room: *jaw and shoulders relaxed, lips flat, spine straight, and attitude vicious.* I repeat it again, making sure each body part follows suit. More straight. More relaxed. More vicious.

"Aria!" My concentration is broken by the raspy, familiar voice. "Aria!" she calls again.

Slowing down, I look over my shoulder to see Lore's bright yellow tail glistening as she swims closer to me, her chartreuse braids wrapped around the top of her head tightly.

"Lore, I'm late for the queen's assembly," I say quickly, already turning to follow Lyre again.

She tugs on my hand, soft fingers wrapping around my own. "I know, and I won't keep you but… I *miss* you. It's been a while since we've had some time together."

My shoulders sink and my stomach twists as she speaks. Lore and I met a few years ago at the annual Summer Solstice celebration. We bonded over the expectations thrust upon us by our mothers—though I wasn't very detailed with her on what those expectations were. Still, we had found a sort of camaraderie with each other. And later that night, as we writhed against one another in bed, we found a different solace there too.

Lore squeezes my fingers again, her eyes lingering on my body.

"I'm sorry, Lore. Things have been crazy lately. I will find you after the assembly, and we can chat, okay?" I pull my hand from hers tentatively. She nods her head, eyes gleaming with hunger, before I spin back around and bolt to the throne room.

There is another large gathering of sirens here again. Only, instead of revelry, they will be asking for the queen's favor. The decorations have been taken down, returning the room to how it normally feels—bare and cold. *Spine straight. Jaw and shoulders relaxed. Lips flat. Attitude. Vicious.* I scan the dais as quickly as I can while moving up the center aisle. Counting only five bodies, I nearly sigh in relief. *I'm not the last one here.*

My mother sits on her throne of bones and decay, her dark purple tail draped delicately over the seat of the chair and brushing the floor of the dais. Once I reach the base, I keep my eyes downcast as I tread the water, holding my bow to my mother as steadily as I did last night.

"Late again, Aria. I'm starting to wonder if you're trying to send some sort of message. That perhaps you don't value your family enough to show up when you are supposed to." I grit my teeth together, my heart pounding so hard in my chest that I'm sure she must hear it. But I stay silent, bent over and frozen with the exception of my tail moving just enough to keep me in place. "You may rise, Daughter."

"Thank you, Your Majesty." I unfold and swim up the dais stiffly, hoping my mask is still in place despite how I feel my blood rushing through me like an icy waterfall.

Allegra floats next to my mother, her malevolent eyes on me as I make my way to the end of the line. Next to her is my third oldest sister, Dyanna. Most of her time is spent running the palace library and researching everything from ancient artifacts to treaty deals that have been put in place since the Spell. Our mother uses Dyanna as her own personal resource center. The only sister missing is Sade herself, which isn't surprising considering she forsake her royal status to instead lead my mother's legion.

It's then I realize that I *was* the last one to arrive today. *Shit.*

I keep swimming until I'm at the end of the line next to Lyre. Colorful eyes bore into me from the gathered sirens below us, the swirling of their floating braids a kaleidoscope in the water.

"My beautiful sirens, it is a wonderful day to hear from you! Please, one at a time, tell me how I may serve you better." My mother's voice is tranquil today, brimming with power and ancient wisdom. She sounds genuine in her offer too—like a truly benevolent queen. Like someone who didn't have two of her own kind murdered in this very room not even a day ago.

It is quiet for a moment before the first siren swims up the center aisle, bowing for a full five seconds before lifting up and addressing the queen. The female starts talking, and I try my best to focus on what her request is. It doesn't matter what she's asking for, my sisters and I will rule the same as our mother.

So eventually, I let my eyes wander around the throne room, my mind going far away.

When the female stops talking, she drops into another bow as she waits for my mother's decision. With a tap of her trident, my mother grants the female's request. Allegra voices her agreement as well, and down the line it goes, our "yes's" ringing out loud.

Time ticks by slowly as one by one more sirens come up and one by one my mother either grants or denies their requests. I roll my shoulders back, once again paying attention right as Lyre voices her agreement to whatever it is the latest siren has requested. I mimic her, continuing this pattern for what feels like forever until, *finally*, the last female is before us. Her braids are cut short, the light blue of her scales beautiful against her dark skin. She bows, but it's noticeably shorter in length than it should be. I try not to bristle—hoping the queen doesn't notice what I have to believe is an *accidental* slight.

"Your Majesty, it is an honor to come before you to make this request. I am Nia Adanna," she announces. *Why does that name sound familiar?*

"Adanna? Now *that* is a name I haven't heard since before the war," my mother says with an air of curiosity.

"Yes, Your Majesty. I believe my aunt was friends with you prior to The War Of Five Kingdoms," Nia says, and the recognition finally clicks into place. The Adanna line was one that was close to the Crown for a long time, each descendent friends with my own ancestors. They were trusted enough to live in the palace—until the war. My eyes dart nervously between her and the queen.

"That she was. Your aunt, Themu, was my mother's closest friend." Nia relaxes her shoulders and goes to speak again but is interrupted by my mother's harsh voice. "Until she betrayed the Crown. Why have you come here? To reminisce on the ways your ancestor was a deceiver? A coward? A *liar?*"

"N-no, Your Majesty, I simply came to make a humble request of you and your court," Nia stutters, eyes flicking down the line of my sisters until they reach me. Her gaze holds mine for a moment, her icy blue eyes nearly penetrating before she finally flicks them away. And I know why. She lives on the outskirts of Lumen with the others my mother has labeled as descendants of traitors. Though I have never seen Nia before, she *must* know that I visit them. I force my palms flat against my sides as my eyes bounce from Nia to the queen.

"Then state your business so we can be done," my mother snaps.

"As you know, my family has been living in the seamounts that line the capital since the war—"

"Yes, as punishment for your aunt's indiscretions," Allegra interjects.

A few sirens *growl* in approval of this consequence. The caves the sirens have hand-dug into rock can't accurately be called homes. They are crude at best, deadly at worst.

Nia clasps her hands behind her as she adjusts her posture. "I understand, but I come before you to ask if some of us might be allowed back into Lumen to live. You see, we've outgrown the space in the seamounts."

It's silent in the throne room as my mother contemplates her ruling, and I force myself to relax my jaw though my rapid pulse flutters beneath my skin.

"No," Queen Amari says simply, the single word echoing out.

"Y-Your Majesty, if you might reconsider—"

"I won't. Your family is one of forsakers and oath breakers. Your aunt tainted your entire family line. I cannot, in good conscience, allow that sort of stain back into the beautiful city that is Lumen."

"But we have no more room. No way to fit all of the other families that are forced to live there. We—"

"Daughters," the queen interrupts again, "what is your ruling? Do you agree that we should not allow the descendants that so ruthlessly betrayed your grandmother and myself to live among us? Or should we heed her supposed pleas that an entire *mountain* is no longer habitable?"

Allegra barely lets our mother finish her sentence before she says "no." Dyanna sounds bored as she also denies Nia's request. With each answer, Nia's shoulders round further as all the confidence she came into the throne room with begins to vanish right before us. Nia is not requesting much, not requesting anything beyond the right to basic and safe housing. Yet, because of a slight her *aunt* committed two hundred years ago, she is being denied.

I hear Lyre's soft rejection next to me, and I bite down on my tongue. I want badly to say *yes*. I want so fiercely to turn to my mother and tell her that this is unfair. That treating her subjects this poorly isn't what good rulers do. But I can't. Nia holds my gaze, her eyes imploring, but all I can do is shake my head and say a quiet "no." A small part of me dies at my cowardice, flaking away like rotting skin from a corpse.

That's what being in this queendom does to anyone with a light spirit and soft heart. It doesn't matter your station or your good intentions. If you don't have the same beliefs and thoughts as the queen, then your ideas and input are inconsequential. *You* are inconsequential.

"You have your fair ruling, Nia Adanna—relative of a betrayer. You may leave now." The words seem like a request, but the tone suggests that this is nothing less than a command.

Nia hesitates for a second, her mouth dropping open to speak, before she bows quickly and swims out of the room.

"Thank you all for coming to your queen with your concerns. You humble me as always with your trust in my rulings. If you'll excuse us, I need to discuss some matters with my daughters."

My throat tightens, but I keep my position steady, going over my mental list to try and calm myself. The moment the last siren leaves and the sea glass door closes, Allegra is swimming down the dais quickly, Mashaka—who must have been hiding behind the throne—right on her fin.

"How *dare* she come in here and attempt to embarrass you that way!" Allegra shouts. "It is a disgrace to ask for such an accommodation to be made for the bloodline of a forsaken!"

"Calm yourself, Allegra. She will be dealt with once enough time has passed. When is your next group of sirens going out hunting?"

"Tomorrow at dawn. We've gotten word from our scouts that there should be a few supply ships crossing the waters from the Mortal Kingdom to the Fae Kingdom."

"Good. I want you all going on this hunt tomorrow morning. We need to make sure our line of succession is secure. I have no doubt that there are others out there who sympathize with Nia. Who think that a weaker queen is what they want to see rule our realm. We cannot let that happen." My mother swims down from her throne, Allegra coming into position behind her and to the side. "You all represent a long line of fierce rulers who do not waiver in their duties. It is on *you* to ensure that you help uphold the values of our queendom to keep our people safe." She gives everyone a hard look, lingering on me the longest. Historically, sirens weren't expected to begin going out to find males until they reached twenty-two years of age. Under my mother's reign, that rule has been bent and younger females are now being told they have the "great honor of fulfilling their duty to the queendom" sooner.

"You are all dismissed. Except for Aria."

I swallow roughly as I fight the nausea now churning in my stomach. Lyre glances at me quickly—that small look relaying her anxious feelings—before she takes off with everyone else until I am alone in the room with my mother.

"Aria, why do you insist on making me look bad in front of our people?" she begins, her trident held tightly in her hand at her side.

"I'm sorry, Your Majesty. It is not my intent to do so." *Shoulders and jaw relaxed, lips flat, spine straight...*

"There are only so many times I can hear you say that before I begin to realize it isn't the truth." The silence between us is heavy, as if the ocean is slowly freezing solid and entombing me here. But it's just terror icing my veins and making my body stiff. "Come with me, Daughter. Let's see if you truly live for your queendom or for yourself."

Chapter Twelve

NOX

"It's been two fucking days," I murmur to the healer, the green light of his magic glowing over Rhea's forehead. I try to keep my frustration—my *terror*—in check, but with each hour that passes, with each moment that she hasn't so much as wiggled a finger, it's becoming harder to rein myself in.

This is all my fucking fault. I should have been honest with her so much sooner. I tried to rationalize with myself that prolonging the full truth until we were back in my kingdom—far enough away from King Dolian—meant she would have the safety and space to process it however she needed to. That she would be able to see with her own eyes what I was trying to protect.

When I thought about all the scenarios that could have unfolded when Rhea found out I was the crown prince of the Mage Kingdom, none of them had accurately portrayed how terribly it would go. Of course, there was no version I thought of where Councilman Osiris was the one to tell her. I didn't see that one coming at all. But a part of me knows that I was also delaying it because I was a coward. I was too afraid that, when she learned about my involvement with Alexi's death, it would be too much. She wouldn't be able to look at me in the same way after that.

Your words mean nothing to me now.

I didn't know what true heartbreak was until that moment, when her red-rimmed eyes met my own and I saw in them the depths to which I had just destroyed her. I have never seen her angry like that—not even on the night that she thought I was making fun of her and kicked me out of the tower. *I* brought that out in her.

The last thing I ever wanted was to make her hurt. To be another person who failed her. Another reason for her to bottle her feelings up because sharing them proved to be too dangerous. Lying to her this entire time felt like forced suffocation—I *hated* it. And the longer she lays here motionless, those perfect green eyes remaining hidden behind closed lids, the further my heart is pummeled.

"She is uninjured and by all accounts healthy, Your Highness," Galen, the palace healer, says as he lifts his hands from her head and his magic flickers out in his palms.

My magic pushes hard beneath my skin, filling me to the brim until I snap, "Then why isn't she waking up?" Galen startles at my outburst, his dark gray eyes widening. I draw a hand down my face as I blow out a breath before continuing, "I'm sorry, Galen. I don't understand why we can't get her to respond. *It's been two days.*"

"Tell me again what happened," Galen says as he slowly strides over to the chair placed at the corner of the bed in my room.

My gaze leaves his and goes back to her—always to her. Her hair is braided into a thick plait that drapes down over her shoulder, Sarai having done so after she washed Rhea with a warm cloth. While I would only go as far as the sitting room, I did give my mother's lady-in-waiting the privacy to carefully clean and change Rhea from her travel-worn clothes into a pink silk robe.

Drawing in more air, I answer, "We were practicing using her magic. She hasn't had much training with it, and she just passed out after expelling some." It is a bald-faced lie, but I don't care. When it comes to Rhea's safety, there are only five people I trust with the truth of who she is and what she can do: my parents, my sister, my best friend, and myself. Though a lie, it encompasses enough of the truth that Galen should be able to heal whatever is wrong with Rhea.

"It is possible that without the proper training, she likely used too much too quickly, and her body is now recovering. Give her time, Your Highness. She just appears to be resting. Let her do so."

I force a smile to my face as I nod. "Thank you, Galen."

The old mage dips his chin, then stands and walks to the door, closing it quietly behind him. I get up from my own chair and stretch my arms overhead before interlacing my fingers behind my head.

It's been two days.

My eyes catch on the dead plants in the corners of the sitting room just beyond, and a shudder rolls through me. The memory of the moment I watched them wilt, life drawn from them in mere seconds, ripples to the forefront of my mind.

Your words mean nothing to me now.

She had screamed that at me from where she knelt on the floor, and like the lighting of a candle, something within her had ignited. But it wasn't warm nor was it light. It was power—raw, unfiltered power—that turned her eyes completely black. Then the screaming started. The sound was so tortured that I thought I might die right there. I saw her magic begin to light her palm, but it wasn't that brilliant, beautiful, luminescent white I was used to. Glittering black shadows balled larger and larger in her hands, and I barely had time to throw my own magic up as a shield when it burst from her palms.

Despite my magical strength, *I* had nearly faltered under the weight of *her* power. I watched through a grimace as the plants in my room went from vibrant green to deathly black within seconds. Then she collapsed, her magic gone like a puff of smoke. I crawled to her, my hands shaking as I tried to wake her, but her skin was wan, her lips so fucking pale, and she was silent. I would take her anger and her hatred of me over that numbing silence.

This newfound quiet is soul-shatteringly unbearable.

That wasn't the first time her eyes had turned black, and it wasn't the first time that she had drawn out the life of a living thing. I'm not sure how the hell I'm supposed to broach that subject with her.

A knock sounds at my door. Crossing the distance from the bedroom to the sitting room, I crack it open enough for me to glimpse who is there. My shoulders relax when I see it's my father.

His voice is low and filled with concern as he walks in and asks, "How is she?"

The powerful outburst of both of our magic had drawn the attention of those in the palace, including my parents who had rushed into my room a few moments after Rhea collapsed. The entire evening was chaotic between my parents coming up with a reason for the expulsion of magic to give to the council and my insistence that only Galen and Sarai be allowed to tend to Rhea.

"She is the same," I croak out, my hand running through my hair and holding the strands there. My father stands next to me—not quite shoulder to shoulder—and folds his arms over his chest.

"What did Galen say?"

"That she is healthy. That she expelled too much magic and needs to continue resting." My gut sinks at the idea that she could be like this for a while, that she could wake up somehow different. Or maybe my fear is that she will wake up the same—falling apart into pieces because of me.

"Son, I can see the worry on your face. What do *you* think?"

"It's my fault," I rasp, allowing emotion to seep out for the first time since I confessed everything to Rhea. "My secrets did this to her—brought her anger to the surface and caused her magic to explode from her too quickly." I didn't have a chance yet to tell my father all about who Rhea is to me—who we are to each other. How I'd walk away from everything if she asked me to. I'd burn entire worlds down—starting with the Mortal Realm and its bastard king—with only a whisper of command from her lips. She wouldn't ask me to do those things. It wasn't in her nature to, but gods, did I fucking want to. There is something primitive inside of me that sings in approval at the thought—my magic hooking onto the idea that I could end any person who even *thinks* about harming her.

"I can feel your magic surging," my father says, his hand coming to grip my shoulder. "Breathe, Nox." Together, we inhale deeply and hold it there for a few seconds before slowly blowing the breath back out. "You haven't lost control like that in a long while." He surveys me, his fatherly intuition seeing more than eyes ever could.

He moves to sit on one couch, and I take the other, able to see Rhea in my bed from where I'm seated. The need to be closer to her is ever-present—never once dulling in the three months we've gotten to know each other. I thought I loved my kingdom and my family to my fullest potential, but then I felt what it was to love *her*, to be loved *by* her, and it changed me. A well deeper than any I had felt before was open within me, and all I wanted to do was fill it with everything made of her.

My father crosses an ankle over his knee as he leans back on the couch. "Did I ever tell you about the time your mother stabbed me?"

I jerk my head back in surprise, making him chuckle. "What? Never."

His smile is wide as he settles in a little more, like he's preparing for a great retelling. "Of course, you know that my marriage to your mother was arranged—"

"Yes, and you were enraptured from the start," I interrupt, folding my arms over my chest. My parents' love story is one that's been told over and over since my childhood.

"We were lucky to have found a lot of commonality at first with each other, especially for a pair of hormonal teenagers. But that doesn't mean that our relationship wasn't without faults or that we didn't have to suffer through trial by fire to figure things out."

"Did you ever lie to her about who you were though?"

He barks out a laugh, making me raise a brow in question. "No. I did not do that, but I *did* lie to her in an attempt to push her away."

Entirely confused, I stare at him, gesturing with my hand for him to continue.

"Your mother has grown into her role as queen of the Mage Kingdom, and she has done so beautifully. You cannot tell me that there is anyone else out there more fit to stand beside me, to help me lead and make decisions. But this was not always the case. When we were younger, she was a soft, free spirit. She hated the politics of court and of posturing to gain the approval of old men that only cared whether or not she could give the kingdom a strong heir."

He tilts his head up towards the ceiling, smiling as he reminisces.

"We had been officially courting for two years, following all the guidelines and rules put in place for an heir apparent and their betrothed. Everything was planned and laid out ahead of time—where we ate, what we wore, even our conversation topics. We may have been attracted to each other, but it wasn't a natural falling together. It wasn't built on the right experiences. It was a façade of sorts. Which meant that, when things started to get difficult, there wasn't a strong enough foundation to hold us to each other."

I contemplate his words as I look over at Rhea. Her face is a mask of calm, her coloring more like its normal glow today. *Sunshine.* She truly is the embodiment of the sun—warm, radiating, and life-giving.

"I was serious about my duties as the crown prince, and Alexandria was a distraction from those things. A beautiful and easy-to-fall-for distraction," he recalls.

"So what happened?" My gaze lingers on her for a moment longer before I finally pull it away and look at my father.

"There was a formal dinner and ball to be held in our honor, and your mother, gods, was counting down the days with absolute dread. She didn't want the eyes of everyone on her. She didn't like the way her father basically confined her to only their home and schooling, lest she accidentally embarrass him with her 'wildness.'"

I didn't know my grandfather on my mother's side, as he passed shortly after I was born, but I hate the idea that anyone would try to confine her in that way.

"I could see how stressed she was. How every time we were forced to parade around the kingdom together, she became less and less present. I couldn't watch her deteriorate like that. My attraction to her had morphed into something else—something deeper—but for her, she was so lost in the burden of what it meant to be married to the crown prince that I thought she didn't feel anything for me besides what was necessary for appearances. I knew it wasn't fair to her, what she was being turned into. What she was giving up. So I concocted a plan. I would make her hate me, and I would pretend to hate her, so that our impending marriage would look too tumultuous, too unstable to continue in the eyes of the council, and she would be free."

"That's an embarrassingly stupid plan."

His laugh is light, coaxing a small chuckle of my own. "Love makes you do stupid things sometimes. And lack of experience. I had both of those going for me and thought I knew the answers. So I spent the months leading up to the dinner being a complete asshole to her."

"And so she stabbed you in anger?" I ask, trying to picture my mother angry enough to do so.

"No," he replies softly. I tilt my head as I look at him, watching as his smile slowly drops and the corners of his mouth tip into a frown. "She was devastated. It wasn't in her nature to interrogate me, to force me to explain why I had begun to push her away, but I saw it. Every time she looked at me with a spark of hope in her gray eyes and every time I snuffed it out with my actions, it nicked away a piece of my heart. And hers."

I swallow roughly, unable to help the way my fingers twitch with the need to hold Rhea's.

"It was the evening before the dinner, and we were both in a space of devastation. I knew that if I didn't do something with all the pent-up energy and anxiety flowing through me, I'd make a dumb decision. So I walked to the training grounds and began throwing daggers to blow off steam. Your mother found me there."

My father uncrosses his legs and stretches them out before him. The room is quiet as he thinks, only the sounds of my guilty heart beating in my ears competing with the rise and fall of Rhea's steady breathing in the bedroom.

"She was furious. She begged me to tell her what was really going on. I tried to ignore her and the way I felt like I was going to vomit at the thought of never getting to be with her again. She grabbed a dagger off of the table and walked up to me—more passion and *anger* than I had ever seen from her before. She told me that if I was truly done with her, I'd better stab her in her heart right now because it would hurt less than watching me pretend to be something I wasn't."

"Gods." I huff out a breath.

"I laughed at her, at the ridiculous picture she had painted with her fury. And then the tears started flowing down her cheeks and she told me that she loved me. It was the first time either of us had said it, and the moment she did, I knew I couldn't lie anymore about how she was the very air my lungs needed. I rushed to her, pulling her body to mine and kissing her with every ounce of emotion I could. But because I was an idiot, I completely ignored the very sharp dagger she still had pointed at me until it became embedded in my stomach."

An actual hearty laugh scrapes up my throat as I gape at him. "So you stabbed yourself?"

He waves his hand in front of him as he says, "Semantics. From that night forward, we were inseparable. When I became king, I asked the council to change the rules—both for her and for our children. So you would have the choice to lead the sort of life you wanted without the parameters set in place by people who truly should have no opinion on what you do."

"It's a good story," I reply, leaning my head back on the couch as I stare out the window in front of me into the forest beyond. "But I don't see how it relates to what I've done."

"Ah, my son, so focused on the bigger picture that you forget the smaller details."

"Like how you forgot the dagger?" I tease, bringing my gaze back to his.

He laughs, nodding his head in agreement before resting his hands over his crossed knee. "Precisely. I thought I knew what I was doing, and I made the wrong call. It was a painful lesson to learn, but in the end, it was worth it. Do you know why?" When I'm silent, unable to see what he's trying to show me, he jerks his chin towards Rhea. "Do you love her?"

"Yes," I answer without hesitation.

My father nods, the look on his face one of genuine knowing. "You do not fall in love with someone only because they make grand gestures or declarations of that love. It's the smaller, more intimate moments that are woven throughout your time together that make your love grow stronger—that build that foundation. That's what I learned with your mother. When we started being completely honest with each other, our foundation became unshakable." He's pensive, his gaze lost in memory when he continues. "In the same vein, it is not merely one large moment that usually breaks a couple. It is repeated small ones and lessons not learned that can crack the love you've built."

"Dad, I was—I *did* something awful to her. Someone she cared about died because of *me*. She is in this state because of *me*. How can we come back from that?" I drop my gaze to my lap, shame and misery coating me.

My father stands and walks to me, his fingers finding my chin and lifting my head up to meet his softened gaze. "When you are in the throes of love, it's easier to be brave. To find courage. To hold strong. But like all things, there is a balance, and sometimes, being in love can drive us to be more fearful. To hold too tightly to the point that we aren't holding on anymore to protect that love, but instead, we are suffocating it. In those moments, we see that love can cost all that we are and all that we will ever be. But it's also only the honesty of love that has the power to set us free. Because where there is love, there is acceptance and understanding." His smile is tender as he drops his hand back to his side and adds with a small shrug, "Where love shines, forgiveness can bloom."

Chapter Thirteen

RHEA

*S*WEAT PLASTERS MY HAIR *to my temples as my eyes flare open and I suck air in with heaping gulps. He's not here. I repeat the phrase in my mind, coming up to sit and placing a hand over my racing heart.*

"It's alright. It was just a nightmare." The woman of the Middle's voice is tranquil as it cradles me from all sides. I swear I feel the weight of her arms around me, pulling me in close. The scent of jasmine is strong as I try to take in a deeper breath.

"Will I ever stop seeing him when I sleep?" I rasp. These nightmares, the memories they pull from real life or sometimes create anew, are exhausting. I know King Dolian is hunting me, and I know he believes me to be only his. He's a monster, a beast dressed in finery preying on someone who was never meant to be by his side. But there is a part of me that knows that deep down, I'm a monster like he is.

"Why would you think that?" she asks, hearing my thoughts as I hug my knees to my chest and rest my cheek on them. My magic—that other magic—awakens again, my guilt and remorse along with it.

I stare out at the black and purple and blue universe of stars and galaxies swirling all around me as I answer, "You know why."

The silence between us is gentle, like a trickle of water leading away from a raging river. Finding its own path amongst the chaos. The stars around me seem so close, yet when I reach a hand out to touch them, my fingers only brush empty air. It's all an illusion. Peace. Comfort. Love. None of it is real, at least not for me.

"Do you want to know what I see when I look at you?" she asks. She lets a few moments pass in silence before she continues. "I see a child who was so terrified that she turned inward to find a place that was safe enough to exist as she was. I see a girl who had to navigate what it meant to grow up—all the emotions and feelings and changes—all by herself. Yes, you had Alexi, and thank the gods for that, but one hour visits are not enough for *any* person. I see a young woman who finally allowed herself to know what it is to be cared for and is now withholding it from herself as punishment for a wrongdoing she did not commit."

I feel the tears, hot and heavy, as they pool in my eyes until everything blurs.

"I see someone struggling to stay afloat in the tumultuous sea of suffering into which she has been tossed," she adds on even more gently.

"It sounds like you see someone incredibly sad and foolish and hopeless," I breathe out, wetness streaking down my cheeks.

"Oh, it is quite the opposite. I see someone resilient. I see someone stronger than she knows. As the waves keep crashing into her, as the tide tries to pull her under, she stays afloat. She treads the waters of despair because she has tenacity. Because she must believe, deep down and buried beneath the broken pieces she is so sure she is made of, that she deserves more. That she is worth the effort of forcing herself to stay above water. That she deserves the love of a man willing to risk his kingdom for her."

"Perhaps," I murmur, swallowing down the thick knot of emotions threatening to choke me. "Or maybe she used to believe that there was something better for her outside of her tower. Let herself fall in love with a man that turned out to be nothing more than a fraud. And now, amongst the destruction of the truth, all she wants is to let go. Perhaps I'm tired of always keeping myself afloat. Maybe now I just want to sink beneath those waters and into something dark and calm and... permanently numb." I hate the way the words form in my mouth so easily, but there is truth in them—in the way I feel like there is no purpose for me anymore. "A person can only take so much before they begin to wonder if an existence in a brutal and terrifying life is better than no existence at all."

The woman hums sadly. "You, my sweet girl, were made for so much more. Though it may not seem that way right now, you are on your journey to finding out what that is if you have the strength to persevere."

I'm not sure that I do. "Can you see the future?" I ask, changing the subject as I reach out my hand this time to trail through the sparkling specks of white and gray that float around me.

Minutes seem to pass before she answers. "I can see glimpses and pieces but not a full picture."

I swallow roughly, wiping my eyes before taking a deep breath and asking, "Am I still with Flynn—I mean Nox?" I wasn't sure how I wanted her to answer that question. Thinking about him was like picturing the withering of a once tall and strong tree. Our love was the roots, made rich by all of the small moments that had brought us together. All the times he showed up for me, slowly breaking down my barriers until I let him in. But those roots had been fed by a manufactured dream—nothing but false intent and unspoken words.

My next inhale is forced while my chest squeezes in on itself. Gods, how was it possible that my trampled heart still loved him so fiercely? Why did the image of him confessing everything replay in my mind not as a memory of anger but one of desperation and insurmountable guilt? I didn't like the idea of him thinking himself culpable. It made wanting to hate him for what he did nearly impossible. Yet I didn't think I could hate him, not ever.

"I cannot answer your question, for that would pull on the strings of fate until they are nothing but a tangled web. But I can show him to you, if you'd like. I can show you his present and his past."

I lift my cheek from my knee. "What do you mean?"

"Would you like to see what Nox is doing right now? At this moment?" she asks, a tinkling, delightful lilt to her voice. "Or perhaps you would like to see what he was doing as he courted you in your tower?"

"I don't think he was courting me." The word implies that he was getting to know me merely for the sake of being interested in who I was.

"Rhea, you are too skilled at reading people to have me believe that you think everything he did was nothing more than a farce. Would you like me to show you the past?"

Yes, I think, while speaking the word "no."

The woman laughs—a legitimate laugh that makes me break out in goosebumps. The sound of it is a recognition, a calling back to a different time I have no memory of but feel distinctly connected to. I must truly be desperate for any sort of joy if a single laugh from a magical woman makes me somehow feel less alone.

"Don't fight your curiosity. It is one of the things that will help guide you. Let's see what your guard is doing." Her words feel poignant, but I'm too weary to try and understand what they mean.

"He's not *my* anything. Not anymore," I whisper, the lie slipping easily between my lips.

"You know that I can hear your thoughts and feel your emotions, right? Why do you insist on lying to yourself about him?" Her tone is one of incredulousness as I imagine her brows furrowing together. I don't answer, choosing to lie back down on my side instead, my knees drawing into my chest while I force my eyes to close.

"Rhea, you cannot hide from this. You need to talk about everything you are keeping locked away. The weight of those burdens is too much for one person to bear. Let him help you. Let *me* help you," she pleads.

I believe the small amount of fear I hear woven into her voice is true. *This* is too much for one person.

And that's the point.

I tried letting someone in. I tried giving them access to the things I keep so deeply buried that it took great personal trust to get them out. And in the end, it only resulted in more pain. More disappointment. More regrets.

So why not let myself be crushed by it all? Why fight it anymore? Hopes and dreams? They were as meaningless as a single blade of grass in a giant meadow. Let me be destroyed by all the consequences of the decisions I had made over the past three months. Let me succumb to it all. Let me be numb.

Chapter Fourteen

Rhea

My eyes open at the deep voice that echoes out into the Middle.

"You cannot tell her any more than that. It will upset the balance of things. You know this." His voice is dominant and commanding yet beautiful at the same time.

"She will suffer! She is suffering," she pleads.

"This is her path," he replies matter-of-factly.

The woman growls, and even though I can't see her, I feel her presence come closer to me while the male fades into the background.

"Hello, Rhea," she says with gentleness, despite her argument with the man.

"Who were you speaking with? I've heard his voice before, the day I nearly drowned." The glimmering silver and white flecks twirl around my fingers delicately, their movements like that of a small snake. The woman doesn't answer, and I have to halt the sarcasm of my own response. *"Let me guess, you can't answer that."*

"I'm afraid not."

There is a tickling at my ankles, and when I look down, I'm surprised to see my body draped in a silky black and white dress. The fabric sinks into my curves, and I drag a hand down it, nearly sighing at its softness.

"This is new," I say, gesturing to my body.

She hums in response. *"Would you like to see him now?"*

My eyes close at her question, and I abandon my interest in the stardust and dress. *"No."*

Honey-thick quiet—one filled with only despair—settles in, seeping into invisible corners as it threatens to drown me.

"Were you ever real?" I rasp, lying on my back as I stare up at the infinite sky and changing the subject not so subtly. Flynn's joke about how terrible I am at that scratches at my heart, the sensation painful, so I banish him from my mind.

"I assume you mean: have I ever lived on Olymazi?"

"Yes. Where did you live? Which kingdom?"

She seems to silently weigh the question before answering, *"I can't tell you."*

I huff out a breath. Of course. I am so tired of hearing how I can't be told things—how others make decisions for me instead of trusting me to handle whatever truths need to be spoken.

"There are other things I can help you with—other things I can tell you about. You just have to ask the right questions."

I scoff, shaking my head. *"The right questions? How very convenient for you."*

Despite my frustration, there are things I wish to know, but I'm afraid to seek out the answers. Afraid to peek behind the curtain and find out if what is there will be something that helps or hurts. It has been so much of the latter that I'm starting to wonder if I was made simply to suffer.

"Your purpose, Rhea, is so much grander than—" Her words are cut off by the sound of choking. I sit up with a start, looking around me despite knowing that I won't see her. Only the stars and faraway worlds stare back at me. *"The magic didn't like what I was about to say,"* she gasps, clearing her throat multiple times.

"How long are you cursed to stay here?"

"It is not a curse. I chose to forgo my final resting place so that I could be here. And I'll be here for as long as I am needed."

That definitely sounded like a curse.

The woman exhales roughly. *"If you are going to continue staying in this place, you will have to make a choice. Being here has a cost, both to you and your magic."*

My brows knit together. "A cost?"

"You have very little understanding of all that you are capable of." Her pause is unsettling, curious in a way that feels like a secret kept. *"Your magic is what is holding you here. And though it is nothing but a trickle in the well of power that you might eventually call your own, you haven't trained at all with it in order to handle visiting here* and *staying present in your physical body."*

"You said I had expelled some of my *other* magic before. What did you mean?"

"The magic you possess is two halves of a whole. You have consciously used one and unconsciously used the other. That is what happened in the moments before you came here."

My palms glide down my dress anxiously. "So, that ancient darkness I sometimes feel, that *is a part of me? A part of this magic I hold?"*

"It is."

I freeze as dread trickles into my veins. That magic doesn't have the same comfort as my healing magic does. That one feels more chaotic, more unpredictable.

"Where did my magic come from? How did I end up with it in the Mortal Kingdom?"

"Unfortunately, those are questions I cannot answer for you."

I let out a noise of frustration. I expected secrets from the king but never from Alexi. Never from Flynn—Nox—and certainly not from an omnipotent, otherworldly woman who knew all but was unwilling to share. How ironic to sit here in another plane of existence with millions of worlds and stars surrounding me, and yet I can be told nothing of value.

"You are at a crossroads, Rhea. You must decide if you will continue to be trapped within yourself or if you are willing to break the chains that bind you to find reprieve on the other side. This existence—these experiences—are not unique to only you."

Her last words sting as they settle over me. "You think I'm being selfish."

"No. What has always set you apart from the very beginning is your heart. The kindness you push to the forefront so easily. The way you care for others. Those are not weaknesses; they are strengths. Give some of that to yourself. You deserve—"

"Nothing. I deserve nothing. Hasn't that been proven? Over and over again!" I bitterly seethe. "Every time I have thought that way, it has always resulted in something bad. If I was so strong, I would have been able to defend myself against a maniacal king. If I was so strong, I would have been able to heal Alexi in time." Tears drip off of my cheeks and down into the darkness below me as I bunch my hands into fists, frustration darkening my vision. "If I was so strong, I would have been able to save Bella! I—I would have guarded my heart. I would have let the ice that encompassed it become impenetrable so that I could never know what it is to love someone so profoundly that a betrayal from them feels like I'm being cleaved in two!"

My screams somehow echo out, despite being surrounded by only space, and I feel my magic come to a sharpened point. Looking down at my hands, I watch as glittering black gathers on top of my palms to form what looks like daggers. It calls to me—a dark song, ancient and powerful, beckoning me to flood this magic out into the world and silence it all. Like being lost in the onyx chasms of my mind, I feel nothing and no one as I begin to let that darkness seep from me.

I'm walking a path of solitude, and with each step I take, I feel what it is to be fueled by nothing but anger. And pain. And a sadness so intense it blankets my tongue with its acerbic taste.

You aren't alone anymore.

His voice comes to me unbidden, and my steps falter.

Let me help you.

My body trembles as I feel him here with me. His warmth and his scent and the way his hands gently cup my face.

There is only you.

A sob rips from my throat as I fall to my knees, the obsidian daggers dissolving into shadows waiting for my command as they writhe around my hands.

I don't want to know of an existence without you.

I scream out into the unyielding darkness. Into the corners within new worlds and the spaces between stars.

If you're in pieces, then I want every fucking one of them.

In the distance ahead of me, a small flame ignites, the heat slight but mighty. I reach my shaky fingers towards it, needing to feel that kernel of life within me. Despite the pain, despite it all, I still yearn for that light.

I want you, in any way you can give me. No scenario changes that.

The shadows begin to retreat back within me, slowly. Reluctantly. No. They aren't retreating. I am calling them back.

I love you. Wholly. Inexorably. In a way that exhilarates as much as it frightens me. With everything that I am or could ever possibly hope to be, I love you.

Relentlessly, I'm pelted with the memories of his words and the moments he spoke them. I see his eyes shining with the truth of each one, and I become undone. I let my grip on my magic release, and like a flame consuming oxygen, everything around me explodes. The shadows disappear, but I know where they've gone. Hiding in the darkness within me—always present, always watching. Every time I shoved an emotion into a mental box and locked it away, that darkness grew. Over and over, I had tucked all my hurts—big and small—into the back of my mind because dealing with them, acknowledging the pain they brought and the despair they smothered me with, was more than I could handle.

And then he *came into my life. And he begged me to let him in. To help shoulder the invisible pain that he somehow managed to see. There is no rational reason for him to have done that—to have treated me with such kindness and respect and love—unless those emotions were true for him.*

Unless I was more than a mission.

I love you.

"She isn't supposed to be here like this," that dominant voice booms, his power shaking my body.

"She needs the space to process."

I love you. I hear his voice again, but it isn't in my head this time. It's all around me.

"She is tempting fate. Her magic is—"

"Please. Just a little longer," the woman implores, her voice shaking.

My ears begin to ring, and my hair rises around me. The last of those shadows pull back into me and settle deep down in my stomach. The sensation is jarring, causing my vision to spin as I collapse onto nothing.

I love you so fucking much.

I scream again, covering my ears with my hands, as the boxes I've kept so closely guarded and frozen in time within me rattle and shake. My tears are a turbulent ocean in which I have become adrift. And one by one, those locks burst—lids flying off.

Here—in a space between life and death, past and future, nothing and everything—I become unmade.

Chapter Fifteen

Nox

The light of the setting sun pours in through the open windows of my room directly onto her soft face. For the last four days, I have watched her sleep here in my bed. I have been too afraid to go far from this space, wondering if she will wake up when I'm gone and then thinking that maybe it's better if I leave so that she can.

But for her, I am selfish. My heart beats discordantly in my chest, but still, it's a song that is only meant for her to hear.

"Fuck," I whisper, my hands cradling my head as my fingers push into my temples.

"Have you tried talking to her?" Cass asks from where he sits in a chair next to me. I look over at him, watching as he uses one of his daggers to carve something into a piece of wood. He's abandoned his guard leathers and, instead, wears simple black trousers and a bright green short-sleeved tunic, his light blond hair tied away from his face. When I don't answer, he elaborates, "You know, telling her a memory or a story that she hasn't heard before."

"No," I answer, lifting my head from my hands and turning my gaze back to her. "Do you think it would help?"

"It wouldn't *hurt*."

I sigh, running a hand through my hair. There are so many memories of our time together to choose from. I keep them tucked into my mind like books tightly packed on a shelf. The first time she smiled at me. The first time I truly heard her laugh. The way she trusted me enough to talk about Alexi, and then the guilt that immediately flooded me after she had. The first—and only—time she told me she loved me. And the way I felt reborn because of it.

"Surely you can think of *one* moment you want to remind her of?" Cass questions skeptically, cutting into my thoughts.

"I remember them all. Every word, every lingering glance and soft touch of our skin. She is imprinted on my very soul, Cass." The words rasp out of me as I fight the urge to let every emotion vying for dominance inside of me spill out. The noise of metal on wood ceases, and I can feel the weight of my friend's stare on the side of my face.

"You're in love with her?" His shock is so blatant that it nearly pulls a laugh from me.

"You don't have to sound so surprised about it," I grumble.

"Bullshit. You want me to ignore the fact that you show up back here with a gorgeous woman in tow—one whose magic feels as strong as yours does, by the way—and I'm just supposed to pretend that this is normal?"

"Preferably."

Cass curses under his breath as he leans forward. "I still don't understand how this happened. When did you have time to fall in love while working as a guard and sneaking around the castle?"

I wince a little at the fact that I haven't told him everything yet. Normally on my visits home, Cass and I would spend the first few days catching up after I had relayed everything I knew to the council. Something they are currently *still* waiting for me to do. My father has been able to hold them off, telling them that I need rest. That I need to readjust after so much time away. Only the healers and Sarai, who are sworn to secrecy, know that Rhea is here with me. And only my parents know the reason that I won't leave.

Magic stirs in my chest, a fierce need urging me to make sure that no one else knows about Rhea. That she is protected at all costs. I have to fight against the harsh yank of that invisible chain, clenching my jaw as I do so. "It's a long story. The important part you need to know now is that I will do *everything* in my power to assure that she is safe here. I may need your help to do so. I won't ask you to do anything you're not—"

"Yeah, I'm going to stop you right there," he interjects.

I turn to look at him, my heart beating more harshly. Cassius is practically my brother. We grew up together and were inseparable through all stages of life until it was time for me to leave and search for the perceived magical threat to our kingdom. On my short visits home, it took days for me to shed the fake persona I had adopted as Flynn, guard in the Mortal Kingdom. But Cass had been there for me every time I came back frustrated and defeated and so godsdamn tired of pretending. His wit and humor—his ability to tell me when I was acting like an ass—always felt like a reset. I was able to find my true self whenever I spent enough time with him—the self I had buried deep within for fear of getting caught undercover. The only other person who had the same effect on me was lying silently in my bed, her golden hair flowing out around her.

"You know that whatever it is you need, *whatever it is,* I'm here for you. And if you need me to extend that same level of trust and protection to her, then I'm here for that too. I knew she was different the moment I saw you two interacting. You have *never* looked that way at any woman." His eyes dance with mischief as he grins. "Well, unless you do it in the bedroom, in which case I wouldn't fucking know."

"Gods above," I say, shaking my head in annoyance and breathing out a sigh of relief. "You're right." When his eyes widen and a choked scoff sounds, I reach over and shove his shoulder. "Idiot. I *mean* that you're right about her being different."

His gaze moving to Rhea, he says, "Tell her that, then. Tell her what's in here." He taps a finger over his heart, a wry grin pulling at his lips.

"That is surprisingly deep for you."

He snorts, shrugging his shoulders while he stands up and brushes the wood shavings off of his lap, pocketing whatever he was chiseling. I watch with a frown as he slides the dagger back into its sheath at his thigh, my gaze moving from him to the now dirtied floor.

"It's not like *you* have to clean it," he remarks when he sees where my attention is. "And yes, I can be deep. In fact, I've heard I can go *very* deep."

"Get the fuck out," I mumble though my lips do curl up at his laugh. I walk Cassius out of the room and into the sitting area, stopping there as he continues to the door. Pausing his steps, he turns to look over his shoulder at me.

"Just talk to her, Nox. Wherever she is, wherever her *mind* is, she appears to be safe there. Remind her that it's safe for her to come back here too." His words settle some of the anxiousness in my chest though guilt still rages like a brewing thunderstorm on the horizon.

"It's weird when you're serious."

He flips me his middle finger and turns to leave, shouting, "And make sure you eat something! Wouldn't want you to lose those vanity muscles before Blondie wakes up!"

Huffing out a laugh, I walk back into the room and carefully lie on the bed next to Rhea. Her lily scent wafts towards me while I tuck an arm under my head, settling into the smallest sliver of space that I can. I study her profile as it glows in the sunlight, the rays soaking into her skin like they can't help but be drawn to another source. If she is in competition with the sun, she is undoubtedly winning.

Cass said to tell her what's in my heart, and that should be easy enough, as it's entirely consumed by her. So, after fortifying myself with another breath, I let the love I feel for her pull the words from me.

"I hope you can hear me, wherever you are. Know that nothing, and no one, will get to you here. I will make sure of it." I swallow roughly, my fingers tapping the top of the comforter. "The first time I saw you, something deep within me seemed to *recognize* you. I know that sounds insane—it made me *feel* insane—but there was this tug in my chest that seemed tethered to you. And I couldn't stay away. I found every excuse I could to be near you, even at the beginning when you wouldn't open the door. I could still feel you. I felt you on the bridge in front of the tower. Your magic was a pulse that beat in time with my own heart. I started to feel you in the guards' barracks all the way on the other side of the damn castle. There was nowhere I could go without there being an overwhelming sense of *you*."

I could never forget those initial few weeks, when silent games turned into passing notes and I got to see the first glimpse of her personality. Then, when my visits became more frequent, I loved the way her face would light up every time I stepped through the door to her tower. Like I wasn't the only one counting down the minutes until we could be together again.

"I remember the moment I realized I was falling in love with you," I say thickly. "We were sitting in the library, taking turns reading from that filthy romance book. I wondered if maybe you had chosen it with the hopes of making me read the more dirty scenes, so you can only imagine my fucking delight when it turned out that you were the one who had to." My smile widens as I recall the way she used the book to shield herself, her voice wavering as the story progressed. "If I'm being honest, it wasn't the words you were reading or the image they were painting that had me clutching on to that bench for dear life. It was the fearless way you read them. It wasn't lost on me that you had never done that with anyone before, and yet there you were, reading those words out loud *with me*. Then you had the courage to ask me if I was with anyone else. It was ludicrous to me then, because anyone who is lucky enough to spend even ten minutes with you would forget all others."

I allow myself to reach out and play with the ends of her hair, twisting the soft strands between my fingers.

"You infiltrated every thought. Your face was all I could picture, both awake and in my dreams. It still is. I should have told you everything that night at the inn. I wish I had because knowing that I hurt you fucking *kills me*. You deserve so much better than that, Rhea, so much more than what I did."

I pause to take a breath, to push away the emotion welling in my eyes that I don't deserve to have there, when I see her hand twitch.

"Rhea? Can you hear me?" I hold my breath, waiting for her to respond or to move her fingers again. Maybe I was just imagining it. Maybe—

Her magic begins to swell, its presence *pushing* on me. Her magical signature is unique, different depending on which power she is calling up. The healing, luminescent magic feels warm and alluring, as strong as the sun itself. I get the distinct feeling that it yearns to be used while her other magic, the one that makes her eyes flash black and creates those glittering shadows... *That* one has an eagerness to it that makes my stomach churn with unease. Like it's using *her*. And that is the magic that is currently pulsing in waves around her. Panic rises within me as that otherness floods in, its darkness a presence that robs me of my breath.

"Sunshine, if you can hear me, you're okay. I'm here with you."

I don't know if I am trying to reassure her or myself. My magic rises in response as it recognizes her power. Kneeling and gently cupping her face, I jolt in surprise when Rhea's skin turns icy right beneath my fingertips.

"Rhea?"

Her eyes jerk side to side under her closed lids, her body stiffening as her magic pulses steadily. I grit my teeth, my hands flying from her face as a strong surge of her magic nearly throws me off the bed. Pressure builds beneath my skin, the urge to shield myself fed by my own power. The air feels thick with static electricity, like the moment before a lightning bolt strikes. Rhea's face contorts into a grimace as her hair begins to *float* around her. Terror strikes me when her back bows, her chest lifting sharply and her mouth opening in a silent scream.

I bring up my magic, a shield of the deepest purple laced with black covering me as I push against the black magic pouring from her in strengths I have never felt before. My arms strain and my hands tremble as I go back to framing her face.

"I love you. I *love* you," I rasp, aching at the way my heart feels as if it's being shredded apart. "I love you so *fucking* much." I repeat the words over and over again, my voice wobbling as I all but plead with any gods listening that she hears them.

Her shadows begin to dissipate, her body straightening out and relaxing back onto the bed. I call my own magic back, watching as it lingers on the parts of her it can touch before it flows back inside me, all while my thumbs gently caress her cheeks. Wetness seeps from the corners of her eyes, the sight of tears trailing down her cheeks might as well be a dagger to my chest. Her breathing evens out, her face returning to a mask of calm.

"Please open your eyes. *Please,*" I beg.

The silence settles back in, somehow more foreboding than before.

The door to the sitting room swings open, my father standing in the doorway with his chest rising and falling rapidly. "What was that?" he asks as he steps in, my mother rushing behind him and shutting the door. They take in my position on the bed, how I'm cradling Rhea's face with my own breaths labored, before their eyes find mine. "Was it her?" my father questions again, his brows reaching towards his hairline. But I'm speechless. I can't form words as my gaze falls back on her.

"My star, what is going on?" my mother asks softly, coming to my side.

I shake my head, my hands still trembling when I pull them away from Rhea and sit back on my heels. "I don't know what happened. She just—" My voice falters as my mother wraps an arm around my shoulders.

"It's alright," she whispers, looking behind me to where my father must be standing. "We need to find a way to explain what that was."

Terror courses through my veins as I stare at the keeper of my heart and soul and find her once again completely still.

Chapter Sixteen

Rhea

*T*HE TENTATIVE QUIET *is strange enough to draw me from sleep. I stretch my fingers and toes, my body aching in a way it never has before—like I've completely drained myself. My memory is foggy, my thoughts tangled together as if in a web of overgrown vines. I focus on the fact that I'm still in the Middle and still alone. Well,* nearly *all alone.*

"You could pretend I'm not here," the woman says with a small bit of mirth.

I snort, pushing myself up to sit. "I enjoy your presence, but I could do without you reading my mind and emotions. Though, in all my visits here, I realize I have never once asked for your name."

"And I have never offered it," she acknowledges with a resigned sigh.

"Does that mean you can't?"

"Indeed." She pauses, thinking something over. "It isn't my real name, which I am forbidden from telling you, but it is a name I have gone by in the past. You can call me Selene."

Goosebumps break out on my skin, and a line forms between my brows. "That name... It feels"—I hesitate, trying to find the right words—"comforting. Am I feeling your emotions?"

Somehow, though there is nothing in front of me, I can see the faintest outline of her shadow in the corner of my eye. It's gone when I try to look at it head-on. "I think perhaps spending so much time here has started to alter your magic."

My body tenses in anticipation of her next words.

Selene senses it as she sighs heavily again. "I don't think you have to go back, not yet, but we should talk about your magic and what you felt as you last wielded it."

Suffocating anxiousness clogs my throat. What I did, what I felt... I'm not sure I want to remember who or what I became in those moments. The power that I could feel hadn't just come from me, but it had overtaken me. Claiming free reign over my emotions and thoughts and body. I felt completely pulled under and overwhelmed and not myself—until I heard his voice.

I wanted to question Nox's love for me, but his actions didn't line up with the doubts that played in my head. He had still lied, still kept important truths from me, but he had also saved me. Kept me safe. Loved me.

"Does it make me foolish?" I ask Selene. "To want to forgive him? To want to try and start over without the lies? Without the confinement and secrets?"

"No, Rhea, it does not make you foolish. You both found love at a time and in a place that it was unlikely to blossom. One on a mission to ensure his kingdom's safety. The other so sunken into her grief that merely breathing was a chore. Yet, despite everything working against you two, your hearts still managed to become linked to each other. That is not something to balk at."

Pressure pushes behind my eyes as I toy with the ends of my hair. Confronting Nox about where we went from here is, at the very least, not something I have to deal with right now. Selene huffs out a breath at that, but before she can lecture me on it, I quickly ask, "Can you see Bella?"

I have tried to avoid all thoughts of her, the pain so fresh that merely speaking her name feels like scrubbing salt into a wound. But, much like how I needed to know Alexi was with Alanna after his death, I want to know if the visions I picture of Bella—free and running through a forest—could be true as well.

"I can see her, yes. She still thinks of you."

I can't quite say it's relief that I feel at that revelation, but my heart swells knowing that, even in the Afterlife, she hasn't forgotten me. A warm tear traces down my cheek while tension of a different kind fills the spaces between my bones. It's the kind that screams of my culpability and stupidity. My guilt and naivety.

"Do you want to talk about any of those things that plague you? I have an excellent listening ear." Her playfulness doesn't mask her earnestness, and though it's strange for me to want to open up to anyone about the darkness I hold within me, with Selene, it inexplicably feels different. And I'm tired, so fucking tired, of having to keep everything held in. Even in the moments between confessions of love and Bella's death, Flynn and I were always trying to maneuver through an ever-changing maze of complicated situations. In our haste to leave the tower, I still hadn't told him about all the things King Dolian had done to me. The abuse and mental torture, yes, but also the fact that he wanted me to wed *him*.

So easy it was to blame Nox for keeping secrets, and yet here I am, holding on to a malicious and barbed part of my history because of the shame I feel over it. But maybe here, in this space where there is both nothing and everything, I can begin to unravel the tangled mess of a person that I am. There is certainly room—and time—to do so. And, in all honesty, I have nothing else to lose.

"Where should I start?" I ask as red creeps up my neck and stains my cheeks.

But Selene sends a jasmine-laced caress over my shoulders, ruffling the silky black and white dress that I still wear. "Let's start with something that is easier to talk about," she suggests.

I close my eyes, forcing myself to pull up memories like one would go digging through an old dresser drawer. Brushing off the cobwebs of fragmented moments in time when I was not exactly happy but content. When the dust settles, I see Alexi, sitting in his green armchair across from me in the living area of the tower.

The glass balcony doors are open, glittering stars and glowing moonlight shining high above in the midnight sky. Candles flicker over the tea table, whole and not yet cracked from King Dolian's abuse. Discarded playing cards lay in a messy pile covering it, and across from Alexi on the small black couch, an eleven-year-old version of me sits. Her hair is lazily pulled back from her face, her green eyes calculating as she looks at the cards in her hand and then back up at Alexi. He smirks, gesturing for her to lay her next card down. She gently brushes a fingertip over a card—what I remember to be the second highest card of the deck. Her smile grows as she lays it down, already basking in her impending victory.

"Little One, remember that playing cards is more than just being impulsive when you think you have a winning hand." He folds his cards down on the table, his hands lingering on them as he looks at her.

I drink in every detail of Alexi in this memory—the salt and pepper of his hair and his broad jaw. The way he seems to have not aged from this moment to the last one I had with him.

"But there is only one other card that can beat mine. The odds are better that I will win." Her voice is the higher-pitched cadence of a child, and her fingers tap on her knee as she looks at our guard. *"I think you just don't want to admit that I won."*

"I would happily lose to you, Little One, but there is a valuable lesson in this game too."

Younger me rolls her eyes. Alexi was always trying to turn simple things into lessons, always trying to teach me something even when all I wanted to do was play. I miss that—miss him.

"I suppose you will delay my victory by telling me all about this lesson,*"* she groans, folding her arms over her chest.

"Such a brat," he says through tilted-up lips. *"Playing a game of cards can be just as multifaceted as life."* He lifts up the last card she played and flips it over so it's now face down in a new pile. She opens her mouth to protest this, but Alexi shoots her a look over the candle flame that tells her to be patient. Sighing, she leans back against the couch. *"It is easy to think that we can predict what will happen in life. That we can get enough information in the present to see the outcome of the future. But so rarely is that ever the case, as there are often things we can't or don't see."*

The child's eyes drift out to the balcony, a calling to look at her little star friends drawing her attention.

"Little One."

She snaps her head back towards his, *"I'm sorry. Cards and life—I'm listening."* She gives him a big smile while tucking her long hair behind her ears.

"Gods above, this girl," he says under his breath. She giggles, and though it is at his expense, Alexi softens under the sound. He leans back in his chair, his hands interlacing under his chin. *"You think you have predicted the outcome of this game because of a single card—a single moment—correct?"*

"Yes, because there is only one card in the entire deck that can beat mine."

"And do you know for sure that the card that can beat yours has been played already?"

"Well, no," she concedes, leaning forward slightly. *"But the odds are pretty good that it has."*

Alexi hums, coming to rest his elbows on his knees, his dark eyes keen and wise. "You are incredibly smart, Rhea. You possess an intelligence beyond your years, but sometimes, you can be impulsive. Reactive before you have all of the information. It is not a fault, not something that you should feel bad about. It's a lesson we must all learn as we grow." He holds her gaze as he says this, ensuring younger me understands that it isn't an insult. "There will be times in your life that will inspire that impulsiveness, though the severity of them will grow as you do. You won't have control over those moments, but you will have autonomy over how you react to them. And the best piece of advice I can give you, Little One, is to remember that, oftentimes, when we think we have seen everything at face value, there are still pieces lingering in the dark."

He then flips her card over, laying it on top of the pile again. Picking up his discarded hand, he plucks a single card from it and lays it down. She groans when she realizes it is the one card that could beat hers.

"People are just as layered as this stack of cards. Life is as unpredictable as trying to guess the cards your opponent has."

The memory fades, my smile wavering as I think about how that very lesson had played out tenfold with Flynn—Nox. But I don't feel all that angry anymore, and maybe it's because I understand that I still don't have all the pieces. At face value, Nox hid something from me, but I hadn't exactly explored all the reasons why. I had been impulsive in my reactions.

I snort, smiling out at the galaxies above. "Still teaching me something, even now."

"Indeed. That was a lovely memory."

I nod and lean back on my hands as I stare out at the swirling and twinkling colors. "In the end, before he died, he could tell that I was about to show my hand. That I didn't care whether King Dolian knew I had magic if it meant saving him. He refused to let me do it, and I've resented him for that," I whisper. The truth of those words, of that emotion, was never one I've admitted before. Not even to myself. "I hated that he made that decision for me. That he was resigned to his fate. That he didn't fight back."

"Alexi couldn't have known what his death would usher in, but he must have believed that, whatever would happen after, you would make the best of it. He must have hoped, at the very least, that you would choose yourself. After all, that's what he did. He chose you."

"Do you think I am worthy of his choice? Of his sacrifice?"

There is no hesitation as she responds, "Yes. And I know of another who would agree."

I know she speaks of Nox. But I'm not quite ready to delve into him yet, instead letting my mind drift to more memories of my time with Alexi.

"Show me another one," Selene says reverently. So I do. *I replay treasured moments with the only father I've known—ones that come to me easily and ones that I'm convinced I can only remember because of the magic of this place. When exhaustion of a different kind weighs heavy on my eyes, my tattered heart swollen with a memorialized love, I allow myself to try and lay to rest that resentment and guilt I feel.*

Though I'm not sure I will ever be worthy of the sacrifice he made for me, I now find that I want to be. I want to try to somehow live a life that could attempt to accomplish just that.

This is not where your journey ends. Promise me. *Those were Alexi's final words to me. And I finally see with clarity just how multifaceted they were.*

"The first step, when you get back to the Mage Kingdom, has to be training with your magic. Learn as much as you can about wielding it," Selene says after I wake up again. *I have no inkling at all how long I've stayed here in the Middle, as time itself feels suspended.*

"What *can* you tell me about the shadows?" *Trepidation once again makes me question just how much I actually want to know about this part of me.*

"They have always been there, the mirror to your light magic. Unfortunately, there is a bit of a limit to what I can say about it—bargains made and all—but I will remind you again that there is someone who *can* help you."

I laugh, shaking my head. "I suppose you want me to talk about him now. I am curious what you think I can tell you that you don't already know."

"It's less about information gleaned and more about you having a space to talk through your feelings for him, complicated as they may be."

"That is one way to put it." *Though it isn't in actuality. I feel like things* should *be complicated. That when it comes to Nox, I should be more angry and bitter. Instead, a persistent thread seems to be twisting around us. One that doesn't give much leash for feelings of betrayal and deceit to grow.*

Selene is silent, even though I know that she can hear my thoughts, which leads me to believe that she wants me to decide where the conversation goes. My exhale is long, and I let my eyes flutter closed at the image of Nox's face in my mind.

"He is... Well, he is everything," I start, trying to put into words what he means to me. "I sometimes have to think of him in terms of past and present because he has infiltrated both so thoroughly. He was the man who saved me from hell, and he is the one who showed me that there was still a new way my heart could break. He was the one who saw things in me that no one else ever did, and he is now the one that I fear could truly hurt me in ways that no one else ever could."

Selene hums—though if it's in agreement or not, I can't tell. "Love is many things," she says after a moment. "Unpredictable. Sometimes unstable and even a little terrifying."

"Is that supposed to make me feel better?" I ask with a lifted brow.

She chuckles lightly. "No, I'm just being honest."

"Have you ever been in love?" I suppose I never really thought much about the life of the woman here in the Middle. What she might have been like and done before making her bargain to stay here. What would possess her to trade away resting for eternity in the Afterlife for a timeless existence in the place between worlds.

"It was love," she replies, answering my unasked question.

"Terrifying, indeed," I retort.

"As I mentioned, sometimes it is. But much like the magic flowing within you, Rhea, there is balance. Love is a mirror of itself; it is two sides of the same coin. So, yes. At times, it is terrifying, but it also can be completely exhilarating. There are moments when it's freeing and consuming and spectacularly beautiful, and I think you've barely scratched the surface of that kind of love with Nox."

His name induces a shuddering breath while I run my hands over the silk dress.

"Why are you so insistent that I try to repair things with him?" I know the moment the question leaves my lips, she won't be able to answer. Remembering how she insisted that I ask the right questions, I try rephrasing it. "What is it about him that you like?"

"Well done, Rhea," she says softly, pride coloring her tone. "And I like many things about him. He's kind to you and devoted. The magic of this place gives me the ability to see with more than eyes, and the Prince of Stars has a great deal of honor and loyalty within him. His love for you is as endless as the space between worlds."

"Prince of Stars?" I ask. And, of course, I am met with silence. Groaning in frustration, I add, "How am I to navigate this new space that we are in?"

"Perhaps you should stop thinking of things as so black and white, Rhea. Fate, in particular, is a curious thing. Remember what Alexi told you while playing cards when you were younger: rarely do we ever have all the pieces we need to try and predict what will happen next. There is no telling what would have happened to Alexi if Nox wasn't the one to point out that he was leaving his post. Just like there is no *guessing how your own fate might have changed had Alexi not brought a bleeding fox to you on the night you discovered your magic.*"

My chin dips as the gravity of her words seeps in. Why had *Alexi* thought to bring me Bella? What if I hadn't called on my magic that day? What if I had stayed hidden when Nox first came to my tower to drop off supplies? I can't begin to fathom how many of the smaller moments in my life had led me down a path towards something more monumental. They weren't always good things, but they certainly weren't all bad either.

"I cannot tell you how to approach dealing with Nox, but I can help lead you out of the fog of indecision that you are lost within."

I'm reminded of the analogy I had used with Nox—at that time, Flynn—about how I felt like I was in a forest with no sense of direction. Selene is offering a compass—a way to guide me through—and after everything, I am eager to take her up on it.

"Tell me."

"Explore who you are and what that means," she says sincerely. "And, most importantly, forgive yourself."

My breath seizes in my throat as my nails dig into my legs.

"Forgive yourself for the things you could not control. For the things that are not your burden to bear. Lean on the ones who would do whatever it takes to keep you safe so that you don't have to add more to that imaginary—and incorrect—list of faults you keep within. Forgive yourself, Rhea."

If it were only as easy as doing that. I had a lifetime of things to work through, to revisit and sort the narrative of. How did I do that without once more becoming undone? I didn't want to always be this shattered version of myself, constantly picking up the pieces of who I was and forcing them to fit together again.

"I don't know how," I gasp.

"Try, Rhea. All you can do is try."

I don't realize how hard I'm crying until my next inhale is a forced sob through my teeth. My hair begins to whip and blow around me, a phantom wind signaling that it's nearing my time to leave. "Wait! Can I stay here for a few moments longer? Just until my eyes close?"

Selene relents easily. "Of course."

I lie on my side and close my eyes, allowing myself to release more than just tears—more than can be measured or seen by the wetness trailing down my cheeks.

"Can you tell me a story?" I say through my heaving. "Just something to help me fall asleep."

With my world crumbling—not to fall apart this time but to rebuild into something new—Selene begins her tale.

"*Once upon a time, a prince fell in love with a magical woman...*"

Chapter Seventeen

BAHIRA

I T'S JARRING TO SEE animals moving about the ship and working as if they were mortals. A shiver works down my body when their heads slowly turn towards me as I walk past them to go to the dining hall. I have no idea what animal form King Kai has, and I suppose that I have no way of telling either. *Unless the shifters can talk in their animal forms?* Gods, I hope not.

The dining hall is empty when I enter, and food has been left out under silver-domed trays on a counter in the back. Lifting each one up, I finally settle on what looks to be a veggie salad with a side of herbed rice and take a seat at one of the many tables that line the room in a grid-like pattern. Sitting in silence has never bothered me before, but there is something about knowing that the only other beings on this ship are currently stalking around as animals that leaves me feeling on edge.

As I eat, I thumb through one of the journals I brought with me. Embroidered on the front is the name Godric, and when I turn to the first page, I see the date is roughly two years before The War Of Five Kingdoms took place. The cursive script of Councilman Godric is elegant, and I easily get lost in the way he describes the historical events that were happening at that time. One particular entry grabs my attention; it details a flame ceremony for a young girl. He talks of how her flame grew to be five feet tall, the glowing show of her magical strength undeniable. The last time a flame was many feet tall was when Nox dropped his blood into the Cauldron of Vires. *So, was this Flame Ceremony before the magic started to decline?* Turning the page, I read about another ceremony for a boy, his flame shooting to four feet. Each of the following entries are much of the same, with no mention at all about magic acting strangely or lessening in any way.

I'm lost in the research, jotting down notes in my own journal with a spelled pen, when a noise from behind startles me. Turning around, I bite back the scream that lodges itself in my throat. Prowling into the dining hall, the dark wooden door swinging behind it, is the most massive wolf I have ever seen. Its steps are slow and methodical, its thick body covered in dark brown fur while its eyes blaze a deep golden color. It continues its leisurely pace in my direction, its massive head tilting as if in observation.

I swallow, setting the journal down as I steel my spine. My fingers curl in on themselves, and a million different scenarios run through my head, all of them ending in me getting ripped to shreds by this massive beast.

The wolf huffs, the noise nearly *sarcastic* in its delivery. It walks past me as if this entire exchange was some sort of test, one I have no idea if I passed or not, when music outside begins to play. I watch the wolf's ears twitch while the hackles on its back rise and its tail goes stiff. The wolf halts and turns to glare back at me.

I'm intent to stare right back when something begins to feel *off*. I stand as the blending of notes—no, a *voice*—resonates in my ears. It is so beautiful and *enticing* that I want to find the owner of such a lovely sound. I brush past the wolf, walking towards the door that will lead out onto the deck. The eerie melody washes over me, getting louder and louder and forcing out every other thought. It begs me to keep moving forward, and I *want* to answer its call. I push through the swinging wooden door, the bright sunlight briefly blinding me as I walk out.

The scent of the ocean—so calming and alluring—is in every breath I take as I step closer and closer to the railing at the edge of the deck. Just a few more steps, and I can sink into the cool waters—I can return *home*. The single voice guiding me is feminine and light, and gods, do I want to be smothered by it. I want it wrapped around me and in me so deeply, so thoroughly, that it's all I can think about. I've never needed something this much.

My hands find the railing, and I peer down into the crystal-blue ocean waters. I see her then—the exquisite creature who calls to me. Her hair, glowing like a ruby, cascades in intricate braids down her head and into the water, floating around her as she swims next to the ship.

My feet step onto the first rung, then the second, as I move to get past this last barrier keeping me from her. Her song stops before I'm yanked back, my heels dragging along the deck as a growl rumbles over me. I twist and turn, my head drowning on the lingering sound of her voice as I'm hauled farther away from the railing until I'm back in the dining hall and deposited onto the floor.

Like the tide drawing back, my mind slowly clears of the film I had felt over it. My hands tremble as I push them into the wooden planks, grounding myself while my temples throb. *What the fuck was that?*

The wolf from earlier gives me a sharp look, the command for me not to move conveyed in its eyes. I'm not inclined to at the moment anyway. I'm too shocked at what just happened, at how my body and mind were not my own. The wolf walks back to the door of the deck, poking its head through and staying still as if waiting for something.

I am standing up on shaky legs, needing to lean on one of the tables for support, when golden light flashes out of the corner of my eye, and then King Kai is striding towards me. A very *naked* King Kai. I stumble backwards at the sight.

"Where the hell did you come from?" I gasp, my hip fully leaning into the edge of the table. My eyes seem to move on their own, drawing a searing line down his broad chest and extremely toned torso. Defined muscle flexes and gleams under his golden-tan skin as he walks, but I force my gaze to move back up before I see too much. It's much harder to do than it should be.

"And why are you naked?" I glance towards the door where the wolf was previously standing, the space now empty. "Fuck," I whisper, as the heat from his body invades my space. Blaming my sudden breathlessness on the fact that I think I was somehow lured by a siren's song seems like the most rational thing to do at the moment.

"Why did it look like you were about to jump off of the boat?" he growls, the wolfish cadence evident now that I know what animal he can shift into. The silence is pressurized—an overfull dam waiting to burst open and drown us both. "Answer. Me," he seethes, taking another very exposed step towards me. His anger is so distinct and sharp that it lures my own out to defend myself.

"I don't answer to you, *Your Majesty*."

"Yes, I am a king. So I can, in fact, command you to answer me."

My eyes narrow into spiteful daggers as I glare back at him. "I would have to respect you enough to give a shit about your title, and I *don't*."

The truth, however, is that I'm not sure enough about what happened to give him *any* sort of answer anyway. One moment, I was staring at a wolf—at him—and the next, I was sitting on my butt in the dining hall, the memory of in between hazy like trying to see through murky waters. I know that something happened with a siren, but I can't remember exactly *what*. That terrifying understanding mixes anxiousness into the already-full pot of anger and confusion I'm operating under.

The king shakes his head, a dark look molding his features into something predatory. "That foul mouth of yours is going to get you killed one day. You are not in the Mage Kingdom anymore, Princess. You're entering a world of beasts and animals. They *will* bite back if provoked, and their teeth are much sharper than yours."

I go to cut him down and remind him that I'm not someone who has to bend to his will, but I stop myself before the words can make it past my lips. Unfortunately, I want answers as much as he does, and that means that I at least have to *try* to work with him.

"I don't know what happened," I grit out. "I wasn't in control of my body. Even my recollection is cloudy."

"Siren songs don't work on females," he states, and I throw my hands up in exasperation. His gaze turns from indignant interrogation to one of pure confusion as his eyes drag down my body, lingering on my chest.

I scoff and cross my arms over myself. "I'm not a fucking male, you *idiot*."

He shrugs though his eyes are slow to move back to mine as the air imperceptibly thickens. "You certainly act like one."

"Why? Because I'm not some simpering fawn falling over myself in your presence?"

"No, because you are brash and don't think before you speak," he snaps, and I do a shit job of hiding my surprise. The shifter king's wide jaw clenches, but it seems he's made his point. "Not going to deny it, then?"

My breaths are quick as I gawk at him, trying to pull words from my brain and into my mouth, but none will come.

"Everything alright here?" Tua asks as he enters the dining hall, his chest bare and a pair of trousers in his hands.

King Kai catches the pair of trousers Tua tosses at him, his eyes boring into mine as he pulls them on, challenging me to look away. Or maybe daring me not to. I might as well be swallowing rocks for as hard as my throat works.

"Everything is perfect, Tua," I respond, turning to grab the journals and pen from the table and then heading towards the door.

Outwardly, my steps are steady and even, but inside my chest, my heart beats furiously. Three months. I have *three months* of this hell to look forward to.

Chapter Eighteen

Bahira

With my stomach ceasing its revolt from being at sea and the shock of the siren attack pushed to the back of my mind, I had decided to spend the morning doing my daily physical and mental exercises, a practiced routine since childhood, before grabbing a plate of food and taking a seat in the dining hall.

Part of the education a mage goes through is learning how to meditate. They say it's because of how our magic works—how *magic flows where intention goes.*

Being without magic, I found meditation to be a way of quieting my mind so that I wasn't constantly overwhelmed by it.

For as much as I appreciate the mental aspect of meditation, my favorite expression of it has always been the physical exercises. The head training instructor, Dilan, is a hard-ass, but he has never treated me any differently for being magicless. If anything, he pushed me harder than the other children. When they would rest and work on manipulating their magic, he would have me running laps or doing extra sparring. For years, I practiced not only at the designated class times but after hours as well. I *had* to be the best: the fastest, the strongest, and the most agile.

Yet, as my peers liked to remind me, it didn't matter how I excelled at fighting if the person I was up against had magic. At the end of the day, magic would always come out on top. I loathed that fact. So much so that the need to find my own magic was a constant itch upon my skin; one that wouldn't be ignored.

A chair screeching across the wooden floor brings my attention back to my plate, risotto and vegetables, and Councilman Godric's journal laid out on the table in front of me. Based on what I've read so far, I'm led to believe that magic was acting normally at this point in our history—a few years before the war. He writes about the queen of Void Magic at the time, Lucia Vasiris, in such a fond way that I've abandoned all pretense of note-taking simply to read his description of her.

Today, Queen Lucia visited the orphanage in Galdr. Though she always glows brightly, being with the children truly made her luminescent. Wrapped on her chest was the newest princess, Aurora, who is only three months old. The princess slept the entire time, allowing the queen to stay quite a while. She showed them her celestial magic, much to their delight.

Afterwards, she met with the council to discuss plans on hosting the rulers of the Fae Kingdom—King Kamon Ryuu and his consort, Lady Jia Ryuu—for their visit to the Mage Kingdom.

A throat clears, and when I lift my head, I find the vigilant eyes of the king's advisor looking down at me.

"Sorry," he says with a chuckle, holding his hands out in front of himself. "May I join you?"

I nod and gesture to the chair across the table from me. While Tua's face is relaxed, there is a noticeable underlying tension in his body. His posture is slightly too stiff, his hands clasped together a little too tightly.

"Is there something you would like to say?" I ask quietly. Though after a quick glance around, I can see that no one else remains in the dining room.

"Am I that easy to read?"

I close the mage journal and place it in my lap—Tua eyeing each movement. "I'm afraid so. Let me guess, it is about what happened this morning."

He sighs, resignation heavily laced within it. "I'm afraid so. I have to ask, what possessed you and the king to openly combat one another in front of the crew?"

I shrug, ignoring the slight prickle of annoyance that flares. Why does it matter that they saw if it was the king himself that engaged with me? "Seemed like a fun idea at the time."

I was in the middle of my practice this morning when the shifter king approached me and challenged me to "let off some steam." We sparred—me with my spear and him with nothing but his fists—and after some back and forth, it had ended with him kneeling before me. I was under no illusion that the shifter king was going easy on me, but when he stood, he whispered only loudly enough for me to hear, "I knew you would be able to handle that spear." His smirk had made me narrow my eyes at him, but then with a jerk of his head towards the watching crew off to the side, he added, "And now they know it too."

I didn't think too deeply about why the shifter king would want to show the others on the ship that I could fight.

"Do you remember what I told you about the unrest on our island?" I nod my head, holding his gaze. "Rumors of our king engaging in these kinds of *extracurriculars* will not boost his image in the way that is needed to ensure our people's trust. They already find him *lacking*, and if you learn one thing about the people of the Shifter Kingdom, Bahira, let it be that maintaining their loyalty is easy. It's *gaining* it that is the hard part."

I fight the urge to roll my eyes. "You should know that it was *your king* who baited me into a fight. If he cannot control even that base impulse, what hope should you have that he can lead an entire realm?"

"That is precisely my point, Your Highness," he says. My shoulders tense at the use of my title. "King Kai is strong and a servant to the crown upon his head, but he lacks refinement. While some like that wild edge when war or conflict arises, the rest of the time someone level-headed is necessary to ensure peace is kept. I will not lie, King Kai struggles with that and, as a result, often has *me* stepping in to do things for him."

My brow arches in question. "Is it normal for you to divulge so much about your king?"

Tua smiles, his dark eyes squinting. "Nothing about this arrangement is normal, wouldn't you agree?"

I huff out a breath at that. I suppose that is true enough. "What would you like me to do? Ignore him when he tries to engage with me?"

"As someone with royal experience, surely, you understand the fine line one must walk in order to appear a certain way to the masses. The Mage Kingdom may be a peaceful, more relaxed one, but I doubt you are without your own issues." He lingers on that statement, long enough to make sure it is heavy in the air between us. "Just as we are not without ours. I simply ask that you keep that in mind should King Kai do something *less* than savory in your presence again." Shadows cast by the flame gems lay across Tua's face as he looks at me, disquiet simmering beneath my skin. Yet I was here to help with the magic problem and nothing more.

"Fair enough, Tua. I will make sure to keep things pleasant and less *aggressive* on my end."

Tua sits back again in his chair, crossing his arms over his chest as he nods his head. "Thank you, Bahira. How are you feeling by the way?"

"Much better, thank you. I had no idea I would be so sick on the water." My fingers tap on the table idly as I debate asking Tua why he didn't tell King Kai about how sick I was, but the door to the dining hall opens and said king appears. I mimic Tua's posture as I watch King Kai grab a plate of food and make his way to us. The way his body moves is one of pure power. Though his tactics during our sparring had lacked the delicate balance that mine possessed, there is no denying that the male knows how to fight.

"See something you like, Princess?" he asks, lifting a brow.

The memory of the naked expanse of his skin when he shifted forces its way into my memory before I can stop it. A retort balances on the tip of my tongue, but one glance at Tua has me swallowing it back down. I wait until he's taken a seat next to his advisor before I gather up the mage journal and my plate. "I think I'll finish this off in my bedroom. Good night, Tua. Your Majes—"

"Kai. Just Kai. I hate the title."

I wince at his word choice, as does Tua, before simply nodding my head. "Kai, then."

Our eyes lock, something heated passing between us before I turn on my heel and leave.

Chapter Nineteen

Bahira

THE DOOR TO MY cabin is thrown open, and I shriek as I come up to sit in my bed, half-dazed and hair strewn about my face.

"Good morning, Princess."

"What the *fuck*?" I pull the blanket up to my chest despite the fact that I am completely decent underneath. "What if I was lying here naked?"

Kai scoffs as he steps up to the foot of the bed, crossing his arms over his chest. The black tattoo that adorns his right arm seems to suck the sunlight right to it, making it stand out even more. He's shaved his face, his golden brown skin smooth and gleaming while the damp strands of his dark brown hair are pushed back. Though his clean scent is subtle, I can still smell him from the head of the bed. "Luckily for us both, you aren't."

I'm going to punch him again. The bastard smiles like he can hear my inner thoughts.

"Why are you here?" I ask, pushing the blanket off of me completely and coming up to stand.

I comb my fingers through my hair, moving the curls away from my face in an attempt to tame them. Kai doesn't answer my question, his gaze lingering on what my hands are doing instead. His body goes rigid, his biceps bulging from the way his hands press into his arms. Yet he stares at my hair as if it's going to walk off my head and right to him.

"Why do you do that?"

My question knocks him from his stupor, his eyes snapping to mine. They look more amber today, perhaps from the way the sunlight shines on them. "Do what?"

I take a step towards him, my hands fisting at my sides. "Why do you stare at my hair as if it personally offends you?"

His nostrils flare as his eyes drag down my body. I'm wearing a thin night chemise, the silky light blue fabric falling to mid-thigh and clinging to my curves. I take another small step forward, forcing his eyes to meet my own.

"You're imagining things."

"Imagining your attention would be a nightmare I wouldn't wish upon my worst enemy. No, I think you stare at my hair because you *like* it." I lean forward, bitterness seeping into my voice. "And you *despise* that you do."

The tension in the cabin is like a raging firestorm, brutal and burning and growing the longer we glare at each other. His body is full of coiled energy just waiting to strike; I can see it in the way his eyes blaze and in the clench of his jaw, the muscle fluttering there. He leans in too, hardly leaving a few inches between our chests as they heave with our strained breaths. "The only thing I *like* about you is that you have the capability to fix the blight on our magic with your own. Beyond that, I have *zero* interest in any part of you."

I still, air ripping from my lungs like the oxygen has been sucked out of the room, at the reminder that he expects me to have magic. That he isn't aware he is bringing someone onto his island who is known for her brain and not her ability to wield magic. *Fuck.* I jolt back, needing space as I think of how to respond.

Something unreadable flashes quickly in his gaze before he turns on his heel. "Dress and pack quickly. We'll be on the island within the hour."

His booted footsteps thud on the wood as he walks out without another word, slamming the door shut behind him.

I close my eyes and tilt my head back, blowing out a slow breath. The tiniest feeling of guilt seeps into my bones as I pace around the cabin. I shouldn't feel bad. The ancient magic of our world *chose me*. King Kai himself chastised Daje for complaining that the magic chose wrong when it settled on me, and yet... I groan, running my hands over my face.

Packing up my belongings is easy considering that I never really unpacked them to begin with. I bring my trunk onto the deck, setting it next to the rest of the crew's things. My backpack carries not only the mage journals and magnifier, as I'm not willing to risk anything happening to them should anyone decide to mistreat my luggage again, but my spear as well. With nothing else to do but wait, I walk to the edge of the deck and lean against the railing, the island nearly upon us.

Though I have seen it to scale on maps in books, there is something quite different about observing it in person. Already, I can tell that it is much more green than any drawing in a book could depict. The color is so vibrant that it glows like a gem amongst the endless blues of the sky above and the water below.

The ship slowly pulls into the port where a handful of others are already docked. Though it's just past sunrise, the heat of the sun causes sweat to bead on my brow. I gather my hair up into a ponytail and then check my backpack to make sure it and my spear are still secure. The humidity of the island is sweltering as I wait for the rest of the crew to disembark before making our way over the creaking planks, the glimmer of the Spell ahead of us. Waves crash up the sides of the dock, misting my heated skin. The salty scent of the ocean saturates the air, but another scent is woven into it—one that's earthier in a different way from back home. It carries with it a zing of citrus and sharply potent floral notes.

Damn it, it smells like the king.

Where the Mage Kingdom is full of verdant green bushes and trees and small sprouting flowers, the shifter isle is lush with long-stemmed plants and leaves of nearly every color. It's so vivid and electrifying in its intensity that my steps falter as I look around.

The shifters ahead of me pass through the Spell effortlessly, but I pause a foot before it. This is the same Spell that lines my own kingdom, that lines them all, but I still harbor apprehension at the thought of crossing. A throat clears behind me, one of the shifter males staring with a brow drawn up when I look over my shoulder. Gripping the straps of my backpack, I take a deep breath and walk forward. From what I have read, those who pass through the Spell know immediately that their magic—or in the case of the mortals, their youth—is dwindling though it can take days before death arrives. I loose a quiet sigh when I cross over and don't feel anything other than the soft sensation of the magic.

Continuing down the pier, I look once more over my shoulder at the shifters behind me, and like an arrow finding its target, I lock eyes with King Kai. His granite features seem even more hardened, no emotion pulling on his face at all. He glares at me with his usual malice, so I roll my eyes and turn back around. We descend a short staircase and step right onto the sandy edges of the beach. The granules are finer than those on mage shores, easier to sink into with each step.

The sand finally gives way to a rocky path, the small pebbles clashing together under the steps of our procession. My eyes bounce from each new plant and tree as I categorize it all in my mind, committing them to memory so that I might be able to identify them in a book. Excitement tingles on the tips of my fingers, my heart beating loudly in my ears as I think of all I will be able to see and learn that isn't related to magic.

We continue walking for another twenty minutes, the humidity so oppressive that, by the time I hear the familiar noises of city life, I'm ready to just walk around nude. Sweat coats every inch of me, my breathing labored even though I'm not exerting myself physically. It's like I'm trying to breathe underwater.

"We are entering the capital," one of the shifters shouts from ahead, probably for my benefit.

My knowledge on the Shifter Kingdom's capital, Molsi, is paltry, only facts like their most popular export and last known populace bounce around uselessly in my mind. Small huts lining either side of our walkway come into view, people surrounding them in small groups. Though "hut" seems like too rudimentary a word to describe the dwellings that are spread out over the landscape. Some are only one story, circular in shape, and made with a mixture of wood, stone, and what looks like dried-out fronds. Others are made of the same materials but stand three stories tall. While the structures back home are whimsical, adorned by the land itself, here they appear more practical. No frill or fanciness, just what is needed to make a sturdy home or business.

The stone used is a brilliant white, and it looks softer than the dragon stone I'm used to, like one could carve into it with a fingernail. Light green ferns dot the ground on either side of what has turned into a central roadway, tiny flowers growing in the spaces between from rich dark brown soil. Plants with wide and glossy leaves in a striated white and green color draw my eye every few feet. The colors of everything here are so crisp that I'm apt to believe they are hues I've never seen before. Rolling rocky hills dotted with trees line the horizon in all directions as I turn slowly to take everything in. Larger homes are built right into some of the hilltops, their white stone stark against the dark rock. I always presumed the Mage Kingdom to be the most beautiful of Olymazi, but even I must admit quietly to myself that this kingdom rivals it.

The capital city is bustling, similar to Galdr in that respect, but there is something about the energy of Molsi that feels *different*. Merchant stalls and free-standing buildings crowd either side of the path we walk. Every shifter we pass gives me a second glance, their eyes all variations of dark gold to deep brown. Can they tell I'm not a shifter? Or is it that I'm the only female in the caravan?

I study them in return, noting how most of the females are dressed in clothing that bare their midriffs, but given the heat and humidity, it doesn't surprise me that they would dress for comfort. I find myself envious of the way they don't seem to be sweating as profusely as I am. The males are dressed in shorts and tunics that are sleeveless, and nearly every single one of them is broad in a way that doesn't anatomically make sense. Almost as if they were stretched just a fraction too wide to accommodate more muscle. For both the males and females, there is no denying that strength is a shifter attribute. And they all have varying midnight-black tattoos adorning their deep tan skin. Some only have one inked on an arm or leg, while others have lines and swirls across every inch of uncovered skin.

Breathing in deeply, the scent of something savory makes my stomach rumble.

"Did you not eat before we left?"

My head jerks to the right, finding Kai now walking beside me. "I was told by an incredibly rude male to dress and pack quickly."

Kai sighs, the sound somehow louder than the noise of the bustling city. People part as we walk, clearing the busy path almost instantaneously, yet nearly *all* of them stare at Kai in an unnerving manner. It isn't one of admiration or even basic respect, but instead, there is wariness in their gazes. Their lips form straight lines, and some of the men in particular look poised to attack—their bodies rigid with tension. I look behind us and find no one from the ship is following. Even Tua has stopped and is talking with a group of males farther back.

"Do you not walk with any kind of royal protection?" I ask quietly.

Kai's lips draw up in a smirk as he cuts in front of me and walks to one of the huts where a delicious scent is emanating from. My steps falter as I splay my arms out to the sides at his back. The asshole just *ignored* me. Intent on giving him a piece of my mind despite what Tua warned, I step towards him, only to be stopped by a tug on my pants. A young shifter female, face covered in what I hope is chocolate, stares up at me. Her amber eyes crinkle against the sunlight coming over my shoulder, so I squat down to get on her eye level.

"Yes?"

"Are you friends with the king?" Her voice is high-pitched as she points to where Kai is still facing the hut.

"I... *know* him, yes."

"Can you ask him when he is going to fix my daddy?"

I huff out a laugh, but it dies the moment that I realize she is being serious. "What is wrong with your daddy?" I ask, but the small female doesn't answer when a shadow instead covers us both.

Her wide eyes grow larger as she tips her head back. I don't have to look to know it's Kai. Though she showed no fear coming up to me, it begins to surface on the little shifter's face the longer she observes him.

"Marida! Come back over here!" a female yells at her, waving her hand quickly. The young female immediately darts off but not before giving me one last look over her shoulder.

I rise slowly, watching as the mother quickly ushers her away and into one of the smaller huts. *What the hell was that?* I look at the king from the corner of my eye, but he gives me no indication if he heard the interaction.

"Come, Bahira," he says before shoving something warm into my hands and walking away. Bewildered, I follow him while the female's words replay in my mind. What could she possibly have meant by "fixing" her daddy? Was this related to the blight? And why the *hell* won't Tua or Kai tell me what it is?

"It's called a samosa," Tua says as he joins me, gesturing with his chin towards the food in my hand.

Looking down, I inhale deeply, and that rich scent from earlier thickens as I unwrap the parchment-covered item. It's a triangle-shaped pastry, one that is clearly filled with savory ingredients instead of sweet ones. I take a small bite and nearly groan at the burst of intricate flavors. It's spicy and earthy yet fresh and decadent. It's one of the best things I've ever tasted, and the king—the arrogant, rude, brash, infuriating king—bought it for me. Because he knew I was hungry. The next bite is tougher to swallow with that realization.

Tua and I walk side by side in silence as we weave through the busy capital. Multiple people come up to him and shake his hand, giving friendly smiles and looks of admiration. And for some reason, one that I don't dare look too closely at, I feel pity for the looming male walking a few paces ahead of us all alone. While he does get a few looks of general indifference, the majority of them are edged—bordering even on cruel. It makes me wonder how Tua can let his ruler walk completely unguarded with so much animosity curling in the air.

Turning down a smaller side road, we continue to the edges of an estate lined with palm trees. It's only two stories, but its expanse is massive, nearly double the width of the palace back home. Tall arches curve between white stone columns that line the outside of the first level in all directions. The second level boasts a wraparound balcony, wooden posts dotting it every few feet with bright purple ivy wound tightly around them.

"Welcome, Bahira, to the Stone Palace," Tua says, gesturing widely at the building.

I take in the gradient green vegetation and sparkling ponds full of colorful fish. A garden, filled with the most unique flowers, blankets the land to the east of the palace. Against the vibrant green of the plants and bright blue of the sky, the white Stone Palace stands out as its own beautiful landmark.

Tua guides me up a small set of steps and through black double doors that already stand open. My eyes grow wide at the white and black stone floors, the pattern like a checkerboard. The walls of the palace are made of sandy-colored wood, the planks stacked vertically, and there are plants in deep green and rich blue tucked into corners or hanging down from the ceiling. Rugs of gold and white lay over the checkered floors, adding an elegance that I'm surprised by.

Tua's pace is unhurried, as is the king in front of us, but I find that my feet are eager to move faster. To drink in even more about this foreign land, and to learn all its secrets.

"You *asshole!*" someone shouts, halting our group. I draw my brows together at the sound of quick-moving footsteps, looking to Tua for any hint of who the owner might be. A female, a little shorter than myself, comes barreling out of a side corridor. "You left without saying goodbye!"

"I told you when I was leaving. You opted to sleep in," he responds with a shrug.

She scoffs, staring at him with narrowed eyes for all of three seconds before a smile breaks out and she jumps onto him, her arms wrapping around his neck. His laugh—an actual *laugh*—echoes out in the hall as he holds her to him and spins around so that he is facing us. Though it makes no sense and goes against every sort of logical reasoning I can quantify in my mind, a spark of jealousy prickles through me. I squeeze my fist tighter around the parchment wrapper still in my grasp. *You are tired and haven't had sex since Max, that is all this is.* I will have to rectify that as soon as possible.

Kai releases the female to her feet, letting her turn around before tucking her into his side, his arm wrapping around her shoulders. She is *stunning,* her features elegant but not dainty. With high cheekbones and full lips, she is not hewn from rock like the shifter king but from glass, brilliant yet no less sharp. Barely giving Tua any sort of acknowledgment, her light brown eyes find mine. Her hair is a lighter shade than my own, thick and wavy with a few braids blended in. She wears the same style of clothing as the females I saw in the city center, baring her golden tanned midriff, but the quality is finer, the fabric bolder in its color and trimmed with delicate ribbon. She eyes me curiously, gazing slowly over my face before turning her attention back to Kai. A taunting smile curls her lips.

Kai clears his throat, giving her a look of warning before glancing back at me. "Tua will show you to your room. Feel free to explore the palace and the grounds, just do not cross the palm tree perimeter on your own."

I offer him a single nod of understanding and watch as he and the female leave, her gaze lingering on me a moment more before Kai leans down and whispers something to her. Their laughter echoes off the palace floors and walls as I watch them retreat, the samosa turning to lead in my stomach.

Chapter Twenty

ARIA

*C*OME WITH ME, DAUGHTER. *Let's see if you truly live for your queendom or for yourself.*

My mother's voice echoes in my head as we swim towards the back exit of the throne room and down one of her private hallways. My tail fin's movements are jerky while I fight to stay in control of the dread rotting thickly within me.

"Did you know that when I was your age, I had already birthed one off-spring?" she lilts, the magical cadence of her voice powerful. I swallow roughly, failing to keep my shoulders from curving in on themselves. I fear that I know where she is leading me, and I *can't* do it again. "Everything I have done—every choice, every seemingly *barbaric* action taken and word spoken—has been for my people. For the siren sisters we share these waters with. But we should have so much *more*."

I know this. It is a declaration she has made plenty of times in the past; it is why things are the way they are for our people. I don't mention that when she was my age, there wasn't a spell cast out over Olymazi. The War Of Five Kingdoms hadn't happened. Our siren song wasn't weakening, and getting pregnant was easier.

There had always been a balance to things. The mortals could easily have children, their numbers robust and plentiful. But they didn't have magic, so their only defense lay in those numbers. The fae had their dragons and extended life, but they conceived at far lower rates than even we did. The shifters had strength and the ability to change forms, but only to one animal, and their lives were not as long-lived as our own. The mages could bend and manipulate the magic of Olymazi to their will, and with a nominally extended life, they were otherwise no stronger or different than mortals. And sirens—we can shift into beings of two worlds. Our song can control the minds of men except that our survival is completely dependant on them. And over the decades, the ability to lure them has begun to dwindle.

The hallway we swim down is dark, the normally brightly lit crystals built into the walls covered in a film of black algae. It leads to an open courtyard, and there in the middle, surrounded by floating stalks of bright green kelp and bundles of neon grass, is my sister Sade. Her scales reflect gold and burnt orange flares all around her on the seafloor as they catch the rays of sun filtering in from the surface. On her lips, her claws digging into his arms so roughly that red blood drips slowly down them, is a male. Though I can't see his face, I already know that his eyes are glazed over, his lips moving at Sade's command as they continue to devour each other's mouths. Through that kiss, siren magic keeps him alive for now.

Sade unseals her lips from his, and my heart jumps into my throat, my talons curling into my palms. This must have been why she wasn't at the assembly.

"It fucking took long enough. Aria, he's all yours," she sings, winking as she swims past me.

My mother smiles somewhat warmly at my older sister before her face settles back into its usual measured indifference.

My eyes bounce back to the male, whose body is slowly sinking to the ocean floor as the magic from Sade's kiss begins to wear off. He looks to be in his third decade, his fair skin dotted with freckles while his longer orange-red hair floats around him.

"Will you honor your people, Aria? Or will you be responsible for this male's death?" I'm already responsible for his death. The only reason he is here is so that my mother can prove a point. Tears well in my eyes, while acidic nausea churns in my gut. *Not again. Not again.* "Hurry up and decide; the magic is nearly gone."

The male's light blue eyes start to clear, that magical veil covering them receding as they widen and look around in panic. I grit my teeth, terror and guilt bleeding together inside of me and keeping me frozen in place. My mother clicks her tongue, swimming to me until she has her gold diamond-tipped trident pointed at my heart.

"This," she says, poking at my chest until a prick of pain clears the wave of emotions holding me in place, "will get you killed. You are not doing this male any favor by not fucking him. The only thing you are doing is proving to me that you do not value your role within this family. Within a queendom that you were *bred* to protect. Mark my words, Aria, if you do not perform your duties as I expect, then there is no place for you here."

She removes the trident, and I quickly swim to the male. The magic is all but gone, and he thrashes wildly as reality seeps into him. I don't open my mouth to sing, as it won't work anyway. My mother may think she knows everything about me, but this secret is one that only one other being is aware of.

It had taken a few hunts for me to realize that my song held no magic. I, a siren princess, cannot lure males in with my song. I can feel the magic build in my throat despite the fact that it doesn't work. If it were not for Lyre always going on hunts with me and using her magic for us both, I'm sure that my secret would already be exposed and I would likely be dead.

So I seal my lips over his, my tongue diving into his mouth and caressing it in gentle strokes. Immediately, his movements calm, his body becoming pliant to my will. At least this part of my magic is effective.

I force my hands to his belt buckle, my talons slicing the leather easily. My gaze stays pinned on the now glassy one in front of me as a tether to reality, even though all I want to do is disappear. It seems more respectful, more dignified—if that could be true at all in this situation—to not close my eyes and pretend I was doing anything other than *violating* him. Even as he moans his pleasure at my touch, it isn't real. It's manufactured and just so horribly *wrong*.

I had fought it the first time Queen Amari ordered me to fuck a male in front of her. I had pushed back and said that I wouldn't do it with an audience. I swore that I was dedicated to this queendom and my role within it, and all that small defiance had done was cause her to bring in more to witness it. The first time I had sex was in front of the cruel jeweled eyes of my mother's vicious supporters, guards, and even a few of my sisters. And *her*. And now, though it is just her and I and this unfortunate male, it feels as if the eyes of the entire Siren Queendom are bearing down on me.

I don't *love* my home, not in the way I think a princess should. I do not want to contribute to our *royal line,* and I absolutely *hate* forcing my body onto someone else. I've wished for more than just the cold writhing of someone under a spell. It is foolish and hopeless and clearly pointless to feel that way, but my yearning heart wants it all the same.

"Aria, I don't have all day." My mother's harsh voice brings me back to the present.

I shift my lower half and yank the male's trousers down. Then I perform what is expected of me under my mother's watchful eyes.

My legs are barely shifted back to a tail when my mother sticks her trident out in front of me, trapping me in place. She doesn't have to speak a word; I know what she wants me to do.

I watch as my magic bleeds from his eyes, replaced instead with all-consuming panic as he begins to thrash. The lack of oxygen slowly deprives his brain, and his lifeless body eventually sinks to the ocean floor. I will the tears to hold off a little bit longer, running through my mental checklist and adjusting my body—hopefully well enough that she will let me go.

All I want is to leave.

With calculated languidness, my mother scrapes her trident against my chest as she withdraws it from in front of me. "It is good to see that your loyalties do, indeed, lie with your people. You will be joining them on the hunt in the morning, and then I have a *special* mission for you."

Her black eyes coat me in an imaginary darkness that seeps from her. It pokes and prods at me like it's looking for a way to corrupt me. What she doesn't realize is that she already has—I am already irredeemable. Nodding my head, I bow deeply, and Queen Amari finally leaves me, a broken shell of a siren struggling to keep her heartbeat steady.

"Surround the ship now!" Allegra shouts as our party fans out around the large vessel. Lyre swims beside me as usual. Both of our faces are grimly set as we move to the far side of the large wooden ship, my muscles straining to keep up with the speed it's sailing at.

Allegra whistles, our sign to get to the surface and start singing. The ship is fast in the water, waves crashing off of it as it moves. But our powerful bodies keep up, streamlining with the current as we were made to. I follow Lyre up, my head breaking through the water as I begin to sing, joining the chorus of the other sirens. Our voices harmonize effortlessly, the chilling melody blanketing the ship from all angles. Magic tickles the base of my throat, while my tail propels me faster.

Lyre moves in front of me, another siren passing behind to go towards the stern of the ship, as I wait to see the males enraptured by our song. Well, not exactly *my* song, but the chorale of my siren sisters.

Two hands land on the railing, and dread fills my veins in anticipation of what I will witness—what I will have to do. Sometimes, I get lucky, and there aren't enough males on the ship. Sometimes, Lyre is able to distract Allegra so that I can sneak away and give the illusion that I've done what I'm supposed to. But a quick look towards my eldest sister reveals her attention already on me. It seems that with my mother's latest punishment, Allegra is more vigilant of my movements. Making sure my *duty* is being fulfilled.

Curly brown hair appears over the railing of the ship, and my eyes widen as I take in the facial features—*feminine* facial features. Our gazes lock, her attention solely on me. My voice falters as I watch her climb a rung of the railing and then another before she is harshly yanked back. I stop singing, my focus moving to Lyre while adrenaline burns through my veins.

I hear Allegra hiss from her position near the front of the ship. "Shifters!" she growls before dipping under the water, our sign to abandon the ship and follow her.

I glance at Lyre, but her focus is on a teal-haired siren swimming on my other side. The female's eyes move from the ship to me, lingering briefly before she ducks her head under the water to follow Allegra.

"Did you see that?" I whisper, catching her amethyst gaze as the ship moves farther away.

"Yes. Come on, we better go." We both sink under the water and follow the rest of the sirens back to Lumen. My mother is going to be furious to find out that we targeted another shifter ship. She may even chastise Allegra for it, but the thought of my eldest sister getting reprimanded doesn't take the edge off of my anxiousness.

Did I nearly call a female into the water? It's impossible. My song, the very magic that is supposed to lure the opposite sex to mate with, doesn't *work*. At least, it doesn't work on males, but is there a chance it works on *females*?

And what will it mean if Lyre isn't the only one who saw me almost call one into the water.

Chapter Twenty-One

DOLIAN

Two weeks prior

MY TEETH GRIT TOGETHER as I watch her run towards the trees, holding *his* hand. The familiarity with which they interacted causes the rage already simmering inside me to intensify.

She is mine.

I am not your queen, she had yelled with more fire than I had ever known her to have. It should anger me, to hear her deny what I know to be fact, but instead, all it does is ignite my yearning for her even further. I knew a certain kernel of defiance was glimmering within her; I had just been wrong that it was only a remnant of her father. No, this brand of rebellion was purely created from her mother's side, and despite my wishes to, I couldn't hate it. I couldn't snuff it out entirely. Not when it reminded me of Luna.

"Do you want me to go with the rest of the King's Guard, Your Majesty?" my personal guard, Jorah, asks.

"Yes. Inform the captain that if he values his head, they will be brought back to me by any means necessary."

Jorah nods before running behind me to find the captain in the throng of golden-armored men.

Turning on my heel, I begin my walk back to her tower, my steps slow and staggered as I try to refrain from limping. For nearly twenty-two years, I have kept her safe and hidden in plain sight. Everyone knows the princess lives, the *heir to the throne*, but they all think that she is nothing more than a woman grieving, lost in the turmoil of her mind. This lie prevents questions from arising about my reign. Unfortunately, it appears Rhea had been keeping things from *me* as well.

She has magic. My grip on my sword tightens as I cross the crushed wildflowers to the base of the tower, the voices of men and clanging of metal fading into the forest. How could she have hidden that from me for so long? All this time I had been waiting...

They will find her and bring her back. And when they do, I will get answers.

Rolling my shoulders back, I open the arched door of the tower, and my boot immediately hits something hard. Lifting my sword, I stagger back and strain my eyes to see into the darkness. "Show yourself to your king!"

A muffled groan sounds out in response, and I allow my grip on the sword to loosen. Stepping forward again, I squat and squint my eyes to try and make out who is in front of me. My free hand reaches out for what must be a gag—barely made visible in the silver light of the moon shining through the door behind me—and yank it down.

"It's me," the man—*Xander*—gasps.

"What happened?" I growl, helping one of my Trusted up.

"There is a small blade strapped to my thigh," he rasps, wobbly on his feet. Finding the blade, I cut the bindings from his hands before handing it to him to remove the ones at his feet.

"Tell me how this happened *now*, Xander." He had been missing for an entire day, and though I was inclined to believe that he was perhaps incapacitated, one can never be too sure when in my position. No matter our personal relationship, I learned firsthand how quickly a man could change allegiances with the right motivation.

"Her guard," he says, leaning a shoulder against the stone of the tower as he runs a hand through his hair. "She attempted to escape yesterday, and—"

I cross the space between us quickly, my forearm coming to his throat as I slam his head against the stone. "What did you say?"

"She tried to escape yesterday," he wheezes, the pressure I put on his neck causing his breaths to become labored.

My anger is a living monster within me, and I welcome the way it turns my impulses into murderous ones, my thoughts all screaming to drive my sword into his neck. Regardless of the blood that flows in his veins. But I *need* more information, so reluctantly, I let him go. His coughing is like nails dragging along stone while I wait for him to elaborate.

"I was talking with her guard—Flynn—on the bridge, and she stepped through the tower door there. I caught her down here. She also had a white fox with her."

My leg burns with pain in response, the bite from that fox flaring back to life.

"I had brought her back to her room and was on my way to tell you when Flynn attacked me. He was able to get the upper hand and then bound me down here." He swallows, his gaze leveling with mine. "He fought differently than how we train our men to fight."

I turn without another word and head up the stairs, leaving Xander to decide if he is going to follow me or not. The steps up to the top are many, and it gives me plenty of time to think about how this could have happened. Somehow, despite the fact that I always had a second pair of eyes on the tower door, Rhea was able to befriend this guard. One that is much younger than Alexi. Than even myself. My steps turn more aggressive as I near the top.

If he so much as touched her... I shake my head and blow a breath out. It matters not because once she is back in my possession, I will make sure she never leaves again.

The wooden door creaks as I push it open and step in, the space feeling empty and cold without her here—though her scent still lingers in the air. *Lilies.* So similar to the flower her mother smelled of. Exhaling roughly, I walk around the main room. Each of my visits here had been purposeful. I never allowed myself to fully take in the space that Rhea dwelled in all day and night. I couldn't. It further crushed a long since shrunken part of me that wanted to nurture and care for her in a different way. But history had proven to me that I would lose her if I did that. If I didn't mold her into who I knew she was capable of being, she would be lost for good. Everything I did was to make her worthy of the title she would gain by my side: Queen of the Mortal Kingdom.

My steps echo against the wood floors as I enter the library. I had already been cut out of Luna's life by the time she was pregnant with Rhea, but even I had heard about her newfound interest in the old guard tower. It's the main reason why I placed Rhea here instead of somewhere in the castle. I hoped she might feel somewhat connected to the woman who curated the space. Despite how things fell apart between us in the end, Luna would always have her fingers wrapped around a piece of my heart.

Walking over to the window seat, my gaze is drawn to the book lying in the middle: *The Little Sun.* Despite myself, I cannot help the small tilt of my lips. When Luna first came to the castle as a maid, she carried this book everywhere with her. I had made her read it to me over and over again in our early days of friendship, and she obliged every time. The memory washes through me, but I allow none of my feelings to latch on to it. That time is long gone, and in the end, she betrayed me as everyone else had. Flipping through the pages, I stop when I see a flash of misplaced paper. I hear Xander come into the library but give him no mind as I read the words Rhea wrote.

Trust the stars over the ancient trees to guide me from the false king. And look to the east for the answers I seek.

I crumple the paper in my hand, twisting my neck side to side to stretch the muscles out as I work to tame the monster inside of me.

"What is it?" Xander asks.

"She is heading towards the Mage Kingdom," I grit out. I know the Mage Kingdom's secret; one they've guarded since the war. With Rhea being part mage, she will be able to pass through the Spell without repercussion. My guards *have* to get to her before then.

I slap the note into Xander's hand before forcing my injured leg to move me across the space to the door and back down the steps. Once I'm finally on the bridge, I find one of the remaining captains.

"They are heading towards the Mage Kingdom border. Send enough men so that, no matter where they try to enter, they fail."

He nods, turning back to run and gather the rest. They *will* stop them, and she will be back in the safety of our kingdom soon enough. Any other option is not acceptable.

Present

"Your Majesty, I have your tea." The maid's voice travels through the door.

"Come in," I command, leaning back in my armchair as I stare out of the floor-to-ceiling window to the gardens below. Each day with no word whether or not Rhea is making her way back to me is nothing short of a flame being held to my skin. I need her here; I need to know that she is safe once more. Now that she is officially twenty-two, I can proceed with my plans of wedding her and making her my queen. I need to *solidify* making her fully mine.

The maid sets my tea on the table at my side, pouring the dark liquid into the porcelain tea cup until it's half full. Steam curls up and over its edge as I reach for the carafe of milk and add a small splash.

"Is there anything else you require, Your Majesty?"

"No, you are free to go." She curtsies, her footsteps nearly silent as she heads towards the door. "Tienne," I call out, my gaze back on the window in front of me while I take a small sip of tea.

"Yes, Your Majesty?"

"Do you have any news to report on our little *side* project?"

After Rhea's escape, I knew that someone had to have been helping her beyond the mage parading as a mortal guard. My grip on the teacup tightens, heat from the steaming hot liquid scalding me.

"Not yet, Sire. As you can imagine, everyone is being very tight-lipped about who worked on her supply orders and if anyone beyond the newest guard delivered them to her."

I smirk at her obvious attempt not to name *Flynn*. Perhaps she *did* notice the way my hands fisted the last time I spoke of him. *Perceptive little maid.* I stand, setting my cup down on its saucer before turning to stride towards her. Her attention to detail means that she should have caught something, should know more about who could have possibly assisted Rhea. Stopping before her, I force the fury I feel inside to show up in the clench of my jaw and glint in my eyes.

"I will find out *who* aided Flynn in abducting the princess. If one of the things I learn is that you helped them or that you are withholding information," I pause, leaning in close enough that I can see the way her pulse flutters at her neck. My voice is a blade honed by years of being on the receiving end of similar words. "I will not hesitate to remove your head. Do I make myself clear?" I devour the way her cheeks flush and her chest rises and falls quickly in fear. Gods, she nearly *smells* like she's afraid, and it would be so *easy* to act on my desire for it. To draw more and more of that dread from her until nothing remains and then force her to draw everything from me with her mouth or hands or body.

But she doesn't look like Rhea, and so I force my blood to cool as she responds.

"Of course, Your Majesty. I will get answers for you."

"Good. Now, get out." Turning back to the window, I once more look upon the garden.

Memories of the first time I had shown it to Luna come to me unbidden. She was so beautiful as she walked barefoot among the flowers, encouraging me to do the same. Our fingers dragged along the delicate petals, the floral fragrance pungent in the air around us, as we talked and laughed. It was nearly a perfect moment—until my father had found us there and punished me for it. For showing any ounce of joy. *For having a friend.*

I close my eyes and grit my teeth, pushing the memories back down. When another knock sounds on my door, I have to fight the urge to shatter the tea set across from me as I scream, "What?"

"Your Majesty, the council is ready for you," Simon, my closest advisor, says through the door.

Swallowing down my annoyance, I walk over to the large standing mirror leaning up against one of the stone walls. I hate the stone—hate how easily it brings me back to that damp, confined space beneath the castle where my father often locked me.

When I became king, I made them cover as much of it as possible with tapestries, paintings, and colorful fabrics embroidered with my sigil. Anything to hide the way that the cold gray seemed to penetrate every inch of this place. I even hired artists to paint directly on it—fantastical scenes of faraway lands and mythical creatures. But it never seemed to stay hidden, the stone's true color finding a way to peek through any of my attempts to muffle it.

My hand smooths down my vest, my attire not showing a single wrinkle. I tilt my head, inspecting my hair to make sure not one strand is out of place and that my beard is neatly trimmed. Satisfied with my appearance, I open the door and join Simon out in the hall. The man was an advisor to my brother during his *brief* reign as king, his age only showing through the silver strands mixing with black in his hair. After Conrad's death, he was eager to show his allegiance to me, even taking a blood oath without question.

"Has there been any word on the return of the guards?" I ask, keeping my gaze forward as we stride down an ornate gold and navy blue adorned hallway. Rugs in the same colors cushion our steps, none of the gray stone visible in this corridor. To my right, golden sconces hold flame gems, the sun shining in through small windows on my left charging them with daylight. I can't be entirely sure, but I believe I have every single flame gem known to exist in the Mortal Kingdom now fixed to some wall in this castle. *Excluding the one that ended up in Rhea's tower.*

"No word yet, Your Majesty. But if you sent the King's Guard to the Mage Kingdom border, we wouldn't expect them to be back until today at the earliest."

I force out a breath at his explanation. He isn't wrong, but two weeks is a long time to wait for my future bride to make her way back to me. I have spent the entire time since her abduction working out how to ensure that, once she is back, she will never leave again. I thought about forcing her to take a blood oath, but without knowing the extent of her magic, I didn't want to chance that she could work around it. As it appeared Flynn had. If that was even his real name. I had combed through every detail that my royal army had on the man, and somehow, he had managed to fake everything about himself well enough that no one questioned him. I would have beheaded every single person responsible for allowing him to infiltrate my kingdom if I could have, but the royal council wouldn't approve such a thing, and I need them on my side for what I am planning to do once I have Rhea back.

I lead us into the large room that houses meetings of the Royal Council. Vaulted ceilings stretch high overhead, coming to a point and making the gray stone impossible to totally cover here—though I have tried my best to do so. The room is regal, full of my ancestors' history and our refined tastes. Golden rugs cover every square inch of the floor, and woven tapestries, the largest in the entire realm, stretch from corner to corner. The images on them are more realistic—paintings surrounding us of the day the realms were separated by the Spell and the war that had ignited it.

A long wooden table is centered in the room, a large candelabra alight in its middle. Though the sun shines in from the many windows on the back wall, there is an ambience that only a dancing flame can provide. One of menace and deeply rooted unease. A subtle reminder for these men before me that, though I may heed their guidance now and again, my word is rule—*is law*. And no one will stand in the way of me getting what I want.

Simon joins the five other men already standing at the table while I take my time walking to the grande chair set at the head, a hand in my pocket as I do so. My fingers clutch the handkerchief with my initials embroidered on it—the remnants of *her* blood still woven within the fabric. It is vile to not have washed it, but it felt like I finally had a piece of her to keep with me at all times. I didn't want to let it go—let *her* go. The men stand at attention, their chins dipped ever so slightly in respect as they wait until I take my seat before following suit.

"Good morning, gentlemen. What updates do you have for me?"

Leopold clears his throat, his blue eyes lifting to mine as he begins to speak about the Cruel Death. I have to force myself to listen, to not let my frustration at being unable to quash that which jeopardizes my sovereignty drown out every word he is saying. "Unfortunately, a total of one hundred men and women have died from the Cruel Death in the past month."

My eyes widen imperceptibly as I level him with a glare. "Were there any commonalities between them? Anything at all?"

"Besides being close in age and the fact that the majority are from smaller cities outside of Vitour, nothing else."

Fucking hell. The room is silent as I rub my fingers over my jaw, my other hand still clutching the bloodstained fabric in my pocket. The numbers are getting worse, the death rate growing, despite my every attempt to quell the sickness. I hadn't cared until it started taking men that were of age to join the guard. Mortals don't have magic, so our strength lies in our numbers, and the Cruel Death was just that—cruel in the way it was slowly thinning us out.

"There is another matter we must speak of, Your Majesty," Paul, the oldest advisor and arguably my biggest critic, croaks from his seat at the far end. Tension lines his withered face, his glassy light brown eyes narrowing.

"By all means, Paul, don't make me wait forever." I gesture with my free hand.

"It is with regard to the princess. And the resources you sent to retrieve her. With our numbers already dwindling, do you think it wise to have sent more than half the guard to scour the kingdom for her?"

Simon, in his seat next to Paul, smirks at the question. I force the corner of my lips to lift as well, the other men adjusting subtly in their chairs because of it.

"She is royalty, is she not? Why wouldn't I send men out to rescue a kidnapped princess?" It was the lie I had told everyone, that her guard had kidnapped her. None of them know the secret of what mages can do—how they can pass through the Spell without consequence. The members of the King's Guard are sworn in blood to obey my every command, including that they not speak of any of the missions I send them on.

"I suppose that I mean why waste resources getting her back? She is inconsequential in the grand scheme of things. She matters not—"

"She matters to me!" I yell, slamming a fist on the table. "I will not have you question what I value."

"My apologies, Your Majesty. I simply meant that she represents a threat to your crown. She is the true heir. What if she is found and contests your rule—"

"You do not know her as I do, Paul. She will come back, and she will do so willingly." His bald head shines with sweat, the look of it churning my stomach, so I turn my focus back on the other men around me. "And when she returns, she will stand behind me while I continue leading this kingdom—as my bride."

While most of the men do a good job at hiding their reaction to my reveal, a few of them cannot help the way their jaws slacken in response. Paul is the only one dumb enough to spew his thoughts.

"Your—your bride, Your Majesty? But she is your—"

"That is enough. Any more discussion of her will result in the immediate termination of your position." And the loss of his life, but he knows the truth of those words without needing them spoken. "Surely, then, you have said everything you intend to on the matter?" My hand lazily gestures towards Paul, my face once again relaxed into an easy one of boredom.

"Of course, Your Majesty. My apologies again."

The door to the council room opens, and Xander walks in, coming to stop at the other end of the table. He bows to me before straightening.

"Your Majesty, the first group of guards has returned."

My body stiffens as I look at him, that seedling of something light and reminiscent of hope sparking within me. "And? Do they have her?" I should have done a better job hiding the eagerness in my voice, but it's too late now.

Xander doesn't do anything for the longest time before he eventually gives one shake of his head.

No. No. No. "Everyone out."

Paul leans forward in his chair and squawks out, "But, My King, there is still much we need to discuss."

I force my gaze to meet his decrepit one. "You're right. Why don't you stay? Everyone else, leave."

No one speaks a word as they filter out until only Xander and Paul remain. I stand from my golden throne and walk down the length of the table to where Xander is waiting, Paul to our right.

"How many more guards are left to return?"

"About half. Perhaps she will be with that group," he suggests though he doesn't sound confident.

"Report back to me the instant they're here." Xander nods, turning on his heel, but my next words halt his exit. "I have need of your sword. Wait outside the door."

My curt command is met with a brief moment of hesitation before Xander heeds it and unsheathes the golden longsword from his hip. I wait until the door closes behind him, watching as Paul grips the armrests of his wooden chair.

She isn't with them.

Somehow, she managed to slip through my fingers and most likely ended up on the other side of the Spell. With *him*.

"My King, I know you are upset—"

"Upset? *No.* No, Paul, that word does not begin to scratch the surface of how I am feeling." My breathing is unsteady as my grip on the sword tightens. I walk around the table until I'm behind the elderly advisor's chair. My eyes close, and

I picture what I'm about to do in my mind. How it will feel to silence this idiot forever. "I might have let you go, even with the way you spoke of your future queen, but to be honest, Paul, I have dreamed of doing this for quite some time."

He gets nothing more than a few sputtered words out before I swing the sharpened blade. It cuts through his flesh easily, his head falling backward and rolling past where I stand. Blood splatters my clothing and shoes, layering over my face and hands.

She is with him.

The thought tumbles over and over in my head, my hand shaking as I turn and walk to the door of the council room. Opening it, I hand the sword back to Xander. "Clean that up."

My skin begins to burn where his blood coats it, but I force my steps to stay steady as I make my way to my rooms and remind myself to be patient. If Rhea has truly escaped to the Mage Kingdom, then I will do whatever is necessary to bring her home. With the right motivation, anyone can be convinced to give up *anything*.

Chapter Twenty-Two

Rhea

Autumn woods and the spicy undertone of earthy leaves fill my next inhale, my body subtly relaxing at the scent. The warmth of the sun blankets my skin, my light magic waking up because of it.

The familiar tingling in my fingers and toes after a visit to the Middle begins, like the scraping of a thousand needles. But then it deepens, those needles pushing into my skin—sharp and unforgiving. I hiss through my teeth, brows drawing low as I try to wiggle my extremities to shake off the pain. The feeling only amplifies as it travels up my arms and legs until it's dripping down into my torso like a slowly building waterfall of pain.

Selene said there would be a physical toll, a cost, for how long I spent in the Middle. She wasn't kidding.

"Rhea?"

His voice. *His. Voice.* Despite everything, the sound is a welcome respite—a shimmering light shone into a dark cave. I try to open my mouth to respond, to say anything at all, but I can't. The sensation continues as the prickling feeling pierces through my skin and muscles and veins, going down to the very bone.

"Rhea, please wake up." His normally deep tenor is nothing more than a shaken rasp against lips.

A groan manages to vibrate in my throat, my mouth still unable to open as I'm plunged further into the pain of being *back*. The weight of his hand covers my own, cloth of some sort between our skin as his fingers tighten around mine.

"Sunshine," he rasps again, "please wake up. I *need* you."

Nox's hand squeezes mine again before he lets it go, along with a strangled breath. Finally, the stinging sensation begins to lessen, retreating out of my abdomen and flooding back through my arms and legs.

My eyes fly open as I gasp, air rushing into me like I've been stuck underwater and have finally broken the surface. My vision is blurry, odd shapes and colors melding together and swirling.

"Nox," I rasp out, but it's hardly a noise as the weight of the world around us begins to suffocate me. Layers upon layers slam into me, and the last thing I hear before darkness once again takes over is Nox calling out my name.

My eyes flutter open, the room I remembered to be lit with sun now draped in night. I immediately wiggle my fingers and find that they are much easier to move, free of any prickling sensation. It's painful to swallow, my throat raw and scratchy. Turning my head slowly, I look to my side and see a figure outlined on the bed next to me. Even with only the light of one of those small flames on the other side of the room, I still know it's Nox. *Nox*—how easy his name now sounds in my head, not quite as foreign as it once did.

I trace his face with my eyes, noting how his body is tense even at rest. Balled fists lay in front of him like he's ready to strike as soon as a threat is revealed. His breathing is easy but not deep enough to suggest that he's fully asleep.

Moving as quietly as I can, I change my position so that I'm lying on my side facing him. Our bodies are mirrored on the bed, not quite knee-to-knee but certainly heart-to-heart. Nox's breathing stays even, his body curled to take up the smallest amount of the bed, which is still almost half of it because he is so big. Tenderly, afraid to disturb the air around him, I lift my hand and gently push my fingers through his hair. Simultaneously, we both release a deeper exhale, as if touching somehow unlocked a breath.

I think about the first time I ever touched Nox's hair during our passionate first kiss. It was the pinnacle of a fixation that seems so silly now. Of all the things I could possibly be obsessed with about Nox—and there were many to choose from—one of the greatest longings I had was simply to run my fingers through his sable waves. It seemed so simple, so banal, but I suppose to someone who had spent her life alone and in a tower, the simplest things sometimes felt the most monumental.

My fingers trail out of his hair and move achingly slowly down his temple, his skin soft under my touch. Smoothness gives way to stubble the closer I get to his jaw. My thumb brushes beneath his lower lip, and emotion constricts my throat.

Staring at him like this, with my touch unhurried, ushers in memories of the quiet moments at the inn. When he gave me a journal; when we confessed that we loved each other. It felt less like an admission and more like an acknowledgment of the inevitable. After my time in the Middle, after the things I had seen there, I could find the truth in that. In the idea that, despite whatever my fate is to be, it might have always led to this somehow—to him and me.

"Rhea?" He says my name roughly as his eyes open.

"Hi," I respond quietly.

Nox shoots up to sit, rubbing a hand over his face as if to wake himself from a dream. His wide gaze never leaves mine while his chest heaves with rapid breaths. I join him in sitting up, my arms a little shaky from the inactivity of however long I've been lying here.

"Are you really awake? Are you really here?" He reaches out to touch me but stops midway.

"Yes." The word is tough with my throat so dry, and it makes something in Nox snap out of his mystified state.

He quickly moves off the bed, crossing out into the sitting room where a small table with a silver tray glints under a dancing flame—a golden pitcher and glass cups stacked on top. Returning to my side, he hands me a glass of water, the cool liquid quelling my aching throat. My hand shakes as I hand it back to him, his fingers lingering over mine.

"I'm okay," I whisper.

He pushes the wayward strands of hair back from his forehead, the movement making a small smile uncurl on my face. "Like hell you are," he says warily.

Turning on the bed, my legs dangle off the edge as I watch him pace in front me. His bare feet are silent, the only tell to his movement the lightly squeaking wooden floorboards beneath them.

"I promise I'm fine." Deciding I want to prove it to him, I try to stand and immediately crumple under my own weight.

Nox moves quickly, catching me before I drop to the floor. "Fine?" he questions, our chests flush together.

"Okay, maybe my legs are a little stiff, but I've been in bed for, what, a day or two?"

Nox's fingers tighten on my back as he holds me, his gaze piercing. "Try six days."

I freeze, my hands holding on to the front of his thin gray shirt causing the fabric to bunch. "That can't be right," I murmur. "You're sure?"

"I have counted every hour—every *minute*—since you passed out, Rhea. I'm sure." His anxious voice hits me harshly, and guilt ties my stomach in knots. "It is the sixth night."

"Have you stayed here the whole time?"

"I wasn't going to leave you. I promised you I never would." I close my eyes and lean my forehead onto his chest, breathing him in. "Only you could ever hold that power over me," he confesses.

"I don't want that power. I don't want to do that to you. And I want to talk about everything, truly I do. But learning I have been laying in a bed for six days has left me somehow more exhausted and desperately wanting to take a bath. And hungry." I realize with a small laugh.

Nox's hand relaxes on my back as it moves in soothing strokes. "Why don't you take a shower, and I'll have some food brought up. And then we can talk."

My head lifts from his chest, our eyes connecting through a chasm of the unspoken. "And then we can talk," I agree.

Nox shows me how to use the shower, the mechanics the same as the one I used in Celatum. Standing under the warm water, I nearly jolt at the realization that Celatum and our entire night at the inn was apparently over a week ago. I had been in the Middle for the equivalent of six nights, and yet it felt like less than half of that. My heart pounds as I turn off the water and grab a soft black towel to dry myself with.

The scent of Nox is everywhere in his bathroom and now on my skin, and I can't say that I dislike it. He had left a pair of sleeping clothes that I think must have been his sister's on the counter, the silk short bottoms and sleeveless top soft against my skin and the color a pretty dark blue.

Running a comb through my hair, my fingers tighten around its handle at the thought of our impending conversation. Confessions sit heavily on my chest, an excruciating weight that threatens each exaggerated breath I take. I know that I love him, that a life without him isn't something I want. But the disquiet whispers that plague my mind and infiltrate my thoughts are hard things to get rid of.

He has an entire other life here, one that I wasn't told of. One that I'm terrified will hold other secrets that may be just as hard to push past as learning the truth about his involvement with Alexi.

I pull my damp hair over my shoulder and quickly brush my teeth with the spare toothbrush that Nox had said his mother's lady-in-waiting, Sarai, brought. Finally feeling somewhat put together again, I turn and reach for the door handle, my hand hesitating in the air for a few seconds before I force myself to grab and turn it. Steam billows out of the bathroom and into Nox's room from behind me. Humidity sits thick in the air, a byproduct of both my shower and the summer air seeping in from the open window.

"How are you feeling?" he asks from where he sits on the bed, his back against the dark wooden headboard. His gray eyes are sharp on me, their awareness causing goosebumps to break out over my skin.

"Better, thank you."

"I had them bring up some food and more water for you." Standing, he gestures to the small table out in the sitting room.

Nodding, I follow him out and sit in front of a platter of fresh fruit—most of which I've never seen before—and some bread. Going for the latter, I then pour myself some water and begin to eat quietly, trying to ignore the sudden awkwardness as Nox sits on one of the couches. I take in the space, the dark colors slowly tugging on memories of when I first arrived. My eyes roam from the wooden beams above to the plush rugs below and then to the corner of the room, where a black and decayed plant sits. *Odd.* I look back to Nox, our gazes clashing before he gives me a barely there smile and then forces his eyes closed, tilting his head back against the couch.

My stomach drops at the movement. "Are you alright?"

His eyes open, and even in the dim light, I notice the dark circles that bruise his skin as if he's been up for days. That guilt rears its head again when I realize that he probably has.

"Better," he says, mimicking my earlier answer though his version sounds less truthful.

Sighing, I push up from the table and walk over to him, ignoring the way his eyes deepen in color the longer he looks at me. I also ignore the way my stomach clenches under his attention. "Let's make a vow," I say, sitting on the couch next to him.

Nox runs a hand through his already-mussed hair and then nods tentatively. It's unsettling to see him so uneasy, to observe his powerful body made rigid with anxious tension and know that, at least in some part, I am the reason why.

"From here on out, there is only honesty between us. No matter how hard, how difficult or *fantastical* that honesty may seem"—he quirks a brow at that—"we only tell the truth."

His head nods in agreement, sending a few strands of raven waves over his forehead again. My fingers twist into the silk of my top, nerves growing the longer we look at each other.

"Are you truly alright?" I ask again.

Nox blows a breath out, his tired expression betraying his words from earlier. "Not really." Then his gaze drops from mine, but not before utter defeat crosses his features.

I yearn to reach a hand out to him, to cup his face and tell him that it's going to be okay, but I don't know if that is exactly true. We are two people afloat in the same sea made up of love and sacrifices and secrets kept, and it feels like we are drifting farther apart.

"Rhea, nothing has ever torn me apart more than keeping these secrets from you, specifically the one about Alexi," he says softly, an admission that I can tell comes from a ragged place within him. "I meant what I said earlier that my plan was to tell you absolutely everything. I just thought it would be better to say it all once we got here. Once we were away from King Dolian and you could see with your own eyes the place and people I was trying to keep safe."

I chew on my lower lip, fear of this unknown space between us working hard to keep my questions locked inside of me. But I had promised honesty, and I meant it. So I break open a box filled with the things I need to know from him.

"How could you look me in the eye and say everything you said, all your professed truths and declarations of love, and still be holding so much of yourself from me? You knew what he meant to me. You *knew* how I had grown up. How naive I was. How sheltered." What started out as a simple question turns into an inferno of accusations within me, sparked by the anger I hadn't realized was still simmering so brightly.

"Everything I said was the gods' honest truth, Rhea—"

"But we aren't really talking about everything you *said,* are we?" My voice is hardly above a whisper, but it strikes Nox like an arrow hitting its target. My magic rises within me, and while it's mostly a warm feeling, there's also a hint of bitter cold.

"No, I suppose we aren't."

The expanse of that invisible ocean between us grows. Perhaps it was foolish to think we could overcome this. Maybe I held too much hope in what Selene had said in the Middle. Could loving someone be enough to bridge a gap that now seemed impossible to close?

"Do you know that I have never *once* been told the entire truth by anyone in my life? Can you *possibly* imagine what it feels like to finally think you've found someone who truly sees you, who says they *love you* as you are, and find out that it was a *lie*?"

"It wasn't a lie," he argues in response, his body leaning towards mine. "Four years ago, I left my title, my friends and family, my *home,* to find what we perceived to be a threat coming from the Mortal Kingdom. I know it doesn't hold a candle to the lifetime of shit you've been through, but for me, those four years felt like trying to walk with heavy chains shackled to my ankles and the weight of my kingdom across my back. *Yes,* I had to pretend. I had to do it every single day, except for the few rare visits I got to make back home, but even then, by the time I finally could relax enough to be myself, I was packing up to leave again." Nox takes a deep breath, his eyes tracing the outline of my face. "I lived in that kingdom, serving King Dolian, with only one thing on my mind: keeping the people that I loved safe. I was willing to sacrifice anyone who stood in my way. I was willing to sacrifice *myself* to ensure it. No matter the cost, I *wanted* to pay it because here, in this place?" He pauses to gesture out with his arms. "It's where *every single thing* that held any sort of value to me was waiting. Waiting for me to find out if they would stay safe or if they had to prepare for an attack I wasn't sure they could defend against. *And then I met you.*"

The last sentence is practically said through gritted teeth, as if that painful realization *broke* something in him. At this moment, it nearly breaks me.

"I remember going up the stairs of that tower for the first time with a damn smile on my face because I was so *sure*—without a shadow of a doubt—that I was going to find what I was sent there for. *Finally,* after four fucking years, I was close enough to get the answer I desperately needed. One that *my kingdom* needed. But then my eyes met yours. You were standing in your loft, looking like a damn goddess of light. You cut through the darkness that surrounded me so easily, so effortlessly. Staring into your eyes, I felt like I could breathe again in a place that was slowly suffocating me."

My eyes widen, my own breaths turning choppy at his admission.

"I knew the moment you came down the stairs from your loft that you were the magic I felt. It was pulsating around you, around the tower, so strongly that I nearly fell to my knees in your presence. It was then that I realized King Dolian had *lied* about you. You weren't some grief-stricken recluse obscuring herself from the outside world. You were beautiful and glowing and *magnificent* in every sense, and that asshole was *hiding* you," he growls. "He hid you and did gods knows what else to you because, even if he didn't know you had magic, he sure as fuck knew you were special. I could tell you that I decided to get to know you purely because I needed to figure out how you had magic or if you were a threat, but that would be a lie. I could say that my feelings for you slowly morphed over time, when our visits became more frequent, but that would also be a lie."

My brows furrow together while my brain tries to play catch-up to everything he is saying.

"It was the moment you called out King Dolian for what he was that I knew—I fucking *knew*—that you were going to change everything," he says, bringing a hand to his chest and rubbing right above his heart.

I replay our first encounter in my mind, the memory surfacing easily. I had snarked that King Dolian liked to make up lies about me and then had panicked at my words, at the frank way I had spoken them in front of a stranger that I thought was bound to serve the king. But Nox had just smiled broadly at me. A smile that was, and still is, beautiful and devastating.

"Visiting you, getting to know you, *falling in love with you*— It was never about completing my mission. Looking back, I think I knew that very first day that I was drawn to *you*, called to you, even if I didn't understand why. It may have been your magic that beckoned me to that tower, Sunshine, but it was *you*—just as you are, magic aside—that kept me coming back. You took everything that I thought I was and tore it to shreds. You did it with the way you looked at me like I truly mattered. You did it with the brief moments I would get a smile or, gods, a fucking laugh. It's like time stood still when your bravery peeked out from under the massive rock of grief you were living under." Nox's breath stutters, his fingers clenching on his knees as his eyes grow glassy. "I had the answer I was searching for, but I didn't realize that the question had changed until much later, and I was absolutely *terrified* by that. Terrified to lose that feeling of being home despite being so far away from the only one I had ever known. Terrified of losing the woman who had ushered in this freedom I was so *desperate* for."

Tears trail down my cheeks as his words dismantle any argument I might have had against them. They completely obliterate any doubt I had lingering that perhaps I really was nothing more than a means to an end.

His voice is rough, and it draws me in until our faces are only a few inches apart as he speaks. "I need you to understand that *nothing* and *no one* is more important to me than you. Not my title, not my crown, and not even this kingdom full of people I would have died for four months ago. You can be angry with me. Fuck, I expect you to be. I *want* you to be angry, but don't question my love for you because, despite everything else, it is the one thing that has always remained true."

My eyes close as his hand cups the side of my face, his thumb gently wiping away my tears.

He takes a deep breath, adding, "And it always will."

Chapter Twenty-Three

Rhea

*C*OWARD.

It is the only thing I can think as I stare at the unfamiliar wooden beam ceiling above me. Utter shame is the only emotion flowing through me while I lay on a bed that is neither mine nor Nox's but his sister's.

After he confessed his side of everything, explained his deeply-rooted love for me, I had just stared at him, speechless. It is ludicrous to find myself shocked at the way he so easily disclosed his feelings. Nox has always been open with me about how he feels, and I know, so deeply within me that it pulls on the edges of my soul, that he is being honest. That lying about who he technically is hurt him—maybe as much as it hurt me. Maybe even more. He is a crown prince, but does that knowledge change who he is to *me*?

What did a title change, anyway? Though I am princess of the Mortal Kingdom, that moniker has no bearing on what makes me who I truly am. It isn't even a title I want. Groaning, I turn on my side, frustration mixing with the wave of emotions crashing into me.

I know that Nox loves his kingdom, and despite what he said earlier, I know he would still fight for them, for their protection. It is ingrained in who he is—a protector. I also know that he loves me and that it is the kind of love that I have read about. The kind I thought might not even exist. A kind so pure and real and *raw* that, even in my quietest wishes spoken to the night sky, I wouldn't have been able to ask for something as good as this. As good as him. I could never have allowed myself to dream of someone like him because I didn't know what it was to be loved like that.

And I am a coward. Because after he confessed *everything*, I had just stared at him, words completely dried up. Anger snuffed out like an ocean's worth of water poured on the flame of a single candle. He gave his heart to me, and I had shored my defenses in response. An intrinsic part of me that is still afraid of getting hurt, the one that screams that I'm a shell of a person not worth anyone's time or love, had won in that moment.

When it was clear that I couldn't—wouldn't—speak, Nox dropped his hold on my face and murmured something about getting some more rest. Then he had led me to Bahira's room, her door just down the hall from his.

Now here I am, contemplating what I am going to do next.

Coward.

Knowing that sleep is a lost cause for tonight, I push off of the bed and walk over to the glass balcony door. The summer air is warm around me as I step out, fragrant floral and pungent earthiness heavy with every inhale. There is no moonlight visible through the canopy of trees, the forest just barely lit by the small flames in glass orbs surrounding the outside of the palace.

My hand absentmindedly reaches out to scratch Bella's soft fur—so used to her being at my side—and I'm met with nothing but empty space instead. My next breath is harsh, and I'm unable to stop my quivering lip as I place both hands on the wooden railing in front of me and dig my nails into it.

Coward.

My head dips back down as my gaze goes once more to the trees in front of me. I remember what Selene had suggested—that I should forgive myself, and that seemed easy enough in theory. But forgiveness had to be earned, didn't it? What had I done to procure that sort of clemency for myself? I had a long list of things I have failed at, another made of matters that I was directly to blame for, and no list of the ways I had atoned for them.

Not like Nox had. He continually risked parts of himself for me because, despite it all, he loved *me*. And when he had professed that love over and over again, when he had laid out his reasons for keeping secrets and then subtly begged me to forgive him for them, I had just *stared*. Silent and dumbfounded. Guilt-ridden and stunned. He deserves my forgiveness; of that, I am sure. And I *do* want to give it to him. A quieter voice whispers that I want to give it myself too.

But it can't be that easy.

Night passes quickly though very little of it is given to sleep. Instead, I sit curled up on Bahira's bed, hugging my knees to my chest as I let myself get lost in memories that now seem to haunt me. Bella's absence has never screamed so loudly as it does now, a phantom in the room that sucks the air from it and leaves me huddled in the mess of the aftermath. Eventually, my lids grow too heavy to keep open, my body uncurling enough to lay down and succumb to the fatigue that calls to me.

I'm awakened by a gentle knock and a voice at the door, the sound causing me to jerk upright, growing dizzy as I do. "Lady Rhea, my name is Sarai. I'm the queen's lady-in-waiting. May I come in?"

Ringing starts in my ears as my heart squeezes in on itself. I don't know who this person is, if they are truly someone who works for the palace or not. *Where is Nox?*

I don't respond, clutching the blankets of a stranger's bed as my magic stretches within me. The silence grows while I stare at the dark wooden door, a trickling of sunlight dotting it from the windows across the room.

Footsteps sound and another voice accompanies a new round of knocks. "Rhea? Are you in there?" Nox asks, and my body immediately relaxes.

Swallowing down the anguish that has taken root in my throat, I quickly cross the room and open the door. The motion feels so familiar, like all the times that I would rush to answer his knock in the tower. But, standing across the threshold now, the man in front of me has traded in his signature smirk for a defeated downturn of his lips. His dark gray eyes roam over me for only a moment before he turns his head. The column of his throat works as he swallows harshly, a hand gesturing to the woman standing a few feet away at his side.

"This is Sarai. She is the lady-in-waiting for my mother and someone I deeply trust. She has some things for you." He steps back, the distance only a foot or so, but he might as well have leapt across a canyon. *Why won't he look at me?*

"Hello, Lady Rhea," Sarai says, stepping into the space Nox left. "I have some new clothes for you as well as some shoes. I can get them all put away for you if you'd like?" She waits for my small nod before she enters, and I watch as she heads down a short hallway that must lead to a closet, her arms full of colorful fabrics and a black sack.

Looking back at Nox, I chew on my lower lip, my next inhale a struggle. "How late in the day is it?" With the sunlight so obscured, it's hard to accurately gauge what time it is.

"Early evening," he answers, still not meeting my gaze. "I am going to let my parents know that you are awake and that we will need some time to figure things out."

My fingers twine together in front of me, my throat burning as I fight to clear it. "Okay." He dips his chin, turning on his heel to walk away from me. "Wait," I croak out, halting his retreat. My mouth opens—to say what, I don't know.

My lack of experience with relationships and interacting with others has never felt like a burden with Nox. He has so effortlessly made me feel like he never finds me inadequate, and yet now, with his back to me and his shoulders rounding under the devastation we both must be feeling, it's like he doesn't have it in him to make up the difference between us anymore. A defeated Nox, a *hopeless* Nox, isn't one I've ever seen. It's one that I'm not sure how to speak with.

"There is a place I'd love to show you a little later if you'd like—"

"Yes," I answer quickly.

Nox finally meets my gaze over his shoulder, and my heart shatters at the way he looks as if he's breaking. At how we both are.

My magic rises, pushing me to go to him. To wrap my arms around him as if that could fix us, but I keep my feet rooted in place, reaching for that space in my mind that I used to hide every hurt within. That *I* used to hide within. It isn't there anymore; not like it was. It's as if being in the Middle somehow gave me a clean slate. I had the space and time and freedom to process every facet of my life, but I didn't know *how* to. And the man that I thought would be the one to help

151

me is looking at me like he'll never see me again. Like I'm already a memory that he's being forced to let go of.

"Take your time getting ready and eating. I'm sure my sister has some books tucked into a bookcase that will help you pass the time until I get back. Or you are welcome to wait in my room." He turns to face me fully then, a hand running through his hair. "I want you to know that you aren't a prisoner, but with your magical signature being so strong, it's safer that you remain on this floor for now."

"Safer?"

"I promise to explain everything," he says quietly. He gives me one last look before turning and heading towards the stairs, and I watch him walk away, a hollow feeling blooming where my heart should be.

Sarai appears from the small hallway, her hands clasped in front of her. I take in her long braid hanging over the shoulder of her emerald-green dress, the brown hair broken up by strands of gray. Wrinkles deepen the corners of her mouth as she smiles.

"All of your new clothing is put away, including your sandals, flats, and boots. We had to guess on the measurements for some of them, so if something doesn't fit properly, just let me know."

My brows furrow as I clear my throat and ask, "What do you mean by guessing the measurements?"

Sarai blinks, as if the question surprises her. "The prince didn't want anyone near you beyond what was necessary, so I couldn't take the proper numbers needed to tailor your clothing. I had to guess. I'm sorry if—"

"Oh, no, please don't apologize. I just..." I drop my gaze to the floor.

"Are you alright, My Lady?"

The use of that title ushers in the memory of Tienne and Erica, their soft voices and even gentler hands taking care of me after Alexi's death. Gifting me dresses because my own collection was so ill-fitting after owning the same ones for the better part of a decade.

"The clothes you brought, where did they come from?" I sincerely hoped they didn't alter Bahira's clothing to fit me. Not because I am ungrateful, but because Bahira didn't seem like the type you wanted to make angry. And I wasn't sure she agreed to let me not only use her room but have her clothes as well.

"I'm sorry, My Lady?" Sarai asks, taking another step towards me.

"The clothes," I say slowly, lifting my gaze. "Whose were they before you altered them?"

She blinks again, giving a small shake of her head. "They were made for you specifically. By order of the queen."

It's my turn to stare in surprise. "The clothes were made for *me*?"

Sarai chuckles, gently patting my shoulder as she walks towards the door. "Indeed, they were. Should you ever need anything, My Lady, don't hesitate to flag me down. I can usually be found on this side of the palace on the second floor. I'm sure His Highness can show you where."

"Thank you," I manage to squeak out.

Sarai smiles warmly at me before continuing down the hall in the same direction that Nox went.

I shut the door to Bahira's room, my heart pounding as I head towards the closet. When I step in, I shouldn't be surprised by how whimsical it looks, like someone carved into the trunk of a tree simply to hang clothes, but I am. One side of the closet is sparse—only a small collection of clothing hanging on metal hooks, most of them dresses. The other side, however, is lined with colorful fabrics and styles I've never seen before. Dresses, yes, but shirts with matching skirts and trousers that have shimmering embroidery also hang from hooks. Shoes line the floor beneath the clothes, and in the corner, the top drawer left slightly open as if to beckon me in for a closer look, is a small dresser. Inside are undergarments, the styles and colors much bolder and *lacier* than anything I've ever owned.

With nothing else to do and my emotions teetering on a sharpened edge, I take a shower and dress, then wait on the balcony for Nox to come.

His knock arrives around an hour later. When I open the door, my eyes widen as I take him in. He's showered, my next inhale full of his clean autumn scent, but he's wearing something *other* than all black. A navy blue tunic is pulled taut across his chest, hugging his biceps and the muscles that are expertly carved there. His trousers are form-fitting and dark brown, tucked into black boots that rise up to his calf. And his hair—*gods, his hair*. Short wavy pieces hang over his forehead and ears, the cut a bit longer than when we first met. I want to run my hand through it, to breathe him in and hold him close and remind him—remind myself—that he is the reason my heart beats. The only reason I have left now.

"You look absolutely beautiful," he says hoarsely.

I tuck my unbound hair behind my ears as I glance down at the outfit I chose. A maroon skirt flows down to my ankles with silver-threaded daisies embroidered in a waterfall pattern all around it. I paired it with a cap-sleeved cream blouse, the hem showing a sliver of skin on my stomach.

"You will need shoes," he says, gesturing towards my bare feet.

"Right," I answer, heading towards the closet. My attention immediately snags on the sparkly pair of sandals, a silver ribbon lacing through black loops that crisscross over the top. Without thinking, I grab them, only to realize halfway across the room that I have no idea how to tie them. My steps falter as I stare at them in my hand.

"May I?" Nox asks as he steps into the room.

It's strange to watch someone you have shared so much of yourself with act as if they are afraid of you. Or afraid *for* you. I'm not sure which one bothers me more.

At my nod, he kneels before me, the heat of his body a familiar comfort. The air around us thickens, and goosebumps break out over my skin, but I focus on lifting my foot and sliding it into the sandal. His touch is gentle—wary—and when he finishes, he stands and gestures towards the door.

"Ready?" he asks, waiting again for another silent nod. He leads me not towards the staircase he went to earlier, the one we took to get up to this level, but in the opposite direction, back towards his room. "This is a secret passageway."

My eyes widen as I stumble slightly, my feet still not used to wearing shoes of any kind. Nox stops in front of a section of the wall, the stone there unassuming. He lays his hand over a stone that has more gray striation than the others surrounding it and pushes. The wall lets out a slow cracking sound before it swings in and cool air rushes out.

"It's pretty dim, and there aren't any flame gems or spelled flames," he says, extending his hand out for mine.

I slide my hand into his, my inhale sharp when a jolt of something passes between us. Nox's gaze flicks down to where we are touching and back up again, his arm now covered with goosebumps. He chooses not to comment, so I don't either.

A tight, narrow spiral staircase made of stone winds down into the darkness, no open center like there was in the tower. My gaze travels over the square shapes of the rock that make up the walls as my pulse begins to quicken.

This place is different.

The temperature is cooler, and the scent of damp air is thick in my nostrils. Shadows are cast from the light of the hallway and down over the steps, making them look a darker gray—like the place that had held me. That had nearly killed me. I had escaped the tower, and it had cost *everything*. I had been handed freedom, but only after I had paid a price that made it feel worthless. I had fallen in love, only to be thrown against a wall of uncertainty. And as my vision blurs and tears trail down my cheeks, I feel the weight of it all come crashing down on me.

"Are you alright?" he asks, his soft voice distorted through the ringing in my ears. "Rhea?"

"I can't—" I say with a gasp, unsure of how to verbalize what I feel. Unsure of everything. I step backwards, my chest heaving as I drop his hand and dig my fingers into my hair.

He searches my face, his eyes widening when recognition strikes. "Fuck, Rhea. I'm sorry. I didn't think—"

"It's okay."

"No, *no*, it's not. I wanted to show you one of my favorite spots, a place where you could go and not worry about being bothered by anyone, but this is the only way to get there. I just didn't think about how similar it looks to the tower." He drags his hands over his face, remorse settling heavily in the corners of his mouth. "Tell me what to do. How can I fix this?"

Wasn't that the biggest question of all? A sob steals my breath as I take tentative steps towards him, my hands leaving my hair to wrap around his torso slowly. I don't have the words to tell him what I need, but he understands all the same. Without hesitation, his arms band around me as I bury my face against his chest.

"I'm sorry, Rhea. I'm so sorry." He repeats the words as a murmur against my temple, never faltering even when I dig my nails into his back. Even when my cries echo in the hallway and I need his help standing, he holds firm.

Just like he promised to do when I lost Bella, he holds my pieces together because I'm too weak to do it myself.

Chapter Twenty-Four

RHEA

I WAKE WITH A start, sweat beading over my temples and drenching the back of my neck at the nightmare. Alexi and Bella's deaths replayed in my mind, only this time twisted into something somehow more horrific.

Dragging my hands down my face, I force the burning in my eyes to stay there. Would it always be this way? Would every thought of her—of Alexi—always feel like a wound made anew? Maybe it is better to try and *not* think of them, but that gaping sensation of loss always rears its head when I least expect it to. Asleep or awake, it doesn't seem to matter. Grief is like trying to fight an invisible enemy.

There's no way to prepare for it—no lessening of the savage way it further pulls me apart. It's a scar ripped open over and over again.

I turn over onto my side and blow out a breath. Nox and I had decided to call it an early night after the staircase incident with the goal of talking in the morning. I don't know if I'm ready to see where that conversation will take us, if I'll end tomorrow even more alone than I feel tonight.

My fingers drag along a skirt the color of twilight. I pick it up and hold it to my body, its flowing fabric—not quite cotton but something softer and more gauzy—drifting down to my knees. I look through the tops, settling on one that matches the fabric of the skirt with buttons that go down the back and sleeves that hang off the shoulders.

After dressing, brushing my teeth, and combing through my hair, I wash my face with cold water, hoping to brighten up the dullness that has taken over my complexion. My hand grips the edge of the counter as I stare at myself in the mirror, little light flares glinting off the glittering gray stone in front of me.

I had wished for a life outside the confinement of a different, colder gray rock. In every fantasy scenario of how I could live if I ever became free, they were always so simplistic. Being free meant being happy; I didn't know how to dream more intricately than that. It wasn't until I was trudging through the forest in bloodstained boots with Nox at my side and a cloud of sadness still blanketing me that I realized that changing my surroundings didn't change who I was. That it isn't quite as easy as just *leaving* and suddenly feeling complete and whole.

Looking back, that oversimplified way of thinking had done nothing but leave me pockmarked with regret. Regret that I didn't question things about Nox sooner—though there is an understanding now that, even if I had, it probably wouldn't have changed where I ended up. Regret over not appreciating my time more with Alexi. With Bella. For thinking that they would always be a constant in my life. Those choices still felt malleable, despite being fixed points in my past. Like I could somehow go back and scream at myself to find another way—to make a different choice. But Selene's words rush back into me, reminding me that the outcome might have always been the same regardless of the path taken to get there.

Unfortunately, that doesn't make it any easier to accept.

I look into my green eyes and try to rally myself for this conversation with Nox. I feel as if I'm sifting through sand, searching for something to convince him that I'm worth fighting for—that *we* are worth fighting for. That I forgive him. *I forgive him.* But the sand keeps caving back in on me, covering up my attempts. Though it was second nature to lock everything up before, to try to move through my existence as numbly as possible, Nox *had* shown me what it was like to have someone to rely on. He begged me to give him some of my burdens, and I had.

Now, as I chew on my lower lip and my reflection blurs from the tears filling my eyes, I hope that he still wants to fill that role. Because I don't know if I can go back to who I was. That version of myself, though only months old, feels like someone I shed. I may not have emerged from this as a beautiful butterfly, but I am no longer a caterpillar hiding in the shadows, hoping to survive long enough to taste freedom. Even if I know now that freedom isn't always sweet.

Selene said I should focus on finding out who I am and everything that might entail. I would like to know more about my magic, and like it can hear my thoughts, wintery cold seeps into my chest, flaring out into my ribs and making me shiver. It is immediately followed by welcoming warmth, the feel of it allowing me to take a deeper breath. These two halves within me are so at odds; how in the world am I supposed to navigate the divide?

And where the *hell* did I even get magic to begin with?

If the type of magic I have is mage, if by all intents I am *considered* mage, then it stands to reason that one of my parents was as well. Or they at least had enough mage blood within them to carry magic down their family line. Was that how it worked? Magic descended through blood? King Dolian had said that my mother had just shown up in Vitour. Could she have traveled from this kingdom? If so, why?

With one last glance at my reflection, I stride through Bahira's room and out into the hall. My steps are heavy, each one feeling more like they are taking me away from a future I hadn't known I wanted and closer to one I don't know how to survive in. Then again, maybe I had to give myself *some* credit—surviving despite my circumstances was my entire existence.

Nox's sitting room is empty as I step inside, the dark blue curtains blowing in the breeze that comes through the open balcony doors. It smells of forest and him, and I inhale both deeply into my lungs.

The door to his bedroom is closed, noises of water running in a sink and something clattering on the counter filtering through it. I silently walk to one of the windows and look out at the densely packed tree line. I smile at the thought of him growing up here, playing and running in the woods. Maybe chasing Bahira or his best friend, Cassius. Or maybe his childhood wasn't as carefree as I am imagining. As the heir to the throne, perhaps he had too many responsibilities to simply play. Sorrow thrums against my heart at the thought that, in a different life, we might have learned these bits of information about each other like any normal, courting couple.

The door to the bedroom opens, and though the sitting room is large, the space between us seems to shrink as we stare at each other.

"Food is over on the table," he says, gesturing to his right.

"Thank you, but I'm not hungry." Not with the way nausea from my nerves roils within me.

He nods, his damp hair glistening in the sunlight trickling through the treetops and windows. "You look beautiful."

"Thank you. It's less jarring to see you in all black," I tease as my hand gestures to his body and the color he's dressed in head to—almost—toe. Only his feet remain bare. I realize then that I didn't put any shoes on either.

"I told you I was boring," he responds with a half-hearted shrug.

Daunting silence settles over us, and I grip my fingers together to fight off the feeling that screams at me to run. That this is too hard—too much work. That *I* am too much work.

"Do you want to talk about what happened last night?"

"Which part?" I ask, taking a step towards him.

"All of it if you want."

All of it. It's the answer I wanted to hear, yet I wonder if the truths I am about to give him are what *he* wants to hear. I had asked him to be completely honest with me and vowed to do the same. The first thing I needed to be honest about is that I am *tired*. I am tired of denying myself the only thing I have ever chosen. I am *exhausted* from straddling the line of self-imposed guilt and all-consuming love.

He mistakes my lingering silence for a refusal to talk and begins to turn away. "We don't have—"

"Nox," I breathe, noting how his body stills at the use of his name. *His real name.* "I forgive you." His eyes widen, and his lips part, shock a palpable thing between us. I'm not sure he's breathing, like the act of doing so might erase the words I've spoken. So I say them again, my voice hard with resolve. "I forgive you."

He runs a hand over his face, holding it on top of his mouth. Finally, he takes a step towards me, reaching as if to tuck my hair behind my ear or cup my face only to drop his hand back at his side. "Rhea, you don't *have* to forgive me. At least not yet."

Disappointment strikes me hard when he doesn't respond like I thought he might. "I understand how forgiveness works."

"That's not— *Fuck*! That isn't what I mean. My fear," he says slowly, calculating each word, "is that you will feel like you *have* to forgive me. Because of who we are to each other and how I helped you. I'm *terrified* you will offer me forgiveness before I've earned it, before you *mean* it, out of some sense of obligation to make me happy." His chest rises and falls quickly, a determined look morphing his features as he drops his voice lower. "Let me be clear. I *have* earned your anger. I will bear the weight of your silence, even. But don't think for one godsdamn minute that I want your false happiness, Rhea. That I want you to give me something I haven't earned."

"But you *have* earned it," I argue as my voice shakes. "And I *do* mean it."

He doesn't say anything, instead allowing his gaze to fall from mine. The way he acted yesterday and what he's doing now, he is purposefully building a wall between us.

"Why are you pushing me away?"

Nox's shoulders drop, his expression a composition of remorse and uncertainty as he shakes his head. "I just want you to be happy. You have more than earned that." My responding scoff has his eyes snapping to mine. His jaw hardens, and he runs a hand through his hair again, holding the strands there. "Rhea, I will not become a second cage for you. I don't want to *suffocate* you. You are free now to explore *all* your options. Just because I brought you here... It doesn't mean that you're beholden to me. I won't be the reason you hurt, not again."

"And I suppose it doesn't matter what *I* want?" Logically, I understand what he's saying, and there is a part of me that even recognizes how devastating it is for him to say those things and *mean* them. But it angers me—this idea that I could want anybody else after knowing what it is to be loved by him. "You have already ruined me," I accuse quietly as a tear tracks down my cheek.

He watches the tear fall, a small frown forming at my insinuation.

"You have completely and *utterly* ravaged my heart so that it will not beat for anyone else. I could not even *conceive* of another marking it the way that you have. It is a broken, jagged thing, and *still*, it beats for you." I take a step towards him, forcing him to hold my gaze. "You broke through the many shields I had placed around myself because *feeling* hurt too much. Exposing myself to *any* kind of love only resulted in my further ruination. Until. *You*!" I gasp the word out, sucking in air through my clenched teeth as I point at him. "And despite *everything*, I find myself unable to stop loving you. Unable to imagine an existence without you in it. You have thoroughly *ruined* me, and for once, it is an invisible scar that I am *happy* to carry. That I *want* to be marked with. And you're telling me now that you don't want me?"

His face softens, his shock morphing into something else—an emotion I can't exactly identify. "Rhea—"

"I'm not done." I begin to pace as I cross my arms over my chest. "There is a place called the Middle. It is space between worlds that, somehow, my magic gives me access to. In this place, I can see billions of stars, millions of galaxies swirling all around me. I've even been told *gods* walk among them. That's where I was—where my consciousness was—these past six days. I was in a space within universes, a magical place not seen here on Olymazi, and still, I thought of *you*." I wipe my tears roughly as I try to gain some composure. It feels like a dam has burst and now I'm awash in the flood, everything I want to say rushing out of me all at once. "And I'm sorry. *I'm sorry* that I ever made you feel like anything less than what you are—my protector. My friend. The only person I have ever wanted to own my heart. The only one that *does*. *You* are my home. *You* are my haven. And I'm sorry. I'm so *fucking* sorry because I understand. I do," I cry, gesturing around the room but referring to the kingdom as a whole. To the people he spent the last four years of his life in a foreign kingdom protecting.

I crave the attention of his star-flecked eyes and the desire I know he can ignite within me. For the touch of his hands and softness of his lips. But even more than that, I ache for the way he looks at me like I truly am the sun. The moon. The stars. I'm *desperate* to be everything he thinks of me. That desperation defies logic and paints my world in a frantic shade of gray instead of clearly defined black and white. Nox had hurt me, and yet I loved him. He had lied, and yet I understood. He is giving me a chance to walk away for something he perceives to be better, *and yet* I want no one other than him.

My words are spoken more softly as I tell him, "I understand why you lied, why you kept secrets, because I have kept them too. But loving you is the easiest decision I was ever given, the easiest one I have ever made." My eyes hold his as I notice the faint tears gathering in them. "*I forgive you.*"

I expect those three words to have a cost when I speak them. The broken and defeated part of my soul says that I need to put myself in a new prison, one where the walls are made up of Bella and Alexi's sacrifices and held together by my need to make sure they weren't all in vain. I know that they wouldn't want that for me though. They would want me to live and to love and to be selfish about both in ways I don't understand but intimately crave. There is only one other person who has ever wanted those things for me too.

"If you still want me, I am yours."

Nox doesn't move—doesn't take his eyes off of me while seconds drip by, each one more painful than the last. Maybe I'm too late. Maybe he has already made up his mind and— He closes the distance between us, his warm hands gently framing my face while my own reach out tentatively towards his chest, our bodies hardly separated by an inch.

"Say it again," he rumbles, the sound sending shivers down my spine. "Say that you're mine."

"I am yours. *Only* yours." I intone it like a prayer—a benediction to a man I've thought was godly on more than one occasion.

His lips only graze mine at first, their softness drawing a small whimper from me. Then his restraint snaps, and we crash together in a maelstrom of pent-up desire and longing and love—so much love. Like the striking of a match, I ignite from my toes to the crown of my head under his touch. It had only been days since we kissed, nearly a week while I was in the Middle, but doing so now is like finding water in a drought. I *need* it, need *him*. Nox guides my lips with his own, his remorse evident with every movement. He's relentless in the way his tongue slides into my mouth and against mine, like he's trying to map out every single part of it. I'm drowning in the way he makes me feel as if there is something worth living for when all I've ever known before him is the opposite. But I'd happily suffocate for this—for him. My hands slide up into his hair and grip tight as I pull him even closer, a soft moan vibrating from my throat.

We separate for just a moment, my lips tingling and chest heaving. "I love you," he says, leaning back in to softly kiss me before his mouth slides over the curve of my jaw. My head tilts back while I arch my neck, giving him access to any part of me he wants. He can have it all. "There is only you, Rhea. *Only you.*"

"I love you," I rasp back, my hands sliding down from his hair to dig into his shoulders. "Nox, I love you."

His teeth find my earlobe, a growl—low and deep—rumbling in his chest. It sends a shock of desire through me, my thighs clenching together as an ache builds in my core.

"My name from your perfect lips is a godsend." His warm mouth moves down my neck, this fervor growing between us the longer he teases me with his teeth and tongue. Each touch from him is kindling to that burning fire within me—even my magic pushes against my skin like it's being drawn closer to him. His hands grip the backs of my thighs, and he picks me up with ease, my legs wrapping around his torso as he squeezes our bodies together. He kisses back up my neck and over my jaw at an unhurried pace, his lips then hovering above my own.

I cradle his face with my hands, each rush of air past my lips fanning the flames of my desire. But looking at him is like peering out at the ocean at night, the stars reflecting on its surface. It's easy to get lost in his beauty.

We're being honest, so though my heart kicks up its rhythm at the thought, I give voice to the words dancing in my head. "I want you."

His smile is so soft, so full of affection, that it draws out one of my own. "You already have me."

"No," I reply, my head shaking. "I want *all* of you."

His brows draw together for a moment in confusion but quickly give way to understanding, his eyes darkening with hunger. "Rhea, are you sure?"

I know he won't continue unless he believes that I'm absolutely positive, and I don't want him to doubt this moment at all. So, forcing myself out of his hold, I grab his hand and guide him into the bedroom. Soft golden light from the morning sun filters in through the windows that line the wall adjacent to his bed, shining directly onto the dark green comforter there. I don't take in much else about his room, my attention fixed on him as I motion for him to sit on the bed and then crawl onto his lap. I kiss his cheek. His jaw. My hands sliding down to his neck and over his shoulders.

"I want this. I want *you*," I say against his skin, my tongue darting out to drag along it. I moan at his taste—earth and spice and *him*. "I wanted you in the tower, when I dreamed of your body pressed against mine. I wanted you when I touched myself and fantasized it was your hands instead of my own." My cheeks heat at my words, at the way my voice doesn't sound like myself.

"Fucking gods." Nox draws me closer to him, the movement giving friction to my core and making me gasp.

Lifting my gaze back to his, my nerve-endings alive and tingling with desire, I push every ounce of certainty I can into my voice. "I wanted you when you gave me my first kiss and showed me what it was to be consumed by passion. On the bank of the river, I wanted you to take me right there on the ground. And at the inn, when I could feel your desire for me so strongly, I wanted you *so badly* that I would have given you *anything* in return. I would have bargained away my very existence if it meant having you in the way I so desperately wanted. None of those feelings have changed. If anything, I want you *more*." My eyes bounce between his, and I hope he can see it in my gaze—the depths to which I love him. "Explore me," I whisper. A summoning. A statement. A *plea*.

Nox breathes out slowly, his hands moving up the sides of my body and resting just beneath the curves of my breasts. I have kissed him so many times, and each of them have felt like a new beginning, but now, as his tongue glides into my mouth and my breath falters with each gentle swipe, I know that this moment might be more pivotal than them all. Desire licks up my spine and entangles with my humming magic.

When we separate again, I'm ready to push him down on the bed and undress him myself. But his expression turns serious, and his eyes become uncompromising. "We stop at any moment you want to. No questions asked." I nod in response, already knowing he will only continue as long as I am enjoying it. His throat works before he leans in close, his lips grazing my ear. "I am going to worship you as thoroughly as you deserve, Rhea, and I am going to take my time doing it. I want to touch you—to *taste* you—so desperately that I'm willing to give up things I never imagined I would."

My heart batters my ribcage at his words.

"But you should know two things. The first is that you are in control here. *Always.*" His eyes hold mine, specks of silver shining in them like a shattered star. "Your first time can be painful."

"I know." I may not have had sex before, but I *had* read enough books to at least understand the physicality of it.

"The second," he continues, slanting his mouth over mine, "is that I have been taking a preventative tonic. But that changes nothing. I'll come when and where you tell me to."

Gods above.

"I want you everywhere."

His smirk is entirely devious as he lifts both arms, bending one and grabbing the back of his collar to pull his shirt off in one swift motion. Words leave me, my mind completely blank, as I stare at the expanse of his tanned skin. My fingers trace over him, moving down his collarbone and lower until they dip into every curve and divot of his abdomen. His sharp inhale fuels my desire to explore him further.

"I can't believe you are mine," I whisper.

Nox smiles before leaning in to kiss me again. "I am yours, and you are mine." I reach back to begin unbuttoning my top, but he halts my hands and replaces them with his own. His voice is a midnight caress against my skin as he murmurs, "I have thought of undressing you slowly more times than I care to admit."

Then he begins to do just that, popping each button free of its loop one at a time. The pace is torturous, and I would think that, as he releases me from the confines of the top, it would get easier to breathe. However, when he reaches the last button, air feels impossible to pull into my chest.

Mistaking my anticipation for nervousness, Nox freezes. "Tell me to stop."

I kiss him hard until he groans, encouraging him to keep going. When the last button is undone, with delicate slowness, he slides the straps of my top down—farther and farther—until I can pull my arms through them, and then he tosses the garment to the floor. I become acutely aware of how naked I am, as if there is a way to become even *more* so.

There is nothing to hide behind, and as he takes me in, I hold my breath and hope that, when reality crashes into the fantasy of me he has in his head, I will live up to the expectation.

Chapter Twenty-Five

RHEA

N ox's breath quickens, my exposed skin warming everywhere he paints his sultry gaze over it.

"You are..." He shakes his head as if the right words simply don't exist.

I see them, though, in his eyes. The reverence. The longing. The love. Wrapping an arm around my back, he draws me forward until our naked skin is pressed together. My fingers dive back into his hair, the soft strands still damp from his shower rustling between them. He kisses me again, the feel of it still hungry and laced with need but also sweeter. More exquisite.

"That night at the river," he breathes, his lips ghosting over my own, "took every *ounce* of willpower I possess. You looked so beautiful bathed in the moonlight, and all I could think about was hearing my name cross your lips in ecstasy."

"It would have been the wrong one," I tease. He captures my mouth again, my words melting into a moan that he eagerly devours.

"Were I a lesser man, I would not have cared," he whispers when we part.

I press myself somehow closer, a rush of warmth gathering at my core when I feel how hard he is. "Were you a lesser man, I would not be so *desperately* in love with you."

Nox leans back to let his hooded gaze roam my face, his subtle exhale dancing across my lips. His expression is one of awe—as if what I've said has unearthed something buried deeply within him.

"I will never tire of hearing you say that." Turning, he holds me to him while moving us farther up the bed. With heart-piercing slowness, he lowers me down, his hips settling between my widened legs and his chest perfectly brushing against mine until my nipples peak from our closeness. Gently, he brushes the hair from my face before leaning down to kiss my forehead, my cheeks, my nose, and then finally my mouth.

It is silly to think that this moment might be one that could heal some of the things I feel about myself. The self-loathing. The unbearable guilt. Yet, as he continues to kiss me like I'm precious, his breathing just as unsteady as my own, I wonder if it *could* be.

"Where do you want me to touch you?" His fingers glide down my neck and across my collarbone, a tingling sensation following in their wake.

My eyes flutter closed, words slow to come to me, but I only need to say one. "*Everywhere.*"

Nox makes a noise low in his throat, pressing himself into me at the same moment his hand drags over one of my breasts. It's guttural, the sensation that floods me as I dig my nails into his back. He slides down my body, the heat of his breath cascading past my neck and then my shoulders. When his lips skim over my nipple once, twice, before closing over it completely, all while he flicks his thumb over the other one, my body succumbs completely to his touch. He moans into my skin, the vibration of it paired with the sliding of his tongue turning my breath staccato.

He kisses his way over to my other side, showing that half as much delicious attention as the first while his hand glides down my stomach, moving over the bunched skirt still at my hips and pausing when his fingers skim the waistband of my undergarments. He doesn't stop the movement of his mouth, but I can practically *feel* the silent question he's asking.

"Yes," I groan, and that's all he needs for his fingers to dive beneath the thin lacy fabric.

He brushes them gently over the sensitive bundle of nerves, blood rushing to my ears as I fixate on his touch. It's the same but also *much* different from the feel of my own hand. I make a strangled noise when he does it again and again, my stomach clenching low and tight. His mouth leaves my body with a soft *pop*, the cool air stinging my skin.

"Rhea, look at me," he rasps, the sound as tormented as I feel because asking me to do anything right now seems impossible. But I manage to open my eyes and arch my neck, meeting his heated gaze. "I want to watch your face when I find out how wet you are for me." Then his finger slips lower until it's pressing right at my entrance. He gently swipes through me, just dipping in enough to gather some of my arousal before bringing it back up, where he begins to move his finger in a tantalizing circle. Nox groans, his forehead falling to my chest as he kisses me there. "Everything about you is so much better than I ever dreamed it would be."

His praise lights me from within, rousing my magic and making it hum in response. I drag my nails up his back and neck until I'm once more gripping his hair, holding onto him as an anchor for fear I might otherwise float away. My panting breaths seem to echo off the walls, and I briefly wonder if I'm doing enough. If I'm doing this *right*.

But his unhurried touch brings me closer to the precipice of release, forcing me to focus only on him and not on my doubts. Nox reaches up to kiss me deeply, his tongue aligning with the movements of his finger so expertly that it claims my breath while leaving me free-falling, the tension uncoiling rapidly within me.

I bite down on my lower lip, trying to silence the indecent moans clawing up my throat.

He notices, his gaze growing lethal as he leans back and *growls*, "Don't you *dare* quiet yourself. I want to hear every single sound you make, Rhea. Those noises are *mine* to claim." As if to punctuate his words, his finger moves faster while his teeth nip at my ear.

The next wave of release peaks, then hangs until I think I'm shouting between my heaving breaths as my heels dig into the bed. I wait for that feeling—the one that ushers in complete relaxation—but with Nox's body still on top of my own, it never comes. Instead, the ache between my legs pulses *stronger*.

"When you dreamed of my hands touching you, was it like that?" His voice is pure velvet, sensuous in a way I've never heard from him, and it turns me utterly *molten*.

"This is better."

A dark chuckle leaves him before he moves to stand.

"What are you—"

My question is halted when he leans over and wraps his hands around either side of my waist, dragging me down the bed until my legs hang off the edge of it. Nox gathers my skirt, and with another look up at me for approval—which I give with a nod—he removes and then tosses it to the floor like he's personally offended by it. The sight makes me laugh, my hand then covering my mouth in mortification.

"Rhea, I meant *every. Single. Noise.*" The cadence of his voice sends my heart skipping and makes my magic press harder at the barrier of my skin.

Lowering my hand, I brace myself on my elbows and stare up at where he stands in front of me, his legs between my knees. "I would have thought laughing at a time like this is a bad thing."

"Not your laugh. *Never* your laugh. I always want to hear it." He leans down and kisses me—first my lips and then the curve of my jaw, my head falling back to give him access to my neck. His sweet words might make me tear up if only I wasn't so overwhelmed by the way his tongue drags across my scorching skin. Nox travels his way down to my stomach, moving slowly like he has to make sure he savors every place his lips caress. "So perfect." His voice melts into me, making my toes curl.

Then he lowers onto his knees, the act igniting my blood. My guard. My friend. My prince. On his knees before *me*. He hooks his fingers into the waistband of my undergarment and, with a restraint I could never replicate, begins to slide them off of me. Time stands still as I watch him, my anxiousness easing a little when I see how quickly his chest is rising and falling too. When I'm completely bare, his eyes fall directly on the spot between my legs. I don't want to be shy about him seeing me this way, but it's instinctual to let my knees fall together.

Nox clicks his tongue, shaking his head and sending his raven waves tumbling over his forehead. Placing his hands on my knees, his lips pull to the right as his gaze pierces me. "I told you I would get on my knees for you." A breathy laugh is all I can manage, words and thoughts wiped completely away by the sight before me. "What do you want, Rhea?" he asks, lowering his body while his hands push my legs apart, his shoulders holding them open.

"What?"

"What. Do. You. Want?" Each word is sharply enunciated, and I gasp again when he plants tender kisses on my inner thigh, moving higher with each one.

For a moment, I don't know how to answer him. I've never been given the opportunity to choose something for myself until the day I allowed him into the tower. That choice had changed everything—*everything*.

So maybe that is answer enough.

"You." Vulnerability makes my lips tremble, the air thick with the emotion. I don't think sex is only about pleasure—it is seeing someone unencumbered. Uninhibited. It is honesty in its purest form. "I just want you."

He presses a kiss right above where I need him. Where I am already so wet with desire. Reaching across my body, he grabs my hand and forces me to partially sit up. Then he guides my fingers into his hair, his grip tightening around my own.

"You will use me to find your pleasure, Rhea."

I stare at him as I feel another jagged part of me smooth over. Despite being inexperienced, he's giving *me* the power in a moment when he could hold it all. That had always been the case with him though. It was almost as if his pleasure was completely dependent upon my own.

The first long swipe of his tongue is euphoric, the sensation foreign and new but so incredibly divine. I hold my breath and watch him lick another line directly up my center, right to where I'm most sensitive. My back arches when he moans, the need for more friction overwhelming.

"I knew you would taste incredible. *Fuck*, I knew it." Then his mouth is on me fully, devouring me in eager and luscious strokes. His eye's meet mine, gleaming in wicked delight while his mouth and tongue—*gods, that tongue*—do something far more sinful.

I'm tumbling off the edge of the world, each ounce of control over my body leaves little by little as he kisses and licks and even drags his teeth over me. His palm flattens on my abdomen, my writhing uncoordinated and led purely by the desire racing through my veins. Nox grabs my legs and places them over his shoulders, the action giving me the ability to use him as leverage. With a hand still in his hair, I hold him to me and roll myself against his mouth, groaning as I do.

"*Yes*, Rhea."

My eyes close as tension builds at the base of my spine. How is it possible that each touch from him is better than the last? That my body both craves *and* is sated by him at the same time? It's enough to make me crazy—to want to lose myself in this madness he creates. *We* create.

"Say my name again." The command in his voice, the *dominance* in it, makes me shudder as my fingers tighten around his hair. He drags his tongue over me again, and I think I could die from this—from the pleasure of him touching me this way.

"Oh gods," I moan, my hips bucking against him, but he forces them back down with his forearm. My eyes fly open, a squeak of protest on the tip of my tongue until I look at him. His lips shine with my arousal, and his gaze narrows fiendishly at the apex of my thighs.

"Say." *Lick.* "My." *Lick.* "Name." *Lick.*

I whimper, each flick of his tongue only edging me closer to release. *His name.* It's not a stretch to assume he needs me to say his name—his *real* name—because it had been so painful for us both when I had first learned it. Maybe this is his way of replacing that memory with a better one. Or maybe it is because he really does like hearing me say it. I honestly don't care if it means he'll keep touching me like this.

"*Nox.*" It's hardly audible, but it pleases him all the same.

He hums, releasing his hold on my hips. "Good girl," he says against me, and *gods,* it's too much. His thumb begins circling right above where his tongue dives into me. The pleasure is relentless, and soon my legs begin to shake, my thighs squeezing around his head. "Come for me, Sunshine."

A scream builds its way up my throat right as my orgasm flares—the intensity of it forcing my shoulders into the bed while my back bows, my body heeding his command. My magic feels like it's bursting at the seams, rushing up and settling into the spaces between my ribs. Stars fracture behind my eyes—in my very *blood*—as I ride out the orgasm he ushers in. Nox's hands caress my stomach, his mouth slowing down while I float back into reality.

"That was..." My lips flutter together while I blow out a breath and throw both arms over my head. I feel him smile against me, placing a delicate kiss inside each thigh before he removes my legs from his shoulders. My entire body is completely languid, as if my bones have become soft, but I know we aren't done. I sit up slowly as Nox braces his hands on either side of my hips, my thighs slick and sliding against each other. "Was that good for you?" I whisper.

He laughs, the sound laced with a shadowy seduction that makes heat burst to life again low in my stomach. "*Good* is not the word I would use to describe what that was, Rhea." His tongue darts out to lick his bottom lip before he traps it between his teeth. "Your taste is one I will forever crave, a pleasure I am now addicted to. I could have my tongue between your gorgeous legs over and over again, every day for the rest of my life, and it would never be enough." He leans in closer, the scent I know as him mixing with one I realize is *me.* "Are you curious to know what you taste like off of my lips?"

My eyes dip down to his glistening mouth. There is something about acknowledging that it's me he's talking about, *me* he is tasting, that further tilts my world on its axis. "Yes."

Nox groans before his hand slides into my hair and he brings my mouth to his. The mixture of us is overwhelming, the taste something indescribable as I devour him, shivering when he groans again. With our chests heaving and hair mussed, he returns to his full height and brings his hands to the buttons of his trousers.

"Tell me to stop," he says after undoing the first one. "It has to be now."

His entire body stills as he waits for me to answer, his self-control evident in the set of his jaw and white of his knuckles. And I know he would stop if I asked him to. Even if lust still flowed through his veins, I know he would do only what I want.

Moving to my knees on the bed, conviction flows through me as my hands go to either side of his face. "No."

Being intimate with Nox in any capacity has always left me feeling powerful when I otherwise felt anything but. So, with his eyes on mine, I move my hands down and begin to undo the remaining buttons on his trousers. He tucks my hair behind my ears as I do so before kissing me again, his adoration for me evident in the delicate way his fingers slide over my shoulders and down my back. How they rest lightly on my hips while his mouth moves to the outside of my jaw.

"You are my everything," he says, trailing his lips down to the crook of my neck. "You are the *only* exception. To every rule, every shield I force myself to carry. To every weakness I try to conquer. I lay it all down and surrender only to you."

My eyes grow glassy, and when Nox lifts his head again as I undo the last button, I can see the truth of those words in his gaze. It feels like a vow, the way he kisses me next, as if just our intention and lips alone can carve the way we feel about each other into stone for eternity. My pulse flutters, the world pausing, as I watch Nox fully undress. His pants slide past his hips, revealing a divot that's somehow sculpted in the muscle there on both sides. Then they fall away completely, and my mouth goes dry. He's glorious and beautiful and—

"Stars above," I whisper.

Tentatively, I start to reach for him but look to him first for permission. His swallow is rough, a muscle in his jaw ticking in time with his heartbeat as he nods his head. My palm envelops silky heat, and *gods,* he looks even more enormous in my hand. It's the desire to touch *all* of him that guides my hand up and down as

I explore every thick inch in my grasp. I don't want to *stare* at him, but my innate curiosity makes it so that I can *only* stare at him.

Damn it, I really should have read another romance novel before doing this.

Nox wraps his fingers around my own, providing a little more pressure as he slides our joined hands in sync. I feel his gaze heavy on me, but I can't look away from how perfect he is. We make it a few more strokes before he lets out a restrained noise and pulls our hands away. "Nope. That is a bad idea."

"I'm sorry, I—"

"If you had any idea what a single touch from you does to me, you wouldn't be apologizing. This will be over before it starts if we keep doing that."

I choke out a laugh which he kisses me through, like he can swallow up the sound and store it within himself. Then he's guiding us farther up the bed until I'm once more on my back with him settled between my legs. A single arm braces his weight by my head while his other hand grazes over my chest and down the side of my body, stopping when he reaches my hip.

"Just so you know, there is no wrong way to do this. Having *you* is all I need." He looks at me like he can see through me—past the skin and muscle and bone and down into the darkest parts of my soul, where my tattered heart beats just for him. "Are you ready?"

It is one last question, one last assurance that I want this. Want *him*. My heart thumps so loudly that I think the entire kingdom may hear it, but I cup his handsome face in my hands, my thumbs brushing his cheekbones in light swipes. "I want you, Nox. *All of you.*"

His hand is then gone from my hip, and I wrap my arms around his neck, hanging onto him and allowing my legs to fall even farther apart. Shifting his weight, I groan when I feel him drag himself—hard and silken and warm—over my core. He brings his forehead to mine, and my eyes fall closed as he guides the very tip of his cock into me. I suck in a breath, my body tensing automatically at the foreign sensation. Nox kisses me slowly—*seductively*—and I drink him in, focusing on the way his tongue dips into my mouth and how his thumb circles my nipple. His hips lift before they roll slowly towards me, and he goes in a little deeper. There is a sharp burst of pain as he stretches me, its suddenness making me gasp.

"Tell me what you're feeling," he murmurs against my lips.

"Pressure—like I'm unbearably full."

"There's... still quite a bit of me to go. Why don't you use your magic to heal yourself?"

My eyes open to stare into his. "No."

"Rhea, you can take away the pain—"

"*No*," I repeat, my chest cracking wide open as I look at him. "I will never get to have this moment again. There will never be another first time. I want to *feel* it all. I want to remember every detail, how sweet and perfect it is. How incredible *you* are. Keep going, Nox. *Please.*"

The wild rhythm of my heart is a song made just for him, each frantic flutter repeating the same chant over and over again: *I love him. I love him. I love him.* It sings out, surpassing this room and kingdom and moving out through space and eons and the Middle. Out into foreign worlds and past the gods that roam among them.

"Okay," he whispers, looking down at me like I might be one of those very goddesses made flesh.

I don't know how much time passes, only that it's measured in the way he moves slowly—*delicately*—his hips rolling and bringing him in and out at a pace that my body can adjust easily to. The discomfort soon morphs into something incandescent, born out of how safe and cared for he makes me feel and cradled by the love burning brightly between us.

He takes small pauses between kissing me, as if he doesn't want to miss a single twitch of my lips or gasp of my breath. And then finally, *finally*, he's inside fully, stretching and molding me. *Remaking* me.

"What do you feel?" he asks again, the dark waves curling over his temple drawing my gaze.

Everything. I feel his breath cascading over my lips, the rush of it in time with my own. I feel the way his heart beats soundly within his chest, reverberating directly over mine, and the weight of his body, most of it held away from me but still blanketing me with his warmth and his scent. I feel him inside me, filling me so entirely—so *wholly*—that I wonder if an emptiness will linger when we're done. If there will always be a part of me that is missing until our bodies come together again.

"I feel *you*," I finally answer. Tears leak from the corners of my eyes, and Nox leans down to kiss them away. "I feel like you were made just for me."

"We were made for each other," he rasps as he pulls out a few inches before pushing back in, the movement still cautious, still tender.

My mind races wildly as I try to understand how he can feel so incredible. How we can fit together so perfectly.

It's a thousand answers to a thousand questions not yet formed.

It's the beginning and the end and the eternity in between.

It's the power of the sun and the moon and every single star in the night sky.

It's bliss and happiness and desire and *life*.

And it's mine. *He's mine.*

I close my eyes as his gentle thrusts grow faster, my body begging to move with his. So I dig my heels into the bed and meet the next roll of his hips halfway. My gasp mixes with his groan, the noises joined by the sound of our bodies coming together.

"*Rhea.*"

My hips tip into his next thrust, the pleasure blinding as I begin to unravel.

"Fuck," he groans.

My brows draw together, the dull pain overshadowed by my unyielding need for him. I don't stop, matching his movements while he gently pulls one of my hands free of his hair to interlace with his, resting them both on the bed above my head.

Visions of glittering white and black tendrils, like loose ribbons billowing in a breeze, fill my mind's eye. It looks like my magic, but there is something else there now too. *Nox's magic.* Shadows of deep purple woven with onyx wrap around it, fusing with it. Not to form something new but to finally become whole. Coming home. As if two star-crossed lovers found each other across worlds.

My breaths turn choppy, and tension coils and curls inside me, my core pulsing and tingling while Nox's own movements fall out of rhythm.

"Tell me that you want me to come," he whispers raggedly, his grip tightening on me. "That you need me to stay inside of you."

"Yes. *Stay.*" Stay inside me. Stay like this forever. Just *stay.*

Nox kisses me hard, his teeth grazing my lower lip. I don't want it to be over yet, but my back arches as my inner muscles clench around him and a groan rips from my throat. Stars burst behind my eyes as I squeeze Nox to me, falling into blissful oblivion. My name is called out as his hips jerk and he finishes with me.

My magic thrums throughout my body, tugging at my chest like it's guiding me towards him—invisible strings looping around us both and pulling taut. For a brief moment, the air around us shifts, electricity building like that of an impending storm. My arms break out in goosebumps as the fine hairs there lift. I force my eyes open, only to see Nox's gaze already on me, a wondrous look in his eyes.

"Do you feel that?" he asks, his body trembling.

Nodding, I take the hand not holding his and push the hair back from his forehead. "It feels almost like static electricity."

Every part of my body aches, none more so than where he is still very much inside of me, but the joy—the utter peace—is something I've never felt this strongly before. With our eyes locked, so tenderly that it threatens more tears, he begins to pull out of me. We both let out a half sigh, half moan when he's fully out before he rests his forehead on my chest and mumbles something into my skin.

"I can't understand you when your face is pressed into me like that," I say, giggling when he responds by planting smacking kisses in the dip between my breasts.

He rolls to my side, only to take me with him so that we are facing each other, my head resting on his arm.

"Better?" he teases, and I roll my eyes at his playful smirk, poking his abdomen. His fingers trail down my side and into the hollow of my waist, his features easing the longer he looks at me. "I love you."

Those words are like sunlight to a flower that has only known shadows. I feel them take root within me, feel them as easily as I feel my own heart's steady rhythm. I smile, wide and unrestrained and just for him. "I love you, too."

Smiling back, his exhale is slow before he asks, "Are you in any pain?"

"I'm sore, but," I pause, kissing the tip of his nose, "I would do it again."

He barks out a shocked laugh, wrapping his arm around me so that I'm flush against his chest, my own laughter filling the room. And how wonderful it is, to laugh so easily while in his embrace. To feel so complete and whole and *loved*, if only for a moment.

"That sensation earlier was our magical signature," Nox says, his fingers draping over my hip.

"What is a magical signature? I've heard you use that term before."

"Raw magic leaves its energy in the air around us. You have to become attuned to it, learn to pick it up out of the chaos of the natural world, but once you do, you will always feel it. Mages both have a signature *and* can pick up on others'." He pulls me closer to him, rolling again until we're off the bed and I'm cradled in his arms. Walking to the bathroom, he sets my feet down on the cold tile as he reaches over and turns the water to the tub on. "And I will tell you more about it *after* you explain to me again what the Middle is."

Part Two

What if healing—whatever that looks like—isn't something that is possible for me?

Chapter Twenty-Six

RHEA

Showering with Nox while I try to tell him all about the Middle and Selene proves to be quite difficult. Partially because I don't want him to think I'm crazy, but also because, when he slides his soaped-up hands over my body, I forget how to speak. Eventually, I find the right words and tell him of my first visit there, what Selene said to me, and my instructions to go east.

"Do you think she specifically meant coming *here*?" I ask him, my eyes closed as he massages my scalp with shampoo.

"It certainly seems that way," he answers, leaning down to kiss my cheek.

I continue, recapping every moment of my time there and leaving out only the details of how I usually went to the Middle after a beating from the king. My fingers tremble when I tell him about that cold, ancient magic. How Selene believes it to be a part of me, a mirrored half to the light magic. He hugs me when I break down over how terrifying it was to feel that magic flood from me, how it didn't wait to be used but seemed to search for a moment of weakness to unleash itself. My voice grows steady again when I tell him that it was his declarations of love that brought me back and allowed me to cease using the shadows. He cradles my face in his hands, his lips finding mine, as he whispers that he's sorry over and over again.

And I repeat that I forgive him.

There is another hurt that lingers in his smoky eyes, one that I know he won't bring up but that my time in the Middle makes me anxious to atone for. "I'm sorry," I say.

Nox frowns, his brows furrowing together in confusion. "You don't apologize to me for—"

I place my fingers over his lips, gently stopping his words. "I know there is an imbalance between us when it comes to, well, *everything*. You've had a normal life—" He makes a snort of derision at that. "Alright, a *more* normal life, even as a crown prince, than I have. I know that I do not always say or do the right things. And I don't think you should give me a pass on any of it just because—"

"I love you?" he interrupts with a curling smirk.

"Yes," I say softly, dropping my fingers. "I can't stop thinking about what I said to you before. How hurtful it was. How, after everything you did for me and *with* me, I didn't even let you explain your side fully without condemning you first. You deserved better than that."

One of his hands moves to tangle in my hair at the back of my head, his hold on me firm. "You were allowed to feel whatever you needed to at that moment. I won't let you be the martyr in a situation that was brought on *entirely* by my actions."

"And *I* won't let *you* bear the weight of something that you had no control over." Nox's eyes close, acknowledging the change in the conversation from me to Alexi. "I do not fault you for his death," I add with a whisper.

He nods, his forehead coming to rest on mine. There's a perceptible shift in us both, the smoothing over of some of the abraded edges of our hearts. I know Nox feels guilt about Alexi's death, but it isn't until now that I recognize how deeply that wound had cut him too.

We finally leave the warmth of the shower, Nox running over to Bahira's room to grab me some clothes while I dry off. Once dressed, we dine together at the small table in the sitting room, my body already void of any tenderness.

"You're curiously calm about the fact that I just told you I subconsciously visit a magical place," I say around a bite of fresh strawberry. The berry might be my new favorite food, its sweet and tart flavor dancing along my tongue.

Nox shrugs, his hand squeezing mine from where he holds it across the table. "It doesn't seem *so* fantastical to me. Our magic is raw—both part of the Continent itself and yet something completely different. Perhaps stronger magic runs in the familial line of whichever parent you got it from." He tilts his head to the side in thought, the movement rustling his hair. "The palace healer thinks that, because you haven't trained with your magic, it's a little more wild and unpredictable. Especially because you are now at the age where our magic peaks."

I trail my fingers over the soft fabric of the skirt Nox chose as I contemplate his words, its dark blue color offset by golden stars embroidered throughout. A matching top, the straps thin and front cut into a V shape that is lower than I've worn before, fits perfectly to my body. Clothes made for me, indeed.

"Whatever the reason, I'm just grateful that the *other* half of my magic has never been used before." It may be a part of me, but that doesn't mean I have to give it any access. As if in answer, bitter cold perks up within me like a chunk of frozen water sliding down my sternum before it settles back down again.

"It has." The words are said so quietly, so *reluctantly*, that it takes me a moment to realize Nox is responding to what I've said.

"What do you mean?"

He lets a few seconds pass by, his eyes scanning my face lovingly and fingers gently caressing my own. "Before I tell you, I need you to know that this changes nothing about who you are. At your core, Rhea, you are *good*. And kind and absolutely perfect."

A different tension makes my heart begin to race as my eyes bounce between his.

"I have seen you use your shadow magic twice. Once was right after I told you about Alexi."

"What?"

"Your magic surged out of you so forcefully, I barely had time to shield against it with my own. It was *strong*. It reached the plants in the corners of the room and sucked them dry, turning them into something brittle and lifeless." My gaze falls to one of those plants still sitting there—dead and completely black. I don't realize that my chest is heaving until Nox leaves his chair to kneel at my side. "Breathe, Sunshine."

I shake my head, my hands trembling in his as I rasp, "I remember succumbing to the feeling I had—this cold, dark power running through my veins. If that's what I did to plants, what would I do to *you*? What if I hurt you, Nox?" Gods, what if I hurt *anyone*?

"You didn't. And you won't."

"What happened the other time?" I ask, already apprehensive of the answer.

Alarm flashes over his features before his throat works with a swallow. "The night we escaped from the tower, when you healed me in the meadow, do you remember what happened with the two guards that approached us?"

"They never reached us. I was able to heal you before they did." I remembered it clearly. I looked back and saw them coming and then started healing Nox's wound. I had found it strange that they hadn't reached us before we were able to get away, but I figured that time had gotten distorted in my memory. That the stress and panic of trying to heal Nox and of exposing my magic to him had perhaps made it seem like time had falsely slowed down.

"No, they made it to us just as you started healing me. They arrived side by side, and one of them laid a hand on your shoulder."

A spark of memory flashes—*a weight on my shoulder, an ear piercing scream*. It's like I have all the pieces of a puzzle scattered out in front of me and I'm left to sort them until they come together and make sense.

"You screamed," Nox continues, "and then your eyes... They went totally black. Shadows exploded from your body in the blink of an eye, there and gone, and the men went flying back."

I drop my gaze from his as another memory comes to light, another piece of the puzzle. This one is of icy cold flowing through me and my vision becoming slightly obscured, like a black veil had been placed over my eyes. "You told me not to look back. Why?"

"Rhea, it's alright."

No. No, it's not alright. "Why did you tell me not to look back?" I sit with the memory—those heart-stopping moments when I healed him.

His mouth opens and closes, words he's trying not to say the only ones that must be coming up as he clamps his mouth shut again. Then, the final puzzle piece clicks into place: the King's Guardsman in the woods holding Bella captive.

You already have two guards' deaths on your hands.

"I killed them, didn't I?" I barely say the words. Afraid that if I speak them too loudly, there will be retribution against me. Or maybe I'm afraid that speaking them aloud will confirm they are true. That it will affirm that there is indeed something monstrous about me. Something that makes me more like my uncle than I ever want to be.

"This doesn't change who you are," he repeats, his eyes boring into mine.

"Did I kill them?"

Nox cradles the side of my face, his thumb brushing over my cheek in reassuring strokes. But it doesn't erase the feeling of a dagger plunging into my heart when he answers, "Yes."

The next few moments are a numbing blur filled with Nox's whispered words of reassurance in my ear, his body holding mine up as I struggle to take breaths between my heaving sobs. I had never wanted magic, this disastrous power that was now running through my veins. I had never wanted this kind of *responsibility*.

Selene had said my magic held balance, but what sort of balance could be found in this? I could apparently *murder*, but I didn't have the ability to give life back? There is no equilibrium in that, no sense of symmetry. How am I somehow supposed to be *alright* with that?

"I will help you train with your magic, help you learn to master it. Everything else will come with time as you begin to explore your freedom, Rhea. Selene is right; you should take as much time as you need to figure out who you are."

It is odd to have him talk of Selene—to reference the Middle—without hesitation.

Nox continues, his voice achingly soft. "This doesn't have to be something that derails you, Sunshine. This can be a moment where you begin to own your power."

So much talk of power—something I had always thought I had none of back in that tower but was now apparently brimming with here. "Does my magic frighten you?" I ask him. I wouldn't blame him if it did. It terrifies *me*. Nox surprises me when he responds by laughing, making me scowl against his chest. "That isn't a funny question."

"No, it isn't. But I think this will help you understand why I'm laughing."

Entirely confused, I let Nox guide me to the balcony off of the sitting room. The summer air hits me, warm and comforting and full of the scent of the trees surrounding us. My hands rest on the wooden railing over the vines of dark purple and green twisting around it. He stands behind me, his hands on either side of mine. Looking out at the forest, my body tingles as fractures of sunlight reach in from the canopies above and cascade down my skin. In answer, my light magic rises up from my stomach like it's reaching for the sun's warmth, delicately humming in response.

"I am the strongest mage in our kingdom," he begins, a faint note of amusement in his voice.

"*Congratulations.*"

He barks out a laugh, wrapping an arm around my waist and squeezing my back to his chest. "Smartass," he says against my ear before gently kissing it. "I'm not saying that to *brag* but to give you a frame of reference. Over the many years—we aren't sure exactly when it started—magic in our kingdom has begun dwindling. Younger mages are now weaker, and older mages are losing their magic like it's being slowly siphoned away. Bahira has been researching it for years, trying to figure out if it ties into where her magic is as well."

I look at him over my shoulder, a pocket of sun giving his light brown skin a golden glow. "What do you mean *where* her magic is?"

"It appears she was born without any. The first in our history," he answers solemnly. "During my Flame Ceremony, when my flame grew higher than it had for anyone else in centuries, we began to test and train my magic right away. Through that, we discovered that beyond having the normal mage abilities—manipulating elements, imbuing items, other small magic—there was something else I could do." Chills break out on the back of my neck, my gaze trapped within his. He leans down and kisses my forehead before gesturing with his chin out to the forest. "Watch."

I turn slowly, looking out at the closely staggered trees. My eyes dart around, trying to find the dark purple and black glow of his magic in the forest in front of me. Movement on the ground catches my attention, a shadow like that of an animal moves on top of the fallen leaves. But something about it looks odd, its shape not elongated in the way a normal shadow cast by the sun high above would be. I lean forward to get a better look and then immediately jolt backwards, bumping into Nox.

"What—" The shadow no longer moves against the ground but, instead, glides in the air—wisps of black swirling around as it comes closer to us.

"The reason that I laughed when you asked if I was scared of your magic, of your shadows, is because you aren't the only one who can wield them." To prove his point, Nox manipulates the pool of shadows in the air directly in front of us, condensing and shaping them into a bird which he then lands on the balcony between my hands.

I'm momentarily stunned, my body tense as I watch the bird made of shadows hop and flit about as if it is *real*. "Can I touch it?" I ask, my hand already lifting to do so.

"Yes, it won't hurt you. Only if I will it to."

My forefinger grazes the top of the shadow bird's head, the sensation bitingly cold but also jarringly smooth. "It feels like—like *stone*," I sputter. The fake bird hops closer to me, my yelp of surprise making Nox chuckle.

"It does. When my magic gathers the shadows and makes them into something tangible, it feels like stone. When I keep them more fluid, they feel more like a thin layer of water." The shape of the bird melts away before my eyes, the shadows turning back into something more translucent. They then slide over the top of my hand, the temperature still like ice, but they feel exactly as Nox said—a barely there caress of something smooth as silk.

"Can your shadows do what mine do?"

Maybe this is why Selene was so insistent that Nox train me. If his magic is unique like mine, then he would be the perfect person to do so.

Nox gently turns me around, his shadows floating in the air behind me now as he places both hands on my shoulders. I marvel at how he can command them without even calling the magic to his hands.

"They aren't exactly *my* shadows, as I can't create them like you can. I can only wield ones that are present, and they can only act as any physical object might. They can't *drain* life in the same way yours do," he says, cringing at his poor word choice. I sigh, my gaze dropping in defeat. Nox places a finger under my chin, tilting my head up to look at him. "You will learn to control them; just as I had to learn to control mine."

"I don't want to use them *at all*," I argue. "That magic is dangerous—*deadly*. I can't imagine any scenario in which I would need to learn how to wield them."

Not here, far away from my uncle who can't cross the Spell to get to me. Even then, I am not sure I *could* use that magic on him. Would the sting of finding out I murdered someone hurt less if I thought that person *deserved* it? Or did that line of thinking make me no better than my uncle?

"Rhea—"

"*Please*, Nox. Don't make me use that magic," I beg him, my panic growing with each heave of my chest.

To learn what I had done to those guards was hard enough thinking about—breathing through. I didn't trust that magic, and I didn't trust *myself* yet to attempt controlling it.

Nox grits his teeth together, his eyes growing darker as that feeling that I had learned was our magical signature thickens the air around us. It is like the brushing of someone's fingertips along my skin. Only, instead of breaking out in goosebumps, my magic pushes harshly at my *bones*.

"I will never make you do anything you don't want to. *Ever*."

"I know," I respond, gripping onto the front of his dark gray tunic.

His magic pours off of him in waves, the strength of it making me feel dizzy now that I know how to sense it. Nox lets out a low curse before he takes a deep breath and kisses the top of my head, his lips lingering there while I feel the swell of his power lessen.

"I'm sorry, Rhea." Wrapping my arms around his waist, I lay my cheek on his chest, breathing him in deeply. "I will never force you to use it, but Selene is right when she says that magic requires balance. It's something we are taught, even as children. You might be able to learn how to wield your light magic efficiently, but completely suppressing the shadow magic... That will have consequences."

Foreboding pokes at my mind and twists my stomach into knots. I can live with an imbalance of magic and whatever repercussions might come of that as long as the price to pay only affects *me*. But more death at my hands? I don't know if there is a way to come back from that.

I don't think my soul would survive.

Chapter Twenty-Seven

ARIA

M Y BODY IS STILL vibrating with dread after our failed attempt to lure the shifter ship—where a female aboard had nearly jumped into the water because of *me*. At least, I *think* it was because of me. My song isn't effective against males, but could it be with females? If so, has that always been the case or is it something... *new*.

"Try to remain calm, or mother will know something is up." Lyre gives me a small squeeze of reassurance before letting go.

My lips purse as I stare at my sister. "She always seems to know anyway when I'm trying to hide something."

"Well, she hasn't figured *this* out yet," she says firmly, looking out in the direction of Lumen. "Have *you* even figured out what is going on?"

"No," I say with a resigned groan. "I don't know why I can't be like everyone else. Why I'm *cursed* to not just be a siren but a terrible one."

"Aria." She says my name like a reprimand, but I know that she's only worried about someone overhearing us.

"I am lucky to have you, Lyre," I whisper, drawing my gaze up to meet her lavender one. "I don't think I would still be alive if I didn't." Without Lyre, there would be no one for me to commiserate with. Though I haven't told her *everything*, like the fact that I'm only attracted to females or about my secret cave, all she would need to effectively end my life is to share the secret about my song with our mother.

Lyre is quiet before gesturing for us to continue swimming. We move past schools of orange and white striped fish and small pods of miniature manatees. The seamounts come into view up ahead, the dark jagged rock stark against the bright blue of the ocean.

"When I was the youngest siren, before you were born, it was *torturous*. Allegra assumed her role as my personal tormentor right away. Sade had already joined the Queen's Legion by then, so I think she was just bored. I may have been able to hide my emotions more quickly and easily than you, Aria, but I had *no one* else to lean on. When Dyanna was born, I was so excited to have someone to interact with that wasn't tainted by the brutality of our queendom yet."

The longing in her voice causes my own to catch in my throat. She's never told me before what it was like to watch Dyanna grow up and how she went from an impressionable young siren to an unfeeling female.

"Dyanna was so curious and sweet as an offspring. She loved learning and would lay completely still if you promised to read her a book. Mother saw that softness in her, even when she was so young, as weakness. So she tucked her under her wing and didn't let go. That docile disposition quickly gave way to indifference and apathy. I had to keep pretending that I wasn't watching the destruction of innocence right in front of me. I learned to act as if I was proud of her—like her transformation was one to be *applauded*. And then you came." She slows us down until we are floating in the water, hovering over the seamounts as she lowers her voice. "I protected you as much as I could, all in the hopes that you could preserve a part of yourself without their corruption. You are special, Aria. Not because you are my sister. Not because you are a princess of the Siren

Queendom, but simply because you are *you*. I would not change any part of who you are."

She holds my hands in both of hers tightly.

"I know it is difficult to constantly hide, but just remember, you have one person who truly cares about you. No matter what the queen or Allegra make you do. No matter how you might beat yourself up about it afterwards. You are *good* and *humane*. Don't let those things get lost in the fray of everything else we have to pretend to be."

Tears of understanding mix into the surrounding waters as I whisper, "You know about yesterday."

My sister tightens her grip on me. "I'm sorry. It should have never happened again." Swallowing is difficult as I struggle to put into words just how grateful I am for Lyre. How *lucky* I am to have her as a confidant. She smiles at me before withdrawing her hands and turning to look in Lumen's direction. "I need to get back and return my books before Dyanna has my head. Are you going to visit them?" She nods to the seamounts.

"Yes. The young sirens will probably want me to play games for a bit, and I could use the distraction. Mother says she has a mission for me. Do you have any idea what it might be?"

Lyre's brows furrow together as she shakes her head. "I haven't heard anything. Whatever it is, I'll help you as much as I can." Her eyes linger on mine as she smiles and then dips her chin, turning to swim back towards our home.

I watch her for a moment, willing her sweet words to replace the anxious ones in my mind. Once she is out of sight and I feel my heartbeat steady, I swim down to the base of the seamounts. I'm met with complete silence when I reach the bottom, the lack of sound sending a wave of unease up my spine. I try to peer inconspicuously into the homes that are carved there, but not a single crystal gleams with light within the dwellings, making the darkness and quiet ominous as I continue swimming.

"What are you doing here?" The familiar voice causes me to startle as I quickly look behind me to see Nia floating there. "You are no longer wanted here."

"What?" I question, my surprise growing when I see colorful eyes catch the light of the sun streaming in from above. Dozens of sirens swim out from their hiding spots, their expressions ranging from apathy to pure disdain.

"Did you think after what happened yesterday that we would *want* you here again?" Nia's voice is vicious and her anger palpable as she moves closer to me, her fingers bent and claws poised to strike.

"Nia, I'm sorry."

She scoffs, her light blue eyes alight with fury. Her anger is not misplaced, I just wish there was more that I could do.

"You are a *princess*, Aria. That holds weight. It holds value to the other sirens that blindly follow your royal family. If one of you were to speak up, were to show others that there was a possibility of someone disagreeing with *Her Wickedness*, it would create a waterfall effect. Others would follow suit."

"It's not that simple, Nia. I can't disagree with her. She will be no less brutal in her punishment of me than she is with anyone else. It does *not* matter that I am her daughter."

"That's a pathetic excuse, and you know it." She moves so that she is directly in front of me, her teeth bared until I can see the points of her canines. Despite the appearance of her soft blue hair and scales, she is nothing less than a predator—hungry for retribution.

"I care about *all* the sirens of this queendom. A fact I would have thought proven by my spending time here. I do not want you stuck in this life, but I am only *one* person. And your aunt—" My words are abruptly halted when Nia slaps me across the face. My hand flies to my cheek, tears welling in my eyes as I bring them back to her.

"You will not utter one *single* word about my aunt. She was twice the female you or your pathetic excuse of a queen could ever be. She told me what actually happened, you know. What your mother and grandmother did during the war. We are doomed to a life in the seamounts under the barrier of the Spell that *they* are the cause of."

Confused, my eyes bounce from her to those gathered behind her. "Nia, how is that possible?" It is well known that her aunt died during the war in a battle fought on the surface.

She scoffs. "I wouldn't dare utter any word to you that I don't want the queen learning. Leave, *Your Highness,* and do not come back. *You* are not welcome here."

With that, she dismisses me, backing up to join the now large group of sirens gathered around me. My eyes roam theirs, trying to find a friendly face—someone who might explain why my presence here matters—but no one speaks up. In a twist of sharp irony, I am now the one wishing someone would defy Nia's orders and stand up for *me*. I take one last look, my eyes finding the small ones of Tiana and then Karina hovering behind her. I don't linger long, especially as Nia growls low from behind me. But I give the young sirens my most reassuring smile and then turn and swim up towards the surface.

While I didn't consider the seamounts a place of refuge, visiting the females there felt like the one *good* thing I was doing. For once in my entire existence within the confines of whom I was born to, I felt like I was making a difference. Without that, who was I really? Just another face upholding the savageness of a female scorned two hundred years ago.

Here or not, it didn't seem to matter. No one other than Lyre would even care anymore if I were to disappear.

The small pieces of sea glass before me glisten under the faint sunlight from above. The bright blues and vibrant greens are sorted out, a few pinks and yellows in their own little piles as well. Normally when I work on a new glass art piece, I have a vision in mind, an image that will imprint itself in my brain until I get it out through the placement of the colored glass. But today, there is nothing.

"Aria, are you in there?" Lyre's voice outside my door is a welcome surprise.

"Yes, come in." She opens the door, and I look up from a small pink table carved from the coral growing in my room. My fingers abandon the sea glass when I see the tension lining her face, worry swirling in her lavender eyes. "What is it?"

"Mother has asked that you meet her in the throne room. Allegra and Mashaka are there, as is Sade."

I wonder if I am truly heading towards my own demise as Lyre and I leave my room. If I am, I cannot say that it wouldn't be a welcome event. I try to focus on my mental checklist, but the closer we get to the yellow sea glass door, the harder it is for me to wear that mask of calm.

We enter the room to complete silence, my mother sitting upon her throne of decayed bones and rotted seashells. She watches us come down the middle aisle, Sade and Allegra hovering in the water on either side of her. Sade has opted not to wear her tritonelli seashell armor, instead letting her burnished orange and amber scales show. The deep brown of her skin makes her orange eyes glow, their intensity matching the tension in the room.

Lyre and I bow before our mother, my gaze focused down on the green scales at the bottom of my tail.

"Rise, daughters," she commands. Lyre doesn't spare me a look before she swims up the dais to Allegra's side. My mother lifts her chin slightly as she stares down the steps to where I wait. "Aria, you have been keeping secrets."

My chest constricts as I hold her unnerving gaze. I don't dare speak first, unsure of which secret she is referring to. She rises from her throne, her massive golden trident in hand.

"It appears that I have underestimated just how *much* you don't value your position. Are you aware of how many sirens would *kill* to be in your place? They might even kill to *take* your place, and yet you betray your family out in the open." The queen moves down the dais until she is only a few inches in front of me, her tail propelling her higher so that I have to tilt my head up to look at her. A horrific truth lies in the depths of her demeanor, one that she makes sure I understand. I am not her daughter but prey standing in the way of what she wants. I remain silent, both out of fear and from some tiny spark of self-preservation burning within me. "I know that you have been visiting the traitors of the seamounts. Giving them royal attention," she hisses, dropping down in the water until there is nothing more than the width of her trident between us. "Giving them coin. Entertaining the young sirens there, as if they are not descendants of *treason*."

"I just feel bad for them—"

"Your bleeding heart can be *sent* to them, then, if you so wish, Aria!" she shouts, backing up until her trident is pointed at my chest. The jagged edges of the diamond tips push against my skin, right on the edge of cutting me open. "I will *not* have you be the weak link in this family. You have two jobs: enforce my rule and add to our family line. So far, you are failing at both of those, and I'm starting to feel inclined to agree with Allegra that we either banish or kill you."

My talons dig into my palms as I look Allegra's way, immediately regretting that I do. There is no recognition or familiarity in her dark blue eyes—only a gleeful rage that she is all too eager to act upon.

"But I have another way that you can atone for your transgressions. A way for you to earn your keep and convince me of your value." My eyes are drawn back to my mother's as she drops her weapon from my chest. Water flows more easily through my gills though my heart still rattles my ribcage. "I need something that is being stored on the Northern Island. You are going to go get it for me."

I draw my brows together as a stuttering noise of confusion tumbles out of me. "You—you want *me* to journey to the Northern Island?" The journey is perilous and time consuming, taking five weeks alone just to *travel* there. Though having that much time out from under the thumb of my merciless mother and sisters sounds like a wish come true, uncertainty roars within me. "Surely, one of my other sisters is more appropriate to task this journey with?"

"Let me make myself clear, Aria. This is not a request but a *demand*. If you refuse, I will punish you by destroying the traitors of the seamounts."

Her threat hits deep, and I betray myself by letting my emotions seep out to the surface. She would kill her own people just to be rid of any who *might* think ill of her, and she'll *happily* put the blame on *me*.

"I cannot make this trip on my own," I say around the quivering of my lips.

To my surprise, she nods her head in agreement. I'm afraid to move—afraid to hope that perhaps she will let Lyre accompany me. But the thought dies before it has time to settle with my mother's next words.

"Mashaka will accompany you as your travel companion and enforcer—should you get any ideas about not returning. If that doesn't sway you, remember this: the lives of the sirens in the seamounts now rest on your shoulders." The queen's lips curl up into a monstrous smile. "If you fail to return, I will slaughter them all."

Chapter Twenty-Eight

BAHIRA

WHEN TUA HAD BROUGHT me to my room, I had barely given it a second glance before quickly showering and passing out on top of the bed.

When I woke up this morning, I spent some time exploring it. It is rather large for a guest suite, bigger than even my own bedroom back home. I was shocked to discover that behind a wide expanse of curtains was a wall made of glass. It looks out to the back side of the palace, over a field of grass that is dotted with palm trees and walkways made of tan-colored stone. In the distance, creating a skyline of its own, is the jungle. Its green is bold in color, the plants and trees growing without any space between them. It stretches for as far as the eye can see, and the curious side of me longs to traverse it. To see what mysteries it holds and how different it is from the kingdom back home.

The rest of my room is elegantly designed in the same light-colored wood as the first level. The large bed I slept on is centered against one wall with the bathroom tucked into a carved out section of the adjacent one. Fluffy rugs of white and gold are laid out on the floors, and sconces of glass holding flame gems dot the shimmering white stone walls. My favorite feature is the wall that has a built-in bookcase, the dark wood pulling attention to it in the otherwise airy space. There hadn't been any books on it until I unpacked the mage journals I brought and stacked them on the lowest shelf.

It isn't home, but it will do for the next three months.

On my first full day on the island, I spent half of it in my room and the other half exploring the floor I'm on. The entire palace is massive, and I marveled at the fact that I walked nonstop for ten minutes before I made it to the other side from where my room is located. Other than a few curious glances from finely dressed males and females, I didn't interact with anyone. I also didn't see Kai. Wherever he is staying, it must not be near my room.

I found what I think may be the royal library, located centrally between my room and what appeared to be a wing full of nobility, but the two guards stationed in front of it kept me from going inside.

The next few days were spent exploring the first level and the grounds of the palace. I found mostly palace staff rooms and other unexciting spaces on the former, though there *was* a second library. It was small, its shelves packed messily with books that were coated in dust.

I wandered past the gardens and fish ponds, going right to the edge of the palm tree border that Kai warned me not to cross. What would he do if I were to disobey him? Would he even notice? I haven't seen him—or the female that greeted him upon our arrival—at all. My restless energy only builds the longer I'm forced to wonder when I will get to work on what I came here to do.

At least there is Lana, an older female who works for the palace. Every day she brings me my meals accompanied with small tidbits of information about what is going on in the palace. She also brought me some more island-appropriate clothing, the thinner fabrics excellent at wicking away sweat caused by the humidity.

Today, I sit cross-legged on the bed, flipping to the last page of an account written by Councilman Godric and tapping my spelled pen on my own journal. Every Flame Ceremony and interaction he catalogs from the time has no mention of dwindling magic or anything out of the ordinary. They were still preparing for a visit from the fae rulers, which seems fitting to read about now that *I* was a visitor of sorts to the Shifter Kingdom.

Setting the ancient journal aside, the pages now all read, I reach for the next one when there is a knock at the door. Swinging it open, I meet Kai's eyes over the threshold, my stomach stupidly dipping at the sight of him.

"Oh, it's you. What do you want?" It's nearly been a *week* since I arrived, and I'm eager to do something other than explore by myself. I hope the sentiment is relayed in my bitter tone.

Kai's expression remains brooding as his arms fold over his broad chest. The laces of his dark green tunic are undone in the center, showing a hint of his chest beneath. My gaze roams over to the intricate dark lines of the tattoo on his arm, the upper portion hidden by the tunic's sleeves.

"There is going to be a dinner tonight."

We stare at each other as a few moments of silence pass before I arch a brow at him. "Dinner *is* something that usually occurs nightly. Is this one special, or are you just excited to tell me?"

His flat look of annoyance draws a dazzling smile of my own as I lean against the door frame and mimic his position. I ignore the way his eyes travel over my body, lingering before he lifts them to mine once more.

"I doubt you've ever experienced a dinner like this before. I'd advise you to be on your guard the entire night. The nobles all know you're my guest here at the palace, but that won't protect you from their advances. You should keep a low profile. You can tell them that you are from Honna, which is a small village on the other side of the island, if anyone asks."

I twist a piece of hair around my finger, and Kai tracks the movement. "If I didn't know better, I'd say you are looking out for me right now." When he stares at me like I've said nothing of importance, I shrug and flick my hair over my shoulder. "Either way, while I appreciate whatever this is," I say, gesturing between us as I right myself and step back into the room, "I can take care of myself."

And then I shut the door in his perfect face.

"Can you tell me what to expect for the celebration tonight, Lana?"

She hands me a bundle of lavender fabric before she huffs a breath and gestures for me to head to the bathroom to change. I watch as she rummages around in a bag she brought, pulling out brushes and serums and cosmetics.

"I am capable of getting dressed on my own."

"The only thing you seem *capable* of is making yourself late with your chatter. *Move.*" Her hands gesture once more for me to change, and I laugh as I heed her instruction. "The celebration is to honor the former king, Kai's father. It's his birthday. Though, between you and me, the male had nothing about him worth honoring."

I'm taken aback by her frankness as I change into the outfit she's given me. The top is in a halter style with the straps tying at the base of my neck and then dangling sheer fabric down my back. The skirt is long, going down to my ankles, with a slit that goes all the way up and stops a few inches beneath my hip.

"Should you speak of the former king that way? What if I tell someone what you've said," I quip when I finish dressing. The skirt moves easily as I walk, the warm and sticky air of the room brushing against the bare skin shown off at my midriff.

Lana mumbles something under her breath before turning to me as I walk back in. "*Aye,* you clean up well. He won't know what to do with you."

"Who?"

She gestures for me to sit in the vanity chair tucked into one of the corners of my room. "First, I am not worried about you telling anyone. I am beloved around here, so no one will believe you." Her accent thickens as she speaks while her fingers gently comb through my hair. "And I am talking about His Majesty of course."

I scoff, the noise exaggerated as I look at her through the reflection of the oval-shaped mirror. "Lana, I am not here for the king, nor do I care what he thinks of how I look."

She lets out a string of tuts, grabbing a comb and sectioning off my hair. "I can tell there is something between you two."

I move to turn and look at her, but she lightly smacks my shoulder so that I am forced to face forward again. Pulling my hair into two braids on either side at the top of my head, Lana continues the plaits back a few inches before she ties them off. The rest is left unbound and flowing down my back.

"You can't possibly tell there is something between us when I have not spent more than two minutes in the company of the king since arriving." Lana overturns one of the bottles of serums onto her palms, its fragrance delicate. Rubbing them together first, she then runs her hands through my curls, making them shine. Though I try to bite it back, my curiosity wins, and I add on, "Besides, he is already with someone."

"No, he isn't," she answers immediately, her lip twitching with amusement. My fingers dig into the fabric at my knees as she moves from my hair to my face, highlighting my cheeks with a lovely scented oil and adding a crimson-colored stain to my lips.

"He is. I saw them when I first arrived here," I comment, wrinkling my nose.

"You saw his sister, Jahlee. There. You are finished." She backs away from the vanity while I study myself. My hair looks richer in its color, my skin glowing as if I've spent a summer beneath the island sun.

Annoyingly, my thoughts draw once more to Kai. "He has a sister?"

"Yes, a wild thing she is, too. Sweet, but very strange." Lana cleans off the vanity while I get my sandals on and give myself one last glance in the mirror. "You look good. Now go. The sun has dipped in the sky already, and you don't want to be late. The party is back there," she says, gesturing to the back of the palace that I can see through the large floor-to-ceiling glass window.

"Thank you, Lana."

She begins humming to herself as she tidies around the bathroom, effectively dismissing me. I shut the door behind me as I leave, walking over to the stairs and descending two flights where music is already floating in the air. Finely dressed shifters mill about the lower level, some glancing my way as I pass. I offer them benign smiles before turning down a long hallway that is painted brilliantly in the orange light of the setting sun pouring in through a wall of glass. It makes the golden frames surrounding portraits of what I assume are past rulers glow. I slow my steps to examine the art, wondering if any of them are Kai's father.

"A big art fan?" a deep voice asks from farther down the hall.

I don't answer, instead watching as the male walks casually, his steps measured and perfectly paced. Though not quite as large as Kai, his stature is like that of all shifter males I've observed—broad and powerful. Tattoos swirl down both arms, at least from what I can see below his rolled-up sleeves. I turn back to look at the portraits, my head tilting to the side.

"More a fan of males with pompous hair, it seems."

He snorts, joining me in looking at the pictures, all of which show males with their hair coiffed and puffed up. "Unfortunately, the artists of the past preferred that rulers looked more refined and less like the wild animals we can turn into."

I glance at him out of the corner of my eye, taking in his cut jaw and broad cheekbones. His hair falls just past his shoulders, a few shorter pieces framing his face. He's handsome, and also currently dragging his own gaze over me.

"I'm Kane." He extends his hand out for me to shake.

Firmly clasping it, I offer my own name. "Bahira."

"Bahira," he drawls, like he's tasting each letter. "Are you looking for the party? I'd be happy to escort you. Unless you need more time with these ancient males." He gestures towards the paintings with a hubristic smirk.

My own lips tug up to the right. "You may escort me, then, Kane." He offers his arm out to me, his red tunic straining around his muscles.

"Are you new here?" he asks as he leads me down the hallway, turning right into a space that opens up into a large foyer. A chandelier of sparkling flame gems hangs from overhead, each one dripping down like a small waterfall of golden yellow drops pouring from the ceiling and suspended in air.

"I am."

Kane chuckles as he guides me through a set of open double doors and under an arch of woven vines, bright orange flowers in blossom all around it. The air is thick with the cloying scent of something smoky and savory. Males and females mingle with each other, holding drinks in their hands as they talk. Flame gems line walkways, and lit torches cast writhing orange and yellow light over the party goers.

"You're going to make me work for more information, aren't you?" he asks.

My smile widens as I look at him. I had lamented about needing someone to cool the fire that Kai seems to stoke within me every time he is near. Kane would work well enough. "Are you afraid of putting in the effort, Kane?"

His voice rumbles like a deep purr in his chest. "You'll find that I can be quite *dedicated* in my efforts."

I hold his light brown eyes, flecks of gold shimmering in them. *Just like Kai's.* I scold myself for letting my thoughts once more go to the shifter king. *Idiot.* Turning my gaze forward, I take in the rest of the party and let go of Kane's arm.

Long dark wooden tables connect to form a u-shape, wooden chairs packed in tightly all around it while dark green leaves and blooming white and purple flowers decorate the table centers. A throne of white and gold sits directly at the center, pretentiously overlooking both sides. I snort at that as I continue my perusal. People dance in an open space to the right of the tables, their sensuous movements in time with the heavy beating of the drums from a band on the opposite side.

"Save me a dance for after dinner?" Kane croons near my ear.

"I am not much of a dancer, I'm afraid."

"Perhaps I will convince you."

I glance at him in question, but when the music comes to a halt, he leads me towards the tables, rounding the outside and—much to my surprise—bringing me to one of the sides that is nearly adjacent to Kai's throne. Kane drops into a chair on my right while a single seat remains empty to my left. I take in the crowd as males and females filter into their own seats, a few studying me with open curiosity.

The drums start to sound again, their beat low and slow, each pound of the mallets reverberating out into the evening air. Everyone around the table stands, and I watch as Kai, Tua, and who I now know is Jahlee emerge from the double doors and descend the palace stairs. The beat picks up, the sound demanding everyone's attention on the king. I may have snickered at him were it not for the fact that he looks absolutely miserable. His lips are drawn in a thin line, his teeth clearly gritting from the scrutiny. Upon his head rests a metal crown of what looks like thickly cut branches twisted together. Each branch curls up into a point at the front, mimicking the look of horns. The dark ensemble he wears fits him impeccably—form fitting enough to show the ridges of his muscles in a tantalizing manner.

Forcing my gaze away, I move to study Jahlee instead. Her wavy hair is left to cascade down her back, its simplicity contrasting with her detailed outfit. The material is the same as my own, only teal in color. Her top goes over one shoulder, tendrils of fabric tying together there and draping over her arm. Instead of a skirt, her bottoms are sheer and loosely cut, a long slit in the wide legs going from the jewel-cuffed ankle and up to the sparkling, threaded waistband. Her wrists are dressed with bangles of gold, each step making them jingle loudly. Where her brother looks put off by the attention, Jahlee is drawing it towards herself. Daring anyone to look her way and then flashing them a cunning smile when they do.

Kai walks behind me and then rounds the corner of the table, straight to his throne. Tua takes up the empty place between the king and I, his eyes widening for a fraction of a second when they meet mine before he schools his face in a placating smile. Leaning forward, he looks past me at someone farther down the table to my right, but my own attention is stuck on Kai. If he is surprised to see me seated amongst the highest of the nobles here, he doesn't show it. His face is one of pure stone, but then his gaze leaves mine and works *slowly* down my body. By the time his eyes make their way back up again, something has changed in his expression. My own heart beats at a pace matching the drums banging quickly behind me. I break whatever is happening between us first and train my attention straight ahead; unfortunately, I'm now staring directly at Jahlee, who appears to have been watching us. Her eyes bounce back and forth between her brother and me before a wide grin splits her lips. *Fuck me.*

Three beats of the drum—harsh and loud—signal that it's time for everyone to sit, and I follow suit. Servants from the palace spill down the steps, bringing plates of warm fish, fresh salads, and steaming rice. As the meals are laid out before everyone, Tua stands, clinking his glass with his fork and getting the crowd to quiet immediately.

"Tonight, we honor the late King Noa and his influential rule on our glorious island. Under his reign, we knew prosperity like no other, and through his son, we shall continue to see it grow."

The crowd claps politely, but a quick scan around the tables shows tight mouths and furrowed brows. I uncomfortably shift in my chair, drawing Kane's attention.

"Are you alright, Bahira?" he asks, sliding a hand over my own. I clench my jaw and remove myself from his touch.

"Quite fine, thank you."

His gaze lingers on me before he flicks it in Kai's direction, the corner of his mouth quirking up. "Glad to hear it."

The music starts up again as everyone begins to eat. A group of people—each holding a long stick with large rounded ends—enter the open space between the tables and form a straight line. The firelight dances over them, showcasing the males' broad naked chests and the females' minimally clad bodies. Black fabric is wrapped strategically around them, and even in only the glow of the nearby flames, it's impossible not to notice their muscular statures.

"They are fire dancers," Kane supplies, leaning in close enough to brush his arm against my own. "They will provide tonight's entertainment as we feast."

My meal is abandoned as I focus my attention on the dancers.

They move in unison, falling to one knee and striking a long match against the sides of their sandals. When they rise again, they each light the ends of their sticks, balls of fire now glowing against the night. They twirl their fire sticks like batons in feats that seem entirely magical though none is being used. The beat of the music aligns with their movements, the orange glow of the flames illuminating their golden skin and stark tattoos. They perform throughout the entire meal, never once faltering in their steps or showing signs of exhaustion. Occasionally, my gaze clashes with Jahlee's across the way, and every time, she responds with a wide, terrifying smile.

We all clap when they finish, the dancers turning to Kai and bowing in his direction before exiting the center space. The drums pick up once more, the sound a little softer and the beat back to a slow and sensual cadence. Leaning back in my chair, I truly take in the beauty of the night sky for the first time since being on the island.

"It is a beautiful view," Kane says softly from my side.

"Indeed," I respond, turning to look at him.

His eyes dip down to my mouth, his own curving up into a bright smile. "Do you want to dance, Bahira?"

"You said you'd try to convince me." I fold my arms over my chest, tilting my head as I stare him down. "So do it. *Convince* me to dance with you."

Kane laughs, turning in his chair until his knee brushes against the side of my leg. "Where are you from?"

"Honna," I reply as Kai instructed me to.

He hums, nodding his head as if this answers some unasked question. "They don't have parties quite like this there."

I shrug and gesture with a hand to the party attendees now heading out to dance. "There's dinner and dancing. Entertainment. Seems like a generic party to me."

"But they don't dance like this back in your small village." When I send him an incredulous look, he juts his broad chin out. "Watch."

Indulging him, I observe the crowd gathered on the dance floor. The females grab onto the fabric of their skirts, lifting them to their knees as they sway their hips to the sultry beat. The males are no less fluid in their movements—some dancing alone, others with hardly a space between them.

Kane's fingers trail up my arm slowly, his touch delicate—too much so. "Look at how they become one with the pulsing of the drums," he whispers near my ear. "Do you see how they all move together? How in sync they are?"

Sure enough, my gaze snags on a female pressed between two males, each one giving her ample attention as they writhe to the band's beat. Heat curls low in my belly as I watch them, my nails tapping on the table. I didn't consider myself inexperienced in bed, but I'd never been with two men at once. What would that be like? To have Kane's mouth on me at the same time Kai—

I stand abruptly, gripping Kane's arm. "Let's dance." I don't look back at the king as I lead us both into the throng of people. While everything about the trip to the island and my arrival thus far has been less than ideal, the only thing that has completely thrown me off is Kai. I can't fathom why I react to him the way that I do, like a pathetic moth drawn to a flame.

Kane's body envelops mine from behind, his hands gripping tightly on my hips as we nestle between the other people dancing. It doesn't take long for me to mimic the movements of everyone around me, my body relaxing more with every melodic beat of the drums. Kane pulls me closer to him, my back completely flush with his front as we move together. I lift my arms up above me, my head resting back against his chest as I twirl them slowly in the air. His scent rushes over me—earthy with the smallest hint of something floral. It's not a *bad* smell, but I have to fight the urge not to recoil. It isn't the one I want.

Unable to help myself, I search around the dancing shifters until I find Kai, still seated on his throne. His eyes glow golden in the flamelight as he watches me, the act sending a shock of desire to my core. Kane's hands tighten on my hips, guiding them in synchronicity with his. Yet, even with the male behind me moving his body so closely with my own that the fabric of our clothes between us may as well be inconsequential, I still can't look away from the shifter king. From the way his eyes bore into mine until I feel that deep heat once more curling within me. My thighs strain to squeeze together, my breaths coming at a wild pace. *It's only because I haven't had sex in a while.*

Kane spins me around and pulls me close, his erection pushing in on my stomach. "Tell me you want to go somewhere private?" he growls, his eyes brighter despite the pocket of darkness we inhabit amongst the other dancing bodies.

My lips part, indecision a momentary flicker before I snuff it out and answer, "Yes."

He wastes no time, pulling me harshly through the crowd—sweaty bodies gliding past us until we reach the steps outside the palace. "Where is your room?"

"Second floor to the right."

"The royal wing? That's a surprise."

The what? Why had Tua put me in the royal wing of the palace?

We round the corner of the split staircase, going up the next set of stairs and making it a few steps before Kane backs me up towards the wall. He crashes his lips onto mine, his tongue spearing into my mouth as his hands begin to roam my body. My fingers grip onto his hair, and I yank him back from me, holding him in place with another hand braced on his chest.

"*Don't* kiss me like that," I growl, tugging harshly on his strands before pulling him back in and taking control the way *I* want to.

He's momentarily stunned but it quickly gives way to his desire. Cool air slides against my bare leg as I wrap it around his hip, the slit in my skirt making it easy to do so. I pull him closer to me, until I can feel his cock nearly lined up with where I want it. He groans as he explores my mouth with his tongue, each flick from it drawing a matching sensation in my core as I grind myself over him. His fingers dig into the flesh at my backside, the opposite hand skimming the side of my breast.

A means to an end is all he is, a way to find release for my body so that I can keep my mind distracted and off of—

"Kane!" Like I've summoned him, Kai's voice snaps down the hallway like a whip. Kane and I separate enough for me to drop my hands and leg though his grip tightens on my ass.

"What do you want?" Kane asks through gritted teeth. I raise my brows at the bold way he speaks to his king.

"She is off limits." Kai's steps eat up the distance between us in hardly three strides, his broad body towering over Kane's by at least six inches.

My anger flares, and I push Kane off of me, moving closer to Kai and jabbing my finger into his chest. "Excuse me? What makes you think you get to decide if I am off limits? I don't *answer* to you."

"Maybe not," he says, leaning closer until I have to strain my neck to look up at him. Kai's eyes slide over to Kane. "But he does."

Chapter Twenty-Nine

Bahira

THE KING AND KANE stare at each other for a few seconds, the air so charged that I'm sure they'll start throwing punches. Or shift into animals and fight that way.

Kane huffs out a breath, casting another glance my way before straightening his tunic and glowering up at Kai. "As you say, *Your Majesty*."

He brushes past us, his shoulder bumping into Kai's arm as he passes. Kai and I wait until he rounds the corner to the stairs before we turn and look back at each other.

"What the fuck was that?"

"You tell me," he responds, his voice a menacing growl. "You're here to work, not fuck your way through my court."

I don't think when I move to strike his face with my left hand. Kai catches my wrist right before I make contact and walks us backward until my back hits the wall. His massive hand pins me there, the other slamming into the wall next to my head—the vibration of it rattling my skull—as he leans over me. "I'm getting tired of you hitting my face."

"It's *none* of your business who I decide to sleep with." At my words, Kai's lips lift in a sneer, and my heart bruises my chest with how hard it beats.

There is no point of contact between us other than where he holds my wrist, and yet I've never felt so ignited within. Anger mixes with desire, the blend making my pulse race even faster. I want to rebel at the idea that this male—so clearly disliked and unwanted by his own kingdom—could rule over my body and desire in such a way. It makes me feel powerless, and that is one thing I can *not* allow. I have spent sixteen years scraping together parts of myself to try to fill the gap that being magicless left. I refuse to lose *any* of it to *him*.

I hold his gaze, bitter determination flooding through me as I start to slide my right hand down my stomach. Kai's eyes dip to watch the movement, his brows drawing up the smallest amount when I slip my hand under the waistband of my skirt.

"What are you doing?"

I wouldn't call his question breathless, but I wouldn't say his voice is steady either. Knowing that watching me touch myself sends the smallest fracture through his stone armor is enough to fuel me to keep going.

"You stole an orgasm from me," I respond, my chin lifting as I dare Kai to stop me. "I'm taking it back." My fingers travel beneath my undergarments, finding the wetness already coating my sex. My next inhale stutters as I push a finger inside myself and then draw it back out, before plunging two back in—deep enough to draw a gasp. My desire is sharp, sending pinpricks of lust that sink deeply into me. "I *detest* you," I rasp, pumping my hand harder. "You—"

"*Stop talking*," he commands, and damn him, all it does is coil that tension tighter. His fingers flex around my wrist, a quiet moan slipping free from me with the movement. He doesn't touch me anywhere else, doesn't even lean in any farther, but I don't want him to. I want to come around my fingers with his eyes on me, and then I never want to think about him this way again.

The heel of my palm rubs against my clit, and my eyes threaten to close from the friction, but I force them to stay open. To stay on him and show him that the power he thinks he can wield over me is *useless*.

My panting fills the hallway, our bodies cast in the shadows between the flame gems hanging from the walls. Kai's breathing grows labored, his inhales and exhales long and exaggerated, but still, his deep brown and gold-speckled eyes lay siege on my gray ones.

I climb and climb, each flex of my fingers and slide against my palm bringing me closer and closer to that edge. Then Kai's nostrils flare, his head dipping a little closer, and it's enough to shove me right over. My orgasm unravels fast and hard as my head kicks back and my thighs squeeze together, a hum of pleasure vibrating past my lips. My arousal coats my fingers and palm, a heady sensation of weightlessness causing me to lean my weight against the wall. Kai's eyes stay focused on mine, his gaze brutal and scrutinizing.

When my breathing evens out, I remove my hand from underneath my skirt, intent to leave now that I've done what I needed to, but the king's other hand snaps out and grabs it, bringing my wet fingers into the small space between us. It could be the post-orgasm endorphins or something equally as stupid to blame, but I can't help the way I study his handsome face. His edges are sharp and broad, meticulously carved from stone. He's a predator in every sense of the word.

But so am I.

Neither of us moves as his gaze focuses intently on my fingers, his arms bulging though his grip on me is no tighter for it. Then, with a snarl, he releases me, stepping back and running a hand through his hair. If looks could kill, I'd be struck dead from the pure fury pouring off of him.

"Don't ever do that again."

Turning on his heel, he walks down the hallway, not towards the stairs but in the opposite direction. He opens a door across the hall from mine and then slams it shut, shaking the glass orbs holding the flame gems.

With my ears still ringing, I enter my room and huff out a rattled breath. My motions are automatic as I undress and make my way to the bath, hoping to wash away how his touch felt like a flame against my skin and how his scent only brought me closer to my climax.

Yet, as the night goes on and sleep eludes me, the only relief I receive is when I come twice more by my own hand. The most troubling part of it all is that when I close my eyes, my fingers pumping between my legs, all I see is *him*.

The next morning, I sit in a dark blue armchair in my room, eating a breakfast pastry brought up by Lana. She had stared at me for a moment before her lips widened and she started cackling. I sent her out of the room immediately after that. How the old hag seemed to know that *something* happened between Kai and I, I don't know. I also don't know how to quantify exactly *what* happened last night. Or why it didn't ease any of the ache I feel when I think of the way Kai's eyes lingered on my slick fingers.

After eating, I dress for the day, intent on finding a room that can double as my workspace to set up my magnifier. I find a pair of blue cotton trousers and a lightweight white sleeveless tunic. My hands braid my hair loosely, and then I slip on some sandals that I brought from home.

Home. The word rattles me enough to pause as I think about my family and all that I'll miss in the next three months. I reminisce about Daje, his birthday only a few weeks after the Autumnal Ball which is near the end of my stay here. His sapphire eyes shine brightly in my mind, the memory of him begging me not to accept Kai's proposal.

I snort out loud at the word. Two different proposals by two men who could not be more opposite, and yet I had accepted the one from the male I didn't know but still loathed beyond comprehension—*and am most inconveniently attracted to*. Daje had stripped me of the very little power I had by taking away my choice and throwing an ultimatum at me instead. Pick him and sacrifice my heart or choose myself and lose the man I've called my best friend for the majority of my life—neither option was ideal, and neither one seemed *necessary*.

Shaking my head as if I can clear the looming deadline that will alter my life, I roll my shoulders back and stand, walking to the door. I shriek at the dark brown eyes staring down at me from across the threshold when I open it.

"*Why?* Why are you lurking in front of my door?" I shout.

Kai's pupils flare for a moment as if his mind has betrayed him with thoughts of last night before his face once again becomes impassive. "It's time you start what you came here to do," he orders.

I scowl at his tone, at how chastising he sounds, as if I haven't been waiting for *his* instructions on what I should be doing. "Of course, *Your Majesty*," I cajole sweetly, enjoying the way he bristles at the title. "Just tell me where you have need of me, and I'd be happy to get out of your hair."

The animosity between us burns, turning any of my lingering thoughts of desire into ash. Kai breathes deeply through his nose before relaxing his jaw, the heat in his eyes cooling.

"Tua has asked around the capital for any families willing to let us speak with them, so you can see firsthand what the blight is doing. We leave in ten minutes."

He doesn't give me a chance to respond before he's already walking towards the stairs. I stare at the now empty space in front of me, exhaling an exaggerated breath before stepping back into the room to gather my journal and spelled pen. Swapping my sandals out for boots, I drop my supplies into my backpack and stride towards the stairs.

Kai leans against a wall on the first floor, his eyes snapping to mine once I'm within a few feet. Dressed casually in a tan tunic with short sleeves and black trousers tucked into dark brown boots, he'd blend in with the rest of the shifters milling about were it not for the fact that he's a head taller than most of them. We proceed out of the palace and down the path we followed when we arrived from the docks, the noise of Molsi growing louder in the distance.

I scour the faces we pass, looking for signs of discontent. Kai's presence draws every gaze, their eyes bouncing from him to me and back again before they reveal whether or not they despise him. As a creature who hides behind her own makeshift armor, I'm beginning to understand why Kai's disposition is less than *pleasant* most of the time. My own people may have hurled cruel words at me as a child and then levied looks of pity my way as an adult, but it was rare to see someone so openly loathe my existence back home. Not like with Kai and the shifters of Molsi.

I look at him from the corner of my eye as a different feeling stirs low in my stomach. Not the normal lust or animosity that so easily toggled back and forth between us but something gentler, more understanding.

"What do your tattoos mean?" I blurt, needing the distraction.

Kai swings his head in my direction, a somewhat surprised look on his face like he's forgotten I was walking next to him. Looking back ahead, he mutters, "They mean many things."

When he doesn't expand on that, I remember *why* hostility is one of the emotions I feel towards him, and we continue walking with only the shouts from merchants and clamoring of shoppers between us.

Kai follows a path that leads away from the very center of Molsi and, instead, goes to where a collection of small homes made of stone and wood are gathered. Smoke blends into the air above the huts from their chimneys, while lanky trees with wide dark green leaves stretch far above them. We halt a few feet in front of one of the homes, a large paw print and snake symbol carved into the light-colored wooden door.

"Here you will see how the magic of our kingdom has changed," he says vaguely, folding his arms over his chest.

I nod, observing the home once more. It appears to be normal, no odd noises or sights anywhere for me to even *begin* to guess what he is talking about as Kai knocks on the door.

The wooden door creaks open, and I look down to find a young female shifter, no older than eight, staring up at us. Her light brown hair is braided haphazardly, the long plait draping over her shoulder. Kai stares at her, his hands opening and closing at his sides slowly like he can somehow yank the words he wants to say out of the air.

When another few seconds pass and she begins to shrink away, I clear my throat and squat down to her level. "Hello. My name is Bahira. What's yours?"

"Mira," she squeaks, her eyes—brown with stripes of golden yellow—moving from Kai to me.

"Hi, Mira. The king and I are here to visit. Are your parents home?" I ask, looking past her shoulder and into what I can see of the small living room.

She nods her head, her small hand twisting the fabric of her skirt. "My mom is always home now."

My head tilts as I dissect her answer before a bare-chested male appears in the doorway. His tattoos run up his arms, pouring over onto the front of his body as well. Part of the pattern is covered by his unbound straight black hair, but the swirls and lines are hard to ignore, especially as I wonder if Kai's chest is adorned with similar ink.

"Majesty," he says by way of greeting to Kai before looking at me. "And Lady…"

"Just Bahira."

He motions for us to enter his home, Mira tucked into his side tightly. The living room is modest, just a few pieces of furniture adorning the space. A tiny kitchen is to our left, a dining table that seats four set in the middle. Draping from wooden shelves attached to the wall are potted plants, all of them varying in their stages of decay as if someone has forgotten to care for them over time.

"My name is Haloa," he says, laying a hand to his chest and tilting his head forward. "You've already met Mira. Thank you both for coming. Come, my wife is back here."

Kai and I follow behind Haloa and his daughter, going down a short hallway and into a bedroom. The room is narrow, only a bed and a dresser holding a glass case filled with plants making up its contents. I cast a curious glance Kai's way at the empty room when he gestures with his chin to the dresser. Together we move towards it, the wood floor beneath us creaking loudly from our steps.

My fingers grip onto the edge of the dresser as I follow Kai's gaze to what rests on top of it. Small plants and grass grow from the black soil tightly packed in the bottom of the glass box, rocks and twigs spread out in a thin layer on top. A large chunk of wood is set in the middle, and residing atop it, nearly camouflaged in its environment, is a small green and black striped snake. I suck in a sharp inhale, realizing that this isn't just a glass case; it's an *enclosure*.

The symbols on the door—a paw print and a serpent—were not sigils or random carvings but a representation of the shifters that reside here. One of which I was staring at.

"Can she no longer shift back?" I ask Kai quietly under my breath. His eyes hold mine, and he doesn't have to speak for me to understand. *This* is the blight. "*My gods.*"

"She shifted nearly two weeks ago," Haloa states from behind me, forlornness woven in his voice. "I've been doing the best I can with Mira, but I have to work both the day and night shifts now that my wife—" He takes a moment to compose himself, and I have to squeeze my eyes shut at how *desperate* he sounds as he tells Mira he is alright. "Can you help her?"

No. This is beyond what I was prepared for. Beyond anything I *could* have prepared for. And the fact that the king knew this and led me in here blind anyway *enrages* me.

"Excuse me," I say sharply, tearing my gaze away from Kai's as I leave the bedroom.

I open the front door too roughly, having to then catch it before it slams into the wall. My teeth grind together, and I feel the pressure of hot tears sting the backs of my eyes. *Failure.* The word burns as it lands in my thoughts, Daje's voice pushing it deeper into me.

"Bahira," Kai grumbles from behind, his heavy footsteps catching up to me quickly. He grips my arm and pulls me to the back of one of the nearby homes, keeping us out of sight. "What is wrong with you?"

"You led me in there *completely* unprepared."

Kai drops his hold on me to throw his arms out to the side. "What did you think you were going to see, Bahira? What were you expecting to find? We are *shifters,* and something is wrong with our magic."

"I didn't think—" I bite down on my tongue as I run a hand through my hair. *I didn't think it would be this.* Naively, I had assumed that it would be a problem similar to the one back home.

Kai's eyes flash golden, his expression sharpening the longer he watches me. "Are you saying that you don't think you can help?" he questions, his hands bracing on his hips.

I know what's at stake—for both kingdoms—if I fail. Though Nox had said that Rhea was responsible for the magic we felt, they both ran from the king of the Mortal Kingdom, and I have no idea if he knows they ran to the Mage Kingdom or if he will retaliate in any way. Part of me suspects that if he had a magical niece under his nose all this time, then there is a chance he might have other magic hidden within his kingdom. We still need the protection that King Kai is offering, and the only way to keep it is to ensure that I stay on this island for as long as possible.

"I will do it—*can* do it," I say, standing up taller. "But I'm going to need you to start giving me more information. I will need your help, *Kai*, and a space in the palace that I can work in. Somewhere I can set up all of my equipment and have access to any books or research I deem necessary."

Kai's hardened expression eases a little as he contemplates my request. The sun shines directly onto him, the exposed skin at his neck and collarbone gleaming in its light as we stare at each other. "You will have it," he finally says.

A rush of surprise catches me off guard, but I give him a nod and swing my backpack around, opening it as I search for my journal and a spelled pen. Once the pack is back on, I gesture with my hand, and Kai leads us back into the house.

Chapter Thirty

BAHIRA

K AI AND I VISITED five families affected by the blight yesterday. Our walk back to the palace had been quiet while I read over the notes I had taken from each household. The king had walked beside me, his presence imposing but beginning to feel normal. Loathe as I was to admit it, I had paid attention to how he interacted with the shifters we visited. He wasn't overly kind or amiable, but he was very respectful and attentive. Even when one older female droned on and on about how she thinks his bloodline is tainted and that these problems started with his grandfather, Kai kept eye contact with her and simply listened, absorbing her barbed words like he thought he deserved to hear them.

I didn't want to find a single thing about the king to like that was beyond the physical, because at least my own carnal desire for him could be explained away by the part of my brain that was guided more by instinct than rationale. The part that saw a male who nearly exceeded seven feet tall and was hewn from a mountain and then carved by the gods into something that seemed exclusively made to torture me... I could deal with the repercussions of that. Yet to find myself growing a seedling of respect for him? A modicum of admiration? No, that only spelled disaster.

Kai kept his word, coming to my room this morning and taking me to what he called a "waste of space" but then amended to clarify that it was an abandoned workroom his father once used for his own experiments. When I asked what kind, he said he didn't know.

The door Kai stops in front of is unremarkable, its wood dark in color while its handle is a worn brass. He pulls out a matching brass key, unlocking the door before handing it to me. I tuck it into the pocket of my black trousers and follow Kai into the dusty space.

The room itself is simple, unadorned and basic in its presentation. The walls are made of vertical slats of wood, each beam a slightly different shade as if the leftovers from other projects were used to construct it. Two large windows are cut into the farthest wall and look out to the jungle. The furniture in the room is simple: one large wooden table in the center with a smaller desk off in the corner. A standing rectangular mirror with an intricately detailed golden frame is pushed to the side, a canvas sheet haphazardly covering part of it. *Is this where he keeps his kingdom's Mirror?*

One side of the room contains shelves built into the wall. Most of them are bare except for a few books randomly stacked together in the center, their colorful leather spines covered in a layer of dust. The other side of the room has a counter with cabinets and drawers stacked underneath and a small basin sink tucked into the corner.

"I take it no one has been in this room for a while?" I ask, turning around to find Kai studying something on the desk in the corner. He picks it up, thumbing through the pages of what must be a journal or book before laying it back down on the desk.

"No. Have you explored much outside yet?" he asks, changing the subject.

I turn from him and set my pack on the table in the center of the room, the sunlight gleaming through the windows showcasing the different scars and indents left on it from past usage. I wonder again what Kai's father experimented on.

"Not yet. Though Kane did have a *lovely* note sent to me this morning offering to show me around the city. I'm thinking—"

"Stay away from Kane." His sudden proximity behind me sends shivers down my spine as I spin to face him, leaning back against the table. He plants his hands on either side of me, lowering down so that we are nearly at eye-level. "Do you hear me?"

"Why?" When he doesn't respond, I shake my head and lift my chin. "I will see whoever I want."

"You would do well to remember that you know nothing of this island and its politics. You know *nothing* of who is friend and who is foe," he murmurs, his gaze antagonizing me as I grip the edge of the table harshly. Unbidden thoughts of us in a similar position on the ship flash in my mind, except he was completely naked then.

"And which are you, Kai? Friend or foe?" My nipples peak under my shirt at our proximity, at the heat radiating off his body and onto mine.

Kai's nostrils flare, and he leans in even closer until our noses are nearly touching. "To you? Neither. And stop looking at me like that."

I can't help but grin deviously as I tilt my head. "How am I looking at you?"

"Like you want me to fuck you," he says as though it's a reprimand. His head moves to the side of mine, his breath tickling my ear. "Like you know that I'm the only one who could do it properly."

It's a battle to keep my breathing even as I stay perfectly still. I don't want that—*can't* want that.

"But I don't touch taken females."

I jerk my head in surprise.

Kai backs up a few steps, plastering his well-worn mask of indifference on. "Let Tua know if you need anything else. I will see you tomorrow morning to visit another round of families." His long legs bring him to the door quickly and out of the room before I even have a chance to reply.

"Taken?" I mumble to myself, drawing on any memory that might give Kai the impression that I am with someone.

I go over every moment since the shifter king came to the island to pick me up, and other than my rendezvous with Kane, there's nothing that comes to mind. Until I remember what Kai said when we were leaving the beach of the Mage Kingdom. *You'll see your boyfriend soon enough.*

"Fucking Daje," I groan. *Of course.* Even an ocean away, there is no escaping what awaits me the moment I return to the Mage Kingdom.

Huffing out a breath, I carefully pull my magnifier out to set on the table, as well as the bottle containing the leaves from my last experiment. My journal with notes taken from yesterday lies next to it, the spelled pen holding the page open.

"Did you know that talking to yourself is a sign of insanity?"

My attention snaps to the door where a female stands under the doorframe, her hands planted on either side as she leans in until her arms are straining. I recognize her warm brown hair and the same golden tan skin that Kai has.

"You're Jahlee."

She smiles wide, her full lips parting to reveal perfectly white teeth. "To you, yes."

Snorting, I walk to the side of the room where a few chairs are stacked and take one back to the table. "You sound just like your brother."

She straightens from the doorframe, practically *waltzing* into the room as she drags her fingertips over the canvas sheet covering part of the mirror, tugging it off completely. "I don't get that a lot. I wish I did. He's actually why I'm here. I saw him storming out looking extremely *flustered*, and I had to see why."

I narrow my eyes as I take her in. She's shorter than I am but built similarly. There's a litheness about her that seems to be something all females from this island have in common. The top half of her hair is tied up into two tiny buns while the lower half drapes over her shoulders in subtle waves.

Mint green gauzy fabric wraps around her chest in a crisscross pattern, tying at the back of her neck. A matching long skirt with a slit that stops mid-thigh glows against her skin, and black hard-soled slippers complete her look. She has a regalness about her, unlike the roughness her brother so often exudes. She also doesn't have a tattoo of any kind, at least not one I can see currently.

"You get under my brother's skin," she says, facing me as she sits atop the table and examines her nails.

"If I do such a thing, it's only because he makes it *so easy* to." She laughs wildly at that, the sound jarring and loud.

Giving her an incredulous look, I carefully uncork the bottle holding the leaves that were brought back to life and take one out, setting it on a glass slide for the magnifier. Jahlee hops off the table and walks with her arms swinging at her sides until she is standing right next to me.

"He is rather prickly at times. I try to lighten the mood whenever we are together, but he seems reluctant to experience *joy* of any kind." She reaches out to touch the jar of leaves, but my hand snaps out and catches her wrist.

"Please don't touch that. It's important to me, and I can't let anything happen to it." I release her from my hold, expecting a curse or for her to threaten going to her brother, but instead, she smiles somehow even wider, the sight completely unsettling.

"You have fast reflexes for someone who doesn't have shifter in her."

I still, my hands falling flat on the tabletop.

"Would you like to?" she asks, leaning her hip against its edge.

"Would I like to *what*?"

"Would you like to have some shifter in you? I know quite a few males who are already smitten by your arrival if the court gossip can be believed." Her brown eyes grow serious as her lips flatten into a straight line. The tension between us grows awkward until she bursts into a fit of laughter, her hands going to her stomach while she doubles over. "You should see your face right now," she huffs out between gasping breaths. "Oh my gods, that was funny."

What. The. Fuck.

"I can see why my brother likes you," she says with a sigh, nearly patting herself on the back for her perceived joke.

"Now *that* is funny," I reply, clicking the first glass circle into place and peering down the magnifier's scope. "I think your brother is only keeping me alive because of our *deal*. Which I assume he's told you about?"

She hums and then grabs a chair of her own, dragging it slowly over the floor. The wood-on-wood scraping sound makes me wince the entire time she moves it, and I'm forced to look away from the magnifier and watch her until she's back at my side. She sets the chair way too close to my own, and before she goes to sit, I push it a little farther away with my foot. Grinning, she takes a seat and leans her elbows on the table.

"So, what are you working on?"

"Do you not know why I am here?" I ask cautiously.

"Oh, I do. At least I've been told by Kai why he brought you here. But I want to hear what you are working on. What you think. I'm so fucking bored of having only Kai for company. He's not much for conversation if you can imagine."

"There's no imagination needed for me to believe that."

That curling smile returns, her eyes eager as she scoots her chair a little closer to me. I recall what Lana said about Jahlee, how she called her *strange*—a title that seems underwhelming for the reality of the female next to me. I look away from her and peer back down the scope.

"Back home, I had been experimenting on plants to help with a problem we've been having. I had no success until right before it was time for me to leave for your island." Clicking another glass disk into place as I speak, I watch the hexagonal-shaped cell walls bow with the plump chloroplast, those familiar red organelles still attached to a few of them.

"Fascinating," she says earnestly. Drawing my journal towards her, she begins to read the notes I took from visiting the families. "And do you think this research will help you figure out what is wrong with *our* magic? Why our people are getting stuck?"

I lean back in my chair as I think on my answer. "I believe so. Each experiment I do is like water eroding away a layer of rock. Eventually, I'll find the layer where the truth will be revealed, and though this may not be *directly* related to your magical blight, I think in the end it will still help."

"Can I help you? With your research?" she asks.

Other than sending me an oddly timed wink, her face betrays nothing more than morbid curiosity. I prefer to work alone, but having someone familiar with the island and its people, as well as the blight here, is valuable enough to give up my solitude for.

"Alright."

"Yes!" she cheers, clapping her hands together before wiggling her fingers at me.

Gods, this is a mistake. "What can you tell me about the blight? Any idea when it started? If it's always presented this way?"

"It's been going on for a while but seems to be worse now," she says, drumming her nails on the table. "Most of the time, shifters are getting stuck in their animal forms, but a few of them are also unable to shift from their mortal forms. That's all I really know."

"That's helpful." It's at least more information than her brother deemed worthy of giving me. I'll need to research as much on shifter history as I can since my personal knowledge on the subject is lacking. I had already explored the library on the first floor, but the books were slim and mostly fiction. "The library on this floor, are you able to take me there?"

She bolts up from her chair, hitting the table with her knee and causing the magnifier and the glass bottle of leaves to shake.

"Gods, you are a disaster waiting to happen," I mumble, my hands reaching out to steady the items.

"That is rude," she chastises, pointing a finger at me. "But fair. I'd rather be a disaster than boring, though. Come on, I can get you into the library."

I stare at her, getting whiplash from the way she bounces between emotions, but when she exits the room, I hop up from my chair and follow. "Wait, I need to lock the door." Taking out the brass key, I wait until I hear the lock click into place and then turn to follow her.

"In case no one told you, the first floor of the palace is mostly for palace staff, the kitchens, a few guest quarters, and then random rooms that honestly serve as places for people to fuck in secret during parties. Oh, and a ballroom." The corner of my mouth twitches at her descriptions. "The second floor is only accessible to those approved by Tua. Which is mostly just *nobility*," she says with a mocking tone on the last word. "Some reside here in the palace and are relegated to the west wing. Others stay nearby."

"Don't you mean guests approved by Kai?" I ask.

Jahlee dances down the hallway more than she walks, her movements light and filled with the kind of bounce that I'm not sure I could ever possess.

"It *should* be Kai, but Tua is all too eager to take any tasks he deems *unnecessary* for Kai off his plate." I arch a brow at her tone again, but before I can question her on it, she points to a door as we pass. "This door leads to the king's bedroom."

"I thought the king's bedroom was back that way," I question with a thumb over my shoulder, remembering the room Kai entered that was near my own.

Jahlee's eyes sparkle with mischievous delight as she spins on her toes and looks at me. "How do you know which room is Kai's?"

I level a flat stare at her. "Because I saw him enter the room while standing *firmly* in front of my own."

Her laugh is bright and, once again, entirely too loud as she rotates back around. "So defensive," she chides. "And Kai chooses to stay in the room that would be delegated for a prince, were he to have offspring. I'm assuming *you* are in the room meant for a princess."

I bite down on my tongue to avoid responding to that. Not many shifters seem to be bustling about as we walk, and the ones that are make sure to glare at us as we pass. Much like how I felt when Kai and I were in the heart of Molsi, it makes me curious to know the reasons why everyone seems to dislike this family so much. Do they really blame them for the magical blight? Or is it something more? My initial opinions of Kai aside, he doesn't appear to be a cruel ruler. More aloof than anything else. And for all her quirkiness, Jahlee doesn't seem to be deserving of the glances she's getting either.

Rugs of dark blue quiet our steps on the hardwood floors as I glance over the art decorating the wall. Most are depictions of scenery—beaches and jungles. As if seeing such sights outside wasn't enough, they had to bring the vision inside as well. We pass arched windows and balcony doors that line one side of the hall, the sunlight so abundant that the golden-framed pictures on the walls flare brightly.

The jungle outside the palace is vibrantly green—tall trees and large plants in varying heights ripple in the wind like their very own ocean. We reach the end of the hallway where the library is, its door made of glass and framed by dark wood that stretches up nearly to the ceiling.

My curiosity gets the best of me, and I ask, "Wouldn't that have been his room? As he *was* the prince?"

Jahlee hums as she guides us past the guards and through the library entrance. "Kai didn't grow up in the palace."

"What?" My voice carries loudly, garnering a few looks from the people that are dispersed throughout. I roll my lips together, my interest in Kai unfortunately renewed once more.

The library is airy and whimsical, its composition one more likely to be found in the Mage Kingdom than this one. A large twisting tree grows in the center of the space, its white and black wood swirling together and going up its massive trunk. Shelves have been carved into the tree, books stacked deeply into it. The top of it fans out over the ceiling, each branch reaching for the edges of the room like there might be more sunlight just beyond it.

While the perimeter of the library holds traditional-looking bookcases and shelves mounted to the walls, dug into the center of the floor is a long rectangular pool of crystal blue water filled with lily pads, orange fish, and tiny floating flowers.

"Odd to have water *inside* of a room filled with books, don't you think?" I ask Jahlee under my breath. She lets out a laugh, quieter than her previous ones at least, as she rounds the long pool and takes us to a section titled *History in the Shifter Realm*. When we are hidden between rows of books, I ask her to explain more on Kai. "So, if you didn't live in the palace, where did you grow up? Wouldn't your father have wanted his heirs—"

"The king wasn't my father," she interjects. The expression on her face is cool, a talent she shares with her brother, but her hands curl into fists at her sides, giving away her unease.

"You don't share the same father?" If Kai's father was the king, then Jahlee not being of his bloodline would mean that she isn't technically royal. The stares I've observed her receive make marginally more sense. She reaches for a random book on the shelf, the red leather crinkling softly when she opens it and pretends to sift through it.

"No. Kai and I had the same mother."

"*Had* the same mother?"

Jahlee's demeanor changes. It's nothing more than the quick rounding of her shoulders, but the air is heavy around her for a fraction of a second before she moves to another aisle, seemingly unable to stay still. "Yes. She died after she gave birth to me," she answers quietly. "When Kai's father murdered her and my birth father."

My eyes widen as I watch her. Admittedly, there wasn't much information to be gleaned back home about the former shifter king. The Spell had already separated the kingdoms by the time he took his rule, making most of our history books with information on the shifter island obsolete within a few decades. Particularly as Kai's father, according to my own, had never reached out to talk other than trade deals and schedules for boats to arrive at the docks in the Mage Kingdom.

"I'm sorry for your loss."

Jahlee clasps her hands behind her as she nods her head and moves on light feet to the next aisle. "It was a long time ago, and Kai's father is dead now, so all is right with the world. Well," she pauses, turning to face me, "except the whole magic thing."

I huff out a laugh, meeting her gaze. "And the fact that your people don't exactly seem very happy that Kai is their king."

"That's because they are all idiots. These people don't have any idea how lucky they are to have Kai as a ruler. Especially considering who they almost got as the alternative."

"Who?" I ask, watching as she drags her fingers along the spines of the books packed tightly together.

"Kane. He was supposed to be next in line for the throne."

Chapter Thirty-One

Rhea

THE LIBRARY IN THE palace is absolutely breathtaking. Deep brown wooden bookcases line the walls from floor to ceiling, only broken up by three large arched windows, their points decorated by blooming flowers of different sizes and colors. Vines grow on the wall around them and work up to the corners where they meet the ceiling, some even stretching across to the other side of the massive space. On the right, passageways between the bookshelves lead to a maze of different aisles. Small wooden signs with cursive script identify the different genres and subjects, and ladders attached to metal rods aid in seeing the books on the top shelves. With the living vines and bobbing glass balls of spelled flame that float in the air, it is the kind of library that feels like it should exist only in a fairytale.

The scent here is familiar, like leather and old paper, though there's also something unique mixed in—woodsy and fragrant. A small pang of yearning hits me for my library in the tower, the only place from that prison worth missing.

When Nox told me this morning we would be venturing to the library, I was hesitant to leave the comfort and safety of his room. Especially after learning from him that not only had the council of advisors been summoning Nox since we arrived from the Mortal Kingdom, but also that he had been ignoring their calls. His father had come to speak with Nox briefly about it while I had been washing in the shower. He told me they were currently occupied in a meeting with the king, so we didn't have to worry about them finding us here.

My eyes are still wide with wonder as Nox leads me around a corner and between the aisles, the signs identifying these bookcases as ones filled with works of nonfiction. I wrinkle my nose, something he notices and chuckles at.

"Don't worry, Sunshine. I think we're heading to the romance section, but I've never actually ventured to that part of the library before," he says quietly. My smile widens, and I lean into him, kissing his arm. "Tomorrow, we should meet with my parents. If only to discuss what we should do with the council."

Though I nod at his casually spoken words, I can't help but tense. It feels easy to rejoice how wonderful it is to be out of the tower, to not have to worry about the watchful eye of my uncle and to move about freely. But with the council wanting to question Nox—question *me*—my freedom seems more of an illusion. Maybe it is foolish to worry that it might be a recurring theme in my life, but I find myself silently hoping that it won't be. That there might be a day where I can walk about the palace, the kingdom, whenever I want without fear of someone questioning who or *what* I am.

Deep in the labyrinth of shelves, Nox finally finds the books dedicated to love stories. The minimal natural light that had blanketed the library near the entrance is non-existent here. Instead, floating flames in glass bowls bob in the air above us, making the center of the space glow yellow while the corners of the shelves still hold shadows.

"I'll give you time to look around. I'm going to go say hello to Rayna, the main librarian here. The old bat gets cranky when she knows I'm back home and haven't checked in with her."

"Okay, take your time."

His lips find mine, that spark of heat that's always present near him flaring to life for a moment before he pulls himself away with a quiet groan. His steps are nearly silent against the thick rugs, and I watch him go until he rounds a corner and is out of view. Blowing out a breath to cool myself, I turn and examine the books in front of me as I tuck my unbound hair behind my ears. The selection is overwhelming, and I'm not sure how much time passes as I browse, only that, eventually, I have a stack of eight books in my arms.

I try to backtrack to the front of the library, but with how similar the shelves look and the overwhelming number of aisles, I quickly get turned around. My heart pounds soundly against my ribcage as a familiar tension begins to creep into me. *I'm not in the tower. I'm not in the tower.* I can't explain why or how quickly it rises—the fear. Fear of being trapped and left here, even if I *know* it's a library and not a stone prison. Fear that I'll be found by someone who wants to take me back to my uncle.

My throat grows tight, and my chest compresses as air trickles to my lungs. Stumbling over my sandals, my feet still clearly not used to being dressed, I smack my shoulder into one of the bookcases, and all of the books I'm holding go flying, scattering onto the floor in front of me. My hand trembles as I bring it to my chest, the frantic racing of my heart making it heave.

"Excuse me, are you alright?"

Whipping my head around, I meet the gaze of a woman with copper hair, the color exaggerated by the spelled flame she's standing under. Her gray eyes move quickly to the carnage of books on the floor and then back to me, pausing on my shaking limbs. Before I can respond to her question, she kneels beside my mess.

"I'm *always* stumbling into things. Especially when I don't have my glasses on." She doesn't look back to me but, instead, points to the glasses on her face as if I wasn't aware of where they were. One by one, she stacks my books up by her knees. "My parents say it's because I have a bad habit of reading while walking, but sometimes a book is too *good* to put down, you know?"

I try to slow my breathing down, remembering all the times that Nox has helped me do it. *In and out. In and out.*

"And because I walk *everywhere*, I have a lot of time to kill. So why not get lost in the pages of made up worlds and fantastical characters?" she continues, picking up a blue leather-bound book, the title embossed in gold over a picture of two people kissing. The woman gasps loudly and turns to me. "Have you read this one?"

The fog that had been clouding me seems to part enough for me to at least shake my head in answer.

"Oh, it's incredible! It's about a princess who falls in love with the captain of her guard, and they have to hide their romance, but she's also forced to be betrothed to her best friend, and then the friend betrays her and nearly kills the guard, and—" The woman sucks in a breath, a look of annoyance on her face as if offended that she's interrupted her own explanation of the book to do so. "Anyways, chapter thirty-two will absolutely make you *sob*. Full on crying with snot and everything." Standing with my books now stacked in her arms, she turns to me fully, her round black glasses sliding down her nose.

"Thank you," I mumble, reaching out for the books.

"No problem. Are you new here? I've never seen you in the library before. Not that I know *everyone*, but I spend a lot of time here, and I'm pretty sure I would remember you."

I stare at her, the weight of the books in my arms making my shoulders round. A few awkward seconds tick by before I clear my throat. "Yes. I'm new to the palace." My eyes widen at what I've said, how I'm admitting to this stranger that I'm not from here. Scrambling, I blurt out possibly an even worse admission. "I mean, I'm new to the kingdom." *For the love of the gods, Rhea.* The woman's brows draw together, her pert nose wrinkling in confusion. My mouth opens and closes three times before I finally settle on, "I *mean*, I'm new to Galdr."

Her laugh is light as she shakes her head. "It's okay! Sometimes I talk faster than my brain can keep up with. Want me to walk with you to the front desk? It can feel like a maze in here until you get familiar."

Nerves cause my palms to sweat, but I force out a shaky reply, "Alright."

The woman smiles wide, a small gap showing between her two front teeth. "I'm Elora, by the way."

"I'm Rhea."

It feels like we endlessly turn corners, books all blurring together and the signs identifying them ranging from *Queens of the Mage Kingdom* to *The Care of Flowers and Fauna* and a particularly jarring section titled *Death and Creation: Where Do We Come From?* which only housed a few books on a single shelf.

I keep a half step behind, my gaze continually sliding towards her even at the risk of tripping again. Elora is dressed in comfortable-looking clothes: loose tan cotton pants and a white button-up shirt that is tucked into the front, the back billowing out. Though the outfit is casual, it does nothing to hide her voluptuous curves underneath them. Her sandals are similar to my own, strappy and black. When I catch her watching me, I scramble for something to say—*anything* that will help me not seem so awkward. So out of place.

"So, do you like to read a lot of romance novels?" she asks, saving me from myself.

"I do. They are my favorite. So much better than the boring history books N—" I make a heinous choking noise to interrupt myself before I say Nox's name, heat rising up my neck and face.

Elora laughs again right as we finally break free of the labyrinth of books and approach two light-colored wooden desks that are set in front of the large square window, the forest beyond a thickly woven sea of trees. Vases of small flowers in dark purple and blue dot the front corners of each desk.

"I don't mind reading some of our older tomes that talk of magic and life centuries ago—before the Spell and war. The newer stuff, however..." Elora shivers from whatever she deems unfit about those texts. "Anyway, I can check out the books for you." She rounds one of the desks, the other occupied by an older woman—her hair white as snow and tanned face set in deep wrinkles—who must be Rayna. She hums to herself as she flips casually through the pages of a book, not sparing Elora or I a single glance.

I grunt as I set my books on the desk, making the vases shake. Elora opens a small drawer, pulling out a pen and a large notepad. The pages are lined, scribblings of what I think are names and possibly titles of books written on each one. She takes a seat at the desk, writing the titles of my books and giving me little summaries of each one and what chapters were her favorite—an odd number of them involve her being brought to tears.

"Okay, Rhea, what is your last name?"

I swallow, my eyes flicking to hers. I don't know if I should give my real last name, but I hadn't even considered asking Nox about creating a fake one. *Should I have given a fake first name?* She tilts her head expectantly as she watches me, her pen lifting from the paper so as not to make the ink dot that had grown while she was waiting any bigger.

"Just put it under my name." His voice immediately relaxes my shoulders and ushers in a deeper inhale.

Elora's eyes widen, her mouth comically falling agape. "His Highness. I mean, *Your Highness*, Prince Nox. What are you doing here? Sorry, what am I saying? You can be here whenever you want!"

Elora laughs again, the noise higher pitched as her cheeks turn bright pink, nearly drowning out the freckles that dot her fair skin. Nox sets two books down on the desktop, his arm wrapping around my low back with his hand resting on my hip. Elora's eyes grow impossibly larger, moving from me to Nox's hand and then back to me.

"You two—"

"Elora, stop gawking at them and give them their books!" the older woman chastises, not even looking up from her own book.

"Right." Elora pinches her lips together, flicking her plaited copper hair over her shoulder as she writes out the titles for Nox's additional books as well as his name. "There. You guys are all set!"

Nox grabs all eight of my books, shooting me an incredulous look at the amount I have chosen.

"Rhea," Elora says, standing from her chair and walking to the side of the desk, her hands sliding into the pockets of her trousers. "If you ever want to talk about books, I'm here most days. If I'm not here, I'm at our bookstore in the central shopping square. It's called The Overflowing Bookshelf. If you are ever free, I mean. I'm sure you're probably busy most of the time." Her eyes dart to where Nox is waiting a few steps behind me.

I study her face, her smile genuine while her gray eyes sparkle with an eagerness that makes me want to say "yes." To *try*—as Selene suggested and as Alexi and Bella would want—to live a life worthy of their sacrifices.

"I would like that," I say, and I mean it.

Chapter Thirty-Two

Rhea

My heart thunders in my chest, and my palms grow clammy as we reach a door where an image of a massive, tangled tree under the stars is burned onto its front. The king and queen are waiting in the room on the other side, and I'm not entirely convinced that the nausea burning in my stomach won't expel itself at any moment.

"This is the queen's dining hall. It's the smaller one of two in the palace and reserved just for our family," Nox informs me, perhaps mistaking my unease for curiosity.

A few palace workers pass us in the hallway, their eyes scanning where Nox holds my hand before widening in surprise. It seems to be the reaction of everyone who sees us together, which admittedly hasn't been many people since we've kept mostly to his room.

"Wait," I screech, tugging on his arm while his opposite hand reaches for the door. "What if— I mean, you know what I am like and my history. I'm not exactly someone worthy of a crown prince. What if they don't want us to be together?"

Bewilderment pulls Nox's brows high on his forehead before he wraps his arms around me. "Sunshine, there is so much wrong with what you just said. First, you are literally a princess—"

"Hardly! Only in title." Even then, I wasn't exactly sure I could claim that title anymore after running away. Not that I necessarily *wanted* it.

"Fine," he says, huffing out a laugh. "Excluding the title of princess, my parents will love you simply because I do. But even if—for some ridiculous reason that I can't fathom—they don't, their opinions or anyone else's are inconsequential."

"You can't mean that."

"I absolutely do." When I don't seem persuaded that this meeting won't be a complete disaster, he adds, "We don't have to do this if you don't want to. We can always wait until you're ready." He smiles down at me, but doubt still lingers within me.

"But?"

With another short laugh at my coaxing, he continues, "*But* they might have an answer for how we can move around here without so much attention brought to you. I can mix my signature with yours when we are near each other, but that means I'd have to go everywhere with you."

Pinching my lips, I exhale slowly through my nose. I hear what he isn't saying—that while he'd happily do what I ask, it will hinder *me* to do so. *I don't want to be another cage for you.*

It takes a few moments for the bravery to seep in, and I nearly convince myself that I should run back to Nox's room before it does. But Alexi and Bella flash in my mind, and eventually, enough courage wells within me, so I give Nox a small nod.

He opens the door, and we step into the dining space. I take in the glittering white stone walls, made brighter by the two gorgeous three-tiered chandeliers above glowing with small flames. The portraits decorating the space draw my eyes, but I don't get the chance to study them before a throat clears. Nox squeezes my hand in comfort and leads us to the long table centered in the space, his parents standing on the opposite side.

"Your Highness, it is wonderful to meet you," Nox's mother says as she lets her gaze roam my face.

Her curly brown hair is twisted into an elegant updo on her head, her beauty classic and regal. Forest-green fabric lays delicately over her brown skin, layered in a crisscrossing pattern that accentuates the curves of her body. Gold roses embroidered in small patterns trail down the length of her dress. Next to her, the king is dressed in a similar shade of green, the sleeves of his tunic rolled to right below his elbows.

I'm caught up in wondering if my own flowing skirt and matching pink top are too informal when I realize that she is addressing *me*. "Oh, you don't— Just Rhea is fine." Then, remembering who I am speaking to, my eyes grow wide, and I add on a quick, "Your Majesty."

"I have a feeling," his father drawls, a familiar smirk on his lips as he gestures for us all to sit, "that there is nothing *just* about you, my dear." My chin dips, my hair a honey-colored curtain that falls around me for a moment before I force myself to look back up. "And I am happy to drop all formalities. My name is Sadryn, and this is my wife, Alexandria. We are incredibly happy to meet you, Rhea."

Nox pulls out my chair before taking his own. Where his posture is completely at ease, I sit perfectly straight, my muscles straining.

"Our son told us a little about you, that you are from the Mortal Kingdom and that you were held prisoner by King Dolian," Sadryn says, his hand wrapped around his wife's and resting on the table between them. I nod my head as I work to swallow down the thick knot in my throat at the mention of my uncle. "My condolences to you. I can't even begin to imagine how difficult that was."

"It must have also been challenging to discover you have magic," his mother adds, her voice gentle as she studies me. "Training for those with magic begins at eight years old in our kingdom, so I can only imagine how terrifying it was to feel something so unfamiliar for so long."

I simply nod again, my hand assuming a death grip on Nox's. It is strange to talk so openly about my magic when I've kept it hidden for so long. In the course of three months, I had gone from one person other than myself knowing to innumerable more. Nox, my uncle, the members of the King's Guard, now his parents... It is disheartening trying to reconcile the fact that Alexi died so that this part of me could stay hidden.

"For the sake of honesty, I'm going to be blunt, Rhea," Sadryn says, leaning forward and placing his elbows on the table. Nox tenses, the movement more felt from where I hold his hand than actually seen. "Did Nox explain magical signatures? How we can sense the magic around us?"

"Yes," I croak out, heat flooding my cheeks. Nox's thumb gently drags across the back of my hand.

"The magic in our kingdom is dwindling, for lack of a better word. Each generation of mage has become weaker with it, and while I won't bore you with the details of the other changes that have been happening, the point I'm making is that, with the exception of our son, no one else has a signature as strong as yours. It's going to draw attention and questions."

Nox sits up straighter, his free hand forming a white-knuckled fist on the table. "They will not have access to her."

"That isn't what your father is saying, my star." I smile at the term of endearment Alexandria uses for Nox, and he gradually relaxes his stiff posture. "We have something that we think can help."

His mother reaches for a small black pouch hidden by a flower arrangement in the center of the table. Opening it, she pulls out a silver chain necklace with a small shiny black pendant dangling at the end.

"Do you know anything about dragon stone, Rhea?" she asks, holding the necklace up.

"No. I've never heard of it."

Alexandria hands the necklace to Sadryn, the dainty jewelry nearly lost in his large hands. "We trade the Fae Kingdom for their dragon stone because it makes for incredible building material, as you can see by the walls and floors of this palace." His free hand gestures to the space around us, the stone reflecting many glittering flares of light as if in gratitude to his compliment. "But it also is an excellent conduit for our magic. Dragon stone has the ability to hold magic that is imbued into it without the magic diminishing over time." He reaches over and passes the necklace to Nox. "Only if the stone is broken will it release the power it holds."

Nox holds it up for me to look at, and when I see what the pendant is, I'm unable to stop the smile that grows. "It's a dragon." Nox's eyes move to my lips, his own curling upwards.

"The necklace is an heirloom, one that was passed down from the last queen of Void Magic. But we think if Nox spells it to dampen your magical signature, it should quell any inquiries as long as you're wearing it," Sadryn says.

I inspect the pendant, the tiny dragon carved in exquisite detail. It looks as if it is gliding through the air—its wings spread out wide with tiny linear divots chiseled into the wingspan. Its tail curves back and forth while its mouth is open as if in mid-roar. I run my thumb over it, marveling at the coincidence of getting something dragon themed given my deep fascination with the creatures.

"If my spell lessens how her magic is sensed by others, will it also affect how *she* wields it while wearing this?" Nox asks.

"Yes, it will put a damper on it," his father answers.

"Is that a good idea? To have something that doesn't let her access her full power?"

"Unfortunately, it is the sacrifice that must be paid in order to hide the magic she does have from everyone else. It's the balance that is required," his mother responds.

Nox's jaw clenches tightly as he thinks over her words.

"Maybe, when it is just you and I, we could take the necklace off?" I suggest.

If our magic is so similarly strong, then he would need to be the one giving me more extensive training with it anyway. He runs a hand through his hair, the shorter strands up front flopping back over his forehead in a cascading wave.

"Alright. If this is the best way to keep anyone from looking too closely, then I agree with you, Sunshine. We'll take the necklace off when it's only you and me." His magic rises to his palm, the dark luminescent purple mixing with wavy lines of pure black. It pulsates when he lowers the pendant until it's submerged.

"Not too strong, Nox. We don't want her to be completely cut off from her magic," his father insists.

"Something like that is possible?" I ask.

"There is a way to temporarily block a mage from accessing their magic." Seeing the look of trepidation on my face, Sadryn adds, "Though it would take a group of people to overpower either of you."

Nox's magic fades back into his palm, and his gaze finds mine again, tight lines framing the corners of his mouth. At my encouraging smile, he motions for me to turn around. I scoot to the edge of the wooden chair, twisting my body to the side and giving Nox my back. His hand gently pulls my long hair over one shoulder, and then he fastens the necklace around me.

A humming sensation blankets my skin, the feeling not unpleasant but still jarring. My magic rises in response, and for a moment, I wonder if the necklace is doing anything at all. Then, as if someone has poured water onto fiery coals, my magic settles within me. It's still there, smoldering under the surface, but I can't feel it as strongly.

I turn back to look at Nox. "It's working. My magic feels *quieter*."

He doesn't exactly look pleased by this update. "I can't feel you as strongly now," he says, his hand reaching out towards mine.

A small door off to the side of the dining hall opens, and a man carrying two trays of food walks in, a line of people following behind him. They set the table—plates and forks quickly appearing before me. Already conscious of my lack of knowledge regarding different foods, Nox quietly begins to explain what everything is and then assembles my meal with the foods I give a little nod at. I catch Alexandria and Sadryn watching their son closely, small smiles and curious eyes expressing emotions I don't quite understand.

"We have two more matters we should discuss," Sadryn announces about halfway through the meal, his hands casually interlaced over his plate. "One being the backstory for how Rhea came to be in the palace, and two being how she came to capture the heart of the crown prince." My fork freezes on its way to my mouth, my eyes darting over to Nox.

"The kingdom already believes that I was out enjoying an adventure before stepping into my role as heir apparent," he says, leaning back against the chair. My brows furrow at this information. "We can just tell them I met Rhea in one of the small villages at the border."

"They didn't know you were in the Mortal Kingdom?" I question.

Nox rests his hand on my thigh, his thumb drawing small circles on the side of it as he shrugs a shoulder up. "We didn't want to cause a panic. Not when it was already so unusual to feel such strong, pulsing magic."

"It is an easy enough story; I assume you two can work out the details in private then?" Sadryn asks, a brow lifted towards us. We both nod in agreement. "I will remind you again, Nox, that because you are interested in Rhea, the council will be as well. They do not have a say in who you marry, but they will still want to meet the woman who may become their future queen."

"Oh, I'm not—" I press my lips together to halt my rebuttal. If Nox and I were to *eventually* marry, of course I would become queen. I can't explain why the full weight of those words and what they mean suddenly cascades over me. Nox leans forward, an inquisitive look etched into his face, but I force my gaze away and down to the table.

"In any case," Sadryn drawls, pulling my attention back up to see the hint of a smile on his lips, "it is something that the two of you need to be aware of and prepare for. The council is antsy about why you haven't spoken with them yet, Nox, and when they find out that you have come home with a new paramour, they will have even more questions."

"If they don't have an official say in who I choose to marry, then why would they even bother questioning Rhea?" Nox argues, an edge to his voice that thickens the air. Or perhaps that is his magic I feel.

Sadryn and Alexandria share a glance with each other, neither seeming to want to speak but Alexandria finally conceding.

"They would care because they know that you and Councilman Borris' niece are friends." Nox's hand goes lax on my thigh. Alexandria nods, a wince crinkling her face. "They are planning to talk to you about a betrothal to Haylee."

Chapter Thirty-Three

RHEA

"Come on, Sunshine. Take it off," Nox begs a few days later from where we lay on our sides facing each other, his arms wrapped tightly around me as he holds me to his very warm and very *naked* chest. "Please?"

Kissing the skin above his heart, I throw my leg over his hip in an attempt to distract him. We both slept in later than usual this morning, and when the smattering of sunlight eventually warmed my face through the windows, making my eyes flutter open, I couldn't fight the urge to touch him. To let my fingers trail over every perfect square inch of him as a reminder that he was here with me. I had expected that he would wake up hungry to take advantage of our slow morning, but training with my magic appeared to be the only thing on his mind.

"Why can't we train with the pendant on? Since that is how I'll be for the majority of the time."

"Because that wasn't the deal we made when I spelled that little necklace." Pulling back, he looks down at me, his brow raised in emphasis.

"Did you know that you're very handsome?" I ask him sweetly, batting my eyelashes as I attempt to change the subject.

"Yes, and I believe you called me out on that awareness in a scathing letter."

I scoff, pushing a hand at his chest as he lowers his head towards me. "That letter was not *scathing*. Though perhaps it would be a good idea to knock your ego down a few notches, *Prince*."

His chuckle is a caress of velvet, and I can feel the curl of his lips at my ear when he breathes, "I do love when you call me that."

My thin undergarments do nothing to obscure my desire for him or his responding want of me as I push myself closer. He presses soft kisses to my jaw and my neck, a hand sliding into my hair to cradle the back of my head.

"Rhea."

"Yes?" I rasp, my fingers digging into his firm muscles and heart rate rising with each quick peppering of his lips.

"No more until we practice your magic," he murmurs against my neck.

Groaning, I fling myself onto my back and stare at the wooden beams of the ceiling above. The morning birds sing and chatter outside, providing the only sound in the room until Nox asks a question I hoped he wouldn't.

"What are you afraid of?"

"Isn't it obvious?" I snap before squeezing my eyes shut. "I'm sorry."

"It's alright," he says gently. Too gently.

It sends fissures through a remaining wall I know I shouldn't have, but one that is there so that I don't have to think too deeply about what I've done. I can begin to grant myself forgiveness for the way Bella and Alexi died because I finally realize that it wasn't *my* hands that carried their blood. The same cannot be said for the two guards whose lives were drained in an instant by my shadows.

"Your shadow magic saved us that night, Rhea. It bought us time for you to heal me. It protected us when I couldn't. Those are not *bad* things, just as that half of your magic isn't inherently bad."

I shake my head and open my eyes to look at him. "My life is worth no more than anyone else's, let alone the lives of two people who were just following orders."

Nox sits up, the expanse of his tanned skin fully on display as he grips onto the dark green comforter. "Your life is *infinitely* more valuable. For a multitude of reasons. You cannot hold the choices that others make against you as a moral measurement. If it comes down to your life or someone else's, you have to choose yourself. Every time."

I join him in sitting, only a thin silk lavender chemise covering my body. "You can't ask me to do that," I argue, my hand reaching up to clutch the tiny stone dragon.

Nox huffs, but his eyes sharpen into daggers, the silver in them intensifying. "I absolutely can and *will* ask you to protect yourself. And to kill, if need be, in order to do so. Would you not ask the same of me?"

Our chests heave in tandem as my gaze falls, tears lining my eyes before I blink them away. "Of course I would," I relent.

His finger gently hooks under my chin and pushes up until my bright green eyes find the cooler gray of his. "Don't ask me to not want the same for you. Being prepared to protect yourself is not the same as agreeing to end lives at the first chance given. You still have free agency—you still have autonomy over those decisions—which is all I want for you. To have a viable choice. But not training with your magic isn't freedom, Rhea, it's just another cage."

I try to force my resolve to harden, but a small part of me knows Nox is right. Selene had even expressed the same urgency to not simply train but to train my magic fully. I know that I need to have more than one way to protect myself. But we have time—time for me to slowly build up to working with that magic. Time for me to reconcile with the death I caused and to be absolutely sure that I won't accidentally do something like that again.

"I am not ready to touch the dark magic yet. I want to learn how to manipulate elements and heal more efficiently and defend myself. I can do that with only the light magic. At least for now."

He takes a moment to answer but then concedes. "For now," he echoes. "Before you take the necklace off, I'm going to cover you in a shield of my magic. The pendant has been suppressing your power for a few days, and it might overwhelm you at first."

"Great," I mutter, earning a chuckle from him. I wait until his magic surrounds us both before I steady my fingers and unclasp the necklace. Handing it to him, I hold my breath and wait for my power to wash over me. Yet nothing happens. "I don't think—"

As if the gates guarding my magic have been forced open, a warm sensation followed by piercing cold begins to unfurl within me. My body goes rigid, and my vision blurs, air nothing but a plea from my screaming lungs as my jaw locks. My ears pound with a vicious drumming while terror bleeds into my veins. Nox's face is in front of mine, but I can't understand what he's saying as my surroundings bleed to a shade of gray. The memory of my shadows unleashing in the Middle pushes to the forefront of my mind, and I immediately look down at my hands, noticing how one glows black and the other white. They flicker, like flames of a candle dancing in a rogue breeze.

It's happening again. I'm going to lose control. I'm going to hurt Nox or worse. There will be no redemption for me then.

"You are okay. You are not hurting me." Nox gradually comes into focus, his body illuminated by the dark glow of his magic. I shake my head, fear keeping my voice locked tightly in my throat. He repeats himself more slowly, grasping just above my hands and holding them up in front of me. "Look, Rhea. You aren't hurting me."

I stare, and I stare, my heart furiously pounding against my bones though I swear I can also hear a calmer echo of the sound in my ear. The stable rhythm gives me something soothing to focus on.

"There you go, love, *breathe*. Like me."

The grayscale vision begins to retreat as I force air in and out to the pattern Nox sets, his steadfast presence preventing me from sinking back into the panic. When the rise and fall of my chest is less like I'm sprinting, he releases my hands. My magic feels *swollen* inside me, like an overfilled cup with nowhere for the extra to flow. I must voice that out loud because Nox nods his head.

"You need to expel some of your magic."

"You know what this feels like?" I rasp.

His hand cups my cheek, and he brushes his thumb gently over it. "Think of our magic as water that is nestled in a well deep within us. Expelling that magic is like lowering a bucket into the well and taking water out. Our bodies then replenish what is taken. For most in the kingdom, that happens slowly. A few have the ability to replenish small amounts fairly fast. For me and, I suspect, you, our wells get replenished instantaneously. But it's not a perfect system. Our magic is tied into our very lives, and we use small amounts without realizing we have."

Nox removes his hand from my face and extends both arms out to his sides. Without so much as a twitch of his eye, he removes the barrier around me and expands his magic out to coat every crevice of the room.

"Now imagine that you blocked access to that well but water was still being replenished within it. Once you remove that barrier, the water is going to come rushing out with force. That's what happened when we took the necklace off. Your magic *overflowed*."

"So what do we do now?"

"Now, you need to expel what's been pent up, and to do that, I'm going to tell you the first thing we're taught when we begin our magic training—*magic goes where intention flows*. It means your mind is the key to controlling your magic. Think about when you healed Bella, when you healed me. What were you visualizing in those moments? What were you seeing in your mind?"

My thoughts had been frantic and— No. *No*, I had been *focused*. "I pictured my magic flooding into your bodies and healing you both. Replenishing blood and closing up veins."

"Exactly, Sunshine. Your magic obeyed your call because, in those moments, your intention was so abundantly clear. It's the same thing when we are manipulating elements or using our magic to imbue items. If you're truly set on not using your shadow magic, then focus wholly on the other one. Try letting it flood out into the room. You don't need to guide it to do anything other than fill the space like mine has."

His instruction seems way less daunting to manage. So I close my eyes and reach for those tendrils of bright white healing light. Continuing on with Nox's well metaphor, I imagine a divider splitting the vessel holding my magic into two halves. I shut out the shadow half and, instead, let the light half pour out.

"Slowly. *Good*. Visualize your magic nestling onto mine. Layering on top of it." I do, feeling that invisible pressure within me lessen more and more with each passing moment. "Open your eyes."

"Stars above," I whisper with a gasp as I look around Nox's room. Glittering white and resplendent purple make the room shine like we're lost in a sea of stars. Our magic pulses together, two heartbeats settling into perfect rhythm. "It's beautiful."

"I've never seen anything like this." It's the awe in his voice that draws my gaze back to him. "Normally, when there are two magics present, they don't *react* like this. They try to repel each other, but our magic seems to—"

"Blend together," I interject, smiling at him, his face lit with the white glow of the magic in my palms.

"Exactly. Now, sever your control. Like a pair of scissors slicing through thread, guide your intention into releasing your magic."

I close my eyes again and sense my magic, the way it all anchors back to me even from the farthest corners of the room. With a deep breath, I imagine letting it all go, as if the tide of my magic has pulled away from me until there is nothing left. When I open my eyes again, the room is back to normal.

"Do this as often as you can so that your magic doesn't get too pent up," Nox suggests, his fingers tucking strands of hair behind my ear. "I don't say this nearly often enough, but I'm so proud of you, Sunshine."

A nervous laugh bubbles out of me as I drop my gaze to my lap. "Why?" I wasn't doing anything but scratching the surface of what someone my age *should* be able to do.

"Because of how brave you are. It would be so easy for you to not *want* to experience new things, to not want to try and push yourself. But you do, and getting to watch you shatter the invisible barrier that has been kept around you for so long..." I look back to him when his voice catches, and he has to work a swallow down before continuing. "It only makes me fall deeper in love with you."

"Nox." Craving his touch, I push the blanket off of me and crawl onto his lap. His scent and warmth cradle me, but it's his words and heart, the way he so effortlessly breathes life and love into me, that make me feel like maybe I *can* accomplish anything.

Home. He's home.

"I can only do those things because of you."

"No. These are not my victories to claim. They are yours. Let them fuel you like a different source of sustenance, one that will remind you of how far you've come. You are incredible, Rhea. I've known it since the very first moment I laid eyes on you."

And what could I even say to that? How could I respond with anything other than a display of how much *he* sustains me? So I kiss him, and when my body demands more, I slowly undress him. And when we are finished and Nox carries me to the shower, I tell him how much I love him. Over and over again.

Chapter Thirty-Four

DOLIAN

I clench Rhea's handkerchief in my pocket, my boots echoing against the moss-covered stone floors deep beneath the castle. My hatred for this space is more palpable than the dank air I breathe. Each step that brings me closer to the cells is fuel for that monster inside me that demands I burn this place to the damn ground. However, kingdoms need dungeons, and despite my history with this one, it is currently serving *many* purposes.

Xander walks a step behind me, his presence a necessary annoyance. The few prisoners that are here are quiet as we walk by, knowing better than to try to plead to their king when there is no mercy to be found. They'll rot here for as long as I command it, and only when I have decided that their worthless lives are no longer of value to me will I let them succumb to the relief of death.

"Has she said anything during your interrogations?" I ask him.

"No, she refuses to speak."

I clutch the handkerchief even harder. Flame gems light our way every few feet—not enough light to keep the menacing shadows away, but enough to faintly make out the outline of the metal bars. I finally reach the end of the passageway and turn to face the cell holding the one person whose value is, unfortunately, too high for me to kill right away. She huddles in a corner, and my nose wrinkles at the foul odors coating the space around her.

"You could free yourself from this torture. You could once more taste fresh air and feel sunlight on your skin. All you have to do is answer my questions." My voice reverberates off the darkened stone, and though I can't actually see the color in the dimness, I *know* that it is gray. "Tell me what you know."

Her head lifts from where she had it resting on her drawn up knees, her hair filthy and tinged red and brown. Her face fares no better, but even through the dried blood and grime, she has a youthful appearance. She might not even have reached her second decade yet.

"I would rather die a slow and painful death at your hands than tell you anything you want to know." She then bares her teeth at me, a low growl rumbling from her throat.

Disgusting.

"Be careful what you wish for, you *vile* creature. I will happily peel the flesh off of you bit by bit."

Her eyes harden, the golden glow of the flame gem lighting them a similar color, and her next words are spoken through gritted teeth. "*Do it, then.*"

"You would do well to remember who you are talking to," Xander snaps. The woman's eyes narrow into slits at him before she turns them back on me.

I take a step closer to the bars, careful not to touch any part of the filthy metal. "How often did you watch from whatever corner you were hidden in? Yet you did nothing." Her muscles bulge in her arms, my blood heating as her nails dig into her bare legs like claws. "You want to paint me as the villain, and maybe I am, but you had the capability to help—to stop it—and you. Did. *Nothing*. Now you will die here, and whether you tell me what I want to know or not, it won't matter. Not to *her*."

She launches up from her corner faster than I would have thought possible. I'm not quick enough to back away, and my stomach threatens to heave up my breakfast when her blood-crusted fingers wrap around the sides of my black and gold vest.

Her eyes shine bright, even in the absence of light, as her lips lift in a snarl. "I will *kill* you."

Xander shoves her and sends her stumbling backward, my clothing slipping from her grip. I stare down at the fabric, bits of rust red and dark brown now smudged on it. My fingers tremble as rage seeps into every pore. *Filthy. Disgusting. Disappointment.* My father's words pummel me, his voice everywhere in this familiar dungeon despite having died before Rhea was born. I back away from the cell, bumping into Xander as I do.

"Get the information out of her by whatever means necessary. For every question she refuses to answer, cut off a finger." I don't hear his reply before I turn and stride down the passageway, counting to one hundred in my head. When I get to ninety-three, the stairs that climb up to the main floor of the castle come into view. I take them two at a time all the way up until I burst through the door and slam it closed behind me. *Outside—get outside.*

A lifetime of living in the castle is the only awareness that guides me to the glass doors that lead to the gardens. Once the sun hits me and the warm air of summer pushes at my skin, I'm able to loose a breath.

I will kill you.

I grit my teeth together, walking deeper into the rows of hedges and flowers. She could try. Same as that mage bastard, Flynn. I'll slice them down and make Rhea watch as I do it. I'll make her kneel in their blood to remind her that there is no one in this world who could love her as I do. Who could make her as powerful as I can, even with the magic flowing in her veins.

My cock grows hard at the thought of her drenched in crimson, and my vision blurs as the fantasies of bloodshed and rage dance through my mind. The noise of flesh on stone sends birds flying from their perches as I pummel my fist into a carved bench tucked between the flowers. I don't stop when I see the first smattering of my blood. I don't stop when the pain begins to leak into my consciousness. No, I wait until I see the vision of Flynn's face smashed beneath me, nothing but a mangled mess of brain matter, blood, and broken bone.

Falling to my knees, I cradle my throbbing hand while I close my eyes and try to steady my breathing. Each inhale erases the smells of the dungeon below, replacing them with the fragrance of iron mixing with the flowers—heady rose and delicate jasmine. And lilies. I breathe in deeply again—the rage simmering to the background where it lingers, waiting to be unleashed once more. *Lilies.* Standing, I stroll out of the garden and shout to the guards to find Simon.

"The women are lined up in your chambers, Your Majesty," Simon says from where he walks behind me as we leave another Royal Council meeting, the men in attendance ignoring Paul's absence.

"Ready the Mirror in the throne room. When I'm finished, I'll meet you there."

He says nothing but dips his chin in response, breaking away from me to stride down an adjacent hallway. I've resisted reaching out for help, but it can't be avoided now. The longer Rhea is away from me, the harder it will be to get her back.

Pausing in front of the door to my chambers, I flex my bandaged right hand before turning the door handle. My room is warm and lit in a soft orange from the flame gems and flickering candlelight. The corners of my mouth draw up when I take in the six women standing in different-colored silk robes right in the center, their gazes all fixed on the floor. I immediately dismiss three of them—one that is too tall, one with breasts that are too big, and another with hair that isn't the right shade. Once the door is shut, I observe the ones that remain as I unbutton my vest, tossing it onto the back of a nearby armchair before moving on to my shirt.

I circle them, scrutinizing their features before I come to stand at their front. "I want each of you to repeat the phrase 'As you say, My King.' Now."

"As you say, My King," the woman in pink says, a slight quiver to her voice.

I nearly groan at the sound but force myself to hold it in. I step in front of the woman in the middle next.

Her eyes lift up to meet mine, a lush smirk extending on her pretty face. "As you say, My King." Her sultry voice does nothing to arouse me further, and with a flick of my wrist, I dismiss her.

The final woman, her purple robe tied tightly around her as if to hide from me, keeps her gaze pinned to my boots. I curl a finger under her chin, my smile sharp when she flinches under my touch. "Say it," I urge, my voice deceptively soft.

Her lip trembles, her light blue eyes wide as she rasps, "As you say, My King." My grip tightens as I scan her more thoroughly. Her face shape is similar enough, if a little more pointed at her nose and chin. Her hair is a near-perfect match, going down to her mid back. *Yes, she will do just fine.*

"Go," I say to the one with the pink robe, chuckling when she all but sprints from the room.

Removing my shirt and laying it with my vest, I turn and lean against the back of the armchair, my hands gripping it tightly enough to make the wood beneath the fabric creak.

"Are you frightened, darling?"

As if the words are a knife dragging along her skin, the woman shivers. "Yes, Your Majesty."

I hum, my blood nearly boiling as I slide my palm against my hardened cock from the outside of the trousers. "Good. Take off your robe."

She obeys immediately, the silky fabric sliding delicately from her body. I take in her soft curves—the small flair of her hips and perk of her breasts. Her petite frame is perfectly suited for my hands to grip, just how I know Rhea's will be.

She avoids watching me undress the rest of the way, but it does nothing to lessen my hunger. In fact, it feeds into the burning desire that courses through me, tangling with my constant, deep-rooted rage. The monster inside me may be a self-reflection born and bred from the torturous beatings of my father, but I've shaped and molded it to become something that serves a purpose now.

Walking over to a vase of freshly cut flowers, I pluck a lily out and turn towards the woman who will fill my needs *for now*. "Do not speak at all. Do not turn around," I tell her while dragging the lily down her cheek and neck, over the slight curve of her breast and lower. Her skin breaks out in goosebumps, but she nods at my command. "You have a role to play, and if you do it well, you will be rewarded."

Tucking the flower over her ear, my fingers lightly grip her elbow. I turn and guide her towards the bed before coming to stand behind her. The first skim of my fingers down her soft skin makes me moan, and I stare at the way her blonde hair hangs down her back—so lovely and perfect. Forcing her chest to meet the bed, I adjust the strands of her hair so they stay splayed out in front of me.

"You are mine."

The meeting of my hand on her ass rings out into the room, followed by her cry of surprise. The monster within me pushes to be let out, to take control, but I wait. Patience pays off; it always has. Another smack, another cry—the sound a perfect symphony to my ears. Again and again, I mark her skin until it's swollen and red. Gripping my cock, I position myself at her entrance.

"You have *always* been mine."

I imagine it's Rhea's muffled cries singing out into the room, Rhea's delicate hands gripping onto the comforter so hard her knuckles turn white. I open the monster's cage and let him command the feral pace I take.

Soon it will be her. *It will be her.* I just need to have patience.

The walk to the throne room is short, the silence much needed while I decide what I am going to say to the being on the other side of the Mirror. Simon meets me outside of the golden double doors, a roaring lion carved in the middle.

"I want that one to stay close by for whenever I have need of her," I tell him.

"Of course, Sire. I shall arrange a room for her."

"Remain outside until I call for you."

Simon nods and stands perfectly straight against the wall, his hands clasping behind his back.

This room was the first I changed when I became king, summoning every artist from Vitour to completely alter the space. Still, I hated it almost more than I did the dungeons. Pushing the heavy door open, I glance up at the golden tapestries that hang from the rafters of the arched ceiling as I walk down a rug of the same shade that lays in the center of the room. Gold had been the antithesis of what was there before. My brother, Conrad, could have changed the sigil and the colors when he became king, but he opted to continue the revolting red and white as if it was an honor to do so. I suppose that, to him, it was. He only knew kindness from the king. Only knew the gentle hand of an adoring father. He never saw the other side. I had hoped that Luna might have remembered our conversation about how much I loathed the colors and what they represented when she became queen. That she would recall the late nights we had spent sprawled on a blanket outside, looking up at the stars and wishing on them. In the end, she betrayed me as everyone else had.

My hands slide into my pockets as I reach the first step of the dais, turning to look down at the Mirror placed before it. Its rectangular shape is basic and unassuming, much like how I imagine others feel about the Mortal Kingdom.

It has been decades since I've last talked with any ruler through the Mirror. Ironic that, of the four other monarchs that rule in Olymazi, it'll be the same one that I spoke with over twenty-two years ago that I'm summoning tonight. The same one who I technically still owed a favor to. Clutching Rhea's handkerchief in my hand, I clear my throat and speak their name out loud.

Chapter Thirty-Five

Rhea

His fist meets my side before I crumple to the floor, the cold wood biting into my knees and palms. Sweat beads at my neck, my magic flaring beneath my skin—pushing and prodding—begging to be released. But what can it do? What can I do?

"I will make you worthy, Rhea. It would all stop if you just showed me that you understand your role." He's so angry—he's always so angry with me. Tears leak down my cheeks as his fingers yank back on my hair, my sharp yelp of pain lancing the air of the tower. His hazel eyes are illuminated by his fury—like he's got a flame *inside of him that is burning so hot, it needs to destroy anyone else that comes too close as well.*

He looms over me, an imposing force that I'm powerless against. His face inches closer, the cruelty not a mask he wears but his truest self. The warmth of his breath hits my face—my nose. His lips are so horrifyingly close, and I try to jerk away, but I can't. His chuckle is foreboding, reverberating into my bones as lips graze over my own.

"Oh, Rhea darling, the things I can do with you now."

I gasp for air, launching up to sit, the remnants of my scream still echoing in the room.

"Rhea? What's wrong?"

I rub my face with my hands, holding them over my eyes as I try to banish any thoughts of my uncle back into whatever dark corners of my mind they leaked from. "I'm sorry," I mumble against my palms. "I didn't mean to wake you."

The sheet and comforter rustle as Nox sits up, his arm going around my back while his other hand gently pulls on my wrists until my bleary eyes meet his. "Sunshine, what's wrong?"

I know I have to reveal how my uncle tortured me in that tower and how he continues to do so in my nightmares. What his plans for me were and how I fear that he won't ever give up trying to get me back. I thought there would be a perfect time for those confessions, a clear moment where I could reveal all the oily parts of me that are tainted by *him*. But I didn't realize how often I only dreamed of terror.

I turn my body to face him, my hands trembling as I grip the comforter gathered at my waist. Gray and silver-flecked eyes lit only by the scant moonlight inspect me, Nox looking for a wound that can't be seen.

"I was fifteen the first time it happened."

I can feel the questions—the confusion—radiating from him, but he doesn't speak, instead interlacing his fingers with mine and squeezing my hand tightly.

"King Dolian always had a horrific temper that only grew worse the older I got. He rarely visited me before I entered my teenage years, and as a small child, I was too frightened by him to do much but cower on the sofa while he walked around the tower. As I grew more into... *myself*, apparently looking more like my mother, it seemed to light a fuse within him. He'd yell at me so loudly that my ears would ring, claiming I had to earn my title and become worthy of it. I still don't know what he means by that, as the title of ruler in the Mortal Kingdom is—*was*—mine."

"It still is yours. And if ruling the Mortal Kingdom is something you want—"

"No," I interrupt, holding his gaze. "That isn't what this is about."

I can't tell if he looks relieved or not by that answer, but he gestures for me to continue.

"It was the day after my birthday, and he had come up with his Trusted as he always did. I don't remember what I said to set him off, but suddenly, there was a stinging burst of pain on my cheek and I was on the floor. He walked towards me so slowly that I should have had time to brace myself for the next hit, but I was so shocked that he had actually slapped me, that I didn't do anything to defend myself against the next one. Or the next. Or the next." Somewhere in my retelling, I start to cry. Shame-filled tears run down my cheeks and plop onto our joined hands. Nox is unnervingly still, only his eyes bouncing back and forth between mine indicating that he's absorbed everything I'm saying. "I woke up still on the floor, my head aching and my face completely bruised. Nearly every time he visited, the outcome was the same. I sometimes showed defiance, but most of the time, I let it happen because I knew I couldn't fight back. That it wouldn't matter if I did."

Nox's eyes darken, and his magic pulses thickly from him. It brushes against me, my own magic surging to answer its pull even with the spelled dragon pendant resting over my heart. He drags a hand through his hair, pulling the dark waves away from his face. "That time I found you, before we escaped the tower, that wasn't the first time he laid a hand on you?"

"No," I whisper, another tear falling under Nox's watch. "I don't know how many times the king hit me. Nearly seven years of those visits meant that I stopped keeping track when the number grew to a point that I simply didn't want to know anymore."

Nox's breathing gets loud, and his chest rises and falls with the force of it. "Did Alexi know?" I don't answer, but the slight rounding of my shoulders tells him enough. "Gods, I should have gotten you out so much sooner," he mumbles more to himself than to me, letting go of my hand to stand from the bed.

"There is more," I whisper, shrinking under his stormy gaze. "The day you found me, King Dolian had revealed his plans for my future. After Summer Solstice, I was to become his bride and—" My voice breaks, and I can't force the rest of the words out. The rest of the vile things he said.

Nox doesn't move, his body rigid with anger. "I shouldn't have spent so much time fucking around. *Everyone* failed you, Rhea. We failed you, and you suffered more than you ever should have."

I blink, stunned at his words and the sharpness of his tone. "Alexi didn't fail me," I respond firmly, but Nox doesn't hear me.

"I knew Dolian was *vile*. When he fucking kissed you after I had been stabbed, I should have unleashed my magic then. I should have let the shadows kill him and then ripped everyone else apart who stood in my way."

"Nox." I shuffle forward on the bed, trying to reach for his hand, but it's like he's stuck in a trance as he pulls away from my grasp. The shadows cast on the dark wooden floor shift. They slither towards him and gather around his legs as if he's walking through churning dark water.

"Ask me why I didn't just kill him when I had the chance." His eyes are wild, the silver in them bright as his magic fills the room. When I don't answer, he shakes his head. "It's because I was a fucking *coward*. I didn't want to leave the Mortal Kingdom in chaos, despite the fact that it's better off without him. I didn't want you to hate me. I made a terrible call because I was terrified you'd choose to stay there. That you'd find it to be the lesser of two evils. I replay the moment that he held you against him, when you *begged* him to let me go, all the damn time. *All the time.*" His voice drops down to a dejected rasp. "And then he fucking *kissed* you, and it took everything in my power not to show my magic because I didn't want you to think I was a monster. But I'm starting to believe that I am, Rhea, because I would choke this world in shadows if it meant you were safer for it. I should have already—"

"Nox! *Stop.*" Climbing off the bed, I grab his hand and pull him towards me, his shadows wrapping around my lower half like an icy wind. They are soft in their touch though, oddly comforting both to me and my magic. My hands frame his face, and I force him to look at me. His body shakes under my grasp while his eyes— It is as if liquid starlight is reflected in them. I lower one hand from his face and glide my fingers down his arm, his attention focused on my touch. Once I reach his hand, I force his arm to wrap around me. I do the same to the other side until he pulls me closer and I can feel him begin to settle. "There is nothing you *or* Alexi could have done. He was bound by the blood oath not to help me escape. Anything else would have resulted in his death. You know King Dolian never visited without his guards. I didn't tell you any of this on purpose because I was ashamed. *Embarrassed.*"

His fingers flex against my back, his breathing still ragged.

"And maybe you could have convinced me to leave earlier with you. Or shown your magic to me sooner, killing Dolian like you said. But there is no guarantee that it wouldn't have resulted in something worse happening. Or that we would even be here together right now. We can play the 'what if' game every day until we are one hundred years old, and all it will do is rob us of the present. For the first time in my life, I *want* to live in the present. We both made mistakes, and I do not fault you for anything, Nox. I just want to be here with you." My thumbs brush his cheeks as his head tilts forward.

"I'm sorry," he sighs, kissing my forehead. "For then and for now. Lately, my magic writhes furiously within me whenever I think about someone hurting you. I—" He pauses, replacing his lips against my forehead with his own as his eyes fall closed. "I have never felt this way about anyone. *Never.*"

I believe every word that pours from him because it isn't the first time he's said it, but also because I've felt it to some degree as well. Despite putting on the spelled pendant, we've spent most of our time since here, in Nox's room. Wrapped up in each other and simply getting to know one another better. We did visit the library again—much to Elora's delight—and Nox also took me on a walk hidden amongst the trees. Even with the block of my magic, I can still sense this connection we have—like a whisper of string tied around my heart. It doesn't feel like a restraint but more like a tether home. Something I could simply tug on if I lost my way.

"I have never been in love before you, but if reading copious amounts of romance novels has taught me anything"—his relaxed snort tips my lips into a smile—"it is that we just take it day by day. Together. I *love* you, Nox, and not just because of what you did to help me, but because I know what is in *here*." I place my hand over his heart, feeling it beat soundly against his chest. He squeezes me closer to him, until my ear is resting next to my hand.

"Promise me that you will tell me if I am suffocating you. If I'm hurting instead of helping," he whispers. I draw back to look at him, my brows furrowed in confusion. His large hand cups my face as his thumb traces underneath my lower lip. "Promise me." All I can do is nod, watching as the final bit of tension that lines his body melts away. "There is one more thing we should discuss."

I groan, pulling him towards the bed as exhaustion begins to weigh on my eyelids. Nox smirks, sitting at its edge before pulling me into his lap, his hands lazily moving on my back. Wrapping my arms around his neck, I kiss both cheeks and his chin, working slowly down his jaw. When it stays silent, I pause, my lips still on his skin. "Nox."

"Right," he huffs with a laugh. "I need to look in your eyes when I tell you this." Kissing my way back up, I give him a quick peck on the lips before leaning back. "I don't think I can or should ignore the council any longer, especially knowing what they want to plan with Haylee."

We hadn't talked much about what Sadryn and Alexandria had told us—how the council would propose that Haylee and Nox get betrothed. Nothing beyond

Nox ensuring me that either I would rule at his side or he would give up the throne all together. I wasn't sure how I felt about either option yet.

"Are you saying it's time we venture out of this room and actually *do* things?" I tease.

"Partially. I mean, *yes,* we should do things. And as you know, Cass is anxious to officially meet you."

I laugh at that since Nox's best friend Cassius had been to the door a few days ago shouting for "the lovebirds to stop fucking and come out." He then told Nox that he was losing his pretty muscles by not training. I had seen those pretty muscles in the flesh *many* times and found that I disagreed completely.

"But more than that, I want this kingdom and the council that helps rule it to know who you are to me and that there is no one else that I will stand beside. That you are mine."

My heart beats a little faster as I search his face, already suspecting what he might say.

"I want to officially announce that we are courting."

It was early morning when Nox had gently kissed my shoulder and told me he was going to meet Cassius for training. I was still mostly asleep, murmuring that I loved him before curling deeper into the blankets.

Now awake, leaning back against the headboard with my journal resting on my thighs, I replay our interaction from the night before. At the look on my face when he said the word "courting," he assured me it wasn't a proposal. Not yet anyway, he had added with a devious wink. Instead, it was a way for me to move about the palace and kingdom with protection by association and for him to shut down the council's idea right away. He also told me a little more about Haylee, that she was simply a family friend and someone they had grown up with. That was a relief, at least, to know I wasn't walking into a situation where someone believed Nox to already be theirs.

My nerves about becoming *more*—consort and queen—stem from the fact that I'm not sure I *can* be those things. What made a good queen? I thought it might be someone who was innately good with people, one who ruled with heart, wisdom, and decorum. I didn't have experience with any of those. I hadn't even been able to rule over *myself* in my first twenty-two years. What hope—no, what *business*—do I have reigning over others?

The door to Nox's room opens, and my heart leaps in my throat as I watch him kick his boots off, setting two swords down against the wall before crossing the sitting room to his bedroom. His hair is disheveled, sweat curling the strands hanging around his temples. His chest—his very *bare* chest—gleams as sunlight hits it at just the right angle, contouring his already sculpted body with well-placed shadows and light.

"Good morning, Sunshine," he says with a smile, pure happiness radiating off of him. My throat constricts more tightly the longer I stare at him.

"You're not wearing a shirt."

"Afraid someone might enjoy the view as much as you do?" he jokes, walking over to the bed and squatting down by my side. When I don't answer, my eyes instead narrowing on his, he only smiles wider. "Are you jealous of those hypothetical people?"

"I—" I freeze, rolling my lips together. I *am* jealous. Even subdued, my magic hums frantically at the thought of anyone else seeing, let alone touching, Nox. *Gods above, what is wrong with me?* I have felt jealousy before but only in the context of what I knew I was missing out on in life. Freedom. Friendship. Love. This, however, feels different. Looking at Nox's perfect face, the only word that pierces through my mind and stabs into my heart is *"mine."*

He places his hands on the bed, leaning forward until we are only a few inches apart. "It's okay if you are. Gods know I have to swallow down my own possessiveness when it comes to you. When I think of others watching you experience new things for the first time."

I relax at his admission and lean forward to kiss him. He smells like the woods, spiced earth, and salt, and I have to squeeze my thighs together to appease the ache that builds between them. "I was expecting you to be exhausted," I tell him when we separate.

He chuckles as he comes to a stand, his abdominal muscles flexing with the movement. My toes curl into the bed.

"Training has always been a release for me, a way to shut my mind off for a little bit." That intrigues me, as the only time my mind ever truly quiets is when we are intimate with each other. "Cass is a talented fighter, especially with daggers and short swords, and I haven't been practicing like usual the past few weeks. So, much to his satisfaction, he was able to best me six out of the ten matches we sparred."

I giggle at his look of chagrin. Maybe it's because of my previous nightmare and my confessions about feeling completely helpless, or maybe it's because Nox looks so *alive* right now, but I'm surprised by my desire to attain the same level of elation.

"I think I want to train." For some reason, my cheeks heat at the admission, but Nox's eyes sparkle with what looks like relief—the emotion perhaps also mixed with pride.

"Of course, Rhea. Anything and everything you want to do and learn, you will." He turns, heading towards the bathroom. "I'm going to take a shower, and then I was thinking we could start to explore Galdr if you want."

He doesn't make it more than halfway across the room before I'm leaping off the bed and following him, exploring something entirely different under the warmth of the shower.

Chapter Thirty-Six

ARIA

S ITTING WITH LYRE ON my bed, we both stare at the aged book between us. She had come by my room after the queen had dismissed me, a large tome in hand that she had stolen from the library after overhearing what our mother wanted. I am leaving tomorrow morning to journey around the Continent to the Northern Island, a small plot of land technically part of the Siren Queendom, to retrieve an old set of rings that are supposedly enchanted by a past queen.

"Enchanting items isn't a magic we possess anymore, but millennia ago, one of our queens did. I found an archive of some of the items she enchanted," she says, flipping the pages as we pore over the different items listed.

There are books and swords and jewelry documented, all ranging in magical capability. Some magic was small, like armor that never nicked, while others were more grand, like a necklace that could be worn to soothe an aching heart and swords that gave the wielder immunity from our song. I turn the page, scanning it for anything that might mention rings.

"Here," Lyre says, pointing at one of the listings. The details of the rings it describes are slightly different from what my mother told me—silver instead of gold, diamonds instead of pearls—but perhaps the enchantment would still be the same. "The bearer of the rings, so long as they have royal blood, will be able to command the magic of it. Placing the ring onto another will yield control over their autonomy to whoever the bearer wishes, whether that be themselves or another. Only can one of royal blood break the spell and end the enchantment for all who wear the rings."

My brows furrow as I click my talons together. I can't at all think why my mother would want such a thing when she already controls everyone by fear alone. Lyre must think the same, as she shakes her head, looking up from the pages to me.

"Why? Why send you, of all people, to retrieve this?"

"She threatened the sirens of the seamounts if I don't. It's just another way to control me since I'm not producing heirs as she wants." Lyre flutters her lips, her exhaustion showing when she yawns heavily. "Go, sister. It's late, and we both have to be up early for my send off."

She closes the book and tucks it under her arm as she swims for the door. "I will try to keep her attention elsewhere while you're gone," she says, looking over her shoulder at me. Her eyes sparkle in earnest, but guilt chews on my conscience.

"I can't have you do that, Lyre, nothing that will draw her focus to you."

Her lavender brow lifts in challenge, the corner of her mouth rising to match. "I have been alive far longer than you have, Aria. I know how to handle myself." Sending a wink my way, she says goodnight and shuts the door behind her.

I continuously circle my room in the minutes after, little bubbles fluttering around me as I do. It will take me over two months to travel around the Continent and return. And if I didn't come back on time...

A knock on my door startles me, and assuming it's Lyre, I rush to open it. Lore hovers in the hallway, her long yellow braids pulled together into a thick plait that lays over her shoulder. Her dark skin gleams in contrast under the light of the crystals.

"Lore, what are you doing here?" I ask, my heart plummeting to my stomach.

Bright yellow eyes caress my body as she interlaces her fingers in front of her. "I was hoping we could chat." She pulls her lower lip into her mouth, dragging her teeth along it while I hide farther behind the door.

"I don't know, Lore. I have to leave in the morning, and I—" My words are forced to a stop when she rushes forward, weaving her hands into my hair and drawing me into her.

"You look like you need to relax, Aria. And I want to help you do that. Please, let me help you." Her voice is soft and melodic, not with magic but from her own lust.

"I am leaving tomorrow morning," I whisper, my eyes darting out into the hall. My mother had not said I had to keep my departure a secret, and when I asked her what she would tell people about my absence for so many weeks, she merely laughed.

If Lore is surprised by my news, she doesn't show it. "Then let's make tonight worth it." Her fingers drag slowly down my shoulders as she crowds me, guiding me backwards towards my bed. "Come on, Aria, you and I both know this is what you want."

I start to recoil, the word "no" bubbling up my throat, but when she is in a mood like this—so clearly ready to take from me, whether it's being offered or not—I don't know how to deny her. When her hands drag over my breasts and descend, her eyes lifting to mine expectantly, I don't bother trying to delay the inevitable.

Legs and feet replace my tail fin, and my scales retract until there is only a shimmer of their pattern on my skin. Lying back, my gaze stays unfocused on the pearlescent ceiling above me. The first lick of her tongue flat against me sends a shiver through my legs.

"So responsive," she hums, her grip on my inner thighs bruising.

My heart rattles in my chest, forced desire and lingering fear warring with each other between my ribs. I wonder if it is normal to always feel a coating of dread during moments of supposed intimacy.

Lore was my first female sexual experience, and the only one since. She knew my body—my likes and dislikes—better than even myself. Our early encounters were passionate and heated, with Lore exploring every part of me in exquisite detail, and I had liked it then, those first few times. I had thrived under the attention she gave me and the way her eyes lingered on parts of me that left my cheeks flushed. She treated me like something precious—a treasure found amongst sand.

Then my choice had been taken from me in front of an audience—one which Lore was a part of. Though I knew she couldn't have said anything, there was a part of me that hoped, when my panicked eyes found hers, that she would. That she would find me worthy of speaking up for. It seemed like I was always waiting for someone to find me worthy of *something*. So far, no one truly had. Not in any way that mattered. Not when the cost was their flesh versus my own.

But was I any better?

She continues her movements, my hips rocking of their own accord, and though pleasure curls and spikes within me, I feel nothing else. This moment is just a blanket over the memories of what came before. It doesn't make the fear and pain and guilt go away; it simply covers them for a time, hides them from view. I force my eyes shut and ride the wave of her ministrations until I am languid but not relaxed. I'm never truly at ease.

When it's over, Lore's need satiated, I curl on my side and wait for the quietness of sleep.

The light of dawn crests over the water, the sky painted a soft lavender and blue. I had expected to see Lyre before I had to leave, but Allegra was at my door as the first peek of the sun rose over the horizon, and Lyre had not come outside the palace to say goodbye. Mashaka swims circles around us slowly, his beady black eyes catching my gaze every time he moves in front of me.

"If you have not returned within ten weeks' time with the rings in hand, you know whose lives you will be condemning." My mother's grip on her trident is light, her body at ease as she elegantly undulates her tail in the water. There is a tightness to her mouth, a quiet zeal churning in her dark eyes. She doesn't just *want* these spelled rings; she *needs* them. And I can't even begin to imagine why.

Turning towards the east, my fingers grip lightly around my eelgrass woven satchel.

"Do not fail me, Aria." With those parting words, the queen turns and swims back in the direction of the palace.

Allegra looks down her nose at me, her lips lifting into a sneer. "Mashaka will not protect your life over his. So don't do anything that will give him the choice because you will lose, every time." She glances towards her delphinidae, narrowing her eyes until he barely treads the water. A muscle trembles in his side, his own eyes wide and focused. When Allegra finally decides to leave, Mashaka relaxes a fraction.

"Okay then, let's go."

Somehow understanding me, he darts off into the water, his sleek form gliding easily against the current. I trail behind him, my gaze lingering on Lumen beneath us until it fades away.

Hours pass while the sun moves higher in the sky. I keep to my quickened pace, following behind Mashaka as he continues to guide the way. Calcified rock juts out from the sand while bright yellow and orange anemones flow gently in the ocean's current. Coral in varying shades of pink and blue and green grows in the crevices of the rock, their spindly hardened veins reaching up towards the surface. It's in one of those coral that a glint of silver catches my attention.

My swimming slows as I cast a glance towards Mashaka, but the delphinidae is yards ahead of me. I only linger on the decision for a moment before my curiosity wins out, and I dive down to the coral. My claws gently work to free the shining object, sending tiny blue crabs scattering over the rock. When I lift it up, I see that it's a small dagger, the hilt cool and heavy in my hand. There is no embellishment or adornment on it except for the initials L.V. in pretty script carved onto the side. Inspecting it closer, I notice that the hilt is marbled with a faint color of brown, reminding me of decaying bone. It's a fine-looking weapon, only partially rusted from its time in the water. Carefully laying it in my bag, I look up to find Mashaka nowhere to be seen. I dart higher into the water, quickly swimming in the direction I last saw him.

In my urgency to catch up, I don't take in my surroundings fully. I don't notice how the coral is fading away or how the sand is darkening in color. It isn't until I feel the unmistakable drop in temperature that I realize where I am.

The Tula Ledge.

The sandy ocean bottom eventually ends, nothing but a pit of black in its place. A chill skitters over me as I look down into it. My mother has utilized these depths and its monsters as a way to dispose of the bodies of sirens who have met her wrath. I've only ever visited the ledge once before, fear and trepidation enough to send me traversing the other way. Now, as I float above it—far closer than I should be—my skin crawls with the feeling of being watched.

Mashaka comes back into view farther ahead, and I hasten my pace over the ledge's menacing opening. My hands grip onto the strap of my bag while I bounce my eyes from beneath me to up ahead where even the vicious delphinidae waits, not willing to cross so low to the opening of the ledge.

On my next glance beneath me, something moves. It's wrapped in shadows and extremely quick, but I think I see the glint of a claw or tooth. My hips roll faster as my tail whips up and down in frenzied movements. Mashaka freezes in the water, his beady eyes focused in my direction but not on *me*.

A scream rips from my throat as an oily black creature darts from the darkness of Tula's pit and right towards me.

"Help me!" I yell to Mashaka, my heart thrashing against my ribcage.

He doesn't move beyond his eyes shifting from the monster to me. The grotesque creature's mouth unhinges, opening widely enough to bite me in half. Rows of razor-sharp teeth make my blood run cold as I change direction and dash towards the surface. Perhaps if the sunlight hits this beast from the deepest pit of the ocean, it will be enough to stop its pursuit of me. I swim faster than I ever have before, my heart beating so soundly that I feel it rattle my skull. I can faintly hear the squeaks of Mashaka, but I'm too afraid to look behind me.

The creature slashes the tip of my tail fin, just enough to sting as I hiss through my teeth. The sun is shining brightly, and still, the creature persists. I glance back quickly and immediately regret doing so. Bony arms that end with long, skinny claws reach towards me, its black skin shiny and covered with patches of silver scales.

I stretch my hands out in front of me and, with a powerful whip of my tail, launch myself into the layer of the Spell before breaking through the water's surface. I hear the monster behind me follow, its screech ringing out over the open air. The hair on the back of my neck rises as I arc above the water, my body tilting until I'm in a dive. The moment my face is back underwater, I don't look behind me. Instead, I shoot towards Mashaka where he swims back and forth at the other side of the ledge.

"Go!" I shout as I close the distance between us.

He waits until I'm only a few yards away and then turns and scurries off. I push hard, ignoring the way my heart pumps much too quickly and the muscles in my tail ache. A cramp forms in my side, and still, I continue to swim. I'm far past Tula's Ledge when I finally stop feeling the presence of something behind me. It isn't until the sun is setting, vibrant orange and pink tainting the sky above, that I allow myself to slow down. The adrenaline fueling my pace begins to fade away, replaced instead by bone-weary fatigue. I haven't eaten at all today, and I'm too exhausted to go hunt for anything now.

"Mashaka, wait," I groan out, searching for somewhere safe for us to rest for the evening.

I find an outcropping of calcified rock just taller than me with an indent at its base big enough for Mashaka and I to hide together in. My movements are lethargic while I sink down onto the seafloor and push myself into the small carved out portion of the rock. I examine my fin, happy to see that there isn't much more than a small scrape against it. Curling in on myself, my eyes are nearly shut when the soft whirring of the current is interrupted by a high-pitched squeak.

A silver and white striped fish dangles lifelessly from his jaws as Mashaka all but plops down next to me, the weight of his body shifting the sediment around us until I have to blink away the sand from my eyes.

"I suppose you aren't going to share that, are you?"

He whips his head towards me, and though he can't say the word "no," I hear it all the same. My stomach rumbles in response, and Mashaka squeaks again before giving me his back. I sigh, returning my head to my folded arms as I allow my eyes to close to the sound of Mashaka enjoying his meal.

Day one down, and I only *almost* got eaten by a sea monster.

Chapter Thirty-Seven

BAHIRA

After interviewing three families in Molsi this morning, I had been surprised when Kai offered to explain more about the magical blight over a bite to eat instead of treading back to the palace. Side stepping a vendor selling grilled meats, I catch the shifter king looking down at me from the corner of his eye.

"What?" I ask, pausing my steps to let a small shifter run ahead of me on the stone pathway.

"Do royalty in the Mage Kingdom always dress so casually?" At the look he sees on my face, he adds, "I don't mean it as an insult. I just assumed—"

"That dressing down is frowned upon? You seem to allow it in your own court," I interrupt, dragging my gaze down his body.

Kai keeps his attention trained ahead but the flex of his hand at his side betrays him. He wasn't really asking me about clothing, he was comparing my kingdom to his.

"I choose clothes for comfort, as is generally the case back home, excluding official royal events." Kai's eyes flick back down to mine. "Though if your assumption of me was that I'd be a docile female prancing around in flowy garb, then I'm happy to have destroyed the illusion."

Kai snorts, shaking his head before looking forward. "Always so quick to think the worst of me."

I suppose I couldn't refute that. He leads me to a small hut set a few feet farther back from the other businesses, a male leaning against it while a group of young shifters chase each other nearby. The male's curly black hair is pulled back, a few of the shorter strands hanging loose from his ponytail.

"Your Majesty," he says, dipping his chin as he rights himself. "And Lady..."

"Just Bahira," I answer. We stop right as the most delicious smell coats the air, the savory herbs and spices making my stomach growl.

"I am Adrian."

"What is that incredible smell?"

The male smiles broadly, his arms spreading out wide. "The king can attest, I cook the finest food in all of Molsi! The usual for you, Your Majesty?" I look to Kai, who nods, his lips still set into a grim line. "And for you, Bahira?"

"Whatever is your favorite to make." Adrian hastens into the hut, and a young male breaks from the group he's playing with to follow him. "He seems happy to see you," I say, somewhat surprised by such an outright display of excitement towards Kai when I've only seen the opposite so far.

Feeling my stare, he turns his head towards me, and immediately, my throat tightens. I hate the way he draws a reaction from me without even trying, my own curiosity begging me to etch away at every layer of armor he hides behind.

"He's a good male." His eyes leave mine to roam my face, my hair, and then my body, the act more like he's studying something he doesn't quite know what to do with than it is sexual in nature.

"Here we go!" Adrian's voice breaks our connection, both of us drawing in a deep breath.

"Thank you, Adrian," Kai says gruffly, grabbing two paper bags from him and paying him for the food before turning to walk in the direction of the beach.

"It was nice meeting you," I say with a wave.

Adrian waves back, his other arm going around the small male who went into the shop with him. "And you, Bahira. Enjoy your meal!"

I jog to catch up with Kai, the stone beneath our feet eventually giving way to sand. He guides us towards a shaded spot between two shorter palm trees, taking a seat and setting one of the bags out in front of him. He waits until I sit down before handing the other to me. Quietly, we dive into our food, each of us holding a different wrap filled with warm vegetables and grilled meat. Kai's is nearly twice the size of my own. The first bite I take draws a low groan unbidden from me as I tilt my head back dramatically.

"This is *fantastic*."

"I've been going to Adrian's since I started living at the palace full time."

"And how long has that been?" I ask.

"About ten years."

"Have you been king for that entirety?" I'm embarrassed that I don't actually know.

Kai shakes his head, waiting until his bite of food is chewed and swallowed before answering. "No." He gives me nothing else.

We eat in silence for a few more minutes before I tell him I officially met Jahlee.

"She told me," he responds, taking another bite.

Unsurprised, I laugh as I tilt my head. "She is—" His eyes snap to mine in warning. "*Vivacious*," I settle on. The corner of his mouth lifts for a moment before falling into that straight line once more.

When our food is gone, I stare out at the rolling waves, opting to change the subject. "So, tell me what I need to know about the blight."

Kai only hesitates for a second before he launches into what he knows. He isn't entirely sure when it started, as the reports of those getting stuck grew gradually over time during his father and grandfather's reign. He adds that those near the edges of the island are more highly affected than shifters who live near the center.

"Jahlee said that it's not just those who get stuck as animals but that sometimes people can't shift at all?"

He nods, resting his elbows on his bent knees as a salty breeze ruffles through his hair. "It's more rare, but it is happening."

"Are there any similarities for those that are affected by one or the other?"

Kai mulls over my question before his gaze slides in my direction. "I cannot be sure that this is the case for *everyone,* but of the shifters I have been made aware of, I think those unable to shift into their animals are older and those stuck as their animal are of prime age."

I pinch my lips together, my fingers drawing in the sand next to my hips. "We'll have to interview as many shifters as we can who are affected by both parts of this blight to try and find more common ground, then."

"We can only talk with the ones who are willing. That is what Tua has been doing this past week."

"It took him *all week* to find a handful of families willing to talk with us?" At Kai's nod, I scoff, shaking my head. "Why would they be so reluctant to receive help?"

"You are smart. I know you've noticed that I'm not exactly *revered* as a leader."

"Feelings on you aside, they must know your intention as ruler. That helping them and wanting to find a solution for the blight is *your* idea."

Kai chuckles, the sound as solemn as the look on his face. "In the Mage Kingdom, do the people separate the ruling of the crown from the male who wears it?"

Fair point. "No, I suppose they don't." Still, there must be more to Kai as a ruler than what I'm seeing. Something worth all of the derogatory glances sent to both him and his sister.

"We should head back."

He stands, offering his hand to help me, but I'm already up at his side. My instinct is to stiffen, waiting for the sigh of annoyance or muttered comment I'm so used to Daje giving me in a situation like this. Instead, Kai's cheeks lift with the faintest smirk before he turns to walk back towards Molsi. I keep a few steps behind, pushing down the confusion stirring in my chest as I follow him.

We're about halfway through the capital when a scream rises above the normal clamoring of the busy city. Mere seconds pass before there's a loud *boom,* my ears ringing as Kai yanks me behind one of the street vendor's carts. The single scream is replaced by a symphony of them, flashes of light sparking around me as males and females shift into their animals.

"What was that?" I shout, turning to look past the cart and to the cloud of black smoke rising in the direction we had just come from.

Kai is silent as he moves back onto the main road, people and animals running past us in panic. He doesn't look at me as he begins to walk towards the chaos. "Go back to the palace."

"There could be people who need help," I counter, brushing against his arm as I jog past him. "There's no fucking way I'm going back."

He doesn't argue, and together, we sprint towards the unknown danger.

Adrian's establishment is all but gone, only the charred husk of its frame remaining. Goosebumps break out over my skin, not due to the still smoking building or the scent of burnt wood in the air but to Adrian's screaming.

His keening wail saturates the air in anguish. My chest heaves from my run here, but it's what Adrian is cradling in the ashes of his business that forces my heart into my throat. He sways as he holds a small body to him, the young shifter's clothing melted to his skin from the heat of the flames.

Kai steps up to me, power radiating from him in a way that I've never felt before. "His son?" I ask him quietly under my breath.

"Yes."

His gaze stays locked on Adrian while my eyes scan the gathered crowd, some holding onto others for support as tears draw down their cheeks. Others stare in open shock, their attention not on the grizzly scene but on the message written in black coal on the tan stone walkway in front of the remains of Adrian's place.

I lean in closer to get a better look, tilting my head to read what it says. A single word, the letters all capitalized, makes me blink in surprise. *USURPER.*

"Clear out the area, everyone. Come on, make some room." I recognize Tua's voice behind me, the crowd beginning to disperse at his command. "Miss, are you— Oh, Bahira. What are you doing here?"

I don't answer him, my focus still on that single word and its implication. I turn, eager to ask Kai what's next and if there is something I can do to help, but the space where he was once standing is empty. A quick look behind me shows his looming figure heading towards the edge of the jungle. "Where the fuck is he going?" I ask Tua.

The king's advisor sends me a morose look, his lips tugging down into a frown. "I'm assuming to try and hunt the people down who did this."

I grit my teeth as I look back to Adrian, his cries quieter now as a few people kneel at his side with their hands on his shoulders. "Shouldn't he have people he can send off to do that for him?"

Tua ponders the question, his hands clasping behind his back. "I suppose he should, but Kai has never done well in situations where a gentle voice is needed to lead. That's why I'm here. Why don't you head back to the palace and wait for His Majesty there?" Giving me a curt smile, he walks towards the carnage left by the rebels and kneels with the other shifters, their teary eyes meeting his in gratitude.

My gaze roams over the people still gathered here, catching the wary glances of those who know my face isn't a familiar one in the capital. So, despite my instinct to stay and help in some way, I do as Tua suggested. I know that he must care about his people—my being here is evidence of that. Yet Tua's warning to me on the ship rings clear. If the goal is to try and better Kai's image with his people, then Tua is failing as his advisor. Either that, or Kai is simply ignoring his suggestions. If I am going to try and learn as much as I can about the blight, I need the people to trust in Kai—in *us*—and to share with us as much as they can.

As the palace comes into view up ahead, the leaves of the palm trees lining it swaying in a gentle breeze, I realize that I *have* to help with much more than just fixing magic.

I need to fix a broken king.

Chapter Thirty-Eight

BAHIRA

The air is thick with humidity as we trudge through the forest to a village right outside of Molsi. My eyes drag over Kai's body where he walks ahead of me, noticing his broad shoulders and back and the way his waist tapers in only slightly. *Everything* about him is substantial—his legs, his arms, his stupid jaw, probably another appendage that I am furious with myself for thinking about.

"I can feel your eyes on me, Princess." His voice is smooth, coating me as easily as the mist in the air.

Godsdamn it.

"Just wondering how an oaf as big as you can move so gracefully." He snorts, holding a low-lying branch up so that I can pass under it without ducking. "Thank you." His eyes widen as he lets the branch go and falls into step beside me. "What?"

"I wasn't sure you knew those words."

I roll my eyes, adjusting my backpack as I check where my spear is tucked into its loops. "I don't generally offer them when the bare minimum is met, but considering manners don't seem to be your strong suit, I figured I'd reward you with acknowledgement."

I keep my gaze on the trail ahead of us, the soil darkened from the moisture in the air which causes my boots to sink in with each step, and ignore the way I can feel Kai's gaze on me. It burns into the side of my face, causing heat to slowly build in my core.

"Does sarcasm come easily to you, or is your sharp tongue simply another defense mechanism?"

"Anything regarding the use of my tongue is intentional, Kai, and in this kingdom? Everything I do *must* be a defense mechanism. I could be attacked by a wild animal." My smile is mocking as I add, "Or a more domesticated one."

The quirk of his lips sends a jolt of excitement through me. It isn't quite a smile, but it's more than he's ever given me before. "Only *you* would so openly insult the king of another realm by calling his shifter form *domesticated*."

I look up at him then, noting the way a few short strands of hair have broken away from the rest and hang over his forehead. The dark brown gleams against his dewy golden skin, matching the color of his eyes. Eyes that are currently watching me with mild amusement.

"I can't decide if you are brave or just stu—"

"Don't finish that sentence if you want to walk the remainder of the way without a limp," I interrupt, patting the side of my spear.

Kai chuckles before we fall back into silence. He had given me a skeptical look when he saw that I had packed the spear, but I simply shrugged and said it would be foolish to travel anywhere without it. Especially after what I witnessed with Adrian and his business, a topic I still haven't figured out how to approach Kai about.

The sky above has changed its hue from blue to gray, and white clouds puffy with the incoming rain perch around the mountains in the distance. We continue trekking through the heavy vegetation, the plants and trees closing in on us the farther we go. Something rustles over the dead leaves on the jungle floor to our right.

"It's just a small monkey," Kai says.

"How can you tell?"

"Its scent," he answers, and my nose wrinkles in response.

"Does your shifter form ever coexist with your mortal form?" I question, wondering if he can call on certain abilities without having to shift fully.

"All shifters have increased strength, eyesight, and sense of smell while in their mortal forms. Those are the only things most can access until they shift fully. Then they gain the nuances that are unique to their animal."

"Does one form feel better than the other?" He turns towards me, a brow raised in question. "I mean, is one form *easier* to exist in? Do you feel called to one more than the other?"

"I can't speak for anyone else, but for me, it's like having an itch I can't quite scratch until I shift. It's underneath my skin and buried deep in my blood. I imagine that is how your magic feels as well? If you don't use it for a while?"

My silent pause is an imaginary scream out into the jungle. It isn't supposed to be a secret that I don't have magic, at least within my own kingdom. Had Kai or Tua *truly* not heard whisperings of it on the docks when their ships dropped off supplies?

"I suppose so," I respond, warring with myself about telling him.

Historically speaking, I've never been one to delay making a decision, mostly because I've usually picked it apart until I've found an answer that has more pros than cons. But lately, my decisions aren't as easy to decipher.

"How did you learn that mages can pass through the Spell?" It's a question that I've been dying to learn the answer to.

"The short answer is because my father knew."

"And the long answer?"

Kai exhales, long and full bodied. "The long answer is a story for another day."

Fine. That's *fine*. I've got weeks and weeks here to get it out of him.

He continues ahead, pushing the thick leaves of overgrown bushes out of the way until we step out of the jungle completely and right into the village. The homes are larger than those in the heart of the capital and more spread out, the style the same round shape made of dried palms, stone, and light wood. It's busy, people meandering around as they carry long planks of wood on their shoulders or baskets of food against their hips.

"What is this place called?" I ask quietly, leaning closer to Kai, my hair accidentally brushing against his arm. The muscles there tense, rippling under the skin adorned with the lines of inked black.

"Leeta," he answers while adjusting his body so that he is no longer touching any part of me. "The capital may be the center of the island, but places like Leeta are its heart."

Kai's reception here is vastly different from that in Molsi. Everyone who passes gives him a respectful acknowledgement, and even Kai himself looks more at ease, the tension normally riding his shoulders mostly gone.

He leads us between a row of homes—the scent of flora, tilled soil, and fired meats thick in the air—to a door where a small monkey and an eagle are carved into the wood. Kai knocks three times, and the door is swung open by a female dressed in an oversized long blue dress, the material ragged at the ends.

"Your Majesty," she blurts out, eyes wide as she attempts to form a curtsy while the baby on her hip pulls at her hair.

I offer my hand out to her. "Hello. I'm Bahira. The king and I are here to speak with you about the blight."

The female's shoulders relax as she exhales, her hand folding over my own. "That's right, I almost forgot. I'm Magda. Come in." Magda's house is cluttered, each corner filled with piles of trinkets and random collections of trash and torn-up leaves. "I'm sorry about the mess. He can't help it, and with working as much as possible to earn enough coin in his absence, I don't have much energy left to clean."

"It's alright," I assure her, turning away from the largest pile of odds and ends. I take my backpack off and set it down, grabbing my journal and spelled pen from the biggest zipper. "Is it your husband who has shifted?"

She nods, a frown drawing her thin lips down. Exhaustion lines her forehead and colors the skin darker under her eyes. "He shifted about three weeks ago, and—" Her sentence is stopped abruptly when her baby yanks a chunk of hair harshly. She struggles to get his little hand free of the now tangled mess while her eyes begin to water.

"Go offer to hold her baby," I say to Kai under my breath.

As if startled by my suggestion, his head snaps towards me, his brows drawn high. "Excuse me?"

"Go. Offer. To. Hold. Her. Baby," I enunciate slowly. When his features remain stupefied, I grumble a plea to the gods above while laying my journal and pen down on the floor and walk over to Magda. "Let me help you."

I work to remove the last remaining strands from the baby's little chubby hand, his amber eyes wide on me as he decides whether or not he is going to cry in my presence. Once his mother's hair is free, I look to her for permission to hold him. She nods gratefully, handing him over in a smooth motion. Returning to

Kai, I bounce the little one on my hip, his toothless smile bringing out a grin of my own.

"What is his name?"

"Sione," Magda says as she braids her long hair back.

"Hello, Sione. Let's see if you can make the grumpy shifter king smile." I hold him out to Kai, his little feet kicking in the air between us, but the king doesn't move. "This is the part where you take the baby from my hands, Your Majesty."

"I have never held a baby. They are too small—too fragile. I don't want to hurt it."

"Him. You don't want to hurt *him*. And you won't. Come on, take him." When Kai still doesn't move, I let loose a laugh. "Don't tell me that you are afraid of a being a tenth of your size?" I let my eyes drag down his body deliberately, knowing he can tell when I linger on some parts longer than others. "No, more like a fifteenth of your size." The small smirk he gives me leaves me feeling oddly victorious.

"You will not hurt him, Your Majesty. Babies are far more durable than most think," Magda adds.

"See? You'll be fine. Hold him."

This time, Kai acts, lifting his hands—albeit *slowly*—to take Sione from me. He keeps his arms straight out in front of him, his large grip taking up Sione's entire torso on both sides.

I laugh as I pat his arm. "There you go."

"What do I do now?" he asks, but I'm already picking up my supplies.

I meet Magda in the small kitchen on the other side of a half wall made of wood and covered with potted plants that divides the home. I take a seat at the small four-person table in the middle of the room, dwindling sunlight streaming in from the window on the farthest wall.

"Can I make you some tea?" Magda asks, already rushing to a cupboard above the counter.

"Yes, please."

She gathers our mugs and fills a kettle with water. "Rangi, my husband, is normally the one who makes the tea, so I apologize if my brew is weak." Her voice quavers as she speaks, her sadness over her husband undeniable.

"What can you tell me about the day he shifted?" I pull my journal closer to me and open it up to a blank page, my pen hovering over it.

"It was a normal day. We've been wary about shifting, as we have seen the blight spreading to more and more homes. But, as you know, we cannot control the call of it."

I nod my head at her back. I may not be a shifter, but I can at least understand in theory what it is to be unable to deny yourself something that feels so intrinsic. It is how I feel when it comes to finding my magic.

"Anyway, he shifted and was gone for a few hours after I put our offspring to bed. I knew something was wrong when he came in through this window still in his animal form. Normally, he shifts outside the front door and walks in."

She continues as I take notes, writing down questions I have to ask Kai about later on. Like if shifters of different species can communicate with each other in their animal forms.

"The longer he stays as he is, the more, well, *animal* he seems to become. I'm afraid that by the time we end this blight and figure out a way for him to return back to normal, it will be too late. He won't be able to be saved."

The kettle whistles, the noise hiding some of the woman's quiet weeping. I study my notes, my resolve to fix the blight deepening the longer Magda speaks. When she sits down across from me and goes on to talk about her struggles operating as essentially a single parent, I ask her if anyone in the village helps her.

"They do as much as they can," she answers, taking a small sip of tea. "But it would be easier if the Crown hadn't denied my plea for aid."

My brows pinch together as I stop writing and lift my gaze to hers. "What do you mean?"

Her eyes nervously dart behind me, where I know she is watching Kai hold Sione.

I drop my voice low and lean in closer. "You needn't worry about him. I merely ask for my own understanding."

Magda blows out a steady breath. "A few weeks after Rangi became stuck, I wrote a letter to the palace asking for help. With my offspring still so young, I cannot work enough to cover all of our expenses. But last week, I received a letter back claiming that they could do nothing." She sighs as she takes another sip of tea and winces. "This really is weak."

I grip the pen more harshly before grinning at her and closing my journal. "Thank you for your time. I promise—" Surprise at my own words temporarily halts any more from coming. I can't *promise* anything. At least, I certainly *shouldn't*. "I will do everything I can to try to solve this as soon as possible."

For the first time since I entered her home, Magda's eyes gleam a little brighter, something like hope seeping into them. We join Kai back out in the living room, the king now surrounded by a gaggle of small shifters climbing all over him like the mountain of a male he is. Despite everything I just learned, I have to swallow down a laugh when his eyes meet mine in desperation.

The next four homes we visit go much like Magda's did, though no one else mentions being denied aid from the Crown.

It's nearly sunset by the time we begin our journey back to the palace. The clouds are fully gray above us, the scent of rain and the feeling of an impending storm thick in the air. I pull my hair up into a ponytail, the curly ends tickling my shoulders as we walk. My thoughts run rampant, mostly on why Kai would deny help for his people. The farther we walk in the jungle, the more my irritation with Kai over this revelation grows.

I thought he genuinely cared about his people, but *this*? It is not what a good king does. They are the actions of one that is malevolent. I could take dealing with an asshole brute who just didn't know how to communicate. I was not, however, willing to work for one that only wanted to heal his people to make them suffer in other ways.

When my anger crests within me, I step abruptly in front of Kai on the trail and stop his advancing step with a hand to his chest. "Why are you denying aid to families of those stuck in their shifter forms?" I ask, working—and failing—to keep the ire out of my voice.

"What?"

"You heard what I asked," I seethe, pushing harder against his chest.

"I did, and I'm still fucking confused. What are you talking about?" His hands flex at his sides, but he doesn't try to remove my own.

"Magda told me that she wrote to the palace asking for help and her plea was denied. So, I ask again, *Your Majesty*, why?" I expect him to bark back a response, to try to justify himself or perhaps even blame others for what is happening. But there is no denying the genuinely confused look on Kai's face as his dark brows draw together.

"I have never heard of this happening."

My hand leaves his chest as I step back, rolling thunder sounding above us as rain begins to sprinkle. "Who is in charge of bringing those things to your attention?"

His eyes narrow as he folds his arms over his chest. "Tua handles most everything of this nature at my request. But I don't see why he would deny something like that."

I huff out a sarcastic laugh and mirror his stance. "You can't just *give* him the responsibilities you don't want."

Kai tilts his head to the side, the air fraught with tension that I'm not sure can be blamed on the storm. "Why not? He's a better fit to handle those things than I am. I'd say it makes me a conscientious ruler to acknowledge that."

My eyes roam over his face, his confession of feeling inadequate tugging at me but not enough to stop my next words. "No. It makes you a *blind* one."

He goes to respond when his head whips to the right, his eyes narrowing on the darkness gathering between the thick vegetation. "Get your spear out." His tone leaves no room for argument as I reach over my shoulder and slide the spear from its loops in my pack.

"What is it?"

Kai *growls* as he scans the area to our right, my mouth parting as I watch his irises turn golden. I wipe the gathering rain off the skin of my brow and grip my spear with both hands in front of me.

"I need—" He hisses, his hand shooting up to his neck and yanking something out of it. "Fuck!" he grits out, dropping to one knee.

"What's wrong?" I stand in front of him as the rustling of leaves reverberates out into the quickly coming night. "Kai!"

On his hands and knees, his breathing is labored as his head hangs between his shoulders. "Rebels. Poisoned," he huffs out slowly, holding what looks like a tiny vial attached to a dart.

Ice invades my veins as steps sound, and I look over my shoulder to watch three figures emerge from the jungle and onto the path ahead of us. It's what covers their faces, however, that halts my next inhale. *Skulls.* They are wearing fucking animal skulls for masks. My training overrides the fear winding through me, and I change my stance to put myself between Kai and the rebels.

"Ten minutes," Kai grunts.

"I've got you," I say back before he fully collapses onto the ground.

"We don't want to hurt you," the shifter in the middle shouts, his voice deep and booming over the rain. "We just want the king. Move aside, and we'll leave you alone." He steps forward, the sound of metal sliding from a sheath cleaving between us as he swings the short sword in front of him.

"How kind of you," I yell back, my grip tightening on my spear. "But you're not going to touch him."

Each of the rebels takes another step towards me, the two on the ends fanning out to form a crescent shape as they box me in.

"He is as inept as his father was before him. We deserve better; the Shifter Kingdom deserves someone with the capability to lead them. Not some feral, half-breed bastard that stole the throne right under our noses," the largest of them snarls.

Of all the things to fucking feel right now as I'm being surrounded by three shifters intent on taking the passed-out king behind me, guilt certainly isn't one

I expected. There's culpability that takes root at the fact that I've called Kai a bastard *multiple* times in my head, and as it turns out, he actually is one.

"Last chance. Don't get yourself killed over someone who wouldn't do the same for you," the shorter male shouts.

I swing my spear out, the metal leaf-shaped tip pointed directly at the largest male in the center. Lightning cracks overhead, and the brief flash of light makes their skull masks glow. I can't quite make out what animal they are, the space between us blanketed in rain, but I think I catch a glimpse of twisted horns and elongated eye sockets.

With the newly fallen night now cloaking the rebels' movements, I brace myself for the incoming attack. *Let them fucking try to hurt me or the idiot on the ground behind me.*

Chapter Thirty-Nine

Bahira

"**T**his won't even be fun," a female says, unsheathing a weapon of her own—*two* weapons actually, the sound of metal against leather the only indication in the dark. "It'll be over before it even starts." Her preemptive deep breath gives her away before the whistling of a blade flying through the air makes me duck quickly. The weapon embeds into the trunk of a tree behind me with a resounding *thunk*, the female growling in frustration as her steps disturb the pebbles on the path.

She swings her second weapon towards me, and I slam my spear up to block her. The rain is slick against the body of my spear, the metal twisted within the cool wood against my palms. We exchange several blows, her movements agile but not lacking in strength. Dancing around her, I split my attention between the rebels, all while diverting her attempts to move me away from Kai.

"What kind of spear is that?" she asks as we separate, retreating a few steps.

"A special one."

The gravel beneath our feet crunches to my right—making me spin and jerk my spear up to block the incoming attack from the male now at my front, bracing it with both hands and crossing it diagonally in front of me. Blood rushes in my ears and my muscles strain as I pant through clenched teeth. Lightning flares, providing a quick break in the dark as the female ambushes me from the side. With a roar, I kick my leg out as hard as I can, connecting with the center of her chest and sending her flying backward as she curses into the rain.

"The masks are really *fucking* creepy," I state, squatting low and avoiding another swing of the male's sword.

He growls beneath his mask, advancing on me again with heavy steps. His silhouette is just barely given form by the silvery moonlight, enough for me to see the outline of his movements. Adjusting my hold on my spear, I leap towards him, spinning in the air as I swing it down at him. He blocks at the last moment, metal clanging out around us against the raging storm. We continue our evenly matched sparring, the other two rebels moving in the shadows somewhere beyond us.

Brilliant light forks across the sky again, thunder rolling behind it and hiding the steps of the second male until he's already barreling into me. I collide with the ground *hard* as I land on my side, grunting out in pain. My spear is knocked from my grasp when the rebel falls on top of me.

"Get the *ki*—" I jerk my hips up, unseating him and forcing a stop to his command as we tumble to the side.

Once again, he ends up on top, my back sinking into the wet earth as he straddles my hips. I stare up at the sockets of the elongated skull, the shifter beneath it tilting his head to the side as he winds his arm back. My arms lift up to cradle the sides of my head just in time to block the first of the barrage of punches he unleashes, strength and gravity on his side. My heart beats heavily in my chest, the sound of the storm around me fading out to give way to the ringing in my ears as I focus on getting myself free. The first attempt to dig my heels into the ground is met with my boots slipping against the slick pebbles. The move costs me a punch to my ribs, my shout met with an answering laugh of menace.

"Not so tough now, are you?"

Behind the rebel, the sky flashes brightly again, highlighting the mud-splattered skull like some sort of grotesque art piece. I grit my teeth together, the force of it strong enough to send pain shooting to my temples, dig my heels into the ground again, forcing my hips up with a shout. The male's eyes widen as he abandons his next hit to brace himself and keep from tipping forward. But his momentum can't be stopped, and when he's close enough, I wrap my arms around his neck and pull him towards me. Bone hits my shoulder, my face narrowly escaping the scrape of the horns as I wrap a leg around his hip, using the other to launch us both to the side.

Rolling off the rebel and reaching for my spear, I chance a look at Kai. The shifter king is still passed out, his face thankfully turned to the side so he doesn't drown in the downpour. Scrambling to my feet, the rain pelts my face as I wheeze through my next breath, pain radiating down my arm from my shoulder.

There is no moment of reprieve, as the larger male is once more upon me, swinging his sword low towards my side. I thrust my spear out to intercept him, the reverberation of the impact making me wince as we take turns blocking the other's onslaught. With the chaos of the storm and the darkness cloaking the jungle between bolts of lightning, the rebel and I are more reckless in our movements. When his footing slips in the over-soaked ground—his arms instinctively stretching out to balance himself—I take advantage and jab my spear forward.

He howls, dropping his guard as the jagged edges of my weapon shred through the skin and muscle of his torso right beneath his ribcage. Holding the spear with one hand, I send a punch into his jaw, dropping him to one knee.

My head jerks abruptly to the side, my teeth knocking together as I stumble back a few steps. The ends of my ponytail plaster to my face from the impact of the surprise punch, and I'm driven backward as I retreat from the attack until my back slams against a tree trunk. Silver glints at my side in the small patch of moonlight glowing through the tree line. The angry storm bursts with lightning again, illuminating the rebel I stabbed with my spear still on the ground, clutching his side. The second male stares at me from where he punched me before spinning around and sprinting towards Kai.

"*Fuck!*" I shout, reaching with my right hand to yank the dagger that was thrown earlier from the tree. Taking a step forward, I wind my arm back and then snap it forward in the direction of the running male. His arm reaches out to Kai right as the dagger hits him, slightly off the mark from where I was aiming but still embedding into his forearm.

Kai begins to stir, his raspy groan catching the attention of both males. My temple pounds above my eye from the punch, but I force myself towards the prone king, holding my spear tightly in both hands.

The female rebel attacks from the side, her steps crashing over the pebbles giving me enough warning to spin away from the swing of her blade. My boot sinks into a muddy pool of water, momentarily holding me in place as she circles behind me.

"Gods, you're fucking annoying," she hisses, yanking my head back with a sharp pull on my ponytail. Her arm wraps around my neck right as I free my boot. With a growl, I kick my leg back as hard as I can, the impact of the hit rattling my body. She screams as she buckles behind me, blindly swinging her shortsword up while I force myself from her grasp. I cry out when the tip of it slices into my forearm with painful precision, the cold rain mixing with my warm blood as it trails down towards my fingers. "We should shift into our anim—"

"No! We'll be identified!"

Kai groans again as he shakily pushes himself up to his hands and knees.

"*Fuck*, he's waking up! We need to go," the largest rebel heaves, his breathing ragged as he cradles his side and stumbles to his feet. The female shouts out her frustration but doesn't advance towards me again, looking to the shorter male who holds his arm to his chest.

I back up until I'm once more in front of Kai, whose head hangs between his shoulders as he sways on all fours. The scent of blood mixes with the rain as lightning continues to roll across the night sky in rapid succession. I get a better look at the masks the three are wearing. The shapes of them are long and angular, the eye sockets large enough to show not only the rebel's eyes but the skin around them. Sticking out of the top are indeed two long horns that twist and curl in different directions.

"What the fuck," I whisper as Kai comes to stand behind me, still very much wobbly, but his presence alone is enough to get the rebels to back up another step.

"This won't be the last attempt. Next time, we are going to kill whoever stands in our way," the female seethes.

"You can fucking *try*," I taunt back.

She bares her teeth at me in response, but then the male cradling his arm—the dagger still sticking out from it—grabs her shoulder and pulls her back. Blood pools at the feet of the third rebel, his gait shaky.

"You might want to get that checked out," I say with a smile, pointing my spear at him. The rain pings off of it, washing away some of the crimson from the tip.

"I'll kill you," he pants, his eyes catching the silver light from above through the sockets of the skull before they all turn and hobble back into the jungle.

I keep my stance at the ready for what feels like minutes, just in case any of them decide to double back. When I'm sure they're gone, I relax my hold on my spear and spin around to face Kai. "Are you alri—"

He steps up to me, his hand wrapping around my wrist as he lifts it up. His eyes are fully molten—the gold shining brighter and illuminating them in a way that isn't *mortal*. "You're hurt," he rumbles as he carefully inspects the cut on my arm.

"I'm fine." There is too much adrenaline in my body at the moment to indicate anything different.

Kai lets go of me, only to bring his hand to my neck. His fingers wrap around the side and back of it while his thumb pushes under my jaw to tilt my face up higher.

"You protected me." He says it like an accusation.

"Yes, well..." I swallow, my heart kicking up its rhythm for an entirely different reason. "Deals were made that need to be kept."

His fingers tighten, pressing into my skin as he pulls me closer until our chests are touching. I can't help the way I lean in, my body curving to the contour of his. The wood and metal of my spear is a hard line between us, the bloodied tip angled only a few inches away from our faces.

"Tell me what you did to them," he demands, low and seductive.

Desire uncoils, pulsing through me as if I've been struck by the very lightning flashing above. It leaves me temporarily paralyzed as I hold Kai's stare. "I think I shattered the female's kneecap," I rasp.

Kai's breathing quickens, his heartbeat a deep thrum against his chest. "What else?"

"I threw a dagger at the other, impaling it into his forearm."

His responding growl is a vicious sound, and I *should* be terrified by it. My traitorous body, however, is nothing but aroused, my core slick with an unsatiated need. Kai dips his head closer to me, his inhale long and deep at the base of my neck. My pulse rages a breath beneath his mouth, while his fingers clamp down even harder. His other hand grips onto my ponytail, slowly wrapping it around his knuckles as he fists it. In one quick tug, he bares my neck completely to him. My nipples rub against the soaked fabric of my clothing, the friction made more rough against his chest. The inferno within me turns blazing when he skates his teeth slowly up the delicate skin of my neck, his groan mixing with a snarl hot against me.

"What happened with the third one? The largest of the three?"

I ache for more of his touch, for his tongue and his teeth to ravage my mouth and my body like I instinctively know he can. My brain is in overdrive as I force another swallow down and wait for him to lift his gaze back up to mine. I need to take some control back because this is too vulnerable. *I* am too vulnerable right now, and that thought scares me more than facing the fucking skull-wearing rebels with weapons.

Kai finally raises his head, his scent intoxicating and everywhere as his mouth hovers over mine. My voice is steady, and I subtly push my chest more into his as I practically groan, "I drove my spear into his side."

"*Fuck*," he growls, his gaze dipping down to my mouth as his tongue swipes over his bottom lip. "You're a godsdamn *curse*."

I get in one quick inhale before his mouth is on mine. The kiss is hot and insistent, sinfully better than I ever could have imagined. He tastes like something primal and powerful, and I suck his tongue farther into my mouth to get more of it. Kai's grip is unforgiving, the squeeze at my neck and pull of my hair only setting me more aflame. Each drive of our tongues and clash of our teeth is a move made to take the other down, but so far, we are evenly matched. I bite down on his lower lip, the tangy taste of iron making me moan as I suck it into my mouth.

"Don't fucking *bite* me unless you're willing to let me mark you in return," he snaps as he pulls back, though his voice lacks any sort of authority and is instead laced thickly with lust.

I free one of my hands from the hold on my spear between us and grip his chin, my nails digging in as I force him back to me. "Don't tell me what to do," I whisper against his lips.

His chest rumbles with the kind of noise that is a precursor to danger, a warning to all that something predatory is coming. And fuck me if I don't want to be his prey.

Kai's lips are warm and surprisingly soft as they press back into mine, the sensation drawing a yearning from deep within me that begs to mark them up somehow. I want to scratch and claw at him until my signature is *everywhere*. I squeeze my hand tighter, surely causing pain from the way my nails indent his skin, but Kai only deepens our kiss, accompanying it with another dark growl low in his throat. His body is hard against my own, his muscles perfectly carved to fit against me. My rationality is gone, and in its place—driven more wild by each flick of his tongue against my own—is a feral desire that I have never felt with anyone else before.

For all the times that we have battled back and forth for dominance with each other, when it really mattered, Kai didn't *question* if I would be able to handle myself *and* protect him. The feelings that arise from knowing that he *trusts* me this way nearly take me out of the moment, but I force them away to be dealt with at another time.

I finally release his jaw, sliding my hand up to the soaked strands of his hair. Threading my fingers into it, I pull hard until he's forced to let go of my mouth, thunder cracking in the sky above us.

"Bahira." He rumbles my name like the curse he called me, like a poison he craves despite knowing it could destroy him.

Which is precisely how I feel. Pulling against Kai's grip on me, I stand on my toes and drag my tongue up his throat, the flavor of salt and citrus and rain exploding over my taste buds and forcing me deeper into this haze where he is the only thing I want to lose myself in. Kai resists when I try to push his head down towards me again, his swollen lips forming a line.

"What would your *boyfriend* have to say about this?" he drawls, halting my movements.

Fucking Daje. I loosen my grip on the shifter king, and he follows suit, though our chests stay flush together. "He isn't my boyfriend," I rush out, my breaths quick as though I've been caught doing something wrong.

Kai lifts a brow, his eyes cooling right before me under the moonlight. "He's definitely *somebody* to you."

"My best friend," I say simply, but that answer satisfies neither of us. Kai can sense there is more to the story, and I *know* that there is no explanation I'm willing to give him right now on it.

As the cool rain stings my skin and pulls me back into reality, Daje, his ultimatum, and the life waiting for me at home floods back in. I pull against Kai's hold, his hands immediately letting me go as I take a step backward. His rigidity returns, the armor he wears in front of his kingdom going on layer by layer as he silently walks past me and down the trail back to the palace. I linger for a moment, closing my eyes and tilting my face up towards the sky before I turn and follow behind him, my words silent but my mind a ferocious discord.

I replay the moment Kai told me to grab my spear. How he didn't look fearful at all as he collapsed to the ground. I can't help but compare it to what Daje would have done. He would have told me to run or tried to drag me away until the poison took effect. He would have stood in front of me until he was no longer capable of standing. All of those things are admirable and heroic, but none of them are things *I* want—*need*—from a partner. I am not a princess looking for her knight in shining armor. This version of myself, the one who fought to piece herself together to be *enough* until I could be *whole*, is a warrior. A work in progress and incomplete, yes, but a warrior nonetheless. One who only wanted to be with someone if they saw that value in me as well.

My answer for Daje becomes startlingly clear. I can't marry him, and if sacrificing his friendship is the cost of that choice, then so be it. I refuse to let the consequences of Daje's own actions slowly tear apart everything I've spent my life crafting.

My inner thoughts begin to settle the farther we walk, and so too does the storm above, leaving only the glimmering stars and a mild breeze in its wake. We arrive at the palace, passing shifters that don't hide their gawking at our disheveled appearance. Climbing the stairs, Kai stops with me in front of my door, the tension between us palpable and made thicker with actions that can't be undone.

"Thank you for protecting me," he says slowly, like the words are being forced from his mouth. I dip my chin but look up at him through my lashes. He studies me for another moment before something makes his expression stony once more. The transformation is unexpected and has my body bracing—though for what, I don't know. "Everything that happened afterwards was a mistake. The ramifications of poison clouding my judgement."

It's hard to deny the way my heart dips, but could I expect anything else? Did I even *want* anything else? Anything beyond the physical attraction between us is a distraction and doomed to fail anyway.

"Of course," I respond, my hand already reaching for the doorknob behind me. "It was a stressful moment, and we responded in kind. No need to make it a big deal." Turning the handle, I step backwards into my room. "It won't happen again."

"You're acting weird," Jahlee says from where she is lying on her stomach on my bed, her feet moving idly behind her. The dark blue fabric of her dress flows out on either side of her, matching a similarly blue pants and top that I'm wearing.

"You don't know me well enough to know if I am acting weird," I reply, flipping through a mage journal while lounging in an armchair adjacent to the bed.

Jahlee had brought breakfast to me this morning—complete with her singing a song loudly enough to wake up the entire palace. We hadn't found much of interest in the library, nothing that would possibly lead to me understanding how this blight started.

"That's true, but I know my brother pretty well, and *he* was definitely acting weird this morning." My fingers twitch on the corner of the page I'm holding between them. "And since the two of you spent yesterday together and you get defensive when I bring him up—"

"I do *not* get defensive when you bring him up." I argue, turning in my chair to look at her.

Her smile is wide, disarmingly so, as she gestures with her hand out in front of her. "I just did, and you were quick to be defensive about not being defensive."

I bite back a groan and turn back around, Jahlee's laugh a boisterous sound that echoes off the walls. "If he is acting weird, it's probably because he and I were attacked on the way back from Leeta last night."

"What?" she yells, shuffling off the bed and appearing at my side with impressive speed. "You were attacked?"

I nod my head, closing the journal. It dates back to the year before the war started and is the first I've read that was written by one of my direct ancestors. He was close to the queen of Void Magic at the time, Lucia, and his writing of her is full of admiration.

"Tell me everything," Jahlee says, panic lacing her tone.

I relay in detail the moment Kai was poisoned and everything that happened after. Well, almost everything. I omit the parts where I was injured, the wounds now hidden beneath my clothing, and how I wanted to shred Kai apart with my teeth and tongue. But Jahlee has an acuteness that I've never seen with anyone else, and after I'm done talking, she silently stares at me for an uncomfortable amount of time.

"Kai wouldn't have been shaken up by that. He gets death threats daily and has been attacked before," she finally says. I sit back in my chair, folding my arms over my chest to hide how uncomfortable that statement makes me. "Still, I'm glad you were there. Where did you learn to fight like that?"

"Training is accessible to everyone back home."

Jahlee nods her head, her finger twirling in her hair. "Kai trained me how to fight growing up. We should spar together!"

"I don't kno—"

"Come *on*, Bahira! Surely, you want to make my brother suffer?" she asks, leaning forward and wiggling her eyebrows at me.

"First of all, I don't care enough about your brother to make him do *anything*, but second of all, why would us sparring together bother him?"

"Aren't you supposed to be smart?" Her bluntness causes my head to jerk back. When I glare at her, she doubles over in laughter, clutching the thin fabric of her dress as she does. "You really don't know, do you?"

"Jahlee, you're speaking nonsense. Either clarify what you're trying to say or *get out*."

She clasps her hands behind her as she tiptoes around the room like some kind of odd dancer. "Kai likes you."

I scoff, rolling my eyes. "He *tolerates* me for the sake of our deal." And *liking* someone had nothing to do with being attracted to them, which my furiously annoying body clearly indicated. She tilts her head to the side, her overtly mischievous grin making me shift in my seat. "Jahlee, I'm here to help solve the issue with the blight on shifter magic—*your* magic. I'm not here to play games with the king," I assert with a hint of bitterness, one not missed by her.

She shrugs, sauntering towards the side table next to the bed where our breakfast still sits on a carved wooden tray. Popping a piece of fruit into her mouth, she turns around and folds her arms over her chest. "Then do it to help me. I could use the extra training." When I keep my face neutral, intent on keeping our interactions to her helping with the magic blight *only*, she pops out her bottom lip like a petulant offspring. "Fine. Don't help me. *Hopefully*, nothing will happen to me, or you will feel terrible."

Snorting, I stand and walk over to the tray of food, grabbing a flaky pastry filled with a yellow jam. "Just shift if you're in danger. Unless of course your animal form is less than helpful, like a worm or a lizard."

She gasps in mock offense, her hand going to her chest. "Be careful making jokes like that. Some of the males here are *very* sensitive about their animals." Her cunning smile tells me she's absolutely made a joke like that to the wrong male before, and I don't need the details to know that Jahlee came out on top of whatever scuffle ensued.

"What *is* your animal?" I ask around the final bite of my pastry.

Jahlee hums as though she doesn't hear me, my curiosity peaking further. Two knocks sound against the door, and she darts towards it before I can even take my first step.

"Kai! What a *surprise* to find you here. At Bahira's door," she drawls, looking over her shoulder at me. My eyes narrow at her as I avoid looking at the shifter king.

"What are you doing here?" he asks.

"Just hanging out with Bahira. You know, *lady things*." Jahlee winks at me, the motion exaggerated and much too slow. "I'll give you guys space to talk. See you later!" she shouts as she pats Kai's shoulder and waltzes out of the room. He watches her walk away, a semblance of a smile on his lips before it falls when he turns to look at me.

"Your Majesty," I say, dipping my chin and rolling my shoulders back.

"Princess," he replies quietly, eyes boring into my own.

We remain like statues in a garden, unmoving as the sunlight streams between us. Is the memory of our kiss and the frenzy it created plaguing his mind like it does mine? Did he spend the night having to find release by his hand at all, or was that a shame only I carried? Kai is the first to break the spell, opening his mouth like he's going to say something only to give his head a small shake before turning to walk away.

"Why did you come here?" I yell out for him, receiving silence in return.

If there are gods watching over us, then I must have done something to offend them. Because not having magic is torture, but finding myself drawn to Kai? Wanting him so fiercely? *That* is a purgatory I'm not sure even *I* deserve.

Chapter Forty

RHEA

I STAND AT THE end of the hallway, the small wooden door before me illuminated only by the spelled flames in glass bowls attached to the wall.

It's the middle of the night, tortuous dreams once more keeping me from sleep. Tomorrow, Nox will resume his meetings with the council, giving them the manufactured story of what he found in the Mortal Kingdom, how we met, and why he is not going to entertain the idea of a betrothal to Haylee. And I will be left on my own for the first time in this kingdom.

My fingers curl into my palms at my sides as I work my bottom lip between my teeth, my attention falling again to the hidden door in front of me. Stepping forward, I push on the gray striated stone, a creaking sound echoing out. My shoulders rise towards my ears, and though it is impossible, as I stare down into the dark expanse of the winding stone staircase in front of me, I swear that I can hear King Dolian's voice. I can feel his fists meeting my body in heavy swings, my chest rising and falling with the anticipation of the next hit.

"This isn't the tower," I whisper to myself, but I can't get my feet to move. Squeezing my eyes shut, I shake my head like the movement is enough to banish his presence in my mind.

You will earn your title. You are mine.

The pain is piercing when I bite through my lip, the sting jolting me out of the spiral. Gasping, I take a step back and shut the door before leaning my forehead against it.

I had failed earlier when Nox took me on an outing to the city center. It was beautiful and lively, and Nox had done his best to keep us to the outskirts of the busy shopping plaza. As he held my hand tightly, offering kind nods and smiles to the people who passed us, he explained how this place compared to Vitour. While he talked of their differences, I reflected on the fact that he had been *desperate* to go home, and yet for three months, he delayed leaving because of me. Eventually, the smell of something sweet had drawn us into a confectionery shop. A bell chimed as we stepped in, and the sugary citrus scent that hung heavy in the air began to feel stifling. It reminded me of a lemon loaf, and as I stared down at the glass case full of chocolate candies, my hands trembling, I was abruptly pelted with memories of Alexi.

Chocolate creams. Two hands of cards on a chipped white table. *This place, this prison, is not where your journey is to end, Little One.* Icy metal stairs biting into my feet as I followed my uncle down them. Alexi kneeling, beaten between golden guards. And blood—so much blood.

Crying and desperate pleading with my magic to save him. *Save him. Save him.* Cradling his head in my lap and his blood pooling around me, cooling as it soaked into my nightgown. My hair. Never-ending screams wrenched from my throat until no further sound would come.

Nox had recognized what was happening and helped guide me out of the shop and into the forest for privacy. He held me to him, murmuring that it was okay if I needed to fall apart. That he would always be there to help me when I did. His voice to anyone else would sound whisper-soft, but to me, it was a shout down into the void of anguish I was stuck in. In his gentle tone, I heard the guilt that ravaged him.

I had felt fine, and then I wasn't. But I shouldn't be falling apart anymore. I am no longer in the tower, no longer in that kingdom. I am safer than I have ever been, and it has been *months* since Alexi's death. Weeks since we ran. Shouldn't time have been a balm to the wounds by now?

I had failed in the city center just as I am failing now. I fail every time I wake Nox up with my nightmares and have to watch as his guilt is laid bare on his face before he remembers to hide it from me. I fail when I don't live the kind of life I had lost so much to gain.

"Rhea?"

I lift my head up as Nox makes his way towards me, only dressed in his gray sleeping pants. His eyes immediately fall to my lip, the wound already closing but the evidence of what I've done to myself present. He looks to the hidden door next as understanding flattens his mouth and makes him exhale roughly. His hand reaches out to gently tilt my chin up so the light of the flame falls over my face. I look away, shame and defeat making my cheeks burn bright.

"Look at me," he commands, gingerly caressing his thumb over my bottom lip. A tear traces down my cheek, my lashes growing wet, as I slowly force my gaze back to his. "I love you."

"Why?"

His shoulders droop with the question, but his focus never strays from me.

"You could be with anyone—*love* anyone. It doesn't make sense—"

"Rhea," he interjects, sliding his hand until it cradles the back of my head. "There is *only* you. There will only *ever* be you. From this day until I draw in my last breath, my heart beats for you and you alone."

"What if I can't be enough?" I ask, the rasp of my voice harsh. "For you. For *them*. For myself. What if this version of me is all I'll ever be?" Nothing but a barely held together mosaic of grief and despair. That fear is an anxious whisper in the back of my mind that has grown louder since I woke up from the Middle. What if healing—whatever that looks like—isn't something that is possible for me?

Nox takes my hand into his and flattens my palm onto his chest directly over where his heart beats in a steady rhythm. "You *are* enough. You could never change from this exact moment, or you could morph into something new every single night, and you would *be enough*. I would still ache to be at your side. Any and every version of you is one that I want."

My next inhale feels like it hits my lungs more deeply, the vibration of his heartbeat beneath my palm urging my own into a similar cadence. "I want to be worthy of you," I whisper to him, closing my eyes when he wraps his arms around me.

"You are. You always have been, and you always *will* be. To me *and* to them." He says it with so much confidence that it's hard not to let myself feel like maybe it's the truth. "But I can't make you feel it about yourself. Only you can do that."

I deflate against him, my cheek resting on his chest. "I don't know how to do that."

He holds me as seconds turn into minutes, his hands stroking in a soothing pattern over my back. Finally, he says in a soft murmur, "I think that all you can do is try."

Our love story allegedly began in a small town near the Mortal Kingdom's border called Santor. At least, that is what Nox told the council. As for the magical burst they could feel from here, he told them it was a spelled crystal in King Dolian's possession and that he decided it would be safer to destroy it. He left out everything about the King's Guard attacking us at the border, about how my uncle likely assumes him to be mage. I suppose the council would have no way of knowing those things anyway.

The first morning he left to meet with them, I kept to his room, reading and writing in my journal. He came back in the afternoon, and after he had relayed what he told them, we spent the rest of the day in his bed together. It was a fantastic distraction.

The second morning, I attempted, and failed again, to go down the passageway to his secret garden, returning once more to his room where I curled up with a book. Nox led me on a tour around the palace when he returned later that day, his fingers firmly laced with mine as we explored the home he grew up in. I didn't know if it was luck or by design that we hadn't run into any of the council members while out.

Our evenings were spent training with one half of my magic, the darker half constantly pushing against the invisible barrier I was trying to build to snuff it out. Nox was patient in his instruction, my fear of accidentally losing control and letting the shadows out again one that he delicately worked around. I had even tried manipulating an element for the first time, attempting to lift water from a small stream that runs through the forest behind the palace. Controlling my magic so precisely was a struggle, and I'm not entirely sure more than a few droplets of water rose from my efforts.

Nox at least lets me keep the pendant on when we are outside, his gentle words coaxing me to take it off once we enter his room again. It wasn't that I didn't understand the importance of learning to control at least *part* of this magic without the safety of his blanketing me. It was that I felt so *disconnected* from that side of me as a whole that I didn't *like* feeling it so strongly.

I can also admit that I am frightened by it—by its strength and the way it seems to grow stronger with each passing day. I fear the darkness that lurks within me and how it might seep out when my guard is down. Despite Nox's warning, this is one subject I refuse to yield on. Maybe once I had more control, I would tackle learning how to wield that *death* magic. So each day he leaves to visit the council, I practice using my light magic while he's gone.

Despite the way tension lingers on him when he returns from the meetings, he is sweet in his encouragement of me, reminding me that with the dragon pendant on, I can explore anywhere I want without drawing attention to myself. That everyone knows who I am to him and this knowledge brings its own level of protection for me.

I am no longer confined to a prison of stone or behind guards with blood oaths. The only person stopping me from living a life I want is *myself*, but I can't seem to get out of my own way. Each attempt I make at stepping past the threshold of Nox's room is met with my breath seizing in my chest and my hands growing clammy.

Even now, I stand in front of his door with my fingers reaching towards the handle, unable to close the distance. Dropping my hand back to my side, I huff out a breath and tilt my head back to look up towards the ceiling. *Try*. It's a word I keep coming back to, one that Selene said to me in the Middle, that Nox had said might be the only way forward. *Just try*. Such an annoyingly simple thing that felt unfathomably difficult to do.

Grinding my teeth, I lower my gaze back to the door. "Try," I whisper to myself. "For them. For Nox." Reaching for the handle again, my fingers grip and twist it, the door opening as I pull it towards myself. "For them. For Nox."

My heartbeat quickens, rattling around my ribcage as I force myself to move. One step. Then two. I practically leap past the threshold, quickly shutting the door. The gold of my bracelet glints beneath a spelled flame, catching my eye. *For Alexi*. With my stomach in knots, I take another step, the soles of my flats quiet against the rug that runs the entire length of the hallway.

Rooms filled with elegant furniture that look like they are meant for friends to gather in glide by in my periphery, but I don't stop to truly look at them. I'm afraid that if I do, I might not be able to keep going.

There's a guard who stands at the end of the hall whose name I had learned is Barron. "Hello, Lady Rhea," he says, dipping his head as his hands clasp behind his back. "Can I assist you with anything today?" His light gray eyes look kind, and the dark brown skin around them crinkles when he smiles.

"I don't know," I reply, clearing my throat when he cocks his head to the side. "I mean, I think I'm going to just go for a walk around the palace."

He surprises me when he asks, "Do you need a guide?" Shifting his position so that his body isn't blocking the stairs anymore, his dark leather armor creaks quietly with the movement.

A guide would be nice, and it would ensure that I don't get lost, but I know that I need to do this alone. Nox said my healing wouldn't be a linear thing, that I might take one step forward and three steps back, over and over again. Eventually, I have to hope that the steps forward will outnumber the steps back. I have to keep *trying*.

"No, thank you," I answer, tucking the loose strands from my ponytail back behind my ears.

"Then I hope you have fun. Should you ever need anything, please don't hesitate to ask," he replies, stepping back a little more to give me space to pass.

I study Barron's features more thoroughly, noting the small strands of gray that are woven into his braids, white also showing in the short beard on his broad jaw. He's an older guard, perhaps somewhere around Alexi's age. I swallow against the sudden burning in my throat. Noting my hesitancy, he holds his hand out, an offer to help me get to the first step. It eases a little of that churning anguish within me. Feeling a little more settled, I continue down the stairs, another guard stationed at its base offering me a tight-lipped smile when I pass.

The foyer to the palace is bustling, and I watch as mages carry trays of fresh food or folded laundry to one of the many other corridors. Others hold conversations with each other while some disappear around corners that Nox had shown me—but that I'm sure I cannot navigate again on my own.

My steps are tentative as I grip onto the light green-colored fabric of my dress, the wide doors of the palace entrance growing larger as I near them. I hadn't studied the carvings on them before, and without any sort of plan now that I'm out of Nox's room, I let my gaze roam over their details.

A tree is depicted, the middle of it perfectly split where the doors open. The tree's trunk is wide and nearly limbless, except for at the very top where branches stretch out in all directions. The roots mirror the branches, growing near the base of the doors and out to their hinges.

Above the canopy of the tree, the carvings look like small "x"s stacked on top of each other in opposite directions. No... Not "x"s. *Stars.* They are carved stars, big and small, made to look like they are flickering. My eyes track to the top right, where a crescent moon is depicted, and then to the left, where a sun with wavy flares sits in exact opposition.

A chill blooms across my skin as I suck in a sharp inhale. "Look to the east and trust the stars over the ancient trees," I murmur to myself.

It is no coincidence that I am here, in this kingdom specifically. Selene couldn't alter my fate, but I realize that she tried to guide me in her own way. I was always *meant* to be here, perhaps even meant to be with Nox. My fingers ease their hold on my dress as the notion that I'm right where I'm supposed to be begins to etch its way into my mind.

With my confidence now higher than when I stepped off of the stairs, I turn and make my way to the one place where I might already have a new friend waiting for me.

I go to see Elora in the palace library.

Chapter Forty-One

RHEA

ELORA HUFFS A BREATH while setting another stack of gathered books onto the desk, shaking the tiered tray of cookies. When I questioned the tray with a raised brow, she had lamented that, "It isn't a proper book club meeting without treats and drinks!" I am not complaining though, as the cookies are some of the most divine I have ever tasted.

"I can't believe you've never had chocolate chip cookies before," she says, dotting the corners of her mouth with a white napkin after taking a bite of the sweet. "They *are* the most basic ones."

I find Elora easy to talk with, her demeanor one that makes up for the lull in conversation that sometimes occurs in my presence. I don't want to lie to her, but I know that for my safety—and Nox's too—I can't tell anyone the truth of where I come from. Of who is likely still searching for me and willing to do whatever it takes to get me back.

"I was very sheltered growing up. This is the first time I've had tea too."

"*What?*" Elora's voice echoes out into the quiet library, making Rayna sigh in exasperation as her gaze meets ours over the top of her book.

"Libraries are to be enjoyed in silence, you two. If you must talk, then do so *quietly*." The wrinkles around her eyes deepen as she squints them at us. I'm fairly convinced the only person she actually likes is Nox.

"Sorry," we both murmur at the same time.

"What are your parents like?" Elora asks, taking a not-so-delicate gulp of tea.

I suppose I don't have to lie to her about this at least. "I didn't know them. They died after I was born," I say quietly, taking a quick sip of tea. Elora's less refined drinking makes me not as anxious about my own, though my fingers tighten around the mug when the memory of my uncle bringing tea to the tower flashes briefly in my mind.

"Oh, Rhea. I'm so sorry. My parents drive me absolutely crazy, but I don't know what I would do without them." We sit in amiable silence for a moment before Elora perks up in her chair. "What is your family name? You said you're from Santor, right?"

Nox and I had discussed changing my last name in an overabundance of caution. Nothing official, just a name that I could tell anyone who asked. Since my lying skills are unrefined and terrible, I chose one that I am already familiar with. "Yes, and it's Selene."

Elora quickly scribbles something on a sheet of paper attached to her leather-bound notepad before she rips it out and then stuffs it into the drawer of the desk. Leaning back in her chair, her gray eyes swirl with mischief before she blinks it away and a playful smile curls her lips.

"So, I have to ask, what's it like dating Prince Nox? It's been quite the gossip since he announced he's officially courting someone. There are quite a few wallowing ladies now that he's unavailable." My cheeks heat at her question as I do my best to feign nonchalance with a small shrug and a bite of cookie. I may be inexperienced, but I'm not blind. I had caught both sexes ogling Nox on our few excursions out. "Oh, come *on,* Rhea! You have to give me something. You are dating a prince! Your story is like a fairytale come to life!" She emphasizes her point by lifting the top book from her stack on the desk and waving it in front of my face.

I laugh and grab the book from her, pretending to read its cover as I trace my finger along its silver-embossed edges. "What do you want to know?"

"*Everything!* Anything. When was your first kiss? Is he a good kisser? He looks like he'd be a *very* good kisser," she says, wiggling her eyebrows as she leans forward.

"He… is a *very* good kisser," I answer before immediately hiding my face with the book.

Elora cackles quietly, so as not to draw another reprimand from Rayna. "I knew he would be. You can't look *that* good and not be. Though good looks *do* run in the entire family. Have you *seen* the king?" She fans her face with her hand as she looks off into the distance wistfully.

"He looks like an older version of Nox."

When her gaze comes back to my questioning one, she smirks. "Exactly." My laugh is loud before I cover my mouth, avoiding Rayna's stare burning into the side of my face. "What? I like older men. Anyway, let's talk about *The Assassin and The Queen*. Which chapter was your favorite?"

Glad for the subject change, I share my thoughts on the latest book I had read at her recommendation. The afternoon passes quickly as we chat and clear out the cookies and tea. Talking to Elora comes easily, her bubbly personality balancing out my own quieter one. I take a look at the stack of books she pulled for me, my fingers running over the spine of the last one.

"What is this?" I ask, tapping the red leather spine with the words *The Mage Kingdom: Life Before The War Of Five Kingdoms.*

"*That* is one of my favorite history books," she trills. At the look on my face, she holds a placating hand out in front of her. "I know, I know. You said you don't like history books, but this one is less about boring facts and more about personal accounts. It was written the year directly following the casting of the Spell and compares what life was like before and after the war."

"Besides the kingdoms not being separated, was life so different then?" I ask, remembering the details in the history tome I read with Bella all those months ago.

"Yes and no. Most of the daily stuff was the same, except you might walk into a tavern and be met with mages, fae, and mortals. Especially here in Galdr. It is fascinating to read about. There are even firsthand accounts of people who had family members living with them one minute and then gone the next after the Spell was cast."

"How did it happen?"

Elora leans forward, her elbows resting on the desk. "While not *overly* common, there *were* beings who fell in love from different kingdoms. Their offspring would then have been born with only one of their parents' magical traits. Like in my family, if you go back to right before the war, one of my ancestors married a mortal. Their child was born without mage magic of any kind. When the Spell went up, both the child and their father disappeared. Weeks later, a letter arrived to my mage ancestor from her husband. The father and child were now bound to the Mortal Kingdom. When it was revealed that mages could pass through the Spell without repercussion, she was left to choose joining them and abandoning everyone and everything she knew, or staying. She chose the former, sneaking out before the king at the time declared that mages should not do such a thing."

I suppose I didn't think about how the Spell could have separated families in this way. "So you have family in the Mortal Kingdom, then?" I ask.

Elora nods. "Not that I'll ever know them."

"Besides your parents, do you have any other family?"

She shakes her head, her fingers twirling one of the magical pens that are always spelled to work in her hand. "Nope, it's just the three of us." Her brow creases as a look of longing crosses her face. "I think about it sometimes. How nice it might be to find more family. How there could be a distant cousin my age somewhere in the Mortal Kingdom."

I always assumed that I felt so alone and incomplete because I never knew my parents and never had the opportunity to be able to form any friendships. Yet Elora had those freedoms, and still, she seems as hungry for those connections as I am.

"Have you ever gone dancing at a tavern?" she asks abruptly, changing the subject. When I shake my head, her eyes widen in surprise. "We *must* go together, then! The cider mead at my favorite tavern is *delicious*, and we can dance to a live band!"

"I don't know what cider mead is, but yes, I would like that." My chuckle at the renewed look of shock on her face is interrupted when my magic rushes up from my abdomen as if answering to a beacon. I grip onto the dragon pendant, my brows drawing together in confusion, but a moment later, Nox rounds a bookshelf, his hands tucked into the pockets of his black trousers. His eyes meet mine, and I have to actively focus on breathing as I watch him near. Is it possible that he's gotten more muscular? Somehow more handsome?

"You guys are adorable," Elora whispers, causing me to break eye contact with Nox to look her way. "You should tell him to grow his hair out like his father's." My hand flies to my mouth as Nox reaches the desk.

"Should I be offended that the two of you are laughing right as I arrive?" he asks, bending down to kiss the top of my head.

"Not at all, Your Highness. Rhea has said nothing but good things about you," Elora croons, giving me a quick wink before standing and sliding the stack of books towards Nox.

His eyebrow draws up as he looks at me. "Merely good? I guess I'll have to try harder."

I think I might be imagining the seduction that flows off his tongue when he speaks, but a quick glance at Elora's widening smile tells me I'm not.

"I'll see you soon?" she asks as Nox grabs the books.

"Yes," I confirm, giving her a small wave and turning to walk out at Nox's side. He glances down at me, his gaze lingering on my mouth as we walk. "What is it?" My fingers trace over my lips, assuming I must have remnants of the cookies on them.

"It's just good to see you smiling, Sunshine."

I kiss his arm before wrapping my hand around it, giving the muscles there a little squeeze. "Was your visit with the council alright?"

Nox heaves out an exaggerated exhale. "They are eager to see me returning to my heir apparent duties. I have a feeling these meetings are only going to increase in frequency. There have been some disturbances that my father is growing more concerned over in some towns bordering the Fae Kingdom." His brows draw together, like he can see whatever those disturbances are off in the distance. Clearing his throat, he blinks the look away and catches my gaze with his. "I'm sorry, Rhea. I truly hoped that I would be eased back into these things so that I would have more time to properly show you around."

"I understand."

Nox smiles as his eyes trace over me before he leans down to kiss the side of my head.

"Do we have any other plans for today? Or can I dive into one of these books," I question, looking eagerly at a green leather-bound book in the middle of the pile that Elora spent fifteen minutes raving about.

"About that," he drawls, using his back to push open the door to the palace library. We turn to the right, walking down a hallway lined with large paintings on both sides. He opens his mouth to continue when a different voice echoes from farther down.

"Hello, Blondie. I heard you are ready to train."

The training grounds are teeming with magic so thick that it's hard to concentrate. The open field filled with thick blades of dark green grass, rolling hills and valleys and small ponds and mud pits dotted throughout, looks as if the finger of a large deity pushed the forest out of the way to make this spot. Trees line the oval-shaped perimeter, the canopied forest left in darkness compared to how brightly the unfiltered sun casts its rays over the open ground. It's beautiful in an unexpected way, and I was grateful when Nox and Cassius didn't bring attention to the audible gasp I made when we first arrived.

On the walk here, Cassius was all jokes and teasing energy as he recounted stories from his and Nox's youth. I wasn't sure if I had ever laughed as hard as I did when he told me about the time they drunkenly bet each other that they could catch a thrown dagger mid-air. Nox ended up slicing his palm deeply, and Cassius had bumped the dagger from its flight path only for the tip of it to slice into the skin at his temple. He had been too drunk to realize it and passed out before healing the wound, so a faint scar now permanently memorialized that night. The teasing mood is gone now though, Cassius' face instead set seriously from where he watches me a few feet away.

Nox's foot taps the inside of my ankle, encouraging me to widen my stance. "Good, Sunshine. Now, keep your knees bent so you have the ability to pivot and move at any moment." His hands rest on my shoulders, slowly sliding down my arms. "Keep these muscles relaxed and lift your guard like I showed you."

I, pathetically, am already huffing, my body coated in sweat under my new training clothes. I had thought Nox might choose to skip training for physical movement of a different kind when he first saw me in them, but after forcing himself to look away from me as he mumbled something under his breath, he turned back around, quickly braided my long hair, and stiffly led us out of his room. Cassius met us at the bottom of the stairs, whistling at me before breaking out into laughter at whatever look was on Nox's face.

Nox walks in front of me, assessing my form thoroughly, like if I fail, the blame will fall to him. "These first few weeks will be about building up your muscle and stamina and learning the different defensive and offensive positions we call Forms. After that—"

"Nox? Nox, is that you?" a female voice shouts from behind as two silhouettes crest a small hill and begin making their way towards us. Their features become more distinguishable as they near, the golden light of the sun making the woman's dark blonde hair glow, her pretty strands braided into a coronet around her head. She wears training clothes like my own—a white form-fitting, short-sleeved top over body-hugging black leggings. Matching black boots go up her calves as well. The man next to her is near Cassius' height with short brown hair and a training outfit of all black, similar to Nox's.

"It *is* you. Welcome home." She throws her arms around Nox's neck, barreling into his body so hard that he's forced to take a step back as they laugh.

"Hey, Haylee. It's good to see you," he responds, reciprocating her hug.

Haylee. The faintest sensation of bitter cold seeps out of the hold I keep on my magic, strong enough to be felt even with the pendant on. *Stupid envious magic*, I curse internally, trying to tamp it back down. I cannot feel *jealous* when there is nothing to be jealous about. Yet, even with those rational thoughts floating in my mind, they are denied the ability to take root when Haylee drags her hand slowly down Nox's arm, her fingers curling around his bicep.

"Your magic is flaring, Blondie. Take a deep breath," Cassius whispers from my side, a gentle hand coming to rest on my shoulder.

I follow his instructions, my ears ringing as Haylee and Nox talk. *Get yourself under control.*

"Daje, glad to see you out and about. Done wallowing now?" The man that came with Haylee looks at Cassius, his deep blue eyes flickering as his lips narrow into a flat line. "Daje here is in love with Nox's sister," Cassius adds on for my benefit.

"Cass," Daje warns, his tawny skin growing pink at his cheeks. Cassius shrugs, his hand sliding off of my shoulder when he feels me take a deeper breath. Daje's eyes bounce from me to Cassius and back again before he extends his hand out in front of me. "I don't think we've met before. I'm Daje."

"I'm Rhea. It's nice to meet you."

His hand is warm around mine, his grasp firm as he gives me a tight-lipped smile. His gaze then goes over my shoulder and up, his hand releasing mine right as Nox rests his own on my back.

"Rhea, I want you to meet Haylee. Haylee, this is Rhea." She steps up next to Daje, my head tilting back so I can meet her gaze.

"Ah, so *this* is the woman who has stolen our prince's heart. A feat no one else can claim if rumors are to be believed."

Daje and Cassius chuckle, but I stiffen at that term—*stolen*. As if Nox did not return my affections and instead was forced to be with me.

"She can't steal what is laid at her feet."

I turn back to look at Nox, my chest flooding with relief at him voicing thoughts similar to my own. Without regard to the small gathering around us, he leans down to kiss me, and everything settles at his touch—the ringing in my ears, the magic writhing beneath my skin, my rapidly beating heart. All answering swiftly to his claiming display. When we break apart, Nox's eyes speak promises of what will come later once we're alone in his room.

"Well, I'm not sure I'll ever get *that* image out of my mind," Cassius teases with a scowl.

My eyes can't help but draw back to Haylee, expecting to see confusion or perhaps even anger given her earlier comment. But her face looks *serene*. As if the attitude I thought was there earlier was imagined.

"You act as if we haven't all had to live through your many public displays with your various lovers," Nox replies, his arm wrapping around my waist.

"Nox missed the spring of Bastian. You both might as well have shared a single shirt for how often you were fused together," Daje chimes in, crossing his muscular arms over his chest.

"Then there was screaming Sorina," Haylee recounts smoothly, causing Cassius to shudder.

"Why was she *screaming* Sorina?" Nox asks.

"Because if they weren't fighting, they were fucking, or close to it, in very public places," she replies, giving Cassius a pointed look.

He shrugs, clasping his hands behind his back. "I suppose you should be glad you weren't here for that one, Nox. She would have tried to convince you to have a threesome with us." He pauses, looking me over as his lip curls up. "A foursome, actually. Not saying I would necessarily have been *opposed* to that—"

"You would fuck anything that welcomed it," Daje cuts in as Nox's hand flexes on my hip.

Cassius chuckles, sending a wink in his direction. "Except you."

"Then it is good that I don't fucking *welcome* it."

I listen quietly as the group continues playfully arguing with each other, my body leaning back against Nox's in comfort. They laugh and talk with the familiarity of friends who have known one another for ages. I'd be remiss not to admit to myself that I'm jealous of that—of the bonds they've formed and the history they have. Even with Nox and Cassius including me in the conversation, I doubt I will ever have the ease that they do while speaking with each other.

After a while, Daje and Haylee say goodbye, and Cassius and Nox go back to introducing me to fighting stances and defensive maneuvers. By the time the sun begins to set, my leg muscles are completely useless. When I express how sore I am, Nox places his hands on my thighs, the feel of his magic sinking into me immediately easing my pain.

"You know I can heal myself," I remind him.

He shrugs before wrapping his arm around me. "Any chance I have to take care of you, I will take."

We part ways with Cassius as we walk back to the palace, and my gaze wanders to the thickly wooded forest, the greens and blues of the leaves around and above us never ceasing to cause a wondrous feeling to bloom inside of me. I lean in closer to Nox, my arm going around his waist. He has felt like home to me for a while, but this is the first moment that the Mage Kingdom feels like it could be home for me too. Like I truly can have a future full of the things I missed out on living in that tower.

Part Three

Wanting to fall to my knees should be a foreign feeling—something only reserved for my crown and my kingdom. But she rules above them all, a goddess that shines brighter than any star, and I crave to surrender only to her.

Chapter Forty-Two

BAHIRA

I TAP MY PEN on the table in the experiment room, my other hand cradling my head as I look over my notes. There doesn't seem to be any discernible traits between any of the shifters that are stuck in their animal forms. Huffing out a breath, my chair scrapes against the wood floor as I push it back and stand, stretching my arms overhead. I head out into the hall and down the stairs, making my way to the courtyard behind the palace for some fresh air.

A few marble statues dot around its border, and I follow a stone path that is cut into the grass to the first one. My fingers trace along its gray and white edges—the bust is that of a male with a broad chin and a crown similar to the one Kai wore at the dinner to honor his father. Leaning closer, I inspect the image carved on the bust's shoulder. It's an animal of some sort with an elongated face, and horns protruding from its head that strike recognition in me.

"Bahira! There you are!" Jahlee's voice startles me as I jolt back from the statue, my hand flying to my chest.

"Fuck, *Jahlee*," I rasp, earning a laugh from her as she walks towards me.

"Why are you studying Kai's great-grandfather so intently?" She lifts a brow, the sun gleaming over her wavy brown hair and the cream and gold dress that wraps nearly sheer fabric strategically around her body, ending right above her knees.

"This is his ancestor?"

She nods, her sandals scuffing against the stone as she attempts to link her arm with mine. I step to the side, sliding away from her and earning a snort. "It is. I keep telling Kai to let the palace sculptor carve a bust of him, but it's like he doesn't want himself memorialized here at all."

I can't say that I'm exactly surprised by that. Kai doesn't strike me as the type of male who cares about that sort of thing. My focus goes back to the carved animal. "What is this?" I ask, pointing to it.

"An oryx. It used to be the old Crown's sigil before Kai's father changed it to the wolf."

An oryx. It isn't an animal I'm familiar with, certainly not one I have read about dwelling in the Mage Kingdom. Why would the rebels wear the skull of an animal associated with the family of the very king they are trying to overthrow?

"You look like you're thinking too hard about something," Jahlee teases, poking my arm. I send her a glare, which just makes her laugh again as she successfully loops an arm around mine and squeezes tightly.

"What are you—"

"*We* are going shopping," she interrupts, tugging at my arm. My feet stay rooted to the ground making her huff out in annoyance.

"*No*, we aren't." With my interest in the rebels once more renewed, all I want to do is ask Kai his thoughts. Or Tua even—if Kai finds that he doesn't want to be in my presence anymore after what happened between us.

"Okay, look. It has been a while since I left the palace grounds during the day. Kai prefers that I go with guards, but it makes me stand out when I do that. He won't get mad, however, if he finds out you are with me."

I level a flat look at her. "Jahlee, I sincerely doubt that he can keep you confined here."

"He can't. Which is why I emphasized that it's been a while since I left the palace during the *day*." Her eyebrows wiggle suggestively at me, and the corners of my mouth can't help but quirk up in response.

"Sneaking out at night? Should I be offended you've never offered to bring me along?"

Jahlee laughs, tugging on my arm and making me relent my stance in staying put. "I thought about it, but I didn't want to interrupt if you and my brother were fucking."

I swing my head in her direction as we climb the steps back into the palace and walk over the black and white checkered floors towards the front entrance. "You don't have to worry about that."

She merely hums in response and then changes the subject to palace gossip. I half listen as we make our way towards Molsi, the other half of my brain pondering the rebels. By the time the city comes into view, I've heard enough about who is fucking who out in the open and who Jahlee believes to be fucking in private. She guides us down different rows of vendors, her confident gait familiar with wherever it is we are going. She doesn't garner as many stares as her brother does, but those who do look seem to share the same animosity about her. Their judgment of her, of Kai, begins to eat at me like an exposed nerve being repeatedly prodded at. Jahlee doesn't seem at all affected by it, her steps light as she keeps her arm linked with my own.

"What can you tell me about Tua?" I ask out of the blue, interrupting her ramblings after the third clothing shop we stop in.

Her eyes dart to mine briefly before she turns them back out to the crowd ahead of us. "What do you want to know?"

"Do you think he is a good advisor? Does Kai listen to him?"

"I think he enjoys running the kingdom *for* Kai. I think he likes striking doubt into my brother's confidence," she answers, her voice low as her fingers curl in towards my arm. "And this isn't a good time to talk about it."

I follow her focus, my gaze meeting the brown eyes of Kane. His eyes flare wide before they relax, and he gives us a stiff wave. Jahlee scoffs, lifting a hand and flipping her middle finger at him before tugging me between two vendor carts.

"Come on, let's finish our shopping and get home."

Standing in front of a large mirror, I admire the way I look. After returning from our shopping trip, Jahlee had informed me that we would be having dinner together. I went to protest, but her eyes sparkled with a defiance that told me that trying to deny her would be useless. She had also insisted that we *match* in some way with our outfits and pulled out the clothing she bought today for us to try on.

Jahlee chose a plum-colored shirt and skirt set, her top barely cinching in beneath her breasts and her skirt sitting low on her hips and flowing down to her ankles. I opted to wear the style of pants she had donned during the dinner party honoring Kai's father. They are maroon in color and sheer from the ankle up, gradually shifting to more opaque the closer they get to my upper thigh. Long slits from my hip to where they cinch in at my ankles split the rich fabric on the outside of my legs, making it so that a large expanse of my skin shows with each step. My top is slightly longer than Jahlee's, with thin straps that go over my shoulders. The entire ensemble has gold accents laced around the edges and chains that droop over my exposed stomach in a scallop pattern.

I have never done anything like this with Haylee, shopping and getting ready together. *Matching* our outfits. I consider her my best friend, one that I told nearly everything to. Yet, reflecting back, we only ever spent time together during training or on a random trip to the tavern for drinks. Rarely had she ever initiated our outings either.

"We are ready, and we look *incredible*," Jahlee sings from behind me.

Smirking, I turn and grab my sandals, slipping them on before we leave. The entire second floor is noisy and filled with people dressed in fine clothing attending to whatever engagements they have. I'm surprised when Jahlee leads us past the stairs and farther into the fray of nobility in the west wing.

"We're eating dinner here?"

"There is something I want you to see," she answers, narrowly avoiding a male with broad shoulders who looks like he purposefully stepped into her path.

A flicker of anger sparks within me at the disrespect. I blow out a steady breath and lengthen my stride so that I'm walking beside her, a feat hard to do with how many people fill the hallway.

"Bastard's sister." This hissed insult comes from a passing female with short onyx hair and a black tattoo that crawls up her neck.

Jahlee's steps halt before she twists around, a frightening smile plastered on her face. "How incredibly original. Did it take you long to come up with that?"

The female bares her teeth, her fingers flexing like claws as she takes a step towards Jahlee—a male and female flanking her sides. Her muscles are firm beneath the chiffon fabric of her silver sleeves, the delicate finery completely at odds with her aggressive stance. I brace myself, my gaze traveling over the trio as I assess them.

"Enjoy your freedom while you can, you pathetic stray. The gods can only hope you and your *mongrel* brother get what's coming to you."

Jahlee goes preternaturally still as her eyes bore into the female. Goosebumps sprinkle the skin on her arms, and I hold my breath as I wait for her to shift. Tension warms the air, the atmosphere so charged that I worry one more anxious second will set it ablaze.

"What's going on here?" Kane shouts as he pushes his way through the crowd lingering to watch the exchange. He has one hand stuffed into his pocket, his gait bordering on a pretentious swagger.

"I am just reminding Jahlee of her and her brother's place."

"You do know that threatening a member of the royal family is a criminal offense, right, Lady Apa?" Kane replies as he steps between Jahlee and the other female. He stares her down, her gaze morphing from unfettered fury to knowing resignation. With a huff, she sends Jahlee and I one more menacing glower and then turns to leave, her retinue following.

"What are you doing here, *Kane*?" Jahlee demands with a scowl as she clenches and unclenches her hands.

"You're welcome for that," he chides, ignoring her question and turning to face her fully.

"Did you forget that it's summer, or did daddy not help you dress today?" Her eyes draw down his body in a scathing manner, taking in his blue tunic with the sleeves going to his wrists while the center buttons are undone halfway down his torso. He wears it over dark trousers and laced-up boots, the latter of which are flaked with dried mud.

"Watch it," he fumes, taking a step towards her until there's hardly any space between them. Jahlee holds firm, tipping her chin up to look at him. "Your brother isn't here to protect you."

"Enough," I snap, shoving my shoulder between them. "We have a dinner we need to get to."

Kane scoffs, his gaze lingering on my lips before meeting my own. "Interesting that you would stand up for them."

Jahlee laughs, the discordant sound like the smashing of piano keys. "*Interesting* that your master gave you such a long leash today. Run along, little kitty. I'm sure you've got some bitch work to attend to."

Oh, fucking gods. Grabbing Jahlee's elbow, I push her forward past Kane right as he makes a noise that echoes out deep and throaty, rattling the glass sconces on the walls. Gesturing for her to lead us to dinner, I wait until we are far enough away before I ask, "What the hell happened back there?"

She tries to flash me a grin, but it doesn't hold the same levity as her usual ones. "I stood up for Kai, that's what happened."

"Okay, and what about with Kane? He was just trying to diffuse the situation."

She barks out a short laugh as she shakes her head. "No, he wasn't. He wants everyone to think he's some diplomatic dignitary, floating about between the people and the Crown and relaying what both need to the other. But the truth is, he's just an asshole."

I snort, glancing at her. "That sounds like your brother."

Her finger digs into my chest as she steps in front of me and snaps, *"Don't fucking say that. They are nothing* alike." Anger burns in her eyes, the soft brown color deepening with it. Slowly, I wrap my hand around her wrist and gently pull her finger away from me. Jahlee goes lax, the tension seeping from her nearly as quickly as it came. "I'm sorry. It's just, *no one* looks beyond Kai's façade. *No one* gives him the chance to prove that he cares, that he is doing the best that he can. Kai *genuinely* wants to help our people. He just doesn't know how."

The guilt that previously sparked within me flares again as I release Jahlee. "Why do so many hate Kai? Why call him a *usurper?*"

Jahlee studies me thoroughly, weighing her answer for a long while before she decides that whatever she has to say is safe with me. "I'm only sharing this because part of the story involves me. Do not ask me for more details than I give you. Kai should be the one to relay the story fully." A line forms between my brows, but I dip my chin in acknowledgement. "Kai was all but *forced* to become king. His father called him to the palace under the guise of wanting to speak to him about our mother. But when Kai arrived, he forced him into the ceremony to become the next successor to the throne. He used me as collateral, threatening to kill me if Kai didn't go through with the ritual."

Her eyes drop away from mine, guilt ravaging her features so thoroughly that I swallow down any of my follow up questions. "Thank you, Jahlee, for telling me." I feel ridiculous offering the words, but something within me twists at the way the weight of that night, of what Kai was forced to do, seems to crush her. We return to walking when something she said to Kane snags my attention. "What did you mean about Kane having a master?"

Jahlee rolls her shoulders back and lifts her chin. "I was talking about Tua."

"Tua? Does he advise Kane as well?" If so, that seems like a flagrant conflict of interest. I don't even know what Kane's official title is, but how could Kai allow his advisor to also work with the man who was *supposed* to be king?

"Tua is Kane's father."

Chapter Forty-Three

BAHIRA

I shoot Jahlee a disbelieving look as we approach guarded double doors, their edges gilded in gold. "So Kane is Kai's cousin by blood?"

Him being tapped as the next king makes more sense, and I'm embarrassed I didn't put it together sooner. With Tua being Kai's uncle, the line of succession would have had no choice but to continue with Kane before Kai was born. Though I still don't understand what exactly happened in Kai's early years, like why he didn't grow up in the palace, I *do* find it curious that neither Tua nor Kai mentioned Kane's relation to them.

Jahlee nods as she links arms with me, but the move feels less like a gesture between friends and more like she's ensuring I don't flee. The reason why is clear when the guards open the doors and we step into the dining space. Tua, Kai, and a handful of other shifters all sit at a long table, their attention snapping to us as we enter.

I clench my teeth together and ask with a whisper, "What the *fuck* is this?"

Though flame gems light the perimeter of the large dining room, pillar candles run in a line down the center of the table, casting the shifters' faces in moving shadows.

"Bahira, Jahlee, what a surprise," Tua says as he stands from his seat, one hand holding a glass chalice of what looks to be wine.

My gaze connects with Kai's as Jahlee drags me towards the table, the look he gives me one that radiates his displeasure at our arrival. Jahlee pulls out the chair directly to Kai's left from where he is seated at the head of the table, acting as if she is going to take it before she quickly darts to the one next to it. "Bahira, you can sit here," she gestures to the seat that is now half pulled out.

Not willing to get sucked further into her antics, I take the chair to her left instead. On Kai's right is Tua, along with every other guest at this dinner, leaving Jahlee and I alone on this side of the table. The split of seats feels significant, and I eye each person carefully before leaning back against my chair.

"Jahlee, I was not aware you would be joining us tonight, let alone with Bahira," Kai states before taking a drink, his eyes half lit with a small golden ring around his irises.

"Oh, Brother. Surely, I told you? If it slipped my mind, many apologies. I just wanted the opportunity for us to spend more time with Bahira."

I stiffen as Kai's eyes flash towards me, his grip tightening on his cup. White plates filled with roasted chicken and vegetables are brought out and placed in front of us by the staff, as well as baskets of buttery rolls and more bottles of wine.

Tua's jaw tenses before he takes his seat again, clearing his throat and gesturing with a hand to the people next to him. "Let me introduce Kai's most trusted court. This is Sir Duarte and his wife, Lady Aisha. They are the Crown's Master of Coin."

My brow arches at that—a husband and wife in charge of where the Crown's money goes is *interesting*. Lady Aisha wears a glittering dress that looks to be pure diamonds sewn onto nude fabric. The jewels wrap around her neck, only to cascade down over her body in a waterfall-like fashion. Her husband's outfit is less reflective, but the satin sheen of his dark blue tunic indicates one of expensive quality. They both have the same golden-tan skin as Kai, but their hair is a rich black.

"Next to them is Sir Adrian, our Master of Sail. He's in charge of all ships coming in and out of port as well as *others* that are currently stationary."

I smirk, unable to help myself at the hidden meaning behind his words. Interesting that he should allude to the fact that they have warships to the one being at this table not of this kingdom. "You needn't censor yourself on my behalf. I'm well aware of what types of ships dock in these waters," I can't help but reply.

Sir Adrian's expression remains deadpan, his dark eyes cast in shadows from the candles. Even his midnight outfit plays into his gloomy disposition.

The corner of Tua's mouth lifts marginally though his eyes hold mine in subtle warning. "Lady Miranda is our Master of Laws, ensuring all are followed as well as putting new ones into place as the need arises," he continues.

She lifts her drink in greeting, the only one of the three positions introduced that offers a genuinely warm smile. Her deep purple dress is accented with silver chains that crisscross down her body tightly, highlighting every curve. Instead of the common dark brown or black hair I've seen here, hers is a lovely white. It cascades over one shoulder in a thickly woven plait.

Tua continues down the line, naming the rest of the shifters with influential roles to the Crown while Kai remains stiff in his seat.

"Bahira, are you enjoying the capital? Tua tells us that you've come from Honna to work on a special research project for His Majesty. It must be quite a change to go from a mud village like that to the beauty of Molsi," Lady Aisha asks, dripping with as much disdain as there are jewels that decorate her dress.

Jahlee bristles next to me, the hand she rests on the table curling inward. The knowledge that she is not technically royal and did not grow up in the palace makes me wonder if perhaps Jahlee is from that village, if *Kai* is. I expect a quip or sharp remark in response, but Jahlee only shifts uncomfortably in her chair.

"The capital is lovely," I say, adopting my most practiced royal voice, "but so is the entire island. I have not been in one place that didn't absolutely take my breath away."

Lady Aisha guffaws, stabbing a piece of chicken with her fork. "If you say so."

The rest of the meal is just as tense and awkward, a vocal few asking questions that are thinly veiled insults to those that do not reside in the capital. Politics back home aren't quite this hostile, at least from the bits I have witnessed. Yes, there are moments when the council members argue and even raise their voices, but my father has always stayed firm in the belief that having an echo chamber full of yes-men is beneficial to no one. Observing the way the members of Kai's court all sit together on Tua's side, I wonder if the chamber is full of blind agreement not for their king but the advisor that sits to his right instead.

"Jahlee, it has been ages since I've seen you at one of these fine dinners. One might think you do not support your brother," Sir Duarte says, the cruel shape of his lips matched by his wife's.

Jahlee shrugs, but the movement is half-hearted. "I have been busy."

He laughs boisterously at that, the sound making me wince.

"Enough," Kai booms, his voice shaking the glassware on the table.

Sir Duarte tempers his impish chuckle, but his eyes still gleam with malicious intent. Everyone's attention draws to him when he muses, "It isn't like you go out for a nighttime stroll in your animal form."

Jahlee takes a sharp inhale, her knuckles turning white from how tightly she grips her fork.

"Get. *Out.*" Kai's words are spoken with deadly precision, but no one attempts to leave. "All of you!" His hand slams down on the table, knocking everyone from their shock.

Maybe shock isn't the right word. Looking at most of them, only Lady Miranda seems mortified by what just happened. The rest poorly attempt to fight off steely smiles. I go to push my chair back, but Jahlee stops me with a hand on my wrist. One by one, the court of the king stands, most eyeing Jahlee and Kai as they leave with looks of unfiltered aversion. Quiet trickles into the room as the door closes behind the last nobleman, leaving Tua, Kai, Jahlee, and I to sort through the tension still lingering.

"That perhaps wasn't the best response, Your Majesty," Tua states.

"I don't care." Kai's gaze is unforgiving as he looks to Tua.

"And therein lies the problem. You *should* care." Tua rises with a sigh, his eyes landing on me as he offers a strained smile, and then he looks to Jahlee, who makes his lips flatten back out.

When the heavy wood and gold doors close again, Jahlee jerks in her seat to turn towards Kai. "They were baiting you, and you fell so easily to what they wanted!"

Gods, this is the most awkward dinner I've ever been a part of.

"You aren't even supposed to be here, Jahlee," he snarls in her direction. "I told you that you needed to *stay away.*"

"I wanted to support you! So that you wouldn't have to go through these dinners alone, you jackass! You think I don't know what they say around you, Kai? How they try to make you feel like you're beneath them? How Tua *lets* them? I came because I *love* you!" Her voice cracks as she drops her hold on me and stands, pointing a finger in his direction. "You are allowed to push everyone else away *but not me!*" She turns and stomps out of the room, leaving me in perhaps an even *more* cumbersome position than before.

Chapter Forty-Four

Bahira

Kai doesn't meet my eyes as he stares down at his plate. "What do you want?"

"I didn't know Jahlee was bringing me here," I offer lamely.

Kai doesn't react. For the first time since I began my stay in the Shifter Kingdom, he looks truly exhausted, as if this ill-fated meal has sucked out every ounce of energy within him. *No one gives him the chance.* Jahlee's words bounce around my head like an annoying fly that is desperate to not be ignored. I groan internally but stand and move two seats closer until I'm sitting next to him.

"I could help you."

Kai's eyes rise to meet mine, frustration and anger reflected in them. "Your job *is* to help me. It's the entire purpose of your being here," he grits out, his head tilting to the side in a movement too smooth to be anything but animalistic. "Speaking of, what are your updates regarding the blight? When will you try using your magic to heal my people?"

"I *meant*, I can help you with court politics," I reply, ignoring his question about my magic. "In case your small brain has forgotten, I am *also* royalty. You—"

"That won't be necessary."

I lean forward and brace my hands on the table. "You *need* the help. Have you talked with anyone yet about what Magda said? How her plea for aid was denied without your knowledge?"

He narrows his eyes as he also leans forward, abandoning his chalice on the table. "That is none of your concern, Princess. You are here to do one thing and one thing—"

"You're pathetic." I stand abruptly from the table, the dishes clinking together from my sudden movement. Kai rises as well, his chest heaving with drawn out breaths. "You are a king, and yet you sit back as if you rule only yourself. You are weak-minded and *pathetic*."

Stepping around the chair, I march towards the door, my hands curling into fists at my sides. *Stupid, infuriating pric—* I jolt as I'm tugged backward, Kai pinning one of my wrists between our bodies while his other arm wraps around my front, his hand going to my neck.

"Did you really think I'd let you insult me and do nothing about it?" he growls near my ear, the heat of his breath and scent of his body causing desire to spark to life low in my belly. He has the strength to end me at any moment—all he would need to do is squeeze—and I'm not sure I could fight my way out of his grip before he snaps my neck. The thought doesn't terrify me nearly as much as it should.

"You let everyone else get away with it," I retort, my lips parting when his hand squeezes more tightly in response.

I catch our reflection in a large standing mirror propped in the corner of the dining room that I didn't notice on our way in. He walks us forward, stopping about five feet away from it. Shadows from the flame gems ripple on its surface, altering our reflections for the briefest second. I take in the image of us—Kai's large presence behind me, the muscles of his arms bulging and the way a few pieces of hair hang over his forehead. His eyes still glow, a haunting beauty to them that has me working hard to swallow.

He breathes deeply, his body going rigid before he dips his head until his cheek is scraping against mine. "You call me pathetic? Weak-minded? Tell me, Bahira, how wet are you between your legs right now?"

I grit my teeth together, my eyes alight with a fury of my own as I try to jerk out of his hold. "I don't know what you're talking about."

Kai's dark chuckle shows his canines, his grin as sharp as any blade. "Your lying tongue can't hide the truths of your body, Princess." With torturous slowness, he releases his hold on my neck and begins to slide his hand down my front, going lower until his fingers tuck under the waistband of my pants. I stare at his reflection, watching as his nose skims over the exposed skin on my shoulder. "I can smell how badly you want me to touch you."

Our gazes clash in the mirror, his hand gliding to where the evidence of my want of him can't be denied. A deep sound rattles between us when his fingers swipe at my slick entrance.

"So fucking wet. Is this *all* for me? I think it is, and I bet you *hate* it."

I don't answer him. I won't—*can't*—give him the satisfaction of knowing that he is right. Keeping my breathing steady is a losing battle—particularly when he plunges two thick fingers into me, his palm beginning to work my clit. He taunts me with his fingers, drawing them in and out slowly enough to draw an eager moan from me. At the sound, he smirks, pumping his fingers faster until tension builds at the base of my spine.

My free arm reaches back, and my nails dig into the hard muscles of his thigh as I struggle for purchase, the arm held behind me tingling from Kai's grip on it. Neither one of us looks away from the other's reflection in the mirror, the energy crackling between us caught between feral lust and unbridled animosity.

Shockwaves ripple through me at his touch—at how the fantasy of my imagination pales in comparison to the real thing. He nips at my ear, the shot of pain making me gasp before he then drags his teeth down my neck. My hips move hungrily with the thrusts of his fingers while need barrels through me, relentless in its intensity. I push my head back against his chest, my breaths quickening as the precipice of release approaches. Just a few more strokes—

He stills, curling his fingers decadently inside of me, the pressure both perfect and agonizing. Speaking into the space where my neck meets my shoulder, Kai's animal is thickly laced within his voice as he growls one word, "Beg."

My voice is haggard as I rasp, "What?"

"If you want to come, Princess, beg me for it."

The fuse of my desire quickly burns away to anger, and I clench my jaw as I dig my nails harder into his thigh. There is no way I'm begging him for *anything*. "Fuck. *You*."

He smiles as his eyes flash a completely molten gold—no remaining brown to be found at all. "*You will*."

His fingers move inside of me again, and I bite down on my lip to stifle my moan. Blood rushes back into my hand as Kai releases it, only to grip my neck once more. There is no pain, only perfect pleasure, and I want to despise that it comes from him, like he said. That my legs are dripping with my arousal, and that his fingers are soaked with it. That he is the cause. But I can't. Not when he's touching me like he's somehow seen into my mind and knows every dark fantasy I've always wanted to try but never trusted a partner enough to explore.

I ignore where the rest of those thoughts lead.

"Beg, Bahira."

I could free myself and walk away right now. I could pretend this never happened and vow to never repeat it. I *should* do that because, if I'm honest with myself, I'm already too invested in whatever this is between us. Instead, I give him what I know he truly wants from me. Not submission but an intensity that matches his own.

"No." I wait until his rumble of annoyance travels down my spine before I reach behind me and palm his cock over the fabric of his trousers. He's impossibly hard, and I groan at the size of him against my hand. "Of course, you're fucking huge," I seethe.

Kai lets out a noise that is somewhere between a laugh and a grunt of surprise as he resumes pumping his fingers—the pace brutal and pressure unyielding. "You're a defiant creature," he snarls. His teeth scrape along my shoulder, sending shivers over my body.

My orgasm builds, climbing higher as heat singes me from within. I continue to stroke him, squeezing more tightly as his other hand does the same around my throat. His breathing falters, the rush of it loud near my ear where his mouth still lingers at the base of my neck.

"Oh gods," I gasp, my thighs involuntarily clenching together right as Kai *bites* down on me. Pain mingles with satisfaction as my climax rushes through me. My eyes slam closed, white spots flaring behind my lids while I shout out into the room.

Kai lifts his head, his cock twitching against my palm. "That was a much better use of that pretty mouth." He licks over his bite as he pulls his fingers out of me, bringing them in front of us.

I quickly spin to face him, wrapping my hand around the back of his head and forcing his lips to mine. Our kiss is a hot and vicious clashing of our tongues and teeth, and I use the moment to quickly untie the laces of his trousers. Once they are loosened, I smirk against his lips.

"That's the least of what this mouth can do." Dropping to my knees, my fingers hook into the sides of his trousers, and I slide them down enough to free his cock.

"Bahira—"

"Suck your fingers into your mouth," I command as I wrap one hand around him, the other digging once more into his thigh. The heat of him invades my senses, everything coiling tightly until I'm nearly trembling with crazed desire. He stares down at me, his fingers still frozen in front of his face. "*Do it*, Kai."

The use of his name draws a deep sound from him, and the moment his fingers brush his lips, I lick the bead of cum off the tip of his cock. We both moan, his salty flavor blanketing my tongue and unleashing me fully. I pump my hand as I tease him, flicking my tongue and gliding my lips over his tip. His fingers curl into my hair, far more gently than I want them to. Sucking him into my mouth, I move in tandem with my hand up and down every perfect thick inch of him. His hips begin to rock with the movement, but I can tell everything is still restrained. He's holding back like he doesn't think I can handle him.

I drag my tongue on the underside of his cock before my mouth leaves him altogether. "I will not make you beg," I say, my breath ghosting over his glistening head while my fist pumps him harder and faster. "But you *will* fuck my face like you mean it, or I'll leave you hard for me and walk right out that door."

He makes a choked sound before his hand tightens in my hair and he guides my mouth back to his cock, submitting to *my* command. Kai is relentless, unfaltering, the size of him making me gag as saliva spills down my chin. And, gods, it's fucking *perfect*. I hum in pleasure at his taste, the vibration making him quicken his pace. Sliding my hand from his thigh to under his shirt, my nails dig into the warm skin of his abdomen. His muscles tighten, the impending orgasm evident in the way his hand loosens its hold on my hair so I can remove him from my mouth if I want. I suck him down harder, hollowing out my cheeks. My own desire grows savage at the way he groans in approval.

"Fuck. *Fuck, Bahira.*" Heady warmth coats my mouth and throat, his cock throbbing as he grunts and jerks his hips to completion. His chest heaves as he watches me draw off of him slowly and swallow, wiping my mouth off with the back of my hand. He helps me to stand before pulling me flush against his chest, his lips sealing over mine and tongue exploring my mouth. The taste of me still lingers on his lips as I'm sure his remains on mine.

The way this male kisses is like lightning striking a forest. I'm completely consumed, unable to fight off the spark of heat and turbulent passion that is left in his wake. When we have to stop and catch our breaths, Kai tucks himself back into his pants.

"It's a bit ironic to be in this position, isn't it? Considering the last time fingers covered with my arousal were between us, you were furious. You must really hate this situation," I jest, running my fingers through my mussed hair.

Kai huffs out a breath, the corner of his mouth lifting the smallest amount—a crack in his stone armor. "I thought you were taken then. And yes, you *are* infuriating and stubborn, like a thorn beneath my skin that I can't quite dig out."

I scoff, my hands going to my hips.

"But I do not hate this," he says, gesturing idly between us. "And I do not hate you. I am *grateful* that you are here. That you are trying to help with the blight."

I don't know how long it's been since I felt butterflies in my stomach over something a male said to me, but I have to fight the urge to lay my hand on top of my lower abdomen when the sensation blooms. "Well, I too find you nearly intolerable. But more like when you step in animal feces and can't quite get rid of the smell." My words get his lips to curl even more, and that thrill returns—the one I only felt before when I riled him up. "For what it's worth, I don't hate you either. At least, not fully." I certainly didn't hate what we just did either.

Kai chuckles, satisfaction rolling through me at the sound. "Fair enough, Princess."

"My offer stands," I say, watching as his shoulders tense. "If you aren't too stubborn to take it, that is."

"Tua has a system for handling the things I am not capable of."

"Who has told you that you aren't capable?"

Kai runs a hand through his hair, settling his features into stoicism once more. "Stop. You've been here for hardly a few weeks and act as if it is your job to fix anything other than the problem I've brought you here to work on."

Rolling my eyes, I point a finger at his chest. "How can I even attempt to fix the magic problem when the people suffering are too afraid to speak up about it? Because they don't trust you or are afraid of the rebels attacking them?"

His eyes snap to mine as his jaw clenches, a muscle fluttering along his neck.

"I don't doubt that Tua has connections; I've seen it in the way he interacts with the people around him," I say more gently. "But he is *not* the king. *You* are. I would also argue that the way he is doing things isn't exactly *working*. So, unless you'd like to abdicate the throne and just *give* it to him—or to your *cousin*—I suggest you change your approach."

"How do you know—" He interrupts himself with a shake of his head. "Jahlee."

"Yes, your sister has a wonderful affinity for dropping nuggets of information at the most inconvenient of times."

He snorts as his eyes roam my face, moving down my neck and then to my shoulder—where he winces. "You might want to heal that." He gestures to where his teeth sunk into my skin, and my fingers lift to trail over the now tender skin there.

Turning, I step towards the mirror and angle my body so that the light of a flame gem glows over the mark. The skin isn't broken, but it will take a few days to completely heal. Like with the wounds I sustained during the rebel attack, I'll have to work to hide this mark until it is gone. He watches me intently, likely waiting to see the flare of my magic. I don't blame him, I would be curious as well if I had sailed across the ocean and risked being attacked by the sirens to get a mage with raw power. I try to keep my heart rate even, knowing that his ears are sensitive enough to pick up any changes. His eyebrow arches, the question so obvious that for a moment I feel panic begin to creep in. *No.* No. I need a distraction, and finally, I think of one.

"Kai, I'd like to contact my family and let them know I am well. Can I speak with them through the Mirror?" I step towards the door, intent on leading him to the mirror in the experiment room, when his hand gently clasps around mine.

His eyes are dark now, the earthy brown taking back over so only small flecks of gold remain. Kai studies me again, and for the first time since my childhood, I fight the urge to shrivel under a male's inspection. My heart leaps in my throat, the weight of my deceit and of what we just did holding it there as I force an inhale. "Of course you can contact your family."

I let loose a small sigh, tugging on his hand to leave the dining space, but he squeezes my fingers once more. Staring up at him in question, I watch as his smirk grows and he gestures with his chin behind me. Letting go of my hand, he walks to the mirror propped in the corner, and I watch in mild horror as the surface of the glass ripples when he's close enough.

"Are you telling me that you fucked me with your fingers in front of the mirror I'm supposed to use to talk with my *family*?"

His answering grin is sinfully devious as he says my father's name, and the Mirror starts to turn cloudy.

Chapter Forty-Five

BAHIRA

I SHOULDN'T HAVE BEEN surprised when Jahlee showed up at barely past sunrise, knocking at my door and asking to spar. I should have been even *less* surprised that when she brought me out to the training yard at the back of the palace, Kai was already there. He was shirtless and gleaming with sweat under the morning sun as he sparred with eight other males at the same time, expertly fighting them off. Jahlee had caught me staring at her brother and seemed inclined to tease me about it every ten minutes.

The sparring had been a welcome distraction after what Kai and I had done to each other, but I still found myself tightly wound at the memories. When one of the males training with Kai took it upon himself to touch my spear where it was lying in the grass near me and *then* proceeded to taunt me with it, I had made an example of him. He had offered to give the spear back if I got on my knees for it. In turn, I kicked him in the balls and sent my elbow into his nose. I received a thumbs up in approval from Jahlee and a look of indifference from Kai before I left the training yard to shower and come to the workroom.

Kai finds me here a few hours later, hunched over my magnifier with my brow furrowed in concentration. And confusion. I've been studying the leaves brought from home, and the once vibrant red organelles that were attached to them have since shriveled into husks compared to the fullness they once held. Even the leaves, though not yet showing any signs of decay, have stopped their growth. Like they've hit some sort of wall and cannot grow past it.

"Am I interrupting?" he asks, knowing damn well that he is.

With a sigh, I sit back in my chair and observe him. A dark green tunic, the sleeves short and cuffed at his biceps, hugs his defined chest, and black trousers tucked into boots simplify his look. He's infuriatingly handsome, and I subconsciously trace my bottom lip with my tongue at the memory of him in my mouth.

"If you've come to reprimand me over what happened in the training yard, I'm afraid you'll be sorely disappointed. I have no regrets."

Kai smirks as he closes the door behind him and then strides to the opposite side of the table from me, his arms crossing over his chest. "Why would I reprimand you for defending yourself?"

I snort and stand from the chair so I don't have to crane my neck as harshly to hold his eye contact. "Defending myself is probably the least of what I was doing with him."

"I'm aware," he replies, his voice dropping deeper. "Everyone on that field was aware that you were just toying with him." His gaze roams over my face before moving down my body, like he's savoring what curves he can see with my clothing on. My thighs ache to squeeze together as he openly devours me.

"It didn't make you angry? Me *toying* with one of your men?"

"On the contrary. It made me eager to see how you'd get all the males on that field to kneel before you."

"Even you?"

He watches the way my teeth work my bottom lip. "You are unlike any female I've ever met."

His words linger in the space between us, and I can't tell if they are meant to be a compliment or not. "So then, why are you here?" I question, forcing his eyes back up to mine.

He leans closer, his hands bracing on the table until he's right over the magnifier. "I—" Tilting his head to the side, he breathes in deeply. "Are you injured?" he asks, studying me in a more assessing manner.

"No?" I watch as his head cants to the side and he takes another sniff. "What is it?"

He doesn't answer, instead looking down at the various glass bottles of leaves I have next to the magnifier. He starts picking them up one by one, sniffing them and then setting them back down so hard that the glass rings in the air as it meets the table.

"Careful," I hiss, my patience thin as I watch him reach for another. His fingers wrap around the last jar as he holds it to his nose longer than any of the others before he looks at me. "What?"

"There is blood in this," he says, handing it to me.

I take the container from him as his words unlock a rush of information. *Blood.* My hand trembles while I stare through the glass that's full of leaves and magic-infused water from home, the ones that sprouted new life, a chill slithering over my skin. Blood. Haylee had cut herself in my workshop back home; she must have bled into the jar before I cleaned her up. It's *blood.*

"I need you to cut me," I state, the rush of adrenaline making the words come out shaky as I move to find a clean new glass bottle.

"And why would I do that?"

New hypotheses and possible solutions roll through my mind, followed closely by a litany of questions. *How did I not realize it before?*

"Bahira."

I grab a new jar and pull the container of dark purple petals Jahlee picked this morning towards me.

"*Bahira*, what are you talking about?" Kai's shadow floods the table from where he's moved to stand behind me.

I sigh and hold up the jar containing the leaves from home. "This jar was part of an experiment I was working on before I was chosen to come here. For *years*, I had zero tangible results. But then, the leaves in this jar *changed*, and finally, I had something new to work with. I thought it had been the magic from one of my test subjects, but you—" I huff out a laugh as I turn to face him. "You just gave me a piece of the puzzle I was missing. The red organelles that I saw under the magnifier weren't something new that had grown from the magic in the water as

I had previously thought. It was *blood*, and the leaves... I think they *fed* off of it." I smile up at Kai in excitement from this revelation.

His eyes bounce from the bottle I'm holding to my lips before reaching my gaze. "And why do you want to cut yourself?"

"I want *you* to cut me with a claw I'm sure you can summon because I want to test and see if my blood will make these petals—" A dark thought forces my words to a halt. Is it possible *my* blood won't do anything? "I'll need your blood too," I tell Kai, moving out from under his shadow to grab another empty glass jar and then dropping more flower petals into it.

It isn't ideal, trying to recreate the experiment without using magic-infused water, but I'm mostly testing to see if blood—*any* kind of blood—will affect the growth of these petals. Based on those results, I can alter the experiment as I need to. When I turn to look at him expectantly, my palm up and ready for him to slice into, Kai narrows his eyes slightly.

"I'm not sure that I understand why you want to do this."

I groan in frustration, trying to slow my thoughts down enough to explain. "Imagine spending nearly your whole life dedicated to discovering something, only to be met with disappointment. It's like you're standing at the shoreline letting the waves batter you until you're soaked and nearly drowning, hoping the next one will stop short of pummeling you. Think of this revelation with the blood as finding reprieve from the water. A shield cast over you so that you can *breathe*." That's what this felt like—a lifeline. If the answer to our magic lies in our blood, then it would crack open a new door of possibilities. "Please, Kai." I would beg for nothing else. But for a chance to gain my magic, to fix both of our kingdoms' magic, I would beg for that knowledge. I would fall to my knees for it.

Perhaps it's the combination of the plea and his name, but his nostrils flare as he blows out a breath. Reaching back, Kai draws a small dagger that must have been sheathed on his belt.

"No claws?" I ask, smiling at the way his lips twitch.

"Unfortunately, we either shift *everything* or nothing. There is no in-between."

The scrape of his calloused hand tenderly cradling mine draws my attention down, freezing my inhale. Kai's motion is quick, digging the tip of the dagger into my palm and dragging for half an inch before he releases me. I squeeze my hand over one of the glass jars until blood, thick and crimson, drips onto the petals. Counting ten drops, I move my hand up and then gesture for Kai to do the same in the other jar.

He repeats the motion on his own palm, letting his blood drip into the second jar until I count to ten. Reaching over, I cup my hand under his, guiding us both to the basin to wash. His gaze is hot on the side of my face as I gently massage the blood off of his skin, watching it trickle down the drain.

"Can your magic heal?" I ask.

"Small cuts like this, yes. Larger wounds take much more time and will still scar."

I let my fingers drag over the back of his hand and up higher until they trace over one of the black lines of his tattoo. "What does it mean?"

His chest rises and falls steadily as I continue my perusal of his warm skin. Up close, I can see that the intricate lines vary in thickness. Some are straight while others curve, lines and swirls moving in alternate directions all the way up his arm.

"Solve the problem with our magic, and I'll tell you."

I let go of his hand immediately, earning a smirk from him, when screaming erupts from somewhere in the palace. My eyes widen as they meet his, both of us drying our hands quickly. The shrieking becomes layered, more and more voices blending into the cacophony.

I add some water to the petals before corking the jars and then bolting towards the door, Kai throwing it open as I follow behind him. It's pandemonium as nobles rush across the foyer and down hallways. Two males halt at Kai's approach, both bowing quickly before straightening.

"What's going on?" Kai shouts.

"A body was found near the palace entrance," one of the males answers, sweat gleaming at his temples. "A message in blood was left for you."

My stomach churns as Kai curses and moves down the stairs. I stay in step with him until we reach the first floor and find ourselves at the edge of a large gathering of people. An eerie sense of dread—as well as the scent of blood—sits heavily in the air, one that only grows as Kai begins to wade through the crowd.

He stops in front of me, and I place my hand on his back as the object of everyone's attention comes into view.

Strung between two stone columns, their white coloring so pristine in contrast to the now crimson-splattered floor, is a female body. Ropes are tied around her wrists, forcing her arms open wide as the rest of her hangs limply. She's disturbingly mutilated, deep cuts stretching from shoulder to shoulder and down the middle have shredded her skin. Blood continues to drip from her toes and onto the floor below, right over a message scrawled out on the tile: *Bastards are not kings.*

"Fucking gods above," I whisper, feeling Kai grow tense beneath my hand.

He walks out of the crowd to two males standing at the side and begins to give orders. The palace staff stare at the body, some crying while others curse out in anger. How did the rebels have the opportunity to string up an entire body on the first floor with no one noticing?

I search for Kai as the guards begin to disperse the crowd, calling more in to help with the body, and find him leaving the palace, his tall frame moving down the stairs quickly.

"He's going to his brooding place before he tears the palace down," Jahlee says as she comes to stand beside me, sadness and shock heavy in her voice.

I take notice of the way she grips the fabric of her skirt in her hands, her normally golden tan skin looking wan. "Are you alright?" I ask, casting a wary glance around us.

"I'm fine. I worry about him though."

"Me, too." I swallow my surprise at those words, at how true they are.

"He does not deserve this," she says softly.

I nod my head in response, and for reasons I cannot explain, I decide to follow him.

The summer sun burns above in a cloudless sky, the light making me squint as I keep a sensible distance between the shifter king and myself. He must know I'm following him—if his heightened sense of smell hasn't given me away, then I assume his hearing has. However, he doesn't order me to leave.

We walk for a while, following a faintly worn path in the thick of the jungle before Kai slows his steps, the plants thinning out as he comes to the edge of a cliff.

Looming in front of us is a large waterfall. The light blue water is stunning as it cascades down from an even higher cliff. Surrounding the water, dark rock and bright green foliage taint the air with the distinct scent of the vegetation and earth.

Kai sits, his elbow propped on one bent knee, the other leg dangling over the ledge. "You should go," he snaps angrily, his head hanging between his shoulders. "I'm in no mood to hear of all the ways I am failing."

Taking a seat a few feet away, I look out over the beautiful scenery, listening to the sounds of the water and the birds chirping overhead in the trees. "I do not think you are failing, Kai, and I have no intention of doing anything but sitting with you. But if you'd still like me to leave, then I will."

Kai doesn't respond. I observe the way his tumultuous energy is swirling within him, but I don't try to speak again. There are no words of encouragement that could help anyway. Regardless of who that shifter is, she died in order for a message to be sent to Kai. The rebels murdered an innocent female to punish this male at my side. Rage and sadness writhe together, my fingers twitching with the urge to do *something*. I may have come to the Shifter Kingdom with the intention of helping with their blight, but that mission has turned into so much more. Taking down the rebels and helping Kai in his role as king feels just as important as fixing the magic.

But for now, I'll be for him what I wish I had for myself—someone to sit in the silence with.

Chapter Forty-Six

BAHIRA

It's late into the evening when we make our way back to the palace, Kai walking at my side this time. I try not to hold my breath as we climb the steps leading to the foyer where the body was found hanging. Thankfully, there's no hint of the brutal display left by the rebels beyond the scent of iron still lingering in the air.

Kai's steps shorten as we near the staircase, and when he speaks, he keeps his gaze fixed ahead. "I need to check in with the staff to make sure everyone is alright before I speak with Tua." I nod my head at his dismissal, already heading towards the stairs when he softly calls out my name. My gaze meets his over my shoulder as he speaks softly, "Thank you. For earlier."

The corner of my mouth lifts as I dip my chin. "You're welcome."

My climb up to my room is slow. As I walk, my hand presses against my thigh and onto the key to the experiment room in the pocket of my skirt. It's likely too early to check and see if the petals have reacted to our blood yet, and with the exhaustion of the day now creeping up on me, I decide to take a shower and head to bed.

My door creaks as I open it, the room beyond blanketed in darkness. *Odd, there is always a flame gem uncovered for when night falls.* Pushing the door open farther to let in the light from the hallway, the hairs on the back of my neck rise. I freeze where I am, clenching my jaw as I study my darkened room. Air stirs to my right, and I instinctively drop down to the floor, sweeping one of my legs around in a kick. I connect with someone in the shadows, their grunt and a solid thud telling me they've hit the ground. Leaping onto the bed, I climb across it to grab where my spear should be resting against the wall. Stretching out, I reach for it and find empty space instead before the intruder's hand grips my ankle and pulls me backward.

"You better hope that you kill me, or this will be the last thing you ever do," I grit out.

They jerk my body closer, and my hand collides with their chest. Gripping onto their tunic, I yank hard until their body crashes against mine.

"I heard you were an eager fuck, but I never expected you'd be this easy," a male voice says against my ear.

I lock my leg around his hip and buck, throwing us off the edge of the bed. We land on our sides with a grunt, and I quickly climb onto his back, forcing his chest to meet the floor as I pin an arm behind him, dragging one of my knees so that it's positioned in between his legs. "Who are you?"

"One of many," he murmurs beneath me.

I draw his arm farther back and lean down over him. "Are you a rebel?"

"I suppose that's what the bastard calls us, isn't it? *Rebels*."

"It's what you *are*. Kai is your king, and you openly defy his rule."

The male twitches his upper body, muttering something under his breath. Instinctively, I lean in, realizing too late the trap he's set. His head snaps back, colliding with my nose.

"*Shit*." White flares behind my lids as my eyes water, my grip on the male loosening just enough for him to jerk free. He rolls to the side, his weight pinning one of my legs to the ground before his elbow crashes into my ribs. I shout in pain as the male rolls off of me and towards the shadowy space not illuminated by the dim light streaming in from the hallway.

Breathing through my nose is impossible as it swells, my eyes still watering as I try to blink the wetness away. Blood leaks down onto my lips, the metallic taste blanketing the tip of my tongue.

Steps shuffle near me, accompanied by the sound of a weapon being drawn. I try to roll away, but the rebel sends a harsh kick to my stomach, a breath wheezing out of me before he straddles my body. He leans over me, squeezing his knees tightly into my sides while he pins both of my hands over my head.

"How angry do you think *His Majesty* will be when we string your corpse up next?" Cold metal presses at my neck, and I force myself to relax as I strain to see the male through the darkness. "Sorry it had to come to this, Princess."

My thoughts halt, dread turning my body leaden. "How do you know that?"

He moves even closer, pushing his blade more harshly against my skin until I grit my teeth at the prickling pain. "We all know who you are, Bahira Daxel. Princess of the Mage Kingdom. Your death is going to usher in the removal of Kai for good."

I buck my hips in an attempt to throw him off balance, but the male doesn't budge. Panic tightens my throat, a strangled noise drawn from me at the sting of his blade. I can barely make out the outline of his head and shoulders, his breath warm as he whispers against my ear.

"We know *all* about you, and—"

His weight is thrown off of me, a growl thundering out into the room. I roll to my side, gasping for a full breath as the crunching of bones followed by a male's whimper sounds. Heavy steps echo, my body bracing to keep fighting until the light of a flame gem is uncovered, revealing Kai. He walks across the room to another flame gem, the golden amber light now pouring into the space and over the body of the male crumpled on the floor.

I stand, ignoring my shaking legs as Kai's gaze traces over my body. He storms his way towards me, absolute fury rippling over every part of him. The male groans on the floor, but Kai kicks him harshly enough to silence him. Standing in front of me, his eyes move to the blood that has only now stopped leaking from my nose and slowly trail down, lingering where the blade was pressed against my neck.

"How did you know to come in here?" I ask, clearing my throat as I drag the back of my hand over the space above my lips.

"I was coming up to speak with you when I saw your bedroom door was ajar and heard whispers. I thought—" He stops abruptly, clenching his jaw.

"You thought what?"

Kai simply shakes his head, running a hand through his hair before he turns and looks back at the male who is now passed out on my floor. Licking my lips, I face the male too and fold my arms over my chest, wincing at the pain in my ribs.

"Do you recognize him?"

"No."

"He knew who I was and said that all the rebels did. He was going to kill me in an attempt to get to you."

Kai snarls at that, causing goosebumps to break out over my body. "That will never happen." I feel the power of his words as they settle between us, his gaze coming back to mine. "Are you okay?"

"Fine enough, thanks to you." The adrenaline coursing through me begins to dwindle, leaving me feeling drained.

Kai's brows draw down low. "I need to bring him down to the dungeons to await interrogation." Squatting down, he tugs on the shifter's body until he's lying on his back. The male's arm flops down at his side, revealing a tattoo on the inner part of his bicep.

"Wait," I tell Kai as I kneel and reach out to twist his arm so it's more visible under the glow of the flame gems. "This tattoo—it's the same as your grandfather's sigil, isn't it?" The oryx.

Amber eyes flick up to mine, a single dark brow arching. "Yes."

Sighing, I drop the male's arm and stand. "Don't you think it's odd that they have chosen this to masquerade under? Literally? They wear fucking oryx skulls as *masks*. If they are so opposed to your rule, why pick an animal that represents the family line you come from?"

"I think they merely hate *me*, not the blood that runs through my veins."

It is stupid to notice the way his voice deepens and how his gaze drops from mine as he speaks. Idiotic to feel that pang of sympathy, not in pity but understanding. Or maybe I'm finally recognizing why I'm so drawn to Kai, why I have been since the very first moment I saw him standing in the Mirror. He's like *me*. We are two halves of the same whole—two people forced to face our shortcomings head-on because the only other alternative is to become the broken down, lesser versions of ourselves that everyone else thinks we already are.

"Well, then they are fools." The words come out more harshly than I intend but still no louder than a whisper. Kai stands slowly before taking a step towards me. His stare is piercing—the feeling of it like having the air squeezed from my lungs. "Stop looking at me like that."

"How am I looking at you?" he asks. I huff out a laugh at how ludicrous this role reversal is, but it only encourages Kai to come closer. Tipping my chin up, my eyes stay glued to his as our chests meet. "Tell me how I'm looking at you, Bahira." He doesn't miss the rapid beating of my heart, how it betrays the mask of calm I try to slip on. His fingers wrap around my neck, careful to not disturb the nick from the blade as his thumb rests over the fluttering of my pulse.

Then his gaze snaps to the door, mine following a second later to see Tua standing there with wide eyes.

"What happened?" he asks, striding into the room before either of us can answer. The male who attacked me moans on the floor, his body twitching as he begins to wake up.

Kai takes a step back and motions to the floor. "He ambushed Bahira."

Tua's jaw works as he glares down at the male. "I'll take him to the dungeons."

"I was on my way to—"

"Stay and"—he directs his gaze to me—"make sure Bahira is alright. I'm afraid I promised her back on the ship that she'd be safe here in the palace. My apologies that the opposite appears to be true." He hauls my attacker up with quick efficiency, throwing the male over his shoulder as he walks back towards the hall.

"Tua," I call out, halting his steps.

"Yes?"

"It might be wise to ask him why the rebels have insisted on using the old sigil as their own. Perhaps it will be a clue as to who is *truly* leading them." Seconds pass before he moves his head in a nod and continues out of the room. I look back to Kai, his focus already on me. "You don't have to hang around," I tell him, gesturing with my hand towards the hallway.

"You're alright being left alone?"

A sharp response dangles from my lips, but I pause at the expression etched into his features. Kai isn't asking sarcastically. He genuinely wants to make sure. My next exhale is shakier, but I dip my chin in confirmation and watch as he only hesitates for a moment before leaving and closing the door behind him. I lock it and then head straight to the bathroom.

My reflection in the mirror makes me wince; dried blood stains my skin in rivulets from my nostrils to my lip. A stream of blood that had dripped down my neck and pooled in my collarbones is now a rusty red color, the offending cut already scabbed over.

Undressing myself, I step into the tub and turn on the shower, making the water the hottest I can take and letting it wash over me. My muscles and head ache, joining the throbbing in my ribs. As I wash the blood away from my body, I recall Kai's face. The way he stared at me as if I wasn't *just* a means to an end but someone *important*. Important to him or only to the kingdom with a blight? I don't know if I necessarily *want* to explore that answer.

When I step out of the bathroom, dried and in my nightclothes, I search for where my spear should have been. I find it under the bed, as if the intruder wanted to hide it before I came into the room. My fingers run along the body of smooth wood and cold metal, my weapon's familiarity not doing much to quell my unease. I can't deny that, after seeing what the rebels are capable of, having their attention on me is more than unsettling.

I'm about to crawl into bed, my spear still firmly held in my grasp, when there's a knock from the hall. Kai's voice follows as he says my name. Unlocking the door, I pull it open and drag my eyes down his body, starting with the damp strands of hair that have been pushed back from his face and moving to the black shirt he wears that clings to the ridges of his shoulders and biceps. Midnight blue trousers hug his thighs, the thin material making it hard to look back up as I lean against the doorway.

"What are you doing here?" I ask, clearing my throat.

His deep brown eyes snap to mine from where they lingered on the hemline of my dark green chemise, and he takes a step towards me, his hands bracing on either side of the doorframe. "I came to check on you."

"I'm fine."

A brow lifts as he pointedly looks at where I'm gripping my spear.

"What? Maybe I like to sleep with my spear next to me." At that, the corner of his mouth lifts slightly before it settles back down. Then he pushes past me and into the room. "Kai, what—"

"Close the door." The command is given with a steady voice, and when I hesitate, he folds his arms over his chest as if prepared to wait me out. Grumbling, I shut the door and glare at him. "I'm staying here tonight."

"Like hell you are—"

"You were just attacked in your bedroom," he starts, stalking towards me, "which is on the same floor as my own. It's a part of the palace that *no one* should have access to." His chest heaves, glints of gold flaring to life in his eyes. "I do not doubt that you can protect yourself, but for tonight, give me this. I will not be able to rest otherwise."

I don't *need* him here to protect *or* comfort me, to make me feel safe. I don't need it, but I *want* it. I want *him*. I swallow roughly, fear of what my desire for him in this way means. But I nod my head anyway and walk to set my spear against the wall by the bed before climbing into it. Kai covers the flame gems with black cloths, plunging the room into darkness. His steps are quiet, and then the mattress dips under his weight, the heat of his body warming my side. I stare up at the ceiling through the darkness for a while, unable to sleep despite the exhaustion pushing down on me.

"Why were you coming to see me?" I ask.

"What?"

I turn my head to look at Kai though I can't see any of his features in the dark. "Earlier, you said you were coming to see me. Why?"

"Does it matter?" he responds.

I frown, but he's right. It doesn't matter. "Fine." I turn onto my side, giving him my back as I force my eyes to close. I'm so acutely *aware* that he's here—so close to me in my bed—that it makes it impossible for me to relax.

He roughly exhales as if the silence he ushered in is now suffocating him. "I came to say thank you. Again."

I stay on my side but turn my head to speak over my shoulder. "Why?"

"I don't know." He hesitates, and I press my lips together. "You are not afraid of me." It isn't said like a challenge or an insult or even a question. Instead, there is a gentleness to his voice, the cadence reminding me of someone experiencing something wondrous for the first time.

"I'm not," I agree.

He makes a noise that almost sounds like a laugh. "I never wanted to be king. Jahlee and I had a quiet life in our small village, and I was keen on it staying that way, despite who my father was. What I hadn't known was that he had taken an interest in me as a teen when he heard rumors of how powerful I had grown." He pauses to inhale slowly, his movement on the bed tugging at the sheets. "He lured me to the palace under the guise of talking to me about my mother, and like the fool that I am, I went. When I arrived, he led me to the throne room where he had set up the ceremony to do a transfer of power from him to me. Kane was there, as was Tua, both furious at what was about to happen though I suspect for different reasons.

"I could have fought back, but then my father threatened Jahlee. Threatened to kill my remaining family after he had already murdered my mother. I was being given a crown I had no idea what to do with, and the bastard didn't care. I had to *ensure* his legacy or some bullshit. Tua stepped up and immediately began guiding me—helping me as best he could. But I already had a reputation amongst the people here as the bastard son of the king. Those who didn't despise me for that fact alone hated me because they wanted to see Kane as king. He had been preparing for the role for nearly a decade before it was pulled out from under him."

Lying on my back, I pinch my lips together in thought. Kai had been through more than I realized, and I could admit to myself in the quiet darkness that I had judged him unfairly when we first met. "I'm sorry that happened to you, Kai," I say, receiving silence in return. "Though, for future reference, I prefer less sad bedtime stories." His chuckle is deep, making my toes curl. My eyes fall closed for a moment before I open them again to ask him one more question. "Did Tua say everyone was doing alright? When you spoke to him earlier?"

"I didn't find him before I decided to turn around and come up to your room."

I yawn and adjust my head on the pillow. "Then how did he know to come here—"

"Sleep, Bahira."

I snort but don't fight him on it because within a few moments, I fall asleep.

I curl farther into the warmth of the bed, the blanket heavy around my waist. There's weight resting between my legs, and when I stretch, the weight slides closer to my core. Readjusting my head on the pillow, the movement pulls at a tender spot on my neck. I lift a hand and run my fingers over the scab there, the memories of the night before rushing to me: the intruder and battling for my life, Kai rescuing me and then wanting to sleep in my room. *In my bed*.

It becomes obvious why I'm so warm and why my body feels cradled by someone else. *Because it is*. He holds my back against him—one of his legs between my own—his face nestled somewhere in my curls. Kai's fingers twitch along my stomach, but his breathing remains heavy and deep. I focus on it, letting myself exist in this sleepy haze a little while longer and pushing the realization out of my mind that I've never laid *like this* with anyone. Not even after sex.

I like this more than I thought I would. More than I *should*. And I think it has everything to do with the male behind me.

Kai is gone when I wake up fully. Sunlight floods into the room between gaps in the curtains, bringing with it a clarity I'm not ready to confront. I climb out of bed and open the window covers fully, stretching as I look out at the jungle in the distance. My thoughts fire in rapid succession, begging me to break down everything that happened from the moment he alerted me that blood had been in the experiments to the way he molded himself protectively around my body as we slept. I choose the former to focus on while I dress, donning a simple pair of tan trousers and a dark green sleeveless top before pulling my hair up into a ponytail and heading out to the experiment room.

Streams of golden light illuminate the dust in the air as I step inside. The door falls shut behind me, and my eyes go directly to the table holding the jars of petals containing blood from myself and the shifter king. Disappointment robs me of my next inhale. One of the jars blooms with new life—green stems and new buds growing from what were only dark plum-colored petals before. I force my feet forward, my heart wild in my ribcage as I observe the other jar. Changes deform the petals in that container as well but in complete opposition to its companion. The petals have begun to decay, their edges curling in. I know, without having to check the labels, which jar contains Kai's blood and which one has my own. I clutch the key to the room so tightly that it bites into my palm.

My mage blood had done nothing to promote the growth of the plants, yet a *shifter's* blood had. What could that mean? *How* could that be?

"Focus, Bahira," I chastise myself before grabbing my journal and dragging a chair out from the table to sit in.

The magic-infused water had only sprouted new life in the leaves back home for a few minutes before they began to wither away again. Some lasted longer than others, but still, the decay was rapid compared to how long the leaves lasted when tainted with blood.

I cradle my forehead in my hand as my fingers drum along the page of the journal. I had never thought to test with blood because of what we are taught in our schooling. A cautionary tale was drilled into us about a group of ancient mages who had done experiments with blood that ended in devastation. But I can't deny the fact now, as I look over at the jar brimming with new growth, that there is a connection between magic and blood. I also can't refute the evidence that, as of right now, there isn't the same level of magic in my own blood. Not enough to affect any change amongst the petals anyway. *Not enough.*

I shake my head, refusing to allow myself to wallow. Flipping to a fresh page of my journal, I write out today's date. I have only seen the blood while it's interacting with the plants, but perhaps I need to look at it on its own first under a magnifier.

With my resolve renewed, I stand from the desk and walk back towards the door, intent on finding a few shifters to take some blood samples from.

Chapter Forty-Seven

ARIA

THE NEXT CHUNK OF our journey is uneventful, a fact I am grateful for. Mashaka keeps to his habit of swimming a few yards ahead of me—though I think it's more to avoid my company than it is to warn me of any danger. With the memory of the Tula Ledge monster still fresh in my mind, I appreciate his presence either way.

We should be getting close to Eersten, the first siren outpost beyond the capital. It is southwest of the Continent, partially between the Shifter Isle and the Mortal Kingdom's beaches. The sirens that still reside there do so not out of banishment but because they have been there for generations, long before my mother started her reign.

When I was younger, I would dream about escaping to a place like Eersten, hoping it would be far enough away from the cruelty of my mother and sisters. Now I'm certain no distance would ever be great enough.

Mashaka lets out a high-pitched squeak, my attention going to him as he waits for me to catch up. The sun is swallowed up by the thick gray clouds in the sky, leaving the outline of the floating white structures in the distance to blend in with the shadows of the darkened ocean.

"Have you been here before, Mashaka?" I ask once we reach them, looking over to him. He squeaks in response, and though I'm not entirely sure, I'm assuming that means he has.

We move cautiously between the looming buildings, and I marvel at their construction. Lumen is built on a part of the seabed that is not, comparatively speaking, very deep beneath the surface. But Eersten's ocean floor seems to drop here, the depths beneath the town black with the lack of sunlight. Yet, somehow, the town floats.

"There are no sirens out," I note, Mashaka squeaking quietly in response.

The outsides of the structures are pearlescent, and oddly shaped cutouts dot around them. Some are small, as if their only intention is to allow a single pair of eyes to peek out. Other holes are large enough for a siren to pass through.

Mashaka heads towards a building with a clamshell bed carved into it. When he's close enough, his nose softly taps the dark blue sea glass door that is surrounded by embedded crystals of different colors. I follow up with a harsher knock of my own, earning a glare from him.

"What? We want them to actually *hear* us out here." He snaps his teeth together and pokes me in the arm. "Ouch, Mashaka!"

Letting out another squeak of defiance, he turns to face the door as we wait. And wait.

I click my talons together nervously at my sides, gazing in both directions at the hauntingly empty town. Suppressing a chill, I knock on the door again before crossing my arms over my chest. Hairs rise on the back of my neck, the sensation of being watched from the shadows cresting over me. Even Mashaka tenses, his beady gaze narrowing. I strain my ears to try and detect any sound, but I only hear the gentle current of the water moving around us.

"Perhaps—"

"Don't move," a female says as something sharp pokes my back. Mashaka lets out a low-pitched noise and attempts to turn around, only to be halted with a glistening silver spear at his side.

"Please don't hurt him," I plead, my hands rising up in front of me in surrender. "We are looking for somewhere to rest for the evening. I'm on a mission on behalf of the queen."

"We know who you are, Princess Aria," she snarls. "We have already had a visit from the legionaries this month. The numbers haven't changed since then."

What? I try to turn around and face her, but she jabs me again with her weapon, actually breaking through the skin. I yelp, my pulse quickening as the presence of a larger entourage bears down on me. "I don't know what you are talking about," I reply, my voice shaking.

Tense silence descends, the water nearly chilling from the icy stares I can feel at my back. "How do we know that is the truth? You could be here—"

"She is telling the truth, Ryn," a deeper voice says. I relax my shoulders, grateful to have someone standing up for me until she continues speaking. "Princess Aria's reputation is one of disappointment to the queen."

When Mashaka squeaks at my side, I have the distinct impression he is laughing at me.

"Turn around."

I wait until the weapon is pulled away before I turn, keeping my hands up in front of me. A crowd of sirens surrounds Mashaka and I, all of them with weapons that look handmade. Nothing like what the Queen's Legion carries.

"Repeat to us what your mission is," one commands; I think she's the one who spoke to the siren named Ryn. Her teal braids are sectioned down the middle and tied back on either side, gently brushing her shoulders and matching her scales in color.

"The queen has sent me on a mission to retrieve something from the Northern Island. Mashaka is my companion for the journey. I promise, we are only here to rest. I don't know of anything else you spoke of."

She studies me, the cunning glint in her eyes not giving away any clue as to if she believes me or not. Finally, she dips her chin. "You may stay one evening, provided you keep Allegra's delphinidae with you at all times. He is not welcome to wander alo—"

Already moving in protest, Mashaka pushes between the sirens and swims until he's hidden in the shadows of two buildings.

I offer a rueful smile. "I'm sorry. He only listens to Allegra."

"Izel, you can't be serious." A flash of bright pink catches my attention as a female pushes forward and bares her canines at me, her lighter pink eyes brimming with unease—and *anger*.

"Ryn, do you or do you not trust me?"

Ryn turns her head to the side, cursing low. "I do."

"Good." Teal eyes move back to me. "My name is Izel." She reaches behind me and knocks twice, pausing for a few seconds before knocking four more times. The door immediately opens, a female with tangerine braids wrapped around her head backing up to let us in. "This is Princess Aria; she is in need of a bed for the night. And I assume a meal?" I nod my head as I clasp my bag, reaching around the dagger within to grab some coins. "No. Anyone who comes from the royal family is permitted to stay here free of charge."

"Oh, I'm happy to pay—"

"Unless you want your mother to take our heads in retribution if she ever finds out, it's better that you don't," Izel bites out, stilling my hand. She doesn't say anything else as she glares at me for a moment longer before leaving, shutting the door behind her.

"Come on, then. I'll show you to a room."

I follow the orange-haired siren up a winding lustrous ramp made of crushed seashell. Sky blue and golden yellow crystals no bigger than my thumbnail line the middle, glowing softly to guide the way. White, shimmering walls reflect the light back as we go higher until we reach the fourth level.

"We have no other sirens staying here right now, so you'll have the place to yourself for the night, unless a new guest shows up."

"Thank you." I chew on my lip a moment before I ask, "What were they talking about? About legionaries already visiting?"

The female snorts as she stops before a green sea glass door. "You're either bold or stupid to assume that you can just ask that," she reprimands, looking over her shoulder at me before opening the door. Swimming past the threshold, I take in the small room with a moderately sized clamshell bed stuffed with thin-bladed dark blue grass and silky yellow-green kelp. "We have a fresh catch of salmon I can bring you as well as a loofah to wash up."

"That would be great, thank you." She closes the door behind her, and I immediately collapse onto the bed. My thoughts swirl in circles as I stare up at the glistening crushed-seashell ceiling. Voices rise from outside the inn, the murmuring of the females catching my attention. I move to a small cutout in the wall to my right, the space only large enough for my eyes to peer through.

"What if she is here to spy on us for the queen? We cannot trust her!" Someone, Ryn perhaps, warns, her voice carrying.

"I highly doubt that is the case. Aria is not known for anything other than being a hindrance to the queen," Izel replies. Her words bring a stinging heat to my cheeks as their voices drop to a murmur.

I know that I am nothing but a pawn for my mother—worthless unless I do the things she asks of me. But to hear that my reputation as such has reached the ears of those outside of the capital ravages my heart in an entirely new way.

Tears come, despite knowing better than to be upset by this. I choke on them, the rush of our journey the past few weeks and the biting unhappiness I feel finally catching up with me. Night grows outside, the crystals in the room flaring a pretty pink, but I close my eyes and wish for a peace that I don't think exists.

After Talla, the owner of the inn, brought me dinner, which Mashaka *conveniently* showed up just in time for, I tried to sleep. But Izel's and Ryn's words nag at me until I find myself completely restless, the itch to get out of this room forcing me to quietly swim off the bed and to the door. My talons scratch at the knob, and I cringe, hoping not to have woken Mashaka. When he doesn't stir, I slowly pull the door open and peek my head out.

The inn is dark and quiet, and an uncanny fear rolls over me with the water's current as I follow the lit ramp back down to the main floor. Pausing at the bottom, I make sure no one is there before darting towards the exit. I move cautiously, hiding between the shadows cast by the floating buildings. Like when we first arrived, I find it odd that the town looks all but empty, and feels it too. Except for the voices I can just faintly make out in the distance. Voices and *music*.

I near what looks like a tavern, its front framed by three white pillars. Sirens dance inside to a mixture of string and conch horn instruments as others gather around tables and talk. Ducking behind a cluster of coral, I reach for my braids and gather them into a knot at the base of my neck to get them out of the way as I watch. I spot Izel's teal hair next to Ryn's bright pink, both females engaged in conversation with each other. Despite seeing hardly any sirens earlier, the tavern is *filled* with them now.

"Snooping, are we, Your Highness?"

I jolt back at the voice, catching only a glimpse of bright blue hair before I'm forced to face forward. "No, I—"

She squeezes my arm tightly in her grasp, forcing a whimper from me. "And they said you wouldn't be a problem. Let's go."

Pushing me forward, she forces me across the waterway and into the tavern, the sirens occupying it turning towards me as the music rapidly fades. The small smile Ryn had as she talked with Izel falls completely when her light pink eyes meet mine.

"I caught her hiding around the corner, Iz, like she was trying to listen in on your conversation," the female holding me announces.

I tense under her hold, the others around me hardening their gazes as they study me. There is no point denying what I've been caught doing, so I nod my head. "I couldn't sleep and needed to burn off some energy. I followed the sound of voices and music here, but I didn't think you would welcome me in."

I must sound pathetic because Izel's gaze turns softer for a moment, her shoulders relaxing as she leans her elbows on the tall table in front of her, her tail swishing beneath it to keep her afloat.

"And did you hear anything?" Ryn asks with a sneer as Izel shoots her a warning glance.

"No."

I fear what Izel is thinking when she tilts her head to the side, her full lips pulling up to the right. "How about an exchange of information, Princess Aria?"

"What?"

Murmuring grows loud from everyone around us, but Izel lifts her hand to silence them. "I want information about what your mother is doing."

My eyes widen as fear takes root in my stomach. "I don't know anything about her plans."

"You can tell us what kind of mission you're on, and in return, I will tell you what I *know* you asked Talla about." A few disgruntled females hiss, but Izel shakes her head. "It is clear that she is not close with her mother. I won't tell her anything that we can't easily disprove should the queen be made aware," she says with a pointed stare in my direction.

I scan the tavern warily, finding no allies or friendly expressions. I don't even know what my mother is planning with the rings, only that they exist and she wants them. Surely there is no harm in telling them that? "The queen asked me to retrieve some spelled rings that are being stored on the Northern Island."

"Siren magic can't *spell* items," someone from my left shouts out. "You're lying."

"You remember the tales passed down from our elders, don't you?" Izel questions, looking around at the sirens. "The stories of the first queen transferring parts of her magic into items in exchange for favors from her subjects."

"Where are all these spelled items, then? Surely, they can't *all* be held on the Northern Island?" Ryn asks at her side.

"It's been many millennia, Ryn. Who knows. They could be anywhere." Her eyes go to mine again. "I assume you know nothing of what these rings can do or why your mother might want them?" I shake my head. "I figured."

Shame once more curdles my blood. Should I have questioned my mother more? Would it have even *mattered*?

"Long before Queen Amari began her rule, we had a sense of sovereignty ourselves. Yes, we still answered to whoever called herself queen, but we were never expected to give more than our pledge of allegiance. That changed about a year ago when a legionary sent by your mother showed up and demanded to know how many of our sirens were with child."

The crowd growls in unison, some of them looking at me like I issued the order myself.

"We gave them a number, and the legionary left. The next month came and so did another from the Queen's Legion. This time, they were not satisfied with the number given and, despite our protests, they forced a siren of only eighteen to leave with them. Each month, a legionary returns, and if we have not met whatever the expressed quota is from your mother, they steal one of our sirens to place into the Queen's Legion." I blink. And blink again, sure I must have misheard. "You look surprised," Izel muses.

"I *am*. That is so *young*. I knew she was forcing sirens out to hunt at younger ages but to join the legion too? Can you not tell her no?" I know the words are a mistake as soon as I say them, but the angry hissing that reverberates in the tavern confirms it. There is no such thing as telling my mother *no*. I know that better than anyone.

"She's already threatened the wrath of her legion against us if we disobey. For now, we have no choice but to bend to her will, for the good of all of those that reside here."

"There *is* another choice, Iz. We have her daughter. Perhaps we can bargain with her. Try to get ours back," the siren behind me says, her voice vibrating over my shoulder. "How many lives is one princess worth?"

"We'd have to have a princess of *value*, Nisha. And we don't. But even then, the queen would make the exchange and then raze the town down. If we are no longer obedient, she will destroy us."

Nausea churns in my stomach as I try to understand this information in a way that makes *sense*. The legion has always been something that sirens have the option of joining. It's never been something forced upon them, at least for those in the capital. Maybe that is not the case for those outside of it.

"Get some sleep, Princess Aria. When the sun rises, you will have to go. Though I believe that you have no ill will towards us, the same cannot be said of your mother. We do not want any more unwanted attention than we already have."

The siren behind me—Nisha—begins to pull me out of the tavern. I fight against her, shouting, "Wait!" She pauses, and I drop my gaze at garnering the attention of every siren. "I'm sorry. That she is doing this. I—I wish I could do more."

There are some noises of disdain, but Izel speaks above them. "Despite what you may think, Your Highness, you *could* do more," she says quietly, pushing away from the table to approach until she is right in front of me. "You choose not to."

Her words ring in my ears hours later as I still try and fail to fall asleep. It's so similar to what Nia said when she confronted me at the seamounts before telling me to never return. I don't understand what they think *I* can do though. They *themselves* know that I'm barely considered one of the queen's daughters as it is.

One person cannot inspire a movement. One person of no power cannot take on the most powerful. I am not strong or clever or fierce like my other sisters. I am a pawn better suited to being molded for the plans of others than trying to stand on my own.

I am nothing and no one.

Chapter Forty-Eight

RHEA

My eyelids flutter open, the edges of a dream fraying away as I focus on the sitting area that's visible through Nox's open bedroom door. My breaths are easy, and my heart beats in a slow and steady rhythm. How long has it been since I've woken up feeling so at ease? Have I *ever* felt that way before? I had moments of being content in the tower, days where nothing unexpected would happen. Where my uncle wouldn't visit and Alexi would. But there was always an underlying current of anxiousness within me, rocking me as if I was driftwood in the sea. Reminding me that any moment of calm was nothing more than the eye of a storm and that the chaos of tumultuous waters would soon find me again—leaving me broken and battered on the floor.

Like he can sense the direction of my dreary thoughts, Nox curls his arm more tightly around my waist, the warmth of his body pressing into me from behind. Since Bella had come into my life, I had only slept alone for a handful of nights. There were the few after I had asked Alexi to free her from the tower—before she came back dying and my magic saved her. Then there were the two nights I had slept in Bahira's room. Maybe it makes me weak or a pathetic excuse for an adult woman, but I like waking up knowing that I'm not alone.

I interlace my fingers with his, taking in a deeper breath. *The moon may have the stars, but at least I have you.* The phrase rings in my head, and I wonder if it will always be meant just for Bella or if there will be a day when my heart might be okay with saying those words to Nox. I think of my happier memories of Bella. How she brightened my days when it would have been so easy to live in darkness. How she saved me from completely spiraling into a despair so deep after Alexi's death that there would have been no return. And, for a moment, I feel the weight of that permanent grief that sits so heavily on my chest lighten a fraction. Maybe pushing the memories away, trying to force myself to become numb to them, only keeps that boulder in place. What if, instead, I could chip away at it by keeping that part of my heart that is exclusively hers unguarded and free? The guilt and sadness might never disappear completely, but maybe they could dwindle down to the size of a pebble. Still there, still something jagged and rough, but smaller—more manageable.

Warm lips meet my shoulder, Nox's gentle kisses causing my skin to break out in goosebumps. "Good morning."

Butterflies take flight low in my stomach at his sleep-roughened voice. "Good morning to you." I wriggle again but still my movements when I feel him hard against my low back.

"I had a particularly *rousing* dream," he murmurs into my hair, his fingers flexing beneath my hand.

A blush pinches my cheeks as I huff out a laugh. "And here I thought it might be because of me." *Bold.* It is so unusually bold of me to speak this way, but if fear and meekness thrive in oppression and anguish, then the opposite might be true in freedom and safety. While I won't say that I'll ever be completely fearless, in this moment, it isn't trepidation that is making my toes curl and need light up my veins.

"Who do you think the dream was about? It's always because of you, Rhea." My legs clench together as his fingers move idly on my bare stomach beneath my satin chemise. "Did you think *you* were the only one who thought about the other's hands on them? That I might not think of you in sleep as often as I do awake?"

"You've never hinted otherwise," I tease, arching more into him.

Nox chuckles, and the sound is as silken as the wetness growing between my legs. "I'm a gentleman. I wouldn't *dare* speak of such things." The tips of his fingers dip beneath the waistband of my undergarments, causing my breath to catch.

"I recall you saying something about *not* being one during a game of naughts and crosses back in the tower."

He kisses my shoulder again before leaning in closer to my ear. "Do you want me to be a gentleman now?"

My eyes go straight to his as I turn my head, the silver in them blazing bright. I find I don't care that it's the first thing in the morning or that I probably look a mess. All I can think about is his touch—the warmth of his skin and softness of his mouth. Our lips brush, and I move the hand still holding his farther down to where I'm aching to feel him.

A small gasp from me separates our kiss when his long fingers reach that sensitive bud. He moves them deftly, gathering every ounce of pleasure until it all pools low in my stomach. I can't help the moan that leaves me when—after teasing—his hand drops even lower and one of his fingers slides delicately inside of me. His groan from behind rattles my back, satisfaction in the sound at the wetness he finds waiting for him.

My own hands grip onto anything I can to brace myself—one on the sheets in front of me, and the other reaching around behind me to dive into his hair. Nox's mouth is on me the entire time. Sometimes showing my neck attention, and sometimes tangling his tongue so perfectly with mine that it draws out the memory of the *other* things his tongue can do.

He takes his time, murmuring his appreciation for how my body is reacting to his touch. Adding a second finger, he coaxes me past the brink of release over and over again until I feel completely boneless and I'm not sure where my body ends and the bed begins. When he removes his fingers, my arousal shining along them, he sucks them into his mouth, and I forget how to *breathe*. There is nothing but the longing to join my body with his again, to be the beginning and the end of each other.

I muster enough strength to sit up, pulling my chemise off eagerly and throwing it to the ground. Nox laughs, the sound cascading over me, before he pulls me on top of him, my knees straddling his hips. I brace myself on his broad chest, leaning over to kiss him.

"Tell me what you want, Rhea," he says against my lips, his voice husky and deep.

I gasp at how hard he feels beneath me, his hands guiding my movements back and forth along him. "I want *you*," I answer.

"Where?"

I suck his lower lip into my mouth before dragging my tongue along it. Nox likes hearing me tell him *exactly* what I want, even though I know that he has no trouble deciphering it on his own. At first, I thought it was because he wanted to make sure I never felt like he was taking advantage of me. Then I thought it might be his way of making me feel more comfortable with my desire, with being vocal in an intimate situation. But now I think he simply finds pleasure in me telling him what I want—what I *need*—and knowing he is the only one who can give it to me.

"Inside of me," I whisper, smiling when he curses in response.

His touch is searing as his warm hands slide up the sides of my body, his thumbs tracing a delicate path along the underside of each breast before moving over my peaked nipples. I rock myself over him, the exhilarating anticipation making my entire body burn bright and my magic hum against my bones. When we're both panting, the air thick with our magic, he effortlessly flips us and quickly removes what remains of our clothing.

"Say it again," he murmurs against my neck, his fingers moving over my breast before gliding down to the warmth between my legs. "Tell me where you want me. *Only* me."

Stars above, I love when he's like this, when it seems like he can't get enough of me. The first time he had ever said that I was *only his*, he froze as soon as the words left him. It was as if he hadn't meant to say them out loud. I could see that an explanation of what he meant—or worse, an apology—was on the tip of his tongue, but I only pulled his face to mine and kissed him until I felt him relax. I love his possessiveness of me because it doesn't feel like possession. It feels like longing and desire and... *love*.

I graze my hands up his torso, my breath faltering when I feel the slick tip of him brush against my thigh. "I need you inside of me, Nox. *Please*."

I have had him every day since our first time, sometimes multiple times a day, and it never gets any less magnificent. The desire he draws out of me is only sated for a time before I begin to crave him all over again. I swear that every time we join, I discover something new. About myself. About him. About how our bodies meld and peak and fall apart together.

He doesn't hesitate, and I don't think either of us is fully breathing when he pushes in slowly, letting my body gradually adjust to every perfect inch.

"You feel so good," he groans into my heated skin once he's seated to the hilt. "Fuck, every time, you feel *perfect*." He moves slowly—consciously—measuring each thrust of his hips.

The fire that simmers low in my belly is begging for *all* of him. I want him as uninhibited and lost in this moment as I am. "More," I say with a gasp, my nails scraping down his back. His breath stutters in response, the arm bracing his body flexing near my head. "I need more."

His eyes lift to mine, tendrils of his raven hair dancing above his eyebrows as his self-control disappears. The cadence of his hips slows, but each pump hits me deeper and deeper until I'm writhing beneath him. I groan out his name, praying to him with my body—my breath.

He snaps upright so that he's on his knees with my legs thrown over his shoulders, his arms wrapping around my thighs until he's hugging them to his chest. His thrusts are calculated and drawn out, the deeper angle torturously perfect. He's a conductor, and my body is his choir as it hums and sings to his every command. My fingers reach to grip onto his knees while my back arches as pleasure, hot and sweet, rolls down my spine. Shouts that might be his name or a cursing of the gods or something in between leap off my tongue as my muscles flutter and spasm, my climax unraveling within me.

Nox tilts his head back, the sunlight caressing the column of his throat and his chiseled chest as his hands squeeze my legs tighter. All I can do is watch as the muscles of his powerful body contract as he joins it with mine. He separates my legs, brazenly looking at where we are connected. The sight alone draws a breathy moan from me, but then he pulls out, the fullness of him gone. I don't have time to protest because his mouth is quickly on me—his tongue *inside* of me—all while his hands slide up my body to my breasts.

"*Oh gods*," I rasp, stars bursting behind my eyes as I cover his hands with my own. It doesn't take long under the ministrations of his mouth for me to become undone again. Through the buzzing of my satiation, I hear him chuckle quietly, moving his lips intimately against me before crawling his way up my body. His mouth crashes onto mine, stealing my oxygen. My sanity. *My existence*. There will never be enough of this—*of him*.

Pulling back, he gently brushes the hair away from my face as his eyes roam over me. "I am so *fucking* unworthy."

"No more unworthy than I am," I reply, though a small spark within me flares in defiance at that thought. *No.* I *am* worthy of this moment, of *him*—of whatever I can make of this life in newfound freedom. If I dare to believe it, perhaps I am worthy of even *more*. And so is he.

My name is a tortured sound paired with a deep thrust as he fills me to the hilt again. I move my body with his, content to watch him come undone as I swallow his groan of pleasure with a kiss when he finishes. The room falls mostly quiet, nothing but our heavy breaths and joined magic sizzling in the air. Nox kisses my forehead as he slowly pulls out, murmuring his love for me before tucking me into his side when he rolls to his back.

"Will it always be like this?" I ask him, my body perfectly aching and languid.

His fingers drag back and forth on my shoulder as he takes his time to answer. "I will try my best to ensure it is."

I smile as I look up at him, his face reflecting the same contentment I feel in my soul. "I think this is my favorite part," I whisper after a moment, kissing his warm skin.

"I don't know if I should be offended that it's *after* sex that is your favorite."

I laugh, lifting up slightly to adjust so that my arms are stacked on his chest with my chin resting atop them. "Oh, I like the sex too." His eyes heat as he bends his arm back and rests his head in its crook. "I just mean *this* moment. Where it feels like the world pauses just for us."

He stares at me, that all-knowing gaze piercing me until my cheeks begin to flush. "Come closer." His hand reaches up to wrap around the back of my head while he pulls me gently into a kiss. "I love that feeling too. Though, if I'm being totally honest, the little gasps you make as you come are my absolute favorite."

Our laughs mingle together between more sweet words and the pressing of our lips. I don't know for sure what happens in the Afterlife, but I can't imagine it's anything more blissful than this.

We've gotten a short reprieve from the council summoning Nox daily to talk about his time in the Mortal Kingdom. I know that he's creating a barrier between their questions and me, but I can see what he won't confess—it's starting to wear him down.

"If the council wants to meet with me, I will do it. Not doing so makes it feel like we have something to hide," I tell him as we walk to the training grounds.

"We *do* have something to hide, Rhea, and that is *precisely* why I don't want them to interrogate you."

"Do you not trust me enough to know how to respond to their questions?" I try to keep my tone light, but it's impossible to deny the pinprick of hurt in my chest. I know everything Nox does for me—*everything*—comes from a place of love and needing to keep me safe, but talking with the council seems like an easy way to eliminate one of the major worries I know he holds.

"Hey." His voice is gentle as he lays a hand on my forearm to pause our steps. "That's not it at all. It has nothing to do with you and everything to do with the fact that I *know* they will pick you apart. There is a reason they wanted to suggest the betrothal to Haylee. Her uncle is on the council, and he is an affluent member of the kingdom. On paper, *to them*, it strengthens the kingdom to have the two of us as rulers."

I swallow a bitter knot down as I nod my head. "And on paper, it's less so for you to marry a supposed commoner."

His head tilts to the side, a concerned look drawing his brows together. "You know I don't care about that. I don't love you because you happen to be a princess, and the council can do nothing about it but annoy me with their questions. I don't want to subject you to that. They will not be kind about it." He speaks as if from experience, and my stomach sinks at the thought of him enduring their tongue lashings at my expense. He forces a smirk to lift the corner of his mouth as he glides his fingers down my arm. "Don't give me that look, Sunshine. It's not anything I'm not used to, nor is it anything that keeps me up at night."

"But it makes sense for them to want to question me, doesn't it? For safety? You could help prepare me for it. I just— I don't like having to lie more than we already do. If interviewing me gets the council off your back and makes them feel more comfortable about our *arrangement*, then I don't see why I shouldn't do it."

His smirk falls slowly as he studies me, likely trying to think of a reason that will convince me that it's better to let him carry the weight of this invisible burden. But I can't let him do that, not after what we promised to each other.

Rising up onto my toes, I cradle his face in my hands. "Nox, I'm not interested in standing by and letting life happen *to* me anymore. I know you want to bear this responsibility on your own, but you can't ask me to let you in to help if you aren't willing to do the same for me."

I had already done so much in the weeks since I woke up from my time in the Middle that I never thought I would. I felt bolder than ever, *stronger* than ever.

Which wasn't exactly saying much when the bar of measurement for those things was so low, but it felt like it could be enough to do this too.

"I don't deserve you," he whispers as he wraps his arms tightly around me, squeezing me to his chest.

"You are more deserving than anyone in this existence. There is *only* you." I repeat his words back to him before grazing his lips with my own. Our kiss is gentle and sweet, a language spoken and understood that is all our own.

When we separate, Nox nods his head in concession. "Okay. I will help prepare you to meet with the council."

Cassius meets us on the training grounds, and we spend the rest of the day working on my Forms. I'm waiting for that moment where I feel as good as Nox looks after one of his own sparring sessions with Cassius, but so far, all I've managed to feel is exhaustion.

After a ten minute cool down, which mostly involves Nox rubbing my sore muscles and infusing his magic into them to take the pain away, I'm led towards a table of different weapons that Cassius set up before Nox and I arrived.

"Okay, Blondie," he says, clapping his hands out in front of him. "Everyone in the Mage Kingdom goes through basic weapons training where they learn to handle each of these with beginner-level skill. However, many choose to hone in on a specialty. Bahira's is the spear, while Nox is a master swordsman. I, myself, am not too bad with daggers." He slips a short dagger from its sheath on the broad dark leather strap going across his chest. Most of what Cassius wears is leather armor, the material covering all the major points of contact on his body—shoulders, torso, and thighs. He also has leather vambraces that lace up from his wrist to his elbows. Beneath the leather, he wears tunics of varying colors—today's is dark green—and black trousers. He flips the dagger across his knuckles before catching it by its metal tip and then extending it out hilt first to me. "See how it feels in your hand."

Impressed, I wrap my fingers around the silver and black stone handle, the slender dagger uniquely beautiful.

"I could teach you the art of slashing your enemies up close. It's an intimate way to watch the light leave someone's eyes." His eyebrows tip inward towards his nose, a feline expression pulling the corners of his mouth up.

My eyes widen as I stare at him until Nox barks out a laugh and shoves Cassius in the shoulder. "The only thing Cass has ever witnessed dying is his own pride every time he fails to woo a potential partner."

"Hey!" his best friend shouts, throwing his arms out to the side.

I laugh, holding his dagger back out to him. "Maybe something a little less *intimate*," I suggest, turning back to the table. There are swords of all sizes—some so long that they might be two-thirds of my own height.

"Shortswords might be a good place to start," Nox states, seeing where my eyes have gone.

But those don't exactly feel right either, the glistening blades too similar to the weapons used by the King's Guard. Despite Cassius' teasing, I don't want to train with a weapon purely for the ability to kill someone. I want to learn so that I can defend myself. Maybe it is stupid to think of those things as being distinctly different, but to me, they are. I take note of the many intricate daggers, some have pommels filled with sparkling multicolored jewels and swirling designs in different hues of metal. There are wooden clubs that look like they weigh more than I do, short axes and hammers, and even a spiked metal ball attached to a wooden handle by a chain. I am drawn to none of them, and it isn't until I reach the very end of the table that I find something that sparks my interest.

My fingers brush against the feathered end of an arrow as Cassius leans his hip against the table's edge, his eyes dancing with glee. "A bow? I like it," he says with a playful nod, picking up the large curved bow and handing it to me. "Yes, I think this is a very good choice. Don't you, Nox?"

My gaze lifts to his as he dips his chin, a glorious smile on his handsome face. "An archer. It's perfect, Sunshine."

They spend the remaining daylight hours teaching me all about how to nock an arrow, swapping the larger bow for one that looks like it's fit for a child. My feeble arms are still too weak to draw it back very far. Despite how poorly my attempts start, there is a sense of rightness within me at learning to wield this weapon. Maybe it is intuition, or perhaps even Selene guiding me somehow, but as we pack up the weapons, the sun now resting for the day and the moon high in the nighttime sky, I can't help but feel a trickle of pride work its way into my heart.

Chapter Forty-Nine

Rhea

SUNSHINE,
LEAVING YOU THIS MORNING WAS NEARLY IMPOSSIBLE. I'VE FOUND THAT WAKING UP TO YOUR KNEE DIGGING INTO MY SIDE AND YOUR HAIR SPLAYED ACROSS MY FACE IS MY FAVORITE THING. I'LL BE WITH MY FATHER MOST OF THE DAY TODAY, BUT IF YOU NEED ME, LET BARRON KNOW. HAVE FUN TRAINING, AND I'LL SEE YOU LATER TONIGHT.
I LOVE YOU.
ONLY YOURS,

NOX

Smiling, I lay the letter back on the table at the side of the bed and stretch my arms overhead. The council's reprieve did not last more than a few days before they proclaimed that Nox should return to his duties as heir. Apparently, there is a lot to catch up on from the four years he was gone and the advisors are eager to make sure Nox does so.

Moving from the bed, I walk into the sitting room, grabbing some stationery from one of the bookcases and taking a seat at the larger square table. Tapping my pen on the corner of the paper, I smile as I remember all of the notes we passed when he was still a nameless guard and I was a lonely prisoner.

Nox,

How absolutely lovely it must be to wake up that way. I'm sure you meant that with no sarcasm at all. I, too, am spoiled by sleeping next to you, but for far nicer reasons. You make me feel safe. Waking up and knowing it's your body that warms mine and your heartbeat beneath my ear provides me with a sense of security I've never felt before. If I forget to say it, let me remind you now: you are my home.

Tonight, I was thinking of meeting Elora at her family's bookstore and then going with her to a tavern. Maybe you can meet us there?

I love you too.

Forever Yours,

Rhea

I dress in my training clothes and boots, slowly tying them the way Nox showed me, before pulling my hair back into a low ponytail. Tucking the dragon pendant under my shirt, I grab the note and leave Nox's room, softly shutting the door behind me. My steps are quiet on the red rugs that line the hallway, the scent of blooming flowers and tilled earth heavy in the air from the open windows down the hall.

Barron stands near the top of the stairs, his smile wide as he greets me. "Lady Rhea, good morning." The guard has become a welcome, friendly face each morning that I leave.

"Good morning, Barron. How are you?"

"I am doing well, thank you."

"Nox said if I need him that I could let you know?"

Barron nods, already moving to take a step down the stairs, but I reach out and gently touch his shoulder.

"I was just hoping you could give him this letter," I say, waving the folded cream-colored paper in front of him.

Barron chuckles, gently taking it from my hand and placing it into a leather pouch attached to his belt. "Of course, My Lady."

We walk down the stairs together, parting ways when we reach the first floor. More people than usual pass me in the foyer as I make my way to the exit, and I remember that Nox had told me today was public forum day, a time when those of the kingdom could come and talk to the king and queen. Rushing towards the doors, my mind occupied with thoughts of Nox, I don't have time to stop when a man abruptly steps into my path. My body crashes into his with a grunt, but I'm able to brace myself against his forearm to keep from falling over.

"I'm so sorry, are you alright?"

I look up and find blue eyes and a vaguely familiar face. It takes me a second to remember his name. "Yes, I'm fine. You're Daje, right?"

He nods his head and grins before his eyes dart over to a man who steps up beside him. The older mage's facial features are harsher than Daje's though they share the same skin tone and shape to their lips. He eyes me curiously before clearing his throat. Daje hesitates another moment before he gestures with his hand to the man. "Rhea, this is my father, Councilman Kallin. Father, this is Rhea. She is—"

"Courting the crown prince," he cuts in.

I offer him a smile, but it falters under his scrutiny. His gray eyes pore over every part of me, criticizing what he finds with a downturn of his lips and a pull of his brows. His tawny skin shows signs of age—wrinkles lay on his forehead and around his eyes—while his head is balding of the dark brown hair present. His magic is a heavy presence, not as strong as Nox's but one that feels as if it's sitting on my chest.

"We have been trying to meet with you, but the prince has been reluctant to do so. Any idea why that might be?"

I try to answer, but only a sputtering noise comes out. The way the councilman is looking at me, it's as if I truly am a threat to the safety of this kingdom. I choke on my own anxiety, unable to answer him beyond the opening and closing of my mouth.

The councilman humphs in disappointment before turning to look at his son, dismissing me entirely. "I've got meetings most of the day." He walks away without another word, going down the long hall that I know leads to the council room.

I watch him until he is gone, my fingers trembling at my sides as my heartbeat pounds loudly in my head. If that was my first chance to show Nox that I could handle myself in front of the council, I have failed *miserably*.

"I'm *sorry* about that. My father isn't one for easy chit chat," Daje says quietly before pursing his lips.

I manage a small huff of breath in response. We stand awkwardly in the center of the palace foyer, the swell of people here forced to move around us.

Finally, Daje gestures towards the doors. "I'm heading to the training grounds."

"Oh, so am I."

"Would you like to walk together?" Waiting for me to nod, he turns and leads us through the double doors and down the steps at the front of the palace.

If I thought that standing in the middle of the foyer was awkward, the silent walk to the training grounds is even more so. My gaze keeps darting his way, tracing the side of his face and the tension that lines it. He catches me on the last look about halfway to our destination.

"You can just ask," he says with a sigh.

Confused, I look down at the leaf-covered stone walkway. Perhaps he means that I can ask him for help preparing to speak with the council? It isn't a terrible idea, as he might have more insight into how I should prepare for a meeting with them.

"You want to know about Bahira. I assume you've heard what happened between us."

"That you *like* her?" It doesn't exactly seem like information that needs extra clarification, and that thought must be painted across my face because, for a moment, Daje looks completely caught off-guard.

"You haven't heard what happened at the Summer Solstice celebration?" When I shake my head, Daje snickers to himself. "You must be the only one in the kingdom who hasn't."

"And, of course, I'm now *wholly* curious about it," I tease, earning a small laugh from him.

He runs a hand down his face before letting it fall to his side. "It's not that interesting. I proposed to Bahira, and she was taking some time to answer. Then the magic chose her to go to the Shifter Kingdom, and she left—our future hanging somewhere in the balance."

Well, I certainly wasn't expecting him to say *that*. "How did you propose to her?" I can't imagine someone needing time to answer a question like that. Even with my anxiousness at becoming a future queen of the Mage Kingdom, if Nox proposed to me today, I already know that I'd say yes. When I cast a glance his way, he is grimacing like the memory causes him pain.

"Maybe *proposed* isn't exactly the right term. I gave her a choice."

"A choice? I suppose that's one way to word asking someone to marry you."

"It's not— We have *history*, and Bahira seems so intent on making herself suffer when she doesn't have to."

My mouth twists to the side. "No one *chooses* to suffer. Or at least to do so without reason."

The training grounds come into view up ahead, the grass bright under the unobstructed sunlight. Warmth caresses my skin as we step past the shade of the trees, my magic stirring in response.

"It's hard to explain. Bahira is smart—brilliant, actually. She's tenacious and driven, her mind as beautiful as she is. And she *is* beautiful. In a garden full of flowers, she would stand out amongst them all. Nothing compares to her."

"Did you tell her all of that?"

"Of course I di—" Daje chokes on a breath, inhaling deeply before dropping his gaze from my own. I watch as a range of emotions flickers over his face, each one a little more devastating than the last.

We continue trodding across the thickly bladed grass field to where Cassius is waiting, a small gathering of curious children surrounding him. His blue magic glows in his hand as he lifts water from the small pond next to him and shapes it into different animals mid-air, all to the children's delight.

"If you didn't know about Bahira, then why did you keep looking at me like you wanted to ask something?" Daje asks quietly at my side.

"Oh, it was actually about your father. I was going to ask if you had any tips on winning him over when it's time for me to speak with the council."

He laughs nervously as his hand rubs the back of his neck. "If I ever figure that out, I will let you know." I blow out a breath and smile slightly, our steps slowing as we near Cassius and his group. "How did you convince Nox to let you talk to them, anyway? The council, I mean. He seemed pretty dead set on not letting that happen."

I shrug as I look up at him, his sapphire-blue eyes rivaling the beauty of the sky above us. "I just told him why it was important to me that I try, and he listened."

The children surrounding Cassius are from the orphanage in Galdr, a place that Cassius has special ties to. He told me that his mother had grown up there and that she had spent a lot of her free time volunteering any way she could until her death when Cassius was fifteen. He tries to give the children there as much of his free time as he can as a way to honor her memory.

They were practicing making shields with their magic, and when one little girl was left without a partner, I volunteered to step in. Truth be told, I needed the practice as well. The little girl, Starla, had been *less* than enthused by our partnership. She let her displeasure show with her sharp tongue and by occasionally blasting past my flimsy shield to pelt me with her magic. Despite her fiery disposition, she carried a sadness that seemed much too heavy for a child her age.

"Do you know her story?" I ask Cass after the lesson ends and the children leave with the other instructor, Dilan.

"Her mother died two years ago from an illness. No other family came forward to claim her, so she went into the orphanage."

"No father?"

Cassius uses the leverage of his arm on me to guide us towards the archery area. Wooden targets with blue and red paint are stationed at increasing distances across from the table that holds the bows and arrows.

"No one knows who he is. When her mother started getting sick and neighbors stepped in to help, they tried to get any information they could from her, but she was apparently very tight-lipped. Starla says that her mother told her what he looked like and that she would know it was him when she saw him. Of course, Starla is keeping that information to herself. Honestly, it seems like a shitty thing to tell a child."

My fingers drag along the smooth wood of one of the curved bows as I think his words over. "Perhaps she just wanted Starla to have a memory of him. In case someone ever came forward?"

"Maybe. Still seems like a lot of unnecessary pressure," he says, rolling his shoulders back and then gesturing with his toe where he wants me to stand. "I'll be going to the orphanage to hang out again in a few days if you want to come. I'm sure they'd love to see someone other than me show up."

"I'd love to." Choosing a smaller bow, the curves of its light brown wooden limb arched so that it looks a bit more heart-shaped than the others, I grab a quiver and meet Cassius at his imaginary line. "Maybe Nox can come too? I'm sure the kids would love to see their prince."

"He always comes when he can, though I imagine his days will only grow more hectic now. He's got not only his own duties as prince but obligations to the council to fulfill as well. Nock your arrow like I showed you."

Cassius has been beyond patient in helping me learn the basics of preparing to shoot an arrow from a bow. Tucking away my thoughts on the council, I extend my left arm forward, gripping the bow in the middle where it curves back towards me. Laying the shaft of the arrow in a small divot in the wood, I line the nock up on the string and begin to pull it back to my jaw. My arms strain from the tautness of the bow, my hands already wavering. I haven't even been able to release the damn arrow yet because my muscles still aren't strong enough to hold everything steady in order for me to aim it.

"You're shaking less than you were before, Blondie. It's progress."

"I guess," I huff.

"Don't let your shoulders round in—pull them back. Good." He walks around me, critiquing my form and telling me to make small adjustments while I keep the string drawn. "Okay, for fun, let's release the arrow today."

"*For fun.*" I mimic his voice, causing him to laugh.

"Just try," he insists. Blowing out a breath so harshly that my lips flutter, I eye the closest target in front of me. "Shooting an arrow has a bit of an instinctive element to it. Slow your breathing down. Focus less on how your muscles might be fatiguing and more on where you want the arrow to go. Think of something that makes you happy to quiet your mind as you focus on the target."

I heed his instructions, images of all the things that make me happy playing in my mind. Warmth rises inside of me as my light magic flares, the darker half still hidden within that imagined well. At least my practice with keeping the shadows suppressed has gotten better. I suppose I could be proud of that. Taking a slow and steady inhale, I hold it for a few seconds as I stare the target down, before releasing the arrow with my exhale. Despite the prep and the small bit of confidence I was feeling, I tilt my head back and groan in defeat when I see the arrow sticking out of the ground a few feet short of the closest target. Over and over, I nock an arrow and release it, only for it to repeatedly fall short. The muscles of my shoulders, back, and arms scream in pain, but I keep going at Cassius' behest until all the arrows in the quiver are gone.

"It's alright, Blondie," he cajoles, patting me on the top of my head twice. "You can only get better from here. Besides, there is no time to fret about it because you and I are going to go for a run."

"What?" I shout, but he is already jogging backwards, waiting for me to join him.

I sigh again, laying the bow and quiver down on the table and then falling into stride with him, which he's obviously altered so that his long legs take shorter steps. We jog for what feels like years—having to slow to a walk multiple times instead—yet my exhaustion is married with a sense of accomplishment. I am not barred inside a stone cage anymore. I am free to move and explore and *live*, and for that, I will *always* find a way to be grateful for this torture.

Though, to be clear, it *is* torture.

After running, Cassius finishes our session with a series of Forms until I'm left lying in the soft grass and gazing at the sky above with my entire body coated in sweat.

"How much do you hate me?" he asks from where he sits next to me, his elbows resting on his knees. His bright blond hair gleams under the sunlight where it's gathered on the top of his head messily. Long tendrils that have fallen from the ponytail frame his handsome face, his eyes as light as chips of ice.

"I don't hate you at all, Cassius."

"Cass. Please call me Cass. Only my father calls me Cassius, and it's usually when he's scolding me." He flashes me a big smile, bumping my boot with his own.

"Okay then, Cass, I don't hate you. In fact, I wanted to thank you. I'm grateful to you for taking the time to train me, for always being so kind." I look back out at the bright blue sky above us, tracing over the small white clouds streaked across it. "What has Nox told you about me? About where I come from?" I don't know why I feel compelled to ask, why it matters to me if Cass knows my history.

"Nox is like a brother to me," he starts, drawing my attention back to him, "and I know him as any sibling might know another. He is different after meeting you. In a good way," he quickly clarifies, holding his hands placatingly out to me. "But I could tell something was wrong between the two of you when you arrived at the palace. Then, when you went into that deep sleep and days passed, he needed someone to talk to. Someone who he knew wouldn't judge his decisions but also would tell him their honest opinion." I move up to sit as his expression grows more serious. "He's told me what is surface level about you—your true title and where you come from, what you escaped. He only told me those things because he needed me to vow that the fierceness with which I protect him, both as my brother and as my prince, would get extended to *you*."

Nodding, I tuck the loosened strands of hair from my braid behind my ear. "I'm not upset that he told you about me. I trust in his decisions, in *him*. And I trust you." I look down and play with a blade of grass as a blush blooms across my cheeks. "On the many lonely nights in my tower, when all there was to do was daydream, I would often wonder if making friends was an art that was lost to me. I had spent my entire life isolated and alone. Before Nox, my only companions were a guard in his fourth decade who could only visit for an hour every few days and a fox who I had to keep hidden. But you've never once made me feel odd or different or questioned why Nox might be with someone so clearly unequipped for... just *life*," I say with a forced chuckle.

"Give yourself some credit, Rhea," he counters, and I startle at his use of my actual name. "I'm not being kind to you because you happen to be with my brother. I like you because you are a *good person*. Because you see Nox like no one ever has before. The more I've gotten to know you, the easier it is to see how and why he's so in love with you." My smile wobbles as my watery eyes hold his. A moment passes before he clears his throat and hops up. "Shall we make our way back?" he asks, extending his hand out to help me up. My muscles ache, but I direct my magic to soothe them as we enter the cover of the trees. "Any plans for tonight?"

"I'm going to go to a tavern with my friend Elora. I invited Nox to join us, and you can come along too if you want."

"Which tavern?" he asks, the question going unanswered because I realize that I never bothered to get that detail from Elora. Cass chuckles after a moment of my silence, his elbow gently bumping my arm. "Don't worry, I'm sure Nox will be able to find you, Blondie."

Chapter Fifty

Rhea

"Mom, I'm leaving early!" Elora shouts to the back of the bookstore she runs with her parents. The Overflowing Bookshelf is just that, an entire store filled top to bottom with more books than I have ever seen outside of an actual library.

Elora and her mother shout a few more things back and forth to each other while I browse the black shelves that line the entire circular space. It smells exactly how I imagined a bookstore built inside of a tree would—leather and aged paper and earth.

After my walk back home with Cassius, I had showered and then stared at my collection of new clothes, which seemed to grow weekly and had been moved into Nox's room. What did one wear to go out to a tavern? After much debate, my anxiousness had grown to be too much, so I shouted down the hall to Barron and asked if he could get Sarai. Within a few moments, the lovely dark haired woman had arrived and guided me towards a pale pink dress with a fitted bodice and a loose skirt that stopped just under my knees. Sheer ribbons tied in a bow held the dress at my shoulders. She paired the look with white sandals and then worked on my hair, giving it a small trim at my request before using her magic to twist it into soft curls.

"Okay, are you ready?" Elora comes bounding around a corner, her own dress of a similar fashion to mine except in a lovely shade of dark green that makes her copper hair and fair skin glow.

"You look beautiful," I tell her, letting her link arms with me as she leads us under the yellow glow of the spelled flames and out the front door where the fragrant floral air greets us.

"Thank you! You do as well! Do you know when the men will join us?"

I had been nervous to tell Elora that I invited Nox and Cassius, perhaps misunderstanding if she wanted this evening to be just for the two of us. But she had been excited instead and broke out into a song about how "more was merrier."

"I'm not sure, actually. They might not show at all, considering I couldn't tell them which tavern we were going to," I confess.

Elora chuckles as she guides us down the side of the busy city center. There are many people out grabbing dinner or shopping, some even chatting together in the middle of the stone road around various statued fountains that line the way. My pulse elevates, but I keep my focus on Elora as she describes the tavern to me.

"There is only one establishment in all of Galdr that is worth going to in the evenings, and that is The Gilded Cup. If they're smart, they'll know to come here." She tugs on my arm, our laughs mixing with music coming from the second story balcony of the large tree that houses The Gilded Cup. Elora pushes the swinging arched door open and comes to a stop as my eyes widen. Lining the edges of the tavern are tables and chairs, men and women sitting in them to drink and eat and engage in conversation. The center of the space has been cleared out of furniture for people to dance in.

"I've never seen anything like this," I say to Elora. She smiles and squeezes my hand, her look of understanding calming my nerves.

I try to take in all the details as we start moving again. Instead of a chandelier like the palace has, long ropes with glass orbs holding spelled flames dangle every foot or so from the true ceiling of the tavern. It lights up the center space brilliantly, casting the edges where the tables are in a soft glow.

Elora holds my hand and pulls me through the dancing bodies until we emerge on the other side where a long counter separates us from a man and a large collection of colored glass bottles behind him. "Evren!" Elora shouts over the music of the band playing behind us from the floor above.

He looks up from the glass he is cleaning and smiles wide, shaking his head and sending his curly blond hair out of his eyes. "Elora, I didn't know you'd be here tonight! Do you want the usual?"

Elora nods, bringing us up to the counter. "This is my friend Rhea. She's never had cider mead before, so let's get her started with one of those too."

Evren's gaze lingers on Elora for a beat before turning to me. He extends his hand out to shake mine, his wide smile lifting his cheeks. "Rhea, I'm Evren. I'm honored to pour you your first cider," he says with a chuckle, his cheeks warming to a light pink.

"It's nice to meet you," I shout back. He turns to start preparing our drinks, and I look back out over the dancing bodies. The band plays a jaunty tune, the sound of drums, string instruments, and singing echoing off the walls within.

"Here you are, ladies. Two ciders," Evren says as he sets two glasses filled with light golden liquid onto the counter.

Elora drops some gold coins onto the counter before handing me one of the glasses, clinking hers against it. "Cheers to new friendships and books!" she yells before bringing the glass to her mouth. I slowly follow suit, remembering Alexi's words about how he hated the taste of mead. Yet, when the drink floods my mouth, the sweet taste of apples dances on my tongue, a fizzing sensation bubbling down my throat as I take a large gulp. "It's good, right?"

"It's delicious!"

Elora laughs as she sets her glass down. "Evren! Watch our drinks, will you? Rhea, let's dance!" She doesn't wait for either Evren or me to answer before her fingers lace with mine and she guides us into the crowd of people.

"I don't know how to dance," I tell her, looking around nervously at the way everyone is moving.

"Neither do I! Just let the beat of the music guide your body. Tune everyone else out." Elora raises her hands in the air and begins to shake her hips side to side.

I gaze back around the crowd of people and observe how they all seem to be doing the same thing. Keeping to themselves and dancing in whatever way they want. So, for the first time in my life, I throw my hands up in the air and I dance.

We take breaks to go drink our mead, Elora insisting that I alternate with water as well so I don't get drunk. I do feel a pleasant hum in my body, one that isn't caused by my magic. We return to dancing, Elora spinning me out and back to her as we laugh. The band picks up the beat of the music, the glass bowls holding the spelled flames on the walls shaking from it. My heart races, the people surrounding me blurring, but all I feel is joy and happiness and *freedom* as I smile. Warmth lifts up from my stomach, my magic stretching like a waking cat. It heightens my focus for a moment, and I can't help but look towards the front door of the tavern.

"What is it?" Elora asks, gasping for air as she slows her dancing to follow my gaze.

The tavern door opens, and though I can't see their faces because of the people surrounding us, I just *know* it's Nox. "He's here!" I tell her, smiling widely.

"Who's here? What are you—" She stops mid-sentence as the crowd begins to part and we watch Nox and Cassius head in our direction.

Nox's gaze roams over the entire space as Cassius greets a few mages with friendly smiles and handshakes. My heart leaps into my throat when Nox's eyes finally lock with mine. He looks incredible—trading in the all-black training gear that he wears most of the time for a dark blue button-up tunic, the top few buttons undone and showing a swath of his tanned skin. The long sleeves are rolled up to his elbows while the bottom of the tunic is partially tucked in at the front. Black trousers and calf-high black boots draw my eyes down his body, but when I bring them back up again, I can't look away from his hair. He's gotten it trimmed, the waves a little shorter on top than before. His face is clean shaven, though I've learned that he prefers it that way. He looks regal and devastating and absolutely, utterly *mine*.

"How in the Five Realms did you know he was here?" Elora asks at my side. I don't have an answer for her because I'm not sure, other than my magic seeming to awaken at his proximity. I assume it's because his signature is so strong.

Nox easily cuts through the remaining crowd, his broad, tall frame making him stand out and garnering more than a few eager stares. But his eyes are entirely focused on me as they leave a searing trail down my body. "Beautiful isn't a descriptive enough word for how stunning you look, Rhea," he states, his eyes darkening under the low light of the flames. His hand finds its way to my hip, his fingers flexing there as he leans over to kiss my cheek while I grip onto the front of his tunic.

"Okay, okay. Enough of that," Cass chides playfully as he comes up next to us, a hand planting on each of our shoulders.

Laughing, I reach back and grab Elora's hand to draw her up closer to our group. "Cass, this is Elora. Elora, this is Cass." They exchange greetings, Elora also saying hello to Nox before she announces that it's time to dance again.

I lose count of the number of songs that are played, my dance partners cycling between Nox, Cass, and Elora. When a new tune starts, the crowd cheers before they separate, men going to one side and women going to the other. Realizing it's some sort of choreographed dance, I opt to watch, encouraging Nox to stay while I head back to where Evren is and take a seat next to the counter. The music picks up its tempo and the two groups surge together in the middle, their steps light and beating in time to the rhythm.

"Would you like another cider, Rhea?" Evren asks, blowing a blond curl away from his forehead.

"I'm good for now. Thank you, Evren."

He grins and then walks towards the other end of the counter where a man has taken a seat. A stony face looks my way, the man lifting his new drink in salutation. I dip my chin and then move my gaze back over the dancing crowd.

I find Nox as he pairs up with a familiar head of dark golden blonde hair. Haylee takes his hand, her smile wide as together they follow the choreography with everyone else. I rub my finger over Alexi's bracelet while I watch them, trying to force down the odd feeling in my chest. As if she can feel my gaze on her, Haylee's gray eyes connect with mine, and I think her lips give the smallest twitch. Though the moment only lasts a few seconds at most, I feel my stomach sink when she leans in towards Nox, their bodies nearly chest to chest before he spins her. The men and women shift again in their dance, Nox partnering with an older woman and Haylee with a different man, a brilliant smile once more painted on her face.

I shiver, shaking my head before looking down at my hands. My magic hums warmly inside me, but for the first time in weeks, I can also feel the prodding of something icier. I blow out a frustrated breath.

The song ends, both lines bowing to each other before they disperse and the band starts a different tune. Elora is the first to make her way to me, wrapping an arm around my shoulders. "Are you alright?" she asks, leaning into my body.

"Of course! That dance looked like fun!"

Elora reaches for her drink, downing the last few dregs before holding it up in a signal to Evren. "It was. I'll teach you the moves so you can join us next time."

Nox abruptly tugs me up from my chair, spinning around until he's sitting in it and I'm standing between his legs. I wrap an arm around his shoulders, running my hand through his hair and tugging his head back gently to look up at me. "Who would have thought that princes were taught tavern dances in addition to waltzes?"

He shrugs, his hands sliding in a distracting line up and down my sides. "I'm a man of *many* talents, as you are well aware."

Though warmth builds in my core at his words, I tap my finger on my chin, feigning ignorance. "I'm not sure I know what you're talking about. You might have to show me later."

Heat sparks in his eyes as he brings me even closer. "How should I demonstrate for you, Sunshine? With my fingers? My tongue?" His voice is a gravelly rumble as he nips at my ear, making me gasp at the sensation. "Or how about with my c—"

"Hey! Daxel."

My head whips around to the man standing behind us, the same one that had lifted his glass in my direction earlier. Nox's demeanor shifts instantly, his face settling into a bored expression. I turn around and sit on his thigh, staring up at a tall man with short blond hair—his light gray eyes narrowed in our direction. His appearance is disheveled, the red tunic he wears is wrinkled and partially unbuttoned down his chest.

"Arin, it's good to see you," Nox replies coolly, his tone one of indifference. His hand wraps possessively around my hip, and the man, Arin, glances briefly at it before his lips curl into a malicious sneer.

"*Bullshit.* You've been hiding since you've been back. Though I suppose the rumors why are true enough." He turns his gaze to me, something dark swirling in it that makes my magic creep up my torso. Nox's fingers tighten on my hip as shadows seep towards us from the corners of the room. The band continues playing, but those closest to us halt their dancing.

"Ah, Arin. Glad to see you're still making terrible decisions," Cass says as he moves in close from the dance floor and rests his hand on Arin's shoulder.

Arin shakes himself free, stumbling as he does. "Shut the hell up, Cassius. This is between Nox and I."

"And what *exactly* is between us?" Nox asks.

"I want a rematch," he growls, the light above glowing directly on him and showcasing better how red his eyes are. *A rematch?* "While you've been gallivanting around the kingdom—doing gods know what—I've been training. Getting stronger. Stronger than even *you*, and I want a rematch."

"No, Arin. I'm not going to fight you again, and I'm *certainly* not going to talk about it here. You're drunk—"

"Did you not hear what I said?" he interrupts, his face growing more flushed. "Or are you too afraid now that you might *lose*?"

"Gods above, let it go," Cass says with exasperation, taking a step so that he is between Arin and Elora. Arin shoves at his shoulder hard, but Cass hardly seems to register it, as his body barely moves.

Nox tenses beneath me as he sits up straighter. "Enough, Arin. Go home." Tension crackles in the air from the rise of everyone's magic. Arin's hands begin to glow a dark green, and another flash of black writhes on the floor towards his feet.

"Arin, what are you doing?" Haylee shouts as she pushes through the crowd and comes to stand in front of him. "Are you drunk?" Arin shakes his head but wobbles from the movement. She huffs out a breath and pushes him roughly towards the exit, completely unafraid of the magic still glowing from his hand—unbothered by the death glare he's giving Nox. Haylee tosses a small wave and a sympathetic look over her shoulder at us before shoving Arin out of the tavern.

"What was that all about?" I ask, turning to look at Nox.

He sighs, kissing my temple and drawing me closer as his magic settles. "Arin has always had some weird grudge against me. I've never quite figured out why, only that he tries to antagonize me any opportunity he gets. Before I left for the Mortal Kingdom, he challenged me to fight in front of Dilan."

"And you won," I surmise, watching Nox's lips twitch.

"Uh, he didn't just win, Blondie. He kicked Arin's ass *easily*, even without the use of his magic," Cass claims, elbowing Nox in his arm.

"You did?" I ask, my gaze shooting back to Nox's.

He lifts a single brow, a smirk slow to grow. "You don't have to sound so surprised." And then, leaning in closer, he whispers, "Do you not find my body to be that of a warrior's?"

I melt from the seduction in his voice, the pure desire in his gaze when he draws back. "Maybe I need you to show me again."

Nox chuckles darkly while Elora pushes around Cass to stand in front of us. "Well, that was... *whatever* that was," she says, referring to Arin, "but can we please get back to dancing now?" Her hand extends out towards me, but I send a questioning look at Nox.

"Why don't you go ahead, Rhea," he answers, placing a soft kiss on my lips. "This warrior's body needs a rest."

I laugh and then grab Elora's hand, letting her lead me back out onto the dance floor—where we spend what feels like hours laughing and dancing together.

I hum as I walk hand in hand with Nox after leaving the tavern, Cass having gone with Elora to make sure she makes it home safely. We pass different statues and water features built around the center square, one in particular drawing my eye enough to tug Nox towards it.

A beautiful woman, her hair long and wrapping around her hips, stands in the center of a pool, the water shooting out from the perimeter towards the middle. She wears a crown with a flaring sun centered on it, two mirrored crescent moons on either side, and stars filling in the gaps between them. Carved on her in exquisite detail is a long dress that clings to every curve, a line drawn down the middle of it. One of her hands is extended in the air, as if offering the city of Galdr whatever is on her palm, though I cannot quite make it out. The other palm is drawn down, something round in the middle of it that has darkened with time.

"This is the first queen of Void Magic," Nox says at my side.

A sweet-smelling breeze ruffles my hair as I stare at the woman, her expression carved into one of soft happiness. There are no words etched onto the statue, nothing to indicate who it is other than the lore of it having been here for a very long time.

My finger reaches out to drag along the cold stone of her arm. "She's beautiful."

"Indeed," he answers, but when I look to him, he's staring at me.

We continue our walk back to the palace, the two guards stationed at the front doors opening them as they bow to Nox. The inside is quiet, not much more than the late night shuffling of steps by the palace aides, until the sound of voices carries down the hall and into the main foyer.

Nox stops, his head tilting to the side before his cheeks lift with a smile. "Bahira," he says, looking down at me. "I think my sister is talking through the Mirror with my parents. Can we say hello?"

"Of course." Nox had previously told me what the Mirror was and how it worked, the magic of it linked to the land and blood of the current ruler.

He leads us down the hallway towards the council room, knocking on the door in a rhythmic pattern before opening it. Sadryn and Alexandria stand together in front of a tall oval-shaped mirror near the head of a long twelve-person table. Their gazes turn towards the door, and Alexandria motions for us to come over. I can feel Nox's excitement as his parents take a step to the side to make room. Through the glass of the Mirror—which looks as if it's liquid—stands Bahira with her curly brown hair pulled up into a high ponytail, the long strands dangling past her shoulders. Her arms are crossed over her chest, and even through the faintly distorted image, it's impossible to miss how beautiful she is. And, once more, how intimidating.

"Hello, nerd," Nox says, leaning back against a chair and wrapping an arm around my waist.

"Hello, idiot," Bahira responds, someone on her side of the mirror chuckling deeply at her response. Her eyes narrow as she turns to look to the side before focusing back on us—on *me*. "You must be Rhea."

"It's a pleasure to officially meet you, Bahira," I say, a bit shakier than I would have liked. Her smile is small but genuine, and I get the feeling that she doesn't offer brilliant wide ones to anyone until she is sure about them. I understand that to my core.

She updates Nox and their parents on her journey so far in the Shifter Kingdom, detailing the experiments she is running and things she is doing, even from afar, to hopefully help the Mage Kingdom and its people get their full magical capabilities again. The conversation eventually dwindles to goodbyes, Nox squeezing me more tightly to him. As Bahira steps back from the Mirror, a woman's sing-songy voice calls her name out followed by another deep chuckle. The glass gets cloudy, like an impending storm, before it settles back into an unassuming mirror.

"She looks well," Alexandria says to Sadryn, wrapping her arms around his waist and laying her head on his chest.

"Are you surprised?" he replies in a teasing tone, rubbing his hands down her back.

"No, no, of course not. But I can't help but worry."

Sadryn kisses the top of her head and whispers something only she can hear before lifting his gaze to Nox. "I'm glad you were able to—"

"King Sadryn of the Mage Kingdom," a voice, slightly altered, abruptly booms through the Mirror. I stiffen, my magic rushing to my throat.

Nox holds me closer to him, his voice soft as he says, "It's okay. This is how the rulers communicate through the Mirror. It's probably King Kai using it for Bahira again. She must have forgotten to tell us something."

Sadryn steps closer to the Mirror, the glass altering as the magic runs through it. But it isn't the fact that a phantom voice rang through the Mirror that has my heart beating at a frantic pace. It's the cadence of the voice, the note of malice within it. I *recognize* that voice deep within my bones. It is one I still hear in my nightmares, one I'm afraid I'll never fully be free of.

My fear is confirmed when the image on the Mirror settles and King Dolian's face is there.

Chapter Fifty-One

NOX

"SHIT," MY FATHER STARTLES, stepping back from the Mirror with a jolt.

My gaze is still on Rhea's, watching as she grows pale and her body becomes rigid. My magic pushes at my bones, feral in the way it seems to *beg* to be unleashed.

"King Sadryn, I'm glad to see you've *finally* answered my call." His voice is like rusty nails scraping down my back, and when I look at him, the cunning smile he has painted on his vile face falters. "*You*," he snarls as his hands clench at his sides.

Drawing his attention back, my father responds, "Well you have my attention now, King Dolian. What can I do for you?"

Dolian looks between my father and myself, seeing more than I ever wanted him to because he's starting to put the pieces together—the ones that tell the story of who I am and what I've done. "You sent your *son* to infiltrate my kingdom?"

"I'm afraid I have no idea what you're talking about," my father replies smoothly, taking a step forward to try and block out some of what Dolian can see.

It's too late, however, because the vile bastard isn't even looking at my father anymore. He's staring at the trembling woman in my arms. Shadows lift from the floor and come rushing towards me as I use some of my magic so that I don't take this entire palace down from the way rage boils in my blood.

"Hello, my darling Rhea," he purrs while shoving a hand into his pocket. "Are you having *fun* on your little adventure away from home?"

A growl erupts from my throat, but Rhea lifts her head and stands taller. "The Mortal Kingdom is *not* my home."

King Dolian laughs, the sound completely at odds with the macabre contortion of his features. "Don't you remember what I told you? You can run and hide, but I will *always* find you. You belong to *me*. You always have, and you always will."

"*Enough*," my father commands, his voice dripping in disdain. "Lady Rhea is not a *thing* to possess. She is a person who has chosen to stay in *my* kingdom. She is protected here, King Dolian, and there is nothing you can do to force her to go back." My chest swells with pride as I glance at my father, my grip on the shadows now swirling around the room relaxing a fraction.

"She was *stolen* from me!" he bellows, his teeth bared as his hazel eyes grow wide with fiery anger. "Rhea, I want you to listen *very* carefully. You are *mine*, and I will stop at nothing to bring you back to where you belong. If that means showing you the depths of what I'm willing to do, then so be it. But it will be *your* hands dirtied with the blood of the sacrifices you're willing to make so that you can play pretend with that lying *prince*."

"I am going to *kill* you," I vow again, eager to end the monster whose blood I will *gladly* coat my hands in. I command the shadows to rise until they are swirling at my shoulders, cloaking me in their darkness as I glare at him. They protectively curl around Rhea as well, her small gasp at the feel of them making Dolian sneer.

"When she is back at my side and I have her in every way *you* cannot, it will be you who dies a slow and painful death." His cold eyes then turn to my father. "Enjoy the safety of your people while you have it, King Sadryn. One can never be too sure when such a thing might be ripped away." He steps away from the Mirror, his gaudy red and gold throne coming into view before the image distorts as the magic fades and the glass returns to its solid mirrored state.

"He is *atrocious*," my mother hisses.

The hair on the back of my neck rises, and I whip my head around to find Daje standing at the door, his wide eyes transfixed on the Mirror. *Fuck.*

With a deep breath, I unspool the shadows from around our bodies and turn Rhea so that she is facing me. Her eyes are glossed over, the color still leached from her face as I cradle it in my hands. "Sunshine, look at me," I say gently, tilting her head back to meet my gaze. She does, her shaking fingers wrapping around my wrists. "I want you to head upstairs to our room. I'm going to handle this, and then I will be right there. You are safe here. Always. I won't let anything happen to you."

She nods, a tear leaking down her cheek. My magic turns volatile, the urge to feel Dolian's neck snapping beneath my fingers spurred on by the sight of that solitary tear. He'll pay for ever causing her a single *ounce* of pain. Clenching my jaw, I walk Rhea to the door of the council room. Daje's eyes meet mine as he swallows roughly, Rhea brushing past him in a daze. When she rounds the corner, I gather the shadows and wrap them around Daje until they become solid ropes as strong as stone.

"What are you doing *here*?"

"I thought I heard Bahira's voice," Daje grunts out against the tightening confines. He doesn't try to fight his way free though; instead, his dark blue eyes stare directly into mine. "I was coming to see if it was her when I heard—"

"What *exactly* did you hear?" I ask, heat flaring in my palm from the magic that glows there.

"Nox, release him," my father urges from my side. My mother stands next to him, her fingers resting at her throat as she moves her stunned gaze from me to Daje.

"Not until he tells me what he's heard and what he plans to do with that information."

Daje's father isn't just on the fucking council—he is my father's *lead advisor*. He cannot know who Rhea truly is or where she comes from, *especially* if that information comes with also finding out that King Dolian all but threatened the Mage Kingdom if Rhea doesn't return. Councilman Kallin's duty is to our kingdom—one that he takes seriously and one that, under any other circumstance, I would be happy of his steadfast dedication to.

"I heard everything," Daje replies cautiously. I tighten the shadow ropes around him until the muscles in his neck flex. "But I'm not going to say anything. To anyone. Not even my father."

"Nox. Let him *go*."

"I swear it, Nox," Daje rasps, and though it goes against every instinct lighting up my body, I release my magic and send the shadows back to where I gathered them from. Daje falls to his knees as he struggles to catch his breath.

Squatting down next to him, my voice lowers until I'm sure it's deep enough to rattle his bones. "I'm choosing to trust you because you are my friend and because I know Bahira does. But if I find out that you have betrayed me in *any* way—that you have betrayed *Rhea*—I will kill you without a second thought."

I wait for Daje to nod his agreement before standing and striding out of the room, feeling my parents stunned gazes heavy on my back. I take the steps up to our room two at a time, anxious to reassure Rhea in any way she needs that she will always be safe with me. I don't even make it all the way up before my magic sharpens within me. Like a needle finding true north, I can feel exactly where Rhea is. It's how I found her at the right tavern this evening.

Barron's worried gaze greets me at the landing, but he simply nods his head in understanding at the pained look that must be on my face, stepping out of my way and then moving back into position as I pass. I quicken my steps, my hand pushing through my hair as I finally reach the door. I allow one slow and steady inhale before I open it—finding Rhea pacing back and forth in the dim light of a single spelled flame, her hands twisting nervously into the fabric of her dress.

"Daje won't say anything," I tell her, hoping to ease some of the anxious tension that has filled the room in my absence, as I close the door behind me.

I expect her to immediately ask how we can be sure—a question I don't exactly have an answer to—but as she makes her way towards me, it isn't curiosity that swirls in her eyes. Hunger, desperate *hunger*, floods her gaze and flushes her cheeks, the emotion making me question if I'm seeing her correctly. Her fingers begin to fumble with my belt buckle, and I'm stuck between growing arousal and utter confusion as I watch for a moment before laying my hands on top of hers and halting her shaky movements.

"Rhea?"

"I need you. I need to *feel* you. To know that we are here. Together. That nothing will *ever* separate us," she rasps, her gaze full of the truth of that desire as her eyes bounce between mine. "Please, Nox."

It feels as if I'm being strangled when I look at her. I love her so fucking much that it physically *hurts* to see her so frightened. So unsure. With a hand on her hip and the other weaving into her hair, I walk her backwards into our bedroom. My gaze catches on a folded-up note lying on top of the side table next to the bed. *You make me feel safe*, she had written in her own letter to me this morning. Now that safety, one that I thought was impenetrable given that we are an entire kingdom away and behind an enchanted border, has been compromised.

I tilt her head back until her eyes meet mine. "Whatever you need is already yours," I whisper as I glide my lips against hers. My cock grows harder at the sound of her breath hitching, at the way her hands go to my tunic this time and unbutton it with a softer urgency. I love the way her desire for me is always one gentle touch away, one light caress from igniting fully. My own hand slides down her neck and over her shoulders, reaching behind her to the buttons lining down her back. I kick off my boots, her sandals falling next to them. Together, we shed what remains of our clothing, the action fueling the steady slow burn of desire growing inside of me. My gaze drifts down her body as I reverently savor every inch of skin, every freckle and curve.

Wanting to fall to my knees should be a foreign feeling—something only reserved for my crown and my kingdom. But she rules above them all, a goddess that shines brighter than any star, and I crave to surrender only to her.

Particularly with my tongue.

I let her guide our next movements, swallowing my own eagerness to taste her in favor of whatever she wants—whatever she *needs*. Her warm hands run down my chest slowly, her green eyes acute as they drink me in before she turns us around and walks *me* backwards until I'm forced to take a seat on the bed.

"I need you close to me," she rasps, straddling my thighs with her knees as her hands wrap around the back of my neck.

I'm not going to last long like this, not with her taking control. Not with the way her scent hits me when she's so close and how her hair frames her face in sweeping strands. She is my fantasy and my ruination, perfection created specifically for *me* to worship. One of her hands leaves my neck to wrap around my hardened cock, guiding it to her entrance with a confident touch. *Shit, I definitely am not going to last.*

Gritting my teeth, my hands find the soft divot of her waist, slowing her down so she doesn't hurt herself. "Careful," I murmur against her neck, the cover of darkness hiding the way I have to squeeze my eyes shut as I begin to fill her.

Sex was never something for me to linger on before her, nothing but a momentary pleasure. Yet the first time with Rhea had been different. Maybe it was stupid to expect anything else when it came to her, because she had been nothing but an axe to every preconceived notion I had since the moment I met her, but I was still surprised by the emotion I felt. How every second spent inside of her was like uncovering parts of myself that had been hidden strictly for us to find together. Like this, we aren't two beings lost to distance and kingdoms divided; no, we are an inevitability.

Her breath stutters as she adjusts to my size, the feel of her nails digging into my shoulders making my own falter. "Are you okay?" I ask, kissing her jaw and working my way around to her mouth.

"Yes, are you?"

I smile against her lips, that ever-present ache for her thrumming in my blood. "Always."

She opens to me, and my tongue slides against hers, our moans echoing in the room as I flatten a hand on her back and pull her closer. Shocks of pleasure coil down my spine at the feel of her soft skin against my chest, of how wet and ready for me she is. I'm completely overwhelmed by her, my body strung tight as she moves desperately for friction in my lap.

"Tell me I'm yours," she commands, her voice a husky cadence that threatens to unravel me right then, my cock twitching in agreement. "Tell me that you need me, Nox."

"You know that you are and that I do."

"I need to hear you say it. I need—" She chokes on her words as her arms wrap around me more tightly.

My heart pounds to the refrain of anger, my magic wild as it dances to the chorus within me. She needs me to say it because, despite knowing to her core how I feel about her, there is a scar that has built up over time from someone else trying to say that she was *his*. I kiss her forehead, her cheeks, and the tip of her nose before bracing myself with one hand on the bed as I wrap my other arm around her waist, right above her hips. I need to make sure she *feels* the surety of my words everywhere. That whenever she thinks of them, she's brought back to only this moment between us and nothing else.

"I could say that you're mine and that I need you, but that isn't exactly true." She leans back slightly to look at me, an adorable frown tugging down on her lips. "It isn't true because *need* isn't a big enough word to explain how I really feel." I push my hips upward as I hold her in place, the thrust of my cock moving inside her making her gasp. "None of it explains how you consume me in a way nothing else ever has. It doesn't explain how I would give up everything that previously held value in my life just to see you smile. How I'd lose it all to gain a *moment* of holding you close."

I thrust again, Rhea's back arching as she groans and tilts her head up towards the ceiling. The soft light of the spelled flame moves over her naked skin, highlighting the curve of her breasts and her peaked nipples. My mouth waters at the sight of her. *Gods,* she's so fucking beautiful and so fucking *mine*.

"It doesn't explain how you burn me from within when we kiss, a branding I'll willingly take over and over again. But, since other words fail me, I'll say that I need you. That I *crave* you." Again and again, I pump deeper into her while pulling her hips down in time with my movements, her cries of pleasure skating over my skin like a silken taunt. I want to fill her not only with my body but with my devotion—so that no part of her is left to fester in fear and doubt. "I wished for you before I ever knew that you existed. And now that you're here in my arms, I know that I'd destroy each and every realm, including my own, to keep you close. To keep you safe. Do you want to know why, Rhea?"

She drops her gaze back to mine as her hands twist in my hair, gently tugging the strands and tipping my head back. Her voice is soft, her perfect lips parting when she asks, "Why?"

I kiss the hollow of her throat, whispering the words against her skin and imbuing them with a different kind of magic. "Because you are my universe. You are my infinite sun and my endless sea. You are more than I've ever deserved, but you are *mine*, and nothing will ever take you from me."

Her chest heaves and her hands move down to cradle the sides of my face as she begins to rock her hips back and forth. "You have every piece of me," she rasps, her breaths coming faster. "All of me is yours."

She crashes her lips to mine, sealing our words together as our bodies move in synchronicity. I feel her magic surge—I can *taste* it, sweet like morning dew and honey. Her teeth nip at my bottom lip before her tongue smooths over it, and it's too fucking much. We become frantic, a medley of ragged breaths, sliding hands, and whispered pleas. Her inner muscles squeeze tightly around me, and my entire body tenses as desire crashes through me in fiery waves, each one stronger than the last. I am consumed by her—her scent, her body, her voice, her *love*. It all surrounds me until I'm moaning her name, my blood pounding in my ears as I spill into her.

Rhea collapses against me, our hearts lined up as they beat together—the flesh and bone separating them inconsequential. Possessiveness seeps into my every pore, holding me captive until I wrap my arms tightly around her to quell it. I wonder if she feels the same when her hands slide to my back and she squeezes us impossibly closer together. Trailing my fingers through her hair, I savor the way her body melts on top of me as I lay us back onto the bed with me still inside of her, unable to end that connection just yet. Our breaths slowly even out until I'm sure Rhea has fallen asleep, but then she lifts her head to kiss my chest before she rests her chin on it.

"My favorite part," she whispers with a sleepy smile.

Chuckling, I carefully, *gently*, slide out of her and move us so that she's lying at my side, her head still resting on my chest as our legs tangle together. Sleep pushes down on my eyelids, sweet darkness rolling in on the corners of my mind as my lips find the top of her head. Though the words aren't enough to truly encompass how my soul calls to her, I say them still. "I love you."

She snuggles in farther, her exhale a soft puff of air against my skin. I'm nearly asleep, perhaps even imagining it, when I hear her whisper back, "The moon may have the stars, but at least I have you."

Part Four

Lies and secrets do not make impenetrable shields. At some point, they are going to turn into weapons; ones that we may no longer wield.

Chapter Fifty-Two

Bahira

It was Magda. The mutilated body delivered by the rebels had been Magda—a mother just trying to survive. A female doing her best as a single parent who wasn't quite so, and she had been murdered so viciously that my stomach churns every time the image of her hanging from the columns comes into my mind. I think of little Sione, of her other children now forced to grow up in an orphanage, and have to swallow down my rage.

Kai had been reluctant to invite the people of his kingdom into his home to air their grievances and have their voices heard after the rebel attack. I pushed back when he initially declined my idea because I thought he needed to hear what the people's actual issues with him were if he was to make any progress on gaining their trust. After what happened with Magda, it seemed like the right thing to do. Yet, three days into hearing mostly the same accusations from the mouths of shifters who are all too eager to point their fingers and wag their tongues, I am beginning to believe that I have made a mistake.

It would be one thing if their comments held value, but the majority blamed Kai for the blight on their magic simply because they *could*. Or they blamed his father. And the king, for all the bite and fury I had seen leak from him in our private moments, sat there and took it. Over and over, his subjects yelled and condemned, and Kai might as well have been a statue for how little he reacted. Too few actually gave reasons for their anger, but when they did, Kai always responded with interest and a promise to fix what he could. I no longer believed him to be an apathetic ruler, and this show of restraint as he was belittled and verbally stoned was proof of that.

A persistent, aggravating voice nags at me in my head, scolding me for being so *wrong* about him. Another voice, less annoying and more urgent, doesn't like that rebels had breached the palace so easily. Then there is the fact that the rebel who attacked *me* somehow escaped from the palace dungeons. Tua wasn't forthcoming with any information when I met him in private, asking for a sample of his blood to study. He told me that it was being handled and that he'd make sure guards were stationed at all the palace entrances. Kai had been less reluctant to tell me that the rebel had killed one of his guards down in the cells and escaped before Tua could interrogate him. The information sat heavily on my chest. I collected a sample of Kai's blood as well—and Jahlee's later on, much to her morbid delight—before returning back to the experiment room to work.

The public forum was the next step on a long list of ideas I had worked up with Kai following the rebel attack, before we learned whose death would now weigh on my soul in a way I could never have anticipated.

One thing we had *not* talked about was how we had ravaged each other in the dining room before I used the Mirror to speak with my family. Or of how he slept in my bed. Even with our avoidance of those topics, there is no denying the cracks in our armor that have formed because of them.

"I swear to the gods, if another person blames Kai for something so obviously out of his control, I'm going to fucking lose it," Jahlee whispers at my side, her arms crossing over her chest as she stares at the long line of shifters still waiting to say their piece.

I nod my head, my gaze going above to the wooden rafters. The light, sandy-colored beams extend the entire length of the rectangular throne room, long fabrics in the colors of the kingdom's sigil—black, gray, and white—draping between each one. The air smells of salt and flora and the incoming rain storm, which makes the humidity mixed with the many bodies in the room feel stifling.

"Perhaps it was too much to make Kai do this for three days," I respond with a grimace.

Jahlee snorts before baring her teeth at a male waiting in line who is glaring at her. He shakes his head in annoyance but is slow to draw his gaze away. "I'm going to fuck him later," she whispers, elbowing me in my ribs.

I arch a brow, my eyes flicking between the male and her. "He looked like he'd rather fight with you."

"*Those* are the best males to bed. Their dumb brains can't handle it when their anger gets mixed with lust." I want to laugh at that, except it hits a little too close to home. "Anyway, did you find what you were looking for in our blood?"

I force my jaw to stay relaxed as I tilt my head to the side. In truth, I didn't exactly know how to answer that. While examining Kai's blood under the magnifier, I zoomed in as far as it would allow and watched as the cells moved within the liquid, nothing seeming out of the ordinary until I saw a glint of light. A flash—no bigger than the tip of a needle—there and gone before I realized what I was looking at. It happened one other time as I peered down the scope, the look of it like a faraway star flashing brightly for only a second. I might not have been as disturbed by the sight if I had seen that hint of light in anyone else's blood. When I studied Tua's, Jahlee's, and my own, I only observed what I had expected: blood cells and plasma and platelets—though there was a distinct difference in the shape of the shifter cells versus my own. The notes I had written in my journal reminded me that I had seen that spark of light before, but it was while peering at the leaves in magic-infused water.

Jahlee elbows me again, staring at me expectantly.

"She would be so *disappointed* in you!" A loud female voice cuts through the room, drawing our attention while everyone else falls silent. "To see what you've let them turn you into is a disgrace, Kai Vaea."

Jahlee and I glance at each other before our quick steps take us up to the front of the line, where an older female with short white hair stands at the bottom of the dais. Tua is posted on the stairs, splitting the distance between the female and Kai, his face set in a grim line as he holds his hands behind his back.

"Iolana?" Jahlee gasps, walking towards her.

The female turns, her head cocking to the side before a smile softens the edges of her face. "My Jahlee!"

Running to embrace her, the crowd murmuring louder at the sight, Jahlee asks, "What are you doing here?"

Iolana growls low, her head turning to look back at Kai with narrowed eyes. "There are rumors that your brother is denying aid for his own people." Her body shakes as she shouts.

"Come, Iolana. Let's talk about this over some tea," Jahlee suggests, guiding her away from the line.

Iolana grumbles something but lets Jahlee lead her to a door.

"We're done for today," Tua announces, walking down the steps with his hands raised over his head. "I appreciate you all coming out to speak with our king, and I promise I will make sure that your voices are heard."

My eyes narrow in on him, watching as Tua continues to ply the crowd with words of reassurance. The words scrape like thorns beneath my skin. Those should be *Kai's* promises to make to his people. I search for said king, startling backward when I see him barreling towards me after having stepped off his throne. "Godsdamn it, how do you move so fast—"

"Is this what you wanted? To have a line of people day in and day out pointing out how ill-fitted I am to be king?" He stares down at me with a cold expression, despite the hot fury of his words.

"Are you blaming *me* for whatever *that* was?" When he doesn't answer, instead brushing past me to continue down the dais and to the door Jahlee exited through, I grind my teeth together and follow him. "Kai, stop."

Of course, he doesn't. The asshole moves as if he doesn't hear me. I trail behind him down a small corridor that leads to an outdoor garden. Vibrant flowers in a variety of shapes and colors grow taller than my hip as I brush past them and down the rocky path to catch up with Kai's long strides.

"Do you honestly think I am trying to humiliate you? *Why* would I do that?" My blood rushes in my ears when he ignores me *again*. "You know what? Fine." Without warning, I kick the back of his knee hard, the sudden movement making him stumble and fall. His animalistic growl rumbles the ground beneath me as he looks at me from over his shoulder, his dark irises sporting two rings of gold. "Are you going to talk to me now?"

He snarls at me, his hand snapping out faster than I can react as he wraps it around my ankle and pulls hard until my back meets the ground. Kicking out at his chest with my free leg makes him grunt, but he doesn't let go of my ankle, instead rolling us off the path and into a patch of flowers growing off to the side.

He finally releases me with a growl when I stomp on his hand with my free foot, and I snap upright to straddle his hips before he has a chance to get up. My hands press into his chest as I hold him down.

"Get off of me, Bahira," he orders.

"Why do you think I'm trying to sabotage you?" I ask, feeling his heart race beneath my hands and mirroring the pacing of my own.

"Get. *Off*." He bares his teeth, canines elongating as fury ripples over his features and his eyes become lost to that bright golden color.

"I'm not afraid of you, Kai." I stress my words while leaning in close so that my face hovers over his. "I am *not* afraid. So tell me what is really wrong because you know *damn well* that I am not trying to hurt you!"

Heated seconds pass, Kai's jaw working as if he can chew the words he wants to say and swallow them down, but they break through anyway. "I will *never* be the kind of king that this island needs," he growls between gritted teeth, his façade cracking for only a second, but the hurt there is enough to make my heart skip a beat.

"You care about your people. I *know* you do."

"And that is not enough. You see what they say, how they *hate* me. I cannot be who they want me to be!" His eyes ignite anew with fury, and my own bounce back and forth between them as his fingers wrap tightly around my wrists.

"You are enough," I tell him, the words hoarse as they scrape up my throat. Kai stills, his top lip still pulled back over his teeth as his eyes grow wider. "You are *enough*," I repeat with added emphasis, my nails digging into him. "And if the people you have surrounded yourself with do not reaffirm that at every opportunity, then they are the *wrong* people to have as your council."

"They are the *only* reason I'm not already removed from the throne. Or dead."

I swallow as I shake my head, ready to voice what I know he won't want to hear. "I think you have a traitor in your court—"

"Be careful of what you say next," he says with a dark edge to his voice.

My brows draw together, and I push myself off of him, stepping away from where he's still lying amongst the flowers. "You may not want to hear this, but the way Tua behaves as your advisor is not *normal*. He acts as if it's his job to personally woo the court and nobles and people when he should be helping *you* do that." I swallow my anger down as I take another step back. "You're right. You can't be the kind of king your people need because you are letting *someone else* do it for you."

Turning on my heel, I leave Kai on the ground and make my way back to the palace.

※ ✦ ※

Kai avoids me the following day. And the next. I should know better than to lament over a male choosing to ignore me, but instead, I'm drowning in my thoughts about him.

Blowing out a frustrated breath, I focus my attention back on the mage journal in front of me while Jahlee clicks another disc into place on the magnifier scope she is looking through. The journal is mostly mundane, detailing Queen Lucia's days after the visit from King Kamon Ryuu and Lady Jia Ryuu of the Fae Kingdom. Apparently, they had gifted her a prized necklace as a token of friendship. I skip down the page to where I see talk of a Flame Ceremony, the descriptions of it indicating nothing wrong with the magic at that time. I nearly decide to quit reading for the day, but a capitalized word catches my attention.

On this final day of summer, the night before the Autumnal Ball, Queen Lucia visited the clinics of Galdr to bestow upon some the magic of Cessation. There were ten in all who waited for her arrival, clinging to life though they should not have been. They were of an age, ailing, and past the point of our healing magic being able to provide any comfort.

My brows crinkle together as I try to remember what I know of the Void Magic that queens of the past were blessed with. It is ancient magic and only given to one at a time whose soul was found *worthy*. Though how that was determined, no one but the gods themselves knew.

The celestial symbols of Void Magic are carved all over the place back home: doors leading into the palace, statues, tapestries, and places of business and worship. Everyone knows what those symbols mean and who they belonged to, but I can't recall a time when it was detailed how those powers *manifested*. In our schooling, we had been taught about how Queen Lucia used this magic to put the Spell up and effectively end the war, but there had been no heir found through any Flame Ceremonies since. It seems that lessons on such magic have devolved until they do not include information about what a Void queen could actually do outside of normal mage magic.

Maybe that is a flaw. Over two hundred years had passed since the war, but we had slowly been shaving off more and more information until only the barest of bones were left. Was it done intentionally? Or had it been the product of a complacent kingdom with a new family of rulers at the helm and no reason to change the status quo? As I try to pry deeper into my memory for anything at all detailing Void Magic, a new question tainted with unease pushes to the forefront—what all could be lost under the illusion of impenetrable safety?

"You're looking mighty contemplative," Jahlee sings from across the table, her brown eyes focused on me. "What are you reading about?"

Closing the journal, I stack it off to the side of the table with a collection of others and lean back in my chair. "Are you familiar with the queens of Void Magic from the Mage Kingdom?"

Jahlee cocks her head to the side, squinting her eyes as if sunlight is shining directly into them. "A little. Most of our education, at least in the place Kai and I grew up, was localized to this kingdom. We didn't learn much other than it was a Mage Queen who cast the Spell in retribution for the war starting."

"What? It wasn't in retribution. She cast it because the Mortal Kingdom, Siren Queendom, and *this* kingdom were warring with each other. Then the fae showed up on their dragons ready to end everything and everyone, so she made the decision to send everyone back home to stop the fighting."

Jahlee gives a fake and hearty laugh, clapping her hands slowly as she stands from her chair. "Is that what they teach over in *mage* school?"

"Yes, because it is the truth," I defend.

Jahlee drops her hands to the table on either side of the magnifier. "I suppose that from *your* point of view it is."

Pointless, this conversation is *pointless*. Shaking my head, I stand up and take a few steps towards her before leaning my hip at the edge of the table. "Who was the woman that yelled at Kai the other day? The one you ushered out of the room."

"Iolana is from the village we grew up in—Honna, right at the northern edge of the island. I was surprised to see her in the capital."

"Did you find out why she was upset?"

"Well, you heard what she said in the throne room. Apparently, a few shifters with family members that are stuck reached out to the palace for aid and were denied. She thinks Kai is to blame. I told her he wouldn't do such a thing, but she thinks he's lost touch with his roots. That the vultures—figuratively, not literally—of Molsi have corrupted him." Jahlee's features are tense while she thinks about the people affected from her home. Perhaps she even knows of some who can't shift back. She doesn't let the serious look last long, however, and a mischievous grin grows as she says, "But she scolded Kai even worse when he met us later that day. He didn't tell you any of this?"

"No, I haven't seen him since—" I pinch my lips together. Spending so much time with Jahlee over the past few weeks has taught me that she is incredibly clever, and I consistently walk into her verbal traps whenever it comes to Kai.

"Yes, he was in a rather *foul* mood when he met with us. I figured it had something to do with you," she teases.

I ignore her gibe and instead ask, "Did it not bother you, the way she was speaking about him?"

"Oh, it did," she says, her eyes darting to the door as she twirls away from the table. "But that's the thing about family; they tend to get away with things that most others don't."

"Family?"

"Iolana is our aunt. Our mother's younger sister." Before I can respond, the door to the room opens and Kai walks in. "Brother! You are looking *much* better today. Does it have anything to do with the female I saw leaving your room this morning?" I turn sharply at Jahlee's words, my jaw clenched until I see the pure amusement rippling over her features. She cackles as she looks at me, bowing at the waist before giving me a wink. "It's too fucking easy, Bahira."

Anger and embarrassment rush through me, propelling my feet towards her. But she darts away, giggling as she pushes Kai towards me to block my path.

"Have fun, you two!" she shouts, running to the door and slamming it behind her.

"There might come a day when I murder your sister, and I just want you to know that she will have earned it," I warn.

To my surprise, he only smirks, folding his arms over his chest as he leans a hip against the table. It's another cloudy day on the island, the sun hidden behind their dreary shades of gray, and still, Kai's skin glows as if he is creating sunlight himself.

And here I am, waxing poetic about it like some love-struck fool. Stuffing the thought down, I ask, "What can I do for you?"

His gaze travels over my face, flicking up to my hair before settling once more on my eyes. "We have another visit to make."

Chapter Fifty-Three

BAHIRA

Honna is just under a day's trip when traveling on foot, something Kai has made sure to mention twice since I met him down in the palace foyer the following morning. "If you want to shift into your wolf, I'll happily ride you so we can get there more quickly," I had offered, only to get an annoyed—albeit heated—look in response.

The sun has already crested its highest point for the day, descending down towards the horizon as we make our way on a path forged through the jungle. Humidity lingers in the air, my curls wild around my face as sweat beads on the back of my neck. I've already complained to Kai about it more than once, earning only snorts or amused grunts in return.

Our conversation is light, both of us avoiding the topics that are harder to navigate. I have always easily detached my feelings from intimacy. It comes as naturally to me as training with my spear does, so it's even more unsettling that, from the very beginning, I have struggled to keep my emotions in check around Kai. Even when those emotions were teetering on the edge of pure disdain, I hadn't been able to reel them in.

"Tell me of your experiments," Kai insists. We walk side by side, the trail barely wide enough to do so—leaves and other fauna brushing against our arms as we pass.

I look over at him, my gaze traveling up the expanse of his tattooed arm until they meet his dark eyes. "How about an exchange? I'll tell you what I've found with the blood, and *you* tell me what your tattoos mean."

Kai, to my everlasting shock, doesn't hesitate. "Deal, Princess. You first."

I smile, one that is perhaps wider than usual and not managed by caution nor tainted with sarcasm. It makes the shifter king misstep as he kicks up the small pebbles that line the dark soil of the jungle path beneath our feet. My hand shoots out to steady him, feral delight dancing in my expression.

"Fucking jungle," he grumbles under his breath, drawing a small chuckle from me.

I launch into the retelling of my experiments from home, only leaving out our kingdom's own magical decline. Kai questions if this is why I am so reluctant to try my magic on his people, and all I can do is nod before quickly changing the subject to what I found in his blood.

As we hike, I explain that his blood looked *different* under the magnifier, that it reminded me of something I had seen from home, but I didn't know *why* that was. This fact seems to intrigue him as much as it does me.

A shrill scream interrupts our conversation, and I automatically reach for where my spear is attached to my pack, but Kai holds his hand up to stop me.

"It's not a shifter." His eyes scan the path ahead, his jaw relaxed as he takes in the other sounds that echo out in response. "We should keep moving. Honna is still a few hours away."

I stay in step with Kai the rest of the way, burnt golden light from the setting sun painting the foliage around us. We enter the outskirts of the small border village, and I eagerly take in the place Kai used to call home. It's reminiscent of the other places he and I have visited over my time here, but there is a noticeably different *feel* to it. The sound of the waves rolling in from the nearby shore is louder, while the chatter of people talking is more like a low hum. There are fewer people out mingling though animals of all species dart behind the homes, moving along the edge of the jungle in skittish steps.

"Can you communicate with *real* animals when you shift?" I ask, the back of my hand accidentally brushing against his. The path had widened as we got closer to what I assume is the village center, large structures with carved signs hanging from their doors dotting either side. Yet Kai and I remain close to each other, his warmth at my side different from the one that surrounds us—even with the sun nearly gone.

"*Real* animals?" he asks sarcastically.

I wave my hand in exasperation in front of me. "You know what I mean."

Kai laughs as he looks down at me from the corner of his eye. "No. I can *sense* animals when they're near, but I can't communicate with them. Nor can I speak with another shifter while they are not mortal."

"Well, that's a relief."

He huffs out another noise of amusement as he guides us to a two-story building, a bear paw and butterfly wings etched into the door. It creaks when Kai pulls it open, the yellow light of flame gems placed equidistant around the foyer illuminating every corner. Kai talks with a female who sits at a desk in front of a wall of wooden cubbies, metal keys on braided ribbon strips stuffed into each one.

Our rooms are on the second floor, the doors facing each other from across a skinny hallway. Walking into mine, I sigh in relief at the clean and quaint space, dropping my pack to the floor. White pillows and a rich burgundy comforter beckon me to collapse onto them, but I immediately head to the bathroom for a cool shower.

Once the sweat from our journey is washed off of me and I'm dressed in clean clothes, I open my door to head to meet Kai and find him already waiting for me in the hall. He's showered too, the longer strands of his hair on top pushed back from his face while a few shorter ones hang over his forehead. Even wearing a simple short-sleeved white tunic, the material thin enough to see the black tattoo lines underneath, there is no mistaking the power he exudes. No questioning that this male is not just any predator in a land of beasts but the apex. The one all others should bow to. If only he could see himself in that light. His gaze travels over my own outfit, slight surprise glinting in his eyes at the green dress I chose, the shade reminding me of the dark-colored leaves on the albero trees back home.

"I didn't know if dinner would require a nicer outfit. I can go change—"

"No," he cuts in, moving towards me and reaching out his hand. "I will find myself quite angry with you if you change."

I snort to hide the way those words spark heat between my legs and place my fingers into his waiting palm without hesitation. We still have so many things to talk about, but giving him my hand is a choice that doesn't require much forethought. He guides me towards the stairs, the width of them just enough for us to descend side by side.

We step out into the cooler evening air, glittering silver stars shining brightly above us along with a nearly full moon. Kai gives me a brief tour of Honna's village center. The people milling about smile warmly at him, a few even come out of their stores to speak with him, shaking his hand before introducing themselves to me. Some glances linger on the place where our fingers are interlaced, and each time it happens, I try to wiggle my hand free. Kai responds by squeezing my hand more tightly. Eventually, I give up the pointless act and instead offer a small smile at the questioning looks that get sent my way. The truth is, even if these people asked outright, I wouldn't know how to explain why he is holding my hand. Or why I enjoy it so much.

I keep watch of the gazes that land on us, noticing a haggard few outliers that keep to the shadowy corners of the shops. One includes a male, his hands resting on two young females—their clothes dirtied and hair messily gathered behind them. They watch us warily as we pass, like they aren't sure if we're a threat. They make no attempt to speak with Kai, so I don't bother pointing them out to him.

We walk all the way to the edge of Honna, where a two-story business stands. The windows are open on the first floor to reveal a gathering of people laughing and singing and talking.

When Kai opens the door and guides me in with a hand on my low back, every gaze in the establishment lands on us. Then a cheer goes up and glasses clink together, and despite myself, I can't help but smile. The people here don't send Kai menacing looks or secret glares. They don't snarl in his direction or whisper as he passes. Instead, they offer genuine conversation and revelry, and something about that—about knowing that there is a place on this island that doesn't harbor ill will towards him—makes my stomach feel pleasantly warm.

"You owe me an explanation of what your tattoos mean," I say around a bite of food, the salty ocean breeze pulling more strands of hair from where I've tucked them behind my ear.

Kai's fingers drum along the stem of his wine glass, the red liquid nearly gone within it. He extends his arm on the table until the entire top of it is bathed in moonlight. "Let me see your hand." I reach across the table, and he wraps his fingers around mine, setting them over the first band of ink that is lowest on his wrist. "There is an ancient ritual that all shifters must go through before they are considered an adult. They can request the ceremony at any age past seventeen. Only when they master the challenges can they get their first tattoo and begin the tableau that will detail their lives." His skin is warm beneath my fingertips as he drags them up to the next tattoo.

"When did you request your ceremony?" I ask, my gaze fixed on our point of contact.

"The earliest moment I could."

"And when did you get your first tattoo?"

I can hear the pleasure—and pride—in his voice when he answers, "Seventeen."

My eyes find his then, only to dip down to his lips. His smile can't be described as wide or brimming compared to someone like Jahlee, but for Kai, it is like watching the exact moment the sun dips past the horizon or a star winks to life in the night sky. It's rare and *raw*.

Clearing my throat, I gesture to the next set of lines. These are more intricate than the band, a V-shaped pattern filling the space between two thick black borders. "What does this one represent?"

"My mother," he says thickly. His fingers twitch around mine, but when I look at him, his attention stays focused on his arm. My thumb brushes the back of his hand in a gentle swipe, and the corner of his mouth lifts a little in response. I push my fingers farther up, tracing over the next tattoo. It covers most of the rest of his forearm, the design one of black whirls like cresting waves that meet at the midline of his arm. The melancholy that surrounded him seeps away as he explains that this larger piece is dedicated to Jahlee.

"I imagine that she loves having such a large focal point devoted to her on your skin," I tease, earning a deep chuckle from him. "Do any of these represent a past lover?"

Not that I had ever asked, but neither Kai nor Jahlee ever mentioned anyone from his past that he might have been romantically involved with. I suppose I hadn't really noticed, between the general stares of disdain or disinterest he received, if there were also those who looked at him with open hunger. He is an attractive king, his strength and fortitude only adding to his appeal. I had to imagine that there was no shortage of females—and males—wanting to drag their mouths over his body. Wanting to watch him crumble beneath them. Or over them.

"No." His one word answer draws my focus back up, and I arch my brow in question. In a movement that makes him look younger, he drags his hand through his hair and holds it there, his voice a touch quieter as he says, "There have been lovers but never anyone important enough to ink permanently on my skin. I have never *allowed* there to be."

I nod, understanding his need to self-isolate in this way. He goes on to explain what the other swirls and intricately woven lines mean. Some represent his animal form, others pivotal moments in his life. He casually mentions the first time he killed a rebel who attacked him, showing me where the short marks of ink that are on his upper arm are dedicated to the life lost. Our elbows rest on the table as we lean in towards each other, Kai letting my fingers drift over his arm as he tells the story of each one. It really is a tapestry of his life, one that only he truly understands but is willing to give me pieces of.

"Thank you for telling me," I say quietly, my fingers cold without his touch when I lean back in my chair. He dips his chin and drains the last bit of his wine before we leave the restaurant and make our way back to the inn, our conversation shifting to the events of the public forum.

"I want to apologize to you for that," he states as we climb the steps to the second floor. We stop in front of my door, Kai's towering frame in front of me as I lean back against the wood.

"And what *exactly* are you apologizing for?" I ask as my lips curl. "There is the fact that you thought I was sabotaging you. You could apologize for ignoring me for days—"

"Let's assume that the apology extends from the moment I stepped off the dais to now," he interrupts with a wave of his hand. "It was not easy hearing what I already assumed to be true from the people of this kingdom. It was as if the whispers that caressed my back became screams pelting my front." He shakes his head, apprehension pulling down his brows and sending a hint of vulnerability into his gaze. "There are not many people I trust, but I am loath to admit that I trust *you*. So, I'm sorry."

His sincerity pulls my breath from me even as guilt slithers like a serpent in my veins, making my heart pound beneath my ribs. "And if I don't accept your apology?" I deflect, focusing instead on the desire taking root when he glares down at me.

"Of course you would make this more difficult." He closes the distance between us, his chest rising and falling only a few inches away from my own. Despite his words, his eyes devour mine, eager intent gleaming within them.

"You did call me a thorn under your skin. And a curse," I remind him, maybe to appease my own conscience. "I suppose you need to ask yourself if the poison you believe me to be is worth consuming in order to earn my forgiveness."

Leaning over me, his thumb brushes my lower lip followed by the caress of his breath. "You will accept the apology, Bahira."

My name on his lips draws a shiver from me as I tilt my chin up to hold his gaze. "*Make me.*"

Kai meets my challenge with feral intensity, one hand wrapping around my hip to pull me closer while the other one opens the door to my room. He walks me backward, his mouth devouring mine while I dig my nails into his shoulders. I moan at his taste, his tongue sliding into my mouth in a manner that's neither gentle nor sweet. The door slams behind us, and he brings his other hand to my neck, gripping it as he pulls me closer to him.

"How badly do you want this?" I ask, my hand roaming down to stroke his cock over the fabric of his trousers, smirking when his grip tightens on me. "How badly do you want *me*?" It's an unfair question, one he has no way of answering truthfully while I am *lying* to him. However, those rational thoughts lose out to the desperation that slices through me. For the first time in a very long time, I crave being told that I'm *wanted*. And not just by anyone, but by *him*.

"Frustrating creature," he breathes, dragging his teeth over my bottom lip. "The things I want to make you do. The things I want to do *to* you. Of course, I want you."

I clench my legs together, need already pounding headily through me, as I grip onto the edge of his tunic and force him to let me go so he can take it off. Light from a nearby flame gem blankets the contours of his muscles, my tongue darting out to lick my bottom lip as I take him in. Gods, he is so fucking *perfect*. Muscles I've never seen so defined before ripple beneath his skin as he reaches for my own clothing.

With quick hands, he takes my dress off while I slide my undergarments down my legs, stepping out of them when they hit the floor. The veins in Kai's forearms protrude as he undoes the laces of his trousers, the fraying of his restraint making his fingers shake. Intent on torturing him further, I lay back on the bed, propping on my elbows before spreading my legs out wide and digging my heels into the comforter. Cool air sweeps against my sex, and my lips twitch at the frenzied look of hunger on his face. Gold flashes in his gaze, the thinnest ring appearing around his irises and signaling what I've learned is his animal trying to break through.

He stands before me completely bare, his hand wrapping around his impressive cock as he begins to stroke it. "You will be my undoing," he groans, his focus on the glistening arousal gathering between my legs. The power dynamic between us shifts in his direction as my attention falls to the way he works himself. Unable to stop myself, my fingers trail down my stomach to my aching clit, lust rushing through me harshly enough to part my lips with a gasp at the first searing touch.

I swirl my finger faster, my focus bouncing between Kai's golden gaze and the rough pumping of his hand. Breaths rush out of me as I build to my climax, and the moment my head falls back, my release only another few strokes away, Kai rushes to me. He yanks my hand away from my body, ignoring my yelp of protest as he uses his forearms to pin my hips to the bed. I cry out at the first swipe of his tongue against me. Kai buries his face between my legs, the sensation of his mouth working me sending me to a blinding cacophony of whimpers and groans.

"The *taste* of you, Bahira. Burning hell."

So close. I'm so fucking close. My fingers grip onto his hair, pulling his head towards my core despite the fact that his tongue is already exploring it thoroughly. He gives me one long luxurious lick up my center before he lifts his head and crawls over my body, settling his hips between my legs.

"What are—" The question is stopped as his lips claim mine, my arousal flavoring the kiss.

"You can come when you accept my apology," he taunts as he pulls back, sliding his mouth lower until he drags his teeth over one of my nipples.

My breaths come unevenly as my heart flutters like a caged bird. *Control.* I need control. In two swift movements, I wrap my leg around his hip and jerk us to the side, Kai's weight making us flip positions with my knees now straddling his hips.

"Bahira," he rumbles, the vibration of it traveling down his body and into mine as his hands find purchase on my waist.

"Do you have any idea how often I've touched myself imagining it was you? How hard I come with your name slipping past my lips? You won't *stay out* of my fucking head." Leaning over to nip at his ear, I moan at the way his grip tightens enough that I know there will be bruises marking my skin in the morning. "I should make you beg," I muse, sex drenching every word. Delirious pleasure radiates from his expression, and though I wish to draw out my torment of him, my body is too eager. Reaching down to position his cock at my entrance, I gradually sink down a little onto him before drawing back up. Repeating the motion, I watch Kai's breathing quicken, my nails digging into his heaving chest.

"I'm going to make you regret teasing me." It's the only warning he gives before he thrusts up in one harsh motion, stretching me and filling me to the brim.

"You *assho*—" I begin to shout, but he pulls me down in tandem with his next thrust, effectively silencing me. We both moan, Kai's gaze heavy on me as I arch my back, sliding my knees farther over the bed so that I can take him in as deeply as possible. He feels so good—*so fucking good*—that I can't help but rock my hips, the angle and force of his own driving up unleashing a cry from my throat. Heavy panting fills the air, the tension between us thick as we move in perfect harmony. "Oh gods," I gasp. My eyes close, but Kai's hand shoots to my neck, his long fingers wrapping firmly around it.

"Watch who is fucking you, Bahira."

I force my gaze to his, sliding my hands over his chest and down the rigid muscles of his abdomen. His warm skin and scent work in tandem with the thrust of his hips to expertly unravel me. My breathing changes when the hand holding me in place tenses, and my orgasm rushes through me so harshly that my legs shake as I come. He immediately sits up and cradles my face, claiming my lips with his.

"Kai." I try to fight out of his intimate hold on me. I need to gain control again—I *have* to—but his grip is unyielding, his predatory eyes feasting on me until I surrender to his mercy. Kai rumbles his approval at this and kisses me again, this time more slowly, his mouth exploring me in exquisite detail. My movements are impatient, *needy*, my body craving the friction that only he can give me, but his hands leave my face and plant on my hips to hold me in place.

"Get on your hands and knees."

The command is given roughly, and I respond in kind, fighting to push him back down on the bed. But he's so much stronger than he's ever let show, and I'm weaker around him than I ever thought possible. So when he gives the order again, I crawl off of him and move onto all fours.

"You are exquisite," he whispers, trailing reverent, delicate kisses down my spine.

My breath catches from the act, my thighs growing more slick as I feel him coat himself in my arousal. Holding on to my hips, he squeezes once in warning before he fills me again. His size stretches me to the edge of pain, the prickling sensation making me groan. The pace he sets is devastating, and my hands slip from the force of his thrusts until my chest meets the blanket and my arms stretch out in front of me.

"Is this what you *need*, Bahira?" he asks, a hand gliding down my skin until it's wrapping into my hair and tugging my head back. *Yes. No. I don't fucking know.* The bow of my back and arch of my neck sends a rippling sear of pleasure through me, my inner walls clenching tightly around Kai as each snap of his hips brings me closer to release. "Say it."

I call out his name, aching pleasure rushing into every vein. Kai slows his thrusts down, letting go of my hair to wrap an arm around my waist. He hauls me up, my back smacking into his chest as my sharp gasp echoes out at the angle change. I reach up and slide my fingers into his hair, tilting his head down so that our lips meet in a blistering kiss.

More. More. More. It's the only word that forms in my mind as I suck his tongue into my mouth, the need to taste him and *feel* him overwhelming every part of me. It's chaos—a world-ending churning of pleasure and pain and bliss and agony. He's orchestrating both my demise and my awakening. I know that I am feeling too deeply, and yet I can't find it in me to stop this.

But Kai does.

He stills our hips, moving his hand down until his thumb flicks over my clit. I cry out, trying to wiggle for friction again, but he keeps me pinned in place against him and completely at his mercy. Sharp teeth meet the shell of my ear, sending waves of desire over every sensitive nerve. "Say it, Bahira."

"I despise you," I growl, but it doesn't come out with the gravity needed to make the statement believable. Kai's chuckle is a tantalizing scrape against me, his thumb playing as if he can't help but taunt me despite his own command. "I accept your apology. Now make me come again, or I swear to all the gods, I will punch you."

His lips skim over my shoulder as he resumes his merciless pace. One of his hands finds mine and flattens it against my stomach, laying his on top. He moves them lower, spreading my pointer and middle finger apart and placing them on either side of where he is fucking me, then draws them closer together until I can feel him sliding in and out.

"You take me so well," he growls in my ear, the words lighting me up as I lean my head back against him. "I knew you would. Do you feel that? Do you feel how only *I* can fuck you?"

"Kai," I whisper, his name a desperate plea. I said I would never beg him for anything, and twice now, I've broken that promise to myself.

His voice is softer than I've ever heard it before, even though he moves as if he's angry with me. His body doling out a punishment mine is all too willing to take. "I thought about you too. Just like this. Come for me, Bahira. Drench my cock with your sweet release." He buries himself to the hilt again, and I do as he says. I give it all to him, his name on my lips against his mouth as my body tightens. Kai pulses inside me, and together, we become undone. Resting his forehead against my temple, his hands hold me in place—perhaps knowing that the moment reality hits, I might crumble.

It's never been like this before. The ludicrous thought tumbles around in my head when Kai pulls out of me, carefully helping me off the bed so that I can head to the bathroom to clean up. *It's never been like this.* I can't even define what *this* is. The sex itself? The emotion in it? Kai's words and the way I never once found myself wishing for more or different or *other*? All of those statements are true, and all of them turn my stomach to lead because this place is not my home. *He* is not my home. He *can't* be.

He's still on the bed when I come out of the bathroom, my steps faltering as I take in each muscular plane and divot of his naked form. He studies me, acknowledging the inner turmoil that must show on my face. "I'll go," he offers effortlessly, as if understanding that I've never done *this*. Maybe he hasn't either.

My throat constricts as I watch him stand and walk to where our clothes are still lying on the floor. "Stay." He freezes, his eyes finding mine across the dark room as something new and *soft* forms between us. "If you want to." *Stupid. What a stupid fucking thing to say.*

But Kai gestures for me to get in bed as he climbs in too, this time going under the covers and reaching for me. He pulls me to him until my head is lying on his chest, the steady beat of his heart pounding beneath my ear and softening the tension in my body.

"Goodnight, Princess."

I allow my eyes to fall closed, my fingers uncurling until my hand is flat against his stomach and my breaths grow lazy. "Goodnight, Kai."

Chapter Fifty-Four

Bahira

Unlike the morning after the rebel attacked me, Kai is still in bed when I wake. Soreness lingers between my legs and on my skin where he gripped me tightly, but all it does is make me want him again. So I wake him up with my hand on his cock, replacing it with my body until we are both panting in the early sunlight.

After showering together, Kai goes to his room to dress and I meet him down in the brightly lit foyer. The female behind the desk offers me a polite smile, the same one she gives to Kai, and then we are off to the village to speak with more families. While most of the residents dwell within view of the village center, a few we have to trek a short distance through the jungle to visit. On our way back, after meeting a rather terrifying lion shifter stuck as their animal, a painful wailing fills the air, jolting us both as Kai snaps his head to the right.

"It's an injured animal," he states, turning and pushing his way past the lower lying plants.

I follow behind him, keeping up with his quick pace while positioning one hand within easy reach of my spear. He sucks in a harsh breath as he kneels. A beautiful bird, with colorful feathers—green, yellow, and blue—lays with its wings sprawled out on the ground, nearly hidden by the decaying leaves it's half buried under. Blood leaks from its long curved deep orange beak, its eyes wide and filled with terror.

"What kind of bird is this?" I ask, kneeling at Kai's side.

"A toucan," he replies, gently tilting the bird's body to the side where a large gash has shredded it. The toucan lets out another keening sound.

"How can you tell that it's purely animal and not a shifter?"

Kai's silent for a moment, not like he's ignoring me but trying to phrase his answer in a way that I will understand. "It's a *sensation* that I feel. Around other shifters, the feeling is thick, as if there is fog in the air. When a being is just an animal, it feels more like a soft caress against my skin." It sounded similar to how mages could detect the magical signature of other mages. He inhales again before turning to look at me. "I suppose your magic cannot help him?"

I swallow roughly, giving him a curt shake of my head. He sighs, reaching back to unsheathe the dagger from his belt. The same one he used when he sliced our palms open to bleed onto the petals. *Blood.* The word bounces around my mind as I watch more of it trickle from the toucan's mouth. *Blood.* My blood had done nothing to the petals, had no reaction, but Kai's—

"Wait." I gently grip his wrist, halting his attempt to put the bird out of its misery.

Mistaking my hesitation for sympathy, Kai's eyes soften. "Bahira, we can't leave it to suffer."

"I know, but I have an idea. It might not do anything, but if you're willing to try..." I fight to keep my chin drawn up, so used to the criticism and skepticism over my experiments. But as he studies me, those dark brown eyes full of intrigue, he simply nods and pulls from my hold to sheathe his dagger. "No, we'll need that." Fortifying myself with a deep breath, I lay my hypothesis out for him. "Your blood had a reaction with the petals. It gave them *life*, making them sprout healthy stems and new flower buds. What if the same principle could be applied to this animal? What if—what if your *blood* could heal?"

Kai's eyes widen in disbelief before his focus moves back to the toucan, the poor bird's breathing growing more labored by the second. His finger delicately strokes the top of its head as he considers what I've told him. "Okay, let us try." *Us.* I feel the invisible noose around my throat grow tighter. "What do I do?"

"Same as before, I think. Slice your palm enough for the blood to bead." Kai sets the bird down carefully and cuts himself, bright red filling the small crevices of his palm before he brings it above the toucan. I look at the open wound that is killing the toucan and guide Kai's hand to it. "Try dropping your blood there."

He nods and then tips his hand, crimson dripping right into the bird. The flow of his blood begins to slow, his own healing properties closing the cut fairly quickly. Kai draws his hand back, and together, we wait in silence. The bird cries out again though it's quieter and less panicked. Time flows slowly like trudging through quicksand, each step forward a work of glacial effort. I don't know what to expect, but it guts me all the same when it appears as if nothing happens. Kai's head falls between his shoulders, his exhale rough as he reaches out for the bird to prepare it for burial.

The lively squawk it gives surprises us both, Kai jolting back so harshly that he nearly knocks me over. In awe, we watch as the wound disfiguring the bird begins to sluggishly knit itself back together. There is no flash of light, like when a mage uses their magic, no dramatic or quick turnaround. But still, the bird's pupils return to their normal size, and it looks around as if it is confused about how it ended up on the ground. Kai wastes no time gently picking it up and cradling it in his arms.

"We'll bring it back to the village healer where she can finish mending the wound."

I nod, my eyes wide as they bounce between his. "That worked," I whisper, excitement prickling my scalp and making my lips lift with a smile. "That actually *worked*."

"You are brilliant," he replies, and *fuck*, that's admiration in his tone. "Absolutely *brilliant*."

I laugh, because I don't know how to respond or what else to say as my mind reels with this data. *This new data*. We continue back to the village center, both silent as I think, Kai recognizing that I need the space to work things out. *Blood*. It is something in every living being, something that binds us all together. If Kai's blood could heal a fatal wound like this on an animal, then what else could it do? What could a mage's blood do?

In school, we were taught that incorporating magic and blood was forbidden. Historians said that it was attempted in the past with catastrophic results. It's why I never had blood at the forefront of my mind when I discovered the red cells under the magnifier. Could it be that what we were told was *wrong*? Could the answer to the problems that plague me be found in the veins of those with magic?

I tell Kai my idea after we drop the toucan off at a healer's quarters. His face is a mask of calm, but I can tell that he is working out the details of the data I'm giving him, weighing the risk of trying such a thing on his people. To his credit, I can't guarantee what will happen, good or bad. He'd have to trust me blindly, something I wouldn't fault him for not doing—even if that annoying fluttering sensation in my stomach says otherwise.

"Kai, it's alright if—"

"We'll try it," he interjects, folding his arms over his chest. My mouth hangs agape, the processing of his faith in me slow. He snorts as he tilts his head to the side. "You did not think I would agree to it?"

"I... *No*." I endure the way Kai's stare seems to see right through me. He takes a step towards me until the space between us is gone and his fingers are playing with a loosened curl from my ponytail.

"Tell me what you need me to do."

Everything happens fairly quickly. Kai and I meet a handful of families, and I explain to them what I'd like to do, giving them a condensed briefing of the blood and magic hypothesis. The first few decline to participate, but the fourth family—one with a shifter stuck as a small mountain cat—agrees to let us try.

"There is no guarantee this will work," Kai says solemnly from where he is sitting next to me on a small couch in the family's living room.

An older male, his black hair peppered with streaks of gray, nods as he looks over at who I assume to be his adult daughter. Her gaze is focused on the animal lying at her feet, its fluffy gray and brown streaked tail lazily swaying back and forth. "It is worth it to try," he says.

"We will need to create a cut, to drip the king's blood in," I say, noting the female's frown at that. "Just a small one, but you will likely have to hold..." I pause, my cheeks reddening at not having asked for this shifter's name. Not even knowing if they are male or female.

"Eliza," the female says, her dark brown eyes glassy as she finally looks at me. "Her name is Eliza."

I nod and stand with Kai as the female and her father kneel on the ground next to Eliza. *Two years.* That is how long it's been since they've heard Eliza's voice. Since she's walked on mortal legs or sang a song or enjoyed a meal with her family.

"I will cut her—"

"Let me," the female interrupts, holding her hand out for the dagger. "I can do it."

Kai looks unsure, his eyes darting to mine in a silent plea, to which I answer with a small nod. He flips the blade so that the hilt is facing out and hands it to the female before unsheathing a second blade from his belt behind him.

"It doesn't need to be large, but it does need to be deep enough that the two bloods will be able to mix," I say.

Kai squats down and holds his hands directly over Eliza, the small beast now stirring as it looks around with curious eyes. She doesn't move when the female shifter rests a hand on her hip, nor does she seem concerned when the older male's fingers curl into her fur at her shoulders. It isn't until I kneel down on the ground too that Eliza's nostrils flare and panic creeps into her gaze.

"Now."

The female doesn't hesitate, taking the dagger and plunging the tip in at a fleshy part of Eliza's hip. Kai drags the other blade over his palm, blood beginning to pool as Eliza lets out a snarl. "I'm sorry," the female says, dropping the dagger to hold Eliza down. Kai tips his hand over, most of the droplets making it into the wound, while a few dot Eliza's fur.

"How much longer?" the older male asks.

I don't know how to answer him, having only ever tested this theory on the toucan. It seemed to happen more quickly then, but this isn't the healing of an outer wound. This is healing something that can't be seen. Not really. The inability to shift back into a mortal form is the consequence of the blight, and I have to hope that Kai's blood can fix that without knowing what is causing it in the first place.

Kai looks to me with expectant eyes. "Just a little bit longer," I plead. *Please.* He hears the unspoken word and flexes his hand to draw out more blood, though his magic is already beginning to heal his wound. As the dripping blood slows, my heart races faster. There is a relentless chant in my head, one that is begging for this to work. One that refuses to let me accept defeat, even when it has become painfully clear to everyone else. Kai sighs, sitting back on his heels and giving a nod to the two shifters holding Eliza down. They let go, and she immediately bolts out of the room and through the open front door. The female collapses into her father's arms, her chest heaving as she cries. The sound quietly screams of resignation and heartbreak and a sadness so devastating that I can feel it in my bones.

I don't fully register that I'm moving, my feet taking me outside in disjointed steps. My fingers curl into my palms, the sting of my nails not clearing the fog of melancholy and disappointment.

"Bahira."

I hear Kai call my name, but I don't stop. It's hypocritical of me, knowing how angry I got when he did the same, but I can't stop. I might fall apart completely if I do. My mind is in chaos, and there is no choice but to sit in this failure. In the missteps of my past and the uncertainty of my future.

Chapter Fifty-Five

ARIA

IN THE WEEKS THAT followed our departure from Eersten, Mashaka and I had found ourselves in an uneventful blur of swimming through endless open blue waters. My muscles ache from overuse, and the urge to shift into my mortal form has grown until it feels like I'm trying to keep another being stuffed beneath my skin. I suppose, in a way, I am. Relaying that to Mashaka, he squeaks in annoyance or protest or maybe even agreement, though I doubt very much it's the latter.

"I am not fully a sea creature like you are. I *need* to shift, or my body will be forced to do it. Can you imagine how much slower we'll be if I have to swim by only kicking my legs?" Tiny black pupils glare at me before he darts a little farther ahead as if he can't even bear to be next to me. As if it's *my* fault. Rolling my eyes, I swim up to the surface in search of a place to safely change and rest.

Swimming through the thick layer of the Spell, I raise my head just enough so that my hazel eyes can scan our surroundings. The beaches of the Mortal Kingdom stretch far and wide in front of me. I follow the long line of tan sand at the water's edge, my disappointment growing when I don't see a place suitable for my needs.

Sinking back under the surface, I'm about to voice the setback to Mashaka when he darts around me until his long snout pokes at my back. "What are you doing?"

He swims out in front of me and squeaks, the sound distinctly one of exasperation, before he takes off, leaving me to follow. He moves leisurely, and I wonder if he's also feeling as exhausted as I am. Minutes pass before Mashaka pivots to the right, heading towards the Mortal Kingdom's shore.

"Wait!" I shout, but of course he doesn't listen. My apprehension grows the closer we get, and I scan the waters looking for anything that might be a threat. The bottom of the seafloor nears, gradually lifting towards us. Only then does he slow, spinning around and letting out a lower-pitched squeak. My gaze slides from him to the shore in the background. "You want me to go there?" I ask, pointing. He doesn't answer, just swims past me and back towards the deeper water. "Wait, take my bag please!" Mashaka keeps swimming, and I'm half convinced that he's going to ignore me again when he abruptly turns and makes his way back. I slide my bag over him, letting it hang mostly from his dorsal fin. "You look adorable!" He snaps his teeth at me and then races back out into the sea. Turning to face the shore I mumble, "There is a fifty percent chance he's leading me into a trap," I mumble to myself while I swim as far as I can before shifting into my mortal form and lifting my head from the water. Though I suppose at the beginning of this journey that chance would have been closer to one hundred percent, so I guess I should be happy for the progress in our relationship.

The sand in front of me gives way to a rocky alcove, the gray and white striated rocks creating a natural arch that blocks the sun's rays. I try to stand and immediately stumble, saltwater stinging as it shoots up my nose. I'm sent into a coughing fit as I crawl the rest of the way, my legs wobbly from the lack of use in this form. Finally reaching the alcove, I check again to make sure I'm alone, before spinning to lay on my back with a huff. In my full mortal body, my braids give way to tight ringlet curls, the strands fanning out as water skims over them. The trapped feeling slowly eases away with the gentle tide, and I close my eyes, the sound of the waves lulling me into further relaxation.

I always feel different above the surface—not necessarily like I *belong* here, but like I am grasping at a freedom that I can't gain beneath it. If there were a way I could live as a mortal, completely forsaking my siren form, I think I would do it. That's my final thought as I begin to drift into sleep, the warm air blanketing my nude skin as the water softly laps around my body.

I wake just before the sun sets, lavender and wisps of pink coloring the sky above. The beach is still empty though a few ships have set anchors down in the distance. Crawling through the shallow water glimmering with the Spell, I wait until I'm deep enough to transform. Ruby-red scales cover my breasts and sides, gradually turning into golden yellow as they move down my forming tail and ending with a rich emerald green that stops at my tail fin.

The waters are calm as I search for Mashaka. My exploration draws me closer to one of the ships bobbing on the water, more dotting the surface nearby.

"Where are you, you little sea monster?" I grumble, pausing about twenty feet from one of the smaller boats. Though it's difficult to spot them, I can just barely make out the long and wide nets that the mortals on the vessels above have cast into the water to catch fish. It would be my luck to accidentally get caught in one of those, so I'd much prefer that we hurry and leave this area before that happens. "Mashaka!" I shout as a glint of silver scales catches my eye.

Spinning to the right, I watch a small school of tuna swim in my direction, chased by none other than Mashaka. I pinch my lips together, watching as he viciously snaps his mouth and tries to catch one of the zig-zagging fish ahead of him. The school changes direction, but Mashaka is quick and powerful and pivots with them. It isn't until the shadow cast by one of the boats moves that I see they are swimming directly towards one of the nets.

"Stop! Stop, Mashaka!" I scream, darting to intercept him.

But he's too focused on catching his dinner, and as the tuna pivot again, they lead him directly into a net, the impact of them all smacking against it causing the boat above to rock.

"Mashaka! No!"

Dread feels like an anchor of its own within me as I watch him get twisted within the net. I dart towards him while the mortals above begin to haul the netting up. I don't know if they'll release him. Gods, they might even *kill* him so he doesn't scare away the fish they are here to catch. I finally reach Mashaka, his bound body only a few feet beneath the bottom layer of the Spell.

"I'm here," I tell him, trying to cut the net open with my talons, but the frantic movements of both him and the caught tuna makes it difficult to find a spot to tear at. "Mashaka, calm down!" He squeaks out in terror, his black eyes wide as the voices of the men hauling him grow near. "Mashaka!" I shout as loudly as I can, the sound reverberating against the bottom of the boat and finally knocking him out of his panic. He stills, his gaze snapping to mine. "I'm going to help you."

At first, I try to find logical places to slice into the netting that I think will free him with the least amount of pain. But the net is already past the bottom of the Spell and mere feet away from breaking the surface.

"Shit," I hiss, abandoning caution in favor of hastily freeing him.

"What is *that*?" a male voice asks, and though I know the Spell is mostly crystalline, I'm hoping there is enough distortion to cause them to pause.

Mashaka stays still, watching as I shred more and more of the rope holding him. The top of his dorsal fin breaks the surface of the water, both of our terror growing when hands grip the netting next to him. I finally disconnect it just before the entirety of his body breaks the surface. The fish scatter as they fall back into the water, leaving Mashaka to sink—his body still too wrapped up in remnants of the broken net to move efficiently. I wrap my arms around him and guide him away from the boats and in the direction we need to continue on our journey.

"Let's get far enough away that they won't be a threat, and then I will free you." He responds with a series of squeaks that would make me laugh in any other situation. "What would Allegra say to know you almost got bested by a *net*?" I tease. At the mention of my sister, Mashaka tenses and goes silent. I can feel the quick flutter of his heartbeat beneath my arms, and guilt slams into me as we continue our escape. "I'm sorry, Mashaka," I whisper.

He doesn't respond, so I keep going, waiting until the sun has set and the half-moon is shining above us before slowing down. I edge closer to the shore so I can set him down on the sandy ocean floor and begin slicing away at his confinement. It's a meticulous process, some of the thin ropes spun so tightly around him that they have begun to cut into his skin. He squeaks in protest at almost every piece I remove, but eventually, he settles down and lets me work.

I cut the last piece off of him, thankfully finding my bag still hanging from his dorsal fin, and back up to let him swim.

"We should have a quick meal and rest before attempting the rest of our journey." Without a sound, he darts past me and back out into the open waters. "*You're welcome*," I groan as I follow behind him.

We easily catch a few salmon and find a spot to sleep between some phosphorescent anemones and coral, their faint glow brought on by the light of the moon. I curl my tail in and stack my arms to lay my cheek on top of after our meal, closing my eyes and willing sleep to come.

We finally reach the Northern Island roughly four weeks after leaving Lumen—if I'm counting the days correctly. The sun is barely past the horizon, the sky a blend of deep orange and bright blue, when I tell Mashaka to stay close to the shore and then change into my mortal form and begin to crawl towards the beach.

While I'm still not sure I can call the delphinidae a friend, since saving him from being captured by the fishermen, he *has* been nicer to me. Sometimes, he even brings me the first fish he catches before going back out to catch another for himself.

Standing on shaky legs, I trudge slowly over the white sands of the Northern Island, the sight of the beach without the Spell lining it a bit jarring. Climbing over white boulders made smooth by the crashing of the surf, I clutch my bag while I observe the narrow staircase. It is carved into the dark stone that makes up the cliffside, Virgreen Palace sitting atop.

My ringlet hair hangs down past my hips, dripping water and partially covering me as I scale the steps. The dark stone is cool beneath my feet, granules of sand scraping my soles with each step up. I have to stop and lean against the cliffside multiple times, my leg muscles shaking from being used in this way. After what feels like hours, with sweat beading on my brow, I crest the very top of the cliff and drop to my knees as I catch my breath.

Once the rushing of blood in my ears fades, I slowly stand and nearly get knocked back down by the sight of the palace. It's massive, perhaps even larger than the one in Lumen, and instead of pearlescent white, aged tan stone makes up the structure. Though its overall shape is rectangular, four towers of differing heights are built into it, two each at its front and back. Green vines and moss cover much of the palace's front, the plants hanging down over carved stone archways.

There's a ghostly quiet, one that clings to me as I walk towards what I hope is an abandoned manor. Climbing another set of stairs, my hand drags along a smooth stone banister to help me with balance as I enter a small round portico—if my memory of above-ground architectural terminology is correct. The plants are all overgrown, clearly no one visiting long enough to care for the space.

Before The War Of Five Kingdoms, this island was where the siren queen invited other rulers to come for peaceful revelry because, while part of our queendom, it was treated as neutral ground. When the Spell was cast, the island stayed untouched by its magical border. With no enchantment surrounding it, the Northern Island is technically open to all.

The stone beneath my feet softens into something more polished as I enter the palace through a large archway. Sparkling tiles of gradient blue and shimmering silver and gold glint in the sunlight like tiny gems. Above me is a large chandelier, small shells in pale blue and iridescent white hang in long strands from five different tiers. Tall columns in the same dark stone of the cliff line the hallway on either side, images carved into them that are too layered with dust and dried salt for me to decipher. The tapestries between the columns are tattered, age fraying them into unrecognizable strips of fabric that gently blow in the breeze coming in off of the ocean.

My mother had said that the treasure room where the rings would be kept is beneath the first floor, a magical locked door leading the way to the underwater vault. Remembering her instructions, I make my way through the maze of the first level, having to turn back and retrace my steps twice, until I arrive at the door with the sea urchin handle. All the while an eerie feeling makes the hairs on the back of my neck rise.

Now, Aria, you must remember this next step. If you fail to do it, you will die, and I'd rather not have to wait weeks to realize you couldn't complete this simple task. The memory of her words floods my cheeks with heat despite the fact that she isn't even here. Huffing out a breath, I drag my finger along the sharpened points of the handle before pushing down. Once blood beads on my fingertip, I smear it on the center of the urchin, watching in fascination as the liquid seeps *into* the unassuming metal and completely disappears.

The sound of locks sliding out of place echoes into the air, starting near the top of the wooden door and then traveling down until the last lock is opened and the door cracks open on its own. Hesitantly, I push it open a little more, poking my head just past it to see into the room. But it isn't a room that lies hidden beyond; it's a pool of glistening teal-colored water. The walls aren't made of tan stone but dark craggy rock, as if this place was carved here before a palace was built atop it. I expect to be plunged into darkness when I step past the threshold and shut the door, but crystals spark to life all around me. Some are embedded into the rocky walls, while the distorted light of others glows beneath the surface of the water.

"Into the water and through the tunnel," I whisper to myself, recalling my mother's pointed instructions. I dive into the water and transform, my eyes quickly adjusting to the view beneath the surface. The colors of the crystals gleam in pink and purple and yellow, and the temperature of the water is surprisingly warm as it glides smoothly against my skin. I move in the only direction that I can, the pool narrowing the farther I go until rocky edges brush against my shoulders. There are no crystals to light this part of the tunnel, and I'm left to swim blindly in the dark. I stretch my arms out in front of me, fear trickling into my veins and making my heart pound heavily as I wonder if perhaps this is some kind of elaborate trap put in place by my mother to finally kill me.

Out of habit, I begin to repeat my mantra to myself: *Jaw and shoulders relaxed, lips flat, spine straight, and attitude vicious.* Over and over, I say the words, first in my head and then out loud as I swim in the oppressive darkness. Something brushes over my arms and down my body, its texture slimy and inducing a million different horrible images of what it could be in my mind, but I push forward. Light glistens farther ahead, growing brighter the closer I get. A crystal, green in color, finally breaks up the darkness of the tunnel. The same jagged dark rock surrounds me, although moss and kelp line its edges—giving answer to the earlier slimy feeling. The water levels are lower here, and when I pop my head up from beneath the surface, thousands of crystals shine in the rock all around me. Like gleaming stars of every color, they illuminate the dark space in a rainbow of brilliance.

I've never seen so many gathered in one place before, and I'm momentarily so distracted by it that I don't notice all of the other items that are lying on natural stone shelves and stacked against the rock wall. Not until I shift and climb the three steps out of the water do I actually observe everything. Treasures and mementos that must date back to even before my mother and her mother. Older still if the film of algae covering some of the items is any indication.

I walk slowly, my gaze traveling over gold bracelets and necklaces with gems of all colors attached to them. There are conch shell helmets and armor, similar to the style the Queen's Legion currently wears except for the silver metal that has been melted and infused into the material. Three swords lay propped against the rock, their hilts glimmering with what looks like opalescent scales, a round diamond set at the very end of each. A line of dark blue cuts through the shining silver of the blades, a faint magical sensation buzzing from them. In fact, this entire room feels as if magic is coating every square inch of it. I stand on my toes to peek at a shelf. Small daggers and jeweled pins line it, giving way to leather-bound books that don't look decayed in any way. Letting out a frustrated sigh, I squat down lower to another shelf where I finally spot a collection of rings. Sifting through them, I find three that match my mother's description.

While all three rings are gold and carved to mimic a spindly piece of coral, two have a small pearl in the center, while the other has a thin line of dark blue similar to the swords. I can't tell if it's a trick of the light or not, but it almost looks as if the inside of the pearls and the line of blue are *moving*. Like mist is somehow trapped within them. Magic radiates from the jewelry, and despite the fact that it's clearly siren power that is imbued into these items, I drop them into my bag quickly, eager to stop touching them. I take a final glance around the room, grateful I'll never have to be here again, and dive back into the water.

Shutting the door to the vault, I head back towards the entrance of the palace. Perhaps it's the unnerving silence or maybe my own imagination, but I can't help but feel as if I'm being watched. My breaths rush in and out of me as I quicken my steps, checking over my shoulder every few feet. By the time I emerge from the palace and begin my descent down the steps carved into the cliffside, I'm practically running. When I reach the bottom, I sprint through the white sand, stumbling as I go, and back into the water, changing my form when I'm deep enough. Luckily, I find Mashaka a little ways offshore, his squeaks of surprise—or more likely annoyance—loud when he sees me.

"Let's get out of here," I say to him, and together, we begin our journey west towards the kingdom of the fae.

Chapter Fifty-Six

RHEA

"Good morning, Barron," I say cheerily to the guard, the window behind him allowing in a trickle of the early morning sun. His hands are laced together in front of him, and a wide smile brimming with joy greets my own.

"Lady Rhea, good morning to you." I wave a folded-up letter in front of me, Barron chuckling as I hand it off to him. "Never would have taken the prince as one to pass love notes."

Laughing, I shrug my shoulders as we both descend the stairs. "I think people often surprise us with what they are capable of."

Barron hums, his baritone soothing. "Or maybe it just takes the right person to bring out a side of us we didn't know we had."

"Well, that is entirely too sweet, Barron," I tell him as we reach the bottom of the stairs. "Please tell me you have someone special you're using those lines on?"

Barron scratches the back of his neck, a boyish grin making his cheeks lift. "I've been married for ten years now," he says, fiddling with the straps of the sheath that houses his sword, the hilt peeking up over his shoulder. I've never paid much attention to the weapons that the guards here have, but the sun hits the metal of it in just the right way that it highlights the small sun and moon engraved there.

"I hope they appreciate how sweet you are?" I question.

"I think they do."

"Good. Please tell your crown prince *not* to lose this note and that I'll see him later," I say with a wink, turning towards the front doors. Barron laughs at my back, the sound echoing even as he walks to wherever Nox is with his father today. Nox had confessed to me that he misplaced my last note. I was happy that one in particular didn't have anything overtly scandalous in it.

I only make it a few steps into the foyer before my name is called out. My magic surges within me at the familiar voice, and I internally curse at it to settle down before turning to face Haylee.

"Are you off to the training grounds?" she asks as she comes to stand next to me, her cheeks flushed and skin glowing against her all-black training uniform.

"I am. What about you?"

Folding her arms over her chest, she takes a deep breath before shaking her head. "No, I just finished my training for the morning."

"Already? It's barely past sunrise," I say with awe, marveling at the fact that she managed to do anything at all before the sun was up. Nox is lucky if I give him a groan of acknowledgement when he kisses me goodbye that early. Although, with the nightmares coming back in full force these past few weeks since King Dolian's appearance through the Mirror, I wasn't sleeping as well or as much right now. Which means Nox isn't either. My guilt at constantly waking him with my screams of terror in the middle of the night sits heavily in my gut.

Haylee smiles, her pretty pink lips showing off her perfect teeth. "You know how it is. When you want something badly enough, you will do whatever it takes to get there. By the way, you should be aware that you've made some enemies." I blink in surprise as I stare at her, something sharp flashing in her gray eyes. "I'm kidding," she says, placing a gentle hand on my shoulder. "I overheard some of the women complaining that Nox has stopped training shirtless since you two have officially announced your courtship."

"Oh, right," I say around a forced laugh.

"Anyway, I better go say hello to my uncle before the council meeting starts. I'll see you around."

"I'll see you."

Haylee turns on her heel and makes her way down the hallway that leads to the council chambers. Letting a breath flutter past my lips, I shake my head and continue my walk through the double doors and down the steps outside of the palace as I head to the training grounds.

The council. I am meeting with them in a few days, and Nox has been working hard every evening before bed to not only familiarize me with each council member but prepare me for the type of questions he thought they might ask. Things beyond just confirming where we met. *How will you support Nox as king? What type of queen do you envision yourself being? How can you support the council in its endeavors to maintain a peaceful kingdom?* That question in particular always made me stumble, as my very existence here was putting the kingdom at risk.

The memory of my uncle's threat sends a rush of unease through me, my next inhale catching in my throat as I stumble. Knowing that I need a moment, I step off of the stone path and into the forest, leaning against one of the large trees while I shut my eyes. *He can't cross the Spell. He can't get to me here. He can't hurt me anymore.* Though the words are strong, my resolve isn't quite there yet. I picture Nox's face and how, if he were here with me, he'd grip my shoulders and tell me to focus on my breathing. *Inhale. Exhale.* I am safe. I am loved. I am home. I repeat those three phrases over and over again, deepening my inhales and slowing down my exhales, just as Nox showed me to do. My posture relaxes, and I open my eyes, the scent of the woods strong with every breath. While my uncle's voice is still in my mind, it's an echo of what it was. More easily ignored. Uncurling my fingers from my palms, I make my way back onto the path.

When the unobstructed sunlight of the training yard blankets my skin, I smile, my light magic humming deeply within me. In between preparing for the council and trying to soak up every free moment we have together, Nox and I have been training my magic without the pendant on. He hasn't brought up accessing my shadow magic, and though I'm grateful that I've gotten stronger at blocking it out, I can still feel it lurking within me. Like a monster hiding in plain sight.

Cassius waves at me from our usual meeting spot near the middle of the grounds. "Blondie, you're late," he says, feigning a look of annoyance.

"I'm sorry. I got held up talking to Haylee." I keep my tone casual, but if there is one thing I've learned Cass excels at, it's being the opposite of casual.

"And what did *she* have to say?" he drawls, knocking into me gently once I stand next to him.

"She was just being polite. It was small talk."

His eyes narrow as he looks at me, and I narrow mine right back. He bursts out laughing, ruffling the hair on the top of my head. "You look adorable when you're trying to be serious." I scoff, a retort nearly off my tongue, but he keeps talking. "Anyway, we're going defensive today. I was hoping Nox would be able to join us so I could coach you as you two spar, but we'll have to make do." I nod as Cass comes up behind me. "Remember what we talked about yesterday. Just because I'm larger than you doesn't mean you can't get the upper hand. You've gotten stronger. You're building muscle. You may not have the ability to overpower *me* now, but you can *definitely* overpower Nox. His muscles have gone soft."

"Stars above," I choke out, laughing as he wraps his arms around me and draws my back to his chest. "I think his muscles have *grown* since he's been home. At least, they feel like they have."

"Gross."

I laugh at Cass's reaction, my arms pinned at my sides where he carefully has one arm above my chest and one wrapped around my stomach.

"Okay. What's the first thing you do to try and break this hold?" he asks, his chin brushing against the top of my head.

"Change the center of gravity to my benefit," I answer, widening my stance and squatting down low, "and knock you off your feet." I move to step my foot behind his, but he easily blocks each of my attempts.

"Keep trying. Move a little lower." I try, but Cass counters too quickly, blocking my path again. I let out a frustrated groan, my body going lax. He eases his hold around me, making sure I'm steady before letting go completely. "I have an idea!"

That's all he says before he takes off running, leaving me staring at his retreating back. A few moments later, he returns, Daje jogging next to him. When the latter spots me, he slows down, his gaze moving to the ground. I haven't spoken with Daje since he happened to walk into the council room when King Dolian was speaking. I don't know the details of what Nox said to him or vice versa, but I *do* think that he's been avoiding being anywhere near me since.

"Daje is going to spar with you so I can coach you better and see where you're tripping yourself up," Cass says with a huff.

Daje's eyes grow wide as he comes to a stop a few feet away from me. "I don't know if I should spar—"

"Oh, come on, it's *fine*. Nox won't be upset. I just need help critiquing her form. It'll be ten minutes," Cass says, pushing Daje towards me.

But my curiosity is piqued by his mention of Nox. "Why would Nox be upset?" I question, looking at Daje when Cass doesn't answer.

"He didn't tell you?" Daje questions, his eyes flicking from me to Cass.

"Tell me what?"

Daje sighs, his hands splaying out in front of him. "I don't want you to think that I don't understand why he said what he did or the action he took, because I do. I'm not upset with him for it. I just don't want to be on the other side of a threat made by him again."

My eyes grow wide as I take a step towards him. "He *threatened* you?"

Daje shoots a look of pleading towards Cass, who merely shrugs and gestures with his hand for Daje to continue. "For the love of all the gods," he says under his breath. "Look, he threatened to kill me if I said anything about what I heard. But I won't. And it's not a big deal."

"Not a big deal," I repeat quietly, my stomach twisting in on itself. Daje is Nox's friend, his sister's *friend*. Or lover—I still wasn't sure. I knew that Nox had been worried, angry even, that Daje had heard what King Dolian said, but to threaten him? I shake my head. "You don't have to spar with me if it makes you uncomfortable, Daje. I'm sorry."

He looks taken aback for a moment, his bright blue eyes reflecting the sunlight from above as he drops his hands to his sides. "It's alright, Rhea. I'll spar with you."

Cass claps his hands together, seemingly oblivious to the awkward tension now pulled taut between Daje and I as he orders us into the position from earlier so that he can critique my form. I tuck my questions for Nox in the back of my mind and focus instead on training.

Cass is able to properly identify why I couldn't take him down, showing me how to correct the movement and slide my leg behind Daje's so that I can take his out from underneath him. Though Daje takes hitting the ground multiple times in stride, even appearing more at ease than when I first saw him, I internally struggle with what Nox said to him.

When we've had enough sparring, Cass sends Daje on his way. We move on to our daily run and then training with the bow. I manage to land a single arrow on the target at the very bottom, earning a delighted cheer from Cass.

I'm dripping with sweat when we finally make our way back to the palace, the silence apparently giving way to my wary thoughts.

"You're upset about what happened," Cass guesses as we walk.

"I hate that we have to lie. That it's because of me. That Nox can't help but be so protective because he's trying to make sure I stay safe. At what point does it become not worth it?"

"I imagine, for Nox, that day will never come. To him, you'll always be worth it."

Sighing, I take in the palace at a distance, its three stories still not towering over the four massive trees anchoring it on each corner. Green vines and blooming flowers wrap around posts and grow over the verandas. It is so stunningly beautiful. This entire kingdom is, and my presence here threatens that beauty. The truth about my past, my identity, my magic... was that really what my life would always consist of? Yes, I am out of the tower and living with the man I love, but I am still shrouded in words that have to remain unspoken. I ache—my heart *aches*—with the weight of these secrets. How am I ever expected to fully and truly *live* if I constantly have to hide parts of who I am?

Cass and I climb the steps to the palace, the guards at the top opening the doors with a dip of their chins as we pass.

"Will you be heading to Nox?" I ask, gazing up at him.

"Yes, I—"

"Lady Rhea!" Barron comes barreling into the foyer, his boots squeaking on the glittering black stone floors. "I've just been sent to get you."

"On whose orders?" Cass asks, taking a subtle step between Barron and me.

Barron's deep gray eyes hold mine, something akin to panic swimming in their depths. "The crown prince's," he responds, taking a half-step back. "Please, we must go."

Cass and I follow Barron's quick strides, drawing a few puzzled looks from the people that pass.

"Do you think the council has summoned me early?" I whisper to Cass.

"Nox wouldn't let them. I don't think that's what this is," he responds firmly and is proven correct when Barron leads us not to the council rooms but to a door farther along. He knocks three times, pausing for a few seconds before adding an additional knock.

Sadryn opens the door, his features strained as his eyes move to Cass and then me. "Thank you, Barron," he says, dismissing the guard.

Barron sends me a weak smile before leaving as Sadryn beckons Cass and I inside, firmly shutting the door and locking it behind us. The room appears to be an office, but the details of it get lost when I see Nox standing with his back to us, a hand running through his hair. His magic is thick in the air, making my own perk up within me.

I look at Sadryn who gestures for me to move forward but places his hand on Cass's shoulder to hold him back. My steps are tentative, the pounding of my heart making it hard to breathe as I come to Nox's side. "Are you alright?" I ask him, leaning my head farther forward to make out his expression. He finally looks down at me, and I nearly gasp from the look of pure devastation that flattens his lips and draws his brows down. "What is it?" Scanning his body, I find him to be whole and uninjured, the only sign of his discomfort is what is so clearly painted on his face.

He drops his hand from his hair and, with a slight tremble to his fingers, hands me a folded-up paper, his thumb brushing over the back of my hand. "Before you read that," he states, his voice hoarse, "I need you to know that not one ounce of this is your burden to carry. Not one *ounce.*"

My gaze moves from him to the paper, the room deathly silent as I begin to unfold it. My hands still when I see the sigil at the top—a golden roaring lion. "What is this?" I whisper as I scan the elegant handwriting.

"The workings of a madman," Nox responds just as quietly.

Holding my breath, I begin to read.

My Darling Rhea,
Do you remember our last chat over tea? The one where I told you the story of how your mother came to the castle? I'm glad that I could share that tale with you, if only to have it fresh on my mind when I sent my guards into Celatum. I'm sure you and your lying prince felt safe residing there; perhaps he even told you that they kept his secrets over the years. However, a lesson I had to learn in my past—and one that you are going to learn now—is that you can get someone to tell you everything you want to know with the right motivation. All you need is the patience to figure out what it is that you can use against them.
And, my darling, I have patience to spare.
As it turns out, there is a man by the name of Edward who resides in Celatum. His family used to own the only inn there and did quite well for themselves. That is, until a woman showed up about twenty-two years ago and opened her own inn just down the road. It's interesting how grudges can fester over time. How they don't fade away but instead burn deeply until they're an inferno waiting to be unleashed. Edward is a patient man. Even

as business began dwindling, once loyal patrons now giving their coin to his competitor, he persevered. He let his growing anger become fuel. Anger and regret do make for powerful motivation. One that spurred Edward into telling my guards that a beautiful blonde woman and a large white fox were spotted together entering a certain inn.

I was surprised to see such a familiar face hiding in plain sight. I think she was even more surprised to see me when I had her dragged back to the castle. I'm afraid it wasn't a reunion either of us wanted.

I hope you recognize this gift I've sent you for what it is—your first sacrifice. Do you feel the blood on your hands? Can you taste the bitterness of the death you've caused? Will you keep playing pretend and hope no one else dies because of it?

Come home to me, Rhea. For this is your only true home.

I'll be waiting for you,

Dolian

I feel Nox slip the letter from my shaking hand as I lift my head up, tears lining my eyes. Sitting on the desk in front of us is a box of black stone, the dancing spelled flames reflecting off of its sides and top. In my panic to make sure Nox was okay, I hadn't even noticed it there. Now, however, it screams at me like a ghost making its presence known.

"Do you know what is in there?" I ask him, as his hand wraps around mine.

"I do, and I don't think you need—"

"Show me."

Nox doesn't move, doesn't speak until he takes a deep breath. "Rhea—"

"Please," I whisper. I need to confirm what the darkest corner of my mind is already certain of. I have to see it—the unknown consequences of my actions. The cost of my supposed *freedom*. There will be no saving me from this, and despite what Nox says, this *is* my burden to bear.

He hesitates another few seconds before clearing his throat and letting go of my hand to lift the lid off the box. My lip trembles as a rotten stench pours out into the room. Air rushes in and fuels a sob that splinters out of my throat. There, lying on a bed of golden silk as if it truly were a present, is the head of the owner of Immie's Inn. The woman whose name I now realized was short for something else, *Immelda*. She was the lead servant who took my mother in from the streets, according to King Dolian's story. It explains how she knew who I was right away. Alexi had told me that I looked just like my mother, and Immie's recognition of me all but confirmed that.

Tears trace warm trails down my cheeks as I force myself to stare at her mutilated face—her eyes missing and lips sewn shut.

Nox's voice buzzes in my ear, but I can't hear what he says. Not over the way my sadness and guilt and anger scream within me.

Before the sun has risen the next morning, on the ceremonial grounds of mage ancestors and past mage queens, Nox, Sadryn, Alexandria, and I lay Immie to rest. I watch as they sprinkle loose dirt over her small grave, my fingers woven tightly together as I squeeze my hands. They tingle as the blood flows back into them when Nox untangles and holds them in his own. His worried gaze finds mine, but he doesn't offer words of solace. I don't want them anyway.

Nox stands with me, even after his parents leave us, my gaze stuck on Immie's grave marker.

"What are you thinking?" he asks quietly, adjusting his hold so that his arm is wrapped around my back.

"I'm furious," I whisper, afraid the uncomfortable feeling burning within me will ignite the very grounds around us as my world flashes gray for a moment before righting. "I think I *want* to kill him, and that makes me even angrier." Because I don't want to be like him. I don't want to have those feelings.

"One day, you will have your vengeance, Rhea. Whether it's by striking him down yourself or through actions taken as queen. Whatever you decide, we'll do it together."

I lean against him, my hand resting on his chest as I nod my head. Perhaps this anger *could* be the fuel that leads to that. To *vengeance*.

I just needed to be strong enough to follow through.

Chapter Fifty-Seven

RHEA

I HAD ALWAYS THOUGHT of grief as something unchanging, something stagnant. I had so little to hold on to in my life that when I actually lost the parts that mattered the most, it felt like utter anguish. It was like leaping on rocks to avoid a raging river, only to discover that the next one I had jumped to was nothing more than a mirage. I plunge into the icy waters below and get swept away with the current until I'm nowhere to be found.

I was in pieces after Alexi's death. Those pieces shredded further after Bella's. Yet, since then, I have come to learn that grief is just as multifaceted as life. I hardly knew Immie, but I mourn her senseless death. My grief is jagged; it stings the sensitive, still healing parts of me as if it were a dagger slicing beneath my skin and into the scarred muscle below. A woman was murdered because we happened to stay at her inn—because my uncle is *obsessed* with creating the love story with me that he never had with my mother. This sort of grief is different than the kind I feel over Alexi. Over Bella. Different from what plagues me over the two lives my shadows had taken that night in the Mortal Kingdom.

But I am also different now.

I have begun to turn weakness into power and anguish into peace. I have made friends and found a home. I am in love, so *desperately* in love, that I often think that the agony of the first twenty-one years of my life has been worth it if it all leads to Nox. I would relive it over and over again to end up with him. It doesn't erase the way my heart drops when I close my eyes and see Immie as King Dolian's victim, but it does remind me that I've come too far to let this break me.

I mourn Immie's death, but I will not let myself succumb to the darkness that took months to crawl out of. That doesn't honor her life; it just gives my uncle the control over me that he so desperately wants. Never again will I lie down and let a monster devour my soul piece by piece until I fear there is nothing left to salvage.

Never again.

"We don't have to do this today," Nox says as he ties off my braid and wraps his arms around me from behind. He had already postponed the meeting by a few days. "If you need more time, I'll get it for you."

"I know, but I don't want to delay it any longer. It feels like we've been stuck in the shadow of the council for a long time." I spin in his arms to face him, my fingers sliding into his hair as I gently drag my nails over his scalp. "I want to do this for *us*."

Nox brings our foreheads together, closing his eyes as he leans into my touch. "When the meeting is over, I want you right back here in this room with me."

"And why is that?" I ask, a breathless tease to my voice.

"Because," he drawls slowly, kissing my temple and cheek before dragging his mouth to my neck and the space beneath my ear, "it's been too long since I've worshiped you on my knees. Too long since you've come on my tongue—my name on your lips as you do."

"You have the filthiest mouth," I whisper, tugging on his hair until his eyes meet mine. "And it's only been a few days."

"*Exactly*," he rumbles, his husky voice causing goosebumps to rise over my skin. I smile at him before leaning in to join our lips, his taste making a soft moan dance in my throat—drawing an even deeper one from him. "Are you *sure* we can't delay it?" His hands move down my sides to rest on my hips before tightening as he pulls me flush against his hard lines.

"Ravage me *after* I make a bunch of other men like me," I say against his mouth, kissing the corners of it before pulling back.

"Don't joke about that," he growls, but I watch as his gray eyes move from a storm of desire to something more tender. "I love you. Regardless of what anyone else says, that will never change. My love for you will not falter."

My exhale is soft, and it takes a minute to find my voice again. "The moon may have the stars, but I will *always* have you." I had told Nox the importance of those words, how I had never said them to anyone else but Bella. How they became an anchor of love and truth when I needed it most, and now they feel like the only ones strong enough to truly convey how much I care about him.

His responding smile is soft as he places one more kiss on my lips and then takes my hand. We turn for the door and for what I hope will be the first step towards a future where neither of us has to pretend to be anything other than what we are.

Upon arrival, Nox is asked to wait outside the council room. We had figured this might be a possibility, if only because the council recognizes that he is very vigilant over me and, as a result, they are afraid he will interfere if the line of questioning gets too *intense*.

"Are you ready?" Sadryn asks me as he walks up, placing a hand on Nox's shoulder. He's dressed casually just as he always is, his shoulder-length hair pulled back and tied at the base of his neck.

"I think so."

"Good." He sends me a wink before turning to Nox, chuckling at the tense look on his son's face. "She's answering questions in a council room not going on a deadly mission." Nox doesn't smile and instead glares at his father, who laughs again.

Nox turns to look me in the eye as he promises, "I'll be right outside these doors waiting for you."

I nod, giving him one last smile before turning and accepting Sadryn's extended arm. Together, we enter the council chambers.

"Please, come have a seat," Daje's father says as he gestures to an empty chair on his left. I glance at the council—all men with the exception of a single woman—as I move to the indicated seat, the fabric of my skirt shuffling as I walk. My steps seem to echo loudly, the weight of every pair of eyes on me making my shoulders round. The concentration of all the magic gathered here is suffocating, as if my head is being pushed below water.

King Sadryn sits at the head of the table, Daje's father to his left and the other eight council members spread out on either side so that the only empty chair remaining is directly across from me. As I take my seat, I look out at the rest of the room. I'm not necessarily surprised to see Daje sitting in a chair against a wall given who his father is. He nods his head sharply, a small grin accompanying the movement, before his eyes dart back to his father's. I am, however, surprised to find Haylee at his side. She avoids meeting my eyes, instead staring off to my left.

"You'll have to forgive Councilwoman Mora; she is out ill today and unable to attend," Daje's father says, his voice deep as he focuses entirely on me. "My name is Councilman Kallin, and I am the king's lead advisor and head of this council. I will be asking most of the questions, but the other council members may ask any additional ones they have as well. Do you understand?"

I nod in silence.

"Before we begin, can you please confirm for the record what your name is?"

I look at Sadryn, the corners of his mouth rising as he subtly nods his head. "Rhea Selene."

Councilman Kallin's gray eyes bore into me from my right. "And where are you from, Miss Selene?"

"The town of Santor," I answer, fighting the urge to nervously chew on my lower lip. *I can do this. I will* do this.

"And where did you and His Highness meet?" I answer the question and a handful of similar ones, feeling myself grow more at ease. We had prepared well so far. When I finish explaining how Nox asked me to come here to Galdr with him, Councilman Kallin gestures to the other council members. "You may ask any questions you have."

An older gentleman with kind brown eyes and graying-black hair sits up taller in his chair to the right of Sadryn, his elbows leaning on the table. "Hello, Lady Rhea. I'm Councilman Hadrik. We've heard the logistics of how you and Prince Nox came into your courtship, but I'd like to hear more about what drew you to him. What was it that made you fall in love?"

The councilman sitting to my immediate left scoffs, his hand running over his bald head. "The girl needs to answer questions that are *actually* relevant, Hadrik."

Councilman Hadrik tilts his head, his lips curling up the slightest bit. "*Lady* Rhea has indicated that she was not aware Nox was the crown prince when they met. I think it is *relevant* to have her prove to us that this is true by listing what she does in fact love about him. The entire existence of this line of questioning is to make sure someone isn't marrying into the royal family for the *wrong* reasons, is it not Councilman Borris?"

The other councilman grumbles under his breath but gestures for me to continue. I look around the table at the collection of faces here—some observing me like I'm something of mystery, while the majority study me as if I mean them harm. But thinking about the reasons I fell for Nox is easy because I *did* fall for him before I knew that he was a prince.

"It was his kindness," I start, willing my breathing to calm and my heart to beat steadily. "It was the gentle way he spoke to me and how he made himself aware of the things I didn't or couldn't verbalize that I needed. He is selfless and sweet and funny but also brave and incredibly smart. He loves his kingdom, his people, his family and friends. And he isn't afraid to show that love or to make it known. He is... *everything*."

The room is silent when I finish, so I flash another look to Sadryn, who sends me a wink in what I hope is approval of my answer.

"Hmm," Councilman Hadrik says, leaning back in his chair. "A lovely answer."

"Our current queen is quite involved in leading the kingdom with His Majesty. Should you and Nox marry, what kind of queen do you see yourself becoming?" the lone councilwoman asks from farther down the table to my left. She looks to be about Sadryn's age, her long black hair braided back from her face and resting over her shoulder in a style that's similar to my own.

I had thought long on this question, often writing down my thoughts in my journal on the rare mornings I would wake up early enough to do so. "I would hope to be the kind of queen that leads with heart. One who understands what it is to not always make the right choices but to persevere despite the mistakes made. One who is brave."

The councilwoman smiles as she laces her fingers together on the table. "You speak of bravery, yet you avoided this council meeting for a long while. Is the burden you placed on Prince Nox by doing so an example of how you will *support* him as his queen?" The man next to her—Councilman Osiris, I believe—snickers from where he leans back in his chair.

My mouth opens and closes, soundless words gathering behind my teeth that I can't voice. How could I explain that we needed time to prepare? That I *was* mage but *wasn't* from the Mage Kingdom?

"Councilwoman Naji, there is no need for this to get contentious," another councilman tuts, his seat next to the empty one across from me. He's younger than the others, his blue eyes and blond hair making him stand out amongst everyone else gathered here. He stares at me with a look of commendation, a small smile tugging on his thin lips. "We are all here because we care about Prince Nox and the future of the kingdom, isn't that true Lady Rhea?"

I nearly let loose a small sigh of relief as I nod my head. "Yes, it is." His grin widens as he twirls his light blue magic in his hand. The sight is distracting, as I've never seen someone just casually *play* with their power before.

"You have quite unique features for a mage—something I can relate to," he says with a chuckle as he gestures to his paler skin. "I am from Galina, are you familiar?"

"I'm sorry, I can't say that I am."

The councilman nods his head in understanding, the blue in his eyes reminding me of a winter morning. They are darker than Cass's but brighter than Daje's. "It's another border town, similar to Santor." His voice is gentle as he talks, my nerves easing as he continues to twirl his magic over his knuckles as if he were rolling a coin. "Because of where I grew up, I have a *soft* spot for those who come from the smaller cities, and I've done my best to get to know the people from them. In fact, just yesterday, I attended the Flame Ceremony of a young girl from Santor." Something shifts, in his gaze or in the air or perhaps both. Studying the councilman, I no longer feel like I am speaking with an ally. He draws his bottom lip between his teeth, letting it pop free before continuing. "Why don't you tell us of *your* Flame Ceremony? It's such a memorable time in a mage child's life; I'm curious to hear what you recall of it."

"Is that necessary, Arav?" Sadryn asks, attempting to sway the conversation. Nox hadn't told me much about Flame Ceremonies, only that they were performed to determine the strength level a mage would reach. "I don't see how it is relevant to Lady Rhea dating my son?"

"Oh, I believe it's *quite* relevant, Your Majesty. For one, it will give us a little more insight into Lady Rhea's magical strength and how it might pair with someone as powerful as Prince Nox. But, also, I'm always curious to learn the perspective that one takes away from the ceremony. Particularly if their magic is, let's say, *weaker*. As I'm assuming Rhea's is, or we would have heard about it.

Although I'd be happy to comb through our records until I find her ceremony to verify, if you would prefer not to answer the question, My Lady."

Oh Gods. There is no record of my Flame Ceremony. There is no record of *me* in this kingdom. My mouth dries out and swallowing becomes impossible, but I force out an answer. "I'm afraid that I don't remember much of my ceremony. Just a small flame." I had no idea if a small flame was a better or worse thing to say, but it seemed like somewhere in the middle.

Councilman Arav dissipates his magic, his hands clasping together. "Do you remember the sting of the knife as it dragged along your palm?"

Daje shifts in his chair, the squeaking drawing both my and Haylee's gaze. She gives him nothing more than a passing glance before turning to look at Arav, whose scrutiny of me makes my cheeks burn.

"Yes, of course I—"

"Enough, Arav. This has nothing to do with anything other than your own odd curiosity," Sadryn interjects, saving me from myself. Yet, despite the fact that I hardly got four words out, the councilman's blue eyes dance with intrigue at my answer.

"Of course, Your Majesty. I'm finished."

"Let us test your knowledge, then, girl," the man sitting next to me huffs.

"Councilman Borris, if you call this young woman a *girl* again, I will insist you see the healer to have your eyes checked."

The brashness of Sadryn's voice draws my shoulders up towards my ears. Any confidence or self-assurance I had is slowly being chiseled away, picked apart like a scab revealing the harsh truth underneath—they don't like me, and they don't want me with their prince.

Chapter Fifty-Eight

Rhea

"MY APOLOGIES OF COURSE," Councilman Borris says—though I don't know if he is apologizing to me or the king, as he doesn't meet either of our eyes. Only when a few seconds have passed and Sadryn nods his head does he continue. "I'd like to reference section ten, article two of the royal laws that bind our kingdom."

My voice seizes in my throat as a cold sweat breaks out on my neck. *The laws?* Nox hadn't prepared me for that. We hadn't even *discussed* them.

Councilman Borris' dark gray eyes gleam when he takes in my discomfort and my silence. "Perhaps you need your memory refreshed? Haylee, dear niece, come here."

My stupid magic surges, warmth permeating my chest and going all the way to my shoulders before I grip the dragon pendant and force out an exhale as slowly as possible to calm it.

Sadryn holds his hand up, halting Haylee as she begins to stand from her chair, an apologetic look written on her face. "The side members are here merely to observe *silently*." Haylee hesitantly sits down again, while Daje looks like he'd rather be anywhere but here.

"I'm afraid that I must contradict you, Your Majesty," Councilman Kallin says, looking from his son over to the king. "It is written in the Code of the Council that during the questioning of a potential consort to the heir apparent anyone present in the room is permitted to speak." I squeeze the dragon pendant even harder, its hard points digging into my skin. When Sadryn doesn't respond, his stare made of ice, Daje's father adds, "I'd be happy to pull the codex out for your reference if you prefer, Your Majesty."

A muscle in Sadryn's jaw flutters before he shakes his head, his eyes remorseful as he looks at me. "That won't be necessary. Proceed."

"Wonderful. Come, Haylee." Her uncle beckons her to the chair across the table from me, and though confusion still contorts her features, her steps are sure as she pulls it out to take a seat. "Please, remind us all what section ten, article two says."

"That section states that, above all else, the ruler of the Mage Kingdom must put their people before their own desires and wants. That, together with the council, it is their responsibility to keep the kingdom a safe and prospering one," Haylee recites, her gaze finally landing on me. "And that anyone who abuses that role should no longer be fit to rule."

"Thank you, Haylee," Councilman Borris praises before turning to look at me. "What I believe we have here, Your Majesty, is someone who wants the finery of life that comes with being married to a king. She has no discernable education or talents or abilities that make her worthy of being queen."

Each insult knocks breath further from me until my lungs are screaming for air. He isn't wrong about the list of faults, and perhaps that is the truth that hurts most of all.

"And with how *enamored* your son is, I believe it pertinent to this council to question what her real intentions are."

"I have no intentions other than to love Prince Nox—"

"But it takes more than that to be a queen!" he interjects, his voice booming into the space and hand smacking the table, making me jump. "It is why this council has suggested that Nox wed my niece! She was raised from birth to lead this—"

Shadows lift from the corners of the room, rushing over the stone floor like a wave of onyx, as the door to the council chambers is thrown open. The sound of it cracking cleaves the room into stunned silence. Nox's silhouette fills the doorway as the shadows he's called climb up his body, writhing around him in furious movements. His eyes catch the light of the spelled flames above, making the silver in them glow as he takes a menacing step forward. Magic pours into the space as if it were a thundercloud all its own, but even under its stifling presence, I feel Nox's power caress me gently. He glares at the men and women at the table, his eyes narrowing when he sees Haylee sitting across from me.

"Who yelled at her?" His voice slices out like a blade, making nearly everyone at the table jump. When no one answers, Nox's eyes flare with barely restrained fury. "*Who yelled at her?*" he asks again through gritted teeth.

Sadryn moves to stand, his hands slipping into his pockets as he takes a step towards his son, but Nox holds a shadow-laced hand out towards him, halting his movements. Wreathed in darkness, he looks less like the prince of the Mage Kingdom and more like a god of the underworld.

"If perhaps my voice was louder than I intended, I'm sorry," Councilman Borris answers, voice quavering.

"*Perhaps?*" Nox questions, taking another step towards the table until he's standing behind Haylee.

Her chin rises, regal and poised even as she clenches her shaking hands. As I observe the picture they paint together, I can't deny that she does look like she belongs there—at his side and ruling over a kingdom. My magic *burns* me from the inside at the thought of them together.

Daje stands, his chair squeaking as he does. Deep purple begins to glow in Nox's hand, his head snapping to the side at the movement.

"Nox, it's okay," I say quickly, drawing his attention away from Daje. I stand and make my way around the table, laying my hands over his. "It's alright."

"Speaking to you that way is *never* alright," he insists, his gaze lifting above me to once more glower over the table. I turn and look to Sadryn for help, his own features a mixture of uncertainty and shock.

"Nox, let's go for a walk and cool down." Sadryn wraps an arm around Nox's shoulders, and though the tension of unmistakable fury still keeps him rigid, he releases his hold on the shadows and calls his magic back. His eyes fall down to mine again, and I nod my head in reassurance.

"I'm fine. Go. I'll meet you back in your room." I watch as Sadryn all but forces Nox to leave, the heavy pressure of magic dissipating as they do.

"This is all *your* fault, girl," Councilman Borris seethes as he stands abruptly from his chair. "I know you—"

"Enough," Councilman Kallin shouts, rising from the table. "Daje, take Rhea out of this room. *Now.*"

My next few steps are automatic, Daje gently placing a hand on my lower back and guiding me out into the hall and past the broken door of the council room.

Not brave enough. Not talented or smart enough. Not good enough. Not. Enough. Without even knowing me, the council was able to prey on my insecurities with little effort.

"Rhea." Daje's voice breaks through my dejection, his image blurring through my burning eyes. "Are you alright?" He immediately pinches his lips together and shakes his head, running a hand over his hair. "No, of course you aren't. That was..."

"Brutal," Haylee supplies, joining us out in the hall. "I'm so sorry, Rhea. My uncle asked me to join, and I had no idea he would call on me." She clasps her hands in front of her, shoulders rolling forward as the corners of her lips tug downward.

"Do you want me to walk you to your room?" Daje asks sincerely, extending an arm out towards me.

Being alone with my thoughts is the last thing I want. I remember that there *is* someone else I can talk to, and she should still be here in the palace. "No, thank you. I think I'll go to the library."

Daje lingers as he observes me, his gaze flicking to Haylee and then back to me. He gives me a small nod and then turns to head back into the council room, carefully pushing past the busted door.

"Can I accompany you on your way to the library?" Haylee asks.

I want to say no, that having her so near makes my magic harder to control. That after what just happened, I'd prefer to walk alone. But she looks concerned, and I have *no* reason to not like her. "Of course."

Together, we move down the hallway, Haylee's light blue dress in contrast to my deep plum-colored one as we walk side by side. She's fixed her posture, her shoulders perfectly level and her spine straight.

"The council will not get past their disapproval of you and Nox," she mutters under her breath, barely loud enough for me to hear though it hits me harshly enough to make me stumble.

"How can you be sure? Today didn't go so well, but there is time to win them over. To try again." *I'm* not even convinced of that. Neither is Haylee, as she slows our pace down when we round a corner.

"I'm privy to much more than you would think, Rhea, and trust me, the council will not change their minds. But it doesn't have to mean that you and Nox can't be together."

I shake my head, disappointment twisting my stomach. "I won't ask Nox to forsake the throne for me. I couldn't do that—to him or the kingdom."

"I don't think there is a need for something *that* dramatic." The door to the library comes into view, and Haylee stops completely, turning her head in both directions to make sure we are alone before she steps closer to me. "What if Nox and I wed for show. To make the council happy."

My head jerks back, glowing white heat flaring in my palms that forces Haylee to take a step back. "Why would you do that?" I snap, my chest heaving with anger and frustration and *jealousy*. The volatile emotions course through me easily at the mere mention of them together. Haylee holds her hands up in surrender, her eyes wide.

"It would be a farce! Only to get the council off your backs. I assure you that I have no romantic feelings towards Nox. Nor would I want to get between you both." I glare at her as I clench my fists, my magic at the ready to do whatever I command of it. "Please, Rhea. I want to help. Listen to what I have to say. *Please.*" Her eyes flick to my hands as she waits for me to make my choice.

With a weighted sigh, I force it back down inside of me where it coils like a hunting snake. "I'm sorry. This meeting did *not* go how I expected it to. I knew they were curious about me, but to know that they think I'm *dooming* them..." I rub my hands down my face. "I just want to be with Nox."

"I know," she whispers, her hands tentatively reaching out to rub my shoulders. "And I think I can help. Let Nox and I marry for show. You two could still be together, spend every moment you can with each other. Hell, even have children that I will pretend are mine when we need to. He'd be yours in nearly every sense of the word."

"I don't think I can do that," I reply hoarsely, dropping my hands to my sides. "I don't think I can only have him in secret while you get him in public. Even if you don't love him as I do."

"And I don't," she reiterates. "He is a friend—nothing more. But I do want him to be happy, and I *do* believe he would be the best king. You know how powerful he is. You know what kind of security that brings to a kingdom whose magic is slowly being drained from them."

"He would never agree to it."

Haylee tilts her head to the side. "He would if you asked him to."

"No," I vehemently deny. "He wouldn't—"

"Rhea, I've seen the way he acts with you. How he *looks* at you as if you hold the very world in your palm. Don't deny the power you hold. It's the kind of power over a man that other women merely dream about." Her gaze turns pleading as her hands slide down my arms to grasp my own. "If you told him how important *you* thought it was that he do this, I have no doubt in my mind that he would."

She may be right, but why does this feel so wrong? Why does the very idea of him marrying anyone else, even just for show, make me want to burst apart? My heart feels made of glass, fracturing further the more the idea starts to burrow into my mind.

"Just think about it. You have *some* time before the council will get more aggressive in their pursuit to change Nox's mind. You can save yourself the anguish—save *Nox* the anguish—and pretend to give the council what they want."

I don't say anything in response, don't even look at Haylee, as she gives my hands one more squeeze before releasing them. My steps towards the library are a blur, and for the first time since waking from the Middle, I *wish* for the old Rhea. The one who could box up this pain and pretend it was something I could deal with later. The one who could be numb.

When I finally make my way to the desk where I know Elora will be waiting, the tidal wave of my despair leaks down my cheeks and I have to gasp for breath. Elora lifts her head from the book she's reading, her smile widening when she sees me. "How did the council meeting go?" She studies me, her grin dropping as she stands and sets the book down on the table. "What's wrong? Are you hurt?"

A broken whimper sounds as my hands cover my face, Elora rushing to me and pulling me in for a hug.

"Did Nox do something? I've never beat a prince up, but I'd do it for you."

For some reason, that only makes me cry harder. I need her to know the truth. Elora is my friend—a friend that *I* chose. Not because she knows Nox. Not because we are forced to be friendly with each other. But because there is something within us that calls to the other.

And I trust her.

Pulling back, I wipe my eyes and then stare into hers. "I need to tell you something."

Chapter Fifty-Nine

RHEA

I TELL ELORA NEARLY everything. Who I truly am and where I come from. How Nox and I met. I tell her about Bella. About how Nox lied to me and how we reconciled. I leave out any talk of my magic and the Middle only because I still have so many questions about those things myself that I can't really explain them to her yet. I share with her about the council meeting and Haylee's proposal afterwards.

Lying on our backs hidden between two bookcases, I stare up at the wooden beams that cross the ceiling and sigh. "I'm sorry that I kept everything from you." When she stays silent, I turn and look at her. "Are you mad?"

She meets my gaze, her freckled cheeks rounding with a small smile. "No, of course not. I understand why you had to keep things secret. I understand why Nox is asking that of you. And I *also* understand that I now need to keep this secret."

"I won't ask you to lie. It is not your responsibility to—"

"I already knew that you weren't from Santor," she interrupts.

My lips part in surprise as I push up onto my elbow. "What?"

Elora mimics my position, playing with the ends of her hair before twisting her lips to the side. "Do you remember during our first book club meeting when I asked you to confirm where you were from? And what your last name was? It's because I wanted to research if anyone from your family line might still be alive. Maybe a distant cousin or something. I was going to surprise you if I found anything, but the orphanage I contacted had no record of you."

I drop my gaze to the floor and swallow roughly.

"And then I reached out to the records person in the town, and *they* had no information on you either. I figured someone with your unique eyes would be remembered, so that had to mean you weren't actually ever there."

"How long have you known? And are my eyes really that unique?" I knew the majority of mages had some variation of gray eyes, but I had seen shades of blue and even brown too. However, Nox had never once said anything about my own other than the fact that he loved them.

"A few weeks now. And yes, I have never seen anyone else with green eyes. I've hardly seen that shade mentioned in any of our history books." She shakes her head in disbelief. "It should make finding your ancestry pretty easy if that is something you want to do. One part of you, at the very least, is mage. If that part comes with the side that gave you green eyes, I think we'll be able to track it. To see if you might have any living family members. Well," she pauses, her cheeks growing red not from embarrassment but from anger, "if there are any *other* than that asshole king."

I want to snort at her reaction, at how her fists ball up as if she can punch my uncle right from where she lies, but I'm still caught up on the fact that she knew I was lying to her for *weeks*. Weeks in which time was spent dancing at a tavern and reading books and talking as if nothing was wrong at all.

"You knew all that time and didn't bring it up? Why?"

Elora sits up fully, smoothing her flowy white top, the sleeves long and growing wider as they near her hands. "I don't know. You only ever talked about your past if I brought it up, and even then, you were reluctant to do so if it didn't revolve around Nox. I thought at first it was because you were kind of obsessed with him"—I can't help but snort at that—"but I realized that there was something else going on. Something you either couldn't or wouldn't speak about. And maybe a part of me hoped that you might trust me enough to open up to me eventually."

"I'm sorry it took so long."

Elora waves off my apology, flicking her copper hair over her shoulder. "Rhea, you've been through enough. You don't need to apologize to me. Just know that if there is ever anything you want to talk about, I'm here. And there are no stipulations attached to that. I'm your friend, whether you tell me every little detail or you pick and choose what truths you want me to know. As long as you know that I am someone you can come to."

I smile at my friend—*my friend*—and she smiles back as if the same words are repeating in her head.

"Though *perhaps* as my friend, you could try every once and a while to *accidentally* have us run into a certain mage king."

"Oh my gods," I huff, our joyful laughter helping to ease my tumultuous nerves. My magic hums within me as a light tugging sensation sends my hand to my chest and my head turning towards the door on the other side of the library.

"What is it?" Elora asks as she watches me stand.

"I think—"

"Sunshine? Are you back there?" Nox calls out right as shadows slither across the floor.

"Yes!" I shout, waiting for Elora to join me as we find our way out of the maze of books and back to her desk. The shadows instantly dissipate as if Nox has released a breath.

"I always forget he can do that," Elora muses as she watches them become stagnant once more. "And I still think it's bizarre that you can tell he's near without seeing him first."

"Isn't it just his magical signature? His is so strong that I figured everyone could tell when he is close by."

Elora shakes her head as Nox's footsteps near. "Signature strengths are specific to each person, but from far away, I can't tell if the magic I am sensing is one individual or many. I can't name the person based on their signature alone without seeing them. Does your magic recognize his?"

"Yes."

"Hmm," she responds, her gaze lost in thought.

My brows furrow at her answer, but then Nox rounds the corner, and I'm taken aback by the look on his face and the way his body moves—by just *him*. Small tendrils of his wavy hair hang over his forehead, the rest looking mussed as if he's run his hand through it multiple times. His magic ripples over me the closer he gets, calling to mine until I feel it blooming right beneath my skin.

"Are you alright?" he asks when he nears, his hands gently cradling my face despite the tension that I can feel radiating off of him.

"Yes, are you?" I question, dragging my gaze over him.

"Better now." His forehead comes to mine, his words quiet and just barely reaching my ear. "You make everything better." He looks *tired*, as if the weight he's been trying to balance since coming home is cleaving him in two.

I turn to look at Elora, an apology on my tongue, but she's already waving her hand. "I'll see you tomorrow?"

"Tomorrow," I confirm, then lace my fingers with Nox's.

He guides us into the hall and up the stairs to his room, our silence only interrupted by the sound of our steps. When he closes the door behind him and turns to lean against it, a line forms between his brows. "I came here after my walk with my father, looking for you."

"I'm sorry. I didn't want to be alone with my thoughts while waiting for you. So I went to see Elora."

He nods his head, a hand diving into his hair as he holds the strands there. "I'm sorry, too. I messed up."

"What do you mean?"

"It was your fear. I swear I could *feel* it when Borris yelled at you. It was like I had no choice; my magic forced me to bend to its will and get to you. I shouldn't have barged into the council room. It played directly into their hands, and now they are convinced you've somehow *tricked* me into being with you. They are officially asking my father to not recognize our courtship."

I hold his gaze, a sinking sensation making bile churn in my stomach. "The questions they asked me... They weren't what we practiced."

"Another thing I've failed at," he grumbles under his breath.

"That isn't what I mean."

"But it's true, isn't it? I didn't prepare you properly. I don't think I've fully convinced them of what I said happened in the Mortal Kingdom. I couldn't save you from more pain caused by your uncle—"

"Nox," I cut in, moving until I'm right in front of him, my hands grabbing his. "You are *not* a failure. You cannot hold yourself to these impossible standards."

"Nothing should be impossible when it comes to keeping you safe," he counters, his voice gravelly. "I *can't* fail at that."

"I *am* safe." At my words, his body softens against mine and he wraps his arms around me. "Do you think we should tell the council the truth?"

He sighs but shakes his head. "I've thought about it, but you saw how they treated you just thinking you were from a small town here in our kingdom." Noting the puzzled look on my face, he adds, "My father told me what they said to you and *about* you." The last two words are growled from between his clenched teeth. My thumbs rub his cheeks as he exhales slowly. "They won't understand. Even knowing that your blood *is* mage, all they'll hear is that you're from the Mortal Kingdom, and they will think even worse about you under the *guise* of safety for the kingdom."

I nod my head though my heart sinks into my already aching stomach. Maybe before today, I might have pushed harder to tell them, but the council already has a person in mind for who they want to be their future queen, and it isn't me. "Then what do we do?"

"I don't know. I hate lying as much as you do, but I think it's our only answer right now. The less people that know the truth, the safer you will be."

Worrying my lower lip, I think about how Nox doesn't know that I have told someone. But Elora is my friend, and she has already proven that she is trustworthy. She could have gone to the council at any moment once she realized I was lying about where I was from, but she hadn't. Even though the logic is sound, the words are still rushed when I say them. "I told Elora."

Nox looks confused before the statement begins to sink in and his lips flatten into a straight line. "Told her what, exactly?"

"Everything. Well, not what my magic can do and nothing about the Middle. But everything else."

"*Why?*" he whispers, not in tenderness but in barely tempered frustration. "I am *lying* through my teeth every day to a council who—" He stops abruptly and squeezes his eyes shut as he shakes his head. "Why would you risk it?"

Stepping back, I create space between us and intertwine my fingers together in front of me. "You told Cassius."

He exhales a short breath while drawing a single brow up. "Cass has been my friend for my entire life. I trust him implicitly."

"Elora is *my* friend. She won't say anything."

Nox moves from the door, his hands braced on his hips as his steps rattle the floor with his pacing. "You don't know her well enough yet to know what her intentions are, Sunshine. You've never experienced someone being polite to your face and then plunging a dagger into your back the moment you turn around."

"She wouldn't do that." I scowl, nervously clutching the dragon pendant as I challenge Nox. "I trust her."

His hands run down his face as he chuckles without levity. "Gods, what if she says something to the council? I need to speak with her and make sure—"

"Like you *spoke* to Daje?" I snap. Both halves of my magic stir to life within me. The dark shadows peek in curiosity from beneath the restraint I have on them, but with a deep breath, I settle both the dark and the light magic back down. The small stone in my grasp seems to hum against my skin.

Eyes stunned wide at first, Nox recovers quickly and splays his arms out at his sides. "Yes! I will say it as often as I need to; I will do *whatever* it takes to make sure you are safe."

"By threatening our friends? *I don't want that!*" My chest heaves with my own conviction, but tears crest my eyelids while we stare at each other.

The hard lines of his expression dissipate as he holds his hands out in front of him. "I will not threaten Elora, but I would like to talk with her."

"Why?"

Magic thickens in the air around us, his *and* mine. His answer is spoken gently despite the harshness of it. "Because you don't *know* her—"

"Just because she hasn't been a lifelong friend doesn't mean she's an enemy!" The room around me begins to blur, my throat growing too narrow.

"And just because *you* think that doesn't make it true." Softly, it's spoken *so* softly. As if coaxing a wild animal into a cage.

I gasp as a thundering understanding pounds into my heart, nearly making me stumble backward. "This has nothing to do with how long I've known her," I murmur, my tears breaking free. "I don't care that you told Cass, not because he's been your friend for a long time but because I trust *you*."

Nox shakes his head, a muscle in his jaw ticking. "That isn't a fair comparison, and you know it."

"What I *know* is that you don't trust my judgment! And that means that you don't trust me."

"You think I don't trust you?" he asks, emotion strangling the words as his face begins to crumble. "Rhea—*gods*—you are my *everything*."

"I do not doubt your *love* for me, but I think *trusting* me means that you would understand why I told Elora. That you would understand we are on an island of our own making, and while we have each other, it's still an *island*." I gasp for a breath, a sob shaking my shoulders as it shatters the tension between us. "I need a lifeline of *my* choosing. I want a friend of *my own* to share this burden with. Just like you have in Cass. And Elora has known for *weeks* that I've been lying to her and has done *nothing* with that information!"

He doesn't say anything at first, his dark gaze flickering as his eyes bounce between mine. "I am just trying to protect you."

"But this doesn't feel like protection! It feels like *drowning*. Like I'm—" I stop myself before I say the word, but Nox reads it on my face anyway.

"It feels like I'm suffocating you."

The anger drains from me nearly as quickly as it came. "Lies and secrets do not make impenetrable shields, Nox. At some point, they are going to turn into weapons; ones that we may no longer wield."

He stills, nothing moving beyond the rough working of the column of his throat as regret shines in his glassy eyes. His devastation is palpable, and it chills me further to the bone with every second that passes.

"You're right," he relents, hardly any sound to his voice. "You're right, and I'm sorry." His gaze falls to my feet as he looses a haggard breath. "Even with years spent living under the ruse of being someone else, I have never felt less in control than I do now. I keep trying to anchor myself back into my role as the crown prince, as a son and a friend. As someone that is strong and worthy of you, but instead, I find myself angry that you can't roam this kingdom as your true self. Angry that a council that shouldn't have a say in our relationship keeps finding ways to. Angry that your bastard uncle has tarnished your freedom by hurting someone who could have given you information about your mother, all because she helped *me*. I am terrified that others might pay that price. Or that *you* will. You have been through so much, and I wanted my home to feel like it could be yours too." A single tear escapes as he lifts his eyes back to mine. "I am angry, and I am scared, and I am *lost*."

My feet move without my command, closing the distance between us until his body is held close to mine. "I'm sorry too," I rasp, squeezing him tightly to me as my arms wrap around his neck. "I'm sorry for pushing to speak with the council, only to make things worse. I'm sorry that I haven't reassured you more that the only thing I need to feel like I am home is *you*." Leaning back, I wait until his eyes meet mine, my hands gently cupping his face. "If you are angry, then let me soothe you. If you are scared, then let me be your comfort. And if you are lost," I whisper, lifting up on my toes. "If you are lost, then let me be lost *with* you. After *everything*, my love for you is not composed of fragile dedication. It is all-consuming, ever-present, and *unshakable*. I don't want you to be afraid to tell me when you are struggling, even if I am the reason why."

"What if this is to be the rest of our life? Fighting with the council and having to hide parts of ourselves from them?" he asks, his arms snaking around me.

I close my eyes and breathe him in. "Do you want to be king?"

A few moments pass before he whispers, "I would like to rule with you."

I smile, softly gliding my lips against his. "Then we take it day by day, remember? And we cannot isolate ourselves. We need to let the people who care about us into our lives too. Without fear."

Nox nods, and though he breathes easier, his body droops as his hands grip onto me tightly. I cannot let him break—not when he's saved me from my own ruination so many times before.

"Come on," I say, my hand finding his as I lead him into the bathroom and start the shower. Steam begins to billow out, fogging the mirror as it surrounds us. My fingers work the buttons of his tunic, releasing each one and exposing his bare chest beneath. When I've reached the end and begin to unbuckle his belt, Nox lays a hand over mine, his brow raised in question. My cheeks heat as I shake my head and admit, "I'm not asking for *that*. I just want to take care of you."

He slowly releases my hand, surprise etched on his face. Has no one ever offered to do that? To care for him in the way he so selflessly does for others?

My undressing of him is tender and affectionate, and when I've peeled all of his clothes away, I gently guide him towards the shower before stripping myself of my dress and undergarments. Nox watches me as I step in and reach for his soap, lathering it on a cloth as the rich scents of earth and spice mix into the warm air. I wash in gentle sweeps over his shoulders, arms, and across his chest before walking around to his back.

"When I first saw you, I thought you were the most beautiful person I had ever seen," I confess, lowering the cloth over his perfect backside and down the length of his legs.

"Well, as you reminded me that morning in the woods, you hadn't seen very many people."

I snort, and though I can't see his face, I can picture the smile that is gracing it. "I've seen more people since then."

"And you now know the error of your ways?" he taunts.

Soap drips down his body as I stand and walk around to his front, gratification suffusing me when I see his lips tilted upwards. "And I still think it's true."

"I was stunned the first time I saw you," he says, his fingers trailing lightly up and down my arms. "You looked so different from the image I had in my head because of the king's lies." He had told me as much in that moment. *You aren't what I expected.* I watch him as he reminisces, reaching up to brush away the wet strands of hair that have plastered to his forehead. "And you were so clearly *terrified* that I didn't know exactly what to do or say to not make you more so."

"I think you handled it well enough, from what I remember." I was still suffocating in the throes of grief after Alexi's death then.

He smiles though there is a somberness to it. His lips caress over my temple, lingering there for a moment before pulling back. "And then, when you came down those stairs, I caught you staring *very* intently at me."

I roll my eyes, slapping his chest with the sudsy cloth before laying it down. Stretching for the shampoo, I stop short when I realize that I can't properly reach the top of his head. "I think you'll have to do your hair."

Nox doesn't hesitate as he lowers onto his knees, his hands resting against my lower back. "Not exactly how I hoped to get on my knees before you today, but where I belong nonetheless," he says quietly.

I run my hands through his hair before leaning down to kiss the top of his head, all while he rests his forehead against my sternum. It's silent once more as I shampoo him before lathering my own hair. Still kneeling before me, Nox washes my body with his hands, his reverent touch coaxing me further into the depths of the emotions welling inside of me—the ones made to glow by what it means to be *his*.

It solidifies the truth that I will never share him with anyone else, even if only in name. I didn't think myself to be a selfish person. But for him? For *us*? I will be. My magic hums happily at the thought.

"Haylee pulled me aside after the meeting." I speak while I drag my fingers slowly back and forth over his shoulders, his muscles relaxing with each swipe. "She offered to marry you for show so that we could be together in secret."

Nox's head snaps up to look at me, sending water droplets flying in all directions. "Please tell me you are joking."

"She seemed very sincere," I continue, the warm water of the shower still raining down over us, "and I can't deny that, in a moment of weakness, I thought about it. I could see the two of you, regal and poised and exactly what the council wants." I do wonder if her earnestness in offering to marry him was truly as she said or if there was another reason she was so *eager* to help me.

He stands, his hands sliding up my body until they are resting below the curve of my breasts. "I don't fucking care how *sincere* her offer was or what the council wants; it will *never* happen."

"I know. I will not share you," I breathe.

"Nor I you."

I can't help the way my lips curve as I respond, "Well, it's not like anyone is out here offering to marry *me* for show."

"That is true. It's a good thing it's not a competition, or you'd be losing." I scoff as he laughs, and stars above, what a beautiful sound it is. "What if there was a proposal to you made out of love?" he asks, his voice low while his hands move a little higher up my sides.

I blink as my lips part, unsure I heard him correctly. "Are you proposing to me in the shower?"

Nox pulls me close as he peppers kisses over my surprised face. "Do you really think I'd propose somewhere that would have others picturing you naked when you told them the story of it? My ego is big, Sunshine, but even I cannot handle that."

I burst into laughter, my forehead going to his chest as the sound reverberates off of the stone around us. I laugh until my stomach hurts, until tears mix with the water and Nox is laughing with me. "You are absolutely *ridiculous*."

"Perhaps, but you love me anyway."

My laughter tapers off as I lift my head and look at him. "I do," I affirm, framing his face with my hands and pulling him down into a kiss.

Though we are pressed together completely free of any clothing, the joining of our lips stays gentle and sweet. When we separate, Nox reaches behind me to turn the shower off before grabbing our towels. Dried and partially dressed—him in a pair of thin cotton sleeping pants and me, curiously, in one of his short-sleeved t-shirts that hangs to mid-thigh—he threads his fingers through mine as we make our way to the bed.

"Is there a reason why my own sleeping clothes were not good enough?" I ask, sliding my leg between his as he wraps an arm around me and pulls me into his side.

"No reason other than it makes me and my magic happy to see you wearing something of mine." I playfully poke his side, garnering a deep chuckle as his lips find my temple. "I am sorry for earlier. I will be better."

I tilt my chin up, my heavy-lidded gaze catching his. "I don't want you to be better, Nox, as that implies there is something wrong with you. Just remember that you don't have to do it all alone." I kiss his cheek before a yawn breaks free as I lay my head back down on his shoulder and close my eyes. "You should probably apologize to Daje though."

His laugh is soft when he replies, "We'll see."

Part Five

Knowledge is a tool, and one that only helps you make the best decisions you possibly can. Hiding from truths, whatever they are, does not help you. It only hinders.

Chapter Sixty

RHEA

*I*T ONLY TAKES THE *hint of jasmine and a tickling sensation against my bare arm to know that I'm back in the Middle.*

"It has been a while," I say, opening my eyes and pushing myself up to sit.

"Don't tell me that you have missed this place," Selene teases, her sweet laugh warming me.

My hands drag down the same silky black and white dress that I wore the last time I was here. "I'm glad to be here under happier conditions. And I suppose I am happy to speak with you again." She laughs, causing glittering specks of stardust to whirl past me. "Why has it been so long?"

"It's harder to reach you when you wear the pendant." There's an edge to her voice, and I swear I can almost see the scowl on her lips in my mind's eye.

"Did you know? What I did the night we escaped? What those shadows were capable of?"

But she does; of course she does.

She answers after a weighted sigh. "Yes, and I agree with what your prince said; the shadows are not inherently bad. That side of your magic is as much a part of you as your healing half is, and you shouldn't deny yourself that power out of fear."

"I thought it would be wise to wait until I had a handle on the magic that won't kill anyone before I start dabbling with the magic that can."

Selene hums in contemplation. "Rhea, the magic you have is the kind of power that is coveted. The kind that others will ki—" Choking sounds fill the air, and I tense as I realize that Selene has said too much. She sucks in a breath in time with one of my own, her gasp traveling on a phantom wind and right past my ears. The hairs on the back of my neck rise as the feeling of another's presence makes my shoulders pull towards my ears.

"You are aware of the deal that you made, yet you continuously test fate with your words," a male says, his voice deep and powerful as it ricochets across the Middle.

I duck my head, my eyes growing wide. "Who are you?"

"Young one, you needn't worry about who I am. It is not relevant to your journey now," he says around a velvety laugh.

"Seems pretty relevant," I grumble back.

The male chuckles again, and I feel it caress my shoulders and weave into my hair. "Yes, I can see I have chosen well. Though I make no mistakes when it comes to matters such as these."

Gods above, what is he talking about?

"She would like you," he says, a deep longing ringing in the timbre of his voice. "Time is a treasure that cannot be bought, bartered, or stolen, Your Highness. You must remind yourself of this often."

"Can anyone in this godsforsaken place please speak plainly?" I blurt out, running my hands through my hair.

His laugh rattles the stars. "This space is anything but forsaken of gods."

"What does that mean?" But his presence is already retreating, his power lifting off of me as if it were never there at all.

"Rhea," Selene says hesitantly, her soft voice soothing, "you still have much to learn about yourself and your magic. You've made great progress, but you cannot stop now. Though the tides have receded, the swell is gathering again in the distance, and it is coming back in full force."

Her words feel like an omen, and they send a rush of worry down my spine as I purse my lips together. "I need more practice with my light magic—just a little more. Then, I promise, I will let Nox teach me how to use the shadows." It is the best I can offer. I refuse to put anyone's life at risk if I lose control again.

"Very well," she concedes. Silence, ancient and boundless, fills the space as I cradle my hands in my lap. "Have you thought about having your own Flame Ceremony?"

I'm confused by the question and tilt my head to the side as I think about the answer. "Not really. I don't need to see the size of a flame to know that my magic is nearly as strong as Nox's."

"It's stronger, and he suspects it."

I snort as I shake my head. "No, the things he can do far exceed my own abilities."

"Because he's had a lifetime to train with it, whereas you've merely had a few months."

"Does it matter?" I ask as stardust glitters past me. "Truly, does it matter that I see this measurement of my magic, knowing how foreign it still feels to me?"

"Knowledge is a tool, and one that only helps you make the best decisions you possibly can. Hiding from truths, whatever they are, does not help you. It only hinders."

I consider her words, chewing on my lower lip. Selene is limited by what she can say and how she can phrase things, the other presence confirming so. If she believes the results of a Flame Ceremony to be something pertinent for me to know, I have to acknowledge that it would be foolish to disregard that.

There's another swirl of splintered stars that dance in front of me, as if in agreement. Then she asks, "Do you want to hear the rest of the story I started the last time you were here? Of the magical woman and the prince?"

I look above me to where a glimmering galaxy in shades of purple glows. "Alright."

"The magical woman had a lovely life as a child. One filled with joy and happiness with a family who loved her dearly, and yet, though she had everything she could ever want at her disposal, she ached for something more. Her parents tried to quell this thirst by giving her every distraction they could think of. Books upon books to read. Training with her magic and with weapons she would never have to wield in battle. She learned how to dance and studied all the variations of the flowers that grew in her home. She made friends wherever she went. But that yearning for more remained.

"As a teenager, she began to push at her boundaries, sneaking into realms that she knew were forbidden. Her curiosity was too strong to ignore, however, and she ventured farther and farther into one of those new realms until, one day, the forest she traveled through gave way to a beautiful city."

The ends of my hair begin to lift while goosebumps break out over my skin. All around me, the stars begin to flicker. "Are you sending me back?" I ask.

"No. His magic is calling you back."

I blink in surprise. "Nox's magic knows that I'm here?"

"Rhea, do you not ponder why your magic reacts with his the way that it does? How it seems to always know where he is?"

"You know that I have."

"Then you have your answer. Your magic is also strong enough to bring you here whenever you want, but only once you've embraced both halves."

I close my eyes as the sensation of plummeting begins to churn my stomach, my chest rising and falling in quick succession. I start to feel heavier, the weightlessness of the Middle fading away with each passing second.

Selene shouts, her voice echoing as if coming up from a deep well, "Rhea, promise me something before you go."

"What is it?" My body shakes as I fall and fall. Though I know I'm close to waking, my ears strain through my descent back to Olymazi to hear her final plea.

"Promise me that you will always remember that you are never alone."

It is hardly a whisper in the tumultuous wind as I vow, "I promise."

And then, there is only darkness.

I wake to find myself half thrown over Nox's body, one knee digging into his side and my hair splayed over the both of us. Carefully untangling myself from him, I reach for my journal, and I begin writing, feeling called to preserve the memory of this visit to the Middle. When I've poured my words out onto its cream-colored pages, I set the journal down and turn back towards Nox. It is not like him to wake up after me, but after last night, I am happy that he is resting.

My eyes trace over him like one would delineate a rare flower, each defining line and soft contour of his body as fascinating the hundredth time I've seen it as it was the very first. Maybe even more so because I've thoroughly explored him now and know the secrets his skin keeps. Like the short scar in a smooth line on his right hip. Or the small mole that dots his left shoulder. When I close my eyes, I see a map of Nox that only I understand.

"Am I *that* devastatingly handsome that you must stare at me as I sleep?"

My cheeks lift as I tickle his chest. "When did you wake up?"

He stretches his arms overhead before turning on his side to face me, his hair a messy collection of waves that fan out in all directions. "While you were writing. I didn't want to disturb you."

My magic is a warm hum along my bones. I can feel the edges of Nox's magic too, the pulsing of his signature tugging on my own. His fingers reach out to trace over my face, tucking my hair behind my ear as he does.

"Sometimes, it hurts to look at you." He says it like a secret, one pulled from the very middle of his heart and laid bare and bloody before me. "You're here, and you're *mine*, and there are moments when I realize that and can't draw in a full breath."

"Nox," I whisper, covering his hand still lingering on my face with my own. He lifts onto one elbow, kissing my shoulder and then my collarbone before he climbs over me and the warmth of his body blankets my own.

"Let's spend all day in bed together," he all but begs, his lips skimming over my chest.

My fingers rustle through his hair, nerve endings burning brightly as heat coils low and tight in my stomach. "What about the council? We can't just avoid them for a day. And your duties..."

His warm mouth moves lower, making my thighs strain to rub together. Dark gray eyes glowing with starlight find mine as he lifts his head from my body. "I'm a prince, am I not? Surely the title comes with *some* agency over how I spend my time."

"Does it?"

He smiles, trailing more kisses down my skin until his hands are gripping onto my thighs and spreading them wide. "If I want to spend all day between your perfect thighs, then I will."

My brow arches as I curl my fingers into the sheets. "Could you last all day?"

A low noise rumbles over me, my skin pebbling as he speaks his answer over my core. "Let's find out."

※※※※ ※※※※

After my shower, I sit cross-legged on Nox's bed and thumb through the pages of the book Elora told me to read. While at first it seemed like something much more suited to Nox's taste, I had admitted to Elora that I was enjoying the stories of what life was like before the war. I'm reading a passage that speaks of Queen Lucia when Nox settles in next to me with a book he plucked from the shelf adjacent to the bed.

"Why was there no queen of Void Magic crowned after the war?" I ask, drawing his curious gaze. Lifting up Elora's recommended read, Nox glances at the title before understanding settles on his face.

"It's not known. She had small children, but none of them had the signature blue flame during their Flame Ceremonies when they came of age after her death. My ancestors took over knowing that, the moment a blue flame was shown, they would need to relinquish the throne, but the gods seem to be taking their time choosing the next queen."

"Is it the gods that choose?"

He tilts his head, a small stream of sunlight illuminating his cheek as he does. "They do. The queens of Void Magic come from a single family line, one that may date back to the formation of Olymazi itself. Their rule is announced if their blood sparks a blue flame at their Flame Ceremony."

"Would you want *me* to do a Flame Ceremony?"

If Nox is surprised by my question, he doesn't show it. "Only if you want to."

I tell him of my latest visit to the Middle and what Selene thinks I should do. In true Nox fashion, he leaves the choice up to me, but there is a certain excitement that dances in his gaze as we talk. Eventually, our conversation moves on to practicing with my magic.

Facing me on the bed now, he hands me an egg-shaped black stone, the surface of it nearly shiny enough to show my reflection. *Dragon stone.* Holding it flat in one hand, I call the white light to my fingertips.

"Focus on where you want the magic to go," Nox instructs gently.

My shoulders rise and fall sharply with my next breath, but I do as Nox says. I imagine the white light filling the dark stone until it glows gray, and my magic leaps from my fingertips and follows suit, settling into the center of the onyx rock. My jaw relaxes at the small release of power, the rest fading from my hand before I hold the stone up and wiggle it in front of his face.

"Another one for the collection," I tease, laying it on my bedside table where a gathering of dragon stone pieces that I've practiced with now sit.

"Well done, Sunshine." He leans over and slides both hands around my neck until he reaches the back. "Now show me your shields without the pendant on." He waits until I nod, then unhooks the necklace and removes it, setting it aside on the bed. I feel the surge within me, warmth quickly traveling up my spine and reaching the base of my throat before I'm able to hold it off. "Good. Breathe through it. Let your intention guide your power back into a relaxed state."

My ears are buzzing by the time I feel that I have full control over my magic. "Why is it so much harder to control now than when I was in the tower?" I had been improving, even with keeping the shadow half untouched, but it felt as if my power was also *adapting*. The more I used it, the more it seemed to *give* me to use.

Nox tucks a strand of hair behind my ear, his hand then falling to my knee. "From what you told me, you didn't ever use it in the tower consistently like you are now. I think your magic became used to being repressed, so it's requiring more effort to balance now that you're drawing on it more. When I was first learning and exploring my magic, it took many months to control it at will. You've only been trying for the equivalent of half a summer."

I nod my head, sure that he is right. I had promised Selene I would train with all of my magic soon, and I will. I just need more time. We continue practicing, Nox helping me build physical shields and then trying to break them with his own magic—a feat that ends up making me laugh as our magic seems to only want to twine together when they are near each other in this way.

When he feels as if we've done enough, Nox clasps the necklace back on me and pulls me to sit between his legs while we read from Elora's book together.

Chapter Sixty-One

BAHIRA

I SWING MY SPEAR down towards her face and Jahlee lifts her shortswords, crossing them overhead and blocking my weapon's path. She's been able to parry most of my attacks, a vast improvement from when we first started training. Kicking out towards her chest, I miss as she evades my boot, spinning with her swords glinting in the sunlight in front of her.

"Good," I acknowledge, spinning my spear until the tip is pointing upwards.

"As good as you?" she asks, dropping her swords onto the grass.

I snort, blowing a curly strand of hair that has fallen out of my ponytail. "You've definitely improved. Well done."

She huffs, giving me a weak thumbs up while reaching for her waterskin in the grass next to her. "So," she says, the word drawn out, "how are *things* with my brother."

I force my jaw to relax at the mention of Kai. Our walk back from Honna had been quiet as I processed the failed experimentation with his blood on the shifter. At least Kai had been able to speak with some additional families before we left, ones who claimed they were also denied aid by the palace.

"*Fine.* How are things with your aunt? Did she leave for Honna already?" Kai had only told her, Jahlee, and Tua about our departure north, the latter seeming indifferent about our journey.

"Yes, she left this morning. She is happier now that she's talked with Kai and has his promise that anyone asking for aid will get it approved by the Crown."

"Did she leave on foot?" I ask, taking a seat next to her and tipping my head back towards the newly risen sun.

"No, her animal is a hawk. She should make it home within a few hours if she stays in that form the entire time."

"You didn't want to go with her?" In our quieter moments, Jahlee had shared that there was more of the island she wished to see. How Kai's fear of the rebels was valid, but that it left her feeling like she was a caged animal bumping into the walls of its enclosure. I thought she might take the opportunity to go with her aunt, if only for a small reprieve.

"No, she prefers to fly. I would have slowed her down with my mortal legs." Her comment catches me off-guard as I tilt my head down to look at her. A moment passes before Jahlee tenses, her gaze flying up to meet mine as if she's just realized what she's said.

I decipher her words, pulling them apart until a realization lifts my brows high on my forehead. I think back to each time I've brought up her shifting, how she changed the subject. I remember the moment she got into an argument with the noble female, and I was sure tensions were strong enough that she might shift, but she didn't. I recount what Sir Duarte said to her at the council dinner and how vehemently Kai defended her.

"You cannot shift," I state gently, the corners of my mouth falling when she nods her head in agreement. "The blight. I had no idea it affected—"

"My ability, or rather *lack* of ability, to shift has nothing to do with the blight," she interrupts.

"You were *born* unable to shift?"

"Surprise," she says, forcing an upward tilt to her lips while wiggling her fingers in front of herself.

"How is that possible?"

Jahlee shrugs, letting her shoulders round as she stares just past me to the palace behind us. "I was born healthy and strong, but when I was well past the age that a child should be able to shift, it became painfully obvious that I couldn't. It's like the magic to do so just *skipped* me."

Quiet stretches between us as I let Jahlee's words settle within me. I understand inherently what it is to be born without something everyone else has. How isolating and lonely it can be. How frustrating and heartbreaking.

"I should get going," she announces, hopping up to stand as she sheathes her shortswords. "There are people to torment and kings to annoy."

"Jahlee," I start, stepping in front of her quickly, "I need to tell you something."

She folds her arms over her chest, a devilish smile curling her lips as the sadness that blanketed her earlier begins to fade. "If you're about to tell me that you're in love with me, I'm afraid I'll have to break your heart—no matter how beautiful I find you. I imagine my brother would explode if the two of us started a relationship."

I roll my eyes and mirror her stance, taking in a deep breath to steady my nerves. The trepidation I feel must show on my face because Jahlee's smile falters and her fingers tighten around her arms. My throat feels like it's constricting, reducing the air flowing to my lungs to nothing more than a slight trickle. Every warning bell in my head blares, and yet the words are begging to be let out, my own guilt a raging entity inside of me that pushes beneath my skin. So I just blurt them out. "I don't have magic."

The statement seems to echo in the training yard as I watch Jahlee's eyes widen. Her arms fall lax at her sides, and her mouth slowly drops open. "But—but you're mage. And all mages—"

"Not all," I interrupt her, building my internal shields back up one block at a time as confusion and shock continue to bleed into her expression. "It appears that I was born without magic. I think it may be hidden within me, waiting to be unlocked, though I haven't figured out how yet."

Jahlee regains control of her features, her mouth tightening into a grim line as she places her hands on her hips. "Kai doesn't know, does he?" she asks, accusation bitter in her voice.

"No."

Jahlee sighs as she studies me, her disappointment coating me with every blink of her lashes. "You need to tell him," she says more gently. "He will understand, Bahira."

I shake my head, moving my gaze to the sky above. "He won't. He brought me here for one purpose, Jahlee. I thought he was aware that I didn't have magic. It's not exactly a secret back home. But then, on the ship, it was obvious that he didn't know, and to be honest, I didn't care. I wanted to stay to see if there was more knowledge I could gain by being here. I wanted the safety he was offering my kingdom. I realized he'd send me home if he knew because he wouldn't find me useful. But then..." The words taper off as I bring my gaze back to hers.

Understanding eases her pursed lips, her eyes softening along with them. "Give him a chance. He might be upset at first, but at least give him the benefit of the doubt. Don't do what everyone else does and assume you know better than him."

I make myself stand tall, my body held rigid by spite alone, and Jahlee, damn her, sees it all. The way I've forced myself to be formidable in all the ways my magic left me wanting—she recognizes it all because she's been forced to do the same. She might be the only person in the entire world who truly understands what it is like to be born missing a part of yourself. Before I can react, she wraps her arms around me and pulls me in for a hug. My body stays tightly wound within her hold, but something within me fractures, another long thin line cracking into the hardened façade of my armor.

"I'm sorry that you understand this feeling, Bahira," she whispers into my hair, "but I always knew that you and I would be close friends. I promise I will not say anything to anyone about this."

"I can't ask you to withhold this from your brother."

She sighs, but it's not out of annoyance. "Unless he asks me directly, I will not give him your story." Leaning back, her hands frame my face. "Is it fucked up that I'm happy to feel less alone?"

I exhale a rough laugh and try to shake my head. "No." It wasn't, because I felt the same way. Jahlee gives my cheeks a squeeze before dropping her hands.

Together, we walk to the palace, changing to a conversation led by Jahlee that goes into extreme detail about how she did indeed bed that shifter she eyed in the throne room. A part of me settles at confiding in her, and it gives me hope that Kai might have a similar reaction. The other side of me, the one ruled by logic and balanced by facts, reminds me that, while they are brother and sister, Jahlee and Kai are not the same. That the sharp and rough edges that make up the shifter king aren't ones that are meant to be flexible.

I have to tell him. I *will* tell him. I just need it to be the right time.

※

Battles rage beyond our borders, the ballad of war carrying on the wind and in through the trees that don't feel as protective as they once did. It is because of the majority of this council that we do not intervene. It is our duty to ensure our own people's safety and to not get involved with a war we want no part in. Though Queen Lucia expressed that perhaps we may not have a choice, the council majority stays firm in the thought that we mustn't sway either side.

Mage magic is too powerful a tool for one side to utilize. It is this councilman's opinion that we will likely see the war resolved between the Mortal Kingdom and the Siren Queendom long before it ever threatens our people.

Our queen looks forward to the visit from the fae king in three weeks' time.

I close the journal and take a bite of the flaky pastry brought up by Lana, who eyed me with a level of interest I had no desire to entertain. I had read through enough journals to bring me to the start of the war, and the tone of this entry leaves me wondering if it was purely neutrality that left the mages of the time unwilling to interfere until the last moment, as I had always been taught, or if it was ignorance. What could have been prevented if those still brimming with their full power had stepped in sooner?

Magic in Olymazi presented in so many different ways, each kingdom and queendom with a unique manifestation. While musing over how to change the past is pointless, I am of the firm belief that there can always be information gleaned by what came before. I wonder if more mistakes were made by the kingdom I call home than what our historians and teachers are willing to admit.

I ponder the subject as I ready myself for the day, intent on visiting the library. The shifter books I have read so far cover a mostly generic history on their people, but I find myself most drawn to the parts that speak of the royal family. Other than the small bits of information Jahlee has given me, I don't know anything else about Kai's father and the lineage he came from. Not that I necessarily *needed* to learn that information, as it wasn't pertinent to anything other than my own curiosity.

Dressed in black leggings and a cream-colored short-sleeved top, the material linen and embroidered with golden thread, I lace my sandals up and draw my hair into a ponytail before opening the door. I find Kai leaning against the wall, his head tipped back and eyes closed as though there aren't people who would try to harm him while he's so unguarded. As if he has no other care in the world but to stand there with his muscular arms folded over his chest, silent and unmoving like a perfectly sculpted statue. Clearly, he handled himself just fine before my arrival, but the thought of him getting attacked makes anger bloom within me. Kai's eyes open when I near, his gaze going right to mine and then down my body in a sensual caress. I feel the weight of it as if it were his hands and fight back the urge to shiver.

"Good morning, Your Majesty," I state, if only to rile him up with the use of his title.

A deep sound rumbles from his throat as he rights himself from the wall and takes a large step towards me, his chest mere inches from my chin. "Princess," he responds, dropping his voice to an octave that does, in fact, make my skin pebble with goosebumps.

The cool depths of his dark brown eyes bore into me, the ever-present golden specks dormant as if he's completely at ease. He curls his finger under my chin, gently tipping my face up while his thumb traces my bottom lip. The soft touch is the first of its kind between us where we might catch an audience, and I know I could move—*should move*—away from it, but the unexpected gentleness and the way my body responds in kind keeps me pinned in place. It's a slow progression, both of us leaning in closer as if to test this unknown space between us. What would it be like to share a kiss here and now? One that isn't a precursor to anything sexual or brought on by high emotions? I have never done such a thing before, never felt so *exposed*. My fingers reach out for his tunic, curling into the fabric as my lips part.

A throat clears a few feet away, the sound halting us. "Am I interrupting?" *Kane*. Kai smoothly drops his hold on me, my own hand coming down to my side as he looks over my shoulder at his cousin. When Kai doesn't speak, Kane chuckles, moving so that he is also in my line of sight. "Quite an intimate moment you were sharing there."

I eye the king's cousin, my gaze roaming over his maroon-colored short-sleeved tunic and the tattoos that go down both arms. The swirling pattern of his right arm is disturbed by a scar, the skin there raised and still slightly pink.

"What do you want, Kane?" Kai growls as we move to stand shoulder-to-shoulder.

"Nothing of importance," he says casually, his head tilting to the side as his gaze goes to me. "Just curious about the comings and goings in the palace. Making sure all is safe after the rebels' *message*. After all, it did happen in broad daylight while our king was still on the premises. They are bold—I'll give them that." He glances quickly Kai's way, the corners of his mouth drawing farther apart as his grin hones into something more cruel.

"You were here too, were you not?" I ask, drawing his attention back to me. "As the supposed liaison between Crown and people, one would suspect that you would have better intel on these rebels. Enough so that an attack in *broad daylight,* as you said, would be nearly impossible." I take a small step forward, Kane's eyes narrowing as I do. "Where were *you* when the rebels came?"

His responding snort is tipped towards the edge of fury. "You're not suggesting *I* had something to do with it?"

"Did you?"

Kane's pupils become framed with gold before his hand shoots out to grasp my arm. "Foolish of you to make an insinuation without proof," he snarls.

My chin dips, and I gaze up through my lashes at him, holding eye contact for a few seconds before I send the heel of my palm right into his nose. He shouts out in pain, his grip tightening on my arm before I latch onto his wrist and twist inward, forcing his fingers to release me. Blood trickles over his lips, the gold in his eyes growing as he bares his teeth at me. I flash mine right back. Kane moves to take a step forward when his gaze flicks to Kai. Whatever he sees there has him inhaling slowly while wiping the blood off of his face with the back of his hand before spinning on his heel and storming towards the palace entrance.

Turning slowly, I find Kai glaring down at me, his own chest rising and falling with quick breaths. Tua's warning to not make Kai look *worse* to his people makes me internally cringe as I watch the palace staff walk by and avert their gazes from us. *Shit.*

"Kai, I'm sorry—"

His hands cup my face, tilting it upward as his lips crash into mine. Burning need pierces my veins as I reach out to claw at him, tugging him closer and wrapping a leg around his hip. He forces my back against the wall while his tongue tastes my mouth, desperation sharpening our edges while the outside world fades until there is only him.

"So defiant," he mumbles as he leaves my mouth to show attention to my neck, scraping his teeth along the delicate skin there. "So indignant." I scoff but arch farther into him as his hands drag down my sides, skimming over my breasts. "But so unexpected," he pauses, licking where my pulse flutters at the base of my neck, "and so fucking magnificent."

Air rushes from me as I squeeze my eyes shut against the onslaught of emotions his words bring. My fingers spear into his hair, holding his head to me so he doesn't see what I'm sure is written all over my face. The urge to tell him the truth about me pokes and prods until it leaves me feeling nauseous.

"We should stop," I say hoarsely though my grip doesn't loosen. Kai immediately lifts his eyes to meet mine, something guarded building in them the longer he looks at me. "Not because I don't want this, but I'd rather not get caught by another person, like your sister."

Kai relaxes, his body slow to lean away. "Technically, Kane didn't catch us doing anything."

"True, but I think the intention was obvious."

"Hmm," he says, taking a step back as he smiles at me. I stare as though I've just uncovered something forbidden, something that I wasn't meant to see. "There is a hot spring near the waterfall you followed me to after the rebel attack. I want to take you to it. I thought we could eat a meal there under the stars."

"Kai Vaea, king of the shifters, are you asking me to go on a picnic date with you to a hot spring?" I enjoy the way his brows draw down, his frown drawing a laugh from me.

"It's not a picnic."

"It is, by every definition, a picnic," I retort, reaching out to grip his arm when he attempts to walk away, grumbling under his breath. "I would love to go with you."

He huffs out a breath but then nods. "I will come to your room when it's time to leave."

We descend the stairs together, he off to check in with the members of his court while I head to the library. But the image of him smiling and the thought that it is because of me, stays cemented in my mind. I wonder if, when I tell him the truth, he will ever smile at me like that again.

Chapter Sixty-Two

BAHIRA

The library is silent upon entry and nearly empty, only the librarian and, surprisingly, Tua occupying the space. I walk up to the small table Tua is seated at, a book splayed open in front of him. "May I join you?"

"Bahira. It has been a bit since we've had a conversation. How are you?" He gestures with a hand to the empty chair across from him.

"Well enough," I reply, taking a seat and leaning my elbows on the table. "And you?"

Tua smiles, the wrinkles around his dark eyes crinkling with it. "I cannot complain." His pause is laden with a knowing glance. "Have you been keeping out of trouble?"

"Not much time left for trouble when I'm helping Kai gain the trust of his people back." I enjoy the way Tua's eyes flare for a moment. I had thought him to truly care about coaching Kai, but it's become abundantly obvious that Tua has his own agenda. What that is exactly, I'm not sure of yet.

"Ah, yes. How do you feel you have fared in those efforts?" he asks, tilting his head contemplatively.

"It doesn't matter what I think. What have his advisors said?" Admittedly, Kai had not told me much about their feedback.

Tua joins his hands together beneath his chin, his gaze biting as he exhales in an exaggerated manner. "They did not find merit in your ideas that he brought forth, and they let him know as much." My eyes widen in surprise. Not that the advisors had not liked the ideas, but that Kai would go against their advice and do them anyway. The realization that follows makes my fingers tremble—he did it for *me*. Tua nods his head as if he has access to my inner thoughts. "I cannot say I blame them. Many of the nobles of the court predicted that it would turn into a disaster, which I hope you can agree with."

A denial and rebuttal rest on my tongue, but I hold them there and cock my head to the side, studying Tua. Though a lot of people had attempted to degrade Kai with their insults and accusations about how he was to blame for the blight, the ones who came to him with problems that were legitimate had their issues resolved. Kai and I talked about the things he had done on our way back from Honna. He had seemed pleased with the results of working closely with his people, and I couldn't help but feel pride in him.

When the silence lingers, Tua closes his book and leans forward, matching my position. "Change takes time. It takes fortitude, but it also takes support. In a kingdom such as ours, not even a king is all-powerful." Conviction colors his tone, the words spoken harshly despite the placid look on his face.

"And he shouldn't be. It is why councils and advisors exist, to help guide the king into choices that better the land he rules over."

"Precisely, Princess. It is important to remember that time is on the side of the plans that have already been put into motion." I clench my jaw at the use of my title, casting a quick glance around the empty library. Tua offers me a pointed smile before standing and pushing his chair in, walking around to my side. I cast my glance upward, his brown eyes now ringed in a faint golden glow. "What are your plans this evening? There is going to be a celebration here at the palace, and there is a theme for the party."

Feigning an ease I don't feel, I lean back in my chair. "I think I might opt to read in my room instead."

Tua chuckles, as though he expected that answer. "Perhaps a wise decision. The gods know that I hate having to mingle at these things." With a knock of his knuckle on the table, he heads towards the library's exit.

I call out to him when he's halfway there. "Tua, what is the theme for the party tonight?"

He halts his steps, barely looking over his shoulder at me. "Masquerade."

Kai and I sneak out the back of the palace. He said it was necessary to do so, as Tua had asked him to meet with the court advisors this evening before the party. He is apparently inclined to avoid them all.

"Should you skip meeting with them? What if they want to discuss everything you've been working on?" I ask, thinking of my conversation with Tua earlier.

"An extra day will not kill them, despite how they may act. Besides, rain is predicted to fall tomorrow, so this is the only opportunity we have to come out here before it's too flooded."

It's nearly sunset, orange and bright pink painting the sky overhead. The temperature is beginning to cool, the oppressive daytime heat sweetening into a slight evening chill. It reminds me of the last days of summer back home, the signal that the Autumnal Ball is nearing.

"What about the masquerade party? We'll be missing that as well."

Kai snorts from where he walks ahead of me, the path only wide enough for us to stay in a single file line. "Do I look like someone who partakes in that sort of revelry?"

"You don't exactly look like someone who is keen on *anything*," I retort.

Kai chuckles, pushing an overgrown plant from our path. The trickling sound of the waterfall fills the air, the temperature dropping even more as we clear the last bit of the jungle. We step out into the open space I saw the day I followed Kai—only, this time, we're on the ground. The waterfall looms in front of me, mist from its powerful flow coating my skin. The water above is the brightest blue I've ever seen, white caps forming where it crashes into the stream below. Unlike the scent of salt that normally permeates the air, the smell that lingers here is one of damp earth and pungent florals. Blooming purple flowers line the banks, and I suspect they are the reason for the perfumed scent.

Kai lets me study our surroundings a little longer before he gestures for me to follow him. We walk for another ten minutes before a second body of water comes into view. Steam curls into the air above the aquamarine pool cradled within a white stone formation in the ground.

"How did this get here?" I ask, marveling at how the spring seems so out of place.

"It's been here since well before my family line held the throne. It may even be as ancient as the island's creation itself." Kai walks around the spring to where the surrounding rocky outcrop has created a small natural cave. "When my mother and I still resided in the palace in my early years, she would often bring me here. I preferred to splash in the water by the waterfall as opposed to boiling in this pool."

Grinning, I round the steaming spring to join him as he pulls off his pack to set it against the stone wall. "How long did you live in the palace?"

"The first five years of my life," he answers.

I set my own backpack down, my spear scraping against the cave wall and causing sparks. "Why did you leave?"

Kai turns to look out over the spring and into the jungle. "Normal shifter offspring manifest into their animal for the first time around the age of two. Yet I made it to five and still had shown no signs of being able to shift. So my father sent my mother and I back to where he took her from."

Shock draws my eyebrows up. "*Took her?*"

Kai nods, his jaw hard as a muscle there tenses. "My father was halfway through a royal tour of the kingdom when he arrived in Honna. My mother helped serve him and his entourage, and he was, according to Iolana, very smitten by her beauty." He pauses, taking a deep breath before turning to look at me. "He demanded for her to be available to serve every meal. He extended his trip and began inviting her on walks or to dine with him in private. My mother had never had so much attention on her, let alone by someone of such importance."

"She got swept up in it," I surmise.

"She did," he replies softly. "He asked her to come back to the palace with him. She knew he was married, but he led her to believe that the queen would be alright with him seeking the pleasure of another, as they hadn't been able to sire an heir."

"Was that true?"

"Partially. They hadn't sired an heir, but his wife was not aware of his *side* activities. When my mother arrived at the palace, she was hired as one of the help and continued to see my father in private." Kai's face is a whirling storm of emotion—sadness and anger are the strongest, but there is also an undercurrent of grief. "Shortly after, she fell pregnant. Fearing his response, she kept me secret for as long as possible before she had to tell him."

"Was he angry?"

Kai shakes his head, an incredulous scoff leaving his lips. "No. He was *elated*. He pampered her the entire pregnancy. She became a lady in the queen's circle—the friends she had made as a palace worker now served *her*. My father doted on her, even taking her out to public events in the city. Everyone came to know her for what she was—the king's favored mistress." His words grow quieter as he speaks until the last one is hardly above a whisper.

When he doesn't continue the story, I don't push him to tell me more, not when he's already given me so much of his history. Sensing he needs a shift in the conversation, I gesture towards the pack he brought. "Are we eating or getting wet first?"

His eyes snap towards me, the pain bright in them receding as his mouth curves into a smirk at the double meaning of my words. He leans in closer until I can feel the warmth radiating from his body. "Dinner first. Dessert later."

Desire coils deeply within me, my core aching in a way I know Kai can detect. His eyes flare as they move down my body, but he forces himself—if a bit stiffly—to squat down to his pack. A red blanket is the first thing he takes out, carefully spreading it onto the surprisingly smooth cave floor. I pinch my lips together as he meticulously places glass containers of food in the center, a bottle of wine and two metal chalices and plates accompanying them. *It's absolutely a fucking picnic.*

When he stands, he looks expectantly at me, gesturing for me to take a seat. At the delighted look I know is on my face, his brows draw together. "What?"

"Nothing. This looks great."

Kai opens the containers, the rich scents of grilled meats, steamed vegetables, and soft rice wafting up from them as we serve ourselves. "The chefs did an incredible job," I say between bites, following the decadent tastes with a swig of sweet wine.

Kai clears his throat, and I *swear* a blush colors his cheeks. "I made this."

My fork freezes halfway to my agape mouth, surprise completely rendering me speechless for a moment. "You can *cook*?"

He shrugs, resting his elbows on his widespread knees. "It's a bit of a hobby." My laugh echoes out in the small space, my surprise at knowing that this beast of a man enjoys cooking makes his blush grow even more. "*Bahira.*"

Though I've come to realize that I like his jagged edges—the anger, the attitude, the domineering way in which he simply *exists*—it also feels good to see a part of him that no one else ever has. "No, no. I'm not laughing at you." It's clear he doesn't believe me, his gaze moving out to the spring as his fingers curl in tightly until his knuckles turn white. Reaching over our meal, I grab his chin and force his eyes back to mine. I choose each of my words carefully, unwilling to have him think I'm anything other than awed. "I am rarely ever surprised, and yet you are nothing like I thought you'd be. Well, that's not entirely true. You are definitely a brute. You're short-tempered, more animal than male sometimes. I've certainly wanted to kill you on occasion." He growls, attempting to jerk from my hold, but I tighten my fingers. "But you have consistently surprised me, Kai Vaea. I must admit, I have never been happier to be wrong."

Small flecks of gold brighten in his irises as he inhales deeply. I release his chin, holding his stare for a moment longer before sitting back and unlacing my boots. Standing, I pull my tunic overhead and then remove my pants until I'm only in my undergarments. I feel the shift in the air as Kai's gaze devours me. He, too, stands and, with torturous slowness, removes *all* of his clothing. The last rays of sun highlight his body, showcasing his perfect skin and sculpted muscles. When he eyes me in challenge, that gruff look sending another core-pulsing thrill through me, I remove my undergarments until I'm fully naked as well.

A deep noise thrums from Kai's chest—akin to the rumblings of an animal either extremely pleased or whole-heartedly not, though I suspect it's the former. He reaches his hand out for mine, our calloused palms scraping together when I take it, and leads me into the springs.

Chapter Sixty-Three

BAHIRA

The water temperature is perfect as is the night sky above, silver stars sparkling against an array of black and blue.

"Do you know much about constellations?" Kai asks, the timbre of his voice soothing as I sink a little deeper under the warm water.

"Nothing beyond where they are and their shape. Of all the areas one could study, the layout of the stars is the least interesting to me."

He chuckles at that, tipping his head back as he leans his elbows against the white stone edge of the hot spring. "Iolana is obsessed with the stars and their alignments. She muses that there are messages hidden within them and we just need to know where to look."

"That's insane."

Amusement graces his face, but it quickly falls with his next words. "I think she's always looking for signs because of what she's lost. Not just her sister—my mother—but a child as well."

"Gods," I whisper.

The quiet stretches into the night as I study him.

"So, when not gazing at the night sky and presumably causing trouble for the lovely people of Honna, what did young Kai do for fun?" I ask, hoping to shift the mood.

"It might surprise you to learn that I was a bit of a recluse." His answer makes me snort, drawing his eyes to mine as he laughs. "Growing up at the edge of the island, I spent a lot of time on the beach looking out at the ocean. I loved watching the pods of whales and delphinidae that would swim by."

"You weren't afraid a siren would find you and sing you into a trance?"

He shrugs as he leans away from the edge of the spring. "I was stupid then. I didn't give a shit, and I thought I was invincible either way. And of the two of us, *I'm* not the one who appeared to fall under the sway of a siren's song."

I send a splash of water his way. I hadn't forgotten what it felt like to be under the siren's thrall—if that's truly what happened.

As if it's an afterthought, he quietly adds, "Then my power began to grow and *change*."

"What do you mean?"

"I didn't shift for the first time until I was nearly twelve, and when I did, I found that I wasn't limited to one animal."

I suck in a breath, leaning away from the edge of the rock with wide eyes. "You can shift into *multiple* animals?" He nods his head as he carefully watches my reaction. "How?"

Kai runs a wet hand through his hair, a few of the dark brown strands breaking free and resting near his temples. "I don't know. At first, I had no control over which animal I shifted into. Eventually, I learned how to subdue the urge and then how to direct it to a specific animal. I am limited to only animals that I've seen."

I shake my head in disbelief. "You can shift into many animals, and Jahlee can't shift at all. That seems…"

"Unfortunate," he supplies.

"Does anyone else know? Besides Jahlee, I assume?"

He smiles, his entire face changing with the expression. There is fondness and contentment there, and I unabashedly observe him, tracing every part of his broad jaw and cheekbones glinting beneath the starlight. "No one else besides the two of you. Because she is nosey, she happened to find me hiding in the jungle as I was practicing switching from one animal to the next."

I laugh at that as I drop my attention to the water, tracing my fingers over its surface. The urge to share something—*anything*—with him is too strong to ignore. Just like every time that I'm in his presence, I lose the battle to keep my emotions steady.

"You once asked about my best friend, the one you saw me with on the beach before we left the Mage Kingdom," I say, and though it isn't exactly the secret I should tell him, I let the words pour from me anyway. "His name is Daje. Growing up, I was an outcast despite being a princess. I was verbally tormented. Told I was too weak, too lacking. That I wasn't a worthy mage. That I couldn't be anything other than a failure. Daje stood up for me, often at his own expense. As we grew older, I could tell that his feelings for me were changing. That they were morphing into something deeper, but like a coward, I didn't acknowledge them out loud, and neither did he until the night of the Summer Solstice."

I look up to find Kai's rapt attention on me, and it makes it a little easier to keep going.

"I've always been singularly focused, driven to find answers to problems that plague not only me but my entire kingdom. Daje didn't—*doesn't*—see the value in that. He believes me to be stuck in a cycle, I think, one of self-imposed masochism, but the truth is, I can't help but be this way. I can't help but look for the right answers, even if—" I pinch my lips together, forcing down the inadequacy that threatens to come out as tears. "Even if there are none to be found. That night, Daje gave me an ultimatum. He proposed to a woman who hasn't existed since our childhood, and I am clinging on to a friend who has undoubtedly changed. All this time away has made me realize that perhaps I've never had anyone in my life who has been able to accept *all* of who I am. The good and the bad. The sharp-tongued warrior and the obsessed researcher. The princess who is trying to live up to the title. I wonder if maybe the combination of things that I am is too much for *anyone*."

Self-consciously, I avert my gaze again as I offer him a little more vulnerability.

"Here, I've been forced to question my desires. My *sanity*. I find myself wondering what exactly I'm going to return to when my time here is up. And what I'll miss when I leave." My hand runs over my chest under the water, my heart aching in a way that makes me draw in a tight breath.

Kai's attention on me feels like a tattoo of its own, marking me until my bare flesh feels raw from the burn of it. The water ripples as he moves towards me, his hand wrapping around the side of my neck as his thumb pushes under my chin to tilt my head up and force me to meet his gaze. His other hand rests on my hip, his fingertips digging into the skin as he draws me towards him. "Only the weak will find you to be too much. Any male who aims to subdue you is not deserving of the same air that fills your lungs."

"And what about you?" I ask, my hands tentatively resting on his firm chest. "You wish I was less of a bother."

"I have no interest in taming you, Bahira." He leans down until his mouth is angled above my own. "And I am no mere male. I am a king. One who recognizes when there is a queen in his presence." Before I can respond, his lips collide with my own while his tongue claims mine in hungry sweeps, narrowing my focus so that I don't dissect his words and the intent behind them too deeply.

My heart ricochets between my ribs, the feel of him in my hands and on my mouth and so near my body ignites every part of me. My need for him is more than wanting to satiate the desire for sex. I want to come undone *with* him. I want to feel our bodies joining until he's stripped of every piece of armor he wears for the world and, instead, is bared to me—*only* to me.

He smiles against my lips, his hands sliding down my slick body to grip my thighs as he lifts me up. My ankles lock behind him, my nails scraping over his shoulders as he carries me out of the hot spring. Our dinner is still spread out over the blanket, and Kai sets me down only long enough to sweep every container to the side. My gaze catches on the dots of neon blue and green glowing on the ceiling of the small cave above us as he wraps an arm around me and lowers my back to the blanket.

Something aches within me when our gazes lock. It demands attention, but I'm too frightened to give the emotion a name. I feel oddly unsure of what to do with my hands, gliding them down his back and then over his shoulders and into his hair. His weight on me is welcome and warm, his body fitting to mine as if it were molded just for me. My equal in every way.

"My undoing," he rasps, leaning in to kiss and nip my neck and shoulder. All I can do is nod in return because I'm becoming undone too.

He slides into me in one easy thrust, my desire for him unrelenting and hot and terrifying. He's everywhere—not just within my body but in my head and in my breath and, further still, in my heart. The stupid thing beats harshly, each flutter of it opening a floodgate of emotions that have no business being here as we writhe together. Our breaths become labored, but unlike our previous joining, the eagerness filling the spaces between us is softer. It's still as desperate, my nails scouring his flesh as his teeth leave an imprint on my own, yet this isn't just fucking. It's everything I've always been too scared to admit wanting. Everything that's lacked with the myriad of other partners I've had.

"*Bahira,*" he rasps my name out, and it sounds like a reckoning. It *feels* like one as my climax twists down my spine and lower, every muscle pulling taut when the tension begins to crest. He grips my thigh in his large hand, pushing it out wide as he buries himself in me. His thrusts become deeper and *harder*, his cock stretching me as my walls clamp down around him. I hold him as I come, breathing his name against his mouth while Kai pulses inside of me, another declaration of my name sworn between us.

My lips tingle though they still search his mouth—content with whatever he'll give me as our chests heave. It's that thought, that utterly forlorn and *pathetic* thought, that tethers me back to reality. The one where I am only a guest in his kingdom and due to return home soon. Where I'm lying to him, keeping him in the dark about what he assumes I can do—what he *values* me for. *That* reality punches me in the gut until I feel the air knocked from my lungs. I slowly slide away and sit up, my breathing labored because I know that there is no escaping what I need to do next.

Kai stands beside me, grabbing something from his pack before exiting the cave. I hear the splashing of water, and then he is back at my side, handing me a wet cloth. We clean up in silence, Kai casting glances my way that grow more and more concerned.

"Your silence is deafening," he finally remarks when we're partially dressed, him with his trousers on and me in my top and undergarments. "Do you regret this?" He asks the question so earnestly—without judgment—that I have to squeeze my eyes shut.

"No, and I'm fine," I lie.

His fingers wrap around my jaw, and he forces me to look at him, waiting until my eyes open again before he speaks. "Say that again but make it more believable." My bottom lip trembles, and the tip of his thumb traces over it. He releases me to tuck my hair behind my ear, his eyes once more holding mine captive. "Do you remember when you asked if I liked your hair on the ship? And I denied it?"

Swallowing, I nod my head.

"I lied. I fucking *love* it."

Then Kai leans forward, his lips gently kissing my temple, and it's too much. I have to hope that he'll understand. That he feels whatever this is between us as strongly as I do and it will be enough to wash away the betrayal. Waiting until he's leaned away, I curl my fingers into my palms so that the nails bite into the skin. Bracing myself, I confess, "I don't have magic."

He looks at me as if the words I've spoken aren't in a language he understands. Nausea rumbles in my stomach and moves up my torso until it's burning the back of my throat. He tilts his head to the side in one sharp movement, studying me like he can see through skin and bones as he searches for something that might not be there.

"You are mage." A statement, not a question.

"I am," I confirm. "But I do not have magic. It's why I was treated poorly as a child. I've been running experiments to try—"

"You *don't* have the ability to wield raw magic?" he interjects, the coldness of his words making me wince. Any optimism I held that he might give me grace vanishes when his upper lip lifts in a snarl. "You lied."

I don't try to explain myself; it doesn't matter. Not as he looks at me like I'm a traitor—a plague within his kingdom, when he had hoped I might be the cure.

"I brought you here so that you could *help* my people. I let you meet with them, hear their stories, and learn their plights. And for what?" His voice grows louder as it echoes off the cave walls and pierces into my heart. I swear the very ground shakes from his fury.

"The magic of the Continent chose *me* for a reason. I can still help—"

"It makes sense now. Why that male—*Daje*—was so insistent that you were the wrong one chosen for the job. He knew, your entire fucking kingdom *knew*, that you would be *worthless* to us."

That word digs under my flesh and deep into my soul, an old wound reopened. *Worthless*. I know that I have no room to defend myself, no moral high ground on which to stand, but I still snap my teeth at him. "There is *no* guarantee that mage magic would have been able to do anything. I *wasn't* lying when I said that my experiments with expelled magic hadn't led to quantifiable results! You don't know for sure that it would have helped at all!"

"I suppose, now I never fucking will!" he barks back, a ring of gold encircling his irises as he stands and roughly grabs his tunic from the ground.

I stand as well, running my hand through my hair and pulling it back from my face. "Kai—"

"Don't." He keeps his back to me as he finishes dressing, grabbing his boots and slipping them on. "This is why I couldn't seem to get you to use your magic. Why you never healed yourself. I thought perhaps you couldn't access it as strongly here or maybe you only used it on rare occasions, but I—"

His chest heaves as he prepares to throw more verbal daggers. I don't shield myself from them because I know that I have earned them. Betrayal simmers thickly in the air when he finally turns around, and I watch him seal any cracks in his armor that he permitted me to see.

"You allowed me to give my people false hope. I let you into my kingdom, into my home, into my fucking *bed*, and you were all too eager to spread your legs to cover up your lies."

Only by sheer will do I not crumble. "I did not *fuck you* to hide anything. I am genuinely trying to help you. I care about your people, Kai. About *you*."

He scoffs, but it's a broken sound. "Like I would ever believe another word from your lips."

"I'm sorry," I croak as he walks past me and out of the cave.

He pauses at my words, looking at me over his shoulder with nothing but uncompromising anger. "Not as sorry as I am." Then he leaves, not bothering to grab the pack he brought with him.

A light breeze scrapes against my face and stings the tears that have yet to fall from my eyes. Like prodding an open wound, Kai knew exactly how to strike me to make sure it hurt. I don't hate him for it. I hate myself for hoping for a different outcome. How had he burrowed himself so deeply under my skin in a matter of months? Why was I stupid enough to allow it, *knowing* that it was only ever destined to fail?

But I already know the answers to those questions. I had seen a part of myself in him. I had found someone who didn't shy away from what—*who*—I am. Even early on, with all the bickering and taunting, he had never once believed me to be weak. To need saving or a new purpose or to change to fit some idealistic cast.

But it doesn't matter now. Not when he considers me to be *worthless*.

I don't know how long I stand and stare in the direction Kai left, only that, eventually, I wipe the tears away and pack up the food as best as I can. Once I'm fully dressed, I head back towards the palace. *Will he force me to go back home early? Do I even want to stay now?* Those thoughts swirl around and around, disorienting me so much that I don't realize I've reached the edge of the palace grounds. It isn't until I hear the screaming, the ominous chorus cleaving through the air, that my attention shifts.

"What the fuck?" I quicken my steps as the screams grow louder, this time joined by a cacophony of roars and chirps and growls. I break into a run, my arms pumping at my sides as I follow the stone pathway through the front gardens. My eyes widen and I skid to a stop when I see the first outline of a shadow past the palace entrance. Tua had said there would be a masquerade party tonight, but these masks aren't normal ones.

A large male stalks down the hallway on the other side of a glass window, a sword in his grasp, and I watch in shock as he arcs it up into the air before swinging it down and into a female. She slumps against the wall, sliding down until she is motionless on the floor and leaving a trail of red above her. The palace rumbles and shakes with more screams and animal noises, some shifters barreling out of the front door and into the jungle.

I drop our packs to the ground and slide my spear from its loops. My steps are nearly silent against the grass as I sprint towards the male. However, his shifter hearing gives him an early warning, and he spins, the shadows of his mask casting onto the wall behind him. An elongated skull with curling horns protruding from the top covers his entire head except for his glowing golden eyes.

"Hello, Princess," the rebel says.

Chapter Sixty-Four

XANDER

The scent of mildew grows stronger the farther down into this hellscape I go. I hate it here in the dungeons, maybe even as much as the king does. It has been longer between visits than I meant for it to be, but *His Majesty* has kept me busy. I slip on some moss on the last step, cursing as I hit the cold stone wall and my stupid fucking golden armor clangs loudly. A few of the prisoners stir, their hands gripping around the iron bars as they begin to plead for help when they see that the king isn't with me. I ignore them all as I walk down the dark corridor, my boots scuffing against the damp stone floors before I stop in front of the last cell. The other prisoners have hushed now, their hope of being set free diminished.

"It's time for you to talk," I say gruffly while reaching for the keys dangling on my belt loop.

The female hunched in the corner with her arms wrapped around her knees lifts her head to glower at me. "*Fuck. You,*" she snarls, her body wobbling as she stands.

I take in her more ragged appearance, and my heart skips a beat as I clench my jaw in regret. *I waited too fucking long.*

"You make this harder on yourself." Finding the key to her cell, I unlock and slide the bars to the side, the ancient metal squealing in protest. She freezes as I enter, her eyes poring over me as if I'm going to attack at any moment. Gripping her arm firmly, I lead her out of the cell, her bare feet slapping on the freezing stone as we walk.

"I'm not going to tell you anything!" she screams.

I don't reply, pulling her towards an adjacent hallway where a single door awaits—made mostly of wood but fortified with metal. She tenses in my hold though she already knows what to expect—or she *should*. I suppose that's the thing with living on the edge of fear for weeks on end. Rationale and logic lose out to what-ifs and hypotheticals. When your mind is the only thing keeping you company, it's easy to get lost in it.

I had assumed Rhea had fallen victim to hers, being all alone in that tower. Well, mostly alone. Her escape with the secret mage prince had taken up *all* of my free time. *The prince.* What a fucking shock *that* had been to learn. I was lucky that I had found something untrustworthy about a guard who worked his way so quickly up the ranks. I doubt him finding out what I had spent years building would have been anything other than disastrous.

Metal hinges creak as I throw the door open, releasing her when she steps past the threshold and out of sight of the other prisoners. Her arms hug her torso as she slowly looks around at the different torture devices filling the room. Swords, daggers, chains, and ropes. Whips and needles and blindfolds and any other thing a man might conjure up in his nightmares—or dreams, depending on how depraved the individual is—can be found. I lock the door after I shut it, ensuring we'll be left alone, before turning to face her.

A single large flame gem is embedded in the ceiling above us, its light shining down on the crown of her head and illuminating her amber eyes. We keep the silence between us as I take a step towards her and reach out my hand. Her hesitation is expected, but it still sends a wave of panic through me when she lingers before finally placing her delicate fingers on my own. Together, we walk back to the corner of the room where an ancient arched door is stationed.

I've oiled its hinges well enough that they are silent when I open it and duck my head, leading us through an old corridor. I have no idea why there is an underground tunnel that connects a now unused wing of the castle to the dungeons; I'm only grateful that, on one of my secret explorations, I found it. The space is pitch black, its ceiling low enough that I have to bend at the waist as we shuffle down it.

I keep my hand wrapped firmly around one of hers. The fingers of her other hand drag across the stone above, creating a whisper of noise that lets me know she won't accidentally hit her head. The smell of dust and mold mixing into the stagnant air is pungent, and when she coughs behind me, I pick up my pace, knowing her heightened senses are only growing more irritated the longer we are in this space. Finally, light frames the edges of another arched door a few feet ahead.

"Wait here," I whisper before letting her hand go and carefully opening the door.

Though I don't expect anyone to be here, I grip the hilt of the dagger strapped to my thigh and slide the thin blade free. Another set of well-oiled hinges keeps the door silent as I pull it open, the light of the flame gem I placed here pouring out into the dark tunnel. When I see that the room is empty of people, I sheathe my dagger, exhaling roughly.

"It's all clear."

"Thank the gods." She steps into the room, and I quickly close the door behind her, locking it in place though we'll only be here for a short time. "Please tell me that you have clean water for me to wash in?"

I snort and walk over to where a canvas cloth hangs from a rafter beam in the low ceiling, pulling it back to reveal a small basin tub I had filled with fresh water prior to retrieving her. "It's not warm—"

"It's perfect," she interrupts, her golden skin flushing before she ducks her head. "Thank you."

I bite back a smile, double checking that there is soap, shampoo, a towel, and a fresh change of clothes for her before crossing to the other side of the room. With my back to the tub, I unstrap the breast and back plates of my armor and set them on the ground before sitting on an overturned crate. Pulling a whetstone from my pocket, I unsheathe a second dagger. Water splashes behind me, and my grip on the stone tightens.

"You do know that it's slightly unsettling that you're sharpening a knife while I'm vulnerable in the bath, don't you?" she asks, sloshing more water onto the wooden floors.

My lips twitch as I continue my movements. "First, if you hear the sound of the blade against the stone, you'll know I'm not trying to sneak a glance at you." She makes a noise that almost sounds like a laugh. "Second, of the two of us, *you're* the least vulnerable. Last time I checked, I couldn't shift into a large fox." She scoffs at that but makes no further comment.

It is progress, though, from the first time I had tried talking to her. She had been brought directly from the border where they captured her to the dungeons, completely naked and with an arrow still sticking out of her thigh. *A shifter*, the guards that shot her had said. The second surprise related to Rhea's escape. How the princess had managed to hide a fucking *fox* in her tower, especially with the king's random visits, I will never know. Though it seems that she was always poised to hold secrets, to *be* a secret—something more myth than real if the king had his way.

I have made my own assumptions about her. Ones that I'm still unsure could be disproven, even with talking to the shifter female. Rhea is technically the rightful heir to the throne of the Mortal Kingdom, which makes things *complicated*. Still, shame coats the back of my throat, and I struggle to swallow it back down. I had made many tough choices over the past few years in my pursuit of something better for this kingdom and its people, for *myself*, and I know that I will have to make even more in the coming future. However, the one that still haunts my dreams, the one choice that may forever be irredeemable, is how I did nothing while Rhea was beaten by—

"I assume you brought something to eat?" Her voice is closer than before. I stop my use of the whetstone, placing it back in my pocket before sheathing the dagger.

"Are you decent?" I ask, hoping she doesn't catch the roughness to my voice.

"I am."

Waiting another few seconds before I turn around, I lift the large satchel from my body and walk over to our makeshift table. Two upended crates are set between two rickety chairs that I'm still not convinced won't snap under our weight. They were left over from whatever this room was used for before it was forgotten.

She towel dries her hair while walking to the chair opposite my own, sitting in it more delicately than she had the first time we came here. The clothes I brought for her had been the head maid Tienne's doing, and luckily, they fit her well. Maybe too well, as my eyes linger for an extra moment on her curves before I pull them away.

"I'm sorry that it took so long for me to come back again," I tell her, taking out a parchment-wrapped sandwich for each of us, two canteens of water, and a few apples. I try to never go more than three days between our visits, but this time, I had nearly doubled that.

"Is everything alright?" she asks, working her snow-white hair into a braid.

I lift my eyes to meet her gaze, tucking a few rogue strands of my own shoulder-length black hair back behind my ear. It's a nervous habit that I can't quite seem to stop around her. "Since I know you're asking for yourself—"

"And for her," she interjects with an angry bite of her sandwich.

I take my seat carefully, holding my hands up in front of me. "Of course. On *both* accounts, yes, I believe things are fine. But the king has been working on something that he's keeping close to the chest, and I haven't been able to get him to tell me yet what it is." Dolian was already paranoid, but Rhea's escape had compounded that madness. He trusts me more than any of the other guards, but that doesn't mean that I am privy to everything. A fact that frustrates me to no end, as it is pertinent that I know what he is planning at all times.

"You don't think it's related to getting her back?"

I shake my head though I'm not entirely sure. "It could be, but he's been very vocal about his ideas for forcing Rhea to come back to this kingdom. He was convinced that the *present* he sent her would do the trick." It hadn't, and when days had gone by with no response from Rhea or the Mage Kingdom, Dolian had raged upon every person he could find, leaving a mess that I was forced to clean up.

"I *will* kill him," she seethes, eyeing me as I take a bite of my own sandwich.

I nod again, but she'll have to get in line.

The first time I had removed her from the cell to bring her here, she fought and screamed every step of the way, convinced that I was indeed going to torture her as the king had suggested from the beginning. Her fiery spirit, even wounded and in captivity, had surprised me. I brought in a healer I trust to clean and patch her wound, her shifter magic helping to at least keep it from reopening. She should be dead—not just from the wound she sustained but because she crossed over the Spell. She's an anomaly, and my next swallow of food is tight in my throat as I study her.

It took *weeks* before she believed that I wasn't going to harm her. More time, and a few secrets of my own, for her to open up the slightest bit about herself and Rhea, but I have no interest in forcing information from her. She has been through enough. They both have. My only goal regarding her now is to help her escape from this place—from the king.

"When?" she asks in a whisper, holding my attention hostage. I lower my half-eaten sandwich to the parchment paper wrinkled on the table, brushing my hands off on my thighs.

"Soon. The last piece of the plan is nearly in place. Once we have that, I will be able to get you on a ship, and the king will never suspect anything beyond an inexperienced guard getting bested by a fierce female."

She grins at my compliment, the expression so rare that I can't help but stare at her full lips, my stomach tightening as I do. But the smile falters, and my gaze draws back up to her eyes—her irises wrapped in gold. "He cannot have her again."

"I know. He won't. He can't cross the Spell. He can't make anyone turn her over from the Mage Kingdom. As long as she stays there, she will be safe." If the princess ever steps foot in this kingdom again, she'll never leave. He'll make sure of it. It's better for my cause and better for her life if she stays where she is. "We'll have to go back soon."

She nods, finishing her meal and then pocketing the rest of the food I brought in her trousers. "Thank you."

"It won't be much longer; I give you my word." I pause, forcing a shaky smile as I stand from the chair. "For whatever that's worth." I imagine it can't be much, considering I had helped the king murder Alexi and had done nothing while he brutalized Rhea.

"It is worth more now than before," she answers quietly, extending her hand out to me. I take it without hesitation, and we make our return back through the tunnel and into the torture room.

"Don't forget to put on a show again; you're *very* convincing when you do."

She chuckles, giving my hand a barely perceptible squeeze before dropping it. "I look forward to your next visit, Xander."

I wrap my fingers gently around her upper arm, her warmth radiating through more than just my skin as I unlock the door, my eyes still honed in on hers. "As do I, Siyala."

I keep my body rigid where I stand guard in front of the throne room. Though familiar faces pass me, none of them look my way. I don't acknowledge them either. It's the number one rule of those who have joined the cause—in daylight, we are nothing but guards, servants, cooks, and workers of Vitour. But when the sun goes down and the castle falls quiet, those ready for something new, something *better*, gather in secret beneath it. Traversing those underground tunnels and utilizing the forgotten wings, we plot how we will take down not only Dolian but his advisors. The men who are letting this kingdom rot away from the Cruel Death.

King Dolian's voice carries through the slender gap in the middle of the double doors, and I take a small step in its direction to try and hear what he's saying.

"Are you *sure* that is what it means?" he asks.

There is a slight pause before a distorted voice answers, its lilt smooth. "If what you said about the shifter female is true, then yes. Do you know nothing of their kingdom, Your Majesty?"

Siyala. They must be talking about her.

King Dolian grunts, the sound of his boots tapping on the floor drowning out his response. I force myself to take a steadying breath, my heart still pounding in my ears as I lean in a little closer. "Fine. We'll do it your way. I'll ready the ship and—"

"Eavesdropping, are we, Commander?" My eyes snap to the owner of the oily voice as I grit my teeth together and glare at perhaps the most vile man I've ever had the displeasure of knowing, including the king.

"Of course not, Simon. Merely stretching." I keep all emotion from my face, something easily done with the many years of practice I've had.

"Good. We wouldn't want His Majesty to regret promoting you so soon or for others to begin to question it, now would we?"

I stare into his soulless eyes, the evil that I know lurks within him tamed for now. But his threat is pointless. Simon is the only person who knows the true connection between the king and I, and Dolian would sooner kill him than have anyone else find out about his *secret shame*.

The doors open behind me, hazel eyes meeting my darker ones briefly as he strides from the room. No one follows him out, his conversation happening within the Mirror, then.

"Xander, when was the last time you spoke with our prisoner?" He doesn't need to specify which one.

"Two days ago," I lie, resuming my position behind him and Simon as we walk down the white painted hallway with floors lined in deep red and gold rugs. Servants and other workers stop and pivot to go in the other direction as they avoid our entourage. "She still hasn't said anything of value, despite my attempts to break her."

Simon snorts, his hands coming behind him as he looks at me over his shoulder. "It doesn't take much to break someone who is already as weak as she is. I'd be happy to use my talents on her if His Majesty is so inclined."

Nausea burns my throat and curdles my stomach, but I force my expression to remain blank. Simon's reputation precedes him when it comes to those *talents*. I'd sooner kill him and then myself before I'd let him anywhere near Siyala.

"That won't be necessary. Her usefulness is nearing its end." The simmering rage in my blood morphs into icy fear at the king's words. "Instruct the other guards to keep her starved for the next few days. I want her weakened for the next part of my plan."

The looming door to the council chambers comes into view, the sigil of the Mortal Kingdom carved into it forcefully drawing my eye as I will myself not to react to his words—*his threat*. Alaric, another member of the King's Guard, opens the doors, allowing Simon to enter. The king stops short, turning to look at me.

We're nearly the same height, my few inches on him something I know he loathes. But that's where the similarities between us end, and thank the gods for it.

"Tell the maids to prepare a large room in the royal wing. It needs to be spotless upon my inspection, or I'll replace them permanently."

My throat tightens as I give a curt nod. "Anything else, Your Majesty?" *What are your fucking plans?*

He smiles, if the ghastly twist of his lips can even be called that. "Patience and persistence always pay off, Xander. Remember that." Then he turns and walks into the council chambers, my stare boring into his back as if it were a dagger. Gods, do I wish it fucking was. My fists tighten at my side as Alaric closes the door.

When the time comes to kill him, it won't be a knife to the back. I may have been forced to take a blood oath that swears I will not harm the king with my own hand, the scar raised on my palm proof of it, but I'll make sure *my* face is the last one he sees when a sharpened blade is plunged into his heart. It's the face of a man he thought he could trust. The face of the man whose mother he killed.

It's the face of his *son*.

Blowing out a breath, I meet Alaric's stare, breaking my own rules to ask him a question. "What ships are docked and ready to leave before the day's end?"

His blue eyes flare widely for a second before he relaxes his expression. "Only one ship is docked that I'm aware of. It's a supply ship from the Shifter Kingdom, and it leaves within the hour."

Shit.

Spinning on my heel, I make my way to the guard's quarters. I've never acted without a plan before, the nature of what I've been building these past few years is too important to risk getting caught. But Siyala's face flashes in my mind, her amber eyes bright with *life* despite what she's been through. There is no fucking way I'm letting my father, or that bastard Simon, add to that list of hurts. She'll be pissed that the ship is going to take her back to her home island and not to where Rhea is, but maybe that's for the best.

Regardless of what the king has planned, a revolution is knocking on his doorstep. One that is likely to bring chaos until it ushers in peace. So, even though it makes a longing I've only ever felt around *her* rush through my veins, I throw open the door to my room and begin grabbing items Siyala will need to make her journey back to her true home.

Chapter Sixty-Five

Rhea

Dust motes float in front of my face in the light given off by my magic. While I hold one hand wreathed in glowing white out in front of me, the other is pressed against the damp cold of the stone wall. The staircase down to Nox's hidden garden has been a small thorn in my side ever since he showed it to me.

I understand well enough that this staircase is different from the one that twisted away from my room at the top of the tower. There are no guards in shining golden armor waiting to take me back. There are no maniacal kings to surprise me when I reach the bottom. There is only a special place that Nox wants to share with me; one that he had only told me a small amount about because he insists it's better that I see it.

And I wanted to. *Gods,* did I want to run down these stairs and burst out into a space that only he and I could access. Something that was special to me *because* it was special to him. Yet my feet remain frozen on the tenth step.

It's progress. Healing isn't linear. You're doing great. I can hear Nox and even Cass's encouragement in my mind, and if those were the only voices I heard, I might be able to continue down into the darkness until I reached its bottom. It's the other voice—bitter and malicious—that roots me in place. *You are mine. You always have been. I will always find you.* It's like an evil songbird's trill stuck on repeat, his words drilling into me until they're all that I can focus on. *Come back home where you belong.*

I inhale deeply, dust tickling my nose until I sneeze. My lack of concentration on my magic makes the light sputter, plunging me into darkness for a few seconds. My heart kicks up, soundly hitting against my ribcage as I blink my eyes rapidly and try to refocus my attention. Each inhale is a gasp followed by a hard swallow, my nails digging into the stone walls. I take a step backward, and though my magic finally glows brightly on my palm again, I'm already retreating up the stairs. The door closes softly before I lean my back against it, the light from the hallway calming my nerves as I draw in another breath.

"Damn it," I whisper to no one before I push off the door and walk to Nox's room.

He's already left for the day, the council calling him to an early session. He expressed over dinner together the night before that there has been a disturbing increase in guards going missing in towns near the Fae Kingdom's border. Even though it was on the opposite side of the kingdom from King Dolian, I couldn't help but replay the final words he spoke through the Mirror. *Enjoy the safety of your people while you have it, King Sadryn. One can never be too sure when such a thing might be ripped away.* I wondered if this was my uncle somehow making good on his threat. Based on the look Nox gave me, somewhere between rage and concern, I think he felt the same.

"Honestly, you're embarrassing yourself," Cass shouts at Nox.

Sitting on the grassy field between Elora and Daje, I watch the two men spar. Heckling from Haylee and a man with a broad jaw and a deep voice I had just met named Max add to the sound of clashing metal.

Daje's fingers twitch restlessly where his arm is draped over his knee, almost as if he is itching to spar as well. Nox had spoken with him a few days after our argument. It had been quick as I observed them from a distance, both men standing with their arms crossed and serious expressions on their faces until Daje's softened imperceptibly at whatever Nox told him. They shook hands, and though I wouldn't call their interactions overtly friendly since, neither one seems to be harboring ill-will towards the other.

Cass unsheathes one of the daggers from what I learned is called a bandolier, a row of shining hilts still waiting for their turn. I've watched him and Nox spar in the past, and it never ceases to make my heart leap into my throat. He twirls the dagger over his knuckles in the blink of an eye and flings it at Nox. Somehow, the latter spins out of its path, obtaining nothing more than a small cut in the fabric of his black training clothes.

"See? *Embarrassing.*"

Nox's brows draw low as he adjusts his grip on the hilt of his sword. "Do you just like the sound of your own voice?"

"Who wouldn't?"

Elora and I laugh, Nox shooting an incredulous look my way. "You're not supposed to encourage him."

I shrug as I lean back on my hands, my braid sliding over my shoulder and down my back. Nox tracks its movement and somehow still blocks an advance from Cass. "I thought that you were the strongest mage the kingdom had seen in over two hundred years," I tease. Elora chokes on her next breath, her cheeks turning red from her silent laughter.

"Blondie makes a good point, Your Highness," Cass says, flipping a different dagger hilt over tip in the air and catching it without even looking.

The rest of the group begins to jokingly taunt Nox, but his eyes stay focused on mine. "How long?"

My head tilts to the side, the sunlight pouring over us on the open field and warming my cheek. "What?"

He rotates his sword in his hand as his lips curl to the right. "Let's make a bet. How long do I have to take him down?"

I roll my lips together as I look over to Elora, who grins like this is the best thing to ever happen while she bumps her shoulder into mine. "Five minutes?"

He shakes his head and reaches back behind him to the second hilt peeking up over his shoulder. "Make it difficult, Sunshine." Metal sliding against leather rings out into the air as he draws his second sword, the silver blade shining brightly in contrast to its midnight-black hilt.

"Three minutes."

Cass clicks his tongue this time.

"Okay, one minute!" I shout in exasperation, drawing a few chuckles from the people around me. "Take Cass down in *one* minute."

Nox's smile is cunning as he takes a small step towards me. "And when I win? What do I get?"

"What do you want?" I should have seen the trap for what it was because, as soon as the question is out of my mouth, Nox's eyes darken, and my cheeks begin to burn. He doesn't answer out loud, but based on the way Elora squeals and Daje groans, he might as well have.

"Now that I have the proper motivation," Nox starts, turning back to face his friend, "I'm sorry for what's about to happen." The two circle each other for a full rotation, Cass drawing his second sword, before Nox attacks. I watch how gracefully Nox pivots and counters around his best friend, his movements fluid though I know the swords in his hands must weigh a ton. I hadn't really studied his fighting skills when we were running for our lives from the tower, but out here in the open space of the training grounds, I can truly appreciate how magnificent he is. Cass fights similarly, seeming to block Nox's attacks while the latter is still forming them. A product of their training together since childhood, I'm sure.

"Do you think King Sadryn can fight with a sword like this?" Elora asks. My head snaps towards her. She chews on her lower lip, pushing her glasses farther up her nose as she stares at the two dueling men in front of us. Though I *know* she isn't really looking at Nox, my magic flares in my chest, forcing me to close my hands into tight fists. It draws Elora's attention, her gray eyes flicking over to mine in question.

"My stupid magic thinks you're looking at Nox like..." I'm too embarrassed to even finish the statement.

Elora smiles, looping her arm through mine as the sound of metal clashing draws both of our attention back to the fight. Cass spins, kicking his leg out low in an attempt to sweep Nox off of his feet. But his effort is in vain when Nox leaps over it, landing with agile skill and then swinging his blades down over Cass's head.

"Twenty seconds!" someone calls out, marking the time that has passed.

493

"Have you ever heard of fated souls?" Elora asks in a low voice meant for only me to hear.

I shake my head—my stomach plummeting when Cass fakes moving right only to go left, his sword swooping down on Nox who blocks it at the last second.

"I read about them in a very old book I found shoved to the back of a shelf in the palace library. It is written more like a journal—the account one of a personal nature for some parts. But the author writes about how they were fated to be with their partner. How they knew it was *destined*."

"Forty seconds!"

"And they also write about how their magic *reacted* to perceived threats to their partner. How it wasn't a conscious act but one that seemed to be driven by the magic itself. In an effort to protect the bond between the two."

"I don't perceive you as a threat at all."

Elora nods, squeezing my arm more tightly. "*I* know that, and *you* know that, but your magic... Mage magic is raw, and very little of its complex nature has been mapped out. Millennia have passed, and our knowledge of the power that flows through us is much the same as it was at the beginning of that time. Actually, there is probably *less* known about it now; something to do with being too content to seek out more information, I'm sure. It is interesting—this thought that perhaps you might be *fated* to be with someone. Maybe it's just your magic acting out because you're still learning to control it, or maybe it's something *more*. Maybe you and Prince Nox are fated souls."

A shout of frustration that isn't Nox's draws claps and cheers from those around us. Cass lies on his back, his hands lifted in surrender as Nox's swords hover crossed above his neck. "Official time?" Nox asks, Cass giving him the middle finger.

"Fifty-five seconds," Haylee answers. Nox removes his swords and slides them back into their sheaths before he holds his hand out to Cass.

"Do you think it could be possible?" I ask Elora as we both stand up, brushing the grass from the backs of our legs.

She nods, running her fingers through her hair—its red hue brighter under the sun. "Honestly, I didn't believe it was a real thing until I saw the two of you. What you guys have is *different*."

I smile at her as I feel Nox near. I like the idea that perhaps there is a reason my magic acts so *defensive* around him, beyond being unable to fully control it yet.

"I've come to claim my prize," he says, wrapping his arms around me as he lifts me up until our faces are level, my feet dangling above the ground. My laugh turns into a scream as he spins us, and I squeeze my arms tightly around his neck, burying my face in the juncture where it meets his shoulder as I pepper quick kisses over the warm skin there.

"Seems like a waste of a prize. You can have me whenever you want," I say when we come to a standstill, the movement of dark blonde hair catching my eye over his shoulder.

Haylee walks over to where Elora and Daje are talking. Elora glares at Haylee, murmuring something too quiet for me to hear before abruptly leaving the group. Haylee watches her retreat, her lips flattening before her gaze moves to me. The rest of the world quiets as we stare at each other, her face indecipherable. I had told her today, as Nox and Cass had readied to spar, that I was declining her offer. That Nox was *mine* and mine alone. Her brows had drawn down slightly, but similar to the look gracing her face now, I couldn't make sense of what she was feeling.

"Rhea." I'm jolted back by the sound of Nox's voice as he slowly lowers me back down to the ground. "Are you alright?"

"Yes. I— What were you saying?"

"It was something wildly romantic. Poetic even," he teases, playing with the end of my braid. "Are you ready for lunch?"

Nodding, I tuck myself into Nox's side as he waves goodbye to Haylee, Max, and the others. They wave back, while Elora, Daje, and Cass join us, though Haylee avoids my gaze.

Elora walks beside me, and I can't help but ask her what she said to Haylee. She turns to look at me, the corners of her mouth set in assurance. "I told her to leave you and Nox the fuck alone."

Chapter Sixty-Six

RHEA

As we climb the steps up to the palace doors, the guards on either side push them open, splitting the image of the albero tree carved on them in half. With the sun depicted on one corner and the moon on the other, it's almost like watching the sky cleave in two as we enter. Perhaps that imagery is fitting, as the palace we step into leaves the quiet of the outside world behind. It's buzzing with life, aides and workers shuffling from room to room as they begin preparations to usher in the autumn season with the aptly named Autumnal Ball. Burnt orange, golden yellow, and ripe red are dotted throughout the foyer and hallways in the form of potted flowers, wreathes, banners with tassels, and rugs. The colors remind me that I am anxiously waiting for the leaves on the trees to change into similar hues. The excitement of seeing that happen up close and not from the tower balcony makes my blood sing with anticipation.

"So, I will meet you here after dinner?" Elora asks as we all stop in the middle of the foyer.

I had asked her if she would like to accompany me to my dress appointment with Sarai later today, and she had leapt at the chance, raving about how lovely the ball was and how it was her favorite celebration. What she didn't know was that I had asked Sarai to also fit her for a dress. It seemed like a simple gesture, one I hoped wasn't stepping over boundaries that normal friends didn't cross.

"Yes. Thank you again for agreeing to come with me."

Elora smiles, giving a small shake of her head. "It's what friends do." She pulls me in for a hug, and I return it, scanning the room from over her shoulder. That's when I spot him, his menacing frown easy to make out even from his current post down the hall. Upon seeing us, Councilman Kallin makes his way towards us with purposeful strides, as if Nox might escape his attention if he doesn't hurry.

He isn't entirely wrong.

I release Elora, a warning on the tip of my tongue for Nox, but it's too late. For an older gentleman, the councilman is quicker than expected.

"Your Highness, I'm afraid that we have need of you today," he says evenly, his gaze roaming from Daje to Nox and skipping over me entirely.

"I'm unavailable for the day, councilman, as I *know* you are aware," Nox replies, moving to take a step towards the stairs. Since our impromptu day of relaxing—or rather, *not* relaxing—together in bed, the council has only increased their requests of Nox. They've often kept him sequestered in meetings or on assignments with his father for the majority of the day, Nox all but dragging his feet into his room at night. He told them he would not be available today at both my and his parent's request, our concerns over the dark circles under his eyes a topic of conversation during a shared dinner two nights ago.

"I must urge you to reconsider," Councilman Kallin insists, clasping his hands in front of him as a crooked smile twists his lips. "The council has decided it would be best for you to go and visit the people of Polatos."

Nox stiffens, the movement echoed by Cass and Daje. "And why have they *recommended* that?"

"It is important that an heir apparent be more involved with the realm he is to rule. Not sequestered within the palace—regardless of the reason why." He flicks his gaze my way, making Elora scoff in response.

"And they think sending the crown prince to an area where there has been an uptick of missing guards is... *smart*?" Cass asks, his tone no longer the jovial teasing of a best friend but the hardened resolve of a personal guard.

"Of course. He'll be protected with his usual retinue, as is the standard for royalty leaving Galdr. Let's not forget he *is* also incredibly powerful. It will be good for the people to know that they are being thought of during this strange time. It will be good for them to see the caring face of their future ruler." Councilman Kallin's features settle into a stoic expression. "It might also do wonders with the other more *reluctant* members of the council to see that their prince is choosing his duties to his kingdom instead of what they will perceive as precious time wasted."

Nox's magic swells, its presence stifling in the air. I glance at him, only to find that cool, bored expression he painted on his face when speaking with Arin. My magic hums beneath my ribs, its vibration warm as it presses against my skin, *yearning* to reach out to Nox's.

"Your Highness, using your magic to threaten a member of the council is highly inappropriate," the councilman hisses.

Nox tips his head to the side, his raven waves shuffling while a smirk grows. "You think I'm *threatening* you, Councilman?" His voice is a warning all its own, one that Daje's father doesn't miss.

I watch as the workers in the palace stop attending to their duties to gawk at this open display. Cass adjusts his stance, folding his arms over his chest, while Daje stands perfectly still next to him, his skin paling as if he's seen a ghost.

"Your duty is to give yourself to your kingdom. Anything else, *anyone* else, falls second to that. If that is not something you can do, then perhaps it is time for the council to begin talks of finding someone who *can*."

Gods above. Shadows crawl towards us from the corners of the room, knocking Daje out of his stupor as he curses lowly under his breath. Did the council truly have that power? To just *remove* the Daxel line? Nox moves to step forward, but I stop him with a hand on his wrist.

"Look at me," I whisper as I angle myself between him and the councilman. His gaze drops immediately, his starlight eyes intense as they pierce mine. "Give them this. Any chance we have to try and change their minds about me we should take, right?"

Nox exhales slowly, his denial nearly out of his lips before mine are there. I kiss him softly at first but let him guide it to something fiercer, ignoring the audience around us. Somehow knowing that this, my physical touch, is what he needs. There's something different about this kiss—he *tastes* different. It's like mist and rain, the static air before a thunderstorm. I am eager for more, my *magic* is eager for more, but Cass clears his throat, and we separate, the anger abating only a fraction in Nox's eyes. "I will make it up to you tonight," he says.

Unfortunately, Councilman Kallin refutes that. "I'm afraid that you and a few council members are scheduled to leave as soon as possible. This way you'll have ample time to spend in Polatos tomorrow."

Tomorrow? "How far away is Polatos?" I ask quietly, failing to hide the slight tremble in my voice.

Nox's anger presses to the surface again, but there is a shift in the magic around us as a new person joins the group, his face a mask of remorse.

"Son, I'm sorry for the last minute notice." Sadryn sounds pained, as if he had tried to fight this but lost. Perhaps the council *did* have the power to remove him. "But I do agree that visiting the people is never a bad thing." The placating statement settles the councilman for the moment but seems to only agitate Nox more. With a stern glance at Kallin, Sadryn adds, "And *I'll* be going with you."

"Polatos is a day's journey away," Elora whispers, answering my earlier question.

Nox's focus finds me again, his jaw working while his hands—still resting on my hips—flex.

"I can say no," he states, but it sounds more like a question.

It would be at least three days away from him. We had technically spent longer apart while I was in the Middle, but that was different. *This* is different. Still, Nox has proven time and time again he will choose me, regardless of the consequence. I couldn't be so selfish as to ask him to do it again simply because I didn't want to be away from him. My magic bucks at the thought, clinging to the spaces within me where I let it rise.

"Go," I whisper, nodding my head with a confidence that isn't truly there. "I'll be alright."

Nox looks completely torn, frustration surrendering to defeat as his forehead drops to mine. "Come with me."

My hands squeeze where they are still gripping his shoulders, his breath featherlight over my lips. "I shouldn't. I have to be here to get my dress fitted for the ball, and though I hate their methods, I don't necessarily disagree with what the council is suggesting. About visiting the town, that is."

Nox leans back, his lips quirking as he fights off a smile. "Smart. Fair. Patient. All qualities of a lovely queen in the making." That makes me blush more deeply than kissing him so openly did. Nox heaves a sigh, his jaw hardening again as he flicks his gaze to Councilman Kallin. "I'll pack and meet those going down here in thirty minutes." Without waiting for anyone else to respond, Nox takes my hand and guides me upstairs to his room, our goodbye rushed but no less passionate.

Evening comes quickly, and at Nox's request, I have dinner with Alexandria, Daje joining as well. Councilman Kallin didn't go on the trip to Polatos, but I don't question why Daje is having his meal here with us. I wouldn't want to spend time alone with his father either. The talk is small, my comfortableness around the duo one that I'm grateful to have been eased into. Daje sits to my right, his eyes casting glances to the chair on the other side of him as if he expects someone to be sitting there. His next question reveals who.

"Have you heard from Bahira?"

"Only once since the last time," Alexandria answers, a soft smile on her face. Daje nods, his mouth opening as if to ask another question, but he chooses to bury it instead. Alexandria is observant, however, and adds, "She is doing well, but she is very focused on her experiments there and navigating her new world. I'm sure she will have much to talk with you about when she returns." That seems to answer whatever Daje wanted to know, though his shoulders round slightly.

When dinner is over, Daje and I bid Nox's mother goodnight. "Thank you for the company," I tell him as we exit the queen's dining hall and enter the long corridor that leads to the foyer.

"Anytime," he murmurs, his mind occupied elsewhere. On Bahira, perhaps.

Though she seemed less terrifying when I spoke with her through the Mirror, she is still a bit of an enigma to me. Everyone speaks highly of her, none more so than Nox. There is reverence and respect there but also carefully chosen words. Maybe it has to do with the fact that she doesn't have magic, or maybe it's something else. I'm excited to try to get to know her. To pick her brain about Nox and what he was like growing up. To maybe gain a sister of sorts; something I never dreamed I would have.

Elora stands tall in the foyer, her smile growing when she spots us—a quick glance given to Daje that I swear makes her cheeks lift a fraction higher. The flame gems reflect in her glasses, and she pushes them higher up her nose before pulling me in for a hug.

"I'll see you both later," Daje says politely, ducking his chin before spinning on his heel and heading to the palace doors.

"Are you ready?" Elora asks in a rush, looping her arm around mine.

"As I'll ever be." Together, we climb the steps to the second floor of the palace and to the seamstress quarters.

My eyes are wide as I take in the rows of folded-up fabric lying neatly on wooden and stone shelves. Strung pearlescent beads of every color and chains of gold, silver, black, and even lavender hang from rods in a corner. There is a table on the far wall to my left lined with sewing machines, the spaces between them filled with spools of thread. In the middle are round platforms lifted up by two short steps. Right above them hangs a large black and gray chandelier, each of the three tiers lined with small spelled flames dancing in glass cups.

"Go ahead and stand here, you two, while I get some fabric choices that I think would be lovely." Sarai gestures to the platforms, and Elora and I do as she asks, each stepping up onto one.

Elora fidgets, her fingers lacing together before she undoes them and squeezes the fabric of her light blue trousers. A line forms between my brows as I study her. She had gone quiet when I told her of my surprise, her eyes wide as they stared at me.

"Are you alright?"

"Of course!" she shouts, scaring some of the women in the room. Scarlet travels up her neck as she forces herself to take a breath. "I have never had a dress made by the palace before, and I don't know... It makes me nervous. I shouldn't wear anything so fancy."

"What? Why?"

She shoots me an arch look but then immediately softens it. "I'm just a librarian. A regular woman. Not royalty. Not someone important enough for all of this." She gestures to the room.

"You are important to *me*," I whisper, reaching my hand out to her. She interlaces her fingers with mine and squeezes them tightly. "And I am no one of importance either. I'm only here because of who I am to Nox."

Elora silently mouths, "You're an actual princess," before rolling her eyes playfully. Sarai and two other women make their way back to us, their arms full of different colored fabrics.

"I am not one *here*."

"Not yet," Elora responds, giving my hand one more squeeze before letting go.

We spend the entire evening choosing fabrics and accessories that fit the autumnal theme of the ball, Sarai and the other women pinning and shaping them until a lovely dress begins to take form.

"It isn't too much?" I ask out loud, my hand resting over the expanse of skin that will be on display at my chest.

"Princess Bahira has worn things much more *revealing* than this, My Lady," a different woman answers, adjusting a panel that covers my breast to make it a little wider. Elora snorts in agreement from the center of her own gathering of fabric. "Of course, if you are uncomfortable with the design, we can add more fabric or even a colored applique in the middle."

I stare at my reflection. At how the deep color of the dress makes my light complexion glow, my hair in perfect golden contrast to it. Its silky texture clings to my upper body, while its length flows down to the tops of my feet. I've never worn something so lovely before, never had a reason to. I am a princess, in the barest sense of the word, but I have never attended anything so *royal*. It makes me feel a bit like a fraud—a child playing dress-up in grown-ups' clothing. That new voice in the back of my head, one formed from love and kindness and safety, begs me to think otherwise. Maybe I've earned a moment like this, and I'm finally stepping into a role that was always meant for me.

"If it won't cause a scandal, then I should like to keep it as it is," I say finally, smiling when Sarai and Elora clap in approval.

Chapter Sixty-Seven

ARIA

The journey around the northeastern end of the continent feels like the longest of the trip so far. The weather here is brutal, the winds colder and seas more violent. Then there are the dragons.

The Fae Kingdom is a mountainous one, the mist-covered jagged black peaks making up the majority of their terrain. On one of those peaks, miles away from where I poked my head above the water, I spotted my first dragon. Even with the distance between us, there was no mistaking its massive size. Its dark-colored scales glinted in the sunlight, sharp and menacing—relaying to anyone looking that this was an apex predator. While I couldn't be sure, I had the distinct feeling that it was scanning the water. I wasn't going to linger long enough to find out if my red hair would garner its curiosity.

The second time I saw a dragon was after Mashaka and I had rounded the most eastern tip of the continent. The beast was bigger than even what my imagination could conjure as it flew close enough to drag its black claws against the water's surface. It should be impossible for the dragon to see us beneath the surface, but as it glided above the waves, I swore I saw it tip its head to the side and down. Maybe not looking at *us*, but definitely looking for *something*. Mashaka ended up guiding us farther out into the open sea and away from the Fae Kingdom's coast after that, and we have yet to see another dragon in the days that we have continued to swim.

I've lost track of the time we've been out here, long travel days and sleepless nights blending together in my mind. The fear of not making it home by my mother's deadline propels me to keep going despite the aching exhaustion that twists within my muscles. As day surrenders to night, Mashaka and I catch our dinner and settle into a small clearing of grass surrounded by pink and red coral and bright blue anemones highlighted by the soft moonlight. Even though my very bones ache, once more, my mind is too loud to find sleep.

Laying my cheek on my forearm with my tail extended behind me, I look back at Mashaka. "I suppose that when we are back in Lumen, we will be enemies again." The delphinidae stirs, opening a beady eye to look at me before snapping it shut again. I can't help but smile, his grumpiness a little more endearing than when we embarked on this journey. "Even if we *wanted* to be friends, Allegra would never allow it," I continue, grimacing when he tenses at the mention of my sister. "I couldn't have done this trip without you, though, so thank you." He doesn't stir again.

What would life look like once I got back? I am unwanted by the sirens of the seamounts, unwanted but needed in ways that I wish I weren't by my mother. Eventually, I will *have* to bear offspring. I will have to watch them get forced into the same life I was perpetually stuck in. Not returning home seemed so easy, *so tempting*. Yet what would I do? Where would I go? The ocean is vast, but I know that the siren queen's reach is bigger.

Thoughts about leaving, about Lyre and the males that I've killed, rattle in my mind until I'm *finally* too tired for even that. Sleep claims me, but not before I feel Mashaka shift the smallest amount. Just until his warm body brushes against the scales of my tail. A soft reminder that I'm not alone.

There is debris everywhere. The waters just off of the coast churn with chunks of wood and an eerie *creaking* sound that vibrates to us on the current. In the distance, a ship is tilted on its side, part of its deck submerged. Two sirens, their jewel-colored hair bright amongst the destruction, float in the water nearby. Their song hits my ears as we get closer.

"Let's try to go around to the other side by the hull," I suggest quietly to Mashaka. We stay low to the rocky ocean floor, its sharp points causing me to hiss every time I scrape my arm or tail against them while the sinking ship looms to our left. Mashaka makes a chittering sound as he too becomes scratched on his underbelly. But the ship is large enough that, unless we backtrack a few miles, we'll be spotted by the other sirens if we try to go around its front. I'd rather not lose any extra time to unnecessary travel.

The sirens' singing grows louder, their melodic magic calling to my own as it tickles the base of my throat.

I look at the black tar of the ship's hull, a jagged line torn into it from nearly end to end. More pieces of wood float by us along with other bits of torn cloth and items from inside the ship that are too heavy to bob on the surface and instead ride the current. It becomes tedious trying to avoid them. Mashaka squeaks and swims upward, and I follow behind him, poking my head above the surface to look around.

Cracking cleaves the air as more water fills the ship, sending it towards the shallow ocean floor. The ballad of the sirens is close, and even with our song less powerful now than it used to be, I'm surprised that they are still singing and not already off with their captured victims. My stomach sours at the thought, and I continue moving with my head above water and Mashaka at my side beneath it.

We're nearly clear of the massive ship when movement on the surface catches my eye. I freeze, afraid we've been spotted by one of the sirens. Narrowing my eyes, I make out what looks like a bundle of black fabric lying on a large piece of wood torn from the ship, and I swim tentatively in its direction, pushing debris out of my way. A figure takes shape as I near, not a bundle of fabric but a *person*. Lowering my head back into the water, I look around in all directions to ensure that Mashaka and I are alone before coming back up.

Miraculously, they must have either fallen before the sirens song started or jumped, lured in by it, and landed on this makeshift raft instead, knocking themselves out. *Lucky*, I think to myself as I edge my way around it. Red stains the wood by their head and dark strands glisten under the sunlight as they drape over the being's features, obscuring any details I can make out about how old they might be.

Carefully, I lift my hand and retract my talons, using the tip of my finger to move their hair behind their ear. Their *pointed* ear. I gasp and yank my hand back quickly. My lips part as I take in the *female* lying unconscious before me. Not just any female, but a fae one. This is a fae ship; no wonder the sirens had to keep singing. The fae, while not totally immune to our song, *do* have a delayed reaction to it. While they cannot ignore the call of the siren as a shifter can in their animal form, something about *them* makes it so that they *can* withstand it for longer than a mage or mortal. Though that ability always seemed like a form of torture to me. What was the point of delaying the inevitable when, in the end, it wouldn't even matter?

I look over her delicately arched ear, its shape and length smaller than the fae males I had seen. Her full dark lashes lightly brush the top of her high cheekbones, and her faintly pink lips are parted with her labored breaths. Blood leaks from the corner of her mouth, but despite the state of her body, she, like all fae, has a divine beauty to her. My eyes linger on every part of her that I can see, inspecting her for any other injuries, though it's impossible to tell with how dark her clothing is.

Something harsh tugs at my stomach as I stare at this helpless female. Would the other sirens leave her be if they were to find her like this? I doubt my mother would only send a group of two out to hunt, so these are *rogue* sirens, which means they might just kill her because they *can*.

I dip my head beneath the water again, looking around as Mashaka slowly circles beneath my tail. Shadows drift beneath the ship as the bodies of the fae males that have been lured in but abandoned by the sirens sink. When I reemerge, the air is quiet of all melody. We are miles from the shore, but I can take her back there. Let her wake up on the beach near the Spelled border. She'll be safer than out in the open waters. Maybe she'll even be spotted by another fae.

"Please let this work," I whisper, checking one last time before I begin to maneuver the wooden plank in front of me. I make sure it stays as level as possible on the water so the female doesn't jostle too much. Mashaka brushes against my side, either protesting this choice or letting me know that he is following. My panting breaths sound louder than the roiling sea, but I push my aching muscles—so tired from weeks and weeks of nonstop traveling—to keep up our steady pace. The fine hairs at the back of my neck lift, goosebumps breaking out over my flesh, but I don't look back. I don't risk slowing down or taking my eyes off of the unconscious fae in case she tumbles over the side and past the layer of the Spell. She lets out a deep groan, her slender pale fingers twitching.

Even above the rushing of the waves, I hear Mashaka's squeak of warning. Digging my claws into the wood to make sure I'm anchored to it, I plunge my face beneath the water, my eyes needing a moment to adjust before I turn to look behind me. Mashaka's tail is to me as he faces the two sirens who are nearing.

"Mashaka, we need to keep swimming," I yell, keeping my head underwater and propelling myself forward. Urging my muscles to give everything they can and then begging them to give even *more*. The glares of the sirens now following me are a scrape of claws and sharp teeth down my back, making every part of my upper body tense, but I don't stop.

Then the sensation is really there, a scream ripping from me as one of the sirens drags the sharp ends of her talons down my tail and through my delicate tail fin, shredding parts of it into ribbons. I lose my grip on the wooden plank, terror pulsing in my throat as I turn around and face a copper-haired siren whose claws are now painted in my blood.

The other siren catches up to her, her bright green braids coiled on the top of her head in a giant knot. "What are you doing with that fae?" she barks.

"It's a female," I say with a wince, the throbbing of my now deformed fin sending shock waves of pain up my entire body.

The copper-haired siren scoffs as she attempts to swim past me to where the fae is floating. I block her path, yelping in pain with the movement. Sparing a glance, I watch Mashaka dart behind the sirens.

"I know who you are." Orange eyes gleam with malice as a smile wide enough to show her canines lifts her cheeks. She swims until her chest brushes against my own, our scales scratching against each other. "Princess Aria, the disappointment of the Siren Queendom." Her eyes flick behind me, and her smile grows, making her features turn predatory. "Tifala, what do you think our glorious queen would say if she were to learn that her very own daughter was *saving* those from our wrath?"

"It's a *female*," I say, backing up towards the fae.

Cackling travels on the water between us as she tilts her head back in glee. "This is exactly what we need, Tifala, to get back in the queen's good graces. To get back into Lumen." She turns her gaze to me, dipping her chin towards her chest. "Imagine the *embarrassment* the queen will feel to know that you, once again, have disappointed her. What would she give us to keep this transgression a secret?"

Tifala's green eyes gleam with the same eagerness, making a pit form in my stomach. I shake my head, my fingers curling and muscles tensing in anticipation of an attack. "She'd rather kill us all than have anything held over her head like that. She treats me no differently than anyone else under her command." But I can tell that my words don't reach them.

They close in on me until the one that ripped through my tailfin shoots her hand out to cover one set of gills on the side of my neck. Tifala attempts to swim past me, but I lurch in her direction, digging my claws into her arm as I grip on to her. She hisses, slashing out towards me and cutting the strap of my bag where it hangs across my body. I feel the weight of it leave as I struggle to keep her in my grasp. White flares slowly creep in to the edges of my vision, my oxygen intake slowing by half.

"Traitorous *bitch*," the siren slowly suffocating me seethes before her other hand covers the rest of my gills, cutting me off from oxygen completely.

"No," I grunt out, forced to release Tifala.

"I can't *wait* to get back into Lumen. It looks like betrayal doesn't just run in *my* family line. I will use you to gain my freedom back, *Your Highness*."

Pain singes my nerve endings, spots of black now merging with the white and clouding my vision. I can't see the other siren, can't *think* beyond the fact that I've failed *again*. Another death on my hands. Another tarnished mark on my soul.

I stare into those orange eyes, the hatred mingling with desperation, and wasn't that just the existence of sirens as a whole now? No matter which side of the line they stood on, our people were consumed with desperate *rage*.

My fingers begin to weaken around her wrists, my grip slipping as the view in front of me begins to fade.

Screaming. There is screaming. My eyes fly open while oxygen rushes into my body, my gills no longer obstructed. I blink quickly, trying to get my bearings as I spin in a circle. A shadow darts past, leaving small bubbles in its wake as it collides with Tifala. She growls, slashing out with her claws into the shadow's side. A high-pitched wail slides along my bones, the owner of it darting backward before swimming in my direction.

Mashaka.

I rush towards him, but then the glint of orange and red scales flashes above me, and I change my direction to where the siren is lifted partially out of the water, her upper body leaning onto the substitute raft still holding the fae. Anger, hotter than the pain firing down my tail, propels me faster until I'm right beneath her. I don't think, letting some feral instinct fuel me, as I *dig* my talons into either side of the siren's waist. I avoid her scales, instead finding the softest part of her flesh for me to gut. An ear-piercing scream sounds above, but I ignore it as I force my claws to slice deeper into her skin—her muscle—drawing them down towards her middle as dark blue blood leaks out into the water.

My hair is harshly yanked back, my throat bared as Tifala stares down at me. "You will *pay* for that. Go, Zina, I've got her."

Her closed fist, talons retracted in, rains down on my temple, the impact making my vision grow hazy again. I feel a quick jerk through my hands, the warmth of Zina gone as she frees herself from my hold. My head snaps to the side as I'm pummeled with another hit. Disoriented, I reach back to try and claw at Tifala. My movements are too frantic to land, and I watch, horror barreling through me, as she winds her arm back again—her teeth gritted and green eyes glowing with the kind of vengeance that has waited decades to be released. I squeeze my eyes closed, preparing for the pain and the possibility of being dragged back to my mother with the tale of what I've done. But the fist never connects with my skin.

"No!" Tifala screams, letting me go.

I right myself, watching as she rushes to get to where Mashaka has clamped his mouth over Zina's neck. A cloud of dark blue blood blooms like a veil around them, but through it, I watch as the siren claws at Mashaka to no avail. He lets out a deep noise, and then there is a massive *crunch*.

Chapter Sixty-Eight

ARIA

TIFALA'S GROWL IS BEASTLY as she reaches the other siren a second too late. She claws at Mashaka, digging into his shiny dark gray skin until his own scream vibrates through my very bones.

"Mashaka!" My pace is slow, barely faster than the equivalent of a crawl in my mortal form, but I push forward.

Tifala claws and shreds at Mashaka, the now lifeless Zina sinking beneath them to the depths of the ocean floor. New blood—*red* blood—clouds the water quickly. *Too quickly.* Mashaka is able to get his mouth around one of her wrists, clenching down as it snaps her bones. Her hand hangs limply, but she pays it no heed as the talons on her other hand stab into him before she drags them along his side. He wails, the sound like a ballad of death; one that I know he won't be able to come back from. Tears blur my eyes, my magic swelling in my throat from my instincts roaring within me. But our songs don't work on each other.

Tifala is so focused on killing Mashaka that she doesn't sense me behind her. She doesn't have time to stop me when I use every last ounce of adrenaline and strength in my body to jab my talons into the gills on both sides of her neck. I *prod* them inside of her, pushing hard as I *scream* and not stopping until I think I hit bone. Until I imagine that I can feel the tips of my claws touching in the middle of her throat. I scream again—one that forces the ocean into dead silence. Tifala falls limp, and I forcefully snatch my hands away from her, watching as her stiff body drifts towards the ocean floor, a trail of blue blood following.

But she isn't the only one.

"Mashaka!" I cry, my tail moving unsteadily as my hips undulate and bring me towards him. "Mashaka," I repeat, retracting my claws to gently grasp on to him. He's too heavy, and I'm too weak to hold him aloft in the water, so we begin to sink together as I gently roll his body over until I can see his face. "No. No. No."

Though they are open, no life swirls in his black eyes. A sob forces its way out of me while I carefully caress the space beneath them, his silky skin paler in color.

"Why did you help? You were supposed to choose yourself," I remind him, the water growing darker as we sink farther away from the sun's reach. "You didn't stop the Tula Ledge monster. You—" I stop speaking, unable to navigate the words past the sadness lodged in my throat. *In my chest.*

Mashaka is dead. This grumpy, sometimes downright *mean* delphinidae, is dead, and my heart is breaking. Because he had risked *everything* to save me. The only being in my life to have ever done so. I drape myself over his body, his warmth already a fading memory. As my ears pop and pressure squeezes me the lower we sink, I wonder if it's better to just stay here in the icy depths of the ocean. If it's better to succumb to the slow death that seems to linger around me no matter where I go.

An image of the fae lying unconscious at the water's surface flashes through my mind. I hadn't even spared her a second glance when I saw Tifala butchering Mashaka. I have no idea if Zina killed her. And, though I wish it didn't, regret at not checking weaves through me. It sifts into the spaces untouched by my grief and settles in until I know that I have to go check on her. I lift my head and look down below us, but it's impossible to tell in the pitch black how much deeper there is to fall.

"I'm sorry, my friend," I rasp, kissing the top of his head. "I have to go." I release him, my muscles aching with each flick of my tail keeping me afloat. The rip in my fin burns anew, but I ignore it all, waiting with a heaving chest until I can no longer see the outline of his body before turning my head up towards the surface.

It's an agonizing swim, and I use my arms more than ever before to keep myself moving upward. I happen to spot my bag on the way up, the strap stuck to a piece of debris floating in the current. Opening it with trembling fingers, I confirm its contents before tying the broken pieces of the strap together around my waist. When I find the familiar wooden raft above me, I take a final glance in all directions and then swim through the Spell.

Dark eyes—eyes as black as Mashaka's—stare into mine as I break the surface, making me yelp and lurch backward. The fae lifts her top lip into a sneer, her sharp canines showing. "I'll kill you," she croaks.

I sigh, working my way to the back of the raft by her feet. As I begin to push her towards the shore, her legs twitch until one of them swings fully towards me. Her movement is sluggish, and I easily dodge her attempt to kick me.

"*Please* stop. You were in a shipwreck of some kind, and then sirens attacked the rest of your crew."

"You mean *you* attacked us?" she slurs, her leg once more blindly trying to connect with my head. I avoid it again, my claw tips digging into the wood. "I'll get myself to shore."

"You barely have the strength to say those words. I will push you there and then leave you alone."

Again, she swings her leg out, and it snaps something within me. The loss of Mashaka, the exhaustion of my journey, and the unbearable weight of simply *existing* all come crashing down on me. I start singing, unsure if it will actually do anything but succumbing to the call of my magic anyway. Her leg relaxes—her entire body does—as I will her to stop moving. To just *stop*.

We finally reach the beach, the sandy ocean floor moving closer and closer until I have to transform into my mortal body and push her the rest of the way by crawling on my knees. Only then do I stop singing, letting the magic of my song fade away. I suppose there is no denying now that, somehow, my magic works on *females*.

The sun is high and bright in the sky, signaling that it's sometime in the afternoon. Its warmth feels good on my back, and when I can't push the heavy piece of wood any more, I collapse onto the damp sand next to it. It'll take a moment for my magic to wear off, and once I'm sure this female is alright, I'll head home. *Alone.*

She groans after a few minutes pass, drawing my attention away from the jagged angry line cut into the top of my foot. "What did you do?" she asks, attempting to push herself up. I reach over to help her sit, but she jerks herself away. "Don't fucking touch me."

Inhaling sharply, I move onto my knees and sit back on my heels, keeping my hands to myself as I watch her struggle to sit up. The wall of the Spell shimmers a few feet behind us, and if I thought I was strong enough, I might toss her through it myself.

"Tell me what you *did*," she grits out through clenched teeth, her dark eyes meeting mine.

Swallowing, I gesture back out to the ocean. "You were in a shipwreck. Somehow, you fell from the sinking boat and landed on that piece of wood. I found you floating there unconscious."

She snaps her eyes shut, her hand gently touching the back of her head before she hisses and brings it back down to her side with dark red blood dotting her fingers. "What else?" she barks, opening her almond-shaped eyes to stare into mine.

Her tangled raven hair hangs above her shoulders, though its current state does nothing to draw away from her beauty. Each of her features, from her perfectly pointed chin and full lips to the sharp arch of her ear, looks like it was purposefully placed there. It is not a gentle kind of beauty. It's precise and powerful. *Deadly.* Sirens use our looks in tandem with our magic to lure and seduce, but this fae, she could use it and nothing else to make others bend to her will.

"*What. Else?*"

I force my gaze to hers again, digging my fingers into my bare thighs. "Then I brought you to the shore." I leave out the attack from the sirens. The death that followed.

The fae shakes her head, wincing with the movement. "I remember asking you not to bring me here, and then it gets...*fuzzy* after that."

I chew on my lower lip, and her gaze dips down to my mouth before she shoots it back up, her own mouth curling in disgust. "You must have passed back out. Your head is injured."

She doesn't look remotely convinced by my lie. "So what do you want, then?" she asks, holding the side of her swollen face as she makes her way to stand. A black cape drapes from her, the fabric tattered at its edges and stained with salt from dried ocean water. It's attached by bronze chains to plates of black leather layered on top of each other at her shoulders. The leather goes down over her chest, two buckled straps crossing over her breasts before moving around her sides. Decorating one of her shoulders, outlined in that same bronze as the chains, is a dragon. "*Hello*!" She snaps her fingers in front of my face.

I clear my throat as I stand, my weight shifting to my non-injured foot. Her expression is shrewd as she faces me, the hand not holding her face flexing down by her thigh.

Right where a dagger is sheathed.

I remember the dagger in my bag, and though I have no idea how to wield it, I position my hand near it. While my hair covers most of my chest and stomach, I adjust my bag to cover as much of my lower half as possible. Not because I'm being modest, but simply because it makes me vulnerable not to.

"You would kill someone who just saved you?" I ask, limping a step closer to the water.

The fae tilts her head as a cruel smile tips her lips upward. I don't get to inhale again before she's holding the dagger at my neck, her movements so quick that I startle backward. Her hand dives into my hair to steady me, but the touch is anything but comforting. Bicep bulging with restraint, contempt seeps out of her every pore. "Oh, Little Siren, I would love nothing more than to drag my knife across your throat and send your remains to your bitch queen." She presses the cold blade to my skin for emphasis, that smile growing when I gasp out in terror. "Were this any other situation, you'd be dead already." Then she abruptly lets me go, chuckling darkly as I stumble backward. "Unfortunately, I cannot kill you now that I owe you a debt."

My chest heaves as I rasp out, "What do you mean?"

She huffs, sheathing her dagger while she looks down her slender nose at me. "Don't play dumb. Everyone knows about the life debt oath we are held to."

Well, not everyone. I have no idea what she is talking about. "I don't want anything from you."

She grumbles under her breath and drags a hand down her face before taking a step towards me. She's taller than I am, and I have to tilt my head up to hold her onyx gaze. There is nothing in their depths but pure *hatred*. "Trust me, I want for that to be true. But until we make an even exchange, my conscience will not let me rest. I refuse to let it consist of thoughts about *something* as abhorrent as you. So, I will ask you again, what do you want as payment for saving my life?"

I swallow as I drop my gaze again, staring at the tops of my feet. At the permanent reminder of my failure that is now carved into one.

"Can I ask you for anything?" I look up as her eyes narrow on me, her jaw clenching.

"Within reason and of equal value, yes."

This is stupid—*stupid*. She could kill me at any moment. I don't even know how this would work, but I can't stop thinking about how different things might be if I could move through this life with the same kind of physical confidence this fae possesses. I would never be forced to be obedient again. I could escape and know that I could fight back if I was found.

"I want you to teach me how to fight," I confess, my hand gesturing in the air between us.

She is silent for a long while, her head twisted to the side as if replaying what I've said until it makes sense. Then she bursts out into laughter. My cheeks heat as she continues laughing at my expense, her head tilted back with the column of her throat elongated. "Why would you want me to do that?" she finally asks when she calms down.

"It's personal."

Looking back out over the ocean, she shakes her head in annoyance. "No. Pick something else."

"That is all I want," I say back, cringing when her eyes snap to mine.

"Then tell me why you want it. Consider it a show of *goodwill*." She faces me fully, crossing her arms over her chest as her lips fall into a flat line. Her gaze is harsh upon my skin, but her eyes don't stray anywhere lower than my face.

"You wouldn't understand," I reply with a shaky whisper.

"Six lessons," she finally says, the words forced out of her mouth like she'd rather saw her tongue off instead.

My brows draw together as my hands interlace in front of me. "Six lessons? Is your life worth no more than that? I thought the fae lived for like a thousand years." Her face is shaded briefly as a cloud moves in front of the sun, but the anger simmering in her eyes remains. "Can't we leave the amount open-ended? Since it might take me a while—"

"No. The oath requires the details to be laid out specifically. Ten lessons."

"Twenty." I shrink in on myself when she takes a menacing step towards me. "Fifteen, then," I rush out quickly. A gust of warm air pushes at my back so strongly that it knocks me off balance. I fall to my knees, the pain in my foot making me whimper as my palms scrape against the sand.

"Pathetic," she hisses, but it's drown out by the shifting of the wind and the sound of... *Oh gods.*

"Twelve, Little Siren. You get twelve lessons with me, or I'll order this dragon to incinerate you."

Looking over my shoulder, I watch as a midnight-blue dragon, its scales reflecting iridescent in the sunlight, slams into the ground, sending clumps of damp sand and water everywhere and rattling my bones with the impact. Heat blasts my back as I cower over my knees, my hands covering my head.

"Better accept quickly," she drawls, walking until she's at my side.

"Okay, twelve lessons." And then, because I'm not a total idiot, I add, "Twice a week and two hours each."

The fae looks down at me from the corner of her eye, the hot breath of the dragon scalding my skin and clashing with the icy cold of her stare. "One hour and once a week. I don't have an abundance of free time."

I nod and slowly stand, the deep rumbling behind me making my shoulders shoot up to my ears. A male voice chuckles, and my gaze flies to the dragon, wondering if I'm going mad. But a fae male is sitting in the space between spikes on the dragon's back, as if it was born with a spot for a rider.

"Hello, beautiful," he purrs, leaning forward. His hair is black, like the female's, though it's much longer. It drapes past his shoulders and brushes against the dragon's rough-looking skin. The female moves so that she is standing between the flying beast and myself, blocking its giant yellow eye from the side of its face that I can see. I swallow, noting how just *one* of the dragon's claws is nearly half the length of my body.

She extends her hand out to me, the other resting above a second dagger strapped to her other thigh. Like she really expects me to somehow attack her while shaking her hand. "We'll meet here in a week's time."

"This meeting place is too far from our capital. Is there somewhere else on the shore we can meet that's closer to the Mage Kingdom's border?" Even that would take a few hours to get to.

She grinds her teeth together and exhales a sharp breath. "Fine. There is a spearhead-shaped peak about ten miles away from where the mage border meets our own. Will that work?" I nod, grasping her hand. "I have to know your name for the oath."

"It's Aria. And yours?"

She lowers down until she is at eye level with me, drawing so close that my vision is entirely consumed by her hauntingly beautiful dark eyes. "You will not utter my name to a single soul. You will not speak of this deal to any of the rest of your *disgusting* kind. Do you understand?" Her grip is so tight that my bones shift in my hand, and I have to fight back the urge to send my talons out.

"I don't want anyone to know about this either." She smirks but keeps her gaze intently on me. It consumes me from the inside out, both luring me closer and spiking enough fear that I want to pull away.

"Myla." Then she gives my hand one quick shake before dropping it like it's made of prickly sea urchins. I suspect that she might like it better if it were. Striding towards the towering dragon, she climbs up its front leg with practiced ease and settles herself behind the male.

"Father has been looking for you," he says to her, giving me a wink.

"Shut the fuck up."

The male chuckles, and then the dragon crouches low, its claws digging into the sand before it launches into the air and spreads its wings out wide—temporarily blocking out the sun. They beat powerfully, pushing warm air down towards me for a long while as I watch them ascend before they go inland through the Spell and towards the black mountains that make up the Fae Kingdom.

I stand there motionless, letting the water wash up and over my feet as I contemplate what in the Five Realms just happened. Finally, as the sun rests above the western horizon, I walk back into the ocean and begin the last leg of my journey to Lumen.

Alone.

Chapter Sixty-Nine

BAHIRA

I can't find Kai.

Or Jahlee. The first rebel I had encountered in the palace lies dead about a hundred feet behind me. The next two are about twenty feet each after that. I run across the first floor, blood dripping from my spear and sweat beading on my brow, and still, I can't find either of them in the chaos.

It's pure madness, shifters wearing fancy party clothing splattered in blood and animals of all varieties darting in both directions—all of them crashing into each other. If a rebel isn't in their mortal form and wearing a mask, I have no idea how to identify them as the threat. So I leave the animals to attack each other and focus on fighting the shifters that I can, all the while scanning the throng of people for the king and his sister.

A scream changes the direction of my quickly moving feet. Readjusting my hold on the spear, I round a corner and find myself staring down the hallway I first met Kane in. The portraits that had hung on the wall before are now crooked, some lying shredded on the floor. Slowing my steps, I force my breaths in my nose and out of my mouth to steady my heartbeat as I cautiously step over them.

Flame gems are scattered on the floor, the glass sconces that had held them broken into tiny pieces that crunch beneath my feet. The hallway comes to an end, the only option to go left or right. Kane had led me to the right the night of the party, but the shouting comes from the opposite direction. So I turn that way.

The new corridor is dim, light from the fallen gems behind me leaking into it. Rumblings farther down—animal and not—make me shiver, but I keep my steps precise and my spear out in front of me. Passing the open doors lining both sides of the hall, I listen and wait to see if anyone pops out from them. Blood paints the walls, the sight churning my stomach. *Please let Jahlee be alright.* She can't shift. If a hoard of rebels in their animal forms surrounded her—

Growling, low and menacing, sounds from behind me. A spike of fear jolts through me, my shoulders rising towards my ears as I spin and come face to face with a prowling tan mountain lion. A deep noise rumbles from it again, the beast toying with me as it shows me its sharp teeth that are perfectly formed for the shredding of flesh.

A bark rends the air, not from the animal in front of me but from behind again. Chancing a look over my shoulder, I fight back the urge to shout at the incoming *massive fox*. Powerful muscles move beneath its reddish-brown fur as it snarls and bares its canines at me. *Fuck, why could it not be something small? Like a turtle.* I pivot, my back now to the wall with the blunt end of my spear pointing towards the mountain lion and the leaf-shaped tip angled towards the fox.

They keep their pace unhurried as they stalk closer. "I'm warning you assholes to stop. I won't hesitate to kill either of you." Neither one so much as pauses at my words, so I keep my attention split between them both, grinding my molars as I brace myself.

The mountain lion launches into a sprint, the distance between us gone in a flash. I have only enough time to rear my spear back a foot before bashing the black metal cap into its face, my muscles straining from the impact. The large cat screeches, stumbling away and pawing at its now bleeding nose. I turn to see the fox already mid-leap, its jaw wide and eyes hungry. Ducking, I jab the sharp metal tip up, catching the underbelly of the fox near its right hind leg. It lets out a howl as it lands in a crouched position, blood already leaking down its leg. I take a step back, both animals now in front of me. The mountain lion springs at me again, swinging a massive paw tipped with sharp claws that I narrowly avoid. I arc my spear down towards it, watching from the corner of my eye as the fox crouches and leaps. But I don't have time to do anything other than duck while I spin and yank my spear towards me, scraping the jagged edge of the metal leaf against the mountain lion's side, making it roar in pain. Agony sears across my upper back, the fox's claws shredding the skin there.

"Shit," I seethe, the scent of blood rich as it leaks down my back.

Poised to continue their assault, both animals' muscles flex before they pounce at the same time, the big cat hitting me first. It barrels into me, knocking me onto the ground as it snaps its massive jaws at my face. I'm able to get my spear up horizontally over my chest, bracing the lion's weight as it leans forward. Warm saliva drips from its maw and onto my neck, my arms trembling as I scream.

White flares in my vision when the fox attacks my leg, claws and teeth tearing into skin and muscle. Through heaving breaths, I kick blindly with my free leg at the animal, my boot connecting harshly enough to make it whine out in pain as it releases my leg.

The cat on top of me presses harder, its hot breath blasting onto my face as I stare at its elongated canines. My strength wanes and tears leak down my cheeks. I wasn't trained for this—to fight against two massive animals. And I'm going to die because of it.

A harrowing scream rends the air, drawing both my attention and that of the mountain lion. The fox, its eyes wide and mouth hanging open, collapses to the ground at my side with a long sword sticking out from where its head meets its neck. Holding the sword, his long brown hair tangled around his shoulders, is Kane. The mountain lion leaps towards Kane with a vicious growl, swiping its paw at his legs. In two movements, I come up to my knees and drive the sharp tip directly in the cat's back. The mountain lion howls, but Kane is there, plunging his sword into the beast's side until it collapses dead next to the fox.

My chest heaves as I lean back on my hands, my vision going blurry for a moment before clearing. Kane squats by my side, assessing my body for injuries and grimacing at what he finds. "You're bleeding."

"You're naked," I counter.

The corner of his mouth kicks up as he runs a hand through his hair to pull it away from his face. He looks fairly uninjured, only a few angry-looking scratches marring his bare chest. I reach for the end of my shirt, ripping off a strip of it to tie around my bleeding leg, while Kane checks out my back and assures me that, while deep, the wounds there have slowed their bleeding. He helps me up to stand, his arm automatically going around my waist as he squeezes me to him. Shrugging out of his grip—much to his annoyance—I start walking down the corridor in the direction I was heading before I got attacked.

"What the hell is going on?" I ask through labored breaths, the pain in my leg mingling with the adrenaline now draining from my body and leaving me limping heavily.

"Rebels attacked the palace during the masquerade party. Just came in and started slaughtering and demanding to know where Kai was."

My body stiffens as I swing my head towards him. "Have you seen him? Kai, I mean?"

Kane shakes his head, his gaze moving from me to the hallway ahead of us. "I haven't." I try to suck in a full breath, but it won't come. "I'm sure he's fine," he grits out, noticing my clear discomfort.

Fuck, I need to get myself under control. "And Jahlee?" I ask.

He tilts his head, that infuriating smirk returning. "Last I saw her, she was attempting to fight off two full-sized gorillas."

I narrow my eyes at the amusement in his voice as he leads us to the left and down another dim hallway. "And you didn't think to help her?"

He shrugs, moving to put his hand into his pocket, only to remember he doesn't have any. "I found you instead. Besides, she seemed to be doing just fine. The female knows how to fight."

My hand braces the wall next to me as I observe him. "How *did* you find me?"

Kane looks at me, a thin ring of gold forming around his irises. "We should keep moving. We need to get you to a healer before you bleed out."

I swallow down my unease but grip my spear more tightly. We walk in silence for another few minutes, my focus entirely on him and the sword he is holding. I slow my steps as the walls begin to change from elegantly painted wood to cold and rough stone.

"It's a good thing you weren't in your room. I was up on the second floor, and the rebels trashed it," he says as we reach a set of double doors. My steps halt again, fear licking up my spine as Kane slows his steps.

"How did you know I wasn't there?" I ask, watching as he slowly turns, his gaze flicking away from me for a blink before returning to my own.

"Kai was gone," he drawls, his fingers flexing on the hilt of his sword. "It wasn't hard to guess that you'd be with him."

Fair point. Still, the mention of my room... I had only told one person that I'd be there tonight. Something sharp pricks at my neck, making me gasp. Reaching up to the stinging area, my dread grows when I feel not smooth skin but a small vial. I yank it out and bring the dart with the tiny glass bottle attached to it out in front of me.

Swaying on my feet, I look to Kane. "What the hell is this?" Yet he looks just as stunned, his fingers trailing over his neck. I try to stumble away from him, every instinct screaming that something is horribly wrong. An acidic fire rips through my veins, shooting down my neck and over my entire body. I can't suck enough air in, and a dark haze begins to creep around the edges of my vision. Shit. *Shit.*

I go to move another step and fall instead, my hands and knees unable to brace my weight from hitting the ground. Boots step in front of me, and then everything goes black.

Drip. Drip. Drip

The incessant sound drags me from the black hole of sleep and into consciousness. The smell of damp earth and mildew mixes with something lighter, citrus maybe.

My body feels heavy, and my veins are on fire. There's a pulsing pain in my back and leg, a soreness on my chin and palms. I have the vague awareness that I'm sitting with my head lolled to the side. My eyes are slow to open, the clarity of my vision even slower to come in. When it does...

Fucking gods.

Bodies. There are bodies hanging from shackles and *dripping blood* on the wall in front of me. Nausea burns up my esophagus, but I force it down, lifting my hand to cover my mouth only for it to come to a stop halfway up. The rattle of chains startles me, and I turn my gaze down to see that I'm shackled at both wrists.

"What the fuck," I rasp, my throat raw as I wince in pain.

"Ah, she is finally awake."

I turn my head in the direction the voice came from, only to see the blurry outline of a body leaning against the adjacent wall, his legs extended out in front of him. "Kane?"

"The one and only." His speech is slurred, the sound of his own voice harsh as it echoes out into the chamber? Dungeon? It looks like a combination of both. The walls, ground, and ceiling are made entirely of thick dark stone bricks, only illuminated by a small flame gem hanging from a glass orb centered overhead. The light is just enough to make out the gruesome details of the three bodies chained by their wrists across from me. Blood stains their exposed skin, dripping incessantly onto the floor.

"What did you do to them?" I ask, my head swimming as my stomach clenches with unease.

"Afraid I can't take credit for that whole mess. They were already like that when I woke."

Chains rattle, and I look down at my own to make sure it isn't me. "Are *you* a prisoner?"

Kane scoffs as his chains shake again. "We got attacked at the same time, Bahira. Of course I'm a prisoner."

"You weren't leading me into a trap?"

"What? *No*, I told you. I was taking you to the fucking healer."

My head rolls to the side as I stare in his direction. "I thought you were working with the rebels. That you were one of them."

"Well, I'm not."

"You can't blame me for being suspicious," I chide, attempting to stretch out my legs before I hiss in pain. "It's no secret that you hate Kai and Jahlee. And then there's that scar on your arm."

Only the dripping of blood sounds in the chamber for a long while, my eyelids battling to stay open in the murky light.

"I am not overly fond of those two, you are correct. And I don't know what my scar has to do with anything."

"When Kai and I were attacked by the rebels on the way back from visiting Leeta, I threw my dagger into one of their forearms."

He lets out an abrupt laugh that turns into a cough. When he's calmed down, his voice is more hoarse as he replies, "That's surprisingly attractive. Kai probably loved it. But no, I'm afraid my wound is less of an adventurous story."

Kane doesn't elaborate as heavy footsteps alert us to someone coming. I am able to gather my wits enough to sit up a little bit taller, but it's all I can muster before a male enters the room. He stands beneath the flame gem, the golden light illuminating his amber eyes and casting shadows beneath his cheekbones.

"Do you remember me?"

I don't get a chance to answer before he draws his leg back and kicks me in the ribs, sending blinding pain throughout my body. I gasp for breath, my chest heaving with the effort as stars burst behind my eyes. I think Kane says something to the male, but I can't decipher it over the ringing in my ears. Nox's voice filters into my mind with his motto for me when I would get overwhelmed while training when we were kids: *attention goes where your breath flows*. It was a twist on our instructor Dilan's saying: *magic goes where intention flows*. I didn't have magic, but I could control my breathing. I could draw my attention there. Keeping my eyes closed, I force my mouth to close and my next inhale to slow. *In and out.* When I open my eyes again, the pain pushed back into a corner of my mind, the male is squatting in front of me, a feral smile splitting his lips.

"Whatever you did, it wasn't memorable enough. I don't know who the fuck you are." Gods my voice sounds so weak. Even more terrifying, I *feel* weak. The male's smile drops into a sneer.

"Let's see if you remember this." He stands, unsheathing a shortsword from behind him and twirling it in his hand. He begins to pace, looking down at me as his boots leave dried flecks of mud all over the stone floor. I watch his annoyance with me grow the longer I stare at him with ignorance. He growls low in his throat as his grip tightens on the hilt.

Nothing on my lower body is shackled, so maybe if I can get him close enough again, I can try to get his weapon. My hands curl into fists when I realize that I don't see my spear anywhere. "If you think your small sword is supposed to mean anything to me, you're—"

The male moves quickly, leaning in to backhand me across the face. I take advantage of his focus, moving slower than I'd like but still managing a kick between his legs right as he slaps me. My head snaps to the side, my breath once more yanked from my chest.

Attention goes where your breath flows. In and out, Bahira.

He falls onto his side, the sword skidding to my left. I kick out again, the bottom of my boot connecting with the asshole's nose. He screams out in pain, and I stretch out with my other leg to slide the sword towards me. My boot slips, and I heave against the manacles to try and move closer. The tip of my shoe touches the silver blade, and I pull it towards me for only an inch before I slip again. I continue trying, inching the sword closer as the male writhes near my feet.

I finally bring it to my hip, still out of reach from my hands, but if I turn—

"I told you not to get close to her, Niko."

I don't stop my efforts, not even as two more bodies fill the chamber. One walks directly towards me and grabs the weapon before I can. I glare at them and the elongated oryx skull they wear as a mask, the twisted horns of it casting an ominous shadow on the stone floor.

The rebel I kicked, Niko, finally gets to his feet. "I am going to *kill* you."

My responding laugh is more of a wheeze, but his words are a familiar tug in my mind. The night we had gotten attacked by the rebels, one of them had said the same thing to me. I study the shifter—his large build and dark hair. My gaze tracks to his boots and the mud on them. It had been raining that night weeks ago, and he had been wearing the skull mask then, but based on his size alone, I think it might be the largest rebel who had attacked me.

I look at one of the shifters that just entered, their build similar to my own. *The female rebel.*

"I think she's starting to understand," the third voice says, his identity covered by the shadows outside of the single flame gem's reach. I focus on my breathing, my mind calculating how to get out of here while shackled to a wall and without a weapon. "I must say, I'm disappointed you haven't already figured it out. You are, apparently, known for your intelligence."

The rebel's voice halts my thoughts, everything stilling as I wait for him to show himself. Steps sound as Tua finally comes into view. Though he drew my suspicions, I didn't *want* to be right. Not about this. Anger, fierce and burning, floods through me as I stare at him under the light. "You fucking asshole. Kai *trusts* you."

Tua chuckles, folding his arms over his chest while the female rebel and Niko flank him on either side, the former taking her mask off and revealing herself to be the female noble who had accosted Jahlee on our way to dinner with the advisors. "And it will be his downfall."

Kane's voice is shaky when he whispers, "Father?"

Chapter Seventy

BAHIRA

"Kane," Tua responds coldly, not even bothering to look his son's way. Instead, he keeps his eyes on me, taking another step forward. "I'm sure you have questions." His voice burns like the poison did, and I wish more than anything that I could drive my spear into his black fucking heart. "Go ahead and ask."

He's so calm, reserved even, that if it weren't for the abominable glint in his eye, he would be the Tua I thought I knew. The one who explained the island's people to me on the ship. Who said he wanted Kai to appear in a better light. The one who checked in on me when I was ravaged with seasickness.

"How could you do this to him?" It's a stupid question, one that betrays the emotion in my voice.

"Easily," Tua answers, his gaze finally lifting off of me as his face turns pensive. To my utter *horror*, one of the shifters hanging from the wall groans out in pain. Steps sound, the female rebel going to them before there is a grunt, and then it falls uncomfortably silent again. "But, to understand why, you need to understand our history. My brother, Noa, was reckless even as a young child. Impulsive. *Stupid*. He used me as his crutch to make his way through schooling and whatever lessons our father would plan."

Breathe.

I carefully test out the shackles again, noticing that the cold metal encircling my wrist is only *barely* smaller than the widest part of my hand. I might be able to force it off of me, though I suspect I'll have to dislocate my thumbs in order to do it. My stomach grows nauseous at the thought.

"And I'll admit, in the early days, I was fine with that," Tua continues, his lips twitching with the memory. "I was content to help my brother rule. To make the best of it all. Our father officially abdicated his throne, and my brother stepped in. He enjoyed the benefits of calling himself king, even if it was at the detriment of everyone else. As long as he held the power, held the riches and everything that went along with it, he didn't care who he trampled on. Who he destroyed to get what he wanted or how his kingdom suffered because of it."

I swallow the bitter taste in my mouth, my head swimming from the blood loss or the hits or, fuck, maybe I've been down here for longer than I realized. I begin to tug against the restraint, fighting to keep my face neutral as the metal digs into my skin.

"Noa got married because it was expected of him, to the daughter of one of the high-ranking nobles at the time. But he was never faithful to her. As the years passed, each one without a pregnancy to name his heir, he came to resent her."

I pretend to lose my balance and flop forward, enough to yank on the shackle. Discomfort flares as the constraint wedges a small amount down my hand. My heart thunders in my head, dizziness once more threatening the edges of my mind.

I need a distraction, a reason to try to yank myself forward again. "You truly relish the sound of your own fucking voice." I snap.

Tua growls, but it's the female who lunges towards me. Her fist hits my cheek, and I tug on my hand at the same time, a scream ripping from me as my thumb dislocates and sends a wave of agony through my hand and up my arm. I manage to catch the shackle in my shaking fingers before it falls, gripping on to it while my upper body wobbles until I'm forced to lean back against the wall.

"I've been *waiting* to do that," she growls as she stands, stepping back behind Tua.

"You hit like a *bitch*," I seethe.

When Niko steps forward this time, I brace myself for the assault to come, but Tua extends his hand out to stop him. "She'll be dead soon enough."

I shut my eyes, inhaling through my nose and swallowing down the dread that rises at that statement.

"I had approached my brother about Kane being the next to inherit the throne. Whether it be due to the gods or something else, Noa wasn't able to sire a child, but he had a willing and able nephew who could step into the role. He was reluctant at first, but I eventually convinced him to agree, and Kane, though only ten, began the duties of the heir apparent. Then Noa met a peasant woman from the small village of Honna."

I begin to tug on the other restraint, leaning my body forward again in an attempt to look off balance. Bile burns up my throat, threatening to spill from my mouth.

"Kai's mother was meek and mild. For a shifter, she might as well have been nothing but a worm under my boot. But she was pretty and clearly wanted him, so he took advantage. Though I will admit, I underestimated my brother. He kept many secrets about this kingdom and what he did to *ensure* Kai would be the strongest among us. To tempt the fates with magic"—his cold eyes find mine, holding them captive—"and blood."

I draw my brows together, icy awareness of his words prickling my neck as I halt my attempt to free myself. "What do you mean?"

He gives a short laugh, shaking his head as he does. "It's funny what people will keep a record of, what secrets they will spill onto paper when they think they will be the only consumer of that knowledge. That's the thing about the written word—the right information in the wrong hands can be deadlier than any sword or dagger. Noa discovered a secret and used it to test on Kai's mother while she was pregnant with him."

"Test *what*?" I clench my teeth together so hard that I expect to hear a cracking noise as I return to pulling against the restraint. It slowly—so slowly—moves, my thumb straining to stay in its socket as tears fill my eyes.

"The details don't matter, at least not to you. The point is, I discovered the same information Noa had, and I also found his own personal documentation of what he did to Kai's mother. Kai has no idea that his father *altered* him before he was even born. Or that Jahlee's inability to shift is a direct consequence of what was done. But I know the truth, just as I also learned your kingdom's secret. One that you've kept since The War Of Five Kingdoms."

"Passing through the Spell," I seethe in answer.

Tua nods his head, squatting down on the balls of his feet until he is at eye level with me. "What a curious thing, isn't it? While every other realm is trapped within their own borders, mages are able to roam free."

"Fuck you," I snap, earning a kick to my ribs from the female. It's enough of a distraction to yank my hand through the shackle with another yelp. Hands freed, I grip on to the metal with the tips of my fingers as I fight to stay conscious.

"We need to make our next move. Kai should be looking for her now," Niko says.

I laugh, a maniacal trill that shakes my entire body as I throw my head back against the damp stone, trying to hide the pulsing waves of pain that now make up my body. "Kai doesn't give a shit about me."

Both rebels begin to argue, but Tua simply lifts his hand to silence them. "You told him, didn't you? That you don't have magic?"

I say nothing, my glower fixed directly on the traitorous bastard.

"It's why, in the six hours since the rebel attack, he hasn't once mentioned to me that you are missing."

Six hours?

Tua nods at the shock in my eyes, the quick slackening of my jaw that I'm unable to stop. "That poison is quite nasty."

"Father, what are you *doing*?" Kane asks, fear and confusion evident in his voice. "You're working for the rebels?"

"I am *leading* the rebels!" Tua's calm façade finally falters as he stares at where his son is chained against the wall. "You've been a disappointment ever since you allowed Kai to live—"

"He was a fucking *child*!"

Tua bolts towards Kane, reaching him in a few strides and slamming him against the wall. Kane's groan of pain reverberates out into the chamber, and I watch the female and Niko's grins widen.

"Exactly," Tua seethes. "All you had to do was eliminate the only threat to a future where *you* ruled, and you couldn't even do that right." Tua slowly exhales, leaving Kane to come back and stand in front of me. "It doesn't matter, however, because in the end, your life as well as Bahira's will still serve a purpose to our cause."

"Whatever you're thinking, it won't work. You might as well kill me because Kai will not care either way. You can't use me as leverage against him." The confession stings, and I squeeze my eyes shut to hide the gathering tears.

"That's the plan," Tua says softly, having the audacity to look regretful about it when I glance up. "Though you *are* a hard woman to kill, Bahira. I've tried three times now, and you've managed to evade them all. I imagine that *this* time, however, will stick." He sends me a wink as he gestures with both arms to the rebels on either side of him. *Fuck,* I need more time.

"Three?" I question, keeping hold of the shackles as I draw my heels back and force myself to slide against the wall and come to a stand, my thighs burning with the movement. All three shifters watch me, Niko stepping closer and lifting his sword.

Breathe.

Tua takes the bait. "Well, there was the attack in the forest, during which you stopped these two and their friend quite easily," Tua sneers, looking from Niko to the female. "Then there was the attempted ambush in your room. Killing that male for his failure was a personal joy of mine." *Of course.* It had been Tua who offered to bring my attacker to the dungeons. "There was also the poisoning on the ship."

"What poisoning—" My mouth snaps shut. Kai had remarked that he didn't know I was sick, that Tua never told him. I only started feeling better once Kai began taking over.

"You didn't think you were merely *seasick*, did you?"

I growl as I slump against the wall, the chains rattling in my grip. "Why bring me aboard the ship if your plan was simply to *kill* me?"

Tua smiles, his hands clasping behind his back. "Who do you think gave Kai the idea to bring a mage onto our island to help? I don't want my people to suffer—a kingdom is no good without people to protect it. But my brother's notes and the magic *experiments* he did intrigued me. The plan was simple: get a mage and have them try healing the shifters before forcing them to recreate what my brother had done. I wanted to make a son *worthy* of ruling over this kingdom. I had heard rumblings from my informants of the Daxel siblings—a son more powerful than all other mages and his magicless sister. I hadn't dared to dream that we'd get your brother, but I hoped a mage with *enough* magic would suffice. Yet, when you were chosen, the timeline to kill you moved up. You were worthless to us without magic, so there was no point in keeping you alive. But I underestimated you, Your Highness. You managed to survive all three attempts.

You convinced Kai to listen to the people, to try and be a better ruler. It was all in vain, of course, but impressive nonetheless."

"You *murdered* a mother. A child! How do their deaths factor into your *interests*?"

Tua's smile stays in place as he answers, "They were peasants who showed allegiance to Kai. I've spent years—*decades*—building my relationships with those of the Crown and court. It is much easier to convince the real people in power to do your bidding when they are promised even more than they have now."

"And the common people? You would have them suffer and call it something *better*?"

He simply shrugs, walking into the darker part of the chamber, just out of my view. "*Better* is in the eye of those with power, and to me and my interests, ridding the island of those who support my nephew is *better*." Just out of view a door opens with a long creak, and then Tua is gone.

The female and Niko glance at each other before the latter takes a step towards me. I hold the shackles more tightly, debating when I can attack. *How I can attack.* I force my breaths to slow, each drag of air into my lungs held for a second before I let it back out. Niko glides his knuckle down my cheek, my glare only intensifying as he does. *Let him drop his guard, let them both assume they have the upper hand.* I glance towards his sword, noticing his lax grip on it.

"Shame that we have to kill you," he purrs, leaning in so that his lips are only a few inches from my own. Desire expands the gold in his eyes until his irises are tinted in the color.

"Niko," the female growls in warning, but I'm already moving. The sword is easy to steal from him, even without the use of my thumb. He doesn't have time to be shocked before I swing the blade at his neck. Blood spurts out, directly onto the female and I, as Niko's head is severed from his body.

Her expression morphs slowly, shock giving way to fury at the same rate her eyes turn fully gold. Moving the sword into both hands, I jab it forward, the tip driving into her chest and going in about an inch before her hands reach out and cover my own. She squeezes, either knowing that I'm injured or just doing it to stop her own demise. A scream ravages my throat as I throw my weight behind the sword, pushing as hard as I can. The female's nails elongate into razor-sharp claws, piercing into my skin. Her body ripples in a pool of shimmering blue light as she prepares to shift.

I have to kill her now. It has to be this moment while she's still mortal—*mostly* mortal—as I'm already too weak to fight off an animal predator. Gritting my teeth together, I dredge up every last ounce of strength, grab onto every feeling of rage and worthlessness and disappointment, and *push*. Tears line my eyes as the image of Nox and my parents filter into my mind. This is *not* when I will say goodbye. I may be made of more failures than victories, but I am Bahira *fucking* Daxel, and I am not done yet.

The shifter's golden eyes widen, the light surrounding her body flickering brightly as her features blur along their edges. Digging into my heels, my muscles scream in protest as my vision goes hazy.

"You've got this, Bahira!" Kane shouts.

"This is for Jahlee."

The female stumbles back a step against the force of my strength, of *me*, and then the hilt of the sword meets her chest. Her eyes glow with the last bit of her magic before it sputters out and she tips towards me with her mouth hanging open in a silent scream.

My hand plants on her shoulder to hold her back before I jerk the sword out, blood blooming down the front of her tunic. Then I step out of the way to let her fall.

Breathe.

It's agonizing to let my lungs take in what they need, my chest rising and falling too quickly. I drop the sword and lean over, placing my hands on my knees before the flaring pain reminds me what I've done to myself. My eyes squeeze together while tears wet my cheeks, my body feeling as if it's made more of agony than flesh and bone.

"That was incredible," Kane sighs.

"Shut up. Just *shut up*."

Time feels like an illusion as I stand there, hunched over myself and struggling to get air in. But I know that I need to warn Kai of what I learned here, of just how many people may be sabotaging his role as king. Of who is trying to *murder* him. I make it a shaky step before the dripping sound rings ominously in my ear.

Turning, I take in the three bodies hanging from the wall and curse. I need to go, to use whatever energy remains in me to get out of here and straight to Kai. Instead, I step towards them and reach my trembling hand out to check the pulse of the shifter closest to me. The tips of my fingers find cold skin, but I still wait for the flutter of a heartbeat. Finding none, I move to the shifter in the middle as I sway, dizziness hounding me. It's faint—the beat so light that I fear I might be imagining it. Gasping, I quickly check the final shifter, only to find that they have passed as well. I eye the shackles holding the shifter in the middle, the male's head lolled down so that his chin is resting against his chest and long black hair shades his face from view.

"Key," I mutter to myself, turning back to stare at the bloody figures lying prone on the floor. Limping to them, I kneel, blood soaking into my pants as I begin to search Niko's headless corpse, and a smile tugs at the corners of my lips.

"It's unsettling that you're smiling right now."

"I'm going to leave you here," I respond, earning a guffaw of protest from him. Digging around in Niko's trouser pockets proves fruitless, so I crawl my way over to the other body. Against all odds, I find a small key in her back pocket, and in seconds that pass like hours, I make my way over to Kane. After unlocking his restraints, I gesture to the middle shifter hanging on the wall. "You need to help me get him down. He's alive."

Kane's eyes widen, but he swallows down whatever retort he has and nods instead. I let him help me cross the room until we are standing in front of the shifter.

"Wake up," I shout, the words sounding far away, as I watch Kane unlock the shackles holding the shifter up.

He falls to the ground, the thud of his body against the stone waking him from unconsciousness and making him groan out in pain. "Go to hell," he mumbles, his deep voice slurring the words.

"I would love to. It's probably better than this, but we need to go." I reach out to grab his arm and help Kane hoist him up, but I stop midway when I take in the state of his skin. "Fuck," I whisper, studying the way his black tattoo is practically flayed off in places, some pieces hanging away from the muscle as new blood oozes from the wounds.

The shifter lifts his head, broad chin and strong brow defined in the single flame gem's light. We stare at each other, recognition slow to dawn for us both. "Haloa?" I ask at the same time he says, "Bahira?" He was the first shifter Kai took me to see in Molsi. The one whose wife is stuck shifted as a snake. "How long have you been down here?" I ask, wrapping my arm around his waist and helping him up to stand while Kane takes his other side.

"I'm not sure. Days, at least. Perhaps longer. My daughter—" he rasps, stumbling a step that nearly takes us all down.

"We'll get her," I promise. "We need to get to the king." I take one last glance around the dim chamber, just in case my spear is here. Finding only disappointment, Kane and I lead Haloa in the direction Tua left. Hidden in the dark is a rickety door that leads to a dank hallway encased in stone. Following that leads to a small staircase barely wide enough for the three of us to stay side by side.

Haloa recounts what he can remember of his abduction and subsequent torture as we climb, abuse perpetrated by Niko and a few other shifters that weren't prominent enough for him to know their names. He had been ambushed while sleeping in his home, and though they treated him like a traitor, they asked no questions. Demanded nothing other than the pleasure they received by causing him pain. "I don't know what they wanted. Or why *I* was targeted."

Swallowing, I lean my weight against the slimy stone wall, grateful when Kane pulls Haloa towards him. "I think it's because you talked with King Kai and me. About getting help. That you trusted us." At Haloa's confused expression, I launch into what I learned of Tua and his involvement with the rebels. I leave out the information pertaining to Kai's father and the complicated insinuations Tua made regarding his mother and magic. I finish right as we finally clear the long set of steps, all of us huffing for breath. Light filters around the edges of a square wooden door in front of us. I look over at Kane as I ask, "Any chance you know where we are? Or where this door leads to?"

His lips form a grim line as he shakes his head. "Afraid not."

"Well, let's hope it doesn't open into the rebels secret lair, or we're totally fucked."

Chapter Seventy-One

Bahira

It isn't a secret lair that we stumble into but, even more surprisingly, a bedroom. A grand bedroom. The kind of sleeping quarters that would be relegated to a king. Haloa whistles, the sound oddly merry considering what we've just escaped.

"I think this room is larger than my entire home," he muses, letting go of Kane and I to lean against a tall wooden dresser.

"I think you may be right." I take in the four-poster bed centered on the wall sharing the door we came through, gossamer cloth in black and red hanging in sweeping arches from corner to corner. On the adjacent wall is the dresser that Haloa leans against and a large balcony, two sets of glass double doors leading out to it. The sun is beginning to rise on the horizon, orange light filtering in and setting a pair of emerald-green tufted armchairs aglow. I limp towards a wide, tall bookcase stuffed to the brim with books of all thicknesses that is situated between two doors on the wall across from the bed. In the streaming light coming in through the glass, dust motes float in the air, and I note the thick layer of dirt on the shelves. "No one has used this room in a long time."

"I think this was Kai's father's room," Kane says. I look at him as he walks around the space, his nakedness more obvious now than it was in the darkness of the dungeon.

"You might want to find something to cover up with," I tell him, holding my side and wincing from the blossoming bruises where the female rebel kicked me. Doing so also irritates one of my dislocated thumbs, and I have to bite down on my tongue to stop the scream that crawls up my throat. Pain radiates down my leg and back, my head still throbbing in a way that makes my steps uneven.

"You okay there, Bahira?" Haloa asks as Kane goes into what I assume to be the bathroom, a towel wrapped around his waist when he returns.

"Never better," I grit out.

Despite being covered in his own blood and gods know what else, he sends a wry smile my way.

Kane reaches for the handle of another door, but I stop him by calling out his name. "Did you truly not know that your father was leading the rebels?"

He takes a deep breath, a bloody hand massaging the back of his neck. "You heard how my father spoke to me down there. I had *no* idea—"

Though it makes white spots flare in my vision, I grip his arm and spin him around to face me, pushing him until his back hits the door. Haloa comes to stand next to me, folding his arms over his chest and causing the mangled one to ooze fresh blood. I doubt we look very menacing, but Kane doesn't try to fight back. My forearm presses against his neck, everything in me begging to just *rest*. I push even harder.

"If you're lying, I will kill you myself. Do you understand?"

He holds his hands out, palms facing me, as he solemnly nods. "I may be an asshole, and I'll admit to loathing Kai and that dimwit—" I let my forearm slide up higher until the pressure causes him to stop talking, his garbled "sorry" barely audible. When it's clear he gets the message, I lower my arm but keep the pressure there. "Gods," he rasps, panting through his teeth. "I swear, I didn't know. I didn't have any involvement with the rebels at all."

I can't tell if he is lying or not, the pounding of my heart rattling my skull too much for me to think clearly. Haloa gently places his hand on my shoulder, giving me a curt nod when I look at him. I release Kane, stepping back with wobbly legs. "Open the door, then. If anyone is waiting for us, you'll be the first one they attack."

Kane narrows his eyes at me but turns and wraps his fingers around the bronze handle, pulling the door open. The sitting room is even larger than the bedroom and just as opulent. Two large leather couches face each other over a burgundy and silver woven rug, the light wood floors beneath standing out in contrast. A wall of windows is to our right, framed by velvet cream-colored drapes. There are gold and silver adornments throughout the room, too many for me to focus on as we all take a collective step into the space.

"I don't remember *much* about my time in the dungeon, but know that whatever you need from me, I'm happy to provide it," Haloa says, speaking as if I am important enough to delegate that sort of thing.

"No. You focus on healing and getting to your daughter. Anything else, I'm sure Kane and I can handle."

"I am indebted to you," he says quietly.

I move to tell him that there is no debt to be paid when voices sound in the hall. The three of us tense, my gaze flying to Kane's. "How close is this room to the stairs?" I ask him, Haloa squaring his shoulders and lifting his chin beside me.

"It's only separated by a long adjacent hallway. We're not far away from your room" he answers, his gaze locked on the door.

I hobble forward, tilting my head to the side as I strain to listen. My inhale is choppy through my nose, my attempt to slow my heart rate down only causing it to speed up instead, the beat reverberating in my skull.

"There's two voices," Kane supplies, Haloa nodding in agreement.

To stay and hide here, where there's a good chance Tua could return with who knows how many rebels. Or to risk leaving and finding wherever Kai is. Despite the way my head and body throb in protest, I take another step forward. Coming to the same conclusion, Kane moves in front of me, his fingers gently gripping the handle.

When I growl at his back, he looks down at me from over his shoulder. "Of the three of us, I'm the least injured. What was it you said earlier? I'll be the first one they attack?" He smirks when I narrow my eyes in response before turning back towards the door to open it.

Kane moves slowly, quietly pulling the door open. I force my body to remain loose, preparing for the worst when the voices grow louder. One male. One female. One whose cadence I recognize right away and another whose timbre sends a shiver down my spine.

"It's—" I'm interrupted when the door's hinges squeak loudly, all of us freezing in place. The seconds tick by, my heart beating at my ribcage so loudly that I swear it fills the room with its pounding. Except the noise falls out of rhythm with my heart, and when Kane lets out a curse and stumbles backward, the beating stops as someone else comes into view.

His presence fills the doorway, his size even larger than I remember. As if it's been months and not hours since I last saw him and I had forgotten. Forgotten the breadth of his shoulders and size of his arms. The way he nearly touches the top of the doorframe, and how his face, each line strong and broad, is perfectly carved. Even when he looks angry. *Especially* when he looks angry, as he does now. His gaze immediately finds mine as a ringing starts in my ears.

"Kai, what are you doing? You're acting unhinged! And that's coming from me! You need to—" Jahlee pushes her brother out of the way and comes to a halt, her mouth dropping open. "Bahira," she whispers, her shock only pausing her for a moment before she runs to me and wraps me in a hug that pulls air from my lungs and sends waves of torturous, fiery misery all over my being. But I wrap my arms around her and bury my face into her shoulder. Her hands squeeze me more tightly while both of our bodies tremble. "Gods, I was so worried about you. I couldn't find you, and I *knew* you hadn't left. I fucking knew it. He did too, but he is such a stubborn *asshole*..."

I lift my head and glance at Kai, only to observe the emotion wiped from his stone-hewn face. His image blurs, tears slipping down my cheeks as Haloa says something to him that draws his gaze away from me. Jahlee leans back, cupping my face in her hands as her shining brown eyes look me over.

"What happened?" she asks softly.

I swallow roughly, shaking my head as I clear my throat. A male grunt shatters my concentration, Jahlee and I both turning to find Kai standing over Kane. The latter is on the ground and holding a hand to his face. "I didn't fucking *do* anything, you *dick*!"

"He's right," I admit, waiting until Kai meets my gaze again. "He was attacked and brought into the dungeon at the same time I was."

"Move, Jahlee." Kai's deep voice sends a ripple of fear and desire and anger through me. Sandalwood and citrus invade my next breath, and I wish I could burn it out of my memory forever. If only to stop the way my heart softens its beat in his presence.

Jahlee steps back, Kai filling in her place as she goes over to Haloa. "I'm going to take him to Lana," she says, and I try to protest, but Kai stops me.

"She'll be fine. The rebels are gone from the palace."

"Where is Tua?" I rush out.

A faint line forms between Kai's brows, his gaze flicking to Kane before returning to me. "He's speaking with the court of advisors on the other end of the palace."

Though I relax my shoulders, agitation stirs deep in my gut.

"Guards are stationed throughout the palace and at every entrance point. Every rebel that partook in the attack is either dead or locked in the dungeon," Kai adds. "She can handle herself."

Jahlee nods her head in agreement and gives me a weak thumbs up that I'm surprisingly grateful for. "I'll take this asshole too," she snaps, pointing at Kane who stands a few feet away, his eyes glowing golden.

"Your generosity knows no bounds," he retorts. Kai growls at him, and Kane wisely lowers his head and lets Jahlee lead both him and Haloa out of the room.

The silence between us, the way I can't get a read on the shifter king, does nothing to relieve my aching head. But I force myself to stay standing, to keep my eyes on his despite the way it ravages my insides to do so.

"You're here," he murmurs, and I don't know if he's relieved or angered by that fact. His head tilts to the side, a small lock of his dark brown hair falling over his forehead as his face remains impossibly placid. "Who did this to you?" he asks, his large hand gently gripping my chin as he tilts my head up higher.

"Does the name Niko mean anything to you?" I question as I jerk away from him. The action makes me sway on my feet, and Kai's hand shoots to my hip to steady me.

He nods, a faint gold illuminating his irises. "He is one of the liaisons for our Master of Sails."

"The rebels want to kill you and replace you with one of their own. You will need to do an entire overhaul of your advisors and the nobles living here," I add, shaking my head. How would he even determine who was truly on his side and who wasn't?

"Who else?"

"Tua." A small flare of distrust flashes in his gaze, hardly longer than a blink, but it's enough for me to take a step back from him. "I'm not lying," I grit out, gripping on to the back of one of the couches for support.

"I didn't say that you were. Am I not allowed to be surprised by that information? By finding out that the man that has guided my journey as king since I was forced into the role has actually been plotting against me?"

"I tried to warn you," I bark back. "Tua told me about your father, claiming Noa did *something* to your mother while she was pregnant with you. He didn't say what, only that the magic *you* possess is a direct result of whatever he did. Whatever he learned. As is Jahlee's inability to shift."

Kai's brows furrow as a desperate look crosses his face.

"I know you won't believe me, but it is the truth. Tua is leading the rebel movement and has been for a very long time. His connections and relationships with your advisors have given him the power that you, as king, should have. Magda, Haloa, the burning of Adrian's business and murder of his son? They were all punished because they support *you*." I draw my hands down my face, hissing in pain as I do. "He's been trying to kill me since the ship left the Mage Kingdom. I wasn't seasick; I was being *poisoned*. The attack in the forest and the ambush in my room were both planned by him. And he knew from the very beginning that I didn't have magic."

Kai grits his teeth together, his features rippling as he fights the urge to shift. I can't imagine how it must feel to be so betrayed by someone who held so much of your trust. My deception had compounded that. I limp over to one of the velvet-wrapped chairs, sinking into it with a grimace. Kai follows and, to my utter surprise, gets on one knee in front of me.

"Do you want me to bring Lana to you? She's our best healer," he says softly, but I shake my head.

"I'm fine."

"Bahira—"

"Don't," I cut him off, tears threatening again despite the fact that I'd rather not feel anything at all. When the silence lingers, I push down the way it slices me between my ribs. "I need to ask you for a favor." Holding my trembling hands out in front of me, I watch silently as he drops his pensive gaze from mine down to them. His brows rise towards his hairline when he takes in the state of my thumbs.

"How?"

I lift a shoulder, my head falling back against the chair. "Shackles were easier to remove this way." A low rumble leaves him and travels directly to my low belly. *Stupid fucking body*. Kai cradles one of my hands in both of his, carefully moving so as not to jostle it more than necessary. I squeeze my eyes shut as my breathing begins to quicken. "What are you going to do about Tua?" I ask, knowing that I have no right to the information but desperate for a distraction.

He gives me no chance to stew in my fear before he pops my thumb back into place. A whimper that I'm too weak to stop slips out as my head swims in stars. Kai lifts my tingling hand up to his mouth, placing a kiss I barely feel on top of my thumb before he lays it in my lap.

"I'll need some time to figure that out."

I open my eyes to find his already on me. "You may not have a lot of it. This seemed to be Tua's final stand, and once he discovers the rebels' bodies, he'll know that I'm the one who did it. He'll immediately be suspicious that I went to you."

He nods and then quickly sets my other thumb. His figure blurs into many bodies before settling back into one while my chest heaves. "You will have to stay hidden." I shake my head and lean forward to argue with him, but the dizziness makes me wobble back. "You and Jahlee will wait in my rooms until you're healed, while I figure out if I have any allies."

"First, you can't tell me what to do." His lips twitch at that. "Second, how do you know who you can trust? What if he tries to kill you while—"

Kai laughs, cutting off my panicked rambling. "Despite what you think, I'm not a *complete* idiot. I'll let Tua think that I'm ignorant to everything. Let him assume that you escaped and left the island altogether."

As *he* had assumed. That unspoken truth settles between us, but neither of us dares to speak it. Kai stands, extending his hand out to me to help me up. He wraps an arm around me and guides us to the door and out into the hall.

"Were these your father's rooms?" Remnants of dried blood from the shifters who were slain in this wing of the palace stain the rugs and walls, the scent of iron still heavy in the air.

"It was."

I refrain from asking why the fuck there is a secret dungeon attached to the king's chambers.

We make our way down the long hallway and turn, Kai holding the majority of my weight as I limp along next to him. We pass the door I recognize as his and head towards mine, the wood splintered and hanging ajar. My stomach sinks when I push the door the rest of the way open to see that my entire room has been ransacked, clothes and papers strewn about and discarded carelessly. Shards of glass litter the floor, as well as the ancient mage journals from home.

"Bastards," I fume, letting go of Kai to kneel down and inspect the journals. Luckily, the magic from home appears to have kept them from any damage.

"Grab some clothes and whatever you want to keep yourself entertained and then head to my room. I'll send Jahlee there next." I nod, gathering the journals in a small stack before standing. Kai's steps crunch over the glass and the debris from the shattered door, but he stops just before exiting the room. Looking over his shoulder at me, sincerity softens his expression. "I am sorry."

I don't know what he's apologizing for exactly, and I can only nod again, both too many words and not enough strangling me into silence. I wait until I hear his steps fading down the hallway before I gather my things, and I contemplate what the hell I'm supposed to do next.

Jahlee is already waiting for me when I open the door to Kai's room. While I'm happy to see her, it's what she's holding in her hands, twirling it irreverently, that has a smile lifting my cheeks.

"You found my spear," I rasp, dropping my items onto the dark wooden coffee table nestled between two sapphire-blue couches and matching armchairs.

"Are you crying?"

"Absolutely not." I clear my throat, fighting the urge to hug the spear to my chest when she hands it to me. "Are you alright?"

"Completely fine, other than dealing with my cranky brother."

I snort as I lean against the chair and take in the rest of the sitting room. Much like the official king's room, it's spacious and contains multiple bookcases, each one packed to the brim. Double glass doors lead out to a balcony, a sheer white curtain drawn over them to filter out some of the sun's light. There are three other doors, one of them opened and revealing a bedroom.

Jahlee follows my gaze and points to one of the closed doors farthest to the left. "Extra bedroom." She moves her finger to the closed door centered in the middle. "Bathroom. And then that one is Kai's room." I nod, taking a step towards the bathroom. I want to take the hottest shower possible and burn the memories of the dungeon from my skin. "All I ask is that when you and Kai fuck, you keep it quiet."

"There will be none of that, Jahlee."

This time, it's her who snorts, her watchful gaze taking in every detail of my movement. "I'll have Lana out here waiting for you. I'm really glad that you're alive. *And* that you didn't leave."

I smile, leaning against the door to the bathroom as I look at her. "And miss all the fun? That would be boring." She beams at me, light coming back into her eyes in recognition of the play on her words from when we first met.

The shower is a welcome reprieve. Enough so that I finally do cry, letting everything out under the safety and privacy of the steaming water. When I exit the bathroom, Lana is sitting with Jahlee, the old female practically crowing from whatever injuries of mine she can see. Within ten minutes, she's covered every wound and cut with a foul-smelling poultice, all while chastising me to eat more food.

When she leaves, Jahlee and I sit across from each other on the couches. "He's going to try to do everything alone," Jahlee muses, sipping on dark red wine from a stemless glass.

"I'm sure he can handle it," I respond, taking a sip of my own drink.

"You can drop the act, Bahira. You don't have to pretend with me."

I lower my glass to look at her. "And what act might that be?"

"The one where you pretend that you don't care about him. That you don't care about what we need to do to help our kingdom."

"It's not my kingdom," I retort soundly—hoping if I say the words forcefully enough, it will make them feel more true.

"Maybe not, but it's *his*, regardless of who might try to take it from him. I don't believe for one moment that you want to see him suffer."

I avoid her gaze and stare out one of the windows. "You don't know anything about what I want." I don't even know if *I* do anymore.

I had come to the Shifter Kingdom with the hope that I could advance my knowledge of magic, that I could have another breakthrough. I suppose that I did to a degree—learning how the blood of those with magic might be a solution to the magical blight—but there is still so much I don't understand about it. I have no answers for the shifters here, no answers for my own kingdom or myself. Soon, I will be heading home, only to lose my best friend when I decline his marriage proposal.

"I know he cares about you. That's why the truth hurt him so much, even if it's hypocritical for him to hold it against you. And, I want to reiterate, it *is* hypocritical of him. But he'll come around."

"Maybe, with everything going on, it *would* be better for me to leave the island early."

Jahlee's eyes narrow on me, her perceptive gaze piercing right to my bones. "I didn't take you for a coward." I stiffen at her words, and though I want to refute them, I can't—even as anger licks at my heart. Jahlee stands, finishing off what's left in her glass before setting it down roughly on the table between us. "I'm going to figure out a way to support Kai. To help him take a stand against the rebels. Leave or don't. *Help* or don't. I just hope that you can live with yourself, whatever choice you *do* make." She glares at me before stomping off to the spare bedroom, the door slamming closed behind her.

Sighing, I place my glass next to hers on the table and curl on my side on the soft velvet couch, my entire body tender and aching. "I hope I can too," I whisper.

Chapter Seventy-Two

ARIA

It takes two more days before the city of Lumen comes into view. In that time, I had minimized my stops as much as possible. Stopping means remembering who isn't here with me. Stopping means I have to restart with a momentum that I don't think I have.

Stopping means reliving my failures.

It's early morning, the sun not quite breaking through the surface of the water yet. I know that I should go straight to my mother and give her the rings, but there is a tugging at my gut that leads me to the seamounts instead. They loom ahead of me, a dark horizon in the water that grows larger as I near.

An ominous quiet washes over me as I swim through the valley cut between the mounts. My chest rattles with the beat of my heart, my ears straining to hear any sound or movement from the sirens that live here. From the offspring. However, as I move into the heart of the mounts, sunlight finally casting it in a subtle glow, I find them completely empty.

I poke my head in and out of the caves carved into the dark rock, finding evidence that suggests the sirens did not just pick up and move. Their *homes* remain intact and full of items. Food caught long ago rots on tables, and items from woven eel grass bags to jewelry are scattered all over. It's as if they had to abandon this place in a hurry.

"Or like they were ambushed," I say quietly with bitter cold realization. My body begins to tremble, shockwaves of sadness and regret drowning me as if I wasn't a being made to live beneath the water. "No," I whisper, shaking my head as my hands fly up to cradle it. *I am too late.* All those lives, young and old... They all died because of *me*. "No!" I scream, pounding my hands into the rock, my braids floating around my head and blocking out the rest of the world.

My attention is narrowed down to this place—this *defeat*—as I scream. Magic tickles my throat, blending into my voice. I *wish* I could use it to *stop* all this cruelty, all this bitterness that stems from the siren queen herself. I just want it all to *stop*. My screams grow long and high-pitched while my talons dig into my palms. When dark blue blood mingles with the water and an ache sharp and fierce pulses in my hands, I finally stop. Leaning my head against the rock, I let my wails quiet until only I can hear their sounds. I wait one more moment, digging deeply into my memory to pull up the list of things I need to remember to be when I enter the palace. *Jaw and shoulders relaxed, lips flat, spine straight, and attitude vicious.*

Pushing away, I turn from the rock and immediately freeze. Two legionaries stare at me, their glinting silver weapons partially drawn from their shell-armored bodies as if frozen mid-strike. My mouth opens and closes without a sound as blood rushes in my ears. Time feels suspended, stretching between the three of us like a taut rubber band until it finally snaps. Eyes of turquoise and garnet narrow predatorily as the legionaries lurch for me, their talons digging into my arms.

"Your mother has been expecting you," the garnet-colored siren says, though she blinks rapidly like she's confused by the statement.

I don't get a word out in response before they are hauling me between them and towards the shining pearlescent palace. I glance back only once to the seamounts, but as before, only hollowness remains.

※ ⁂ ※

The hallways of the palace are as cold and unwelcoming as I remember them to be.

The sirens holding me captive usher me into the throne room, drawing both my mother's dark gaze and Allegra's. The latter sneers at me, the move unsurprising, but it's my mother's smile—a genuine *smile*—as she looks at me that causes me to stop moving for a moment. The colored crystals embedded into the columns lining the walkway up to her dais make the space glow in a rainbow of colors, yet it's what is positioned on the dais next to her ghastly throne that gives me pause: the Siren Queendom's Mirror. In my entire twenty-one years, I have never once seen my mother use it. Shells of every color and variety make up the entire back of the oval-shaped Mirror, while its edges are wrapped in never-dying seaweed and adorned with permanently blooming water lilies.

I stop at the bottom of the dais and bow.

"Aria, you may rise." I do, dragging my gaze up the steps until they meet the nearly black ones of my mother where she floats next to the Mirror. "Tell me you've acquired what I asked of you?" I reach for the bag tied around my body and open it, grabbing the rings and holding them out to her in my palm.

Allegra's sapphire eyes glance behind me as she finally realizes who is missing. "Where's Mashaka?"

"He—" I falter over the words before clearing my throat and trying again. "We were attacked by rogue sirens. He did not make it." I wait for any hint of sadness to pass over Allegra's features. Not much, but enough to show that her favored animal, her companion for *years*, actually meant something to her.

But she rolls her eyes, annoyance obvious in the gesture of her hand as she waves it in front of her. "If he was too weak to fight them off, then he had no business being at my side. Good riddance."

My mother chuckles as she makes her way to me, her hand snatching the rings from my own. "You made it home early. I'm impressed, Daughter."

"Early? But..." I let the thought die as my mother's smile turns menacing. I have to force my hands to stay open, but I can't stop the way my fingers strain. *She killed them*. I had been early, had done what she asked, and she *still* killed them.

Allegra holds our mother's gold and diamond trident out to her, the tips sparkling under the filtered sunlight.

"I have another job for you. One that I expect your bleeding heart will enjoy."

A low growl from Allegra washes over my skin, disquiet creeping in the longer my mother lets the silence between us grow. Finally, she tips her trident in my direction, letting the sharply cut diamonds imprint on my chest.

"Someone tipped off the sirens at the seamounts that the Queen's Legion was coming for them. They were able to escape shortly before we got there." She presses the trident harder, drawing blood as I wince. Her dark eyes take on a murderous glint when she leans in closer to me. "I want you to find them and tell me where they are hiding."

"But Y-Your Majesty, what makes you think that I can find them?" I stutter, my throat narrowing.

My mother tilts her head faintly, not enough to bare her neck but enough to relay her displeasure with my question. "Don't ask questions you already know the answer to, *Daughter*. You will work to find them, just as you worked to befriend them behind my back."

"But—"

"Do *not* disappoint me, Aria," she cuts in, silencing me with more pressure of her trident on my chest. "If you fail in this, if you embarrass me and my royal legacy any more than you *already* have, I will destroy everything you love and hold dear. *Everything*, Aria."

The seconds tick by as her words and the insinuation behind them settle between us. I have no one important to me, no one I love dearly... *except for Lyre*. When my realization becomes evident, the queen simply sends another sharp look of disappointment my way.

"You will join a group of sirens going out tomorrow to hunt for ships." That's all she says before she and Allegra leave, the throne room left in horrific silence. I stay there, my injured tail fin slowly swishing the water as I hold myself afloat. *Find the missing sirens?* It is an impossible task. *Impossible.*

Grinding my teeth together, I do the only thing I can when being in this palace—this court—becomes too much. I head to my cave.

I don't spot any of my other sisters as I exit the palace though I'm only really looking for Lyre.

When I finally reach the cave's hidden entrance, I carefully part the sea kelp gently rocking in the current and enter. I catalog every shelf and corner, confirming that all is as it should be, and finally let some of the tension ease from my body.

"Aria." I turn with a gasp as the familiar voice sends my heart into a furious beat.

"Nia?" I rasp, backing farther into the cave when she pushes past the sea kelp, her lips twisted somewhere between surprise and fury. Her short blue braids float smoothly around her head when she comes to a stop in front of me.

"Well, what do we have here?" Nia observes me for a moment before pushing past to study all the items I've collected.

"How did you find this place?" I ask as my body trembles.

"I've been following you since I spotted you at the seamounts. Your little display of anger was quite impressive to watch. It almost made me think you were the one who tipped us off that the Queen's Legion was coming, but then I remembered hearing whispers of you being gone for weeks on a mission for your mother. What did the queen send you out for?" She keeps her back to me as she slowly inspects the treasures of the dead, sometimes lifting one up to examine it more closely.

"Nia, you can't tell anyone about—"

"No," she interjects, finally turning to face me. Her pace as she moves towards me is slow and calculated, and she waits until she's close enough that I can see the freckles on her cheeks before she speaks again. "You do not get to issue the commands here. It seems I've stumbled onto something quite forbidden, wouldn't you say?"

I shake my head, ready to plead with her to keep this quiet. Maybe if I tell her what she wants to know, she'll leave with the promise to not say anything. "My mother sent me to the Northern Island to retrieve a set of spelled rings. I don't know what her plan is for them; she never told me. Please, Nia, I swear that is all I know," I plead, showing her the palms of my hands.

"Let me see your bag," she demands. I untie it, handing it to her and watching as she riffles through it. The only thing in there now is the dagger I found in the early days of the trip. Nia tosses both to the ground, deeming them worthless, as she turns to look all around the cave. "How long have you had this little space?"

I hesitate, unsure if her knowing the truth would be better or worse. Her head snaps towards me, her blue eyes flaring in warning. The truth, then. "A few years. I started collecting items from the males who were felled by our song."

Nia lifts a brow and smirks. "Morbid. And nobody else knows of its existence?"

"No. I *swear* it. It serves no purpose other than for me to have a space of my own."

"Not anymore," Nia says under her breath, her gaze tracking up to the hole in the rock above us.

Fear keeps its fingers wrapped tightly around my throat as I prepare to keep pleading, but Nia, with a move faster than I expect, punches me directly in the face, right below my left eye. I let out a yelp, my body propelled backward until it slams into the wall. Nia is there, sending another closed fist into the other side of my face. I try to cower behind my raised arms, but she pins them to my sides before leaning in towards me.

"That was for agreeing with your mother to keep us doomed to the seamounts."

My flowing tears mix into the seawater as I stare at her. "I am only *one* person, Nia. And the least influential one at that. It would have changed *nothing*."

Releasing my arms, she slams my head against the rock, wrapping a fist tightly into my long braids. Her figure blurs in front of me as I grip her wrist and try to right myself.

"They're just excuses, Aria. Pathetic, *weak* excuses. But you have the opportunity to make it up to me—to *us*. All you have to do is let us meet here."

My ears ring, my focus waning with the dizziness in my head. "What do you mean?"

"The cave." She gestures with her chin. "When we were tipped off last week about your mother's impending raid, we were able to get the children and older sirens out to Eersten before the Queen's Legion came, but we lost a lot of our weapons and gear that we had slowly been stockpiling. With this cave, I can safely coordinate meetings with the sirens I send out to spy on the Legion. We'll take our weapons back and store them here until the time is right."

"Nia, *please*," I cry, squeezing my eyes closed. "This is the *only* place I have that is safe—"

"And what a fucking luxury that is, you spoiled, stupid brat. You claim you want to help us, that you are *only one person*, yet when I ask you to give me access to the one thing that could help us, you selfishly try to keep it. *No.* If you want the queen left unaware about this little spot, you'll do as I ask." Her forearm presses into my neck, forcing my eyes to open and look into hers. "You will help me find where your mother has hidden the weapons they stole from us and then bring them here. Do that, and I won't let anyone else know about this place. When it comes time to end your family's line, I will allow you to keep your pathetic life. Do you understand?"

Not knowing what else to do, I nod my throbbing head in silence. Nia eases up her hold on me, prowling around the cave one final time before looking at me over her shoulder.

"Pleasure talking with you, Your Highness." She pushes through the sea kelp and leaves.

I sink against the wall, my hands cradling my head, as the weight of what I've agreed to drags me farther down into darkness. The irony of being asked to help Nia find weapons my mother took from her mere minutes after my mother has commanded that I find the sirens of the seamounts has me biting down hard on the inside of my cheek. I am not a spy. I am not some sort of clever sleuth. *I cannot do this.*

Gently rubbing my eyes, I swim to the center of the cave that is no longer my own and curl in on myself, burying my head in my arms.

Every time I manage to close my eyes, I think of all that has happened to me—all that still awaits—and find that I'd much rather be awake. When a familiar, gentle set of knocks rouses me from the glass art I'm working on, I nearly knock it over in my rush to the door.

Lyre lets out a small laugh as I barrel into her, squeezing her tightly to me. "Where have you been?" I ask, my mouth muffled in her lavender hair. I had been home for days and hadn't seen her in the palace or out on hunts. Her arms wrap around me once before she forcefully draws back, her gaze going to the hallway.

"I'm sorry that I haven't been able to see you until now." She offers no other explanation as nervous energy rattles her body. When I back up into my room to beckon her in, she shakes her head. "We've been summoned by her."

I follow Lyre down the hall from our rooms, bypassing the throne room and heading towards the palace exit. "Do you know what is happening?"

"It could be one of a number of things," she responds quietly. After feeling the weight of my stare on the side of her face, she sighs and adds, "None of which I believe are good." My lips draw down in a frown as I fully take in my sister. While appearing on the outside as lovely as she always has—her light purple scales glistening against the phosphorescent lights that glow from the plants on the ocean floor—there is something draining her that wasn't there before I left for the Northern Island.

Shaking off my feeling of unease, we join my mother and the rest of my sisters outside the palace. Allegra ignores me, her gaze sharp in the direction of the Continent's shores. Sade's biceps flex as she ties her orange braids back, her sunset eyes finding mine with a short linger before she diverts them. Dyanna, her pink-colored scales glimmering against her dark skin, twirls a piece of seaweed in her hand, looking more bored than anything else. My sisters and I have never joined my mother like this outside of the queen's assemblies.

"Daughters, it is time to begin the first act of my grand plan to bring us back to the surface." My ruby brows raise in surprise as I glance around our small group to gauge everyone else's reactions. While Lyre shares my confusion, Allegra, Sade, and Dyanna do not. Our mother offers no other explanation as she turns to face north, towards the Continent. "Let us rewrite history."

We swim for a while, the full moon at its highest point in the sky our only source of light. When my mother diverts towards the surface, we all follow, breaking through the water one at a time. I eye the length of the shore in both directions, trying to surmise how far west we've gone.

"Look!" Lyre whispers, pointing straight ahead. My gaze narrows on the darkness beyond the water when there's abrupt flashes of color—green and yellow, perhaps also blue—before it goes dark again.

"It's time," my mother declares before taking off towards the beach.

Part Six

Our love is not a beginning or an end but an infinite constant.

Chapter Seventy-Three

RHEA

"Are you nervous about tonight?" Elora asks as she shelves a book in the history section of the palace library.

"What is there to be nervous about? It's just dancing, right?"

I had spent the past week trading magic lessons in the evenings for dancing ones with Nox in preparation for the Autumnal Ball. While the ball is named after the fast-approaching season, we are still a few weeks away from the official start of it. The ball, Nox had told me as I tripped over my own two feet, is a way to honor the transition from summer to autumn, the withering of warmth and life before the death of winter and rebirth of spring.

"Yes, it's dancing, but as long as you're on Nox's arm, the people who haven't grown used to seeing you around the palace will find you quite fascinating to observe."

I wrinkle my nose, giving her a book from her cart when she extends an empty hand out to me. "Why does that make it seem like I'm an animal on display?"

Elora snorts. "I suppose, in a way, you are. Not the animal part, but the display part." Adjusting her glasses, she extends her hand out again for another book to shelve. "This is the first big public event since Nox has returned and announced your courtship. Even though you guys haven't been shy about the fact that you're together when you're out and about, and for the record, you *aren't* shy about it." She looks over her shoulder at me and wiggles her eyebrows as a blush stains my cheeks. "There's something fascinating about the story that the prince is dating someone supposedly not of noble birth."

"If they only knew," I joke under my breath.

"Have you heard anything recently from the council?" Elora asks.

I let out a resigned sigh. Nox had returned late on the third day from his trip to Polatos. He looked as if he'd been riding all day to get home as quickly as possible. Though my magic had shown its disdain for us being apart, writhing beneath my skin enough that I had to expel it more frequently than my usual daily practice sessions, our time apart had otherwise been fine. I trained with Daje, who stepped in for Cass—the latter having gone on the trip as Nox's guard. I spent time with Elora and Nox's parents. Elora and I visited Starla and the other children at the orphanage, much to the little girl's disdain. Though it felt as if a piece of me was missing, I was proud of the fact that I didn't completely crumple in on myself because of his absence. Nox held me tightly to him his entire first night back, and it took well into the next morning, after joining our bodies multiple times, before both of our magics finally settled.

Unfortunately, the council still seems unwavering in their disdain of me. "No. They have been keeping Nox busy from basically sunup to sundown. He's studying laws and codes and shadowing his father. It's almost as if..." I trail off, not wanting to give voice to the worry that's been steadily building inside of me.

"Almost as if they are trying to keep you guys apart," she guesses.

I nod my head. "They've even suggested moving me to the second floor, as it's apparently *improper* for us to be sleeping in the same room." Nox had met me out on the balcony on the lower level of the palace for tea right after the council suggested that to him. To say he had been frustrated would be an understatement.

"I wish there was something more I could do. I offered to speak to the council again, but Nox said that when he brought it up, they declined."

"Well, you said King Sadryn changed things, so the council has no say in your relationship, right? Maybe they will ease up with time. Seems like such a silly thing to harp on when, in the end, it won't make a difference."

I hum in agreement, reaching for the next book—a tome that necessitates two hands to pick it up. "Gods, why is a book labeled *The Origins of The Albero Tree* so large? Surely its roots don't need this much explanation."

Elora chuckles, reaching for the book only for it to topple out of both of our hands. Within a blink, pink magic surrounds the book, keeping it from smacking loudly into the cart. She huffs out a breath and guides the book to its place on the shelf, her magic as beautiful as a blooming blush rose. "That was close."

When the rest of the books on the cart are put away, we bid Rayna farewell and make our way to the second floor of the palace. Elora links her arm with mine, her eyes taking in every detail of the autumnal decor that we pass. "Thank you for inviting me to get ready with you, Rhea. Normally, it's my mother and I arguing about how to do my hair or which dress I should wear. Though she didn't argue at all when I told her about my custom *palace-made* attire."

I laugh, even as a small pang of longing at the thought of getting ready for something as monumental as my first ball without my mother constricts my throat. With only knowing mere facts about my mother, Luna, and only a handful at that, I think I would have liked her. Or maybe that's just the wishful thoughts of a woman pining for something she's never had before. While I didn't have a traditional mother and father, or family really, I did have the memory of Alexi. Of Bella. I have Nox, Elora, and Cass. Even Daje, a man who is keeping my secret despite who his father is and the power he holds. There are Sadryn and Alexandria, Barron and Sarai, and the countless friendly mages I have encountered in my months here so far. Each of them has filled a part of me that I once thought might always be empty.

I may have lost the family I was born into, but I have made a new one right here. And I am happy for the first time in my life; I can say that with certainty. I am well and truly *happy*.

We pass a door with an image carved into the dark wood—a crescent moon on top of a flaring sun and surrounded by stars. Gold paint fills the carvings, making the symbol stand out.

A woman pops her head out from a doorway farther down, her eyes widening as she beckons her hand to us and shouts, "You're here! Come, it's time to get ready!" Elora yelps as more women appear, and she and I are whisked off to separate bathrooms within the suite.

"What is your name?" I ask the lady-in-waiting who starts the water for the tub.

"Elowen, My Lady," she answers, dipping her chin as her dark blue eyes look up at me from under her lashes.

"Elowen, if it's alright with you, I'd like to do the shower part myself."

Sometimes, in my quiet moments while doing something as mundane as reading or going for a walk, the feeling of the night Alexi died would hit me as if I were back there once more. It always felt more visceral than a simple memory. I didn't only see the blade going through his chest, but I could hear it—smell the iron in the air and feel the wood beneath my knees shake when his body collapsed to the ground. Once, in the shower, Nox was simply rubbing a cloth over my shoulder, and I was brought back to when Tienne and Erica had done the same. It had taken a long while to calm the tremors of my body, to then explain to Nox what had happened and watch his own guilt play out in his eyes. Maybe it was selfish, but I was looking forward to tonight, and I didn't want it tainted by a nightmare from the past if I could help it.

"Of course, Lady Rhea, it is no trouble at all. I'll be just outside the room when you're ready." Elowen bows, the act surprising me, before she leaves. Some of the palace staff treat me as if I am already a princess, an action that I am still unsure how to respond to. Others hardly regard me with more than an obligatory nod as they pass in the halls. Of all the things I had fantasized about happening if I left the tower, the politics of palace life when dating a royal was not one of them.

I take my time in the shower, reviewing the dance moves Nox taught me in the hope that it might distract me as well as improve my actual dancing tonight. Once I'm out, Elowen guides me to sit at a small vanity, Elora already seated at one to my right.

Elowen's magic is a brilliant red, and she uses it to manipulate the air to dry my hair, gently guiding the element so that, when she's done, there is a soft curl at my ends. Then she leaves the room, coming back with my dress in hand.

"It's stunning," I whisper in awe. I hadn't seen it completely finished yet.

Elowen smiles widely before guiding me to a part of the room where a divider is set up, Elora getting the same treatment when her lady-in-waiting comes out with her own gown.

My dress is a rich, dark green with twin panels of soft pleated fabric coming up from the cinched waist to cover my breasts and attach to a cape at my shoulders. The cape flows down nearly to the floor, covering my otherwise exposed back. Though most of the middle of my chest and sternum are free of fabric, a thick embroidery of what looks like the bare branches of a tree dipped in silver starts on one side of the dress and stretches across my bare skin to the other side, offering a little more modesty. I wonder if it's completely irrelevant, however, when twin slits split my dress all the way up to the top of my thigh.

Elowen shows me how to adjust the cape so that it can either come around my shoulders more or stay held back. "Come, you must see yourself."

Walking out past the divider, I take in Elora from across the room, her beautiful russet-colored gown complimenting her fair skin and red hair and showing off her lovely curves. "Elora, you look beautiful," I gasp out.

But she shakes her head while she walks towards me, her eyes glassy as she draws them over me. "Rhea, you are *ethereal*."

Stepping up to a large gold-framed mirror propped up against the white stone wall, my hands tremble as I take in my reflection. My skin holds a slightly darker pigmentation, time spent training outside these past weeks having given it a kiss of a tan. It glows against the dark hue of the dress, my honey-blonde hair curled perfectly and hanging to just above my hips. I had chosen to keep the dragon necklace on, the black pendant shining between the panels of fabric against my chest. Elowen opted to keep my face bare of anything more than a light lip color, the soft pink brightening the green of my eyes. Swallowing, I wait for the familiar feelings of self-doubt to rise—the ones that whisper that I'm not worthy enough to wear something this lovely. But the longer I stare at my reflection, Elora smiling brilliantly at my side, the more that anticipation fades away until all I feel is simply *beautiful*.

"Nox is going to lose his mind when he sees you," Elora cackles, smoothing a hand down the tulle of her own dress and causing the bits of gold to glitter under the light of the spelled flames as she does.

"And is there someone who is going to lose it when they see *you*?" I ask, lifting a brow.

Elora snorts, twisting in front of the mirror to look at the back of her dress which dips low into a V-shape. "I'm sure there are a few who will be excited to see that I have crawled out of my cave of books. We'll see if I decide any of them are worthy of a dance tonight."

We laugh as Elowen walks over to the vanity I was seated at and carefully removes something from a satin pouch. "There is one more piece, Lady Rhea," she says softly, returning to my side. She shows me a diadem made of silver and glittering diamonds, a large flaring sun set in its center while a crescent moon lays beneath it. Shining bursts of stars surround the celestial markers in different heights, making the piece look larger than it truly is. A design of swirling diamonds, like that of a misty sky or churning sea, makes up the bottom portion.

I shake my head, meeting her gaze. "There must be a mistake; I did not request this."

"His Highness, Prince Nox, did," she answers, her lips twitching as she does. She motions for me to face the mirror again, standing behind me as she carefully places the diadem on my head and weaves strands of hair around its sides to hold it in place.

When her hands leave the small crown, there is an abrupt and sharp tugging on my stomach, making me gasp as an image bursts to life in my mind:

A woman, her hair so blonde it's nearly white and eyes a green that matches my own, adjusts the same diadem over her head. The woman hums as she smooths over her black and white silk dress with her hand. A dark-skinned man with black hair to his shoulders comes up behind her, his arms wrapping around her waist.

"Are you ready, my love?" he asks, kissing the shell of her ear. "We can't be late for our very first ball."

She laughs, turning her head to the side to meet his gaze. "I'm so very happy you are here with me. I do not think I could have done this—rule them—alone."

They kiss, and my stomach is pulled on sharply again as the image fades and I find myself staring at my own reflection.

"Are you alright, Rhea?" Elora asks, her fingers gently touching my forearm with concern.

I shake my head, blinking in confusion. "Yes, I—" I'm thankfully interrupted when someone knocks on the door.

Elowen leaves my side to answer it, speaking in a low voice before gently shutting it. "His Highness is here to escort you, My Lady."

I swallow, pushing the odd experience to the back of my mind for now. Elowen gathers the other ladies-in-waiting and heads for the door, Elora following behind them.

"I'll give you guys some *alone* time so he can properly drool over you," she teases, pushing her glasses farther up her nose. "But I'll see you on the dance floor!"

I laugh as I wave goodbye, my smile growing wider when I hear her whistle and compliment Nox in the hallway. And then he steps into the room.

Air is pulled from my lungs at the sight of him, my body going both taut and loose at the same time. "Stars above," I whisper, drinking every detail in with hungry eyes while he does the same to me. The onyx lapels of his jacket shine while beneath it, a deep blue button-up shirt—the top few buttons left undone—shows a hint of his light brown skin. Black trousers and finely made dress shoes of the same color complete the outfit; the entire ensemble is enough on its own to send my heartrate soaring. But it's what rests on top of his wavy black hair, a few rogue strands hanging over his forehead, that leaves me surprisingly coiled with desire. A crown made of black metal, its short triangle-shaped spires inset with large diamonds, holds my attention even as he closes the door and begins to walk towards me. At its center is the same flaring sun as the one on my diadem—except that crescent moons flank either side, facing in opposite directions.

"In all my dreams, I could never have imagined anyone as absolutely perfect as you are, Rhea." His gaze pores over me once more, unabashedly lingering on every dip and curve. I take a step towards him, revealing the slits that show an expanse of skin on both legs, and Nox's eyes become a churning midnight storm, his hands flexing at his sides.

"The diadem was a surprise," I tell him, sliding my hands up the firmness of his chest. Warmth from his fingers permeates my sides as they rest over the exposed skin there. Nox shrugs, as if dressing me in a crown in front of the kingdom—in front of the *council*—was nothing short of expected. "And it matches yours," I add on with an arched brow. This time, the corner of his mouth lifts followed by a gentle squeeze of his hands.

"Is it a bad thing that I wanted everyone to know who you are to me? To this kingdom?"

My own smile wobbles as I search his gaze. "The council won't like the message we're sending." Even if it is unintentional. Though I doubt very much Nox hadn't already thought of any implications that might arise when I show up on his arm adorned in a Mage Kingdom crown.

"They'll get over it," he says much too confidently, then chuckles at the less than convinced look on my face. "It doesn't matter, Rhea. As long as you're mine, everyone else is going to have to get on board. Now, come on. We have two things we need to take care of."

"Two?" I question, interlacing my fingers with his and walking at his side as we exit the room. I knew of one thing that Nox wanted—*I* wanted—to do before the ball tonight. One that I had spent time talking with him about ever since Selene brought it up on my last visit to the Middle.

"It's a surprise." His eyes sparkle, something knowing and excited gleaming in them. I expect to head to the first floor, but instead, we continue up the stairs to the third, my steps slowing when we come to his room. "Not here." He gestures farther down the hall, where the secret door to the garden is. Nox turns us so that we are facing each other, the door like an ominous ghost hovering at our sides.

"I know you've tried going down alone, and unless you haven't told me, I'm assuming that you haven't made it to the bottom yet." I shake my head as I hold his gaze. "I was hoping we could try again, together. If you want."

I turn my gaze to the door, as if it will give me its opinion on the matter. But this decision, like all of the ones I've made while with Nox, lies solely with me. I could feel defeated that I hadn't been able to conquer this on my own, or I could celebrate the fact that I wasn't alone anymore. That I had someone who loved me unconditionally and who knew when to push and when to give me the time and space to figure things out on my own. Who knew me better than I sometimes knew myself, but who never forced me in a direction that I hadn't chosen on my own.

Looking back to him, his face open and gaze soft, I smile and say, "Let's go."

Chapter Seventy-Four

RHEA

THERE'S A DOOR AT the bottom of the staircase.

I had assumed as much, but what I hadn't imagined was how beautiful it would be. Inset in its middle is a stained-glass window with the image of a tall albero tree under a twinkling night sky. My fingers trace over the glass, the temperature cool despite the trickling of sunlight pouring in at its center. "This is stunning."

Nox rubs his thumb over the back of my hand as he nods his head. He never once let go as we descended the stairs. I used my magic to light our way, but Nox moved with the practiced ease of someone familiar with the darkness that lingered there. It was as exhilarating as it was frightening, and my legs shook with every step, but we had made it to the bottom. Together.

I let loose a long exhale at the gentle flowing breeze and the calming light of sunset when Nox opens the door. We step down onto a pristine white stone path that leads away from the palace and winds through the garden, and I gasp as I take in the view. The colors are resplendent, and as I look around, noticing the natural perimeter created by albero trees, I can't help but feel like this is less of a garden and more of a work of art.

Centered between the walkway and a small teal-colored stream is a massive tree. Though not as tall as some of the others that line the forests of the Mage Kingdom, this one is much wider, its branches growing high before forming an arc and drooping back down towards the ground. Beyond the tree, the plants and flowers seem to shimmer from certain angles, their floral scent heady in the air.

I take in another deep breath as our steps click against the stone, the sweet-scented air reminding me of a different place—a different time. "When I was in the tower, sometimes a breeze would carry the scent of flowers up to my balcony. I would close my eyes and daydream about dragging my fingers along their petals, how delicate they would feel beneath my fingertips. What walking in an entire garden might smell like as opposed to getting wisps of the fragrance along the wind." I reach out and carefully touch the velvet-soft petals of a burgundy flower and then a purple one, its petals long and curling. "Sometimes, I'm afraid that this is a dream."

"Which part?"

"All of it. Being with you and living in this place. Having friends and training out in the open with my magic. Living without *fear*."

Nox nods his head, the diamonds of his crown glinting beneath the sunlight and casting white flares on the emerald-green grass. "What convinces you that it's real? That you're really here?"

"Going for a walk and seeing the dots of sunlight streaming in through the canopy of the trees above me. I don't think I could dream up a sight more beautiful than that. Occasionally, it's remembering that Alexi and Bella are gone and that if this *were* a dream, they'd most certainly be here." He squeezes his hand around mine, leaning over to press a kiss to my head. "But the biggest thing, the one that works the fastest to bring me into the present and prove to me that this life I'm living is *real*, is your touch. Your scent. The way you love me. Just *you*."

I hear Nox's breath hitch as he guides us to a shady spot right underneath the majestic tree. Its dark branches stretch overhead, while leaves in lavender and deep blue pour from the ends like mini waterfalls.

"You anchor me. You have since the day you entered my life." We turn to face each other, my hand reaching up to brush a strand of hair off of his forehead before I cradle his face and continue speaking. "I don't think I've ever said this to you, but you saved me, and I don't just mean in the literal sense. You kept me from sinking into a place there would have been no return from. I think I finally comprehend what you mean when you say you choose me over your crown. Because I could be given every treasure, every valuable piece of land or the highest title one can have, and none of it would compare to how it feels to be loved by you."

Nox covers my hand with his own, turning his face to kiss the center of my palm. "Damn it, Rhea," he breathes, blinking the glassy look in his eyes away. "*I was supposed to be the one who gave the big declaration of love today.*"

I scrunch my brows together as he places another kiss on my palm before bringing his hands to my shoulders and slowly spinning me to face the trunk of the tree.

"Close your eyes," he whispers as his hands slowly travel down to my hips, holding me in place. I do, feeling him draw his magic out. "When I was a boy, shortly after my Flame Ceremony, I would come out here to the gardens and test my magic. Test the limits on my own of what I could do as someone with more power than the kingdom had seen in centuries. I understood the responsibilities I would bear, even if I didn't yet know the lengths to which I would go to fulfill them. But, like I told you when you woke up from the Middle, I was happy to give all of myself to protect this place. To protect these people." Nox removes his hands from my body just as the breeze picks up, shaking the leaves of the tree above us. "I have two gifts for you," he says softly, his fingers moving over my shoulders and down to my collarbone, where I feel the shock of cold metal against my chest. He clasps what I assume to be a necklace before his hands leave me once more. "Turn around and open your eyes," he says, emotion thickly laced within the words.

My eyes flutter open, and as I begin to turn around, my gaze catches on the way the leaves are falling from the branches all around us, like a twilight-colored rain. The last remnants of the golden sun before it sets paint the garden with a luminous glow, the scene almost too beautiful to be real. Cool air caresses my skin, the rattling of the leaves and gentle babbling of the small stream heightening the storybook effect of this place.

Nox grabs one of my hands and draws my attention to him, to where he's kneeling on one knee in front of me. "What are you doing?" I ask, smiling at the way his eyes brighten.

"The first gift is hanging around your neck," he says, gesturing with his chin to the necklace. I reach up with my free hand to find a small oval-shaped gold locket layered above the dragon pendant. "In a normal situation, I might have asked permission from your father or guardian first. I might have gone to them and explained all the ways I planned to love you, to keep you safe, to *worship* you as we grow old together. I might have tried to sell myself as someone honorable and worthy of your love in return." My heart beats more harshly, the sound reverberating over my bones, while my magic uncoils from within me and rises to attention. "But our story is not a *normal* one. My love for you is anything *but* normal. While, for you, I will always be honorable, I know that being worthy enough to call myself yours is something I will have to strive for every single day."

"Nox," I whisper, pressure building behind my eyes as I fully take in his position. As the words he's speaking to me finally settle between my ears. "What are you doing?"

There's a slight tremble to his hand, and his inhale is shaky, but when he speaks, his voice—deep and captivating—rings out into the air with conviction. "When I first met you, I thought there was only one kind of love—the kind you would die for. I had been ready and willing to die—and do far worse—because I loved my family and my kingdom. That's what I remember thinking about as a little boy here in this garden, how true love meant you would be willing to sacrifice every part of yourself to protect it. Then I met you, and you showed me what it was to have a love worth *living* for."

I release the locket from my grasp and reach up to wipe away the tears that have gathered in my eyes. Nox's thumb gently brushes the back of my hand in reassuring sweeps as his other hand dives into his pocket and reemerges with a small black velvet box. Everything stills—each tree and flower and star flickering to life in the dusk sky pauses to watch.

"I never realized how deprived I was until I tasted your lips—your skin. I never knew home could be a person and not a place until the day you told me you loved me for the first time. I now understand with absolute certainty that if I were to follow the threads of my soul through the immeasurable distance of time and space—in this lifetime and every other—I would always find yours entangled within them at the end. Our love is not a beginning or an end but an *infinite* constant."

I can picture it, those golden threads of our essence always linked to one another. A subconscious pull towards each other that felt both fated by an unknown force *and* chosen by us. Because I had chosen him. Over and over again. And he had chosen me. *Maybe there is some truth to Elora's fated souls theory.*

"I am yours, Rhea. Every inch of my body and beat of my heart. Every bit of my magic and ounce of my love. Every one of my thoughts and every part of my soul. They all belong to you. *I* belong wholly to you. That is my second gift, and in return, all I ask is that you let me love you the way I know I was made to."

Nox lets go of my hand to reach up and wipe away my falling tears—though more rapidly replace them. Then he curls his fingers around the locket, lifting it from my chest and into the space between us.

"This was the closest I could get to including them in this moment. I hope that it's okay."

I trace the outside of the locket, a drangyea flower with its small bunched-up petals engraved into the metal. With a small *click*, the locket opens, and inside, the details so perfectly meticulous, are portraits of Alexi and Bella.

The world narrows down to this singular moment as my watery eyes meet his. As I take in the love and longing and vulnerability that are laid bare within them. How could it feel as though every heartache and bruise laid upon me—upon my very soul—was not a stain marking my history but a steppingstone towards something better? How is it possible to stare at this man—my friend, my savior, my lover, my *home*—and know that the amount of love I feel for him is more than one lifetime should allow? How could I be so impossibly and unbearably *lucky*?

With his cheeks growing flushed, Nox carefully opens the box to reveal a gold ring tucked into black silk. At its center is an elegant large teardrop-shaped diamond. The gemstone is so clear that it appears kaleidoscopic, reflecting a rainbow of colors in the waning sun's light. Flanking each side of the diamond and trailing down the band are three small light pink diamonds clustered together, followed by a pair of light green ones. Leaves made of gold extend from the band to hold them all in place, like a beautiful twisting vine.

There is no breath deep enough, no way to settle the urgent beating of my heart or the way my magic rises to tangle with Nox's. There is only one word to answer the impending question that dangles from his lips.

"Rhea Maxwell, will you marry—"

"Yes!" I interrupt, falling to my knees on the soft grass while nodding my head as tears cut through my smile. "Yes, I will marry you."

Nox hardly has a moment to slip the ring onto my finger before I seal my lips over his. Our kiss is hungry and devouring, my arms wrapping around his neck as

I draw him in closer. Never enough—there will *never be enough* of this. Of him. *Of us*. The presence of his magic lessens, my own burrowing back within me in a flash of warm light that feels like an acceptance of this moment. Only then do I separate from him, bringing my hand back up between us to examine the ring more closely.

"It's so very beautiful," I marvel.

Nox smiles as he stands, helping me up as well before he pockets the little velvet box. "The diamond was taken from a ring that has been passed down from queen to queen for millennia."

My eyes widen, an incredulous noise slipping out. "You just *took* from another ring? One that was worn by a past queen of Void Magic?"

"Of course. You are to be the next queen, Rhea. You have every right to wear this ring." He grasps my hand, lifting it up higher as he inspects it. "The diamonds on the sides are in the shape of a blooming flower. I thought it might represent our beginning." His cheeks hint at a slight blush while his eyes lift to mine. "Our love blossomed much like a flower breaking through the earth in the spring. It was slow but deliberate. A surprise *yet* as natural as the seasons."

"You are—"

"Insanely creative?" he teases, kissing the tip of my nose before moving on to my cheeks.

"Maybe just the insane part." I laugh when he nips at my bottom lip before pressing a featherlight kiss there.

"Come on. We still have one more place to visit before we make our entrance at the ball."

After righting our crowns and clothes—with a locket hanging from my neck containing pictures of my family and the most incredible symbol of our love adorning my finger—we begin our walk to a temple covered in flowers.

Chapter Seventy-Five

RHEA

Sadryn and Alexandria greet us near the entrance to the public gardens an hour later, in a side corridor tucked away from prying eyes.

"We are so incredibly happy for you both," Alexandria expresses, a sheen covering her dark gray eyes. Dressed in a stunning strapless gown of burgundy with gold accents along the hem, the queen of the Mage Kingdom exudes regal beauty, her hair left loose and cascading down her shoulders. Sadryn stands next to her, his button-up shirt matching Nox's navy-colored one and undone to reveal his chest and a little more. Silver threading in a swirling pattern travels up his sleeves and to his shoulders, while his black trousers tuck into pristine black boots. On their heads are crowns of gold, both larger and with more gems than Nox's but with the same celestial theme etched into the metal.

Alexandria reaches her hand out for mine, her own silver ring glinting on her finger. "We will plan it however you like. Whatever you want and need, you will have."

A wedding. I would be planning a *wedding*. The thought is almost enough to distract me from what had happened earlier at the temple. I swallow down the bit of uncertainty that threatens to extinguish my excitement. Tonight, I will have a good time with my friends. I will celebrate my engagement and spend every moment in blissful happiness. Everything else can be dealt with in the morning.

"Thank you, Your Majesty."

Alexandria playfully scoffs while Sadryn chuckles next to her. "There are no more formalities, my dear, even out here. Use whatever name for us that you feel comfortable with, but know that for Alexandria and me, you are well and truly our daughter." Sadryn claps Nox on the shoulder, a shared look of pride bouncing between him and Alexandria as she squeezes my hand one more time before letting go. The king and queen head off through the open double doors, the herald announcing their arrival to the cheers of their people.

"Does he have any idea what those words mean to me?" I whisper to Nox as I struggle to keep myself composed. *Their daughter.* Not by birth. Not by force. But because they *want* me to be. Because they see how much their son loves me. Nox's fingers glide down my arm lightly, just a sensation of touch before he holds my hand in his.

"I know he speaks the truth. They love you, Rhea." And then, as if he heard my inner thoughts, he adds, "Not because you are mine, but because you are *you*." He brings my hand to his lips, gently kissing the back of it. "Are you ready?"

I blow out a breath and roll my shoulders back. Am I ready to announce to the kingdom that we are betrothed? To deal with whatever the council may say and have every eye on me—friend and foe? *No.* I am decidedly *not* ready. But I am not alone either. I had told Nox that it felt like we were on an island, and until the day came that I didn't have to hide a single part of me, I imagined I would always feel that way. However, with the support of my friends and my new family, with *him*, perhaps an island wasn't the worst place to be.

No longer am I a woman who cowers in fear or in despair. As Selene had once told me, those parts of my life are woven into me like the threads of a tapestry. Up close, the history of it all is tangled and ravaging—hard to let go of. But maybe that is the point. I am not meant to let those things go as if the hurts haven't happened to me at all. I can choose to use them as a point of comparison, a way for me to see just how far I've come. How far I've grown and evolved and *bloomed*. When I step back and look at my life as a whole, at the tapestry that makes up who Rhea Maxwell is, I find that I quite like what I see now. Someone who is strong and determined and unafraid to love. Someone who is far from perfect but who is no longer letting life pass her by. I see someone I am proud to be.

So turning to Nox, his hand tightly holding mine, I reach up onto my toes and plant a kiss on his cheek before facing forward, my lips curving into a triumphant smile.

"Congratulations!" Elora shouts as she pulls me into a hug. I had heard the word over and over again as I passed the partygoers on my way to her.

When the herald announced our arrival, when he shouted our titles "His Highness, Prince Nox Daxel, and his betrothed, Lady Rhea Selene," the gardens had erupted into nothing short of pandemonium. There were cheers and clapping, and though it all became a discordant ringing in my ear, I had looked around to find mostly happy smiles. Only when my gaze met a few of the council members' did I remember that there would be an important few who were *not* thrilled. They were apparently so distraught over the news that they called an emergency council meeting, pulling Nox and Sadryn back into the palace.

"Thank you, Elora. I'm sorry that we didn't have the chance to tell you before everyone else found out."

Elora snorts and waves her hand in front of her face. "As long as I get to be included when it's time for you to start planning, then all is forgiven," she jokes with a wink. Linking my arm with hers, she guides me around the ball where we have polite conversation with some of the patrons before we end up next to the refreshments table.

"This is not as daunting as I thought it might be," I tell her, taking a bite of a small leaf-shaped cookie, the flavors of apple and cinnamon dancing along my tongue.

"Good. The engagement announcement certainly became an invitation to start a conversation with you." Her eyes sparkle under the light of the spelled flames as she takes a sip of her drink. She wasn't wrong. I lost count of how many people cooed or gasped at the sight of my ring. I didn't mind it, however, feeling just as excited to show it off as they were to glimpse it. We finish our fare, and Elora begins to lead us to the dance floor.

"There are some gentlemen over there eyeing us as if they are in need of dance partners." Tugging on my hand, she drags me through the crowd, the strangers' eyes meeting mine and offering warm smiles and dips of their chins. And then her words register, and I stumble over myself as I try to slow down her pace.

"I don't know if I should dance with anyone else?"

"What? Why?" she shouts over her shoulder. "Don't tell me the prince is so possessive over you that he won't let you dance with another man!" Her eyes narrow as she looks around, presumably for Nox.

"No! It's not that. I don't know what the protocol is. Am I *allowed* to?"

Elora stops a few feet short of the men whose eyes have grown wider and turns to face me. "Rhea, you are going to be *queen* of the Mage Kingdom. More importantly, only *you* decide what you want to do. No one else. If you want to dance, dance. If you don't, don't. No one makes those decisions but *you*. And if Nox doesn't agree... Well, prince or not, he'll get a piece of my mind." I huff out a laugh, tucking a strand of hair behind my ear. Elora reaches over and straightens my diadem before placing her hands on my shoulders. "Do you want to dance?"

"I do."

"Then let's dance." We step in front of two men, both bowing before us and holding out their arms to lead us to the dance floor. The man I'm paired up with smiles warmly before placing a hand gently at my side, his touch like a ghost's with how it almost hovers over me. His other hand clasps mine, eyes bouncing between my face and the sparkling crown that sits on my head. I hadn't thought it possible, but he might be even more nervous than I am.

"I have to warn you. I'm not very good at this dance. I only learned it this week," I confess.

That does earn me a chuckle, his stiff posture loosening slightly. "That's alright. I always seem to forget the steps when it's time for me to move."

I laugh as the music from the band crescendos, the sound somehow floating in the air all around us. Whether it's magic or just a testament to the band's talent, the beat is easy to hear as we waltz across the makeshift dance floor set in the center of the garden. I learn that the man's name is Ian and that he is a carpenter that lives in a small town on the outskirts of Galdr.

"I'm sad to say I haven't explored much outside of the capital. I will have to remedy that." While Galdr is beautiful and has everything one might need within a few short miles, there is still so much I haven't seen. But time... I have so much of it now. At least until we ascend the throne. Swallowing, I force that thought away to deal with tomorrow and finish the waltz with Ian, who bows again once it's over. Then a familiar face takes his place.

"May I have this dance?" Evren, the man who works at the tavern, asks as he extends a hand out to me. I nod, and we move into the same waltz as before.

"Are you having a good time?" I ask him, his curly blond hair bouncing with each step.

"I am. Congratulations on the engagement." Our conversation turns into small talk, his eyes darting behind me for most of it. I follow to see what is snagging his attention and am surprised to find Elora dancing with Daje. She laughs at something he says before he twirls her. Looking back at Evren, my curious gaze catches his, and he clears his throat, twirling me as well.

"You should ask her to dance next," I say, watching as his eyes move to Elora again.

A blush stains his fair skin as he lifts a shoulder. "We'll see."

We chat more about his work at the tavern, how his dream is to one day open his own, before the song ends and I all but push him towards Elora. Smiling, I watch as he extends his hand out to her after she and Daje part, a curl falling over his forehead that she reaches to brush out of the way with easy familiarity.

Walking to the edge of the dance floor, I search the crowd for a head of wavy black hair. I can feel him here, my magic like a magnet sensing its match somewhere within the revelry—those invisible strings pulling taut. As minutes pass and my search proves fruitless, I take a step towards the palace in hopes that perhaps Nox is with his parents near their dais, but I am halted when a man steps in front of me.

"Would you like to dance?" He extends a broad hand out towards me, his shaved dark blond hair glistening when the orbs of the spelled flames floating on a magical wind pass above us. They set the features of his face aglow, and I have to pinch my lips together to stop a gasp of surprise from escaping. *Arin*. My throat constricts as I cast my gaze out towards the palace again in search of Nox.

"I was actually—"

"Just one dance, My Lady," he insists.

I stare at his proffered hand, my own growing clammy with unease. When Arin lifts a brow in question, I tentatively place my hand in his and let him guide me to the middle of the dance floor. A cold shiver breaks out over my skin when his fingers touch my side though he's not doing anything different than any other dancer before him.

"You look absolutely beautiful." The words are a low purr in his throat.

I murmur a "thank you" that garners a deep chuckle from him. Avoiding his gaze, I stare at the gold threading of his green jacket instead. It covers the lapels and cuffs of his sleeves, the embroidered design made to look like stars.

"I'm surprised Daxel left you alone out here."

"I can take care of myself." My voice wavers as I speak, an unfortunate thing to happen when paired with that statement. A laugh trickles from him again while his hand flexes, tightening a little more around my waist. The sound of the band begins to get drowned out by the heavy thumping of my heart.

"You know, I was curious when I first saw you on his lap in that tavern. He's so clearly enamored by you that it's honestly pathetic. Whatever you've done to him, I commend you for it."

Embarrassment brightens my chest and neck when his gaze draws down my body and a lecherous smile curls his thin lips. "I haven't *done* anything—"

Arin leans down until his cheek is pressed against my own. He holds me in place against him, ignoring the way my body struggles to get away. "He has a weakness now. I can't wait to see how I can exploit it."

I grit my teeth together against the onslaught of magic boiling beneath my skin. He quickly straightens and then releases me, making a mockery of a bow before he disappears into the crowd. Music comes rushing back in as sweat beads on the nape of my neck. Minutes tick by while I stand there, trying to calm my quickly beating heart.

"Rhea!" Cass calls out to me, motioning with his hand for me to come join him. I glance back to confirm that Elora is still dancing with Evren before making my way over to Cass, my hands shaking at my sides at the memory of Arin's hands on my body and words in my ear.

"Wow," he drawls, giving me a bright smile. "You look like a queen already. Congratulations, by the way."

"Thank you. Look at you!"

Cass throws his arms out to his sides and spins in a circle, showcasing how handsome he looks. Dressed in a brocade-style overcoat in dark plum and silver, Cass' stark blond hair—left unbound and hanging just past his shoulders—shines brightly against it. Trousers of the same deep purple and black boots add to his lavish look.

"And—because I know you're wondering—yes, there are several daggers hidden on my body," he adds, winking at a nearby man who happens to overhear him. I cover my laugh with the back of my hand, my mood improving as Cass holds his own out to me. "I would be honored to dance with the future queen."

Playfully rolling my eyes, I squeal when he whisks me into a surprise twirl, drawing several inquisitive looks from the people around us. "Thanks for that," I grumble when I'm facing him again.

"If it's any consolation, they are mostly staring at *me*."

I laugh again, Cass leading us in a different waltz—one I can't remember all the steps to. He makes up for my lack of refined dancing with smooth movements of his own.

"Did you know Nox was going to propose?" I ask, once more searching the crowd for him.

"I knew it was coming soon, but I didn't know he was going to do it today," he answers. "He's still inside talking with the council."

I can't help my defeated sigh. "They *hate* me."

"Maybe not *hate*." At the look on my face, he snorts. "They're all just paranoid about change, I think." He shrugs, and it's on the tip of my tongue to tell him where Nox and I had gone earlier and how that had the potential to change things even more, but I bite it back down. *Tomorrow.*

Daje and Haylee pass by us as they dance together, the former giving me a warm smile. A grin tips Haylee's lips as well, her hair curled to frame her face while a sapphire gown made of thin silk adorns her body. She catches my gaze and holds it briefly before the dance moves them farther away.

The ending of the song builds, the string and percussion instruments growing louder as they reach the song's peak. The thumping of my heart matches pace, Cass and I finding a rhythm that ends when he dips me in time to the song stopping. There's a tug on my chest, a nudge of recognition, and when Cass pulls me back up, Nox is there, his hands behind his back and an easy smile carved on his perfect face.

"Can I cut in?" he asks, his voice a soothing balm that caresses my entire body.

Cass nods, but before he releases me, I pull him into a hug. I can't say why, other than that I'm grateful for his presence and friendship. He wraps his arms around me, carefully placing his hands over the cape that runs down the back of my dress before squeezing me tightly. We separate, and he flags down one of the palace aides carrying a tray of drinks. Plucking up a glass flute, he gives Nox a two-fingered salute before spinning on his heel and walking farther into the crowd.

"I'm sorry I've been gone for so long," Nox murmurs against my temple as I slide my hand into his.

"Trouble with the council?" I ask, letting him guide us into a slower dance.

"We were correct with our assumptions of how they would react. My parents are still speaking with them now."

"Cass said that maybe they are afraid of change." I let my insecurity bleed into my words, let Nox see the way I frown as I say them.

"If that's the case, then they are fools. Fearing change will only lead to the inevitability of it."

He turns me so that my back rests against his chest, our hips swaying in tandem to the slower pace of the current song. I tilt my head, looking up at the woven branches of the trees—the canopy thick enough in this spot that seeing the night sky is impossible. I know it's there though, the moon and stars calling to me just as the sun does.

"Do you remember the night we danced in the tower?"

Nox spins me to face him again, one hand holding mine between us and his other resting on my lower back. It's so easy to get lost in the way his eyes swallow me whole, how everything about him draws me in.

"Of course. It was my first time dancing, after all."

"I almost kissed you that night," he confesses, leaning in until our noses touch. "I could tell you wanted me to; it was written all over your beautiful face. The way your chest was rising and falling. How you were pushing yourself closer to me. *Gods*, did I want to. I had dreamed about how you would taste—how your body might feel in my hands—for so long. But when the moment came, I hesitated. Then we were interrupted, and it felt like it wasn't the right time anymore. I do wonder sometimes how things might have changed if we had kissed then."

"There is nothing stopping you from kissing me *now*."

Heat sparks in his eyes as his lips hover over mine. "If I kiss you now, I may not be able to stop," he says quietly, his breath warm against my lips. "Because, I need to be honest, the moment you said yes to marrying me, I have thought of only one thing."

"And what is that?" I ask, my fingers digging into the muscles of his shoulder.

"Getting you alone and slowly undressing you from this *very* distracting dress so that you're only wearing my ring." He pauses, his gaze flicking up to my head before dropping back down. "I suppose the crown can stay on too."

"So we *shouldn't* kiss, then?" I ask, pushing myself closer to him as desire pools low in my belly.

"Not unless you're fine with leaving this party."

The song ends, the slow beat replaced by one that's more lively. New couples form and begin dancing around where Nox and I now stand. My hand roams from his shoulder to his collarbone, tracing the indent there until I reach the unbuttoned portion of his shirt.

"And if I asked *you* to keep your crown on, would you?"

He makes a noise deep in his throat, his voice dark and seductive when he answers, "I'll do *whatever* you want me to."

"I want you," I rasp against his mouth, and that's all it takes before he's guiding me through the crowd and back towards the palace.

Chapter Seventy-Six

Rhea

Our steps are clumsy as we stumble into his room, Nox kicking the door closed behind him before bringing his lips to mine.

"Do you have *any* idea how you torture me?" he asks. My mouth opens to his as our tongues tangle together and his hands roam over my backside and squeeze, lifting me so that my legs can wrap around him. His arousal is a hard line between us, and I gasp desperately for air when he grazes his teeth down my neck while his fingers dig harder into my flesh. "I think about you all fucking day. Your eyes and your smile and your laugh. The way you taste. How perfect you feel around my cock. *All day, Rhea.* It's godsdamn torture to be apart from you."

My nails scour the back of his neck, words beyond me as I writhe against his body. The sitting room is alight with the glow of spelled flames, but Nox leads us right to the bedroom, somehow having the grace to give me all of his attention without crashing us into any furniture. Closing the bedroom door, he spins and gently presses my back against it, his hands sliding up my sides as his calloused skin scrapes against mine. My heart soars in my chest, desire a cresting wave building within me with every sweep of his tongue in my mouth and brush of his thumbs on the undersides of my breasts.

"This dress could bring an entire kingdom to their knees for you," he says against me, teasing me when one hand moves lower and his fingers apply pressure to the apex of my thighs.

"I don't need an entire kingdom on their knees for me. Only you."

He growls, and then we're moving lower as Nox does just that. Shadows slide against the floor and up my body, their icy touch contrasting the fire burning within me. Midnight tendrils wrap around my waist and upper thighs and help to hold me in place when Nox places each of my legs over his shoulders, moving the fabric of my dress off to the side while he positions his mouth right at my center.

"Is this okay?" he asks, one hand pressing low on my stomach while he inhales deeply, as his star-flecked gaze peers up into mine beneath his dark waves and the crown resting upon them. "Prince of Stars" Selene had called him, and I find that I whole-heartedly agree.

"Yes." I wrap a hand around the back of his head, my other pressing firmly into the door behind me. He lays his tongue flat against me, my arousal seeping through my undergarments and making him groan in approval.

"So wet—you are always *so wet* and ready for me."

I nod, the ache to have his mouth and that wicked tongue drawing along my flesh, to feel him deep inside of me, nearly unbearable.

"*Nox,*" I gasp, attempting to press closer to him while simultaneously yielding to his control. The pressure of his tongue darting out, only to be blocked by the thin layer of fabric again coils my desire more tightly.

His laugh is dark and rough at my frustrated whimper as he skims his fingers down the inside of one of my thighs, taunting me while his icy shadows dance along my skin in juxtaposition. "Do you need more, Sunshine? Do you want me to fuck you with my tongue?"

"Gods, your mouth."

"Answer the question, love. Tell me what you want me to do."

My chest heaves, and I'm beyond the point of caring about anything but relieving the way my entire body is strung tight. "Put your mouth on me, Nox. *Please.*"

The last word isn't fully out before his finger hooks around my undergarment and yanks it to the side. And then it's bliss—pure, unfiltered *bliss*—as his tongue dives into me. His appreciative groan vibrates over every inch of my body while he devours me like I'm his only sustenance. I clench my teeth together, panting through them as his tongue coaxes me closer and closer towards release. He slows his pace down, practically drinking from me one moment and then speeding up so that my toes curl from sensation the next. Two fingers slide inside of me, Nox pumping them in time to the bucking of my hips as he sucks on that sensitive bundle of nerves.

I have to remember to breathe while I struggle to grip onto any part of him that I can. The back of my head hits the door when my orgasm unravels, sending a tingling sensation over my entire body. His name echoes out into the room on my cries. I expect him to slow down, to pause and come up for air, but he doesn't. He continues wringing me of pleasure until one orgasm moves into the next and I'm practically hoarse from crying out. Only when my lips are numb and body pliant does he slowly take my shaking legs off of his shoulders, sending the shadows back and catching me as I lean forward, unable to keep myself standing.

"So perfect," he whispers at my chest before standing, carrying me with him towards the bed. I nuzzle my face into his neck, melting with each lungful of our mingled scents. "Do you think you can stand now?" he asks, a purely satisfied lilt to his voice.

I smile as he slides me down his body, my hands already reaching for his jacket and helping it off of him. "I suppose that ego of yours feels fairly good after that?" I ask, then work on the buttons of his shirt.

"Lots of things feel good after that," he murmurs, making me laugh. Tucking my hair behind my ears, he kisses me like it's an exploration of my mouth, an infusion of my taste on his tongue. I'm breathless when he pulls back and drops his shirt to the floor before his hands cup my face. "I would do anything for you. *Anything.* You know that, right?"

I nod, my hands gripping his wrists before I slide them down his arms and to his chest. He leans in to kiss me again, but I push him towards the bed. "Lay back," I order quietly, my heart beating in a riotous chorus within me.

Nox's lids grow heavy, his eyes dark pools of desire and feverish heat, but he follows my command. Scooting back on the bed until he's propped up by his elbows, he puts his naked upper body on display before me. I carefully remove his crown and set it on the nightstand, snorting when Nox makes a noise of protest when I also remove my own, and then I crawl between his legs—one hand gripping the comforter by his hip while my other reaches out to tip his chin up to me.

"Nox Flynn Daxel, you will be my husband," I state, my voice wavering on the last word. *Husband.* Bound to each other forever. A part of me wishes we could get married tonight, if only so I could continue to call him that.

His eyes bounce between mine while a smile, soft and sweet, lifts his lips. "Yes."

I kiss those lips before moving to his jaw. "Because you are mine," I say against the warmth of his skin, trailing my mouth until I'm right over his heart. "Mine." His breath stutters, and his hand reaches up to weave through my hair. I continue down his hard chest and farther, lingering over the carved muscles of his stomach. "Mine," I whisper again. A deep noise rumbles from his throat when my fingers find the buttons of his trousers.

"Rhea," he murmurs in a low warning when I free his cock from his pants. Stroking slowly, I savor every inch of heat that my palm envelops, my gaze locked on his. His fingers curl into my hair more tightly when I lower down until my lips are hovering right over his tip, his arousal already leaking from it.

"All *mine.*" And then I claim him, licking a long line down the side of his cock and back up again, smiling against him when he lets out a string of curses as his taste floods my mouth.

"*Fucking gods above.*" Nox's neck arches, his head falling back as the fingers of his free hand dig into the comforter and his chest rises and falls as if he's engaged in battle.

I take my time, exploring how his body reacts to my movements, how his groans change with every slight alteration I make to my speed or how deeply I take him into my mouth. Swirling my tongue over him, I swallow him down, *yearning* for more. I had been too nervous to try this with him before—afraid that my inexperience would ruin the moment, even if Nox promised otherwise.

I have no such fear now.

His stomach muscles contract, another curse slipping from between his lips when he abruptly sits up and reaches for me, pulling me off of him and, instead, placing me in his lap.

"What are you doing?" I ask, heat flaring in my cheeks as I drag the back of my hand over my mouth. "Was it— Did you not like that?" *Oh gods, what if I was doing it wrong?*

Nox's eyes are feral, his hands cradling the sides of my face as he brings our foreheads together. "I was about five seconds away from coming in your mouth, Sunshine."

"So?"

He barks out a surprised laugh, kissing me soundly and stealing every bit of my uncertainty from me. His hands work deftly to slide the top of my dress down until my chest is bared to him. Leaning in, he whispers against my skin. "I'm so fucking in love with you, and I'm not ready for this night to be over. Not yet. I haven't—"

Pounding on the door to the sitting room silences Nox as we both tense.

"Who could that be?" I ask, looking back behind me towards the sound.

"Just ignore it. I don't care who's there." He gently guides my face back around, kissing me again before sliding his hands down my back. I moan as I arch against him, his mouth moving down my body and closing over one of my nipples as I spear my fingers into his hair to hold him there. Melting under his touch, I rock my hips over his length, both of us desperate to shed these final layers. But the knocking persists, this time on the door that leads into this room. Onyx shadows race across the floor and barricade the door, some of them slipping underneath it.

"You have five seconds to explain why the *fuck* you're in my room!" Nox shouts, holding me tightly against him.

"I wouldn't be here if it wasn't important." My gaze clashes with his at Cass's voice. "Send your shadows back. I won't go past this door." Nox releases his hold on his magic but keeps his arms wound tightly around me.

"What's wrong?"

There's a considerable pause, as if Cass is weighing his words before he answers. "There's something you need to see."

We both dress back in our ball attire, leaving our crowns off as we open the door to find Cass pacing in the sitting room.

"What is it?" Nox asks, but Cass shakes his head, opening the door to let us pass before closing it behind him.

"A woman was found wandering the beach by a patrol. She was disheveled and disoriented, mumbling about needing to speak with the king. The guards brought her here, and as they were making their way to a secure room, the woman collapsed."

Anxiety slithers up my spine and my hand grips Nox's more tightly as we make our way down the stairs, passing a stoic Barron as we do.

"Is she alright?" I ask.

Cass' response is slow to come. "She's dead."

When we reach the bottom, more guards than I have ever seen before form a barricade blocking the foyer from being accessed by anyone coming from the gardens or the main entrance. A wall of blue magic further separates the guards from something—*someone*—in the space they are surrounding.

Sadryn stands next to Councilman Hadrik and another guard, the latter's hand resting firmly on the hilt of his sword. When the king spots us coming towards him, he holds up a hand, and Nox halts our steps. Murmuring something to the councilman, he makes his way around the somber guards, the room silent other than the occasional shuffling of feet.

Nox is the first to speak to his father. "What's going on?"

Sadryn's eyes move to me, his gaze softening as he leans in. "Are you sure you want to see this?"

I nod my head as Nox drops his voice lower and asks again, "What is it?"

Sadryn motions for us to follow him with a tilt of his head. He guides us past the guards to where the blue magic is glowing. With a flick of his hand, the magic disappears, and lying before us, frail body pale against the black stone floors, is a woman with brown hair. She looks emaciated, as if the life has been sucked out of her, leaving her just skin and bone. Her cheeks are concave, her pale lips dried out, but there's something about her that strikes me as familiar.

My gaze draws over her outfit, the gray color of her dress and the white apron that covers it. Though dirty and tattered, the clothing too plucks at a memory. There's a note attached to the front of her apron, and I lean in a little closer to read what it says.

I warned you.

Ice churns in my blood as my eyes move to Nox's. Anger and sadness war within them, and his hand trembles with restraint in mine. I look back to the woman, at her delicate fingers and finer features. The truth strikes me, a jagged dagger sawing at my bones, as I gasp. "Tienne?"

Nox nods, having already come to that conclusion.

"Oh my gods, why does she look like that?" Had my uncle been starving her? Or was this the consequence for crossing over the Spell?

"The Cruel Death," Nox says somberly, his free hand running through his hair as Cass and Sadryn give him their attention. "This is what someone who has the Cruel Death looks like."

Sadryn nods, but his jaw ticks, disquiet tightening his features. "She crossed over the Spell and somehow made her way here. Given her condition, it seems nearly impossible that she didn't have help." Nox stiffens as he takes a step closer to me.

The guards break their formation, dark leather armor with metal details gleaming under the massive tiered chandelier above, to let Councilman Kallin and Daje through. The former stares down at Tienne, a flash of what looks like disgust quickly rolling over his face before he schools it back to neutral. I grit my teeth together when he meets my gaze with a dismissive glance.

Looking down at Tienne again, my heart drops into my stomach as I remember just how kind she was to me. How she and Erica brought me dresses and gave me all those gifts. How they helped make sure I had my satchel and boots. Was Erica alright? Why had Tienne crossed the Spell? How had she known to come *here*?

Nox releases my hand to wrap his arms around me, his body blocking Tienne from my view as he moves us a few steps away.

"He did this because of me," I say only loud enough for him to hear, conscious of the ears around us. Tears burn my eyes when I meet Nox's concerned gaze. "He—" A held back sob ravages my throat, and Nox places a hand on the back of my head and holds me to his chest.

"Not just you, Sunshine. I knew Tienne too," he rasps, leaning his head down to speak closer to my ear. "She knew I was visiting you, I think. She somehow seemed to know everything that was happening in the palace. I wonder if King Dolian found out just how involved she was."

"Perhaps the lady should not be here," Councilman Kallin says, assuming me to be distraught merely over the sight of a dead body. Nox's magic thickens around us, his head snapping over his shoulder as he snarls at Daje's father.

"Son, I think we should act as if the threat is still active. We still don't know how this woman managed to cross the Spell in her condition. How she ended up so close to the palace. It might be a good idea for you both to go back upstairs and—"

"We should have a meeting about this, Your Majesty. One His Highness needs to be a part of. If this is a targeted attack against him for his time spent in the

Mortal Kingdom, then we will need a thorough breakdown of everything he knows," Councilman Kallin implores. Daje adjusts awkwardly on his feet as he stares down at Tienne's body.

The king nods, if a bit reluctantly, and Nox sighs as he turns to Cass. "Can you bring Rhea up to our room and stay with her?"

Cass, having gotten his sword somehow, reaches out a hand for me, but Sadryn intercepts him by stepping between us. "Until we have the full details of what happened, I want you to be protected at all times."

"I can take care of myself just fine. Cass is more useful with Rhea."

But Sadryn shakes his head, a protective gleam shining in his eyes. He may rule this kingdom, but he's a parent first and foremost. This has shaken him enough that he wants to make sure Nox is properly guarded, and I can't say that I blame him. I feel Nox's magic rising while his father gives him a warning look.

"I'll go with her." All eyes move to Daje as he carefully walks around Tienne's body until he's at our side. "If it's alright, I'll stay with her until you're finished."

"Daje, you have your own duties—"

"I don't have anything to do here that can't be done by any one of these available guards," he states, interrupting his father. He holds Nox's gaze, determination set in his features. "I'd be happy to help."

I reach up and lay my palm against Nox's cheek, directing his attention to me. "That is a good idea. Let Daje help." *He has already proven that he is loyal in protecting me,* goes unspoken between us.

Nox turns to kiss my palm as his brows draw together. "I will be up as soon as I'm done here." He leans in, his lips grazing my ear gently, and whispers, "This is not your fault, Rhea."

My eyes close as I force air into my lungs. I logically *know* that it isn't, yet the guilt... It still has a home within me. Like some long-buried weed that keeps coming back no matter how many times I try to squash it.

"I love you."

"I love you," I promise, kissing him lightly on his lips before pulling back.

Nox turns to Daje, absolute resolve coloring his voice. "Wait until you hear from me."

Daje nods, and with one last glance at me, Nox joins his father, the two men conversing in quiet voices with Cass and Sadryn's guard at their side. I don't look at Councilman Kallin as we turn to leave, not in the mood to see his scowl turned on me. Daje and I climb the stairs back up to the third floor where Barron is waiting on the landing.

"Barron, can I ask a favor of you?"

"Of course, My Lady," he answers, his hands clasping behind his back as his brows draw low over his eyes.

"If you hear any updates, will you let us know? I have a feeling Prince Nox will be busy for the rest of the night, and I know it's ridiculous given who he is, but I'm worried for him." I'm only now realizing that I never offered Nox the same assurance he gave me—that this wasn't *his* fault either. That we are both trapped within the snare of an absolute monster.

Barron's expression eases into understanding. "Of course. I'll check in periodically, but try not to worry, Lady Rhea. I believe that His Highness is strong enough to protect the entire kingdom if it truly came down to it."

I offer him a grateful smile before leading Daje down the quiet hall, the hairs on the back of my neck rising. We enter the sitting room, the space now seeming too dim with Daje in it. I carefully wrap my magic around one of the spelled flames and carry a part of it over to another sconce, repeating the motion twice more so the entire sitting room glows in golden light. I remember when I first saw Nox do such a thing, how incredible it was to watch him control the flames and wonder if I might ever be able to do the same.

"You've gotten good at controlling your magic," Daje muses, taking a seat on the navy-colored couch and stretching his legs out in front of him.

I shrug, sitting in the leather armchair across from him as I grab the fabric of the cape attached to my dress and wrap it around myself. "It's not anything any of you guys can't do." My gaze travels over his own fancy attire, his tunic one of emerald green with bronze-colored detailing. Dark brown trousers and black dress shoes accentuate his look. "Sorry you got pulled from the festivities," I offer with a slight wince.

Daje laughs, running a hand over the top of his head. "It's alright. I was all but done for the evening anyway when..." He tapers off, gesturing to the door. *When Tienne's body was found.* I grip on to the cape more tightly. "You knew her?"

I contemplate not answering or even lying, but he already knows I'm from the Mortal Kingdom. Any other details pale in comparison to that larger secret. "I did. She was very kind to me after something tragic happened." My throat tightens at the onslaught of memories—at the sights and sounds and smells embedded within them. "I worry who else might suffer because I'm here."

"Why does he want you back so badly? Is he aware that you have magic?"

"He wasn't until the night Nox helped me escape," I answer, avoiding his other question. But Daje quirks a brow, clearly wanting me to explain further. My lips flutter before I turn my gaze to one of the spelled flames. "He was in love with my mother, and she married his brother instead. He thinks I'm his second chance, I guess."

"Second chance at what?" It's my turn to give him an arch look, hoping that I don't actually have to say the words out loud. Daje's brows furrow together for a moment before they rise impossibly high on his forehead, making a sullen chuckle leave me. "But you're his—"

"Niece. Yes, I know."

"Gods," he says in shock, disgust layered in there as well. "And Nox saved you?"

"He did." Understanding seems to dawn within him as he turns his body so he's lying back on the couch, his arms crossed under his head. I draw my legs up onto the chair, settling further into it. "I'm happy he apologized to you," I divulge as a yawn escapes me.

Daje shakes his head, his gaze on the ceiling above us. "He didn't have to. I know what it feels like—that need to do everything you can to protect someone." He opens his mouth like he wants to say more but then shuts it, letting the words hang there.

I decide not to pry about his relationship with Bahira, instead reaching out for one of the pieces of smooth dragon stone Nox left on the table. The circular, flat black rock is cool in my hand, and I rotate it over and over again as nervous energy makes me fidget in the silence.

I blow out a shaky breath as the memories of Tienne unravel in my mind. The pressure grows behind my eyes, and I squeeze them shut to keep the moisture locked there. Another kind person caught in the destruction of my uncle's sick plans. *I warned you.* I knew he was capable of such atrocities, but a part of me hoped he might eventually realize that his attempts were futile. It feels selfish to think that way—to minimize the deaths of Immie and Tienne to nothing more than just endeavors enacted by King Dolian to try and get me back to the Mortal Kingdom.

"I'm sure it won't be much longer," he says, noting my anxiousness without even looking at me. Quiet falls once again as we wait for word from Nox.

Chapter Seventy-Seven

RHEA

D AJE HAS TAKEN TO pacing the room, his boots tapping on the wooden floor in front of the door. He almost fell asleep on the couch, which would have been fine with me, but he insisted on staying awake until Nox was here.

"Any idea how long we've been up here?" I ask, my magic glowing white in my hand as I infuse it into another stone. Though my thoughts are scattered between Nox and Tienne and what else my uncle may be doing, I try to focus enough intention into my magic to make the stone stay glowing.

"At least an hour, maybe closer to ninety minutes." He continues pacing, his arms crossed over his chest.

I watch as my magic seeps into the dragon stone, making it glow gray at its center. When a few seconds pass and the rock stays lit, I set it on the table next to small piles of rocks I've practiced with. The small release both eases my magic and focuses my mind so that I don't sink too deeply into my guilt. My ring catches a glint of the light, and I stare at the back of my hand, smiling while I recall the words Nox said and how I had never felt so inexplicably happy and *whole* because of them.

"I didn't congratulate you guys yet, I'm sorry." I look up to find Daje gazing at my hand—at the ring—a look I can't quite interpret pinching his features.

"It's alright. And thank you." The right corner of his mouth lifts, his dark blue eyes glistening under the spelled flame. We both jump when someone pounds on the door three times.

"Gods," he growls, reaching for the door handle before looking back at me, "Maybe you should go to the other side of the room. Just in case." His magic, yellow like the light of the sun, flares brightly in one of his palms, his signature growing stronger in the air as I follow his instructions. With a nod, Daje faces the door again and opens it slowly, his magic at the ready to attack. But he quickly relaxes as he steps to the side to reveal one of the guards standing there.

"You both have been summoned to the beach by Prince Nox," the guard says as he rocks back on his heels, his long pin-straight black hair hanging over his shoulders.

"The beach?" Daje asks as I walk forward and stand next to him.

The guard nods, his arms crossing over his chest. "His Highness went to investigate it with a small patrol. He needs your confirmation on whatever it is they've found," he says, looking at me.

"You don't know what it is?" I question.

The guard shrugs. "I don't need to. I was just sent to relay the message."

"We should go, then, right?" I ask Daje, already taking a step out of the room. Daje hesitates, an argument with himself warring in his mind, before he eventually nods and shuts the door behind us. "I wonder what it is they could have found." Was it evidence of how she ended up here? It seemed impossible for her to randomly appear on the beach exactly where the capital of the Mage Kingdom is. We follow the guard to the end of the hallway, the landing empty.

"Maybe they found something of hers? Or perhaps another person?" Daje offers grimly, and I have to force my steps not to falter.

We reach the bottom of the stairs and walk into the foyer, all evidence of Tienne's body thankfully gone. The guard stops, turning to face us as the light of the spelled flames casts shadows over his high cheekbones. "I need to meet with the council and let them know you are on your way," he says, waiting for Daje's nod before spinning on his heel and walking towards the council room.

"Let's not assume the worst," Daje offers, turning to me with a sympathetic twist of his lips.

I swallow down my nerves, my heart racing as we make our way to the tall carved double doors. *Please don't let it be another person hurt in my name.* A familiar feeling pulls on my chest, the sensation strong enough that I stop walking.

"What is it?"

"It's Nox," I tell him, my brows drawing together. At his look of confusion, I add, "I can feel his magic."

"You can sense his signature? From all the way at the beach?" he asks, no shortage of astonishment in his voice.

"I guess so," I respond, stepping back as Daje opens one of the double doors, nodding in greeting to the four guards standing on the other side. Holding his arm out to me, we descend the white stone steps onto the pathway that leads to the beach.

The night air is crisp, a slight chill making me draw the fabric of my cape closer together while we quicken our steps, the music from the ball still playing despite the late hour. The rest of the path leading deeper into the forest is nearly pitch black, only a few pools of silvery light from above stream past the thickly woven canopies.

"How late will the ball go?" I ask, goosebumps rising on my arms.

"Either until all the guests have gone home or until sunrise, usually the latter in my experience."

"And yet you were ready to call it an early night?" The fallen leaves around us rustle, some crunching beneath our steps.

He snorts, exhaling loudly. "I suppose that this year is just different."

It's too dark to make out his expression, but needing the distraction, I ask, "Because Bahira isn't here?"

"I—" Daje's grunt halts his response, his body falling to the ground with a horrifying thump as he goes silent.

"Daje?" I call out, bringing my magic to my palm. I take a step forward, turning my hand down and illuminating the path. My gasp is loud as I fall to my knees beside him. Fresh blood gleams as it drips down from his temple and over his unconscious face, pooling onto the stone path and fallen leaves. *Oh gods.* My heart drops at the sight of his injury, and I call up more of my magic, laying a hand on his temple when a searing crack sounds in my ears and pain bursts to life at the back of my head.

I go crashing to the ground on my side, the harsh beating of my heart drowning out the muffled voices that surround me. The presence of magic thickens the air, the sensation lying atop me as if I'm being buried beneath it. Panic and adrenaline shoot like lightning through my veins, begging me to move as I groan, but my *head*—

"I need her ring. *Get it!*" someone hisses, their words slurring in my mind as I try to push myself up, my palms slipping on fallen leaves. A hand, warm against the cool night air, grabs mine, pulling my engagement ring from my finger in one quick movement.

"No," I murmur, the ringing in my ears deafening but my heartbeat even louder as I feel it pulse at the back of my head. I call on my magic, but the moment it rises up my torso, it falters under the feeling of a barricade tightening around my body. *They're suppressing my magic with their own.*

Terror courses through me as I realize that between the pendant and my expulsion magic earlier, I'm too weak to fight them off. I gasp for breath, white lights flaring behind my eyelids while I struggle to reach for my power. For *anything* to help me. *Nox!* I mentally scream out, hoping that whatever connection we have through our magic might be enough for him to feel that I'm in pain. That I *need* him.

"*Gods*, her magic is strong," someone shouts, and I feel that restriction around me falter.

I quickly call up whatever I can—healing and shadows alike. Warm power gathers on one palm as I blindly attempt to lift it in front of me.

"She's still fucking awake! Hit her again, and let's *go*." *That voice...*

"What about Daje?"

"Leave him!"

I manage to open a single lid, bright and colorful magic of different colors holding me in place as it blinds me against the backdrop of the dark forest. Steps rattle the stone beneath me, moving closer until another hit jerks my body, and I succumb to utter darkness.

Chapter Seventy-Eight

KAI

My fingernails dig into the armrests of my throne while I sit and wait for Tua's arrival.

It has been two days since the rebel attack, much of that time spent cleaning up the aftermath and dealing with the fallout. I have kept Jahlee and Bahira in my rooms for the entirety of it, while I figured out what to do after learning of Tua's betrayal. Each of those days, the latter had refused to speak with me beyond what was necessary.

It is better this way, to keep her at arm's length now in preparation for when she's an ocean away later. It is better, yet she still consumes every one of my fucking thoughts like a thunderstorm that won't break. I learned the truth of who she was, and each day since, I find it harder to remind myself why it matters that she lied. Eventually, I do—past insecurities feed into the present, and Bahira's lies become Tua's, and those become my father's, and on and on until I find myself angry with her once again. But the cycle ultimately stalls—usually the moment I step foot into my rooms at the end of the day and see her curled on the couch with a book on her lap, still recovering from her injuries.

My power pushes at me to shift, my neck straining as a slight haze covers my eyes. It had taken every ounce of control not to kill Tua the moment I saw him after I learned what he had orchestrated. What he had done behind my back, yes, but more importantly, what he had done to *her*. Instead, I was forced to listen to his lies with a straight face. I was left in awe of how he held my gaze, his dark brown eyes steadfast, and lied with the ease of talking about the weather.

And he had been doing it my entire life.

At least he never brought up Kane. Haloa volunteered to let my cousin stay with him until I could confront his father. We had thankfully found his daughter unharmed and under the care of neighbors. Both families will be receiving a large stipend from the Crown for the foreseeable future.

Bahira had said that Tua knew of something my father orchestrated while my mother was pregnant with me. In the only conversation that lasted longer than a minute, she had relayed everything she could remember about what he said regarding my parents. Despite her obvious anger towards me and the sadness she tried and failed to hide, there was something eager that lit her gray eyes when she talked of what Tua told her. Of the blood and magic connection he hinted at. Something told me that, even if I didn't want her to, she'd go digging for more.

I had visited my rooms one final time before coming to the throne room, to make sure Jahlee and Bahira stayed put until this was over, only to find it empty. I know better than to assume that either female is incapable of taking care of themselves, but it doesn't make my ire at them being gone disappear. Maybe Jahlee helped Bahira sneak out to board a ship heading towards the Mage Kingdom. Or perhaps they just needed time away from the palace—from *me*.

I recall the way Bahira's face broke when she told me of her deceit. How her eyes begged for a forgiveness I wasn't ready to give her then. One that she doesn't seem to want now. Bahira had been an anomaly in my life since the moment she punched me in the face. Never once had anyone left me both furious and heated in a single interaction, and this female had done so in nearly every moment we spent together.

Both of the wooden doors to the throne room open, and my uncle strides in, flanked by two guards who shut the door behind them and take up posts on either side.

"Everything alright, Uncle?" I ask him, sending all thoughts of Bahira back behind my mental armor as I stare Tua down from my throne.

"One can never be too safe," he answers, clasping his hands behind him. "You've summoned me, Your Majesty?"

Standing, I fold my arms over my chest, letting my power glow in my eyes. "Did you think that I would not discover your treachery?"

His delayed response is the only giveaway to his surprise. "Ah. So the princess lives," he surmises, giving me a small smile. I had kept him too busy to visit the dungeon attached to my father's rooms in the wake of the attack—also assigning males from Honna that I could trust to patrol the second floor so that no rebels could slip past.

"She does. Though I can't say the same for your son." When Tua doesn't react to the fake news about Kane, I take a single step down the dais and add, "Neither can it be said of the two rebels who laid their hands on her."

Tua's power flares in his eyes, his canines elongating as he drops any pretense of civility. "I will *kill* her for this."

Primal rage bleeds into my every cell as I glower at him. She is *mine* to protect. Even if she wants nothing more to do with me. *She is mine.*

"She's already on a ship heading home," I lie. Or maybe it is the truth. If it is the only way to keep her safe, then despite the nausea roiling through me, I hope she really is on a ship.

He growls low in his throat, his animal thrashing beneath the surface.

"How does it feel to know that a female bested you?"

"I suppose I could ask the same question of you," he snarls, taking a single step towards me. I eye the guards, their curled lips and combative positions relaying their allegiance to Tua. "You thought that she would hold the key to solving our blight, that she could fix your idiotic *legacy*. Everyone now sees you for what you really are, Nephew. A failure. Unworthy and undeserving of that throne behind you. When I rule—"

"No," I interrupt, descending the rest of the steps as I bring my power up to right beneath my skin. The urge to shift is overwhelming, setting my veins on fire and nearly choking me of breath. "You will rule *nothing*, Uncle. Except maybe a small cell in the *true* dungeons while I figure out what to do with you."

His laugh is callous as he rolls his shoulders back. "You can't just make me *disappear*. I've already cemented myself as a fixture of stability with the nobles. I've got the support of nearly the entire panel of advisors—nearly the entire *kingdom*! While you have *nothing* and *no one*."

"Now, that's not entirely true."

Her voice makes my stomach clench as I look to the side door that leads to the gardens. Leaning against the doorframe, looking amusingly bored as she examines her nails on one hand and idly swings her spear from side to side in the other, is Bahira. I want to strangle her for still being here. I want to claim her mouth for the same. Burning fucking hell, I just want *her*.

Looking up, her eyes snare mine, and for a brief moment, I think she might want the same. But then she shifts her gaze to Tua. "Surprise."

Tua growls again as Bahira steps away from the door and allows it to close loudly behind her.

"I have a bone to pick with you," she taunts, the leaf-shaped tip of her spear pointing in his direction. "Or, if I'm lucky, perhaps I'll get to carve out a few from your cold, dead body."

"Killing you will be easier than breathing," he hisses. I let a rumbling sound of warning slip out, and Tua's taunting smile grows more so. "And I'm going to make him watch as I do it." His shift happens quickly, a flash of blinding green light glows, and then he's two steps closer to Bahira. Her reaction time is slower than usual, reminding me that she still hasn't healed from her injuries. Wounds that *he* allowed her to get.

In a flash of golden light, I shift into my preferred animal—a wolf—and leap to intercept him, landing in a crouch as we snarl at each other. In his lion form, his head is as large as Bahira's torso. His paws are tipped in blade-sharp claws, and his elongated canines glint in the sunlight. In another burst of golden light, I shift again, this time becoming a lion to match Tua's.

His eyes narrow as he snarls at me, letting out a massive roar and making my hackles rise as we leap towards each other. It's easy work, dodging his incoming strike and then pouncing on his body, my own razor-sharp teeth sinking into his neck as I pin him to the ground. My predatory instincts drive my motions as I clamp my jaw more tightly, Tua jerking and trying to scrabble for purchase to get away from me.

I'm so focused on him that I've forgotten about the other two guards, and it isn't until Bahira shouts out in pain that I realize my mistake. She is trapped between them, her hold on her spear too limp to be effective. Her injuries haven't had enough time to heal, and that truth washes over the both of us at the same time. Her eyes widen as she blocks a punch from one of the guards, the other moving behind her too quickly.

There isn't a moment to think rationally, not as rage narrows my vision. Keeping Tua alive had been my goal, but it is no longer my priority. *She is. Only her.* I bite down harder, letting my canines travel farther into his jugular, before jerking sharply, twisting until there is a snapping sound that rings out into the air. I release his limp body and bolt towards Bahira, tackling one of the guards from behind. He lets out a wail, but my claws dig deeply into his back before I fling him across the room and into the wall.

"Stay there," the other guard shouts, his arm tight around Bahira's neck as he drags her backward—her spear left discarded on the floor. I growl as I lower into a crouch, my eyes pinned on hers. She doesn't look panicked, not even as she fails to get out of his hold. "Shift back, or I'll kill her." He brandishes a small dagger, the metal glinting as the tip digs into her skin.

"You're going to regret that, asshole," Bahira wheezes, her neck straining as her nails dig into his forearms.

I shift back to my mortal form, coming up to stand as I stalk closer to him. "She's right. I might have made your death quick before, but you'll suffer now for touching her." His shaking hand nicks her skin, adding a wound to the many she's accrued here under my watch. *I will not allow another.* With the guard's gaze fully on me, he isn't able to stop the blow to his ribs from Bahira's elbow. He yelps as he leans to the side, his knife no longer indenting her skin.

I charge towards them as she spins, sending a knee up into his gut. He hunches over, and the knife flies from his hands before mine are there, squeezing on either side of his head. My vision grows hazy as the aggression of my animal rises like a sickly wave. Every other sound in the room fizzles away until there is only his desperate wailing as I slowly, *methodically*, crush his skull. The bone begins to shift beneath my hands as he frantically claws at my wrists. I can't stop—I don't *want to*—not when I know that he would have killed Bahira. *She is mine. She is mine. She is mine.* His skull gives out, my hands moving closer together as true silence blankets the throne room. I drop his corpse and watch as blood and brain matter shoot out in all directions from the impact.

Feeling the weight of her gaze, I take my time turning to Bahira, forcing each inhale through my nose to last longer than the one before it. The fog of my magic is nearly gone from my vision when I face her fully. I don't expect fear, Bahira's a female not possessing a fragile constitution, but I do wonder if she'll be repulsed by what I've done. When my eyes meet hers, however, I'm reminded again of just how wrong I've been about her. She watches me with curiosity, her body leaning towards me while I take a step in her direction. Tentatively, I move to cup the side of her face. Right over the small smattering of freckles there, their pattern a constellation I've tried to burn into my memory too many times to count. But my hand is covered in gore, so I let it fall back to my side.

"Are you alright?" I ask, grinding my teeth at the blood dripping from the small cut on her neck. She lets loose a slow breath, her gray eyes as beautiful—as deadly—as any tropical storm. I've come to realize that I am merely the rock which her powerful waves crash against, both of us slowly carving away at the other's shields. Who could I be with a female like her at my side? What could I accomplish with the motivation of someone who knows what it's like to stand tall in the face of adversity? How can I look at her, knowing that her iron will sharpens my own, and call her anything less than extraordinary? Anything other than *mine*?

"I've been better," she answers, her hand going to where my gaze is drawn. The tips of her fingers get stained with blood, but she pays it no mind while she studies me. "Are *you* okay?"

No. I may never be again—not when I know what it feels like to have you. To then lose you. I can't say that, not as I watch her trace over my face and body with concerned eyes. Not after the things I said at the hot spring. So I settle on repeating, "I've been better."

She snorts, gesturing with her clean hand to my body. "You're also naked." The words are breathless, and I nearly groan at the slight shade of pink that stains her cheeks.

One of the doors to the throne room is thrown open, the wood smacking against the wall as Jahlee comes stumbling in. Her hands rest on her knees while her chest heaves with quick breaths before she observes the carnage left in the room. She rights herself, placing her hands on her hips and glares at us. "Damn it, you guys! I wanted to get at least *one* rebel!"

"Then you should have gotten here quicker," Bahira purrs.

"I'm sorry, I was busy gathering our *allies*."

Bahira gives my sister a small smile before she clears her throat, carefully taking a step away from me. "And? How did it go?"

Jahlee eyes the space between Bahira and I suspiciously before tossing her hair over her shoulder and letting out a low whistle. "See for yourself."

A slow trickle of people enter, males and females, faces I recognize from their work in the palace or in shops and businesses in the surrounding villages. As more and more of my people filter in, their eyes holding none of the contempt I've grown used to seeing in so many others, I struggle to keep my emotions tame. I feel Bahira's eyes on me and send a glance her way, my brow raised in question.

"You are still *naked*," she whispers.

"It's not a big deal to not be clothed here, Princess. We lose them when we shift."

She mumbles under her breath, something like, "not everyone needs to see your massive dick," and alters her stance so that she is partially blocking me from the crowd now gathered.

Jahlee snorts, then outright laughs when Bahira threatens her with her spear. "Anyone have some trousers the king can borrow?" Jahlee shouts, the crowd hushing as every pair of eyes lands on me.

Fucking Jahlee. A male steps forward and hands my sister some clothing. Where he got them from, I don't know, but I slip the pants on and fold my arms over my chest, catching Bahira's lingering glance before she notices me watching and looks away.

Jahlee steps right in front of me, her smile as wide as physically possible before she gestures to the shifters now filed into the room. "These people believe you—believe *in* you. You were made to lead this kingdom, Kai. For better or for worse, *you* were chosen. While I know this won't be an easy task, it's a start."

I had fought against the idea that being king was anything more than an unfortunate necessity. I hadn't expected that list of things I cared about to grow beyond Jahlee—certainly not to include the subjects I reluctantly ruled over. While a kingdom of chaos and ashes seems unavoidable now, my hope is that the cost of fixing everything I turned a blind eye to will be low.

"You should address the crowd," Bahira suggests, keeping her eyes straight ahead.

"She's right," Jahlee chimes in.

I clench my jaw at the thought, wondering if perhaps abdicating to Kane would not be as awful as I had previously thought. Clearing my throat, I give an awkward as fuck speech about trying to rebuild the kingdom into something better. Based on the way Jahlee bites back a laugh every time our eyes meet, I assume it didn't exactly motivate anyone.

The next hour passes quickly as I help clean the throne room and assign new roles and jobs to the shifters present. Haloa and Kane show up, the former eager for the opportunity to be one of my personal guards and the latter ignoring me. In a gesture that I hope quells the whispers of him behind his back, I shake his hand and announce that he can keep his position, seeing as he had nothing to do with the rebels. I make sure to squeeze his hand harder than necessary, reminding him that at any moment I will end him if he proves to be anything less than useful.

I leave briefly to go to my rooms to shower and change into my own clothing, returning to join Jahlee and Bahira in the now cleared out throne room. The corner of my lips rises when I see the way Bahira is lounging on my throne nonchalantly.

"Don't move on my account," I drawl, walking to the edge of the dais and gazing up at her.

"I wasn't planning on it," she coos back, and it almost feels like our fight never happened.

"You look good in it."

Her gaze widens as it holds mine before she averts it and stands, stepping away from the very thing she looked so comfortable—so *right*—in. "You need a plan of how you're going to approach this with the rebels. How you'll share what happened with Tua to the kingdom."

I nod, watching as Jahlee steps up to Bahira and throws an arm around her shoulders. "I say we do a clean sweep. Just throw everyone out into the training yard and start questioning them there."

"You won't make any friends doing that."

Jahlee's smile is deviously cunning. "No, but it'll piss off a bunch of the nobles. And that will bring *me* joy."

"We start with who we know to be our allies and go from there," I tell her, fighting off a chuckle at the way her face drops. "It's going to take time, Jahlee."

Haloa opens one of the doors and pokes his head in, gaze searching until he finds mine. "Your Majesty, there is someone who has just arrived from the docks. She is requesting an immediate audience with you."

I run my hand down my face, exhaustion lingering like a fine mist over me. "Did she give a name or what she wants?"

"All she said is that her name is Siyala."

Jahlee's gasp echoes out, my own inhale quick as I narrow my eyes at Haloa. "You're sure?"

"Yes, Your Majesty."

"Send her in."

Haloa nods at my command and leaves so quickly that he doesn't shut the door.

My sister turns towards me, her brows raised high on her forehead. "You don't think—" She swallows, shaking her head as Bahira looks between us. "It's been over four years."

This could just be mere coincidence because the odds that my cousin has miraculously appeared after four years are astronomically low. Though the same could be said of the way she seemed to completely disappear from the island in the first place.

"She's our cousin, Iolana's daughter," I tell a bewildered Bahira while keeping my focus on the doors as the sound of approaching footsteps sends a foreign feeling of hope simmering in my veins.

"The one you said went missing?" she asks. I nod my head again, almost smirking at her murmured "fuck" under her breath.

A cloaked female walks into the throne room, her boots—worn and too big—clomping on the wooden floorboards. My breath sticks in my chest when she reaches up and pulls the hood back. She's obviously older than when I last saw her, a woman now instead of a teen. But as Siyala's amber eyes meet mine, her rare white hair bright against her golden tanned skin, there is no denying that it's my cousin staring back at me.

Siyala's attention moves from me to Bahira, a quizzical look contorting her face, before going to Jahlee, a smile finally breaking her serious façade. "Hello, cousins," she rasps.

"You're not dead!" Jahlee blurts out, Bahira and I both snapping our heads towards her. "Where have you been? I swear, if this has all been some elaborate prank, I'm going—"

"I've been in the Mortal Kingdom."

Jahlee's words choke off, my own voice lost as I tilt my head to the side. Silence once more descends upon the room until Bahira breaks it. "You are a shifter, yes?"

Siyala nods.

I take in her travel-worn clothes, her too big boots and cloak, and the large satchel she has crossed over her torso. "You snuck out of the kingdom and onto a boat," I guess.

"Yes, and I promise, we will catch up on where I've been and everything that goes with that, but there is something more important that we need to discuss."

"More important than where you've been for the past four years?" Jahlee shouts, her arms splaying out at her sides.

"Yes," Siyala answers, and though her eyes burn with the details of that story, she blinks it away as she focuses her attention on me. "I need you to contact the Mage Kingdom."

"Why?" Bahira asks as she studies my cousin.

Rubbing my fingers over my jaw, I gesture for Siyala to continue.

She plays with the hem of her cloak, her eyes watering as she heaves out a weighted sigh. "There is a woman there named Rhea. I believe her to be in danger, and I'd like to warn her."

My gaze hones in on Bahira, her brown skin paling as she stares at Siyala. She sucks in a quick inhale before she says, "Tell us everything you know."

Chapter Seventy-Nine

ARIA

THE OCEAN IS CALM, the rippling over the surface caused by our propulsion of the small boat the only sound for miles. Under the light of the silver moon and the shimmering blanket of stars, an uneasy feeling squeezes my gut.

With our mother leading the way, my sisters and I gather around the vessel, each with a hand on it. Allegra and Sade take one side, Dyanna and Lyre on the other, and I push at the back, my gaze stuck on the woman lying unconscious within. Her blonde hair is fanned out all around her, some of it tainted with what smells like blood. We're already a few miles off of the shore, my mother insisting we hurry though no one seems poised to chase after us.

My talons scrape along the old wood of the boat, drawing Lyre's curious gaze from my right. She gives me a quick shake of her head. I don't know if she's relaying that I shouldn't say anything or if it's more that she doesn't know what our mother's plan is, but it doesn't stop the way that I can practically taste my discomfort. We've stolen something—*someone*—her body passed carelessly to Allegra and Sade just outside of the Spell by a man and woman. Only my mother seems to know who she is, her dark eyes glowing with untampered glee under the moon's light.

"Who is she?" Sade asks into the silence, making me jolt in surprise.

"You *dare* question our mother?" Allegra retorts, flashing her teeth.

Sade rolls her orange eyes, then pins them on our oldest sister. "I believe I'm questioning *who* the knocked-out woman we are transporting over the water is."

Allegra growls but is interrupted by our mother. "If what the king has told me about her magic is true, then she will prove to be quite useful to our cause."

"The king?" I ask at the same time Sade says, "Then why are we giving her to him?" At both of our questions, the queen turns around, swimming backwards without breaking her pace to glare at us.

"Yes, *the king* of the Mortal Realm," she answers, making Lyre's eyes nearly bulge out of their sockets. Dyanna looks on with vague interest. "He has made a bargain for our help. He now owes me *two* different debts."

"And if he tries to betray us as his ancestors once did?" Allegra asks, disbelief flashing for a second on her stern face before she hides it beneath a sneer.

Our mother chuckles, turning back around with fluid elegance. In the distance, an orange light glows against the black of the night sky.

"He knows not what he has. What she *is*," my mother mocks. "I've given him an inkling, enough of the truth that he'll want more answers, and *that* will inevitably lead him back to me. However, even if he tries to betray me, I've learned from our past mistakes. This woman will only ever be a siren's call away."

She says nothing more as we swim closer to the light. The creaking of a ship at anchor, the waves gently rocking it, sends a shiver down my spine. It reminds me of the noises the fallen fae ship had made before the carnage that had taken Mashaka's life.

We slow our pace, the small boat jostling the motionless woman. *What have they done to her?* Magic builds at the base of my throat, the urge to use it confusing me. There is no threat, yet as I stare at her, something makes my instincts go on alert.

Male voices sound, and the orange light morphs into a flickering flame attached to a torch, the person holding it going to the side of the ship as we approach. Ropes are thrown down over a roaring lion that is engraved on the side of the vessel. Allegra and Sade tie them to metal loops attached to the small boat we push, my mother heaving herself up onto its edge as she transforms into her mortal form. Her purple braids release into a cascade of curls, the longest ones dripping down past her hips. Her iridescent scales become flush against her dark skin though still shimmer under the moonlight. She holds a hand out to Allegra, who reaches into the satchel she is carrying and drops something into my mother's waiting hand—the sound of familiar metal clinking making my chest squeeze tightly.

"Wait here," she commands, shooting a deadly glare at Allegra when she attempts to speak up in protest.

My sister bows her head, swimming back from the ship to where the rest of us wait. With a shout from above, my mother and the woman are hoisted up, slowly rising along the body of the ship until they are brought over and onto the deck.

"I don't like this," Allegra seethes as she shakes her head. "We can't trust *any* of them."

My other sisters stay silent, their eyes vigilantly trained on the deck where our mother disappeared. Time moves slowly, the sound of voices dwindles until it's just one male and one female. Then my mother's frame appears as she steps up onto the ship's railing. She stops and says something over her shoulder to the man standing there, his golden crown glinting in the light of the torch he holds, before she dives into the water. We sink beneath the surface to join her.

"What happened?" Allegra asks, Sade joining her at our mother's side.

Queen Amari, already back in her siren form, smiles victoriously. She holds her hand out in front of her, and glinting on her middle finger is a gold ring, a pearl nestled at its center.

"That's one of the rings," I whisper, my stomach bottoming out.

She cocks her head to the side, her smile growing sharper as she examines the pearl-topped ring on her finger. "It is, and one I am saving for another. Soon, daughters, we will rule over land *and* sea."

Chapter Eighty

NOX

"You think this is retaliation for Nox taking the magical item from their kingdom?" Councilman Hadrik asks from his place to the right of my father, his dark eyes shrewd as he looks at Councilman Kallin across the table. "How would they even know that Nox was there undercover?"

I drown out whoever responds, my attention instead on the image of Tienne in my mind. How had that bastard realized that she helped Rhea? Tienne didn't strike me as a woman easily convinced to spill secrets. It had taken nearly the entirety of my four years spent in the guard for her to not look at me like I was a fox in a henhouse, though her instincts *had* been correct. Still, when I took over for Alexi, she threatened to kill me herself if I so much as looked at Rhea the wrong way. How she would know, I had no clue, but I believed she would do it. To see her looking so devoid of the life she had been full of mere months ago was like getting punched in the gut. It knocked the air from my lungs. And Rhea—

"Nox." I glance up from my hands, meeting my father's tired gaze. "Councilman Kallin has asked you a question."

I nearly retort back that I'm fucking *tired* of this bastard asking me questions. It seems that he is never satisfied with my work as heir apparent or my relationship with Rhea. Each question I answer only leads to a handful more. Like pulling on a loose string, I feel myself slowly unraveling under his prattling.

"Apologies for interrupting your thoughts, Your Highness," he addresses me, his hands clasped on the table before him. "I was simply asking if the letter attached to the woman's body had any meaning to you."

"It doesn't." I know I don't exactly sound convincing, but I've reached a place where I simply don't care. The day this council questioned Rhea to the point of causing her anguish is the day they lost any semblance of respect that I had for them. I had offered four years of my life up to ensure our kingdom's safety. Many more before that as they tested me and my magic. I had done everything they asked of me up until I chose to be with Rhea. Though my father insists that they have no say in our relationship, the council seems to be finding ways to do just that. And if our previous heated discussion after Rhea and I announced our engagement is any *further* indication of their feelings towards her, then I can't imagine that telling them the full truth of who she is will fare any better.

Not that she's the magic we felt from so far away or that she's the rightful heir to the Mortal Kingdom, but that she is the true ruler of *this* one. Rhea Maxwell, my betrothed, my love, my *light*, bled into the Cauldron of Vires earlier tonight. Her single drop of blood produced a flame that was leagues taller than my own, its color a rich *cobalt blue*. She isn't just a powerful mage; she is *the* most powerful mage. A queen *in spite* of her impending marriage to me. Over two hundred years had passed since the last queen of Void Magic ruled this realm, and yet there she was, found a kingdom away. Her magic calling out to mine like it was searching for me.

"Should we reach out to the Mortal Kingdom? Ask King Dolian outright what message he's trying to send?" Councilman Borris questions, gesturing to the Mirror that is placed at the back of the room.

Shit. I do send a look of concern to my father this time. My magic abruptly tugs at my gut with enough force that I brace my hands on the table. The sensation of fear trickles into me, making my heart beat out of rhythm. As quickly as it comes, the feeling dissipates.

"No. We wait for him to reach out to us. We do nothing to encourage his antics. We have nothing that he could possibly want that will result in anything good." At the unrelenting tone in my father's voice, Borris submits, his back hitting the chair as he slides his beady gaze my way.

"There is *another* matter that we have not finished discussing."

I cut the councilman a sharp glance, my fingers twitching as my magic pulses in my palm. "I think we've exhausted that conversation."

"Nox is right. Though, for reasons neither I nor Alexandria can comprehend, the council does not approve of Rhea, it ultimately is Nox's choice." The silence rings out heavily in the air, my father's words a dagger hitting its mark. The corner of my mouth kicks up in triumph, ready to finally put this behind me. *Behind us.* Yet, as I scan the room, the expressions of the council before me aren't ones of dejected acceptance. Only Hadrik looks as confused as I feel, a line forming between his brows.

"Unfortunately, Your Majesty, I'm afraid you're mistaken." Kallin's words are spoken firmly, his gaze holding mine while he answers my father.

"Councilman Kallin, what might I be mistaken about?"

"While we may not have a choice in who His Highness chooses as a *potential* future queen, we *do* have the power to veto that choice if necessary." My lips flatten as my eyes narrow.

"Councilman, you were here the day I requested that, moving forward, any heir to the throne retain the power to choose who they want to wed, free of any interference from this very council," my father recounts, his fingers interlacing on the table in front of him. "Don't tell me that your age has begun to catch up with you?" My father's teasing chuckle is met with alarming silence, causing him and Hadrik to share a concerned look. I observe each of the council members, one councilwoman still absent from the table.

"I remember the day quite well, Your Majesty. It was the day after your coronation, and you came to this very room with gusto, ready to take charge and lead this kingdom with great honor," Kallin says, his eyes glazing over as he reminisces. The memory fades, and the councilman tips his chin down to his chest, shadows from the chandelier above slashing a harsh line over his face. "You requested that this council consider a proposal to change how things had been done. That is what we did. We changed the fact that we could not force a betrothal. That an heir apparent be allowed to choose whomever it is they want to court. What we did *not* change, however, is our ability to deny that choice."

My body stills as my magic pulsates beneath my skin, power scraping along my bones and begging for release.

"What do you *mean*?" Hadrik asks, his palms planting on the table. "I was not aware of such a stipulation to the law."

Kallin clears his throat, leaning forward until his eyes move from the shadows. "Do remember, Hadrik, that you did not join this council until a year after His Majesty's coronation, and we have not had an opportunity to *test* it as we do now." Hadrik frowns, his eyes bouncing from my father to Kallin. "As the law is written, the council is allowed to bring the choice of partner given to them by the immediate heir to a vote. Should we find that partner acceptable, we shall vote that way. However, should we find anything about them unfit to rule by the side of the crown prince or princess, then our vote has the power to stop the betrothal."

"Kallin," my father rumbles, his voice laden with his power, "that is *not* what I proposed when I brought the idea forward."

"Oh, but it is. You asked that the council not interfere with the choice of partner prior to *betrothal*. Yet there were no specifics given at the time regarding removing the power of the council once a betrothal *has* occurred. With Nox proposing to Lady Rhea and her acceptance, it is now up to this council to vote whether or not a marriage between them will be beneficial for the kingdom as its future rulers."

"She will become queen either way!" I snap, anger flashing hot in my chest. But, no, I cannot tell them who Rhea is yet. Not until she is next to me to reveal that secret herself. The thought of her causes goosebumps to break out over my skin, my magic flaring wildly in my gut and tugging me nearly out of my chair. I glance towards the door, expecting to see Rhea on the threshold, her long blonde hair hanging over her shoulders as she peeks her head in. The tugging sensation persists, but the door remains closed.

"Not unless this council allows it," Borris chimes in, his smug face spurring the anger lancing through me into an inferno. "That *girl* will not be queen—"

It takes no effort to surround him with a wisp of shadow pulled from somewhere in the room. It binds around his irritating mouth and throat, as if it were a vine growing around the trunk of a tree. I tighten it as he sputters for air, the sound of chairs scraping back from the table louder than his wheezing.

"Nox," my father calls, coming to stand beside me. Ignoring him, I keep rooted in my seat, my hands flat on the table as I let the shadow acting as a gag stiffen into something harsher. "That's enough, Nox."

"No, it isn't," I muse, the other murmurs of protest around me becoming a buzzing noise in my ears. "I have grown weary of this council meddling in something that is *none* of their business, regardless of what the law says." My gaze snares Councilman Kallin, his stare unforgiving as he regards me. "I do not care what the council has to say on the matter, as Rhea will be my queen whether you vote it so or not. I will also not tolerate someone *repeatedly* disrespecting my future wife."

"Nox, this is not the way." It's the desperation in my father's voice that finally draws my attention to him. His eyes shine with something that looks a lot like fucking remorse, and I *refuse* to let that be the case.

By our laws as well, Rhea is the *true* ruler of the Mage Kingdom, so this posturing of council power is fucking pointless. My magic still isn't satisfied with the stunned silence around the table and the watery choking noises coming from the man clawing at the equivalent of a stone rope curled around his neck.

"If you will not accept Rhea as your queen, then you do not accept *me* as your king either." I let the ultimatum slice into the room, every pair of eyes I meet widening over my words.

The door to the council room is thrown open, all heads pivoting to look at who's entered. Once more, I expect it to be Rhea, my magic still on edge as it calls out to hers—searching for her signature in the palace. It isn't until Daje staggers into the room, blood both fresh and dried leaking down his cheek and neck, that I let Councilman Borris go. I bolt upright from my chair, the wooden furniture toppling over with the force of my movement. Daje's eyes widen as they land on me, his pupils swallowing the dark blue of his irises while he stumbles forward.

I cast my magic out wider, searching for her, not quite comprehending exactly why he is here and she isn't. Assuming that perhaps she is in the hall, waiting for me. Only with her magic can my own act like a beacon—looking for that impression of *her*. I brush past a bewildered Daje and step out into the hall, searching it for a pair of bright green eyes. Revelry from the ball trickles in from outside, the attendees blissfully unaware of what horror occurred here earlier tonight. Finding the hallway empty, I try to tame my heart as it threatens to burst from my chest. *She is safe.*

Yelling draws my attention back to the council room, Daje's voice rising amongst the others. Stepping back in, I ignore the way my blood ices over as I study Daje once more. He cradles the side of his head, his hands shaking as he turns away from where he's talking with his father to face me fully. I stalk another step towards him.

"Where is she?" I ask, my voice grating along my throat. The entire room falls into silence, my father the only one brave enough to move towards me when Daje just shakes his head. "Where the *fuck* is she?"

"I'm sorry, we were attacked and—"

My magic rumbles, bursting from me in an explosion of purple and black. I'm before Daje faster than he or anyone else can stop, my hands gripping his tunic.

"Nox!" my father shouts, but I seal Daje and I in a cocoon of menacing shadows pulled from every corner.

"What are you talking about?" I rasp. Tears—fucking *tears*—build in his eyes as his mouth opens and closes without sound. I realize that the fear emanating from him isn't because of me but because of what happened. I scan his face again, noting the bruise that's beginning to form at his temple. "Daje, *where is Rhea?*"

"I'm sorry," he wheezes, a tear falling to his cheek. My power builds, my body barely holding it in, as I watch him struggle to find the right words. "I don't know. I was knocked out, but I didn't see by who, and when I woke, she was gone."

Gone?

"No," I growl, the shield around us flickering as the control on my magic frays, an electric feeling sizzling up my spine while my vision flickers and all color seeps from it for just a flash. Daje's eyes close, his body trembling, but I shake him until he's forced to open them again, making him look at me.

"I'm sorry, Nox. I tried—I tried looking for her when I woke up. We were told you wanted us down at the beach. But then something happened. I don't— *I can't remember.*" He holds his hand out to me, the locket I gave Rhea broken in half, its chain missing. "I found this on the ground next to me when I—"

He doesn't finish his sentence before I lose my grasp on my magic. It bursts from me, shadows and purple light racing in every direction. The council room shakes, colorful shields going up around each council member as they try to protect themselves from the onslaught.

Rage and fear send more of my magic flowing out of me in a way that it never has before. Trapped in a vortex of it, Daje and I watch as the council room crumbles around us and the other mages duck under the table—their faces red while they scream. It happens in slow motion, the Mirror toppling over and slamming into the ground, sending a cascade of reflective glass scattering over the floor as the ancient magic that fuels it releases like a gust of sparkling wind.

My father screams my name, his dark blue magic trying to break through my barrier to reach me. But the chaotic swell of my power is a representation of the way my mind is reeling, only one thought on repeat: she's gone.

She's gone.

I don't remember leaving the palace and sprinting to the beach, looking for any sign of her or her magic. I don't know how long I run along the edge of the water, desperately *searching, searching, searching.* There is no feeling in my body when I collapse to my knees in the sand, a scream ravaging my throat as I surround myself in shadows and magic, her broken locket clenched tightly in my hand. There is only a hollow emptiness where my heart should beat, the absence of her like losing my soul.

Chapter Eighty-One

BAHIRA

Kai's voice booms out in the dining room where the Mirror is located as he calls out my father's name again. Still, only silence answers.

"Is it possible that your father may have moved the Mirror to a spot where they cannot hear it?" Kai asks.

I shake my head as I clench my hands at my sides. "I don't think so. It's been in the council room since you used it to first reach out to us. Even if my father moved it, he would make sure that there is always a guard near it." I finally look in his direction, giving voice to the thought that sends a heavy dread through me. "Something is wrong."

Siyala, the female who had somehow been living in the Mortal Kingdom in her animal form until an injury forced her to shift, had given us a brief breakdown of what she knew of Rhea. Of what King Dolian had done so far to try and get his niece back. My stomach twists in on itself at the thought of what he wants her for—to *marry* her.

"What do you want to do?" Kai's voice is tentative where he stands across from me, Siyala and Jahlee at his side.

I turn my gaze towards the Mirror, the gears of my mind turning but coming up with nothing except horrific scenarios of what could have happened back home. "I think it's time for me to leave."

"Then I will prepare a ship immediately."

It doesn't take long to pack up my belongings—ancient journals, a magnifier, clothes, and a spear are all that I need to take back with me. Jahlee and Siyala meet me on the steps outside the palace, Kai giving us space and waiting a few yards ahead.

"I wish you didn't have to go at all," Jahlee laments while pulling me into a hug, her arms squeezing way too tightly. I squeeze her back just as hard.

"I am going to miss you." It's hard to define what Jahlee's presence—her *friendship*—has meant to me. She is the only one who truly understands what it's like to be magicless in a world filled to the brim with it, and yet she commands a presence about her that dares anyone to call her less than.

"Just remember that when you feel adrift between two worlds, I am in that middle space too. We are only outcasts if we let them make us so." She plants a kiss on my cheek and pulls back, her gaze flicking to her brother. "And perhaps there is still something that might bring you back here."

Unable to sever her hope, I give her a quirk of my lips before turning to Siyala. She has washed up and changed since our meeting in the throne room, but her haunting amber eyes remain fiercely focused on me.

"You will let us know that Rhea is safe?" she asks though it sounds more like a command, her fingers curling at her sides.

"I will."

She sticks her hand out between us, my own clasping hers as she firmly shakes it. "I'm sorry we could not talk more, as I know you have many questions. If I could accompany you on your journey, I would, but..."

"You have people who have waited years to see you, Siyala. Bahira will keep her word and reach out to us as soon as she can," Jahlee says, giving Siyala a waggle of her brows. Reluctantly, the shifter female lets me go. I give them one last parting smile before turning and walking down the steps to the waiting shifter king, my trunk in his hands.

"You do not have to accompany me to the docks," I tell him.

He doesn't offer a response, instead turning and leading the way to where a ship is waiting for me. Blowing out a breath, I follow a step behind him. Kai leads us down a path that doesn't cut directly through Molsi, but one that brings us around its outskirts. I can't help but watch him as he walks in front of me. He will have so much work to do with weeding out the rest of the rebels and truly beginning his reign here as king. Though I no longer underestimate him, I find myself uselessly wishing that I could stay and *help*. If he would even allow that.

"I can feel your gaze on me, Princess."

My lips twitch at the familiar statement, but I swallow back the urge to respond. The rest of our walk is quiet as the edges of the dock come into view. My hands run up over the straps of my pack and back to where my spear is tucked into its loops, nervous energy making me fidget.

The wooden planks, warped from sun and sea and time, creak under our steps as we walk to where a small ship is docked. The boat is a third of the size of the one I traveled to the island on and appears to only be manned by three people, their faces I somewhat recognize from the throne room.

"I trust these men," Kai says, following my gaze. "But if they decide that they want to test that trust, you have my permission to kill them all." He speaks the words loudly enough as we near the boat that all three men turn and look at us.

"Thank you, Your Majesty, for the permission."

Kai sets the trunk down gently, halting us in front of the boat. "Kai. It's just Kai to you." The breeze blowing in off the ocean ruffles his hair, sending dark strands over his forehead, and my stupid heart skips a beat at the sight of it.

"Bad idea to give *your ruin* so much power." He steps closer, and I have to brace myself for his presence—his warmth and scent and just *him*.

"Be my ruin. Be my poison. Be the reason I question who the fuck I am and what I'm doing. The reason I give a shit at all. Be all those things and whatever else you want to, Bahira."

His statements catch me off-guard as does the sincere look on his face. I shake my head, my teeth gritting together as too many emotions knot thickly in my throat. "Please, don't do this," I protest, my voice hardly loud enough to be heard over the lapping waves. I try to take a step back, only for him to pull me closer, an arm wrapping around my waist. My hands splay on his chest, both pushing him away and gripping his tunic. "I have stood firm behind my shields for so many years, and now, because of you, I am *faltering*. I am not strong enough—"

"You are," he interrupts. His finger curls beneath my chin, tilting my face up to his. "People often think of strength as something that's measured in battle—physical combat and mastery of weapons. But they rarely take into account mental and emotional toughness. They forget the will and perseverance it takes to continue on when the world tells them they shouldn't. When it tells them they are *weak*. You are many things, Bahira, but *weak* isn't one of them."

"Kai." The strain on my throat is heavy, my eyes growing wet as I stare up at him. His own gaze searches mine—my face and hair—while his hand flexes on my hip.

"What I said to you that night in the cave is not something that can be unsaid. I deserve nothing from you, and I will not ask you for anything you aren't willing to give me. Nor would I want to keep you from anything—*anyone*—back in your kingdom." He swallows, the edges of his face softening as he adds quietly, "But if there is a moment when you decide you'd like to talk with me again, I will make sure someone is always guarding the Mirror."

I don't let the sob trapped in my chest break free, one that's filled with the words I don't know how to say aloud to him. So, instead, I let him hold me, his hand tangling in my hair as he presses my head to his chest.

With the sun hanging low, a golden glow against the backdrop of a blue and lavender sky, I finally step out of Kai's arms and onto the boat. He gives his parting words to the crew as they lift the anchor and the ship begins to pull away from the dock. I watch Kai the entire time until his figure is nothing but a dot in the distance. My hands grip the railing of the boat, the three shifters moving about the deck as they adjust the sails to steer us over the open water.

With a deep breath, I turn away from the Shifter Kingdom and face the direction of home. Except that, now, home feels more like the place I just said goodbye to.

Salty air caresses my skin through the open window of my cabin, gently tugging on the pages of the journal I'm reading. Needing the distraction, I pulled the ancient record out of my pack after dinner and began thumbing through the detailed notes left by the former council member.

As this one is only about fifty years old, it must have been one I grabbed from the nightstand in my room before leaving for the Shifter Kingdom. My eyes drift over the councilman's words as he recounts the Flame Ceremonies of that particular week. It all seems standard for the time, the flames produced from each drop of blood only a few feet high. A boy from Santor saw a flame just over one foot tall. A girl from Galdr saw one of three feet. Another girl, this one from Galina, was also shown a flame of under two feet in height.

My finger taps on the page as I draw my brows together. Galina and Santor are both small towns that are close to the border of the Mortal Kingdom. Odd that, of the three ceremonies documented on this day, the two of those from these border towns produced a much smaller flame than the one child from Galdr. I set the councilman's journal to the side and reach for my pack on the floor next to the bed, digging through it until I find my own journal. The pages rustle as I flip through them, stopping when I reach the chart that I had created to plot not only the details of the Flame Ceremonies but any mention of magical discrepancies.

I study the graph, most of the x's marked are information gleaned from the past few years. There is a gap in the middle of the graph, that timeline missing because I haven't read enough journals to fill it in. Yet, as I study the markings and find where the majority of the disturbances in magic are noted, the similarities between them become abundantly clear. *Galina. Santor. Polatos. Agarino.* All of these towns are near either the mortal or fae borders, and *all* of them have markings that show not only decreasing magic but a rate higher than any of the other cities that are centered in the Mage Kingdom. Like Galdr. Despite having the highest populace, according to the data I've plotted so far, the capital has the lowest amount of noted magical discrepancies.

Sitting up taller, I let the journal fall to my lap as I stare at the wall of wooden slats across from me. Hadn't Kai also said that the shifters who live near the edges of the island are more highly affected by their magical blight than those who live near the island center?

"*Fucking gods*," I whisper, running my hands over my face.

The blight in the Shifter Kingdom. The decrease in magic in the Mage Kingdom. It isn't some random coincidence. There is only one thing that both kingdoms have in common. Only one thing that would affect the towns more closely located to the kingdoms' borders. My legs shake as I force myself up from the bed, pacing on the squeaking floorboards as the gears of my mind turn and turn until they lock into place. Looking back down at the journals spread out on the bed, goosebumps break out over my arms as a chill runs down my spine.

"It's the Spell."

Chapter Eighty-Two

Rhea

I'M FREEZING.

The cold air of the room I'm in sinks beneath my skin, somehow touching my bones. My tongue feels heavy in my mouth, the need for a drink driving my eyes to flutter open. I wait for the details of our bedroom to come into focus, but when the double vision finally evens out, above me isn't a ceiling made of wood but one of gray stone, sending confusion spiraling through me. I blink several times, the act doing nothing to make sense of where I am. *And my head...* It is as though there is a haze clouding it or it's been submerged in water. I try to shake the sensation off, pushing myself up to sit as my hands cradle my temples.

"Nox," I rasp out, working to clear my throat and feeling as if I haven't spoken in days. Slowly, my memories filter in. Tienne's body in the foyer. Nox staying with his dad and Cass and the council. Daje and I—

Daje.

I had tried to help him when... The thought dies as I look down at my dress, the green fabric covered in dirt and the hem ripped in multiple spots. The slits in the front show my bare legs, dried blood crusted on one of them. My hair hangs down past my shoulder, a rust color dyeing the ends of the strands.

"What happened?" I whisper, finally turning my attention out to the room. It's a modestly large bedroom. The bed I'm in is centered on a wall across from the floor-to-ceiling rectangular window. Curtains, in a light shade of purple, are pulled open and secured to pulls on the wall, sunlight pouring in between them.

A tapestry depicting a field of flowers covers a large portion of the wall to my left, and to my right is a wooden wardrobe—lilies, jasmine, and roses painted delicately on its front. Next to the wardrobe is an open door, and when I lean forward, I see that it leads to a bathroom.

"Nox?" I say again, my voice echoing ominously in the room, that odd feeling of a watery veil still in place. I reach for my magic, pulling at the warm tendrils to heal whatever this *presence* is, but it stops short of my head, like there is some kind of wall around my mind that my magic can't pierce through.

My eyes lift to the ceiling again, to the gray stone. *Gray. Stone.* My magic thrashes wildly in panic as I choke on my fear, gasping for a single breath. No. *No*, it's impossible. I am in the Mage Kingdom. I was with Daje on our way to the beach, and I—

The door to the room opens, startling me as I grip the comforter with both hands. My lips part, a yelp slipping out when a golden-armored guard steps in, his dark eyes boring into me with intense recognition. *Xander.* I shake my head, my body acting on instinct alone as I try to scurry off of the bed—intent on running through the window if I have to. Xander's eyes *scream* at me, the only part of his face that shows any sort of shock. Any sort of emotion at all.

And then *he* walks in.

"No," I gasp out loud, legs tangling in the scraps of my dress as I haphazardly reach the edge of the bed. The moment my feet hit the rug, I spin towards the bathroom door, stretching a hand out for the door handle. Even if it's just a bathroom, I'll lock myself in there forever. I'd rather die there in the dark than live in the light with my uncle again.

"Stop," King Dolian commands calmly. That film covering my mind *flares*, like a wall of water cast out by a tempest sea. It surrounds me until I feel as if I'm on the outside of my own body.

I watch in utter horror as my body obeys his command. My feet stay fixed to the floor, my hand dropping down to my side. *Move.* I send the thought to each limb, visualizing myself stretching my fingers towards that door handle. But I don't go anywhere. *Move!* I scream in terror in my mind, my chest heaving and my eyes beginning to dry out from how wide I hold them open. King Dolian appears in my peripheral vision, walking until he is standing directly in front of me.

"My gods, it *does* work," he muses, his eyes scraping over my face, *my skin*, and making my stomach churn. "Hello, my darling. Gods have I missed you."

"You bastard!" I scream, my limbs like lead. "Nox will *kill* you—"

"You are to *never* say that name again," he snarls, his voice hitting a deeper octave as his lips curl in anger. Power flares again within me, the sound of rushing water filling both of my ears.

I open my mouth, Nox's name on the tip of my tongue in any act of defiance I can muster. *Nox.* My voice echoes in my head, but the word... *Nox!* My mouth doesn't move. King Dolian brings his thumb to my chin, moving higher until he's caressing my bottom lip.

"What is going on?" I whisper, unable to stop the fear that ravages my voice. "What have you done?"

He reaches for my left hand, bringing it up until it's between us. "Do you see this ring?"

Following his gaze, I look down not on the beautiful engagement ring Nox had given me but a different one. The band is gold, carved to look like coral with a small pearl resting in the center, the inside of it swirling as if it's somehow captured the very sea within it.

"Where is my other ring? The one—" I choke, unable to say Nox's name out loud. King Dolian studies me, watching as my eyes flit in panic back and forth between his face and the ring on my finger.

"This is the only ring that matters now," he says gently, as if he's speaking to someone he might love and not someone that he *abducted*. That he beat and tortured and abused for *years*. "It's a very special ring, Rhea. I even have one that matches." He turns his hand around, keeping mine in his grip, as he shows me a gold and blue band on his ring finger.

"Don't touch me," I growl.

Through the haze of confusion and terror and whatever this feeling of submersion around my mind is, my magic writhes furiously. *My magic.* I don't have to hide it anymore. I know how to use it, and I don't need control over my body to call it up and hurt him when he's this close. He tilts his head to the side, his smile growing wider as if he's finally been given everything he wants. My magic quickly heeds my call, filling my palms with bright light. I blast it into him, his body flying back and smacking into the wall before he falls down on his knees. My heart beats fast and hard, and I keep my grip on my power as I try once more to move. But it's as if I am nothing more than a rooted tree. Xander rushes around me, his sword drawn as his eyes briefly meet mine before they move to the king.

"I'm fine," King Dolian growls, pushing Xander away before coming up to stand. "You will *never* use your magic on me again. In fact, you will *only* use your magic when *I* tell you to. Is that understood?"

My mind is drowning again, even as I try to fight against his demand. I picture Nox standing at my side, squeezing my hand tightly. Reminding me that I am not the same woman he found in that tower. I've changed—grown into something stronger. Into a version of myself that will never tolerate the abuse doled out by this monster *ever* again. "*Fuck you.*"

I expect it, but it still stings my cheek when he backhands me. My vision blurs as tears form, the taste of blood filling my mouth. I reach for my magic—ready to hit him again, to hit him as many times as it takes to kill him. To call even the shadows up—as I should have done the first time. But there is nothing except a feeling of emptiness where my power should be. *No. No. No.*

"I see that spending time with that *filthy* prince has changed you, but it's no matter. I'll get you back to how you were," he says calmly, his hand once more wrapping around mine. He kisses the ring on my finger, his eyes pinned to mine as he does. "No, you will be even better than before because now you are *truly* mine to command. Can you sense it? The power my words hold over you? Can you feel the way your body responds to them? How you respond to *me*?"

I can, and I've never been more terrified in my life. "You can't do this," I beg hoarsely.

"Oh, Darling, I can do *whatever* I want. And now," he pauses, interlacing our fingers despite my inability to move my own. Despite how my stomach revolts and how I'm screaming in my mind to stop, stop, *stop*. "Now I can make *you* do whatever I want as well."

This time, the tears that drip down *are* in response to the lethal fear that is poisoning my very blood. My uncle drags his thumb up my cheek, collecting the wetness there and then bringing it to his lips, smearing my tears over them as he smiles.

"Come, I have something to show you." My head wobbles from the cresting of his command within me while my feet move, despite my internal protests. He takes me to the window, and when I peer out, expecting to see the castle garden or perhaps the lake or wildflowers visible from my tower, I'm instead met with a view of the ocean, a large ship bobbing in the water where it's anchored at the dock. My lips part as I drag in a breath, my eyes flitting over the tan sandy beach and small green shrubs that dot its border before the Spell.

Swallowing, I blink through the lingering tears and ask, "Where are we?"

"I thought we might spend some time together before I *officially* introduce you to the court." Gripping my chin, his smooth fingers sliding along my cheek, he turns my head to face him. "We are somewhere *no one* will know where to look."

The insinuation pummels me as if it were his fists, and he smiles at the panic that drains the blood from my face.

"Welcome home, *my betrothed*."

Epilogue

THE WIND WHIPS THROUGH my hair, wild strands pulling on the sensitive part of my scalp and making my teeth grit together from the force of it. I squeeze my legs tighter around the small divot on the back of the dragon, Lan, that my brother and I ride on, that movement making me grimace too. *Fuck*, how far *had* I fallen from the ship? I bring my fingers to my head, checking for blood and thankfully finding that my healing abilities have finally sealed the wound.

"On another one of your *missions*?" Navin shouts from in front of me, the wind just barely carrying his voice past me. His black hair snaps at my face, and I swat it out of the way with an exasperated sigh.

"You could say that." I feel more than hear his responding chuckle, his shoulders shaking with it.

"With all the secrets you hold, it's a wonder Lan here can carry your weight." He trails his hand over his dragon, the dark blue iridescent scales shimmering under the sun as Lan tips his wings forward a small degree and we glide to a lower altitude. Navin's shoulders shake again.

"What?" I yell, kicking him in the boot.

"Lan finds you amusing!" Regardless of the fact that the beast we fly on comes from the savage Nila line—dragons of varying shades of blue with leaf-shaped scales—all it takes is a bit of food and all of your attention, and Lan will become as docile as a pup. His coltish energy matches that of his rider, so I suppose it makes sense that they've bonded.

"You can tell *Lan* that he is nothing more than an overgrown rat." The dragon growls as Navin hunches, the sound reverberating down his massive body as it rattles my bones.

"He didn't like that," Navin yells. I smirk, my grip tightening on the leather strap that wraps around the beast's neck.

My *mission*, as my brother had called it, was supposed to be a quick endeavor. I had snuck onto the ship, intent on questioning the male I had been tailing for a few days before slicing a blade across his throat and tossing him into the sea. Yet my interrogation had been ruined by the siren attack, and with none of the males in their right mind to steer the ship, it had veered too close to the jagged rocks lining the seafloor off the coast. With the hull shredded, the ship began to sink as I scrambled towards its deck. Unfortunately, in my desperation to get there, my attention had been diverted and I must have been hit with falling debris as the ship tipped. While I'm grateful to be alive, to now owe a life debt to a siren sets my teeth on edge.

"What did Father want?" I shout to Navin as I banish the thoughts of the ruby-haired siren from my mind.

"Apparently, you were absent from a mandatory teatime with the queen consort's ladies."

I groan, his shoulders shaking again as he laughs at my expense. I had completely forgotten about fucking *tea* with my mother.

My life as the royal princess of the Fae Kingdom was shrouded in secret. Both by design of the Crown and because of the *alternative* lifestyle I had chosen for myself.

By day, everyone assumes that Princess Myla Ryuu is nothing but a servant to her status. As is custom for our kingdom, nearly all of my face is shrouded by an opaque veil most of the time, only my onyx eyes left uncovered. With the exception of my mother, father, brother, and a handful of servants, no one knows what I truly look like. To the kingdom, I am but a precious jewel to be guarded until I wed. Only then can my face be revealed. My value is whittled down to nothing more than what I can provide between my legs to whichever suitor my father deems *worthy*.

By night, however, I trade in my colorful, tailored gowns and veil and, instead, don my preferred outfit of all black. With weapons sheathed on my thighs and hidden in compartments at my ribs, I am what the sinister shadows of Khargis have come to both revere and fear. While my father does not rule with an iron fist, neither does he provide adequate provisions to those in the kingdom who need it most. He revels in his status, keeping only to the upper crust of society while his lower-level subjects are left to fend for themselves—unless they slight the Crown. Only then do they gain his attention, and it's not the kind of notice anyone would want, as it usually ends with a trip to the dragon fields. No one returns from there.

So, when the sun sets, I prowl the streets looking for those that believe themselves to be exempt from justice. Anyone who preys on the defenseless finds the end of my blade instead. That's what I had been doing on the ship—enacting a deft punishment upon a male who thought it his *right* to corner a female in an alley and take advantage of her.

Navin whistles, drawing my attention back to the present as we soar over Khargis. The architecture of the city consists of gleaming dragon stone and harvested wood from the mountain's many forests. Though our kingdom is mostly one of black mountains and gray mist, patches of brightly colored wildflowers and forests of deep green trees stand out in stark contrast between the capital and its surrounding cities. Lakes and streams, their color an icy blue, look like the veins of the mountain from up here.

"So," Navin drawls loudly.

I kick his boot again, already suspecting what he'll say. "*Don't.*"

His laugh is teasing as he yells over his shoulder. "I was just going to say, if you were stuck making a deal with a siren, that female wasn't the worst looking—"

"*Navin—*" This time, I send a punch into his side, my brother grunting from the impact. Lan growls, and though he's too big to tilt his head back to look at us, he tries anyway, the dragon's anger radiating from the single yellow eye that I can see. "I will find a way out of it. She wasn't smart enough to choose her wording carefully."

Navin nods his head, his hand reaching back to pat my knee. "If anyone can work their charm, it's you," he coos sarcastically, earning another kick, this time to his calf. His chuckle works its way past me again as Lan's powerful wings beat and the looming palace nears.

The siren is the least of my concerns. I'm a being made of many secrets, and one does not go as long as I have protecting them without learning a thing or two about how to manipulate situations to my advantage. I'll meet with her, and when our agreement has been fulfilled, I'll do what I told her I wanted to: slit her throat and send her remains to her horrific queen. Maybe then the sirens will feel a fraction of the pain they have caused my family.

I don't consider myself a sentimental fae, but gods help me, I thrive on the feeling of vengeance. That little siren might just satiate it.

Rhea, Bahira, Aria, and Myla's stories will continue
in book 3 of The Five Realms Series.
Stay tuned to my social media for release date announcement!

Acknowledgements

Oof. How are you guys doing? To say this book was a journey to write would be the understatement of the year. I'm not sure if this is something all authors experience, but the transition from writing HOSAM to COSAT was a difficult one for me, made more so by the fact that so much needed to happen in this book. I mean, we get the reveal that we have a shadow daddy AND mommy (even if she is too afraid to use them), we have a siren whose magic only works on females, and we have our brainy queen figuring out that not only does blood have *something* to do with magic, but also that the Spell is what *might* be wreaking havoc on Olymazi. Yes, I just recapped those points on purpose. Anyways, all of that to say that for as long as this book is, there is an equally long draft filled with parts that I took out or rewrote. I feel like this is the book that showed me what it is to truly embrace this job. The good. The bad. And the downright ugly. I'm proud of the finished product though, and I'm grateful that the writing process unraveled like it did because it taught me a lot about myself.

To my girls, I love you so very much. You are my biggest inspiration and the source of my joy.

To my husband Joe, no one else in the world is more supportive than you. I know it. I'll fight anyone who tries to come for your 'Most Supportive Husband' crown.

To my friend Allie, thank you so much for all the time you dedicate to The Five Realms. So much of this book would have been impossible without you.

To my beta readers Ash, Heather, Katie, Kimberly, and Reenie, thank you guys so, so much for all your amazing feedback. I was so beyond nervous to have you guys read this and your hype and kind words truly meant everything.

Finally, to you, the reader, thank you for reading this book and hopefully loving on this series. Thank you for cheering on a little indie author with big dreams. I genuinely hope you found yourself within the pages of the story, whether it was Bahira's steadfast resilience or Rhea's healing journey. Or maybe you find yourself more like Aria, stuck in an awful cycle that you are desperate to get free from. In that case, please know that I'm rooting for you and I know you will find your path to happiness soon. Fantasy romance is such a wonderful genre because it really can encapsulate what it means to be *human* while in a world where magic, dragons, and sirens exist. Sometimes we feel on top of the world, safe and whole and loved. And sometimes, the opposite is true and that experience is just as real. Just as valid.

If the ending of this book has you grieving, know that I'm already hard at work with book three! I love you all and I can't wait for you to continue the story!

About the author

Jenessa Ren loved reading romantic fantasy so much, she created her own series! When she isn't causing chaos for the world of Olymazi, she's hanging out on bookstagram. You can follow along on Instagram at @jenessalikes and Tiktok @jenessaren

Retailers that carry The Five Realms books can be found on my site, https://jenessaren.my.canva.site/

Made in United States
Troutdale, OR
03/07/2025

29573053R00371